I0627549

ARTHURIAN STUDIES LXXXVII

# A NEW COMPANION TO MALORY

ARTHURIAN STUDIES

ISSN 0261-9814

General Editor: Norris J. Lacy

Previously published volumes in the series
are listed at the back of this book

# A NEW COMPANION TO MALORY

edited by
Megan G. Leitch and Cory James Rushton

D. S. BREWER

© Contributors 2019

*All rights reserved*. Except as permitted under current legislation
no part of this work may be photocopied, stored in a retrieval system,
published, performed in public, adapted, broadcast,transmitted,
recorded or reproduced in any form or by any means,
without the prior permission of the copyright owner

First published 2019
Paperback edition 2022

D. S. Brewer, Cambridge

ISBN 978 1 84384 523 2 hardback
ISBN 978 1 84384 675 8 paperback

D. S. Brewer is an imprint of Boydell & Brewer Ltd
PO Box 9, Woodbridge, Suffolk, IP12 3DF, UK
and of Boydell & Brewer Inc.
668 Mount Hope Ave, Rochester, NY 14620–2731, USA
website: www.boydellandbrewer.com


The publisher has no responsibility for the continued existence
or accuracy of URLs for external or third-party internet websites
referred to in this book, and does not guarantee that any content
on such websites is, or will remain, accurate or appropriate

A CIP catalogue record for this book is available
from the British Library

# Contents

# Illustrations

*Chapter 5. Malory in Print*, Siân Echard

*Chapter 12. Malory and the Wider World*, Meg Roland

The editors, contributors and publisher are grateful to all the institutions and persons listed for permission to reproduce the materials in which they hold copyright. Every effort has been made to trace the copyright holders; apologies are offered for any omission, and the publisher will be pleased to add any necessary acknowledgement in subsequent editions.

# Contributors

DORSEY ARMSTRONG, Purdue University

THOMAS H. CROFTS, East Tennessee State University

SIÂN ECHARD, University of British Columbia

ROB GOSSEDGE, Cardiff University

DANIEL HELBERT, West Texas A&M University

AMY S. KAUFMAN, Independent Scholar

MEGAN G. LEITCH, Cardiff University

ANDREW LYNCH, University of Western Australia

CATHERINE NALL, Royal Holloway, University of London

RALPH NORRIS, Sam Houston State University

RALUCA L. RADULESCU, Bangor University

LISA ROBESON, Ohio Northern University

MEG ROLAND, Marylhurst University

CORY JAMES RUSHTON, St Francis Xavier University

MASAKO TAKAGI, Kyorin University

K. S. WHETTER, Acadia University

# Abbreviations

| | |
|---|---|
| BBIAS | Bibliography of the British International Arthurian Society |
| EETS ES | Early English Text Society, Extra Series |
| EETS OS | Early English Text Society, Original Series |
| EETS SS | Early English Text Society, Supplementary Series |
| JEGP | *Journal of English and Germanic Philology* |
| JIAS | *Journal of the International Arthurian Society* |
| NS | New Series |
| N&Q | *Notes and Queries* |
| OED | *The Oxford English Dictionary* |
| PMLA | *Publications of the Modern Language Assocation* |

# Editions

The chronological arrangement of this list allows the reader to "see" the pattern of the *Morte*'s publication history. It includes translations and some loose adaptations in order to acknowledge the multiple entry points readers have into the *Morte*. The small gap between 1582 and 1634, and the larger one between the latter and 1816, show periods of waning interest in Malory, while the steady acceleration of editions and translations from the middle of the twentieth century to the current moment is also striking. Entries are mostly complete editions in the original language except when noted as incomplete (inc.), translations into English contemporary with the volume (trans.), close adaptations with some departures (adap.), bowdlerized (bowd.), reprinted (repr.), or containing significant additional material (add.). Versions of the Arthurian story in which Malory has been considerably augmented by stories from the Mabinogion, Tennyson, Middle English Gawain romances, etc., are usually so thoroughly adapted as to be entirely new texts, and are not included (this category includes Howard Pyle and Thomas Berger, and Tennyson himself). This list does not include editions that are translations into languages other than modern English.

For a comparison of many of the more recent editions, see Chapter Three, "Writing the *Morte Darthur*: Author, Manuscript, and Modern Editions"; and for a discussion of the longer print history of the *Morte Darthur*, and of the survival of illustration in the early black letter editions, see Chapter Five, "Malory in Print."

c. 1477–80    Winchester Manuscript (British Library Additional Manuscript 59678)

1485    William Caxton, London/Westmestre

1498    Wynkyn de Worde, London/Westmestre (repr. 1529, from Caxton)

1557    William Copland, London (from de Worde)

c. 1582–85    Thomas East, *The storye of the most noble and worthy kynge Arthur*, London (from de Worde and Copland)

1634    William Stansby for Iacob Bloome, *The most ancient and famous history of the renowned prince Arthur King of Britaine*, London (trans., bowd., from East)

1816    Walker and Edwards (publishers), *The History of the Renowned Prince Arthur, King of Britain*, London (trans., from Stansby)

| | |
|---|---|
| 1816 | Joseph Haslewood for R. Wilks, *La Mort D'Arthur*, London (trans., from Stansby) |
| 1817 | Robert Southey and William Upcott, *The Byrth, Lyf, and Actes of Kyng Arthur*, London (from Caxton/de Worde) |
| 1858 | Thomas Wright, *La Morte d'Arthure*, 3 vols., London (from Stansby) |
| 1868 | Edward Strachey, *Morte Darthur*, London (trans., bowd.) |
| 1868 | E. Conybeare, *La Morte d'Arthur*, London (inc., trans.) |
| 1880 | Sidney Lanier, *The Boy's King Arthur: Sir Thomas Malory's History of King Arthur and His Knights of the Round Table, Edited for Boys*, New York (inc., trans., adap., bowd.) |
| 1889–91 | H. Oskar Sommer, with an essay by Andrew Lang, 3 vols., London (from Caxton) |
| 1892 | Ernest Rhys for Scott Library, *Malory's History of King Arthur and the Quest of the Holy Grail*, London |
| 1893–94 | Aubrey Beardsley (illustrator) for Dent, *The birth life and acts of King Arthur*, 12 vols., London (from Caxton, reprinted in one volume, 1909) |
| 1897 | Israel Gollancz for Temple Classics, *Sir Thomas Malory's* Le Morte Darthur, 4 vols., London |
| 1900 | Alfred Pollard for MacMillan, *Le Morte Darthur*, London (trans., from Caxton via Sommer, itself reprinted and abridged multiple times) |
| 1906 | Anonymous for Dent Everyman, 2 vols., London |
| 1913 | Anonymous for Ashendene Press, *The Noble and Joyous Books entitled Le Morte Darthur*, Chelsea (from Southey) |
| 1917 | Alfred W. Pollard, *The Romance of King Arthur and His Knights of the Round Table*, ill. Arthur Rackham, London (from Caxton via Beardsley, inc.) |
| 1932 | Henry Frith, *King Arthur and His Knights*, ill. Frank Schoonover, Garden City (inc., trans., bowd.) |
| 1933 | Adrian Mott (Shakespeare Head edition), *The Noble & Joyous Boke Entytled Le Morte Darthur*, 2 vols., Oxford (from de Worde) |
| 1947 | Eugène Vinaver, *The Works of Sir Thomas Malory*, 3 vols., Oxford, rev. 1967 and rev. [by P. J. C. Field] 1990 |
| 1954 | Eugène Vinaver, *Malory: Complete Works*, Oxford, rev. 1971 and repr. 1977 (from Winchester) |
| 1968 | Derek Brewer, *Malory: The* Morte Darthur *(Parts Seven and Eight*, Evanston, IL (from Winchester, inc.) |
| 1969 | Janet Cowen, *Sir Thomas Malory:* Le Morte D'Arthur, 2 vols., London (from Caxton, repr. 2004) |

1977    P. J. C. Field, Le Morte Darthur: *The Seventh and Eighth Tales*, London (from Winchester, inc.)

1982    John Steinbeck, *The Acts of King Arthur and His Noble Knights*, New York (inc., trans., adap.)

1982    Folio Society, London

1983    James W. Spisak, *Caxton's Malory: A New Edition of Sir Thomas Malory's* Le Morte Darthur *based on the Pierpont Morgan Copy of William Caxton's Edition of 1485*, 2 vols., Berkeley and Los Angeles (from Caxton)

1998    Helen Cooper, Le Morte Darthur: *The Winchester Manuscript*, Oxford (from Winchester, inc., trans.)

1999    Elizabeth Bryan, *Le Morte D'Arthur*, New York, Modern Library (from Caxton, trans.)

2004    Stephen H. A. Shepherd, *Le Morte Darthur*, New York (from Winchester)

2009    Dorsey Armstrong, *Sir Thomas Malory's* Morte Darthur: *A New Modern English Translation based on the Winchester Manuscript*, West Lafayette, IN (from Winchester, trans.)

2010    Peter Ackroyd, *The Death of King Arthur: Thomas Malory's Le Morte d'Arthur*, London (from Winchester via Vinaver, inc., trans., adap.)

2013    P. J. C. Field, *Le Morte Darthur*, 2 vols., Cambridge, UK

2014    Maureen Okun, *Le Morte Darthur: Selections*, Peterborough, ONT (inc., trans.)

2015    Joseph Glaser, *Sir Thomas Malory's* Morte Darthur: *Condensed and Modernized*, Indianapolis (trans., adap.)

# Introduction

## MEGAN G. LEITCH AND CORY JAMES RUSHTON

Who that woll make ony more lette hym seke other bookis of Kynge
Arthure or of Sir Launcelot or Sir Trystrams; for this was drawyn by
a knyght presoner, Sir Thomas Malleorré, that God sende hym good
recover. Amen.[1]

Like its precursor over twenty years ago, this *New Companion to Malory* is a
testament both to the enduring popularity of its subject matter and to the continuing evolution of scholarly debate about, and ways of reading, Malory's
Arthuriad. The 1996 *A Companion to Malory*, edited by Elizabeth Archibald and
A. S. G. Edwards, has proved a valuable and influential guide to the study of
Malory's *Morte Darthur*. However, the two decades since its publication have
seen a transformation and expansion of critical approaches to Malory, as well
as significant advances in understanding the *Morte Darthur*'s milieux – textual,
literary, cultural and historical. Malory is now canonical and widely taught, and
this *New Companion* provides an up-to-date guide to match Malory's centrality
to the university curriculum and to critical discourse. The recent publication of
P. J. C. Field's two-volume critical edition of the *Morte Darthur* (D. S. Brewer,
2013), about which little has yet been said in print but which is changing the way
in which Malory scholarship is conducted, offers an additional stimulus for the
current volume. This *New Companion* offers scholars, teachers and students of the
*Morte Darthur* a new series of essays from established and emerging experts in
the field, together providing a synthetic overview of, and fresh perspectives on,
the range of questions and contexts essential for upper-level undergraduates or
new postgraduates studying Malory.

This is not to say that Malory scholarship did not exist before the 1996
*Companion*; it was, as Larry Benson once wrote, a "critical 'discovery' of the
twentieth century."[2] James W. Spisak wrote in 1985 that his collection, *Studies in
Malory*, drew on twenty years of sustained criticism prompted in large part by a
move away from concerns about biography (who Malory was) and by the unity

---

[1] Sir Thomas Malory, *Le Morte Darthur*, ed. P. J. C. Field, 2 vols. (Cambridge, 2013),
I, 144.1–4; this passage is not in Caxton's edition, but is found on folio 70v of the
Winchester manuscript.

[2] Larry Benson, "Sir Thomas Malory's *Le Morte Darthur*," in *Critical Approaches to
Six Major English Works*: Beowulf *Through* Paradise Lost, ed. R. M. Lumiansky and
Herschel Baker (Philadelphia, 1968), 81–131.

debate.[3] Book-length studies of Malory tend to interpret the whole work, often in isolation, with a few exceptions (for example, Sandra Ness Ihle's 1983 comparison of Malory's Grail sequence with his source, the *Queste del Saint Graal*[4]). Relative agreement on the unity and authorship debates has allowed Malory scholars to turn to topics like gender and the postcolonial, to geography and religion, and to the *Morte*'s place in its author's wider literary, cultural, and political worlds.

## Reading Malory, Malory's Reading: The Function of the Author

Critical perceptions of the text have often been keyed to perceptions of its author. The author of the Arthurian prose romance known today as the *Morte Darthur* is named within the text, in a series of colophons or comments addressed to readers, as Sir Thomas Malory. In the first of these colophons, the author is described as "a knight prisoner," a disclosure that ties in with historical records to suggest that Malory was writing the *Morte Darthur* – or what he seems to have called "The Hoole Book of Kyng Arthur and of His Noble Knyghtes of the Rounde Table" – while imprisoned for his potentially treasonous involvement in the English civil strife known as the Wars of the Roses.[5] Colophons such as this one have been central to critical debates about the nature of the *Morte Darthur*, giving rise to questions about the identity of the author, the unity and divisions of his work, the surviving versions and their relationship to each other and to what Malory may have originally written, and thus about how Malory should be both edited and read.[6] This is particularly so because most of these colophons exist only in one of the two surviving early witnesses to the "Hoole Book" Malory finished in 1469: the Winchester manuscript, written by scribes rather than by the author himself, but pre-dating the other textual witness to what Malory wrote – the version that William Caxton, the first English printer, published in 1485. Caxton's was the only version of Malory's *Morte* known to more modern readers until the manuscript version was discovered by a Winchester College librarian in a safe in 1934. When the first critical edition of the Winchester manuscript version was published by the influential editor Eugène Vinaver in 1947, decades of debate about whether Malory had written one work or many ensued. We see an example of fuel for this sort of debate when, earlier in this same colophon, Malory declares "Here endyth this tale" and "this booke endyth" (143.29–31 / W, fol. 70v): these words are found not at the end of Malory's whole narrative of King Arthur and the knights of the Round Table, but rather, like the other colophons, at the end of what Vinaver therefore identified as one of eight Tales Malory wrote (in this case, the first Tale).[7] As addressed in more detail elsewhere in this volume,

---

[3] James W. Spisak, "Introduction: Recent Trends in Malory Studies," in *Studies in Malory*, ed. James W. Spisak (Kalamazoo, 1985), 1–5.

[4] Sandra Ness Ihle, *Malory's Grail Quest: Invention and Adaptation in Medieval Prose Romance* (Madison, WI, 1983).

[5] P. J. C. Field, *The Life and Times of Sir Thomas Malory* (Cambridge, 1993), 131–2.

[6] For more on these debates, see the chapter by Crofts and Whetter in this volume.

[7] While "tale" and "book" are sometimes used interchangeably by Malory, critics today use "Tales" to refer to the eight sections of the *Morte Darthur* for which Vinaver

a degree of critical consensus on some of these issues had been reached by the end of the twentieth century, allowing twenty-first-century Malory criticism to explore other questions and develop new interpretive approaches, as showcased in the chapters that follow.

Yet while scholars today generally recognise the unity of Malory's Arthuriad alongside these internal divisions, the instruction in this first colophon in the *Morte Darthur* for interested readers to "seke other bookis" if they want to know more about figures such as Arthur, Launcelot or Tristram has, nonetheless, often been taken as an indication that, at this stage at least, Malory may not have intended to write a "Hoole Booke." One of the aims of this Introduction is to reflect on some of the ways in which perceptions of Malory as a reader and a writer (and perceptions of his authorial intentions and abilities) have shaped critical views of the nature and achievements of the *Morte Darthur*, in order to provide students of Malory with a guide to the evolution of the central questions surrounding the text, and the critical debates that are – fruitfully, we think – still visible across and between the chapters in this *New Companion*. What sort of reader of the Arthurian legend we see Malory as being has implications for our own reading of Malory's Arthuriad.

More is known about Malory's life than is usually the case for medieval authors, who are often anonymous. Moreover, in conjunction with his rather colourful biography, scholarly opinions of Malory's authorial abilities and interests have perhaps been premised on what is known of his life and what is presumed about his character even more so than might be the case for other named and historically know-able authors of late medieval English literature, like Geoffrey Chaucer. Sir Thomas Malory of Newbold Revel in Warwickshire (who has been, in recent decades, generally accepted as the author of the *Morte*) is known to have been a country gentleman who was a member of parliament but was also accused of the likes of cattle thievery, rape (at least from the perspective of the woman's husband), and the attempted assassination of the duke of Buckingham, in addition to the later involvement in the Wars of the Roses that landed him in prison for being on the losing side.[8] Where Chaucer's appearances in the historical records as the son of a middle-class wine merchant and a civil servant who travelled abroad on royal business have been invoked as explanations for his interests in class discourses and his access to French and Italian literary models, Chaucer's reputation as a writer of poetry that is both playful and thoughtful, sensitive and subversive originates in his verse. Malory's biography, by contrast, has been used not only to understand his text's interest in gentry concerns such as chivalry, friendship and marriage, and to underpin his presumed exposure to a small library of French and English Arthurian texts that he could translate and adapt while in prison. In addition, Malory's life – in particular, his backstory as a fighting man – has also sometimes been used to support arguments that his

---

posited authorial status in his edition of the Winchester Manuscript, and "Books" to refer to the twenty-one sections into which Caxton divided Malory's work in his 1485 print.

[8] P. J. C. Field, "The Malory Life-Records," in *A Companion to Malory*, ed. Elizabeth Archibald and A. S. G. Edwards (Cambridge, 1996), 115–30.

writing of the *Morte Darthur* resulted more from a need to pass the time while incarcerated than from inclination or ability.[9]

The presumption that the *Morte Darthur* as we have it is the result of Malory having little or no literary ability to start with is visible, for instance, in the introduction to Vinaver's seminal three-volume edition of Malory (printed three times, most recently in 1990, and – until 2013 – the predominant critical edition). Vinaver argued that in translating and adapting his sources, Malory

> evolved, as it were by reaction, his own narrative technique. [...] Through them [his sources] and with their aid Malory was able to discover what he needed above all: his own method of conveying sentiment through fiction. And so his last two works – *The Book of Sir Launcelot and Queen Guinevere* and the *Morte Arthur* – could reach a degree of independence unparalleled in his earlier books.[10]

Here, Vinaver posits that Malory learned as he went along: that he learned from his reading, that his reading guided him to seek specific other books to translate, and that it was only through his reading that he "could" become a more independent writer. All writers are readers, of course, but this characterises the relative independence of the various sections of Malory's Arthuriad as the result *only* of Malory's growing familiarity with his French sources, rather than a product of choice or selective adaptation. Vinaver also argues in his Introduction that Malory wrote a self-contained tale, and only afterwards sought more Arthurian material – material to read in the first instance, and *then* to adapt. For Vinaver, Malory's Arthuriad was an accidental one.

While Vinaver's assertion that Malory wrote eight separate romances rather than (in the end) one unified Arthuriad met with much resistance from other Malory scholars,[11] Vinaver's assumptions about what he terms "The Writer's Progress" have had a more diffuse and lasting influence on approaches to Malory.[12] Vinaver's extensive *Commentary* in the third volume of his critical edition (examining Malory's relationship to his sources, and pointing up differences) often articulates the assumption that Malory "got it wrong" where he

---

[9] In addition, Malory's questionable chivalric conduct and criminal record shaped a view of Malory as lacking what Vinaver termed "moral and sentimental refinement": "If any background of actual experience was needed to awaken interest in [Arthurian literature], it was certainly not one of moral and sentimental refinement; and there is no real reason why a man totally unaffected by the accepted code of behaviour should not have been as sensitive as Malory was to their poetic and human appeal": *The Works of Sir Thomas Malory*, ed. Eugène Vinaver, 3rd edn, rev. P. J. C. Field, 3 vols. (Oxford, 1990), I, xxix. See also Richard Altick, who wrote of the perceived difficulty of reconciling Malory's "flamboyant criminal record" with his writing of "a book celebrating many articles of knightly behaviour which he himself had honoured far more in the breach than in the observance": Richard D. Altick, *The Scholar Adventurers* (New York, 1950), 83–4.

[10] Vinaver, *Works*, I, lvi.

[11] See, for instance, *Malory's Originality: A Critical Study of "Le Morte Darthur,"* ed. R. M. Lumiansky (Baltimore, 1964), to which Vinaver explicitly responds in turn in the revised editions of his three-volume edition (*Works*, I, xli–xlvii).

[12] Vinaver, *Works*, I, lvi.

departs from his French sources,[13] which Vinaver (himself a French scholar) privileged as the definitive versions of the Arthurian legend. This assumption is not generally shared by today's Malory scholars, for whom Vinaver's *Commentary* is nonetheless still one of the most valuable resources, often consulted and cited for the specifics of Malory's originality and relationship to his sources. Yet Vinaver's view that Malory *learned how* to be an author as he went along, in reaction to his sources in sequence, and that Malory became the author of an Arthuriad only by degrees, still often shapes critical perception of how and what Malory read and wrote. For instance, Vinaver rationalises his argument that Malory must have written Tale II (the Roman War section, or The Tale of the Noble King Arthur and Emperor Lucius) first of all the Tales on the basis that this is "the least polished" of Malory's "works," and "had a decisive influence on both the formation of his style and on his subsequent choice of material. It induced him to "seek other books of Arthur" and adapt them into his own prose.[14]

This way of understanding the text of the *Morte Darthur*, as a result of Malory's gradual maturation as a writer, has been influential. As Michel Foucault has famously observed, the function of the author is to shape the interpretation of the text and the relationship between its various components.[15] Foucault observes that in literary criticism, as in other discourses,

> the author provides the basis for explaining not only the presence of certain events in a work, but also their transformations, distortions, and diverse modifications (through his biography, the determination of his individual perspective, the analysis of his social position, and the revelation of his basic design). The author is also the principle of a certain unity of writing – all differences have to be resolved, at least in part, by the principles of evolution, maturation, or influence.[16]

That is to say, expectations of authorial evolution, maturation, and influence (from his sources, and from his own life experience) often precede and shape arguments about the composition, structure, and interests of Malory's *Morte Darthur*. The text's identification of its writer as "knyght presoner, Sir Thomas Malleorré," then, alongside the historical records of this knight's brushes with the law, has certainly fulfilled the brief that Foucault described as that of the "author-function." The epithet "knight prisoner," identifying the author as an incarcerated member of the gentry classes, indicates both the status and the state of the author when writing. "Sir Thomas Malory" is not just a name, then; it is also a principle by which we understand and interpret the *Morte Darthur*.

This *New Companion to Malory*, in foregrounding both recent interventions regarding longstanding questions and new critical approaches, seeks both to provide the most up-to-date overview of contexts for the writing and reading

---

[13] For instance, Vinaver writes of what he terms Malory's "curious misreading" of French sources such as the Prose *Lancelot*, and suggests that Malory "failed to understand the French" text at points where he does not follow his source (Vinaver, *Works*, III, 1419), rather than positing agency – conscious or otherwise – in Malory's adaptations.

[14] Vinaver, *Works*, I, lv.

[15] Michel Foucault, "What Is an Author?" in *The Foucault Reader*, ed. Paul Rabinow (London, 1986), 101–20, at 110.

[16] Foucault, "What Is an Author?", 111.

of the *Morte*, and to encourage a mode of reading that is more conscious of the assumptions we are making as we read. Scholars and students of the *Morte Darthur* are fortunate in the extent of what is known about Malory and his milieux, as this allows us to understand the text's production and contemporary reception all the better – as addressed by some of the chapters that follow. Yet Foucault's author-function also offers a caution, reminding us that we are bringing certain baggage to our reading of a text, as well as allowing the text to shape our reading or interpretation. And Roland Barthes, of course, when arguing (two years prior to Foucault) against types of literary criticism that resort to knowledge of the author's identity to explain the author's work, entitled his essay *"La mort de l'auteur"* ("The Death of the Author"); but while the author may indeed be dead, for Malory studies, he still has his uses.[17] Readers of this *New Companion* are invited to attune themselves to how conceptions of the author shape some of the ongoing critical debates within the field of Malory studies, debates to which this *New Companion* bears witness.

For instance, Amy S. Kaufman's chapter "Malory and Gender" addresses both perceptions of Malory's misogyny (or lack thereof) and representations of women within his text, and seeks to disentangle the two. After all, as the disjunction between Malory's criminal record and his book of high ideals reminds us, an author is not what he writes. Different conceptions of the author and how he composed his work also inform Ralph Norris's chapter "Malory and His Sources" and Cory James Rushton's chapter "Malory and Form." Malory's "Tale of Sir Gareth of Orkney," for which there is no extant source, is one of the cruxes of debate about Malory's composition. Did Malory have a source (whether French or English) for this story of one of Arthur's nephews, who conceals his identity until he has proven his worth and won the hand of his lady (with the assistance of a dwarf and a magical ring) – a source which is now lost, as many would argue? Or, as others suggest, might Malory have created a Fair Unknown Tale of his own to insert into his wider narrative by drawing upon his general familiarity with romance motifs and Arthurian literature? As with many Malorian matters, scholars work around the question without finally solving it. The best approach may be Helen Cooper's: noting that the healing of Urry, like Gareth, has no known source, Cooper acknowledges that Malory may have had sources for these sections, "but both must have been invented by somebody at some stage, and there is no strong reason why that person should not have been Malory."[18]

One vital direction in Malory studies has been the work done to contextualise him within the long fifteenth century, both to explain his text and to expand the number of texts commonly studied.[19] The fifteenth century has a mixed

---

[17] Roland Barthes, "The Death of the Author," in *Image-Music-Text*, essays selected and trans. Stephen Heath (New York, 1977), 142–8.

[18] Helen Cooper, "Introduction," in Le Morte Darthur: *The Winchester Manuscript*, ed. Helen Cooper (Oxford, 1998), vii–xxx, at xx.

[19] See, for instance, Helen Cooper, "Counter-Romance: Civil Strife and Father-Killing in the Prose Romances," in *The Long Fifteenth Century*, ed. Helen Cooper and Sally Mapstone (Oxford, 1997), 141–62; William Kuskin, *Symbolic Caxton: Literary Culture and Print Capitalism* (Notre Dame, IN, 2008); and Megan G. Leitch, *Romancing Treason: The Literature of the Wars of the Roses* (Oxford, 2015), 64–84.

reputation in literary studies, long considered a "dull" period with little literary innovation, dominated by Chaucerian imitators like Lydgate, Hoccleve and Henryson.[20] Malory's *Morte* was in some sense helped on its way into the canon by its historical location, seen as a bright spot in a tired landscape (in much the same way that his fellow canonical newcomer, Margery Kempe, could stand out earlier in the century). At the same time, as Malory's biography reflects, fifteenth-century England is also a politically tumultuous time of civil war, even as technological innovations – notably the printing press – accelerate the sharing of thought.

Perhaps it is time to give Malory's text the same latitude we give Chaucer's writings. At the very least, we might acknowledge that Malory has remained as popular as Chaucer over the centuries, while contemporaries like Gower or Lydgate slipped into relative obscurity. While Malory was briefly out of print in the seventeenth century, it did not take an academic audience to revive him: it was popular presses which did this, the publishers fully expecting the work to sell. Moreover, where Chaucer has long been seen as an author receptive to post-modern approaches – and one in whose writing we should be open to finding irony, humour and productive ambiguity – traces of outdated conceptions of Malory as an earnest, slightly inept redactor have persisted despite the postmodern popularity of his text and the success of recent criticism in opening it up to new ways of reading. Yet perhaps Malory's own ironic sense of humour is visible in moments such as that at which Sir Gareth, having defeated many knights in the hope of rescuing and marrying Lyonesse, and having sustained many wounds of his own in the process, plaintively objects to the lady's standoffishness in not even granting him entry to her castle. Gareth complains – calling up to Lyonesse's window from outside her castle gate:

> "Alas! fayre lady, [...] I have nat deserved that ye sholde shew me this straungenesse. And I hadde wente I sholde have had ryght good chere with you, and unto my power I have deserved thanke. And well I am sure I have bought your love with parte of the beste bloode within my body." (255.15–19 / C VII.19)

Here, a petulant young Gareth voices his sense of what his blood ought to be worth in the market of courtly love, and Malory simultaneously offers ironic foreshadowing of what happens with Gareth's blood later in the Tale.[21] While Gareth thinks he has staunchly suffered enough bloodshed to earn Lyonesse's love, little does he know that even when he does later win the lady's affections, he will be prevented from consummating his love with her by a magical knight wounding him in the thigh and causing him to bleed so much that he swoons – not once, but twice.[22] This serious-yet-silly somatic representation is just one of

---

[20] For a reconsideration of this view, see David Lawton, "Dullness and the Fifteenth Century," *English Literary History* 54.4 (1987): 761–99.

[21] See Megan G. Leitch, "(Dis)Figuring Transgressive Desire: Blood, Sex, and Stained Sheets in Malory's *Morte Darthur*," *Arthurian Literature* XXVIII (2011): 21–38.

[22] On the prominence of swooning in Malory's *Morte*, see Barry Windeatt, "The Art of Swooning in Middle English," in *Medieval Latin and Middle English Literature: Essays in Honour of Jill Mann*, ed. Christopher Cannon and Maura Nolan (Cambridge, 2011), 211–30.

the many ways in which the legibility of the body intervenes in discourses of (for instance) desire, devotion, affect and ethics in the *Morte*.

Attention to the body has also contributed to the ways in which some twenty-first-century approaches to Malory have been increasingly enriched by critical theory. Recent theoretical approaches have productively informed our understanding of matters such as gender, sexuality and emotions in the *Morte Darthur* (to take just a few examples).[23] Here too there is a balancing act between deploying what we know and being open to what we might find. As Paul Strohm points out in his exploratory psychoanalytic reading of Malory's Melleagaunt (who desires Guinevere and envies Launcelot),

> The enemy of good criticism is what might be called "premature knowledge," which I would define as knowledge achieved the easy way, by acceptance of the text's own self-descriptions. [...] Also to be resisted is the subsequent error, which is to become so arrogant about the capacities of one's critical tools that one indiscriminately overrides or reverses what the text seems to be trying to tell us about itself.[24]

Taking the text on its own terms, then, is not necessarily the same thing as taking the text at face value. Questions about the extent to which we might find what we are looking for may attend the application of theory as well as the function of the author, but recent criticism has certainly deepened our understanding of the richness of Malory's *Morte Darthur* and suggested avenues for further exploration. Some of the chapters in this *New Companion*, while offering new readings and syntheses of their subjects, likewise gesture towards understudied aspects of the *Morte*. For Malory studies, then – as for Gareth waiting outside Lyonesse's castle gate – there is certainly more to come.

## *Reading the* New Companion to Malory

This volume seeks not to replicate the original *Companion to Malory* directly, but to offer a new companion commensurate with twenty-first-century scholarship and study. The first *Companion*'s second section, entitled "The Art of the *Morte Darthur*," included chapters for each major section of Malory's text, in order (a structure borrowed from Lumiansky's edited volume, *Malory's Originality*, and one that, of course, also followed the *Morte* itself). This section, in the editors' opinion, cannot be bettered.[25] Instead, the *New Companion* aims to familiarise

---

[23] See, for instance, Kathleen Coyne Kelly, "The Writable Lesbian and Lesbian Desire in Malory's *Morte Darthur*," *Exemplaria: A Journal of Theory in Medieval and Renaissance Studies* 14:2 (2002): 239–70; Amy S. Kaufman, "Between Women: Desire and its Object in Malory's 'Alexander the Orphan'," *Parergon* 24.1 (2007): 137–54; Kenneth Hodges, "Wounded Masculinity: Injury and Gender in Sir Thomas Malory's *Le Morte Darthur*," *Studies in Philology* 106.1 (2009): 14–31; Andrew Lynch, "'What Cheer?' Action and Emotion in the Arthurian World," in *Emotions in Medieval Arthurian Literature: Mind, Body, Voice*, ed. Frank Brandsma, Carolyne Larrington and Corinne Saunders (Cambridge, 2015), 47–63.

[24] Paul Strohm, *Theory and the Premodern Text* (Minneapolis, 2000), 212.

[25] This *New Companion* therefore does not offer summaries of the individual Tales of Malory's *Morte Darthur*; readers seeking detailed overviews of the eight Tales are

readers with the *Morte Darthur*'s polyvalent vitality. Once considered formally clumsy and resistant to theoretical approaches, Malory's text now sustains a variety of approaches even as his artistry is revisited and reconsidered. The first of the three sections of this volume centres on the current state of research with respect to traditional but much-evolved (and still-debated) questions; the second section addresses emerging critical approaches and new directions; and the third offers suggestive analyses of the *Morte Darthur*'s afterlives, showcasing the rich and emerging critical field of Malory and medievalism as well as the text's continued relevance and impact in the twentieth and twenty-first centuries.

## Malory in His Time

The *New Companion* reflects this interest in Malory's world. In addition to Ralph Norris's discussion of Malory's sources, the volume contains chapters by Kevin Whetter and Thomas Crofts on the connections between Malory as author and later editions of his work; Siân Echard on print editions; and Megan G. Leitch on the ways in which the *Morte* is just one of many long-form prose romances with similar thematic concerns written in the period. Meg Roland's chapter suggests that Malory had an interest in the world outside of England, reflected at various points in his work. Catherine Nall situates Malory within his social and political context closer to home, while Lisa Robeson explores connections between Malory's text and contemporary political concerns, especially ideas of kingship. Raluca Radulescu, meanwhile, offers a reading of Malory's religiosity (another important topic in Malory studies, especially since the publication of Thomas Hanks and Janet Jesmok's *Malory and Christianity* in 2013).[26]

## Malory as Artist

As stated earlier, Malory has not always been taken seriously as literary artist, a situation exacerbated by his best-known editors. Cory James Rushton revisits the discussion of the nature of Malory's book in formal terms, a conversation usually subsumed in that of genre. Dorsey Armstrong examines Malory's approach to character, a question also often tied up with that of form and consistency. Amy S. Kaufman looks not only at Malory's ideas about gender, but also at the long critical tradition of assumptions about his essential misogyny, and calls for a more generous and nuanced reading. Finally, Andrew Lynch applies recent critical work on literature and the emotions to the *Morte*, a text long acknowledged as both interested in emotion and capable of producing emotional effect, and which can be illuminated productively in light of the affective turn in literary studies.

## Malory as Cultural Inheritance

Twentieth-century readers turned the nineteenth century's partial rediscovery of Malory into a more thorough engagement with, and canonisation of, the *Morte Darthur*. The early twentieth-century instrumentality and cultural cachet of the

---

invited to consult the original *Companion*, which does not require updating in this area.

[26] *Malory and Christianity: Essays on Sir Thomas Malory's* Morte Darthur, ed. D. Thomas Hanks, Jr., and Janet Jesmok (Kalamazoo, 2013).

*Morte Darthur* had consequences for the subsequent popularity of Malory, both within and beyond academia, witnessed by the inclusion of a "Posterity" section in the original *Companion* consisting of a single short chapter by Edwards on the reception of the *Morte*, in which he highlights the "creative vitality over time and medium, finding expression in verse and prose, in painting, architecture and film and extending as far afield as Japan."[27] The *New Companion* seeks to open up this very line, exploring how Malory has been received around the world (and in the case of Japan, how Japanese scholarly and creative work has broadened our understanding of the *Morte* itself). Japanese interest in and contributions to Malory studies is the subject of Masako Takagi's chapter. Rob Gossedge examines Malory's cultural role in Britain in the twentieth century, especially in the context of the two world wars, while Daniel Helbert offers a reading of American engagement with the *Morte* in the nineteenth century. These chapters offer views of Malory's cultural vitality in the modern world that are illustrative, but not comprehensive; other avenues and cultural arenas, such as those that might be illuminated by a postcolonial approach, would also prove fruitful for exploration.

---

[27] A. S. G. Edwards, "The Reception of Malory's *Morte Darthur*," in *A Companion to Malory*, 241–52, at 241.

# A Note on Malory's Text

Thomas Crofts has suggested that "Malory criticism since 1934 is really a narrative of at least two texts resolutely not being the same book."[1] Certainly few authors exist in as many different forms as Malory does. Loose modern translations like those of Keith Baynes (1962) and Peter Ackroyd (2010), and adaptations which are very close to translation, such as John Steinbeck, brush up against closer but abridged modern-spelling editions like that of Helen Cooper, or editions which contain only the last Tales (Field, 1977; reprinted 2008). Since most people who creatively adapt the legend use some variation of Caxton (as everybody did between the fifteenth and the mid twentieth century, by necessity) or Vinaver's single-volume *Works*, this is something to bear in mind. As Edwards writes in the original *Companion*:

> While most study of Malory since then [the discovery of Winchester] has been appropriately based on this manuscript, it is necessary to emphasize the fact that all responses to the *Morte* down to the twentieth century have been based on versions of Caxton's text and that it has its own culturally inscribed position in the history of the work's reception.[2]

Field's new edition both stabilises and complicates this inheritance.

Field is a brilliant editor and philologist, in Crofts's phrase, "a formidable researcher in textual, historical and biographical criticism,"[3] dedicated to getting as close as possible to Malory's original text. Decades of Malory scholarship, however, are keyed to either the one- or three-volume Vinaver edition. That critical work proceeded according to the rules and impulses of twentieth-century literary criticism. Yet rather than focus on aesthetics or on historical content (what Malory could tell us about the English Middle Ages), as earlier criticism had done, late twentieth-century work focused on cruxes in the text, gaps and fissures which seemed to require or invite explanation. As Elizabeth Edwards wrote in 2001, "I prefer to preserve the contradictions, rather than to neutralize them."[4] However, almost by definition, Field's attempt at an original text is focused on ironing out those gaps and contradictions, making sense at the level

---

[1] Thomas H. Crofts, *Malory's Contemporary Audience* (Cambridge, 2006), 11.
[2] A. S. G. Edwards, "The Reception of Malory's *Morte Darthur*," in *A Companion to Malory*, ed. Elizabeth Archibald and A. S. G. Edwards (Cambridge, 1996), 241–52, at 243.
[3] Crofts, *Malory's Contemporary Audience*, 14.
[4] Elizabeth Edwards, *The Genesis of Narrative in Malory's* Morte Darthur (Cambridge, 2001), 23.

of the text itself. It seems possible that where Field sees a textual corruption, others might see a kind of symptom worth exploring. If those gaps disappear between editions, the flow and direction of Malory studies will see a significant disconnect. In practical terms, Malory scholars will, for the foreseeable future, need to have both the Field and the Vinaver editions in order to navigate the critical conversation to this point, especially as Boydell and Brewer (publisher of the present volume and of the Field edition), Palgrave MacMillan (publisher of both the New Middle Ages series and the Arthurian and Courtly Cultures series), and the journal *Arthuriana* all now strongly prefer use of the Field edition. (The original *Companion* had a smaller version of this problem, and asked contributors to use the one-volume Vinaver but to emend any quotations in line with Field's third revised edition of the three-volume version, at that point a mere six years old.)

Therefore, the editors of this *New Companion* cite the new Field edition while including cross-references to Caxton's book and chapter numbers so that readers with different editions can find passages in their own copies. The Norton Shepherd and the single-volume Vinaver may both prove useful in this regard. The chapter by Crofts and Whetter offers an overview of various critical editions and student editions. Since various spellings of Arthurian characters' names are found in published criticism of the *Morte Darthur*, the editors have not sought to impose the use of standardized versions of these names across this volume; however, when such names appear in the Index, we have used Malory's spellings where this would not interfere with usability (e.g. Lancelot and Guenevere rather than Launcelot and Guinevere).

# I

## The *Morte Darthur*: Text(s) and Contexts

# 1

# Malory in Historical Context

## CATHERINE NALL

In the final tale of his *Morte Darthur*, Sir Thomas Malory describes the disintegration of the Arthurian world, as Mordred, Arthur's son and nephew, whom Arthur had left in charge of the kingdom, usurps the throne. Malory describes the changing political landscape of this realm, as "muche people" choose to side with the usurper and betray their king, even those men, Malory points out, whom Arthur "had brought up of nought," endowing them with lands.[1] At this moment, Malory makes a rare authorial interjection, addressing his readers directly:

> Lo ye all Englysshemen, se ye nat what a myschyff here was? For he that was the moste kynge and nobelyst knyght of the worlde, and moste loved the felyshyp of noble knyghtes, and by hym they all were upholdyn, and yet myght nat thes Englyshemen holde them contente with hym. Lo thus was the olde custom and usayges of thys londe, and men say that we of thys londe have nat yet loste that custom. Alas! thys ys a greate defaughte of us Englysshemen, for there may no thynge us please no terme. (916.34–917.6 / C XXI.1)

Malory's contemporaries had good reason to suspect the existence of a national predisposition to political unsteadfastness. The decades leading up to the completion of the *Morte Darthur* in 1469–70 had witnessed unprecedented civil unrest, popular rebellion, armed conflict, and the deposition of the anointed king, Henry VI. This period of civil turmoil has been referred to as the Wars of the Roses since the nineteenth century.[2] Malory himself was involved or implicated in some of the events of these decades, if we accept that the Malory who wrote the *Morte Darthur* was the Thomas Malory of Newbold Revel in Warwickshire.[3] Indeed his criminal career, which included everything from attempting to ambush the duke of Buckingham to extortion and cattle rustling, exemplifies some of the local disorder and lawlessness which for some commentators, both medieval and modern, was endemic in the fifteenth century.

In what follows, I shall begin by outlining the key political events of the period leading up to, and occurring shortly after, Malory's death on 14 March 1471. I shall

---

[1] Sir Thomas Malory, *Le Morte Darthur*, ed. P. J. C. Field, 2 vols. (Cambridge, 2013), I, 916.28, 32; C XXI.1.

[2] This was in reference to the badges used by the opposing sides: the House of York with its white rose and the House of Lancaster with its red rose.

[3] The chapter by Thomas Crofts and Kevin Whetter in this volume discusses the authorship question in more detail.

then consider some of the ways in which scholarship of the past two decades has sought to situate the *Morte Darthur* in this wider historical context by addressing it in relation to some of the key concerns of the period, concerns which are reflected in Malory's text and which were shared by the gentry, the social group to which Malory himself belonged and for whom he presumably wrote.[4] In particular, the events of this period directed attention to, and prompted discussion of, the issues of loyalty and treason, effective kingship and counsel, and the relationship between outward war and internal peace.

## Sir Thomas Malory and the Wars of the Roses

The catalyst for the problems of these decades, which are the key contexts for Malory's writing, was the deteriorating situation in those parts of France which had been conquered by Henry's father, Henry V: the county of Maine was ceded to the French in the late 1440s and between August 1449 and August 1450 Normandy fell to the French king, Charles VII. In the parliament that met between November 1449 and June 1450, and which was probably attended by Malory who had been returned as member of parliament for Bedwin, Wiltshire, on 14 October 1449, William de la Pole, duke of Suffolk and one of Henry's main advisers, was accused by the commons of having conspired with the French. Although the king rejected the charges of treason, and banished Suffolk for five years, as Suffolk made his way to the Low Countries his ship was intercepted by another ship named the *Nicholas of the Tower*. Its crew took Suffolk prisoner, conducted a mock trial, and executed him. Earlier that year, Adam Moleyns, keeper of the privy seal and bishop of Chichester, had also been murdered by soldiers waiting to leave for Gascony.

The murder of those held responsible for the loss of the lands in France is testament to the degree of popular outrage and discontent in existence during these months. This found its fullest expression in the summer of 1450, in the rebellion known as Cade's revolt, in reference to its leader, Jack Cade. This period is indeed marked by such popular uprisings (see below, p. 19). The grievances of Cade's rebels, outlined in surviving manifestoes, combine the local and the national. The rebels referred to the enforcement of the Statute of Labourers, the practices of "gret extorsiners" in Kent, and purveyance (the payment for the provisions for the royal household – a perennial source of concern throughout the period), as well as to the loss of lands in France, and the arrest and subsequent death of Humphrey, duke of Gloucester, the king's uncle.[5] Here, in ways which resonate with Malory's *Morte Darthur* (see below, p. 30), failure in outward war and the loss of the lands in France are connected to a range of domestic issues. At the heart of these complaints was the perception that the king had been poorly counselled by the men who surrounded him. Such accusations were mainstays

---

[4] Raluca L. Radulescu, *The Gentry Context for Malory's* Morte Darthur (Cambridge, 2003).
[5] Those practising extortion were named as Stephen Slegge, William Cromer, William Isle and Robert Est. Duke Humphrey was arrested in the Bury parliament of 1447 and died in captivity.

of rebel manifestoes in this period, and Malory's *Morte Darthur* similarly raises questions concerning counsel and who ought to have access to the king (see below, p. 27). Cade's rebels identified Richard, duke of York, one of England's leading magnates, as the man to redress these wrongs. Over the course of the following months, York adopted the mantle of reformer. One of the main targets of York's criticism was Edmund Beaufort, duke of Somerset, and the rivalry between these two men was to dominate the politics of the next few years.[6]

The following years witnessed a crisis in kingship, a problem exacerbated by the onset of Henry's illness in 1453. Following the news of the death of John Talbot, earl of Shrewsbury, at Castillon on 17 July, the king fell into a stupor, from which he did not emerge for over a year.[7] In March 1454, York was made protector and defender of the realm. It was a realm, though, plagued by division and disorder. Divisions among the nobility – between the Bonvilles and Courteneys in the West Country, and the Percys and the Nevilles in the North – had escalated into actual violence. Furthermore, that the Neville lords – the earl of Salisbury and the earl of Warwick – supported York, and thus their rivals, the Percys, supported the king, his wife, Margaret of Anjou, and Somerset, meant that these feuds took on a wider significance. When Henry recovered at the end of 1454, Somerset, who had been imprisoned in the Tower of London, was released, and York was removed from office. York's precarious position forced him to take drastic action. On 22 May 1455, York, Salisbury and Warwick attacked the king's forces at St Albans. Somerset and Henry Percy, earl of Northumberland, were killed. The heirs of these men would not rest until their fathers had been avenged.[8] The *Morte Darthur* is similarly concerned with the effects of feud, the difficulties of maintaining peace between powerful magnates, and the potential conflict between the claims of blood ties and political allegiances (see below, pp. 22–5).

By the end of this decade, England was in a state of civil war. Following battles at Blore Heath on 23 September 1459, and at Ludford Bridge on 13 October, the Yorkist lords were attainted for treason at the "Parliament of Devils" at Coventry. On 10 July 1460 at the Battle of Northampton the king was taken prisoner; Queen Margaret fled north with the heir to the throne. The following October, York formally claimed the throne, basing his claim on his descent, through his mother, from Lionel, duke of Clarence, the second surviving son of Edward III. The issue of Lancastrian legitimacy that had been latent since Henry Bolingbroke's usurpation of the throne in 1399 here came to the fore. With some reluctance, York was eventually recognised as Henry's heir in an agreement known as the Act of Accord.

However, on 30 December 1460, York, and his second son, the earl of Rutland, were killed at the Battle of Wakefield. Salisbury was captured and later beheaded. It fell now to Richard's eldest son, Edward, earl of March, to press the Yorkist

---

[6] M. K. Jones, "Somerset, York and the Wars of the Roses," *English Historical Review* 104 (1984): 285–307, at 303–4.

[7] It is not entirely clear what Henry was suffering from. For discussion, see David Grummitt, *Henry VI* (Abingdon, 2015), 170–3.

[8] A. J. Pollard, *Late Medieval England 1399–1509* (Harlow, 2000), 148.

claim. On 2–3 February 1461, Edward was victorious against Lancastrian forces at the Battle of Mortimer's Cross. Later that month, however, on 17 February, Queen Margaret's Lancastrian forces defeated Yorkist forces led by the earl of Warwick at the second Battle of St Albans and regained custody of the king. At this point, London barred her entry, either because of the rumours about the lack of discipline in her army or because it had already committed to Edward's cause.[9]

On 27 February 1461, Edward and Warwick entered London. On 4 March, Edward took the throne: the killing of York, it was argued, meant that Henry VI had broken the Accord of the previous year and thus forfeited his right to the throne. More bloodshed followed. On Palm Sunday (29 March) Edward's forces defeated a Lancastrian force at Towton in what would be the longest, largest, and bloodiest battle of the Wars of the Roses.[10] The king, Queen Margaret, and their son, fled north to Scotland. On 28 June Edward was crowned king at Westminster Abbey.

The main problem facing Edward at this point was the fact that the former king, and his heir, still lived, thus providing a focus for the opposition of any stalwart Lancastrians or disaffected subjects. Much of the military activity of the first part of Edward's reign centred on Northumberland, and the control of the castles of Alnwick, Bamburgh, and Dunstanburgh. Malory, who had been released from prison following the Yorkist invasion in 1460, was present at the sieges that took place in 1462–3, serving under the earl of Warwick.[11] It may well be that Malory's suggestion that Lancelot's castle of Joyous Garde was either Alnwick or Bamburgh reflects his experience on campaign there (937.29–30 / C XXI.12).

By the end of the decade, England had returned to a state of civil war. This was due in particular to the actions of the earl of Warwick, popularly known with some justification as "the Kingmaker." As the decade went on, there were signs of a growing rift between the king and the earl, mainly over the direction of foreign policy. Edward's secret marriage to Elizabeth Woodville, which scuppered Warwick's plans for a marital alliance between the king and a foreign princess, hardly helped matters either. Malory's connection to Warwick may have implicated him in a plot against the king which was discovered in June 1468. He was certainly back in prison from this point onwards. He was specifically excluded, by name, from the general pardons of 14 July 1468 and 22 February 1470. This suggests that his had been a political crime; however, his imprisonment in Newgate,

[9] For the reputation of the Lancastrian forces, see Anthony Goodman, *The Wars of the Roses: Military Activity and English Society 1452–97* (London, 1981), 214–16. Clement Paston's letter of 1461 to his brother, John Paston I, reflects this reputation, as it describes how "pepill in þe northe robbe and styll and ben apoyntyd to pill all thys cwntré, and gyffe a-way menys goodys and lyfflodys in all þe sowthe cwntré, and that wyll ask a myscheffe": *Paston Letters and Papers of the Fifteenth Century*, ed. Norman Davis, 2 vols. (Oxford, 1971–76), 1: 198.

[10] For the Battle of Towton in relation to Arthur's final battle against Mordred, see below, p. 20.

[11] P. J. C. Field, *The Life and Times of Sir Thomas Malory* (Cambridge, 1993), 200.

rather than the Tower of London where other of the known conspirators were imprisoned, does not.[12]

A series of uprisings in 1469, when Malory was completing the *Morte Darthur*, indicates the degree to which Edward's kingship was now in jeopardy. The first was a revolt in Yorkshire, known as Robin of Redesdale's rebellion. A second rising followed, and was quickly suppressed. A third, led by a member of the Conyers family – a local gentry family retained by Warwick – proved more troublesome. As the rebels moved south, Warwick crossed to Calais, with his daughter Isabel, and the king's brother, George, duke of Clarence. On 11 July Clarence and Isabel were married, in clear contravention of royal authority. The king's forces were defeated at Edgecote on 26 July and members of the queen's family were captured and executed.[13] In the wake of news of the defeat, Edward moved south, was captured by George Neville, archbishop of York and younger brother of Warwick, and was imprisoned. At this point, Warwick and Clarence seem to have tried to rule in the king's name, but the king's imprisonment made it virtually impossible for them to exert any authority. Ironically, a rebellion led by the staunch Lancastrian Humphrey Neville led to Edward's release, as Warwick was unable to raise the troops to repress the revolt.

Edward returned to London, but chose not to exact vengeance on the rebel lords. The following spring, however, Warwick and Clarence attempted to stir up rebellion once more. This rebellion failed, and they fled to France. It is at this point that Warwick and Clarence were forced into an extraordinary course of action: on 22 July 1470, Warwick and Margaret of Anjou were formally reconciled, and Warwick agreed to restore Henry VI, who had been imprisoned in the Tower of London since 1465, as king. Further risings occurred in the north of England; as Edward was in York quelling the rebellions, Warwick and Clarence returned to England. The commons of Kent rose once again; Henry was released from his imprisonment, and restored to the throne for a short period that is known as the Lancastrian Readeption. He was king in name only, clearly incapable of ruling at this point.

Edward fled to the Low Countries in early October 1470, where he was received by his brother-in-law, Charles the Bold, duke of Burgundy. The following months were spent preparing an invasion to recover his throne. On 13 March 1471 Edward, as had Bolingbroke, the future Henry IV, in 1399, landed at Ravenspur at the mouth of the river Humber, claiming that he wished only to reclaim the duchy of York. As he marched south he gained support, and on 3 April he and his brother Clarence were reconciled. On 11 April London admitted him. The readepted king, Henry, surrendered to Edward, and Edward marched towards St Albans. On 14 April his forces met with those of Warwick and his

[12] For different views on this issue, see P. J. C. Field, "Malory, Sir Thomas (1415x18–1471)," *Oxford Dictionary of National Biography*, Oxford University Press, 2004; online edn, May 2011 [http://www.oxforddnb.com/view/article/17899, accessed 5 April 2017], and Anne F. Sutton, "Malory in Newgate: A New Document," *The Library*, 7th series, 1 (2000): 243–62.

[13] For the following, see Rosemary Horrox, "Edward IV (1442–1483)," *Oxford Dictionary of National Biography*, Oxford University Press, 2004; online edn, September 2011 [http://www.oxforddnb.com/view/article/8520, accessed 2 April 2017].

allies at Barnet. There, the Lancastrian forces were defeated, and Warwick was killed.

Queen Margaret and her son, Prince Edward, still needed to be dealt with. At the battle of Tewkesbury, fought on 4 May 1471, the queen's forces were defeated, and Prince Edward was killed. By the end of the month, Henry VI was dead, almost certainly murdered on Edward IV's orders. At long last, Edward's hold on the realm was secure. By this point, however, Malory had finished writing the *Morte Darthur*, and was dead and buried in Greyfriars, Newgate.

## *The* Morte Darthur *in Historical Context*

Critics have identified various points of intersection between the *Morte Darthur* and its historical context. For some critics, particular details of Malory's text recall the events, or contemporary descriptions of the events, that took place during the Wars of the Roses.[14] The most extensive overview of such connections has been provided by P. J. C. Field. Field, for example, has suggested that the detail that guns were used during Mordred's siege of the Tower of London (915.24 / C XXI.1) may recall the Yorkist siege of the Tower in 1460, and that Malory's comment in the opening tale that "Thenne stood the reame in grete jeaopardy long whyle, for every lord that was myghty of men maade hym stronge, and many wende to have ben kyng" (6.27–9 / C I.3–5) may reflect "his memories of drifting into civil war."[15] He has also seen a number of correspondences between contemporary accounts of the Battle of Towton and Arthur's final battle.[16]

The *Morte Darthur*, however, resists easy historicisation. Malory rarely encourages his readers to connect his narrative with contemporary events and he rarely comments on the potential parallels between the Arthurian world and his own. Even in the example with which I opened this chapter, scholars are divided about exactly which king Malory is referring to. Is he castigating Englishmen for abandoning Henry or for abandoning Edward? Or is he, as seems more likely, pointing not to an isolated, momentary switch of allegiance, but a more entrenched and long-established English habit of getting rid of their kings?[17] And that address has its own literary history as well. Although it is not present in

---

[14] P. J. C. Field, "Fifteenth-Century History in Malory's *Morte Darthur*," in his *Malory: Texts and Sources* (Cambridge, 1998), 47–71.

[15] Field, "Fifteenth-Century History," 65 and 53. For alternative explanations of this detail, see E. D. Kennedy, "Malory's *Morte Darthur*: A Politically Neutral English Adaptation of the Arthurian Story," *Arthurian Literature* XX (2003): 145–70, at 154.

[16] For example, the presence of moonlight, the pillagers on the battlefield following the battle, and the duration of the battle: P. J. C. Field, "Malory and the Battle of Towton," in *The Social and Literary Contexts of Malory's* Morte Darthur, ed. D. Thomas Hanks Jr and Jessica G. Brogdon (Cambridge, 2000), 68–74. Some of these details are in Malory's sources, while others are common to battle accounts of the period: Kennedy, "Malory's *Morte Darthur*," 154.

[17] This was certainly the politically-useful view of the English developed over the course of the fifteenth century in France, in the wake of the deposition of Richard II. For such views, see Craig Taylor, "'Weep Thou for Me in France': French Views of the Deposition of Richard II," in *Fourteenth Century England, III*, ed. W. Mark Ormrod (Woodbridge, 2004), 207–22.

Malory's sources, it recalls in some ways Geoffrey of Monmouth's address to the Britons in the *Historia Regum Britanniae* (c. 1138), the text that effectively invented Arthurian literature.[18] Indeed, that so much of the material that makes up the *Morte Darthur* has its own prior history means that attempts to historicise the text have to attend to what was and was not already present in Malory's sources, while also recognising that the commonplace, conventional or pre-existing can take on a renewed force and relevance in their own particular historical moment.

One way in which Malory does, of course, encourage his readers to iden- tify with the narrative he presents is by turning the mythic or imprecise land- scape of his sources into a recognisable one. Thus, Ascolat becomes Guildford (804.25 / C XVIII.8); the unnamed river by which the Maid of Ascolat arrives at Westminster becomes the Thames (828.13 / C XVIII.19); and Camelot, we are told, is also called Winchester (804.5 / C XVIII.8).[19] Sometimes these changes seem to have a particular political or topical relevance – for example, Malory specifies that the battle between Uther and "a gret hoost of the North" takes place at St Albans (6.5 / C I.3–5), a detail not in his source. As mentioned above (pp. 17 and 18), two battles were fought at or near St Albans during the Wars of the Roses, and this may have been what prompted Malory to make this addition. But even here it is difficult to establish what Malory hoped to achieve by the allusion or indeed even if he had those battles in mind: he may have got the detail from John Hardyng's *Chronicle*, one of his minor sources, which also makes St Albans the site of Uther's last battle.[20]

Although attempts have been made to read parts of the *Morte Darthur* as referring to specific events and people, the most fruitful approach over the past two decades has been to historicise the *Morte Darthur* by situating it in its wider discursive context, relating it to the wider preoccupations, interests, and discur- sive strategies of both the period and Malory's likely readership. Such a project requires multiple types of contextualisation – knowledge of other forms and texts – and of the broad range of material to which Malory and his readership might have been exposed. Scholarship of the last two decades has thus sought to recover the concerns and interests of the period in which Malory wrote and has

[18] Geoffrey of Monmouth, *The History of the Kings of Britain: an Edition and Translation of De gestis Britonum [Historia Regum Britanniae]*, ed. Michael Reeve and trans. Neil Wright (Woodbridge, 2007), 257, lines 141–54.

[19] Scholarship has illuminated how such rewritings might relate to wider understand- ings of regional political identities, identities and allegiances which were under par- ticular pressure and scrutiny during the period of the Wars of the Roses. For examples of this work, see Robert L. Kelly, "Malory's 'Tale of King Arthur' and the Political Geography of Fifteenth-Century England," in *Re-viewing Le Morte Darthur*, ed. K. S. Whetter and Raluca L. Radulescu (Cambridge, 2005), 79–93; Dorsey Armstrong and Kenneth Hodges, *Mapping Malory: Regional Identities and National Geographies in Le Morte Darthur* (New York, 2014). See also Meg Roland's chapter in this volume.

[20] For discussion, see Field, "Fifteenth-Century History," 50–3. Field suggests that the two battles "were too well-known for him to have failed to notice that he was creat- ing an analogue of recent events" and that "a number of similarities" between the first battle and Uther's last battle "strongly suggests that he had it in mind" (p. 51). Several scholars have demonstrated that Hardyng was a minor source for Malory; for example, Edward D. Kennedy, "Malory's Use of Hardyng's Chronicle," *Notes and Queries* 16 (1969): 167–70; Ralph Norris, *Malory's Library: the Sources of the Morte Darthur* (Cambridge, 2008).

turned to a variety of sources to recover these concerns and interests: the gentry letters which survive, for example, those of the Paston, Stonor, Plumpton, and Armburgh families; the texts and manuscripts owned by members of the gentry; and political discourse, as revealed by manifestoes, parliamentary speeches, political attainders, political verse and chronicles.

Raluca Radulescu's *The Gentry Context for Malory's Morte Darthur*, for example, both situates the *Morte Darthur* in its historical context and explores how Malory rewrote his sources in ways which would resonate particularly with his gentry readership.[21] In order to establish the probable concerns and attitudes of this readership, Radulescu considers the anthologies owned by members of the gentry, manuscript compilations which contained works relating to the issues of good governance, kingship and counsel. Thus, Radulescu illuminates the shared concerns of the *Morte Darthur*, other fifteenth-century reading material, and members of Malory's audience. She establishes that the values of worship, lordship, friendship and fellowship were of crucial importance to the fifteenth-century gentry, and she examines the treatment of these same concerns in the *Morte Darthur*. The situation of Malory's work within a wider reading culture has also been the aim of other scholars over the past two decades, and, in mapping this wider textual culture, critics have contributed to a deeper, more nuanced, historicisation of Malory's work.[22]

In the remainder of this chapter, I shall concentrate on three related areas that have been identified by critics as of crucial concern during the period in which Malory was writing – loyalty and treason, kingship and counsel, and war and peace – and I shall gesture towards some of the ways in which Malory's text has been seen as engaging with those contemporary concerns and anxieties which were all naturally raised by the tumultuous events narrated in the first part of this chapter.

## Loyalty and Treason

Megan Leitch argues that the rise in public disorder and the absence of royal authority which marked the 1450s "gave rise to heightened concerns about instability" and that, for the landowning classes, whose responsibility it was to maintain public order, "social cohesion, and its antithesis, treason, were of pressing concern."[23] She identifies in this period and in its writing – prose romances, political attainders, poems and gentry correspondence – "uncertainty regarding to whom a lack of loyalty was treasonous" and anxiety around being falsely accused of treason oneself.[24] The vocabulary of treason abounds in this

---

[21] Radulescu, *The Gentry Context for Malory's* Morte Darthur.

[22] See, for example, Thomas H. Crofts, *Malory's Contemporary Audience: The Social Reading of Romance in Late Medieval England* (Cambridge, 2006); Karen Cherewatuk, "Sir Thomas Malory's 'Grete Boke'," in *Social and Literary Contexts*, ed. Hanks and Brogdon, 42–67.

[23] Megan G. Leitch, *Romancing Treason: The Literature of the Wars of the Roses* (Oxford, 2015), 8–9.

[24] Leitch, *Romancing Treason*, 20.

period; for example, the bill of attainder of the duke of Suffolk submitted by the commons to parliament in 1450 uses the collocation "falsely and traiterously" six times, and such vocabulary is also pronounced in Malory's *Morte Darthur*, where Malory frequently alters his sources by using terms such as "traytoure" and "traytourly."[25]

Accusations of treason were likewise rife. The bill presented by Richard, duke of York, to the king in 1450 complains of the treatment he had received upon his return from Ireland, treatment which he says stems from the unfounded accusation that he had "come ayenst your entente as your traitor."[26] In a second bill addressed to the king, York laments that Henry was "cunduite by suche unsaciable, covetous thristelowe colde kowghe hertes y broughte up of noughte" ["guided by such insatiable, covetous, thirsty, cold cough hearts brought up from nothing"], and urged the king to charge such men with treason.[27] These bills clearly had a wider circulation.[28] The literature of this period thus reveals "an anxiety about the breakdown of social order and of traditional loyalties" and a concomitant preoccupation with treason, which encompasses both "hierarchical" treason (betraying one's king or overlord) and "horizontal" treason (the betrayal of friends, companions, neighbours or family). The *Morte Darthur*'s preoccupation with treason is most evident in those moments when Malory is narrating "the internal politics of the Arthurian realm."[29] Such an emphasis, Leitch demonstrates, is often added by Malory as he rewrites and alters his source material. She demonstrates that Malory "questions institutional conceptions of what constitutes loyalty to the king and realm," but is also engaged in a critique of institutionalised legal practices, evident in particular in Malory's account of the way that Arthur is compelled to abide by the laws regarding treason when condemning Guenevere to death in the final tale of the *Morte Darthur*.[30] In Leitch's reading, the *Morte* not only responds to contemporary concerns around treason, but also acts in the real world of its readers, attempting to promote "a renewal of personal loyalties and community-focused justice."[31]

Assertions of loyalty were fundamental to the working of political complaint. As is clear from the events of these decades narrated above, this period is marked by popular rebellion and uprisings. Those who took part in such uprisings shared an insistence that they were loyal subjects. Jack Cade's rebels, for example, repeatedly identified themselves as the king's "trew legemen" and

---

[25] Leitch, *Romancing Treason*, 25–6.

[26] Leitch, *Romancing Treason*, 37. The bill and Henry's response to it are printed in R. A. Griffiths, "Duke Richard of York's Intentions in 1450 and the Origins of the Wars of the Roses," *Journal of Medieval History* 1 (1975): 187–209, at 203–4, and in *The Politics of Fifteenth-Century England: John Vale's Book*, ed. M. L. Kekewich et al. (Gloucester, 1995), 185–6.

[27] "Articles of the Duke of York to the King and Council," in *John Vale's Book*, ed. Kekewich et al., 187–8, at 187. A "cold cough" is a cough which derives from a cold humour, like phlegm. Those with a phlegmatic complexion were considered to be cowardly, which is presumably the implication here: see Virginia Langum, *Medicine and the Seven Deadly Sins in Late Medieval Literature and Culture* (Basingstoke, 2016), 66.

[28] Leitch, *Romancing Treason*, 38.

[29] Leitch, *Romancing Treason*, 95.

[30] Leitch, *Romancing Treason*, 111–13.

[31] Leitch, *Romancing Treason*, 130.

his "trewe comyns" in contrast to the "false traytours" who surrounded him; Richard, duke of York, referred to himself as King Henry's "trewe liegeman"; Robin of Redesdale's rebels termed themselves King Edward's "true commones and subgiettes."[32] They thus constructed the criticism they offered as coming from a position of loyalty, motivated by a concern for the common weal, rather than from the pursuit of personal ambition and gain. Malory often emphasises that the people of the realm are Arthur's subjects – his preferred term is that they are his "liege people," meaning that they owe him allegiance. He often also specifies, in a way that his sources do not, that they are his "*true* liege people."[33] Of course, specifying that these are faithful subjects implies the existence of those who are not.

The *Morte Darthur* frets about loyalty: the loyalty subjects owe to their king, the loyalty owed to family, the loyalty owed to one's companions. It depicts a society that it is undone at least in part by the competing loyalties which ultimately work to prolong feud. As many critics have emphasised, as the narrative goes on, more attention is paid to the debts of loyalty owed by virtue of blood relationships, and emphasis is increasingly placed on the knights' familial relationship to one another.[34] Gareth's loyalty to Lancelot, a knight whose company he explicitly prefers over the members of his own family, is established when Lancelot makes him knight – and this is acknowledged not only by Lancelot and Gareth but by other knights as an important bond, one which makes Lancelot's unfortunate, accidental killing of Gareth more horrific.

The destruction of the fellowship of knights is driven by Gawain's need to avenge the death of his brother, Gareth, a need which forces Arthur into supporting his nephew and renders calls for peace futile. But, ironically, it is precisely that familial disposition towards vengefulness which Gareth has rejected in the preceding tales. In the "Tale of Sir Gareth of Orkney" we are told that as soon as Gareth observes Gawain's character, "he wythdrewe hymself fro his brother Sir Gawaynes felyshyp, for he was evir vengeable, and where he hated he wolde be avenged with murther, and that hated Sir Gareth" (285.30–2 / C VII.35). On hearing of the murder of Sir Lamerok, Gareth directly repudiates blood feud and disassociates himself from that familial trait seemingly shared by his Orkney brethren: "I undirstonde the vengeaunce of my brethirne, Sir Gawayne, Sir Aggravayne, Sir Gaherys, and Sir Mordred. But, as for me ... I meddyll nat of theire maters, and therefore is none of them that lovyth me" (553.28–35 / C

---

[32] Variant versions of the manifestoes of Cade's rebels are edited in I. M. W. Harvey, *Jack Cade's Rebellion of 1450* (Oxford, 1991), 186–91; for Richard, duke of York, and Robin of Redesdale, see *John Vale's Book*, ed. Kekewich et al., 189 and 215.

[33] At the beginning of "Balyn le Sauvage," for example, Arthur is told that King Royns of North Wales had entered Arthur's land and "brente and slew the kyngis trew lyege people" (47.9–12 / C II.1). Later on in the opening tale, Arthur promises to protect his "trwe lyege peple" (101.1–4 / C IV.2).

[34] Dorsey Armstrong, for example, shows how Malory emphasises kin relationships in the Grail Quest: *Gender and the Chivalric Community in Malory's* Morte Darthur (Gainesville, FL, 2003), 147–9. Kate McClune explores how "blood relationships repeatedly jeopardize the stability potentially offered by Arthur's alternative chivalric brotherhood of the Round Table" in "'The Vengeaunce of my Brethirne': Blood Ties in Malory's *Morte Darthur*," *Arthurian Literature* XXVIII (2011): 89–106, at 91.

X.58). Gawain too temporarily rejects vengeance following the death of his two sons and his brother Agravain at the beginning of the final tale, but the death of Gareth makes such a rejection unsustainable.

Vengeance and feud are not isolated to the final tale, but are present, to varying degrees, throughout the *Morte Darthur*. The effects of the Lot-Pellinor feud established in the opening tale, where Pellinor kills King Lot, the father of the Orkney brothers, and Gawain in retaliation kills Pellinor, permeate beyond the initial tale.[35] The murder of Sir Lamerok, Pellinor's son, at the hands of Sir Agravain, Gaherys and Mordred, is a continuation of that feud, exacerbated by Lamerok's affair with Morgawse, their mother. According to the account given by Sir Palomydes, the Orkney brothers set upon Lamerok "in a pryvy place" and Mordred "gaff hym his dethis wounde behynde hym at his bakke, and all to-hewe hym" (554.12–15 / C X.58). For Ruth Lexton, this murder functions as the "emblematic treasonous murder" of the *Morte Darthur*.[36] Crucially, justice is not meted out to the perpetrators. The *Morte* registers that it is Arthur's blood relationship to the knights that protects them, by having Tristram and Dynadan say as much: "yf they were nat cousyns of my lorde Kynge Arthure that slew hym, they sholde dye for hit" (553.22–3 / C X.58). Lexton regards the repeated references to Lamerok's murder in the final two tales – references added by Malory – as acting "as testimony among the knights to the failures of their bonds of fellowship."[37] Ultimately, the bonds forged between knights are rendered insufficient, unable to withstand the competing demands for loyalty the narrative makes of them.

## Kingship and Counsel

Across the late medieval period, the issue of who had access to the king – of who counselled him – was a source of concern. This was crucially a question of influence; those around the king could control who had access to him and could influence where the revenue he received was spent. A king's ability to receive counsel and to surround himself with able advisers was an expectation of good

---

[35] For the view that Malory's emphasis on the feud between the Orkney clan and De Galys clan relates to the gentry feuds of the period, see Field, "Fifteenth-Century History," 48–9. Sally Mapstone stresses the importance of the Orkney brothers being Scottish, and relates Malory's presentation of the feud to Scottish politics of the time, in particular the civil war between James II and the Douglases. She suggests that James Douglas, exiled in England and involved in some of the events of the Wars of the Roses, who relentlessly pursued his feud against the king, "would have afforded Malory a potent example of the powerful and disruptive character that a Scottish blood feud could have": "Malory and the Scots," *Arthurian Literature* XXVIII (2011): 107–20, at 113. See also Cory Rushton, "'Of an uncouthe stede': The Scottish Knight in Middle English Arthurian Romances", in *The Scots and Medieval Arthurian Legend*, ed. Rhiannon Purdie and Nicola Royan (Cambridge, 2005), 109–19.

[36] Ruth Lexton, *Contested Language in Malory's* Morte Darthur: *The Politics of Romance in Fifteenth-Century England* (New York, 2014), 143. Lexton considers treason along with other "politically-charged" terms: the commons, justice, counsel, rule, worship, courtesy, service and fellowship.

[37] Lexton, *Contested Language*, 149.

kingship, one which was perpetuated, for example, in the popular genre of the mirror for princes, advisory literature which was addressed to princes but was read by those lower down the social scale too. Who was giving counsel, and the nature of that counsel, were the targets of severe criticism during the Wars of the Roses.

In surviving manifestoes, for example, Cade's rebels complain about the presence of "certeyn persones" about the king, men who were "insaciable covetows malicious pompes, and fals" and, like the men Malory tells us betrayed Arthur, "of nowght browght up" who "dayly enforme hym that good is evyll and evyll is good."[38] The loss of lands and the king's poverty and mounting debts provided the evidence that the king had received "ffalse counsayle." The "traytours" who surrounded him made sure that they benefitted personally from any revenue that came to the king.[39] The king's natural counsellors ought to be nobles of royal blood. Instead, the king was surrounded by low-born counsellors. Such men impeded the progress of law, preventing the king from even hearing about the lawlessness taking place in the realm unless substantial bribes were paid.[40]

These complaints also surface in the poems that circulated in these months. "A Warning to King Henry," for example, states that such advisers "have made the kyng so pore, / That now he beggeth fro dore to dore."[41] Indeed, the issues outlined in Cade's manifesto – of poor counsel, self-interested advisers, and the parlous state of royal finances – continued to occupy a prominent place in the rhetorical landscape of the 1450s and 1460s. Richard, duke of York, reiterated some of these criticisms and indeed used some of the language of the rebels' manifestoes. In another bill addressed to the king he echoed the language of Cade's manifesto, explaining that "it is a grete pite to thinke on that so gracieux and mighty prince for the singularite of the thristelewe, coveitous and colde kowardise I broughte up of noughte, shold cause thise inconvenientes, lossis and pouertie and dissolacions." These same traitors "have caused the losses of his glorious reaume of France."[42]

In the late 1460s, when Malory was finishing the *Morte Darthur*, similar issues were once more at stake. The manifesto issued by the rebel lords on 12 July 1469 offered a transhistorical explanation of why previous kings – Edward II, Richard II, Henry VI – had been undone, with the clear implication that Edward IV would soon follow in their footsteps. The old issues of poor counsel, excessive taxation, the corrupt execution of the law, and the poverty of the king were reprised. In addition, the manifesto singled out specific "seditious persons" about the king, identified as the recently-created earls of Pembroke and Devon, and members of

---

[38] *Three Fifteenth-Century Chronicles: With Historical Memoranda by John Stowe, the Antiquary, and Contemporary Notes of Occurrences Written by Him in the Reign of Queen Elizabeth*, ed. James Gairdner, Camden Society, n.s. 28 (Westminster, 1880), 94–9, at 94.

[39] Harvey, *Jack Cade's Rebellion*, 189.

[40] Harvey, *Jack Cade's Rebellion*, 189.

[41] *Political Poems and Songs Relating to English History*, ed. Thomas Wright, 2 vols. (London, 1861), II, 229.

[42] "Articles of the Duke of York to the King and Council," in *John Vale's Book*, ed. Kekewich et al., 187–8, at 188.

the queen's family – her father, Earl Rivers, and his wife, the duchess of Bedford, and her brothers.[43]

Sarah Peverley has examined the recurrence of the phrase "brought of nought" across the *Morte*, political writings, and the work of some of Malory's contemporaries.[44] She demonstrates its particular political valence at this point. John Vale, who compiled a collection of topical political documents at some point in the late 1470s or early 1480s, includes the phrase "brought up on nought" in his short chronicle of the events of 1431–71, explaining that Henry VI's problems started when he began to be "reuled by divers of his counsele suche as were not be comen of blood roiall, but that were broughte up on noughte."[45] She finds in the first version of John Hardyng's *Chronicle*, one of Malory's sources, which was presented to Henry VI in 1457, a tendency to attribute civil division to the actions of low-born men who had been raised to positions of authority. Malory uses the phrase twice, once in the quotation with which I opened this chapter, and on a second occasion in the book of Sir Tristram de Lyones. In this tale, the phrase occurs when King Harmaunce of the Red City is killed. Tristram, Gareth and Dynadan discover his corpse in a boat, and read the letter he dictated before he died. In that letter, Harmaunce asks the "noble knyghtes of Arthurs court" to avenge his death, and to fight against the "too bretherne that I brought up off nought" who have killed him (556.2–4 / C X.59). In a later episode, the example of Harmaunce functions as a warning to others. Sir Ebell explains that he was "a noble knyght, layrge and lyberall of his expence" but "he was destroyed in his owne defaute; for had he cheryshed his owne bloode, he had been a lyvis kynge and lyved with grete ryches and reste; but all astatys may beware by owre kynge" (560.26–561.4 / C X.59). Harmaunce favoured the two knights to the exclusion of men "of his owne bloode." Malory quotes an old saying: "Gyeff a chorle rule and thereby he woll nat be suffysed" and goes on to say "Therefore, all the astatys and lordys, of what astate ye be, loke you beware whom ye take aboute you" (561.20–6 / C X.61). The contents of the letter are given again, with Harmaunce emphasising that the knights were "of myne owne bryngynge up and of myne owne makyng" (562.10–11 / C X.62). Here the danger concerns promoting men "brought up of nought" and alienating men of noble birth, who, the implication is, will be loyal. In this way, then, Malory's text speaks to some of the key concerns of the period, but not in a way that is unproblematic or straightforward. This example of a good king undone by elevating men "brought up of nought" is in Malory's source, the thirteenth-century Old French *Prose Tristram*. But that it has its own prior literary history does not negate the resonance it must have had for the *Morte Darthur*'s first readers.

[43] John Warkworth, *Chronicle of the First Thirteen Years of the Reign of King Edward IV*, ed. J. O. Halliwell (London, 1839), 47–51.

[44] Sarah Peverley, "Political Consciousness and the Literary Mind in Late Medieval England: Men 'Brought up of nought' in Vale, Hardyng, *Mankind*, and Malory," *Studies in Philology* 105 (2008): 1–29.

[45] Peverley, "Political Consciousness," 10–11.

## Unity and Division, War and Peace

Malory's contemporaries, living through a period which witnessed the loss of the Lancastrian-held lands in France and civil war in England, saw a connection between successful outward war and the maintenance of internal unity and peace.[46] The perceived relationship here was twofold. On the one hand, various sources connected the return of demobilised soldiers and the men and women dispossessed by the cession of Maine and the loss of Normandy (see p. 16) to an increase in lawlessness and a decline in public order.[47] Charges brought against the duke of Suffolk refer to how "pillages, murders and ydelnesse, and cursednesse [were] brought amonge us" as a result of the loss of lands.[48] The author of "Bale's Chronicle," which dates from after 1461, likewise complains that those who had been "driven out" of France, Normandy and Anjou had returned to England and "drewe to theft and misrule and noyed sore the cominalte of þis land spirituell and temporell."[49]

On the other hand, political disunity, even civil war, was judged to be a consequence of an absence of outward war. This connection between lack of outward war and internal division was frequently made during the period in which Malory was writing, with writers often using classical examples or indeed classical texts to demonstrate its proof. The 1408 Middle English translation of the late Roman military manual, De re militari, a text which circulated among members of the gentry during this period, for example, drew attention to the damaging consequences of peace. An anonymous English translation of Christine de Pizan's Livre du Corps de Policie, made in c. 1470, likewise warned against prolonged peace and glossed outward war as positive and beneficial to a realm. The dangers of peace are persistent themes throughout this work; accordingly, "the werres of Rome profyted more to the citee than did ydelnesse. For many worchipfull realmes came to greate vertue by good exercise and to gret reste brought in ydelnesse and myschiefe."[50]

These discussions of the dangers of peace are often imprecise in defining the consequences of lack of outward war: they refer instead, like the examples cited above regarding the effect of returning soldiers, to "ydelnesse" and "slothe" from which various other harms stem. In this way, they recall Cador's speech in favour of war following the arrival of the Roman embassy. In that speech, which occurs in most versions of accounts of Arthur's reign following Geoffrey

---

[46] The following is based on Catherine Nall, Reading and War in Fifteenth-Century England: from Lydgate to Malory (Cambridge, 2012), 139–58.

[47] This view had fourteenth-century antecedents. As Mark Ormrod has argued, in the 1330s, "there was a widespread belief that soldiers returning from the wars were responsible for the increasing level of crime and violence": W. M. Ormrod, The Reign of Edward III: Crown and Political Society in England 1327–1377 (New Haven and London, 1990), 55.

[48] "The Charter Chests of the Family of Neville of Holt in the County of Leicester," Appendix to the Third Report of the Royal Commission on Historical Manuscripts (London, 1872), 279.

[49] "Bale's Chronicle," in Six Town Chronicles of England, ed. Ralph Flenley (Oxford, 1911), 114–52, at 128.

[50] The Middle English Translation of Christine de Pisan's Livre du corps de policie ed. from the MS CUL Kk 1 5, ed. Diane Bornstein (Heidelberg, 1977), 104, lines 16–19.

of Monmouth, Cador argues that God has sent them the Roman challenge to prevent them from falling further into slothfulness.[51] In these texts, as in Cador's speech, it is specifically military activity that is recommended as the necessary antidote to idleness.

These arguments concerning the mutual dependence of outward war and inward peace had particular force and relevance in the period in which Malory was composing his work. A range of texts produced in this period glossed the civil disorders of the 1450s and early 1460s as a product of a lack of outward war while also arguing that a new campaign against France would actively secure domestic peace. As early as 1449, before the loss of the English-held territories in France, there was concern that lack of outward war would have a wide-scale and potentially disastrous impact on the realm. According to a recommendation copied into one of notebooks of William Worcester, secretary to the veteran of the French wars, Sir John Fastolf,

> many English, nobles and others who, while the war in France lasted have been used to living splendidly and might not be able to continue that way of life in England, perhaps would strive to disturb our common weal; and then perhaps many familiar enemies who are currently lurking and deceiving us might rise up such as the Welsh, Scots and others, as much domestic as foreign.[52]

In the late 1460s, when Malory was writing, Edward IV began to consider a new campaign in France: on 17 May 1468 Edward's chancellor, Robert Stillington, bishop of Bath and Wells, announced that Edward intended to invade France. Stillington delivered a speech on this theme to parliament and urged those present to remember "the state and condicion that this reame stode yn" when Edward IV became king:

> for atte that tyme this londe was full naked and bareyn of justice, the peas not kepte, nor lawes duely mynystred within the same, and was also spoilled of the crowne of Fraunce.[53]

Edward intended to recover those lands in France "for the wele, suerte, peas and defence of this lond."[54] Stillington also suggested that outward war was necessary for the internal peace of England, as the "disposition of the people of this lond" meant that "they must be occupied."[55]

This wider context perhaps helps to explain one of Malory's innovations. In the second tale of the *Morte Darthur*, Malory departs from his main source, the

---

[51] In Malory's version, Cador states: "I am nat hevy of this message, for we have be many dayes rested us and have ben ydle. Now the lettyrs of Lucius the Emperoure lykis me well, for now shall we have warre and worship" (147.10–13 / C V.1).

[52] London, College of Arms, MS Arundel 48, fol. 333r, printed in *Letters and Papers Illustrative of the Wars of the English in France During the Reign of Henry VI*, ed. Joseph Stevenson, Rolls Series 22, 2 vols. (London: 1861–4), II, 726; my translation.

[53] *The Parliament Rolls of Medieval England, 1275–1504*, ed. Chris Given-Wilson et al., 16 vols. (Woodbridge and London, 2005), 13: 362. Hereafter referred to as *PROME*.

[54] *PROME*, 13: 364.

[55] *PROME*, 13: 364. These ideas were further developed in the speech delivered to parliament in 1472: see *Literae Cantuarienses: The Letter Books of the Monastery of Christ Church, Canterbury*, ed. J. B. Sheppard, Rolls Series 85, 3 vols. (London, 1887–9), III, 282.

late fourteenth-century poem, the Alliterative *Morte Arthure*, to offer an account of the success and aftermath of Arthur's Roman campaign that is significantly at odds both with that of his source and the majority of earlier insular narratives of this campaign. While in the Alliterative *Morte Arthure*, in a tradition stretching back to Geoffrey of Monmouth's *Historia Regum Britanniae* (c. 1138), Arthur never quite achieves the imperial crown and has to return to Britain to face rebellion, Malory not only has Arthur achieve imperial success, but also rewrites the chronology of the Roman war, moving it back to a much earlier point in Arthur's career and disconnecting it altogether from Arthur's downfall.[56] In earlier accounts of the Roman war episode, Arthur's war against the Romans is linked, either temporally or causally, to his downfall. This implication is most fully realised in Malory's source, which encourages an explanation of Arthur's fall which is grounded in his military activities on the Continent.[57] By repositioning the Roman war in this way, Malory thus discourages his readers from linking successful outward war in Europe to internal rebellion at home. Malory perhaps rewrote his source material in this way, following the position of the Roman war in the Vulgate cycle, as a result of the wider discursive context in which he was writing: one in which external war, far from creating internal division, was seen as promoting internal peace and in which civil war was regarded not as a product of outward war but rather of its absence.[58] This is not to say that Malory was consciously promoting a renewal of the war in France, or that he was suggesting that another war of conquest would have been enough to solve the problems that tear Arthur's England apart, but that he deliberately avoids making successful external war the cause for the downfall of the realm, a decision that may reflect the arguments being made with force in the period in which he was writing.[59]

*

The *Morte Darthur* is not political allegory. It engages with its historical moment in ways which are often suggestive, but rarely unproblematic or straightforward.

---

[56] John Hardyng, in the second version of his chronicle written before 1464, also has Arthur achieve the imperial crown.

[57] See, for example, *Morte Arthure: A Critical Edition*, ed. Mary Hamel (New York and London, 1984), lines 3396–3400.

[58] As previous scholars have noted, the idea of repositioning the Roman war may have been suggested to Malory by his reading of the Old French prose text, the Vulgate *Suite de Merlin*, which was a minor source for both his "Tale of King Arthur" and "Tale of Arthur and Lucius." In this version, the Roman war does not lead to Arthur's death, but is one in a series of major battles that takes place in the early years of his reign: *The Vulgate Version of the Arthurian Romances, Edited from Manuscripts in the British Museum*, ed. H. O. Somner, 8 vols. (Washington, 1908–16), II, 424–50.

[59] The *Morte Darthur* has been read in relation to the context of a proposed new campaign in France by other critics. Robert L. Kelly, for example, has argued that the *Morte Darthur* "portrays England and France as kingdoms whose internal stability and unity depend upon the support of one another," and he proposes that the work as a whole exhibits "pro-French, anti-war" sympathies which "could have been readily identifiable as a Lancastrian critique of King Edward IV's plans to reopen the Hundred Years' War": Robert L. Kelly, "Malory's Argument against War with France: the Political Geography of War with France and the Anglo-French Alliance in the *Morte Darthur*," in *Social and Literary Contexts*, ed. Hanks and Brogdon, 111–33, at 132–3. Kennedy counters this claim by pointing out that the pro-French view is present in Malory's sources: "Malory's *Morte Darthur*," 155.

For its first readers, though, reading the *Morte Darthur* in a context of civil war, it must surely have had an uncomfortable resonance. And of course it would continue to have such a resonance, as the civil strife of the fifteenth century did not end with Edward's recovery of the throne in 1471. Those who encountered Malory's text in its new form as it had been revised and altered by its first printer, William Caxton, would have done so in a renewed context of civil instability and political change, three weeks before the Battle of Bosworth and the accession of Henry Tudor.[60]

Malory opens the final tale of the *Morte Darthur* with an extraordinary inversion of the traditional May topos. This is used elsewhere in medieval literature – in lyrics and dream visions, for example – to frame explorations of courtly love and love longing, and indeed Malory uses it in this conventional sense earlier on in the *Morte Darthur* to introduce "The Knight of the Cart."[61] Malory places his final tale in this same May–time setting:

> In May, whan every harte floryshyth and burgenyth (for, as the season ys lusty to beholde and comfortable, so man and woman rejoysyth and gladith of somer commynge with his freyshe floures, for wynter wyth hys rowghe wyndis and blastis causyth lusty men and women to cowre and to syt by fyres). (870.1–7 / C XX.1)

May is the period of rebirth, of life, of generation and productivity, a time when hearts do what plants and trees do, where every heart "floryshyth" (blossoms, produces flowers) and "burgenyth" (grows, sprouts).[62] Malory uses the natural world here to point to the unnaturalness of civil war, its "unkyndeness" because, in Malory's rendition, May will not see new life, but death; summer may still come with its "fresh flowers," but it will not be enjoyed by "the floure of chyvalry" of the Arthurian world. That is, because it is in "thys season" that:

> hit befelle in the moneth of May a grete angur and unhappe that stynted nat tylle the floure of chyvalry of alle the worlde was destroyed and slayne. (870.7–11 / C XX.1)

For Malory's contemporaries the fear must have been that the "great angur and unhappe" that had defined the previous two decades would similarly not end until "the floure of chyvalry" of their own world had been destroyed.

---

[60] Caxton also engages with this context. In the dream which Arthur has while crossing the Channel in response to Lucius' demands for tribute, he sees a "dredfull dragon" fighting a bear. Caxton famously changes the bear to the boar, which was the badge of Richard III, thus making, according to Field, "a bold political allusion": Field, "Caxton's Roman War", 37, and see also discussion of this change in Crofts, *Malory's Contemporary Audience*, 97–99.

[61] "... the moneth of May was com, whan every lusty harte begynnyth to blossom and to burgyne. For, lyke as trees and erbys burgenyth and florysshyth in May, in lyke wyse every lusty harte that ys ony maner of lover spryngith, burgenyth, buddyth, and florysshyth in lusty dedis" (841.2–7 / C XVIII. 25).

[62] The same collocation appears in relation to trees and plants elsewhere, as above, where hearts similarly "sprout" and produce flowers.

# 2

## Malory and His Sources

RALPH NORRIS

Malory's *Morte Darthur* is often described as a compendium of medieval Arthurian literature. That is misleading, for, although it follows on from a great tradition of medieval Arthurian literature in French and English, it makes no comprehensive effort to represent the texts in this tradition, some of which Malory considered "auctorysed," others he rejected as merely the "favour of makers."[1] Nevertheless, the *Morte Darthur* is built out of its various sources in a way that may be unfamiliar to many modern readers. This method was more characteristic of the Middle Ages, but, even among medieval authors, Malory's use of diverse sources is highly unusual in being both so extensive and selective. This is doubtless why modern scholarship and criticism of Malory began in the late nineteenth century with source study.[2] Perhaps the first contribution of source studies to a greater understanding of Malory was the realization that Malory was more than a mere compiler.[3] Over a century later, Malory is perceived rather as a great literary artist with a sophisticated relationship to his sources. Significantly, as the number of works shown to have influenced Malory has grown, so has the evidence of the independence with which Malory handled these sources. The larger number of these are minor sources, and the appreciation of how greatly the cumulative effect of their use adds to Malory's achievement has been the major innovation in Malory source studies since the publication of the predecessor to this Companion.[4]

Malory produced the first full account in English prose of the life of Arthur, together with the rise and fall of the Round Table, and while "reducing" the story from his major sources, in Caxton's term, he also added a wealth of details taken from his extensive reading. Malory's sources consist primarily of selections from French and English Arthurian literature and are usefully discussed as falling into the categories of major and minor. The major sources themselves can be divided

---

[1] Sir Thomas Malory, *Le Morte Darthur*, ed. P. J. C. Field, 2 vols. (Cambridge, 2013), I, 940.7–12.

[2] H. Oskar Sommer, *Studies on the Sources*, which is vol. 3 of his edition of Malory, *Le Morte Darthur*, 3 vols. in 4 (London, 1889–91); see also what is perhaps the first book-length study of Malory independent of an edition: Vida D. Scudder, *Le Morte Darthur of Sir Thomas Malory and Its Sources* (New York, 1921).

[3] Sommer, *Studies on the Sources*, 8.

[4] See Ralph Norris, *Malory's Library: The Sources of the* Morte Darthur (Cambridge, 2008); cf. *A Companion to Malory*, ed. Elizabeth Archibald and A. S. G. Edwards (Cambridge, 1996).

broadly into the French prose romance cycles from which Malory derived the overarching structure of Arthur's life history and the English poems that provided important episodes within that structure.

This chapter considers Malory's book as a whole and its relationship to its myriad sources. The major sources are discussed together first, before reflecting on the use Malory made of them; then follows a discussion of the minor sources and then the discernible traces of lost and oral sources. To give a sense of the scope of Malory's sources, this chapter includes a table, in which major sources of each tale are set out in boldface. The chapter then ends with a discussion of the contribution of source study to the major controversies in Malory scholarship over the past century and in the past two decades in particular.

## Malory's Major Sources

Malory's *Morte Darthur* is the ultimate product of a complex of medieval prose romances that developed over the course of the thirteenth century, through the work of many hands.[5] It is thought that the most important cycle of this complex, known as the Lancelot-Grail Cycle,[6] was conceived as a unity by a single person, referred to as the architect.[7] However, it too had its antecedents, and later writers responded to this cycle and to each other to produce a series of cycles that could not have been envisioned by any single person. Collectively, these works elaborate on the stories of Arthur and his knights as established by the twelfth-century romances, answering implicit questions that these raised and providing full life histories of a vast array of major characters, resulting in an Arthurian *summa* which itself is set into the larger contexts of both British and biblical history.

The idea of combining stories of Arthur and his knights into cycles seems to have begun with the work of Robert de Boron in the early thirteenth century.[8] Taking inspiration from Chrétien de Troyes's twelfth-century Grail romance, *Perceval*, and its continuations, Robert's work relates the history of the Grail from its beginning in first-century Palestine to its appearance in Arthurian Britain. He then connects the Grail history to the story of Merlin, by altering the older story that Merlin was fathered upon a virgin by an invisible spirit of the air. In Robert's version, Merlin's father is now a demon, and Merlin's conception is an unsuccessful attempt to create an infernal counterpart to Christ. It is usually thought that he wrote in verse that was later adapted, either by himself or

---

[5] For a more detailed discussion see *A Companion to the Lancelot-Grail Cycle*, ed. Carol Dover (Cambridge, 2003), and the individual entries in *The Arthur of the French. The Arthurian Legend in Medieval French and Occitan Literature*, ed. Glyn S. Burgess and Karen Pratt (Cardiff, 2006), 274–324.

[6] This phrase is sometimes used to describe the entire Vulgate Cycle in its final form, for which see below, and sometimes, as here, in reference to the three romances known as the Prose *Lancelot*, *Queste del Sainte Graal* and *Mort Artu*.

[7] This idea was first put forward by Jean Frappier, *Étude sur la* Mort le roi Artu (Paris, 1936), 27–146.

[8] See Rupert T. Pickens, "Robert de Boron," in *Arthur of the French*, ed. Burgess and Pratt, 247–59.

someone unknown, into a surviving prose trilogy.[9] Of the poetic cycle, only the
first branch, *Joseph d'Aramathie,* and about 500 lines of the *Merlin* (both *c.* 1200)
survive.[10] The prose version of the *Merlin,* however, survives in its entirety. In
it, Merlin guides British kings and aids in Arthur's birth in a story adapted from
Geoffrey of Monmouth's *Historia regum Britanniae* (*History of the Kings of Britain,*
1138).[11] This prose version, which concludes with Arthur's coronation, is followed
by a prose *Perceval* (sometimes called the Didot *Perceval* after the name of the
owner of the earliest known manuscript), which may have been likewise adapted
from a lost poem by Robert. The prose *Perceval* also contains a version of the fall
of Arthur's kingdom, and a prose adaptation of the *Joseph* is connected to the
prose *Merlin* to form the first Arthurian prose cycle, intertwining the history of
the Holy Grail with the history of Arthur's kingdom.[12] The prose *Perceval* appears
to have soon been overshadowed by the popularity of later versions of the Grail
quest, but the *Joseph* and the *Merlin* became the basis for the longer versions of the
Vulgate Cycle.[13] Although Malory chose not to include the pre-Arthurian history
of the Grail, Malory's story from the beginning of his book up to Arthur's coronation comes ultimately from the *Merlin* attributed to Robert de Boron.

The urge to complete the narrative of Chrétien's unfinished *Perceval* also
led an unknown author to write the independent prose romance known as the
*Perlesvaus.*[14] It is generally considered to be either one of the first prose romances
and influential in the development of the Lancelot-Grail, or else, conversely, a
late derivative romance; there is no real consensus.[15] If the *Perlesvaus* was an early
creation, it would fill a gap in the history of French prose Arthurian literature
between the prose trilogy attributed to Robert de Boron and the Lancelot-Grail
Cycle. The *Perlesvaus* is a longer story with more interlaced adventures of a larger
cast than can be found in the trilogy attributed to Robert de Boron, but much
shorter and less complicated than the Lancelot-Grail. Also, prominent themes
in the Lancelot-Grail, such as the consequences of Lancelot's and Guinevere's
relationship and the enmity of Claudas for Lancelot, appear as if in a less developed state in the *Perlesvaus.* Whether *Perlesvaus* was innovative or derivative, it

---

[9] For a contrary interpretation of the evidence, see Linda Gowans, "What did Robert de
    Boron really Write?" in *Arthurian Studies in Honour of P. J. C. Field,* ed. Bonnie Wheeler
    (Cambridge, 2004), 15–28.
[10] Robert de Boron, *Le roman de l'estoire dou Graal,* ed. William Nitze (Paris, 1999); and
    Robert de Boron, *Merlin: roman du XIIIe siècle,* ed. Alexandre Micha (Geneva, 1980).
[11] Geoffrey of Monmouth, *The History of the Kings of Britain,* ed. Michael Reeve, trans.
    Neil Wright (Cambridge, 2007).
[12] Robert de Boron, *Le roman du Graal,* ed. Bernard Cerquiglini (Paris, 1981); and for an
    English translation, see *Merlin and the Grail,* trans. Nigel Bryant (Cambridge, 2001).
[13] This cycle is called the "Vulgate" because it was vulgar in the sense of "common" or
    "standard." The Vulgate Cycle is discussed further later in this chapter.
[14] *Le haut livre du Graal: Perlesvaus,* ed. William Nitze and T. Atkinson Jenkins, 2 vols.
    (New York, 1932–37); for an English translation, see *The High Book of the Grail,* trans.
    Nigel Bryant (Cambridge, 2007).
[15] See Andrea M. L. Williams, "Perlesvaus," in *Arthur of the French,* 260–4. For a recent
    discussion of the position of the *Perlesvaus* in the continuum of thirteenth-century Old
    French prose romances, see David F. Hult, "From Perceval to Galahad: A Missing
    Link?" in *"De Sens Rassis": Essays in Honor of Rupert T. Pickens,* ed. Keith Busby et al.
    (Amsterdam, 2005), 265–81.

was known to Malory and was the source of one of the adventures in his tale "Sir Lancelot du Lake."

The next step in the series that would eventually provide Malory with his material was the creation of a prose life history of Lancelot, the aforementioned Lancelot-Grail Cycle (1220–30).[16] It is hard to say to what extent it was influenced by the prose romances that came before. The Lancelot-Grail Cycle itself may or may not have been inspired by the prose trilogy attributed to Robert de Boron; and if an early date for the *Perlesvaus* is assumed, it may have been commissioned to be the Grail quest for this new series but later rejected.[17] This new cycle's central character is arguably Lancelot himself rather than Arthur, and its main theme is the power of noble love, as demonstrated by the great courtly love affair between him and Guinevere. In the first romance of this cycle, the prose *Lancelot* itself, its young hero is brought up in the realm of the Lady of the Lake after the fall of his parents' kingdom to the villainous King Claudas. Lancelot comes to adulthood unaware of his royal status but has a natural instinct towards noble behavior. This leads him to ask the lady to take him to Arthur's court to be knighted, and while there he sees Queen Guinevere for the first time and instantly falls in love with her. Inspired by this love, Lancelot strives until he becomes Arthur's greatest knight. Eventually he saves Arthur's realm from an irresistible invader who surrenders in recognition of Lancelot's superlative nobility. Lancelot also completes numerous adventures that imply that he is the greatest knight in the world, and leads a war to reclaim his father's kingdom.

In the last two branches of this cycle, *La Queste del Saint Graal* (*The Quest for the Holy Grail*) and *La Mort Artu* (*The Death of Arthur*), the great medieval ideal of noble love that is celebrated so much in the *Lancelot* is now brought into conflict with the spiritual ideals of medieval monastic Christianity and with the ideal of loyalty to one's liege. The first conflict costs Lancelot his chance to achieve a full vision of the Holy Grail, the reward of which is a full, earthly communion with God, and the second is an important element in the fracturing of the Round Table fellowship and the destruction of Arthur's realm. Critics have long referred to the double spirit of *The Lancelot-Grail Cycle*, because it celebrates adulterous courtly love and condemns it in turn, but perhaps one might better speak of a

---

[16] This cycle itself may have been preceded by a non-cyclic version of the prose *Lancelot*. See Elspeth Kennedy, "The Making of the *Lancelot-Grail Cycle*," in *Companion to the Lancelot-Grail Cycle*, ed. Dover, 13–22.

[17] See further J. Neale Carman, *A Study of the Pseudo-Map Cycle of Arthurian Romance* (Wichita, KS, 1973), and Elspeth Kennedy, *Lancelot and the Grail* (Oxford, 1986). Two symposiums have been devoted to the problems involved in the study of the French prose cycles, *Cyclifaction: The Development of Narrative Cycles in the Chanson de Geste and the Arthurian Romances*, ed. Bart Besamusca et al. (Amsterdam, 1994) and *Transtextualities: Of Cycles and Cyclicity in Medieval French Literature*, ed. Sara Sturm-Maddox and Donald Maddox (Birmingham, NY, 1996). Carol J. Chase, "La fabrication du Cycle du Lancelot-Graal," *Bibliographical Bulletin of the International Arthurian Society* 61 (2009): 261–80, argues that the romances of the Lancelot-Grail were composed simultaneously.

triple spirit of loyalty to one's lady, to God, and to one's lord, as exemplified by Lancelot, Galahad, and Gawain.[18]

The Lancelot-Grail Cycle was popular enough to cause one or more authors (but not, it is thought, the original architect, nor anyone under his direction) to wish to complete the story by recasting the prose *Joseph* and prose *Merlin* to fit the events it depicts. *L'estoire del Saint Graal* (*The History of the Holy Grail*) connects the beginning of the cycle to its end with a prologue set in the year 717, therefore narrating events subsequent to *Mort Artu* before moving to the chronological beginning of the cycle. *L'estoire* follows the basic plotline of the *Joseph* but augments its depiction of events to set up all of the prophecies, artifacts and characters that figure in the *Queste* and by adding genealogies of the major Arthurian characters that connect them to the cast of the *L'estoire*. A long continuation (in French, a *suite*) was then added to the prose *Merlin* to bridge the period between the coronation of Arthur and the childhood of Lancelot. The Vulgate *Suite du Merlin* occupies itself mostly with the large-scale battles of a protracted series of civil wars against rebellious barons, which Arthur must wage to unite his kingdom. Over the course of these wars, important characters like Gawain reach maturity and are impelled by Arthur's nobility themselves to rebel against their rebellious fathers, eventually bringing the wars to a successful conclusion. The narrative climax of the Vulgate *Suite* occurs when a united Britain faces the challenge of the Roman Empire with a campaign in which Arthur conquers Rome and becomes emperor himself. The *Suite* ends by foretelling the coming of Lancelot, thus completing the most popular of all the prose cycles, which scholars since the nineteenth century have called the Vulgate Version of the Arthurian Romances,[19] or, more briefly, the Vulgate Cycle.[20] The Vulgate gave Malory the main source for his "Tale of the Sankgreal," "Sir Lancelot and Queen Guenivere" and "The Morte Arthur," as well as the majority of his "Sir Lancelot."

In the middle decades of the thirteenth century, this cycle served as the basis for two new cyclic creations. The next development was the production of a prose *Tristan* in emulation of the prose *Lancelot*. Just as the previous work had expanded on the relationship of Lancelot and Guinevere in the context of the ongoing adventures of Arthur's kingdom, so the latter work focuses on the

---

[18] The idea of Gawain as such an exemplar might be surprising to readers who know him primarily through Malory, where, although valiant and well intentioned, he is often volatile and "evir vengeable, and where he hated he wolde be avenged with murther" (285.31–2 / C VII.35). This depiction of Gawain comes to Malory largely from the prose *Tristan*, for which see below. In the Vulgate Cycle, Gawain is a far more positive character, much more comparable to his depiction in Chrétien's romances and in *Sir Gawain and the Green Knight*. For a detailed look at how Gawain's character slowly shifted from a paragon of courtesy to a vengeful hothead, see Keith Busby, *Gauvain in Old French Literature* (Amsterdam, 1980).

[19] Oskar Sommer is often given the credit for originating this designation, but the term must antedate him because in the introduction to his edition of the Vulgate he refers to it as commonly so called already.

[20] The first modern edition of the entire Vulgate Cycle has been published under the title *Livre du Graal*, ed. Phillippe Walter et al. 3 vols. (Paris, 2001–2009). For an English translation, see *Lancelot-Grail: The Old French Arthurian Vulgate and Post-Vulgate in Translation*, gen. ed. Norris J. Lacy, 10 vols (Cambridge, 2010).

parallel story of Tristan and Isode interlaced among other adventures in the court of King Mark of Cornwall. The history of this work is like a microcosm of the Arthurian prose romance cycles, in that it exists in a series of redactions, in this case four major versions and a number of unique versions.[21] Early versions are remarkably consistent with the Vulgate Cycle; the author clearly envisioned the *Tristan* as further adventures in the same fictional world. In its fullest versions, however, the *Tristan* becomes a rival cycle with its own Grail quest and its own version of the death of Arthur.

On the other hand, the cycle that modern scholars call the Post-Vulgate or Romance of the Grail Cycle seems to have been intended from the beginning to be an alternative storyline.[22] In this cycle the ascetic philosophy implicit in the Grail sections of the Vulgate dominates the entire story. This later cycle departs from the Vulgate at the end of the original prose *Merlin* at Arthur's coronation. Instead of the large-scale campaigns of its predecessor, the Post-Vulgate *Suite du Merlin* provides a series of individual quests in the romance mode. The Post-Vulgate announces that it will omit the lengthy *Lancelot* section in order to achieve a narrative in three parts of comparable length.[23] It too has its own somewhat longer Grail quest and death of Arthur sections. However, the tone is very different from the earlier work. The Post-Vulgate calls attention repeatedly to the unworthiness of all of the main characters with the exception of the Grail knights, and the conclusion, in which the villainous King Mark of Cornwall survives the catastrophic fall of Arthur's kingdom to occupy Camelot and break the Round Table, is the most bitter ending of all medieval Arthurian literature. However, Malory's use of the Post-Vulgate concentrates on the early sections; his first tale is based upon the *Merlin* and the first part of its Post-Vulgate *Suite*, as discussed below.

Although scholars have painstakingly reconstructed these discrete cycles from the surviving manuscripts,[24] Malory refers to them collectively as "the French book," suggesting that he thought of the various branches of the various cycles to be parts of a single great whole. Malory's narrator implies that the fact that his source is in French guarantees its authenticity. Perhaps Malory was aware of the relative antiquity of the French prose romances, which to the medieval mind

---

[21] See Emmanuèle Baumgartner, "The Prose Tristan," in *Arthur of the French*, 325–41. *Le Roman de Tristan en prose*, ed. Renée L. Curtis, 3 vols. (Cambridge, 1986); *Le roman de Tristan en prose*, ed. Philippe Ménard, 9 vols. (Geneva, 1987–95). There is no complete English translation; *The Romance of Tristan*, trans. Renée L. Curtis (Oxford, 1994) is heavily abridged.

[22] There is no complete edition of the Post-Vulgate Cycle, which has had to be reconstructed from various manuscript fragments. Its branches, beginning with the Post-Vulgate *Suite du Merlin*, can be found in the following editions: *La Suite du Roman de Merlin*, ed. Gilles Roussineau, 2 vols. (Geneva, 1996); *La Folie Lancelot*, ed. Fanni Bogdanow (Tübingen, 1965); *La Version Post-Vulgate de la "Queste del Saint Graal" et de la "Mort Artu,"* ed. Fanni Bogdanow, 4 vols. in 5 (Paris, 1991). An English translation is given in vols. 8–9 of *Lancelot-Grail*.

[23] *La Suite du Merlin*, 194; and *Lancelot-Grail*, 8: 111–12.

[24] Fanni Bogdanow, *The Romance of the Grail* (Manchester, 1966); and Fanni Bogdanow and Richard Trachsler, "Rewriting Prose Romance: The Post-Vulgate *Roman du Graal* and Related Texts," in *Arthur of the French*, 342–92.

would have been an indicator of their authority. Despite this, Malory also makes use of a fairly large amount of English Arthurian literature. Medieval English Arthurian literature was never as extensive as the French, but it had produced a variety of works, including chronicles, which most would have accepted as of reasonable historical accuracy, and some frankly fantastical romances of different modes and styles.[25] In terms of literary quality, they vary considerably, but Malory knew one of the masterpieces and many of the lesser pieces. Two works in particular served Malory as major sources, the Alliterative *Morte Arthure* (*c.* 1375) and the Stanzaic *Morte Arthur* (before 1460).

The Alliterative *Morte Arthure* is a poetic treatment of Arthur's war against the Roman Empire, originally written in the dialect of the northeastern Midlands.[26] Following the story originally established by Geoffrey of Monmouth, Arthur is challenged by the Roman Emperor and in response presses a prior claim of his own to the imperium. Arthur's forces defeat those of Rome, which are made out to be predominantly non-Christian, giving Arthur's action the air of a crusade. However, this concentration abroad leaves Arthur vulnerable to treason at home. Mordred uses the opportunity to usurp the throne, and, after defeating the Roman forces, Arthur is forced to cancel his march on Rome itself to return and face this crisis. Mordred resists Arthur, and the ensuing war annihilates both sides, bringing the Arthurian kingdom to an end.

The Alliterative *Morte* treats its theme with considerable subtlety. The thrust of the narrative encourages the reader to approve of Arthur's war, and the crusading element lends the campaign the appearance of a struggle against evil rather than a dispute over tribute. However, Arthur is unable to complete his conquest, and when he returns to quell treachery in his home kingdom he succeeds only at the cost of its destruction. Therefore, the Alliterative *Morte* is a sophisticated look at this part of Arthur's history, suggesting questions about pride and ambition without providing any easy answers. Reminiscent of epic and *chanson de geste* in a tragic mode, the Alliterative *Morte* is an impressive piece in its own right, and one can see why Malory would have used it as the basis for his rendition. This choice also affected Malory's book in more than solely narrative terms, for although he rendered this section into prose in keeping with the rest of his narrative, the language of the Alliterative *Morte* had an effect on Malory's writing, resulting in a unique section characterized by a more northern regional vocabulary and heavy alliteration.

Malory's final major source is known as the Stanzaic *Morte Arthur*.[27] This work is written in the London dialect (a dialect of English more familiar for modern readers) and is an adaptation of the Old French *Mort Artu*, the last branch of the Vulgate Cycle. This poem is notable for being one of very few works in English to deal with the theme of the love between Lancelot and Guinevere, although even this one focuses only on its tragic conclusion. The poem is notable for

---

[25] For a detailed overview, see *The Arthur of the English. The Arthurian Legend in Medieval English Life and Literature*, ed. W. R. J. Barron, rev. edn (Cardiff, 2001), which divides the romances into categories of "dynastic," "chivalric" and "folk."

[26] *Morte Arthure: A Critical Edition*, ed. Mary Hamel (New York, 1984).

[27] *Le Morte Arthur*, ed. P. E. Hissinger (The Hague, 1975).

straightening out somewhat the interlaced narrative structure characteristic of the Old French prose romances. Malory apparently favoured this more linear style of narration and further disentangled interlaced episodes in his version of the story. Malory's debt to the poem also includes much of its wording, which he often echoes in his version.

Such is the incontrovertible contribution of the English tradition to Malory's major sources, but English Arthurian sources also had a pervasive influence on the general mood and tone of Malory's work. For one thing, Malory overwhelmingly prefers English forms for the names of his characters. Also, although it would be wrong to say that the French sources lack dignity and gravitas, for many readers Malory's work has these qualities more consistently. Characters such as Arthur and Gawain often appear pitifully ineffective or villainous in the French, but Malory provides a more even characterization that is based on the bedrock assumption of the nobility of all of his major players, in spite of flaws and lapses.[28] This subtle but pervasive difference between Malory's story and his French major sources has been shown to be likely due to the general influence of the English conception of these figures and the English attitude towards the fall of Arthur's realm as a part of English history.[29] Malory therefore may well have had an early acquaintance with Arthur and his knights in the English tradition and later interpreted the French sources in the light of the English background.

## Malory's Originality

Indicating the material that Malory took from his major sources does not illustrate his entire relationship to them; as has been observed, one must also consider what Malory chose to omit.[30] Although naturally it is impossible to be sure, there are reasons to think that Malory knew and perhaps had access to the large parts of the Old French prose romance cycles that he did not include in his *Morte Darthur*. This selectivity is also an important element of Malory's vision of the Arthurian story.

Malory's most significant omission is the story of Lancelot's early life, including the overthrow of his father's kingdom, his childhood as the ward of the Lady of the Lake, his first arrival at Arthur's court, and, most crucially, his first sight of Guinevere and all of the details of their growing relationship. It is often thought that this subject was uncongenial to Malory and that he therefore chose to allude to it only by the analogy of Tristram and Isode. This view has led to the extreme conclusion that Malory would have wished the reader to conclude that the relationship between Lancelot and Guinevere was platonic with the single exception

---

[28] First shown by Robert H. Wilson, *Characterization in Malory* (Chicago, 1934); see also Dorsey Armstrong, "Malory and Character," in this volume.

[29] Edward Donald Kennedy, "Malory and His English Sources," in *Aspects of Malory*, ed. Toshiyuki Takamiya and Derek Brewer (Cambridge, 1981), 27–55.

[30] Terence McCarthy, "Malory and his Sources," in *A Companion to Malory*, ed. Archibald and Edwards, 75–95, at 85.

that occurs during the "Knight of the Cart" segment.[31] One cannot always be certain when Malory omits material whether it is because he has chosen to or because the material was not available to him.[32] In this case, Malory gives a clue in the reference that Lancelot makes to an incident from his knighting ceremony (802.15–21 / C XVIII.8). Although Lancelot's description does not correspond completely to the account in the prose *Lancelot*, this reference most likely demonstrates Malory's familiarity with that material, making the omission of this episode from the prose *Lancelot* appear to be deliberate.

Malory also declined to include large sections from the Vulgate and Post-Vulgate *Suites du Merlin*. In this case, no one has argued that the large-scale warfare contained in the Vulgate and the individual adventures in the Post-Vulgate would have been objectionable to Malory. At least part of the reason here must have been practical. Because Malory had decided to include a Roman War section based on the Alliterative *Morte Arthure*, he would have had to bring the knight errant adventures from the Post-Vulgate to a more decisive conclusion than that source provided. He therefore ended the tale with a series of adventures of his own invention. What is remarkable, however, is the extent to which Malory is able to capture the spirit of both *Suites* by providing representative sections from both the Vulgate (Arthur's civil wars and his war against Rome) and the Post-Vulgate (mysterious adventures of questing knights).

Malory's final significant omission from his major sources is again less an omission than a choice of sources. The third section of the prose *Tristan* relates its own version of the quest for the Holy Grail and of the conflict and wars that result in the destruction of Arthur's realm. In this case, Malory seems to have been motivated by his attitude towards the last two branches of the Vulgate, which he used instead. His treatment of the Vulgate *Queste del Saint Graal* is his most faithful adaptation of any source. In his colophon, he refers to it as "one of the treweyst and of the holyest that ys in this worlde" (789.16 / C XVII.23), and this suggests that he considered the Vulgate form of the story to be definitive.

### Malory's Minor Sources

The counterpart to this consideration of what Malory chose not to include in his story is the recognition of the many details that Malory adds to his story from sources other than his major ones. By the time the first of Vinaver's three-volume editions was published in 1947, a scholarly consensus had largely formed about Malory's major sources and, since then, work in this area has largely concentrated on one of the most unusual features of Malory's use of sources, his use of

---

[31] Beverly Kennedy, "Malory's Lancelot: 'Trewest Lover, Of A Synful Man'," *Viator: Medieval and Renaissance Studies* 12 (1981): 409–456.

[32] For a discussion of the availability of material to Malory see Thomas Crofts and Kevin Whetter, "Writing the *Morte Darthur*: Author, Manuscripts, and Modern Editions", in this volume.

minor sources.[33] As the designation implies, each contribution of a minor source to the overall narrative is rather small, but the cumulative effect is great. It is a large part of what gives Malory's book its distinctive character. The greater number of purely minor sources are in English, and many of the major French sources also serve as minor sources elsewhere in Malory's book. However, some French sources are used exclusively in ways that can only be called minor, such as some of the romances of Chrétien de Troyes. In addition to providing information, like names of people and places, the English sources often reveal themselves in verbal echoes that Malory has left in his writing.[34] Such echoes hint at the breadth of Malory's familiarity with literature. For example, they demonstrate that Malory had read at least several of Chaucer's *Canterbury Tales* as well as Lydgate's *Pageant of Knowledge*. They also confirm the impression given by his usual style of translating, that Malory's use of language, even written language, was very aural. Names, echoes of poetic lines, and near homophones in Malory's writings are reflections of his sources.

The most conspicuous use of the minor sources is for names – names of minor characters and occasionally of places. The French prose cycles had a great tolerance for anonymous characters and unidentified locations. In most cases, these nameless characters play minor roles, and the nameless places are merely part of an indistinct, unreal geography. As they are narrative functions of the story rather than well-drawn personalities or places, it might make sense for a story that already makes great demands on the memory of its audience, as the voluminous prose cycles invariably do, not to burden them unnecessarily with such details. This may be, but it is also true that many of the unnamed characters are far from insignificant, and even the much briefer compositions of Chrétien de Troyes have far more unnamed characters than most modern readers might expect. Malory clearly preferred to specify his people and places; therefore, Malory supplies names for the great majority of the characters and locations. Most of these names come from English sources and follow the natural tendency that Malory had of using English equivalents of the French names that he encountered in his major sources. A fortunate consequence of this tendency of Malory's is the demonstration this gives of his knowledge of many stories that he chose

---

[33] For an overview of the history of the discussion and for the evidence and argument that establishes the minor sources, see Norris, *Malory's Library*.

[34] E.g. these lines from "The Franklin's Tale" which seem to have been in Malory's mind when writing a scene from "Lancelot and Guenevere":

> Love wol nat been constreyned by maistrye.
> Whan maistrie comth, the God of Love anon
> Beteth his wynges, and farewell, he is gon!
> Love is a thyng as any spirit free.
> Wommen, of kynde, desiren libertee,
> And nat to been constreyned as a thral;
> And so doon men, if sooth seyen shal.
> (*The Riverside Chaucer*, ed. Larry Benson (Boston, 1987), lines 763–66)

The echo can be heard in these lines of Lancelot's: "I love nat to be constrained to love, for love must only aryse of the harte self, and nat by none constraynte" (830.12–13 / C XVIII.21). See Norris, *Malory's Library*, for more examples, *passim*.

not to incorporate, stories such as several of the English Gawain romances that could have been used for additional adventures.[35] Perhaps he made no more use of these English romances than he did because, although he may have thought that they contained authentic details, like names of knights and adversaries of Arthur's court, he did not consider them to be a part of the authentic tradition that he was presenting to readers in English.

Malory's most significant minor source, the *Chronicle* of John Hardyng, is an exception to that rule.[36] Hardyng was a near contemporary of Malory who had written a verse chronicle of Britain based ultimately on the story established by Geoffrey of Monmouth, although with a few elements that are more to be expected in romance than in chronicle, such as the quest for the Grail. Malory shows his reliance on Hardyng in characteristic ways in each section of Malory's book that has an equivalent section in Hardyng. For example, the name of Uther's last battle, St Albans, phrases to describe Arthur's coronation as Roman emperor, and Arthur's reaction to the dispersal of his knights on the quest for the Grail all seem to have come to Malory's work from Hardyng. This reliance is noteworthy not least as a demonstration of Malory's appreciation for an author whose poetry is, despite its respectable material, generally considered doggerel today. Apparently, for Malory, Hardyng's depiction of Arthur's imperial greatness and his attachment to his fellowship of knights were more important considerations.

The final important aspect of Malory's use of minor sources is his use of his major sources as minor sources in other parts of his book. This is largely in the interest of consistency, as, for example, the domineering personality of Morgan le Fay as she is presented in the Post-Vulgate *Suite du Merlin* seems to have influenced Malory's presentation of this same character when she appears in a story that he has taken from the prose *Lancelot*.[37] But in other respects, he uses the major sources in exactly the same way as his minor, as when in the story of Balin he borrows the names of two minor characters from the prose *Tristan* to use for characters who are anonymous in his major source for this episode, the Post-Vulgate *Suite du Merlin*.

The number of minor sources is large enough to make it most unlikely that Malory would have had access to all of them during the imprisonment in which he wrote. This suggests that Malory had internalized a great deal of literature that he was able to draw upon from memory. This is particularly likely to be the case with the poetic quotations and misquotations that appear in his prose, but it also raises the possibility that he used his memory of his major sources as he worked, especially when he was using the major source of one tale as a minor

---

[35] E.g. *Gawain and the Carl of Carlisle*, *The Anturs of Arthur* and *The Wedding of Sir Gawain*, each of which Malory drew from in his "Book of Sir Tristram."

[36] John Hardyng, *The Chronicle of John Hardyng*, ed. Henry Ellis (New York, 1974).

[37] However, as Dorsey Armstrong discusses elsewhere in this volume, Malory's Morgan behaves rather differently in her appearance in the ending sequences of the *Morte*, in a section derived from the French *Mort Artu* and the English Stanzaic *Morte Arthure*. The classic discussion of Morgan's character is Fanni Bogdanow, "Morgain's Role in the Thirteenth-Century French Prose Romances of the Arthurian Cycle," *Medium Ævum* 38 (1969): 123–33.

one in another. This realization makes more understandable the occasional contradictions and mistakes in which scholars have caught Malory.[38]

All in all, Malory's minor sources add a plethora of details to his rendition
of the history of Arthur's kingdom. Although as a medieval prose romance, the
*Morte Darthur* cannot be expected to provide its readers with realism as that
concept is understood in relation to literature today, the very concreteness of
the specific names and occasional bits of larger history that the minor sources
provide, particularly Malory's use of English place names to make Arthurian
Britain feel closer to his original audience,[39] gave Malory's work a verisimilitude
that his original readers would have found unusual and compelling.

## Malory's Lost and Oral Sources

Malory also drew upon sources that have been lost over the centuries or were
never written down at all. These lost and oral sources may be considered together
because they are similarly unavailable for scholarly consultation. Obviously,
little can be said with certainty about such sources, which makes the hints about
them in the *Morte Darthur* tantalizing.

Allusions to oral stories of Arthur and his warriors can be detected in all strata
of the development of the legend. Wace and Chrétien attest to the existence of
storytellers who circulate stories of Arthur, and Geoffrey of Monmouth alludes
to oral history in the preface of his *Historia regum Britanniae*. Similarly, the allusion to marvels associated with Arthur in the ninth-century *Historia Britonum*
and the allusion to Arthur in the oldest extant Welsh poem, *Y Gododdin*, imply
the existence of stories of Arthur that were probably never committed to parch-
ment.[40] Malory's work relies, as his narrator repeatedly asserts, on the "French
Book," but even so, some of the details in his story seem to have been derived
from the oral stories of his own day.

The first instance that seems to demonstrate this reliance on an oral tradition
is the oath that all the Round Table knights swear on each Pentecost, apparently
an example of Sir Thomas's life directly impacting his writing.[41] The Pentecostal
Oath is one of Malory's most quoted passages and appears to be based upon the

[38] E.g. the knights Harleuse and Peryne who are killed in Malory's first tale but also
appear much later in the fifth tale; see P. J. C. Field, "Author, Scribe, and Reader
in Malory: The Case of Harleuse and Peryne," in his *Malory: Texts and Sources*
(Cambridge, 1998), 72–88.

[39] As Meg Roland discusses in her chapter in this volume.

[40] The Arthurian marvels are said to be a stone with the footprint of Arthur's dog, Cafal
(Welsh for horse), that will return to its spot on a pile of rocks if removed, and the
grave of Amr, said to be Arthur's son whom Arthur slew, that changes size so that no
two measurements of it are the same: Nennius, *British History and the Welsh Annals*, ed.
and trans. John Morris (London, 1980), 42. In the *Gododdin* a warrior is praised for his
skill in battle, although he is no Arthur: *The Gododdin of Aneirin: Text and Context from
Dark Age North Britain*, ed. and trans. John Koch (Cardiff, 1997).

[41] The standard scholarly biography is P. J. C. Field, *The Life and Times of Sir Thomas
Malory* (Cambridge, 1996), and for a lively, less restrained reconstruction, see Christina
Hardyment, *Malory: The Life and Times of King Arthur's Chronicler* (London, 2005).

formal charges that the initiates to the Knights of the Bath swear to uphold. The inclusion of the oath with its specific provisions illuminates some of the method of Malory's creation of the Arthurian world. Most significantly, it demonstrates a concern for realism in an aspect of chivalric life that his major sources did not have. The prose *Lancelot* mentions that the Round Table knights recite an oath every year, but it gives none of the specifics of that oath. By composing an oath based upon the one that he most likely took himself, Malory brings the distant Arthurian world closer to the world he would have expected his readers to share without destroying the alterity of Arthur's kingdom. However, the specific articles of the oath are never mentioned again, nor is any knight ever punished according to its articles. Arthur himself, in order to be released from imprisonment, fights for Sir Damas in a wrongful quarrel against the letter of the oath (however, he soon sets things right), and Gawain and his brothers murder Sir Lamorak in direct violation of the oath. They are censured but do not lose Arthur's lordship, as the oath stipulates.

The same impulse towards relative realism probably also motivated the two further examples of the influence of oral tradition. The notion that the Holy Grail was a cup containing the actual blood of Christ appears to have been current in the England of Malory's day, and so he transferred this belief into his story of the Holy Grail (68.15–21 / C II.16). Finally, the words of the epitaph on Arthur's tomb, "Hic iacet Arthur, Rex quondam Rexque futurus,"[42] comes from oral tradition or from a lost source (928.28 / C XXI.7).[43] In this case, Malory superseded the exact words of his major source, the *Mort Artu*: "Here lies King Arthur, who by his valour conquered twelve kingdoms."[44] The same epitaph that Malory used appears in conjunction with two other English Arthurian narratives: at the end of the Alliterative *Morte* in the Thornton manuscript in a later hand; and, translated into English as "Heer lith king Arthour, which shal regne ageyn," in the Arthur section of John Lydgate's *Fall of Princes* (1430s).[45] These suggest a common source of some kind, either lost or, as John Withrington suggests, oral.[46] It may seem unlikely for a Latin leonine hexameter to have circulated in oral tradition, but this may have been possible in a world in which virtually everyone had regular exposure to church Latin.

Just as the nature of Malory's oral sources has to be deduced from their effect on the story, so it is with some of his written sources. All of the exact manuscripts that Malory used of his various sources have been lost during the intervening centuries,[47] and some of the actual romances that he drew from failed to survive

---

[42] Latin for "Here lies Arthur, the once and future king."

[43] For an in-depth discussion, see John Withrington, "The Arthurian Epitaph in Malory's *Morte Darthur*," *Arthurian Literature* VII (1987): 103–44.

[44] *The Death of Arthur*, trans. Norris J. Lacy, *Lancelot-Grail*, vol. 7 (Cambridge, 2010), 129; "Ci gist li Rois Artus qui par sa valeur mist en sa subjecton .XII. roiaumes," *La Mort le roi Artu: Roman du XIIIe siècle*, ed. Jean Frappier (Geneva, 1964), 251.

[45] John Lydgate, *Fall of Princes*, ed. Henry Bergen, 4 vols. (London, 1924–27), VIII 3122.

[46] Withrington, "The Arthurian Epitaph," 133.

[47] Scholars have occasionally argued that particular extant manuscripts are the ones that Malory used, but never successfully. William Matthews argued that Malory used the single surviving manuscript of the *Morte Arthure*, in *The Ill-Framed Knight: A Skeptical Inquiry into the Identity of Sir Thomas Malory* (Berkeley, 1966), 92–9, but this idea was

at all. Two of these lost sources are very minor, contributing only names, but the third is the major source of an entire section of the *Morte Darthur*. In the list of knights who attempt to heal Sir Urry near the end of the *Morte*, Malory mentions a Sir Merrok whose wife betrayed him and "made hym seven yere a warwolff" (866.3 / C XIX.12). This seems a clear variation of the tradition embodied in the twelfth-century Breton lai "Bisclavret" by Marie de France. Just as variants of Marie's "Lanval" appear in Middle English versions, the story of Bisclavret appears to have been retold with the name of its hero given as Merrok in a version of the story that has not survived, unless Malory himself had read or heard "Bisclavret" and changed the name either purposefully or mistakenly.

Two more names, odd ones, Playne de Fors and Playne de Amors, are given to minor characters that are anonymous in Malory's major source. Although our fleeting glimpse of him in Malory is the only trace of the existence of Playne de Fors, another fleeting glimpse survives of Playne de Amors, in a list of famous heroes in the introduction to Chaucer's "Tale of Sir Thopas."[48] Although Chaucer could have invented an absurd name as a reference in an absurd tale, all of the other heroes named in the list come from actual heroic tradition or history, so it is likely that Playne de Amors did as well. This conclusion fits with the complementary nature of the name of Playne de Amors's companion, who, therefore, probably featured in a story that has not survived.

Of course, by far the most significant lost source is the major source of Malory's fourth tale, "Sir Gareth of Orkney." Because it alone has no known major source, scholarship has faced the task of determining whether the tale was based upon a source or whether this tale is, uniquely, an original composition by Malory. Although there is general agreement that Malory did have a source, it is not unanimous. At first glance, Occam's razor may suggest that the observable information should be accounted for without positing a lost romance. After all, even by a cautious estimate, by the time he came to write this tale Malory must have had enough familiarity with the motifs of Arthurian romance and enough experience as an author to create a tale of his own that could fit within his wider narrative world.[49] This notion has an undeniable appeal, since it would be a solution to a question that, otherwise, will never be fully answered. However, in my view, such a first glance would be deceptive.[50]

---

refuted by Mary Hamel in her edition of the Alliterative *Morte*, 5–12. More recently, Jonathan Passaro has argued that Cambridge University Library, Additional MS 7071, was the copy of the Post-Vulgate *Suite du Merlin* that Malory used, "Malory's Text of the *Suite du Merlin*," *Arthurian Literature* XXVI (2009), 39–75. However, two articles in *Arthurian Literature* XXIX (2012) severely damage his case: P. J. C. Field, "Malory's Source-Manuscript for the First Tale of Le *Morte Darthur*," 111–19, and Linda Gowans, "Malory's Sources – and Arthur's Sisters – Revisited," 121–42.

48 Chaucer, "The Tale of Sir Thopas," *The Riverside Chaucer*, line 900. The other heroes are Horn, Ypotys, Bevis of Hampton, Guy of Warwick and Libeaus Desconus; the last is actually the *nom du guerre* for Gawain's son Guinglain, who appears briefly in the *Morte Darthur*.

49 The classic statement of the minimum assumptions is Robert H. Wilson, "Malory's Early Knowledge of Arthurian Romance," *University of Texas Studies in English* 32 (1953): 1–13.

50 The notion that Malory composed "Gareth" out of romance commonplaces has been proposed in Wilfred L. Guerin, "'The Tale of Gareth': The Chivalric Flowering,"

"Sir Gareth" belongs to a family of stories known as the Fair Unknown type. For the basis of this tale, Malory must have followed either the structure of this well-known story type, or a particular version of the Fair Unknown. *Le bel inconnu* and *Lybeaus Desconus* are the quintessential Fair Unknown poems that survive in French and English respectively,[51] but neither are close enough to Malory's "Gareth" to have been his major source. Also, "Gareth" contains details from versions of Fair Unknown romances that survive in other languages such as Italian and German that Malory is unlikely to have known of, let alone to have read.[52] The connection between "Sir Gareth" and the romances of the Fair Unknown story type, albeit with a modified ending, a Malory hallmark,[53] establishes that Malory almost certainly had a major source for this tale that simply has not survived. This lost romance would have been in either French or English, more likely in English. Whenever Malory follows an English poem as a major source, traces of the poetry tend to survive in his prose.[54] In "Sir Gareth," remnants of English rhyme and alliteration can be found.[55] These may be verbal echoes of an English poem, most likely the major source.

Alternative explanations could be devised but, in my view, not convincing ones. The correspondence with foreign Fair Unknown romances may all be coincidence, but if so Malory would have had to invent all of the details that "Sir Gareth" has in common with the various Fair Unknown romances he was unaware of, which seems quite improbable. The apparent echoes of English poetry could reflect Malory's familiarity with English poetry in general, but such echoes never appear elsewhere in the *Morte Darthur* except when he is drawing upon an English poem, even in places such as the end of "The Tale of King Arthur" and "The Healing of Sir Urry," in which he is thought to be working without a major source. Thus, the correspondence with cognate Fair Unknown romances suggests that Malory has not decided for once to compose a large section of his *Morte Darthur* without any major source as such. Together these factors justify Malory's most recent editor in saying that there is little doubt that Malory had

---

in *Malory's Originality: A Critical Study of* Le Morte Darthur, ed. R. M. Lumiansky (Baltimore, 1964), 99–117; and Arnold Sanders, "Sir Gareth and the 'Unfair Unknown': Malory's Use of the Gawain Romances," *Arthuriana* 16.1 (2006): 34–46. However, neither addresses the evidence and arguments offered here.

[51] See Penny Simmons, "Le Bel Inconnu," in *Arthur of the French*, 412–15, and Maldwyn Mills, "Lybeaus Desconus," in *Arthur of the English*, 124–9.

[52] For details, see Field, "The Source of Malory's 'Tale of Gareth,'" in *Malory: Texts and Sources*, 246–60, and the headnote to "Sir Gareth" in Field's edition of Malory, II, 185–93. For a recent discussion, see Ralph Norris, "Another Source for Malory's 'Tale of Sir Gareth,'" *Arthurian Literature* XXXII (2015): 59–74.

[53] Field divides the tale into four sections in his headnote to "Sir Gareth" (II, 185). The fourth section abandons the Fair Unknown storyline as established by the other surviving romances of this type as Gareth departs from his lady to have a series of adventures that have no Fair Unknown counterparts, culminating in a fight to a draw with his brother Gawain.

[54] E.g. Alliterative *Morte Arthure* lines 941–4 and Malory 155.24–5 / C V.5; and Stanzaic *Morte Arthur* lines 2842–6 and Malory 912.7–9 / C XX.21.

[55] E.g. Gareth as a kitchen boy, "never displeased man nother chylde, but allwayes he was meke and mylde" (225.33–4), and "thou were as wyght as ever was Wade" (237.24)

a major source for this tale, a lost English poem of the Fair Unknown type.[56] However, only the unlikely recovery of this source could establish with certainty whether Malory adapted it closely or loosely, and whether or to what extent he supplemented it with other sources.

## Malory's Whole Book of King Arthur

Despite the reliance on a vast previous tradition that one can readily see, the book that Malory wrote is different in many ways from anything that came before. This is the paradox of Malory source study; although he invented very little from scratch, Malory nevertheless created something greater than the sum of his various sources. Most likely this was because he began with a vision of the overall story that was based upon his own interpretation, which presumably took shape over years of reading and meditating upon the many versions of the various parts of Arthur's story that he knew.

For Malory, the life of Arthur, his wars, the adventures of the knights of the Round Table, and its fall and Arthur's death were valuable in themselves, rather than as episodes in the history of the Grail or of Britain. From the beginning, therefore, he liberates the central story of Arthur and his knights from the larger historical context given by his sources and presents it as the focus of his overall narrative. He rejects the theme of the Post-Vulgate Cycle of the unworthiness of all except the Grail knights, and this same understanding of the world can be seen in his adaptation of the Vulgate Grail quest. He declines to elaborate on the love between Lancelot and Guinevere and so chooses not to adapt most of the prose *Lancelot*, instead structuring the long central section of interlaced adventures of errant knights from the first two thirds of the prose *Tristan*. When he rejoins the Vulgate version with the Grail quest, he still controls his material with his own interpretation, and his account of the fall of Arthur's kingdom is perhaps more moving than any provided by his sources. Finally, his attention to the myriad details provided by his minor sources adds considerable solidity to Malory's story. Hardly a character or a location goes unnamed, and most locations are also identified with place names from Malory's own time.

The first tale of the *Morte Darthur* begins with the events leading up to Arthur's birth, which come from the prose *Merlin* and follow the Post-Vulgate continuation, ending, however, with a series of adventures of Malory's own creation. The second tale is based upon the first two thirds of the Alliterative *Morte Arthure*, but, whereas the alliterative poem is a tragedy in which Arthur's war against Rome leads to his death and the destruction of his kingdom, in Malory's rendition Arthur's war against the Roman Empire is the greatest triumph of his early career. The Vulgate *Merlin* continuation puts the Roman War at the end of Arthur's early career and makes it a similar triumph, and Malory is likely following its example by placing it at this point. One could thus say that Malory's first

---

[56] Field, Headnote to "Sir Gareth of Orkney," in *Le Morte Darthur*, II, 185.

two tales give an abbreviated and modified version of the material in the prose *Merlin* and both its Vulgate and Post-Vulgate *Suites*.

Malory's third tale, by far his briefest, is taken from the Vulgate's longest romance, the prose *Lancelot*. In this case rather than adapting a substantial part of a work, Malory borrowed a few episodes from their original context and placed them in a frame that he wrote to make a complete tale. However, one of the episodes comes from a prose romance known as the *Perlesvaus*, discussed above. The fourth tale, "The Tale of Gareth," is based upon its lost major source.

"The Tale of Sir Tristram," more properly, the first and second books of Sir Tristram, is based upon approximately the first two thirds of the fourth of the four main versions of the prose *Tristan*,[57] which Malory uses as the long central section of his work, having it replace the function that the prose *Lancelot* serves in the French Vulgate Cycle. Malory states that there will be no rehearsal of the third book of Tristan. Because this section contained the Tristan version of the Grail quest and the fall of Arthur's kingdom, it seems that he chose to retell the Vulgate versions of these stories instead.

Accordingly, "The Tale of the Sangreal" is an adaptation of the Vulgate *Queste del Saint Graal*. In this tale, Malory follows his source much more closely than he does in any other tale. He adapts the entire tale from beginning to ending without adding or removing any key events. However, there is an important difference in tone between Malory's version and its source, which shows the subtlety with which Malory is capable of asserting his independence. The French *Queste* insists on the inadequacy of earthly chivalric ideals compared with those of celestial chivalry, as embodied in Galahad, Perceval and Bors. Lancelot's humiliation in the quest must have been a shock to some in the original audience, as the source of his greatness, his love of Guinevere, is now shown to be a source of condemnation and his earthly glory as the greatest of knights is now turned against him. For the French author, Lancelot's humiliation is a jarring object lesson of the principle of *sic transit gloria mundi*; whereas for Malory, Lancelot is still the greatest of the earthly knights, an honour as far as it goes.

For his conclusion, Malory shows his independence by splitting the material from the Vulgate *Mort Artu* into two sections, rearranging and adding material as he goes. As noted above, he also took structural hints and wording from the English stanzaic poem *Le Morte Arthur*. The first of the two sections, "Sir Launcelot and Queen Guinevere" in Field's edition, is notable for what Malory adds, the story of the abduction of Guinevere and her rescue by Lancelot, which Malory most likely took from the heart of the prose *Lancelot*, and an account that has no known source of a wounded knight named Sir Urry who can only be healed by the best knight in the world. Together these additions show the extent of the adultery between Lancelot and Guinevere and that, despite that, Lancelot is the greatest knight in the world; together, moreover, they create a tense and moving moment just before the final section, "The Morte Arthur." Malory follows the story of the second half of the *Mort Artu*, although he borrows wording from the alliterative and stanzaic English poems.

---

[57] See pp. 36–7 above.

## Malory's Sources

| Tale | French Sources | English Sources | Lost | Oral |
|---|---|---|---|---|
| King Uther and King Arthur | **Prose *Merlin*, Post-Vulgate *Suite du Merlin*,** Prose *Tristan*, *Chevalier au lion*, *Perlesvaus* | Alliterative *Morte Arthure*, Stanzaic *Morte Arthur*, Hardyng's *Chronicle*, Chaucer's "The Wife of Bath's Tale," and "The Franklin's Tale," *Of Arthour and Merlin, Gawain and Yvain, The Carl of Carlisle, Torrent of Portyngale* | Major source of "Sir Gareth" | Charges to the Knights of the Bath, The Grail containing the Blood of Christ |
| King Arthur and Emperor Lucius | Vulgate *Suite du Merlin*, Prose *Lancelot* | **Alliterative *Morte Arthure*,** Hardyng's *Chronicle* | Major source of "Sir Gareth" | |
| Sir Launcelot du Lake | **Prose *Lancelot*, *Perlesvaus*,** Chrétien's *Erec et Enide, Chevalier au lion, L'Atre périlleux* | | | |
| Sir Gareth of Orkney | Prose *Lancelot*, Prose *Tristan, Erec et Enide*, perhaps Chrétien's *Chevalier de la charrette* | *Ipomadon* | **Major source, probably in English** | |
| Sir Tristram of Lyones | **Prose *Tristan*,** Prose *Lancelot*, Chrétien's *Erec et Enide* | *Gawain and the Carl of Carlisle* or *Anturs of Arthur, Wedding of Sir Gawain* | Romance of Playne de Fors and Playne de Amors, Major source of "Sir Gareth" | |
| The Sankgreal | **Vulgate *Queste del Saint Graal*,** Prose *Tristan* | Hardyng's *Chronicle* | | |
| Sir Launcelot and Queen Guenivere | **Vulgate *Mort Artu*,** Vulgate *Suite du Merlin*, Prose *Lancelot*, Chrétien's *Chevalier au lion*, and perhaps *Chevalier de la charrette* | **Stanzaic *Morte Arthur*,** "The Knight's Tale," Lydgate's *Pageant of Knowledge, Sir Triamour*, a version of "Sir Landeval," Chaucer's "Knight's Tale" | Romance of Playne de Fors and Playne de Amors, Tale of Sir Marrok, the Werewolf, Major source of "Sir Gareth" | |
| The Morte Arthur | **Vulgate *Mort Artu*** | **Stanzaic *Morte Arthur*,** Alliterative *Morte Arthure*, Hardyng's *Chronicle, Wedding of Sir Gawain* | Major source of "Sir Gareth" | Arthur's Epitaph, Legend of Arthur's Survival |

Recent work on Malory's sources has underscored the skill Malory demonstrates as he manipulates his sources, deepening critical appreciation of Malory as a literary artist. The author of the *Morte Darthur* emerges as more thoughtful, more selective, more literate and creative than previously perceived. In the late nineteenth century, Sommer thought that adding anything to the story furnished by his sources was beyond Malory's ability,[58] and Vinaver, writing in the mid twentieth century, occasionally gave the impression that he thought of Malory as working with material that he did not quite understand, as when he suggested that perhaps Malory had made no more of the prose *Lancelot* than he did because he had found a single gathering that had fallen from a codex.[59] This attitude is probably why, when Vinaver published a collection of selections from Malory, he moved the abduction of Guinevere from "The Book of Lancelot and Guinevere" to the middle of his collection, thus approximating the position of the episode in the Vulgate Cycle. However, from the perspective of the twenty-first century, following more recent source study's exploration of the extent of Malory's reading, Malory appears remarkably well read, even cultured, with the verses of great poets like Chaucer and Lydgate echoing in his thoughts; a creative artist who used each source with deliberation to create certain literary effects.

## Scholarship, Criticism, and Source Study

The knowledge that source study uncovers can be an end in itself, but, ultimately, source study is also a scholarly tool that also provides information for the benefit of criticism. In this respect, source study has been particularly useful in the great twentieth-century critical debates about Malory's work: unity, authorship, independence, and the text of the Roman War.

Modern critical reception of the *Morte Darthur* was spurred by the first appearance of Eugène Vinaver's edition *The Works of Sir Thomas Malory* in 1947, the first edition to be based upon the Winchester Manuscript, which had then been recently discovered.[60] The publication of this edition was a milestone that allowed the world to see Malory's work from a new perspective. Vinaver's most contentious critical conclusion based on his examination of Winchester was that Malory had written a series of romances that occupied similar fictional universes but that were otherwise independent of each other. In other words, Malory's works were closer to the romances of Chrétien de Troyes than to those of the

---

[58] Sommer, *Studies on the Sources*, 272.

[59] "Commentary," in *The Works of Sir Thomas Malory*, ed. Eugène Vinaver, 3 vols., 3rd edn. rev. P. J. C. Field (Oxford, 1990), 1408.

[60] The manuscript is now British Library, MS Additional 59678; the British Library refers to it as the Malory Manuscript. It lacks its first and last gatherings and three other leaves and has been reproduced in photographic facsimile in *The Winchester Malory: A Facsimile*, intro. N. R. Ker (Oxford, 1976). A digital facsimile of the manuscript and of the preface, table of contents, Book V and Book XXI of the copy of Caxton's original printing of the *Morte Darthur* that is held by the John Rylands Library of the University of Manchester are available online at The Malory Project, directed by Takako Kato and designed by Nick Hayward, http://www.maloryproject.com. For an account of its discovery, see Walter Oakeshott, "The Finding of the Manuscript," in *Essays on Malory*, ed. J. A. W. Bennett (Oxford, 1963), 1–6.

Vulgate Cycle.[61] Unusually among Vinaver's contributions, this idea instigated great controversy and was eventually rejected by the academic community. One of the landmarks of this debate was a collection of essays, one for each of Malory's eight tales, entitled *Malory's Originality*.[62] Together these essays argued that Malory had handled his various sources in a fairly consistent way that tended towards the unity of the overall story. The group that produced this volume had been anticipated by Robert H. Wilson, whose *Characterization in Malory* demonstrated the same point, a decade ahead of Vinaver's controversial conclusion.[63]

Another important discussion in which Malory's sources played a role is the search for the author, that is, the attempt to establish which, if any, of the Thomas Malorys on record in the second half of the fifteenth century was the author of the *Morte Darthur*. The Sir Thomas Malory of Newbold Revel had been the leading contender since the nineteenth century.[64] A major challenge to this conclusion occurred in 1966 when William Matthews argued that the language in the Alliterative *Morte Arthure* was in a dialect that would have been unintelligible to an Englishman from Warwickshire, the location of Newbold Revel, and that, therefore, a Thomas Malory from Yorkshire must have been the author.[65] Expert dialectical analysis has since established that Matthews's theory was mistaken,[66] and the Newbold Revel Malory has been reinstated as the only man of that name of his time who was both a knight and a prisoner and, therefore, the only candidate to be the author of the *Morte Darthur*.[67] Therefore, source studies helped to instigate a debate which led to a more secure identification than had been the case previously.

Source study led Vinaver to the conclusion that Malory had written his second tale, "Arthur and Lucius," first and his first tale second.[68] This idea carried influence for a long time until its foundation was eventually exploded.[69] However, in proposing this idea, Vinaver opened up a discussion of the order in which Malory composed his tales. They appear in the same order in all full editions of the work, but Malory need not necessarily have composed them in this same order. Terence McCarthy later suggested that Malory might have become more independent as he progressed as an author and so ordered the composition of Malory's tales in inverse proposition to their fidelity to their major sources.[70] This would put "The Sangreal" first and his final tales last. Interesting as this notion is, Malory's interaction with his sources shows a greater sophistication and control than this idea would allow. Malory appears to have used each of his

[61] "The Story of the Book," in *The Works of Sir Thomas Malory*, ed. Vinaver, I, xxxv–lvi.
[62] *Malory's Originality*, ed. R. M. Lumiansky (Baltimore, 1964).
[63] Wilson, *Characterization in Malory*.
[64] George Lyman Kittridge, "Who Was Sir Thomas Malory?" *Harvard Studies and Notes in Philology and Literature* 5 (1896): 85–106; Field, *Life and Times of Sir Thomas Malory*.
[65] Matthews, *The Ill-Framed Knight*.
[66] Angus McIntosh, review of Matthews, *The Ill-Framed Knight*, in *Medium Ævum* 37 (1968): 346–8.
[67] See "Alternatives" and "Identification," Chapters One and Two in Field, *Life and Times of Sir Thomas Malory*, 1–35. See also Crofts and Whetter's chapter in this volume.
[68] "Introduction," in *The Works of Sir Thomas Malory*, ed. Vinaver, I, lvii–lxxii.
[69] Kennedy, "Malory and His English Sources," 28–39.
[70] Terence McCarthy, "The Order of Composition in the *Morte Darthur*," *Yearbook of English Studies* 1 (1971): 18–29.

major sources, even those he followed most closely, only so far as suited him, leaving this discussion open.

William Matthews contributed a further controversial idea that occupied scholarship in the last decades of the twentieth century. Noting the very different versions in the two principal witnesses of Malory's second tale, which Field calls "King Arthur and Emperor Lucius," Matthews came to the conclusion that the version contained in the Winchester Manuscript was an inferior version that Malory himself had rejected and revised to create the version that appears in the Caxton incunable.[71] Although this idea was influential for over twenty years, it has been soundly refuted. Again, however, this debate has led to an important advance in Malory studies, in this case leading to a more accurate understanding of the relationship between the two surviving textual witnesses and to a more complete reconstruction of Malory's original version from which both witnesses descend.

Source study, therefore, has clarified Malory's artistic achievement, helped to establish the identity of the author, and helped to establish the text. In line with current critical trends, Malory's work is more often considered in its own right from a variety of perspectives. However, recent critical work also often relies on the findings of source study for an understanding of how Malory's selective reworking of his sources sheds light on the development and emphases of themes in his own work. The study of sources, therefore, remains fundamental, and Malory critics are ill-advised if they make their critical judgements independently from the evidence of Malory's sources. An understanding of what Malory chose to adapt from the vast body of Arthurian literature that preceded him, how he chose to adapt it, and what he chose to omit, is indispensable. Only with the perspective that source study provides can the *Morte Darthur* be seen as that greatest of *desideria* that it is, a masterpiece of literary art that is also a traditional retelling of the lives of Arthur and his greatest knights and ladies.

---

[71] See the apparatus to "Arthur and Lucius" in volume two of Field's edition and Appendix II "The Opening of the Roman War," 2: 843–9 and Appendix III "The End of the Roman War," 2: 850–3. See also Ralph Norris, "Once Again King Arthur and the Ambassadors," *Journal of the International Arthurian Society* 3:1 (2015): 102–19. For an overview of the debate, see *The Malory Debate*, ed. Bonnie Wheeler et al. (Cambridge, 2000), especially Matthews, "A Question of Texts," 65–107; Field, "Caxton's Roman War," 127–67; and Yuji Nakao, "Musings on the Reviser of Book V in Caxton's Malory," 191–216, in which Nakao reviews the statistical linguistic evidence that establishes Caxton as the reviser beyond reasonable doubt.

# 3
## Writing the *Morte Darthur*:
## Author, Manuscript and Modern Editions

THOMAS H. CROFTS AND K. S. WHETTER

Our subject is the author and text of the *Morte Darthur*, a text which was completed in 1469/70 and first printed in 1485. We start with a survey of the debate surrounding which Sir Thomas Malory penned the *Morte* and how he may have accessed or acquired the various source books necessary for such an enterprise. We then turn to an account of the text of the *Morte* in the form it takes in its late-medieval manuscript, its first printing, and the principal modern editions, concomitantly addressing how these different forms shape the meaning and interpretation of the text.

The terms of enquiry in each of these issues are set for us by the subjects themselves: the author of the narrative self-identifies, so scholarship has only to determine which Sir Thomas Malory likely did the writing, not attempt the daunting task of creating an author from scratch. Likewise there is only one surviving manuscript of the *Morte* and two surviving early prints. Despite such certainties, there is considerable debate about what to do with the facts at hand, as well as some generally accepted truths. Although we shall endeavour to paint in broad strokes when possible, offering a narrative overview of the issues, several elements of the debate are keyed to the positions of specific scholars, as we shall explain. Despite some of the complexities involved, we hope in this chapter to offer a clear and thematic path through the critical, textual, and historical maze that surrounds the writing of the *Morte Darthur*.

### The Authorship and Library Questions

The names of many, if not most, medieval authors are lost to history. Fortunately, the author of the 1469/70 work known today as the *Morte Darthur* at several points in his narrative identifies himself as Thomas Malory, and as having been both a knight and a prisoner. William Caxton, England's first printer, excised many of these authorial self-references when he printed Malory's text (and gave it the title *Le Morte Darthur*) in 1485, but he did include the final identification:

> *Here is the ende of* The Hoole Book of Kyng Arthur and of His
> Noble Knyghtes of the Rounde Table, *that whan they were holé*
> *togyders there was ever an hondred and fyfty. And here is the*
> *ende of* "Le Morte Darthur."

*I praye you all jentylmen and jentylwymmen that redeth this book*
*of Arthur and his knyghtes from the begynnyng to the endynge,*
*praye for me whyle I am on lyve that God sende me good*
*delyveraunce, and whan I am deed, I praye you all*
*praye for my soule.*
*For this book was ended*
*the ninth yere of the reygne of Kynge Edward the Fourth,*
*by Syr Thomas Maleoré, knyght,*
*as Jesu helpe hym for Hys grete myght,*
*as he is the servaunt of Jesu bothe day and nyght.*[1]

As Malory's original readers probably knew, "the ninth yere of the reygne of Kynge Edward the Fourth" puts the *Morte*'s completion somewhere between 4 March 1469 and 4 March 1470. Since several of the *explicits* in the surviving manuscript version make similar statements about Malory's imprisonment, most scholars conclude that the text was written continuously in one long stretch, near the end of Malory's life, while he was in prison; the time taken to compose the entire narrative is usually estimated at about two years.

Although Malory records his name and knighthood, along with the title and circumstances surrounding his work, it was left to later scholars to determine which of the possible Thomas Malorys alive in the fifteenth century might be the actual author, and where that author resided and worked. This search for a specific Malory is important for socio-political contexts, for possible thematic emphases, and especially (it is often thought) for identifying where and how Malory acquired the sources for his *Morte Darthur*.

Although the sixteenth-century antiquarian John Bale thought this Thomas Malory was Welsh, late nineteenth- and early twentieth-century scholars, many of them following the influential George Lyman Kittredge,[2] generally accepted that our Sir Thomas Malory was from Newbold Revel, Warwickshire, an identity that remained unchallenged until the mid twentieth century. At that point, however, the biographical and bibliographical were deemed to clash. William Matthews in particular objected to the perceived discrepancy between the ideal of the High Order of Knighthood expounded throughout the *Morte Darthur* and the fact that the Newbold Revel Malory was accused of such crimes as cattle theft, sheep rustling, robbery, rape (of the same woman, twice), and the attempted murder of the duke of Buckingham. Partly to explain away this Malory's supposed ill manners, and partly doubting the ability of an English prisoner-author to acquire or access the many French books necessary to pen the *Morte*, Matthews made a lengthy argument for the author being one Thomas Malory from Hutton

---

[1] Sir Thomas Malory, *Le Morte Darthur*, ed. P. J. C. Field, 2 vols. (Cambridge, 2013), I, 940.17–30; C XXI.13; the first volume contains the entire text and the second volume the apparatus. In the *Morte*'s final colophon, line 3 of our quotation, the number of Round Table knights is listed as 140, but this is clearly an error, and Field justly emends to 150 for consistency with other references across the entirety of the *Morte*. The layout and italicisation of the colophon are editorial. Subsequent references to the text of the *Morte* will be parenthetical, using this edition.

[2] George Lyman Kittredge, "Who Was Sir Thomas Malory?" *Studies in Notes in Philology and Literature* 5 (1896): 85–106.

Conyers, Yorkshire.[3] In an effort to address similar problems, Richard Griffith then proposed yet a third Thomas Malory, this one hailing from Papworth St Agnes, Cambridgeshire.[4] While neither the Yorkshire nor the Cambridgeshire candidate finds many supporters today, the theories of Matthews and Griffith did much to sharpen the terms of the so-called "authorship question."

P. J. C. Field responded to Matthews and Griffith with a series of articles and then a book-length biography elucidating precisely why the Warwickshire Malory must be the author.[5] In brief, Field's argument rests on the case that the only Malory alive at the right time and also known to be a knight was Sir Thomas Malory of Newbold Revel; since the author of the *Morte* repeatedly styles himself knight, then only the Warwickshire Sir Thomas Malory can be the author. Accordingly, the original *Companion to Malory* included a chapter by Field giving a précis of Malory's career and the principal medieval records that allow scholars to reconstruct that life.[6] Since 1996 Field's conclusions have been questioned by some scholars, but Christina Hardyment's *Malory: The Life and Times of King Arthur's Chronicler*, which is a blend of scholarly biography and speculative fiction, includes new research – including the discovery of a distraint against knighthood by the Cambridgeshire Malory and the Malory of Newbold Revel coat of arms – that confirms Field's findings.[7] The biographical evidence at the moment does quite firmly support the Warwickshire Malory as the author, and that evidence has been both questioned but also emphatically confirmed over the last quarter-century.

The authorship controversy has turned not only on the moral fibre of whichever Thomas Malory wrote the *Morte* – though by now this ethical criterion has rightly faded from consideration – but also, more significantly, how he read or acquired the many French sources needed to write his own lengthy Arthuriad.[8] Matthews claimed – amongst much else – that no such library existed on English soil; he posited instead that the Yorkshire Malory accessed all of the relevant French sources from the French library of Jacques d'Armagnac (1433–77), duke

---

[3] William Matthews, *The Ill-Framed Knight: A Skeptical Inquiry into the Identity of Sir Thomas Malory* (Berkeley and Los Angeles, 1966).

[4] Richard R. Griffith, "Arthur's Author: The Mystery of Sir Thomas Malory," *Ventures in Research* 1 (1972): 7–43, revised and with sources added, as "The Authorship Question Reconsidered: A Case for Thomas Malory of Papworth St Agnes, Cambridgeshire," in *Aspects of Malory*, ed. Toshiyuki Takamiya and Derek Brewer (Cambridge, 1981), 159–77.

[5] P. J. C. Field, *The Life and Times of Sir Thomas Malory* (Cambridge, 1993). The relevant articles are mentioned in Field's Preface.

[6] P. J. C. Field, "The Malory Life-Records," in *A Companion to Malory*, ed. Elizabeth Archibald and A. S. G. Edwards (Cambridge, 1996), 115–30.

[7] Christina Hardyment, *Malory: The Life and Times of King Arthur's Chronicler* (London, 2005); reprinted as *Malory: The Knight Who Became King Arthur's Chronicler*. Field's position is also endorsed by T. J. Lustig, *Knight Prisoner: Thomas Malory Then and Now* (Brighton, 2013). Although her view is now in the minority, the most significant challenge to Field's argument is that of Christine Carpenter, Review of "*The Life and Times of Sir Thomas Malory*," *Medium Ævum* 63 (1994): 334–6.

[8] This discussion of the debate about Malory's library (and identity) repeats material from K. S. Whetter, *The Manuscript and Meaning of Malory's* Morte Darthur: *Rubrication, Commemoration, Memorialization* (Cambridge, 2017), 65–9. We have made some minor modifications to the original argument.

of Nemours.[9] The Yorkshire Malory, so the argument goes, could have consulted this library as a prisoner of war in the late 1460s. Furthermore, Jacques d'Armagnac's library contained at least one example of a single-volume French Arthurian compilation – the famous Bibliothèque nationale, MS français 112, compiled by Micheau Gonnot in 1470 – which is thematically and structurally cognate with Malory's *Morte*.[10] Griffith for his part also argued for a French library, but favoured instead the one-time royal library pillaged in France by the duke of Bedford in 1425, a library eventually passing through marriage to Bedford's young widow Jacquetta, who subsequently married Sir Richard Wydeville.[11] This former French library – "the one library in England containing the books essential for [Malory's] work" – was in turn inherited by Sir Anthony Wydeville, who, argues Griffith, lent it to the Cambridgeshire Malory, who in fact lived nearby. That Sir Anthony was tutor to the young son of Edward IV – his own nephew, in fact – and that the king insisted on chivalric literature as part of his education, is an important piece of Griffith's argument. The other major crux of Griffith's case is the fact that Wydeville collaborated with William Caxton on certain of Caxton's other publications.[12]

As discussed in more detail in this volume's chapter on Malory's sources,[13] source-study reveals that Malory worked closely with his sources – not from memory only – sometimes translating word-for-word. However, Malory also adapted his sources freely at times, and he need not always have had a source manuscript open in front of him, especially since medieval texts that survive in multiple copies reveal regular evidence of scribes and authors reconstructing texts (with varying degrees of accuracy) from memory or oral transmission. It can also be objected that Wydeville's mother, Jacquetta, former wife of the duke of Bedford and the person from whom Wydeville supposedly inherited Bedford's French library, was still alive when the *Morte Darthur* was being written: the Cambridgeshire Malory died in 1469, the Warwickshire Malory died in 1471, and Jacquetta died in 1472, two or three years after the *Morte*'s completion in 1469/70.[14] But she need not have formally bequeathed it for it to have been in

[9] Matthews, *Ill-Framed Knight*, 139–50.
[10] See Fanni Bogdanow, "Micheau Gonnot's Arthuriad Preserved in Paris, Bibliothèque Nationale de France, fr. 112 and Its Place in the Evolution of Arthurian Romance," *Arthurian Literature* XXII (2005): 20–48. See also Cedric E. Pickford, *L'Évolution du roman arthurien en prose vers la fin du moyen âge d'après le ms. 112 du fonds français de la Bibliothèque Nationale* (Paris, 1960), and Miriam Edlich-Muth, *Malory and His European Contemporaries: Adapting Late Arthurian Romance Collections* (Cambridge, 2014).
[11] Griffith, "The Authorship Question Reconsidered," 171–3.
[12] Three of Caxton's earliest printed books – including the very first printed in England – were translated from French by Wydeville: *Dictes or sayengis of the philosophres* (1477), *Morale Proverbes of Christyne* (1478) and *Cordyale, or Four last thinges* (1479). Caxton reprinted *Dictes* in 1479 or 1480 and again in 1489. On the relationship between Caxton and Wydeville see further Hilton Kelliher, "The Early History of the Malory Manuscript," in *Aspects of Malory*, 143–58, at 153–5, and Thomas H. Crofts, *Malory's Contemporary Audience: The Social Reading of Late Medieval Romance* (Cambridge, 2006), 18–21.
[13] See Ralph Norris, "Malory and His Sources," in this volume.
[14] Carol Meale, "Manuscripts, Readers and Patrons in Fifteenth-Century England: Sir Thomas Malory and Arthurian Romance," *Arthurian Literature* IV (1985): 93–126, at 97 and n. 11.

circulation. Wydeville might still have borrowed books from his mother to lend to whichever Malory penned the *Morte*. But the duchess was not known for her generosity, and, if we rule her out as a resource, or even posit that Malory stole the books (which is not outside the bounds of reason and biography), Griffith's thesis considerably unravels.

Tracing old books and their owners, moreover, can be difficult; tracing which source-books Malory might have borrowed from which owner, and how, can verge on the Quixotic. Fortunately, Carol Meale, who knows more than most about book ownership in fifteenth-century England, points out, against Matthews and his adherents, that books are often not listed in wills, and then rarely by title, meaning it is difficult to ascertain whether a suitable library did or did not exist in England in Malory's day. It is also hard to determine how much or how little of the French royal library actually made it to England or to Wydeville's (and thence Malory's) hands. Equally importantly, Malory did not need *de luxe* (elaborately designed and decorated) versions of the source texts; he could well have found most of his principal sources in a handful of plainer romance anthologies, one or two of which he may have owned himself, and the remainder of which he could easily have borrowed from friends and acquaintances.[15] Roger Middleton's definitive survey of ownership of French Arthurian manuscripts leads to a similar observation and to Middleton's endorsement of Meale's thesis. The common assumption that Malory must have required access to a large library or large number of expensive manuscripts to write the *Morte Darthur* is, concludes Middleton, "a misconception. All the French texts that Malory used could be contained in two or three volumes at most, and there is no need for any of them to have been expensive."[16] (Consider, for example, Gonnot's anthology, mentioned above.) This is equally true, we would add, of Malory's English sources, major and minor. The library question was still a reasonably contested topic in 1996, but with Middleton's endorsement of Meale, the present writers believe that a viable and convincing alternative has been reached.

## The Text and Its Witnesses

Moving from the author and acquisition of sources to the text of the *Morte Darthur* puts readers on much firmer ground, but there are still some controversies. Malory's Arthuriad survives today in two textual witnesses.[17] The older witness

---

[15] Meale, "Manuscripts, Readers and Patrons," 101–8.

[16] Roger Middleton, "The Manuscripts," in *The Arthur of the French: The Arthurian Legend in Medieval French and Occitan Literature*, ed. Glyn S. Burgess and Karen Pratt (Cardiff, 2006), 8–92, at 47.

[17] The original copy-text upon which one bases a modern edition of a pre-modern text (whether a classroom edition or a critical edition) is known as a *textual witness*. These textual witnesses may be authorial or scribal, manuscript or incunable (early print). Confusingly, they may not always agree, as with the different manuscript versions of Chaucer's works; even if there is only one witness, as with the unique manuscripts of *Sir Gawain and the Green Knight* or *Beowulf*, the witness may have gaps or errors. The text, in other words, can be less stable than those encountering it in the classroom, in a modern bookstore or through a tablet interface might realise.

is the late fifteenth-century manuscript now owned by the British Library, and catalogued as "British Library Additional Manuscript 59678."[18] There is, however, some scholarly inconsistency over how to cite this manuscript. Some scholars use (in full or abbreviated form) the British Library's shelf mark. Since, however, the manuscript was discovered in Winchester College in 1934, it is perhaps most commonly referred to as the "Winchester manuscript" (the designation we use in this chapter). Yet other scholars use the title "the Malory manuscript." All three titles refer to the same manuscript, but "Malory manuscript" is potentially misleading since the manuscript is not Malory's holograph (the text as written by an author's own hand) and was not produced until after his death. Nor is there full agreement about who designed the manuscript – a question to which we will return below.

Watermarks on the paper stock allow us to date the Winchester manuscript to approximately 1477.[19] Since Sir Thomas Malory of Newbold Revel died in 1471, Winchester is obviously not his holograph. The mere fact of its existence, however, shows that there was at least some demand amongst medieval readers for copies of an English Arthuriad. (Indeed, as we explain further below, evidence from the copying process reveals that there were in fact at least two manuscripts of the *Morte* in Caxton's shop; there may have been more in wider circulation.) This demand no doubt reflects the general appetite for vernacular Arthuriana evident in the fifteenth-century production or copying of such English texts as the Prose *Merlin*, Henry Lovelich's verse behemoths *The History of the Holy Grail* and *Merlin* (all *c*. 1450), and the copying of the Alliterative and Stanzaic *Mortes* (which date to *c*. 1400 or – for the Alliterative *Morte* – earlier, but survive in later manuscripts).[20] The 1485 printing of the *Morte Darthur* by Caxton, like the two printings by his successor Wynkyn de Worde in 1498 and 1529, further testify to the demand for Malory's Arthur story,[21] a story whose appeal no doubt rests partly on the fact that Malory tells the complete story ("the hoole book") of Arthur and his knights and the ladies who interact with them, and partly on Malory's own thematic and narrative emphases. The Arthurian legend was well established as a pan-European phenomenon by the fifteenth century, existing in stories, and often art, in all major western European countries and languages. Malory, always deferential to what he calls "the Freynshe booke," is careful to disclaim any originality, but he nevertheless crafted the defining medieval English Arthur story, one which Caxton's and de Worde's printings strongly imply had a wide readership.

---

[18] The manuscript exists in two facsimiles: the black-and-white *The Winchester Malory: A Facsimile*, intro. N. R. Ker (London, 1976); and, since 2011, Takako Kato's digital Malory Project at www.maloryproject.com. The British Library also has an online digital facsimile, but it is hard to locate: www.bl.uk/manuscripts/FullDisplay. aspx?ref=Add_MS_59678.

[19] Kelliher, "Early History of the Malory Manuscript," 144–5.

[20] *Merlin: or The Early History of King Arthur: A Prose Romance*, ed. Henry B. Wheatley, 4 vols. (London, 1865–1899); Henry Lovelich, *The History of the Holy Grail*, ed. Frederick J. Furnivall, 5 vols. (London, 1874–1905), and *Merlin: A Middle English Metrical Version of a French Romance*, ed. Ernst A. Kock, 3 vols. (London, 1904–1932); *Morte Arthure: A Critical Edition*, ed. Mary Hamel (New York and London, 1984); and *Le Morte Arthur: A Romance in Stanzas of Eight Lines*, ed. J. Douglas Bruce (London, 1903; rpr. 1959).

[21] On such appeal see further A. S. G. Edwards, "The Reception of Malory's *Morte Darthur*," in *Companion to Malory*, 241–52 (at 241–3).

Presumably some of these early readers were the "jentylmen and jentylwym-men" Malory addresses as his audience in the final colophon (quoted above), though evidence from other romance audiences suggests that the genre appealed to a wide range of society.[22] Much twentieth-century scholarship of the *Morte* was concerned with the inconsistences and – for modern readers accustomed to the novel – seeming vagaries of Malory's timeline, characterization, and even genre,[23] but the existence of at least some (now lost) manuscripts and several early printings indicates that medieval audiences were less concerned by these matters than are modern readers.

The Winchester manuscript of Malory's *Morte Darthur* is unique, meaning it is the only surviving manuscript text of the *Morte*, but it is also imperfect, meaning that it is missing sizeable sections: specifically, the opening and closing gather-ings (of eight folios each), and three other folios. The (modern) folio numbers pencilled in the upper corners of the manuscript and clearly visible in the fac-similes take these gaps into account, so that the opening folio is numbered 9 and the final folio is numbered 484; there survive, then, only 473 actual folio pages, and these include several blanks – probably due to quiring miscounts when the manuscript was being copied. Each folio has a front (recto: abbreviated to "r") and back (verso: abbreviated to "v"), and the majority of Winchester's folios record text on both sides. Winchester is written in two hands, meaning not only two different kinds of handwriting but that two different people were responsible for its copying. Modern scholars refer to Winchester's copyists as simply "Scribe A" and "Scribe B." These otherwise unknown scribes divided up the copying of Malory's *Morte Darthur* between them, but neat corrections in a third hand and ink on folios 22v, 61r, and 215v suggest that they were perhaps under the occasional supervision of a similarly unidentified scribal corrector or overseer.

The codicological evidence indicates that Scribe A and B worked simultane-ously from a sectioned exemplar: that is, they each copied the same manuscript base text, but this exemplar was unbound to allow each scribe to reproduce dif-ferent sections of text at the same time. Scribe A copied most of Tale I, now folios 9–34, though Ker's hypothesis that A also copied the missing sections (folios

[22] This appeal would hold true even if Malory's narrative is not quite a straightforward romance. On the genre of the *Morte* see especially Helen Cooper, "Counter-Romance: Civil Strife and Father-Killing in the Prose Romances," in *The Long Fifteenth Century: Essays for Douglas Gray*, ed. Helen Cooper and Sally Mapstone (Oxford, 1997), 141–62; and K. S. Whetter, *Understanding Genre and Medieval Romance* (Aldershot, 2008), 99–149.

[23] Early complaints regarding Malory's artistry are typified by Ernest Rhys, *Malory's History of King Arthur and the Quest of the Holy Grail* (London, 1886), v–xxxv, and entrenched in Roger Sherman Loomis, *The Development of Arthurian Romance* (London, 1963), 170–5, who goes so far as to suggest that Malory must have been drunk when he composed the May Passage! More favourable readings of the *Morte* which treat it as a proto-novel include George Saintsbury, *The English Novel* (London, 1913), 8, 25, 28–31; *Malory's Originality: A Critical Study of* Le Morte Darthur, ed. R. M. Lumiansky (Baltimore, 1964); Charles Moorman, *The Book of Kyng Arthur: The Unity of Malory's Morte Darthur* (Lexington, KY, 1965), xii, 2–3, 80 and 89. On these and related issues see further Cory J. Rushton's chapter "Malory and Form," in this volume.

1–8, 32–33) is surely correct.[24] For reasons now impossible to determine, both scribes copied parts of folio 35r, with Scribe A copying only the first eight lines, but continuing from the verso until folio 44v. There are then three stubs where folios were removed before the current folio 45r, which again has both scribes at work.[25] Scribe A copied the first six lines, but B the remainder, who then copied Tales II, III, IV and most of V: in total, the narrative found in folios 45–346v. Scribe A, however, helped with the lengthy "Trystram," copying folios 191v–229r. The final tales – VI, VII, VIII – occupying folios 349–484 (and perforce the missing pages) are by A.

The other textual witness to the *Morte Darthur* is the incunable (or early printed book) published by William Caxton in 1485, making it the first Arthurian text printed anywhere.[26] This incunable is commonly styled "the Caxton" or "Caxton's print," in part to avoid confusing Caxton the merchant and printer with the Arthurian book he produced. The Caxton survives in two copies: one perfect copy in the Pierpont Morgan Library, New York, and one, lacking eleven leaves, in the John Rylands Library, Manchester.[27] Because Winchester is missing some pages, and because in other places the scribes made obvious copying mistakes, it has been customary to correct Winchester's gaps and errors from the Caxton. It is of course possible that Caxton's readings are as faulty as the erroneous material in Winchester, but fortunately source-study allows us to correct Winchester – and to reconstruct Malory's text – with a fair degree of certainty.[28]

When a pre-modern text survives in multiple witnesses, textual criticism must decide which of several witnesses is the more accurate. This binary approach to the merits of textual witnesses – in which more correct readings are sought, and corrupt ones, the result of scribal error and accident, are purged – is largely the legacy of biblical textual study, which assumed that only one reading could possibly be correct (or authorial), and that that reading cancelled out all others. Establishing correct readings of biblical texts, whose witnesses are both many and fragmentary,

---

[24] Ker, Introduction to *Winchester*, xiii. Winchester's foliation was inserted by W. F. Oakeshott in the 1930s.

[25] On these stubs see further Whetter, *Manuscript and Meaning*, 13, 56.

[26] French prose romance was not printed until 1488, when the two-volume print of the *Lancelot*, *Queste del Saint Graal* and *Mort Artu* (the core of the *Lancelot-Graal* or Vulgate Cycle) appeared under the title *Lancelot du Lac*. See *Lancelot du Lac 1488*, intro. C. E. Pickford, 2 vols. (London, 1973).

[27] For a facsimile, see *Le Morte Darthur Printed by William Caxton, 1485*, intro. Paul Needham (London, 1976).

[28] Modern source-study of the *Morte* can be said to begin with the third volume of H. Oskar Sommer's edition of *Le Morte Darthur*, 3 vols. (London, 1889–91), but is defined by Eugène Vinaver's Introduction and Commentary to *The Works of Sir Thomas Malory* (see note 38 below); numerous studies by Robert H. Wilson, especially "Malory and the *Perlesvaus*," *Modern Philology* 30 (1932): 13–22, *Characterization in Malory: A Comparison with His Sources* (Chicago, 1934), "Malory, the Stanzaic *Morte Arthur*, and the *Mort Artu*," *Modern Philology* 37 (1939): 125–38, "The Fair Unknown in Malory," *PMLA* 58 (1943): 1–21, "Malory's 'French Book' Again," *Comparative Literature* 2 (1950): 172–81, "Addenda on Malory's Minor Characters," *Journal of English and Germanic Philology* 55 (1956): 263–87, and "The Cambridge *Suite de Merlin* Re-examined," *Studies in English* 36 (1957): 41–51; P. J. C. Field, *Malory: Texts and Sources* (Cambridge, 1998), and subsequent studies, including his Commentary to *Morte Darthur*; and Ralph Norris, *Malory's Library: The Sources of the Morte Darthur* (Cambridge, 2008), and subsequent studies, including those mentioned in n. 87. (This list is not exhaustive.)

is a daunting task indeed. The same is true of Homeric scholarship: beginning in the Alexandrian period the main job of Homer scholars was to weigh the likely authenticity not only of each manuscript, but of each line. But even when there are only two early witnesses, as is the case with Malory, the problems mount up quickly.

The case of Malory's two witnesses is also charged with a certain drama. For several hundred years (most of its known history, in fact), the sole textual witness to the *Morte Darthur* was Caxton's 1485 incunable.[29] The *Morte* proved quite popular for the next 150 years, winning regular reprintings – and thus continued audience demand – until William Stansby's 1634 edition, whereupon it fell into an hiatus until three editions were printed in 1816–17 (see this volume's List of Editions); rediscovered by the Victorians and adapted to great effect by Alfred Lord Tennyson, it has been in near constant print ever since. But all of these prints were, with greater and lesser degrees of accuracy, based on Caxton's incunable. Suddenly, in 1934 – a remarkably late date for such a consequential find – Walter Oakeshott discovered a manuscript of the *Morte Darthur* in a safe in the rooms of the Warden at Winchester College: the Winchester manuscript.[30] It was soon clear that the manuscript pre-dated the 1485 edition, and so had an immediate claim to greater authenticity.

## The Malory Debate

The two witnesses to the *Morte Darthur*, Winchester and the Caxton, are in lexical agreement about 90 per cent of the time, but in the remaining cases they differ in several important respects. Depending on the theoretical persuasion of the modern editor or reader, scholars variously favour a Caxton-based text, a Winchester-based text, or, at least in the Roman War, both texts. Given that the Roman War story recounted in "King Arthur and the Emperor Lucius" (Winchester, folios 71r–96r; Caxton, Book V) is pruned to half its length in the Caxton version versus the Winchester text, this tale has been ever since the discovery of Winchester the *locus classicus* of the Malory debate. The twentieth-century's august Malory editor Eugène Vinaver concluded that Caxton had edited the text, shortening the Roman War section for his own reasons; these changes were not authorial, and therefore counted as a corruption. Vinaver's edition of this tale is thus based upon, and prioritizes, the manuscript text, but includes the relevant Caxton text at the bottom of each page.[31] Nearly two decades later another great Malory scholar, William Matthews, made the shocking claim that the Caxton edition was in fact the more authoritative since its changes reflected Malory's own revisions. (We will return to this shocking claim below.)

The plot thickened in the 1970s when Lotte Hellinga, using an ultra-violet lamp and then an infra-red imaging machine in Scotland Yard, discovered traces

[29] The print history of Malory's *Morte Darthur* is explored by Siân Echard, "Malory in Print," in this volume.

[30] See W. F. Oakeshott, "The Finding of the Manuscript," in *Essays on Malory*, ed. J. A. W. Bennet (Oxford, 1963), 1–6.

[31] *The Works of Sir Thomas Malory*, ed. Eugène Vinaver, 3 vols. (Oxford, 1947 [*O¹*]). See also note 38, below.

of printer's ink offsets on sixty-six folios scattered throughout the Winchester manuscript, revealing that the manuscript had been in Caxton's shop between 1480 and 1483, when the matching type was in use.[32] The presence of a small piece of recycled vellum used to repair folio 243 allowed Hellinga further to establish that Winchester remained with Caxton till at least 1489. Winchester was thus in Caxton's printing house well before the 1485 incunable, but it was not the copy-text for the *Morte Darthur* since it contains none of the compositor's casting-off marks used by early printers to blueprint how much of the manuscript page could be set on each printed page. Caxton, in other words, had not one but two separate manuscripts of the *Morte Darthur*.

In an attempt to explain Winchester's presence in Caxton's printing house, and Caxton's ink in Winchester, Hellinga tentatively suggested that Caxton or someone in his shop copied Winchester to create a copy-text (the text from which he printed the book).[33] This thesis has not won much approval by scholars because the textual-critical evidence disallows it: there are too many passages of the *Morte* that appear only in Winchester or only in the Caxton and that are clearly genuine on the basis of narrative sense and comparable readings in the sources, but which have no counterpart in the other witness. By this reasoning, Winchester and the Caxton must stand in a parallel, not linear, relation, and Caxton must have printed his *Morte Darthur* from a now lost manuscript, not from Winchester. Although the precise number of ancestors between Winchester and the Caxton and Malory has been debated by some critics, current scholarship accepts that the stemma for the *Morte Darthur* looks like this:[34]

M

X

Y     Z

W     C

What all of this means for understanding a modern edition of Malory's *Morte Darthur* is that although Caxton was quite willing to modify Malory's words when it suited, he also took considerable care with his English Arthuriad: so

[32] Lotte Hellinga, "The Malory Manuscript and Caxton," in *Aspects of Malory*, 127–41, at 127–34. Hellinga's findings were first published in *British Library Journal* 3 (1977), and revised for *Aspects of Malory*.

[33] Hellinga, "The Malory Manuscript and Caxton," 135–8. Hellinga's thesis was expanded by Ingrid Tieken-Boon van Ostade, *The Two Versions of Malory's* Morte Darthur: *Multiple Negation and the Editing of the Text* (Cambridge, 1995), and N. F. Blake, "Caxton at Work: A Reconsideration," in *The Malory Debate: Essays on the Texts of* Le Morte Darthur, ed. Bonnie Wheeler, Robert L. Kindrick and Michael N. Salda (Cambridge, 2000), 233–53.

[34] In this stemma, M = Malory, W = Winchester, C = the Caxton print, and X, Y, Z = lost intermediary copies. The textual relations were most convincingly proposed by Vinaver in *Works* (1947), lxxxvi–civ, and continued through Vinaver's second (1967) and third (1990) editions: c–cxx in both editions. Compelling further evidence is offered by Field, ed., *Morte Darthur*, I, xi and xvii, and Commentary (vol. II) on 23.28, 119.35–120.1, and 206.13–14. Field's findings for the edition negate his earlier conclusions in P. J. C. Field, "The Earliest Texts of Malory's *Morte Darthur*," in his *Malory: Texts and Sources* (Cambridge, 1998), 1–13. Cf. Whetter, *Manuscript and Meaning*, 5–10 and 70.

much care, in fact, that he used Winchester as a secondary or consultation copy from which to check and correct difficult or illegible passages in his copy-text manuscript. This care was felicitous, for it means modern editors committed to the Winchester text can (and at times must) use the Caxton text to help fill in Winchester's gaps or errors. Modern research has shown, however, that Caxton also regularly changed the wording of the *Morte*, particularly towards the bottom of pages to save space; thus his text must be tested, where possible, against both Winchester and the sources.

While, on the one hand, the discovery of Winchester long represented a thorny problem for Malory scholars, on the other it is useful to keep in mind that textual criticism has begun to move away from an "either/or" approach, and many contemporary theorists and researchers reject the binary descriptors of "corrupt" and "correct" as applied to pre-modern texts. Bonnie Wheeler and Michael Salda suggest as much when they introduce an important collection of essays devoted to the competing merits of Winchester and the Caxton by claiming that "in thousands of cases of variation spread over hundreds of pages there is no 'better' [reading], there is merely 'different'."[35] This statement is not only an example of the more positive reappraisal of Caxton as an editor which has taken place in the last two decades, but also an expression of the more pluralistic approach to textual witnesses formulated most powerfully by the late textual scholar and theorist Paul Zumthor. Briefly, while Zumthor was studying the multiple manuscript witnesses of the early twelfth-century *Chanson de Roland*, he concluded that each of the manuscripts had an equal claim on the reader's attention: a manuscript's value derived not from its fidelity to a so-called "original" version – no such "original" is historically recoverable in any case – but derives instead from its use and circulation, its *being read* in its historical time. One of the most important clues to a text's use and circulation, then, is the range of variants in scribal versions of the text: the various readings in these "textual states" – along with other, non-verbal signs which accrue in the process of scribal transmission – are an index of a text's vitality.[36] Zumthor called this effect *mouvance* (variously translated as "variance" or "mutability," but often left untranslated), and though it was his observation that *mouvance* was largely found in anonymous texts – texts as subject to a kind of collective authorship – it is something which inheres, to varying degrees, in all scribally transmitted (and early printed) texts, including those of Chaucer and perhaps even Shakespeare. By this account, both the Caxton incunable and the Winchester manuscript may transmit two equally compelling, equally correct, versions of the *Morte Darthur*.

Not all modern scholars, however, especially textual scholars, are content with such a claim, and Wheeler and Salda admit that there are "hundreds of instances short and long" across the *Morte* "where the variation does seem to

---

[35] Bonnie Wheeler and Michael N. Salda, "Introduction: The Debate on Editing Malory's *Le Morte Darthur*," in *The Malory Debate*, ix–xiii, at x.

[36] Paul Zumthor, *Essai de poétique médiévale* (Paris, 1972); translated as *Toward a Medieval Poetics* by Philip Bennett (Minnessota, 1992).

matter."[37] And it is true that scribes (and authors) make mistakes. How do we detect such mistakes, and having detected them, how should we deal with them?

Here is where the different demands of different reading practices creep back into the picture. Some scholars have deep – and profoundly divergent – convictions about which version of the *Morte* is the most authoritative. Even if they disagree about which text has greater authority, they believe that we can recapture what Malory tried to write. And it is through the work of such scholars that we encounter Malory, in the form of the modern critical edition or a classroom or popular edition.

## Modern Editions and the Meaning of the Text

At the risk of belabouring the obvious, the kind of edition depends upon its audience. For our purposes, the main contenders are classroom or teaching texts and scholarly or critical texts. Classroom editions need to prioritize accessibility of text and student learning needs; a critical edition prioritizes scholarship and authority, whether the authority is thought to be closest to the author's intentions and final text, or (in the *mouvance* sense) merely one version of the available texts which is at least as valid as another.

A sense of the distinctions between the two types of edition can be easily illustrated by comparing the standard editions of the latter half of the twentieth century. The critical edition of Malory's *Morte Darthur* from 1947 until 2013 was Eugène Vinaver's three-volume *The Works of Sir Thomas Malory*, a magisterial display of scholarship and textual editing granted three editions.[38] In each of these editions the complete original-spelling text runs to 1,260 pages, preceded (in Volume 1) by Vinaver's Introduction and a further five pages of Caxton's Preface and table of contents; the text is followed, in Volume 3, by several hundred pages of Commentary plus an Index of Names and a Glossary.[39] The level of detail throughout is designed far more for the needs and interests of the scholar than of the average student. Thus, in the third edition (the most recent of Vinaver's critical editions), the Introduction is 107 pages plus a bibliography and prefatory material; the same is true of the second edition. The Commentary in the third edition is just over 400 pages, plus the Index of Proper Names, Glossary, and Field's Note to the Third Edition (itself twenty-two pages). The first edition's Introduction and Commentary are both *slightly* shorter, but the grand total even there remains 1,742 pages. At the other end of the spectrum stands Vinaver's one-volume Oxford Standard Authors edition, part of a series designed to bring classics of English literature to a wider audience, but becoming, especially in paperback, a staple classroom edition.[40] In its well-known paperback format,

---

[37] Wheeler and Salda, "Introduction," in *The Malory Debate*, x.

[38] *The Works of Sir Thomas Malory*, ed. Eugène Vinaver (Oxford, 1947 [$O^1$]), reprinted with some corrections in 1948 and revised by Vinaver for a second edition [$O^2$] in 1967, and revised by P. J. C. Field for a third edition [$O^3$] in 1990 (all with Clarendon Press).

[39] The glossary is by G. L. Brook, modified and corrected in the third edition by Field.

[40] The single-volume Malory, *Works*, ed. Eugène Vinaver, first appeared in hardcover in the Oxford Standard Authors series in 1954, was revised as a second edition in 1971,

Vinaver's one-volume teaching text runs to a mere 812 pages, 726 of which are the complete Middle English text, with the Introduction being perforce reduced to a mere six pages. The Notes and Glossary are likewise considerably condensed.

As of 2018, the three most important critical editions of Malory for the academic reader are the multivolume editions of (respectively) Vinaver (1947, 1967, 1990), Matthews and Spisak (1983), and Field (2013). These are not, however, the earliest. The first critical edition of the *Morte Darthur* can be said to be Oskar Sommer's Caxton-based text, published in 1889–91.[41] Sommer's *Morte* included studies of the sources and a (very good) interpretative essay by Andrew Lang. Sommer's edition, though, was already out of date by the time Winchester was discovered – and the discovery of the manuscript convinced many scholars that the entire Caxton text, although still invaluable, had been superseded. Enter Eugène Vinaver's three-volume *The Works of Sir Thomas Malory*, the edition that stood for over half a century as the authoritative text of Malory's "Hoole Book."[42] Vinaver's edition remains an indispensable treasury of textual analysis and source-study, and is further important for being the edition cited by nearly two generations of scholarship. Notwithstanding its historical significance and continuing value, Vinaver's Malory nonetheless also reminds us that a critical edition is also a critical interpretation. If the discovery of the Winchester manuscript was a bombshell, Vinaver's edition of it was revolutionary. First, the layout and textual divisions of the manuscript, together with occasional plot inconsistencies, persuaded Vinaver that Malory's book was not a single unified narrative, but a collection of tales about Arthur and his knights – hence his title *Works* instead of *Le Morte Darthur*, a title Vinaver rejected as Caxtonian. Vinaver's conclusions about the Arthuriad's lack of unity continued and were strengthened across the three editions (especially in the second), creating a decades-long scholarly argument known now as the Unity Debate.[43] Secondly, Vinaver, whose (profound) expertise lay in the thirteenth-century French prose romances which Malory adapted, was uniquely suited to laying bare, almost word-for-word, Malory's debt to his source texts (both French and English). The monumental edition thus offers not only a scholarly representation of the Winchester manuscript (with its lacunae necessarily supplemented from the Caxton), but something resembling an x-ray picture of Malory's processes as a translator.

---

and offered in paperback in 1977. Unlike Vinaver's critical edition, the one-volume text is still in print today.

[41] Le Morte Darthur *by Syr Thomas Malory: The Original Edition of William Caxton now Reprinted and Edited*, ed. H. Oskar Sommer, with an essay by Andrew Lang, 3 vols. (London, 1889–91).

[42] See note 38. Hereafter, *Works*. The pagination of the second and third editions is the same, though there are in each revision numerous textual corrections and updates to the notes. The third edition also includes extra pages at the end for Field's "Note to the Third Edition."

[43] Although Vinaver never wavered in this conviction, almost all modern scholars now accept that the *Morte* is in fact unified. See especially Robert H. Wilson, "How Many Books did Malory Write?" *Studies in English* 30 (1951): 1–23; D. S. Brewer, "Form in the *Morte Darthur*," *Medium Ævum* 21 (1952): 14–24; D. S. Brewer, "'The Hoole Book'," in *Essays on Malory*, 41–63; *Malory's Originality*, ed. Lumiansky (published in 1964); and Murray J. Evans, "The Explicits and Narrative Division in the Winchester MS: A Critique of Vinaver's Malory," *Philological Quarterly* 58 (1979): 263–81. As the dates of these studies show, the Unity Debate was largely over by the time the original *Companion to Malory* was published in 1996.

Vinaver's *Works* did more than any previous edition to show the massive textual traditions and verbal structures through which Malory, with a skill it was only now possible to appreciate fully, was able to "reduce" his sources into English. It is clear that both medieval and modern readers appreciated Malory's reduction, but only now was that process illuminated. If there is a flaw in this approach, it is in Vinaver's tendency to favour the authenticity of Malory's sources over Malory himself, reflecting, at the same time, a binary understanding of literary and textual merit. Rather than a prose artist in his own right, Malory was viewed as an adventurous and commendable, if at times inaccurate or inattentive, translator of tales whose French versions remained the more coherent expressions, and infinitely the more polished. For Vinaver and other early and authoritative scholars, including Wilson and Field, the *Morte* was a great story despite, rather than because of, Malory's artistry. Scholars of the late twentieth and early twenty-first century have rightly pushed against this negative valuation of Malory's skill.

Not everyone, however, was satisfied with Vinaver's conception of Malory's text. An important recent study illustrates how William Matthews had contacted Vinaver's publisher, Clarendon Press (now wholly part of Oxford University Press), with concerns about Vinaver's editorial procedures and the critical edition of Malory's *Morte Darthur* as far back as 1962.[44] It seems clear from the context that Matthews was hoping to pre-empt the forthcoming 1967 second edition, and that he may well have been angling for Vinaver's position as Malory's modern (at the time) editor. Notwithstanding Matthews's concerns about Vinaver's methods and the resulting text, the Press, after due diligence, went ahead with the second (and eventually the 1990 third) edition of *Works*. Having failed to supplant Vinaver's edition or editorship of the Clarendon Malory text, Matthews then began work on his own Caxton-based edition of the *Morte*, which was eventually completed and seen through to publication by James Spisak. In the meantime, Matthews's views on the superiority of the Caxton text did not become relatively public knowledge until the 1975 Congress of the International Arthurian Society, held that year in Exeter, where a now-notorious conference paper briefly outlining his case was delivered posthumously on Matthews's behalf. Matthews's thesis was not published for another two decades;[45] in the interim, two slightly different unpublished versions of the conference paper were occasionally passed quietly and privately amongst senior circles of the Arthurian community.

Matthews's shocking contention – known to those at the conference or those who were later given access to an unpublished copy of the paper – was that

---

[44] See Samantha Rayner, "The Case of the 'Curious Document': Thomas Malory, William Matthews and Eugène Vinaver," *Journal of the International Arthurian Society* (*JIAS*) 3 (2015): 120–38. This paragraph reworks material from Whetter, *Manuscript and Meaning*, 7–8.

[45] In a special issue of *Arthuriana* (7.1 [Spring 1997]); later republished as the backbone of *The Malory Debate* (in 2000). The key paper is "A Question of Texts," in *The Malory Debate*, 65–107. Matthews's (in)famous conference paper was thus a continuation of the complaint he had raised with Clarendon more than a decade earlier. The 1997 publication of Matthews's papers happened too late to be of any use to the contributors to the original *Companion*, but they re-dramatised the entire Winchester-Caxton controversy, and their ripples are still being felt.

Malory himself was responsible for the considerable differences between the Winchester and the Caxton versions of the Roman War story comprising the Tale of "King Arthur and the Emperor Lucius," Vinaver's Tale II but Caxton's Book V. As a consequence, the Caxton text rather than the manuscript was, for Matthews and his adherents, the more authoritative. When it finally appeared in 1983, accordingly, the two-volume Matthews-Spisak critical edition was quite explicitly an edition of *Caxton's* Malory.[46] In its transmission of the text, this version, too, is an interpretation and a performance. Caxton's edition is granted an authority which, for Vinaver, was rendered suspect the moment the Winchester manuscript was shown to predate the 1485 incunable.[47] For Matthews and Spisak, in contrast, Winchester was negated by the substantial rewriting Malory himself had supposedly undertaken in the Roman War section and elsewhere, revisions which Matthews argued were found only in the Caxton text, what one scholar therefore described as "Malory's second edition."[48]

Although the idea of an edition based exclusively on Caxton failed (reasonably, in our opinion) to win widespread acceptance, a number of scholars over the years have justly critiqued Vinaver's presentation of the text.[49] This critique was considerably buttressed by Carol Meale's important contribution to the original *Companion*.[50] Meale and others highlight, amongst other factors, the various ways in which the layout of the *Morte Darthur* in Winchester occasionally creates a markedly different reading experience, and even a different set of themes, from those foregrounded by Vinaver's layout. An oft-noted and well-justified example is the famous May Passage, a long encomium about "the moneth of May . . . whan every lusty harte begynnyth to blossom" in which Malory talks of love and lovers "and worshyp in armys," contrasts the "hasty" love of "nowadayes" against the "vertuouse love" that "was used . . . in Kynge Arthurs dayes," and concludes that lovers should recall May, and everyone should recall how "Quene Gwenyvere . . . was a trew lover, and therefor she had a good ende" (841.1–842.11; C XVIII.25). Vinaver used this passage to open the episode of the Knight of the Cart, the penultimate episode of the penultimate tale of the *Morte*, and that opening is emphasized by his use of a sub-title page (with a blank verso-page), a list of Caxton's chapter rubrics (with another blank verso), and then the May Passage. In Winchester, no such divisions occur: this narrative moment carefully conjoins

---

[46] The difference was clearly articulated in the title: *Caxton's Malory: A New Edition of Sir Thomas Malory's Le Morte Darthur based on the Pierpont Morgan Copy of William Caxton's Edition of 1485*, ed. James W. Spisak, based on work begun by the late William Matthews, 2 vols. (Berkeley and Los Angeles, 1983).

[47] Vinaver had himself been "nearing completion" of a new Caxton edition when Winchester was discovered. It is a testament to his conviction that, "Without undue regret [he] abandoned [his] original project" in favour of a new Winchester-based text: see *Works*, Preface to the first edition.

[48] Charles Moorman, "Caxton's *Morte Darthur*: Malory's Second Edition?" *Fifteenth-Century Studies* 12 (1987): 99–113.

[49] In addition to the studies mentioned, see especially Evans, "The Explicits and Narrative Division in the Winchester MS"; Murray J. Evans, "*Ordinatio* and Narrative Links: The Impact of Malory's Tales as a 'Hoole Book'," in *Studies in Malory*, ed. James W. Spisak (Kalamazoo, 1985), 29–52; and Helen Cooper, "Opening up the Malory Manuscript," in *The Malory Debate*, 255–84.

[50] Carol M. Meale, "'The Hoole Book': Editing and the Creation of Meaning in Malory's Text," in *Companion to Malory*, 3–17.

the close of the episodes Vinaver entitled the Great Tournament and the Knight of the Cart.[51] Although we are sceptical of Meale's contention that Winchester supports only four major narrative segments in the *Morte* as a whole, she was quite correct to point out how the manuscript version of these episodes actively unites tournament, male companionate love, and heterosexual love.[52]

As the twentieth century drew to a close, then, most Malory scholars accepted that the text of Malory's *Morte Darthur* as preserved in Winchester was more authoritative, even if several leading scholars rightly drew attention to the limitations and occasional errors in the way Vinaver presented that text in his critical edition. The general scholarly acceptance of Winchester's textual superiority was evident in the fact that Clarendon Press undertook a revised third edition of *Works*. Since Vinaver had died in 1979, his mantle of leading authority on Malory and his text – and thus the revision – deservedly fell to P. J. C. Field. Although he had been tasked with revising the third edition of *Works*, Field confined himself to correcting obvious mistakes and updating Vinaver's Commentary; importantly, he also had to stay within the pre-existing page ranges. Hence the position of his "Note to the Third Edition" at the end of the text. One of Field's more noticeable corrections included changing the middle section of the opening tale from Vinaver's "Torre and Pellinor" sub-title to the manuscript's "The Wedding of King Arthur," a title further justified by the episode's closing *explicit*. But Field refrained from modifying *Works* in any more substantial ways to reflect any of his own considered disagreements with Vinaver's editorial principles or textual-critical conclusions.[53] Those ideas, however, were soon being put into practice, eventually appearing as the most recent critical edition, Sir Thomas Malory's *Le Morte Darthur* (2013), the edition cited throughout this *New Companion*.

Within reason and excepting manifest error, Matthews favoured the Caxton text and Vinaver favoured the Winchester text; Field, as he makes clear in his Introduction, quite frequently modifies Winchester in favour of a reading found either in the Caxton or the sources or even Field's own reconstruction. His emendations are consequently much more radical and interventionist than were Vinaver's, often adopting readings that Vinaver had cited only to reject. Field also retitles several of the minor sub-sections of the *Morte* to reflect Malory's focus on character and what Malory himself called "The Hoole Book of Kyng Arthur *and of His Noble Knyghtes* of the Rounde Table" (940.17–18 / C XXI.13; our emphasis).

Field also shortens the titles of many of the eight major tale divisions. This abbreviation occurs noticeably with Tales II and VII, where Vinaver's "The Tale of the Noble King Arthur that was Emperor Himself through Dignity of his Hands" becomes Field's "King Arthur and the Emperor Lucius," while "The Book of Sir Launcelot and Queen Guinevere" is simply "Sir Launcelot and Queen Guenivere." Field also retitles Tale I to the more subject-accurate "King Uther and King Arthur," in contrast with Vinaver's "The Tale of King Arthur." Such

---

[51] Compare Winchester fols. 434v–435v; *Works*, 1114–20, and Field's *Le Morte Darthur*, 840–1. See further Whetter, *Manuscript and Meaning*, 163–4.

[52] Meale, "'Hoole Book'," 8, 13–14 and 15–16.

[53] Many of these disagreements and modifications were revised and republished collectively in Field, *Malory: Texts and Sources*.

changes are justified partly by different editorial visions, but also by Malory's wording and Winchester's layout: Winchester and Malory give two titles to the Roman War, and no obvious title to Tale VII. The full title for Tale I seems the longer and more awkward "Fro the Maryage of Kynge Uther unto Kyng Arthure that Regned aftir Hym and ded Many Batayles." Field's is more eloquent, but wordiness is often a Malorian trait, and some form of this longer title is followed by other recent editors.[54] Field's titles are logical, highlighting the most important characters and kings of the Arthuriad, and they follow Malory's own consider- able emphasis on character. Malory scholars in general have also long shortened Vinaver's Tale II title to "King Arthur and the Emperor Lucius" or even "Arthur and Lucius," so Field's title reflects both textual and critical practice. For all of the merits of Field's edition, however, some readers may well be confused by some of the new titles and their attendant textual differences; indeed, Malory studies will be assessing these textual and editorial events for some time to come, and Vinaver's edition (as noted) remains indispensable for the Commentary and its magisterial source-study. Vinaver's edition will also need to be cited by those brave scholars who wish to dispute any of Field's interventionist readings. Thus, as we go to press, many scholars are avoiding confusion by citing both Vinaver and Field.

Field's new edition – which restores the traditional title *Le Morte Darthur*, and which should not be confused with his earlier stand-alone edition of Tales VII and VIII[55] – is a challenging and daring combination of traditional textual editing whose aim is to recapture authorial intention, coupled with a radical willingness to emend the witness(es) based on a learned conviction that the text as recorded contains some sort of error. Field's critical text thus contains many readings which differ from all previous editions. Our appraisal of Field's edi- tion is based on our own experience and judgement, but is confirmed by the reviews: Shepherd, for example, notes the distinction between Vinaver's text and Field's, hails Field as "*the* editor of" Malory's *Morte*, and likewise emphasizes the "unprecedented degree of conjecture" undergirding the text.[56]

Field's interventionist shifting of the witnesses and sources to reconstruct "what Malory intended to write" will have its critics.[57] Even the authors of the present chapter, two scholars who, in making sense of Malory's book, agree on most things, may differ here. While Whetter cautiously affirms the practice of well-justified editorial intervention according to local necessity, Crofts consid- ers strange readings, and even scribal errors, to preserve the unique texture of a handwritten literary record, and so, for better or worse, might be less willing to intervene. Readers who are committed to the celebration of *mouvance*, then, will be particularly opposed to Field's editorial principles. Yet readers of all persuasions are constantly reminded by the various *explicits* in the Winchester

---

[54] See, e.g., *Le Morte Darthur*, ed. Helen Cooper (Oxford, 1998), 3; and *Le Morte Darthur*, ed. Stephen H. A. Shepherd (New York, 2004), 3.

[55] *Le Morte Darthur: The Seventh and Eighth Tales*, ed. P. J. C. Field; initially published in 1977 as part of the London Medieval and Renaissance Series, and revised by Field and reissued by Hackett (Indianapolis) in 2008.

[56] Stephen Shepherd, "No Vinaver Redux," *JIAS* 2 (2014): 114–20.

[57] His editorial approach is outlined in Volume I's Introduction. We quote I, xviii.

text of the *Morte* at folios 70v (143.29–144.5), 346v (664.9–18), 409r (789.14–18), 449r (869.1–17), and the final colophon of 940.17–30, as well as the apostrophe to Trystram and hunting (at 280v; 538.33–539.9),[58] that Malory's text was written by Malory, not by Caxton or the scribes, and source-study and textual criticism allow us to see where Malory, his printer, or his scribes made errors. The Vinaver-versus-Matthews debate teaches us that the question of how to edit the words of Malory's Arthuriad, like all important questions, can be contentious, but also that no scholarly opinion profits from being inflexible. As Professor Field observes, "it is in everyone's interest to try to see if it is possible to generate less heat and more light."[59]

Given Arthurian scholars' liking for vigorous debate, in fact, the most surprising element of Field's edition is not the intervention but how quickly the text has been accepted by the scholarly world. The typical method by which a modern scholarly work becomes standard – similar to the mainstream acceptance of any artist or work of art throughout human history – is through recognition and cautious or celebratory acceptance by the community of users of the work at hand. For a textual edition, such acceptance, if it is won at all, comes through positive reviews and repeated citation leading to adoption. With Field's Malory, however, the cart somewhat kickstarted the horse: the edition was accepted and lauded by many scholars even before the reviews came in, while immediately upon the edition's publication, the editor of the journal *Arthuriana* announced that all articles on Malory submitted to the journal would cite Field's edition.

Partly, of course, such an unusually quick and positive reaction is a tribute to the learning behind the edition, as well as the fact that many Malory scholars had been anxiously awaiting it for years. There is also the fact that Field could be said to have already passed the normal publication-review process by virtue of a masterful body of work that has helped to define Malory's style, his biography and elements of his text.[60]

The new critical edition does, however, have weaknesses and not all of Field's emendations will be accepted. Most of the textual-critical challenges, we suspect, will however take the shape of offering different textual reconstructions: it is a question of what, where, and how to emend rather than whether emendation should occur. The real limitation of Field's text is thus not so much intervention per se as the fact that so much of the Commentary and apparatus is geared purely to textual-critical matters – Field's textual-critical work is nothing if not minutely documented – and geared so high as to be of maximum use only to the expert rather than the new reader. One reason why the final text is so convincing is because Field has given it considerable thought: much of that thought is

---

[58] Caxton modified or cut all but the final colophon, so even when he kept references to the "I" who wrote the story, he disallowed any mention of "Thomas Malory" at these points; we therefore cite Winchester and Field. The final authorial *explicit* only exists in the Caxton due to the missing gatherings of Winchester. Happily, Caxton did not excise this authorial and biographical comment.

[59] P. J. C. Field, "Caxton's Roman War," in *The Malory Debate*, 127–67, at 127. On this essay, see note 85 below.

[60] See, e.g., *Romance and Chronicle: A Study of Malory's Prose Style* (London, 1971); *The Life and Times of Sir Thomas Malory*; Field's "Note to the Third Edition" of *Works*; and his *Malory: Texts and Sources*.

carefully outlined in the relevant notes, but the novice reader may find the detail overwhelming. On the other hand, readerly accessibility to an accurate text was always one of Field's primary goals, and the new edition, with its lack of on-page commentary or bracketing, allows readers, at times forces readers, to read Malory's prose according to their own understanding. This is no bad thing, and may well result in a redefinition of Malory studies for the next fifty years just as the first edition of Vinaver's *Works* set the direction for Malory criticism for decades after its publication.

Notwithstanding Field's daring conjectures, then, we heartily concur with Shepherd that this new *Morte Darthur* "is the most 'sensible' Malory yet, with many minor illogicalities and incongruities eliminated, and many intimations of codicological wear and tear patched up with remarkable editorial insight and intuition."[61] Helen Cooper likewise praises Field's massive "rethinking" as well as the sheer level of learning and industry; she too concludes that this is a fitting "tribute" to Malory and the "definitive" text.[62]

For all of its merits, the sheer bulk and price of Field's edition make it imprac-tical as a teaching text. A single-volume paperback version of Field's complete, original-spelling *Morte Darthur* (that is, Volume 1 of the critical edition with almost no accompanying *apparatus*) is now available and very reasonably priced; this paperback edition includes a somewhat different Introduction but reprints the text of the critical edition as well as the Index of Proper Names and Glossary. The paperback text has the same pagination as the original, so industrious stu-dents could still make use of Field's Commentary in Volume II of a library copy of the critical edition. It will thus work in the classroom, but will leave most students largely to their own critical resources, with all the advantages and disadvantages of such a system. Vinaver's critical edition was also impractical for teaching, which is why the original *Companion to Malory* was keyed to the (complete) one-volume Vinaver edition as the text most commonly used in the classroom. This was quite true in the 1990s, and indeed the choice to tie citations to the classroom Vinaver is still justified since that version remains in print – in marked contrast to the three-volume critical edition. The one-volume complete Vinaver, however, is often (at least in North America) quite expensive. Cheaper alternatives are available, some quite excellent. Penguin has long had available a good two-volume paperback of the complete Caxton text,[63] but the Penguin uses modern spelling and it is clear by now that most scholars accept the superiority of a manuscript-based *Morte Darthur*. Oxford World's Classics, as is the brief of the series, likewise offers a reasonably-priced edition, one based on Winchester;[64] the edition, by Helen Cooper, offers an excellent Introduction, Explanatory

---

[61] Shepherd, "No Vinaver Redux," 118. Cf. Carolyne Larrington, "Unto me delyverd," *Times Literary Supplement*, 9 May 2014, 13.

[62] Helen Cooper, "Such Werkes," *Cambridge Quarterly* 43.4 (2014): 384–9. Lupack offers similar praise, concluding that Field's *Morte Darthur* "is an invaluable contribution to Malory scholarship and ... the standard edition of Malory's masterpiece:" Alan Lupack, Review of Sir Thomas Malory, *Le Morte Darthur*, ed. P. J. C. Field, 2 vols (Cambridge, UK, 2013), *Arthuriana* 24.4 (2014): 131–3.

[63] Sir Thomas Malory, *Le Morte D'Arthur*, ed. Janet Cowen, intro. John Lawlor, 2 vols. (London, 1969).

[64] As above, note 54.

Notes, and exemplary Index of Characters providing considerable erudition and assistance for the reader. Cooper's text, however, is both abridged and modernized, so its merits come at the cost of the full Malory experience. In comparison to the price of the single-volume classroom Vinaver and the abridged text of the World's Classics edition, the Norton *Le Morte Darthur* edited by Stephen H. A. Shepherd offers a more affordable and complete manuscript-based text.[65] Shepherd's edition is affordable, but not necessarily accessible, for reasons which lead us back to one last and distinguishing feature of the manuscript: its physical design.

## *Winchester's* Ordinatio *and Meaning*

Winchester is not an elaborate manuscript, but it does have one striking visual feature: all character names, quite a few place names, and several object names are rubricated (written in red ink). The effect is so striking partly because of the consistency of the rubrication, and partly by contrast with the dark brown ink used to record the rest of the words. As one of us has observed before, so vivid is the rubrication of names "that, in turning from this manuscript back to the typographical text, one feels as if the lights had gone out."[66] The manuscript also contains, and is partly divided by, 111 coloured initials, as well as eighty rubricated marginal comments together with one further and somewhat unique non-rubricated marginalium and fourteen *maniculae* (small hands drawn in the margins) pointing to certain places in the text.[67] Perhaps because of the lack of the usual sort of decoration such as tracery or scroll-work, illustrations major or minor (and sacred or profane), or explanatory glosses, however, the significance of Winchester's non-textual visual features is still debated.[68] The question of narrative divisions, codicological and textual, was highlighted above. For now, it needs be noted that many scholars in the last twenty years have argued that modern editions of medieval texts should reflect the layout of those texts in their manuscript witnesses.[69]

---

[65] Also as above, note 54.

[66] Crofts, *Malory's Contemporary Audience*, 66.

[67] The marginalium is unique for being non-scribal and especially because it is the only one to correct the text and include a face (or faces) in its surrounding shield-like shape. For the main scholarly positions on this marginalium see P. J. C. Field, "Malory's Own Marginalia," *Medium Ævum* 70 (2001): 226–39, at 231; Crofts, *Malory's Contemporary Audience*, 74–6; and K. S. Whetter, "Inks and Hands and Fingers in the Manuscript of Malory's *Morte Darthur*," *Speculum* 92.2 (April 2017): 429–46, at 435–8. On Winchester's pointing fingers, see especially Crofts, *Malory's Contemporary Audience*, 62–3 and Table 1 (at 65) and the critics cited therein, and Whetter, "Inks and Hands and Fingers," and the critics cited therein.

[68] Manuscript scholars refer to the overall effect of these type of decorative features and how the manuscript is laid out on the page as *ordinatio* or *mise-en-page*.

[69] Examples relevant to Malory include D. Thomas Hanks, Jr, "Textual Harassment: Caxton, de Worde, and Malory's *Morte Darthur*," in *Re-Viewing* Le Morte Darthur: *Texts and Contexts, Characters and Themes*, ed. K. S. Whetter and Raluca L. Radulescu (Cambridge, 2005), 27–47; and Cooper, "Opening up the Malory Manuscript," 273–4; Cooper, "Suche Werkes," 387.

To date, only one modern Malory edition has put this theory into practice; Stephen H. A. Shepherd is thus to be applauded for attempting to mimic
Winchester's *ordinatio* in his Norton edition of the *Morte*. Shepherd uses Lombard
capitals to reflect Winchester's decorated initials, prints the manuscript's marginalia in his own margins, and uses a bold type and old-fashioned font to approximate
the rubrication of names in the manuscript. This printed "rubrication-font" is quite
different from that used for the main narrative, and it has manuscript authority
since Winchester's rubricated names are written in a slightly different script from
what the scribes use elsewhere. Unfortunately, students in our experience find
Shepherd's black-letter font for names all but unreadable, even to the point of failing to recognize (or spell) Gwenyvere's name, let alone the host of minor character
names appearing in Malory's Arthuriad. Since named characters were important
to Malory, this confusion is best avoided. And although it would have been beyond
the editor's control, the paper used in the Shepherd *Morte* is quite thin, allowing
show-through which makes the page, though attractive, difficult to read.

Even before Shepherd's edition attempted to mimic Winchester's rubrication, the layout of Winchester had generated small but significant debate. This
debate is dominated by a select group of important figures. Because of the centrality of the manuscript to the text of the *Morte Darthur* much early criticism
of Winchester was necessarily focussed on textual-critical matters. A detailed
codicological description of Winchester's size, format, *ordinatio* and scribes by
N. R. Ker, the leading English manuscript scholar of his generation, introduces
the EETS facsimile.[70] Ker's descriptions and conclusions were adopted and
briefly expanded by two scholars contributing to two important books of essays
devoted to Malory's *Morte*. The first was Hilton Kelliher in his history of the
manuscript, and the second was Meale in the original *Companion*.[71] Meale's study
of the manuscript advocated (and is used by subsequent critics to advocate) conclusions about the text of the *Morte* as well as the *ordinatio* of Winchester since she
uses these codicological conclusions to critique the page layout and textual divisions of Vinaver's edition. Meale further argued that Winchester's rubrication of
names was typical of late medieval manuscript production, an argument which
requires some scrutiny since Winchester's kind and consistency of rubrication
seem in fact rather unique. Rubrication itself is a common decorative technique
in a diverse range of genres and manuscripts in the Middle Ages, but the rubrication of each name from the beginning to the end of a manuscript and narrative is
in fact found only in Winchester.[72]

Further scholarship continued to examine both the layout and production of
Winchester, linking these issues to the *Morte*'s meaning, author, or scribes. In the
course of a stimulating study, Cooper proposed a shorter stemma between Malory
and Winchester, concluded that the scribes created Winchester's marginalia as an
early and original reader response to Malory's narrative, and posited that certain

---

[70] *The Winchester Malory: A Facsimile* (1976).
[71] Kelliher, "Early History of the Malory Manuscript"; Meale, "'The Hoole Book'."
[72] The manuscripts of Malory's French sources, for instance, were more likely to have
abbreviated and non-rubricated names. On Winchester's uniqueness, see Whetter,
*Manuscript and Meaning*, 23–53.

other features of Winchester's design, especially its basic layout and punctuation and capitalization, could conceivably be authorial.[73] Field responded instead that the marginalia go back to Malory.[74] Other critics urged that at least some of the coloured initials and thus some aspects of the manuscript's design are scribal.[75] Crofts offers a middle ground between Cooper and Field, proposing a thematic reading of the marginalia and layout in the "Tale of Balyn" section, where a differently-styled marginalium is found at folio 23r.[76] In the most detailed study of Winchester to date, Whetter responds to this pre-existing scholarship by using Cooper's suggestion that Winchester's rubrication "may have" derived from the exemplar and Field's evidence for Winchester's marginalia being authorial, together with codicological evidence about scribes faithfully copying manuscript layout as well as text, to conclude that all of Winchester's marginalia and rubrication have a marked thematic function and thus ultimately derive from Malory himself.[77] Whetter argues further, somewhat contrary to Cooper and Crofts, that the unique marginalium on folio 23r is contemporary with Winchester's copying and was done by the same person who drew the *maniculae*.[78]

Winchester's primary value is obviously textual-critical – its witness to the narrative of Malory's *Morte Darthur* – but since the original *Companion* the manuscript has increasingly been recognized as a window onto scribal production and manuscript book culture. For students of literary history, moreover, part of the interest of Malory's Arthuriad resides in the ways it embodies the transition from the manuscript book to the printed book. Malory himself tells readers that the *Morte* was finished in 1469/70, which antedates Caxton's establishment of the first printing press in England by five to seven years. Caxton was a successful merchant as well as a printer, and we might well suppose that "Caxton may have had a scriptorium, as well as a press, and may have dealt in MSS as well as printed books."[79] The notion of Caxton producing and selling manuscripts as well as incunables is sound, but it remains an open question just how Malory's *Morte Darthur* came to his attention. Nevertheless, come to his attention it did, for he printed it within a decade of establishing his press. That he did so brings us to the ultimate cause of the divergent modern editions.

---

[73] Cooper, "Opening up the Malory Manuscript"; Cooper's conclusions about the scribal marginalia are supported by Nicole Eddy, "Annotating the Winchester Malory: A Fifteenth-Century Guide to the Martialism, the Marvels, and the Narrative Structure of the *Morte Darthur*," *Viator* 42.2 (2011): 283–305; and James Wade, "Malory's Marginalia Reconsidered," *Arthuriana* 21.3 (2011): 170–86.

[74] Field, "Malory's Own Marginalia," 226–39.

[75] See Takako Kato, *Caxton's* Morte Darthur: *The Printing Process and the Authenticity of the Text* (Oxford, 2002), 69–73; David Eugene Clark, "Scribal Modifications to Concluding Formulae in the Winchester Manuscript," *Arthurian Literature* XXXII (2015): 123–54.

[76] Crofts, *Malory's Contemporary Audience*, 61–93.

[77] Whetter, *Manuscript and Meaning, passim*. On scribal copying, see A. I. Doyle and M. B. Parkes, "The Production of Copies of the *Canterbury Tales* and the *Confessio Amantis* in the Early Fifteenth Century," in *Medieval Scribes, Manuscripts and Libraries: Essays presented to N. R. Ker*, ed. M. B. Parkes and Andrew G. Watson (London, 1978), 163–210 (esp. 165). Whetter is also explicitly responding to Crofts, *Malory's Contemporary Audience*.

[78] Whetter, "Inks and Hands and Fingers," 435–8.

[79] J. A. W. Bennett, "Preface" to *The Caxton Master and His Patrons*, by Kathleen L. Scott (Cambridge, 1976), ix–xvii (xi).

One issue facing all editors of the *Morte* is how to represent (and perhaps create) textual divisions. The necessary narrative divisions, as already indicated, are both large – distinguishing between, say, the Roman War narrative and the many adventures of and surrounding Trystram – and small – noticing distinctions between the episode of the Knight of the Cart or the healing of Sir Urry. The question of how to present the *Morte* and divide its narrative sections goes back to the original witnesses. With the notable exceptions of the lack of rubrication and marginalia and *maniculae*, the physical layout of the Caxton resembles Winchester in many ways; there are, though, notable differences, especially in terms of narrative divisions. We concur with Vinaver and Field that Malory's many *explicits* and occasional *explicit-cum-incipits* recorded throughout Winchester produce an eight-tale Arthuriad. Most of these tale divisions also come with titles, even when the title comes at the end of the tale. (See, for instance, 189.18–22 / C V.12; 222.16–18 / C VI.18; 664.9–18 / C XII.14; and 869.14–15/ C XIX.13).

All editors since Caxton, however, have felt that Malory's or Winchester's divisions are too few, and have attempted to render the textual layout of the *Morte* in more contemporary fashion. Caxton's common practice as printer was to provide prologues or epilogues to each print edition in which he outlined such matters as his editorial procedures, textual sources, patrons, and the didactic purpose of what he had printed.[80] Thus Caxton informs readers in his preface to the *Morte* that he divided Malory's Arthuriad into twenty-one books and 507 chapters (though there are actually 506). Caxton's narrative divisions have been adopted by all modern editors, even if the book and chapter numbers are only noted in the header and margins. So ingrained are these divisions that even editors of Winchester give on-page Caxton cross-references. So too did the original *Companion*: a practice followed in this sequel to facilitate cross-references between different editions. As most readers will recognize, some modern scholars also give Caxton's divisions in their publications.

Nevertheless, Caxton's book and chapter divisions, it bears emphasizing, are his invention. Winchester, we repeat, has far fewer major narrative divisions: anywhere from four to eight to ten, depending on which critic one consults. We conclude that there are eight *major* tales and seven *main* divisions in the manuscript, and that these divisions have authorial stature. Some of these tales then have sub-sections. This eight-tale division is employed in all manuscript-based editions. Vinaver and Field sometimes give different tale titles, but they follow Malory and Winchester in the arrangement of eight tales. Malory's and Vinaver's and Field's tale divisions are not at all coterminous with Caxton's book and chapter divisions, even though Caxton seems to have taken his cue from Winchester in many places.

It is therefore highly confusing when, as sometimes happens, modern scholars cite Caxton's "Book" and Malory's "Tale" divisions interchangeably as if

---

[80] On Caxton's prologues and epilogues in general, see *The Prologues and Epilogues of William Caxton*, ed. W. J. B. Crotch (London, 1928). For Caxton's prologue (equally often called "preface" by scholars) to the *Morte*, see Thomas H. Crofts, "'Thynges Foresayd Aledged': *Historia* and Argumentum in Caxton's Preface to the *Morte Darthur*," in *Re-Viewing* Le Morte Darthur, 49–64.

they were axiomatically the same. Such, to take two notable examples, is the practice of the otherwise learned and sensible introductions to the *Morte Darthur* by two leading scholars, both of whom use "Book" to refer to the various Tale divisions in the *Morte*.[81] A reference to "Book XIX" causes no problems, since it quickly becomes apparent even to novice readers that there is no Tale XIX; but Caxton's Book V and Malory's (and so Vinaver's and Field's or Cooper's and Shepherd's) Tale V are quite different areas of text: respectively, The Roman War story (in "King Arthur and the Emperor Lucius," Tale II) and the prolix "Book of Sir Trystram." Readers will likewise notice that we put the tale title – "Book of Sir Trystram" – in italics here, but not Roman War. The most common tale titles for the eight major narrative divisions of the *Morte* are based on *explicits* in the manuscript. If Winchester has the textual and authorial weight that we maintain, then such major tale divisions as "A Noble Tale of Sir Launcelot du Lake" or "Morte Arthure" and their fellows deserve to be put in quotation marks: italics are too divisive (despite the practice of some scholars), because italics create too emphatic a narrative division, suggestive of individual stories rather than a cohesive whole, thereby implying that Vinaver was correct and Malory's various tales are independent of one another. To go to the other extreme and not set the major tale titles off by any sort of typographic *ordinatio* likewise seems ineffective. Quotation marks around the eight constituent tales hopefully clarify that they are major parts of the larger whole. The *Morte*'s many minor episodes often do have recognisable descriptive titles: some of these titles, such as the "The Tale of Balyn" or "The Weddyng of King Arthur," are Malory's invention, but many others, such as the Roman War or Fair Maid of Ascolat or Knight of the Cart, are the creation of Vinaver or other modern scholars. These sub-titles and scholarly short-hands (such as Tale VIII or the May Passage) lack manuscript authority; the episodes are there, but not necessarily these titles. Accordingly, these non-authorial episode epithets (as we might label them) should not go in quotation marks. The confusion is once again compounded by a lack of scholarly consistency, making even experienced readers uncertain of how to indicate major versus minor textual divisions or nicknames when citing the text. This sort of inconsistency in scholarly terminology does little to advance consistent practice or student understanding of Malory's masterpiece; on the other hand, knowing that this is the case, the new reader can confidently begin by ignoring such terms in favour of enjoying the text itself, a course we fully recommend.

Not the least of the attractions of Field's edition is aesthetic. Vinaver's pages are thick with marginal notes at the top, bottom, and outer side of each page, and his emendations are marked by a complex system of bracketing requiring no fewer than three different kinds of parenthetical marks, one of which (the square brackets) is used in two slightly different ways, though both denote readings adopted from Caxton. Field jettisons nearly all of this, maintaining only manuscript and incunable cross-references; these were added for practical necessity, but appear only in the header, not in their exact location in the margins. Thus

---

[81] See Felicity Riddy, *Sir Thomas Malory* (Leiden, 1987), and Terence McCarthy, *An Introduction to Malory* (Cambridge, 1991). These examples are chosen for their authority; they are hardly exclusive.

Field's pages, like those of the Winchester manuscript itself, are very clean, foregrounding Malory's work rather than that of his editor. This is good, though readers wishing to locate the precise beginning and ending of the relevant manuscript or incunable pages must hunt a little longer than with Vinaver's signposting. Field emends the text even more frequently than Vinaver, but one must turn to the Commentary to learn how. The resulting text is mostly quite convincing and Malorian, and the modern reader will appreciate the capitalization of "Sir" in references to knights that Vinaver, puzzlingly since they have manuscript authority, refused to adopt. At the same time, Field's tale titles will take some getting used to since most scholarship of the *Morte* for the last two generations has adopted Vinaver's major and minor titles as a scholarly aid with which to navigate Malory's expansive narrative.

As Malory's many invocations of "the Freynshe booke" illustrate, the medieval Arthurian legend is a remarkably intertextual and composite construct. Both the medieval Arthurian legend in general and the medieval method of romance storytelling in particular have accordingly been likened to the art of building medieval cathedrals. Thus, it is said, Malory is merely the last great builder of his Arthuriad, although Caxton considerably touched up – or in places tore down – Malory's edifice, and Vinaver polished the stone and offered a new path to the cathedral.[82] Field, by this analogy, not merely polishes but actively rebuilds parts of Malory's narrative; the restoration is, to our eyes, impressive and convincing. If, with C. S. Lewis, modern readers prefer Malory as he was known from Caxton to Tennyson, a Malory still available in mass-market editions, then they will seek a Caxton-based *Morte Darthur*.[83] On the other hand, readers concerned with authorship and authority, or who follow the balance of scholarly debate over the text of the *Morte*, will seek a manuscript-based edition as the best way forward: that is certainly where our own sympathies and critical recommendations lie.

For the general reader several adaptations and translations of the *Morte* are available, though many of them offer a poor text and even the best are usually abridged. Cooper's abridged edition is perfectly accessible to the interested layperson due to its modernized spelling, and her notes and detailed index are excellent for the generalist or specialist; Dorsey Armstrong's rendition into Modern English provides a complete text and a concise Introduction.[84] For the undergraduate reader, Vinaver's one-volume Oxford Standard Authors paperback (cited throughout the original *Companion*) remains an accessible authoritative text. Shepherd's Norton edition, for all of the limitations created

---

[82] C. S. Lewis, "The English Prose *Morte*," in *Essays on Malory*, 7–28 at 24–8. For another architectural reading of Malory see Sandra Ness Ihle, *Malory's Grail Quest: Invention and Adaptation in Medieval Prose Romance* (Madison, WI, 1983).

[83] Lewis, "The English Prose *Morte*." See further Rushton, "Malory and Form," in this volume.

[84] *Sir Thomas Malory's* Morte Darthur: *A New Modern English Translation based on the Winchester Manuscript*, trans. Dorsey Armstrong (West Lafayette, IN, 2009). It should be added that Peter Ackroyd has made a "retelling" and abridgement into modern English: *The Death of King Arthur: Thomas Malory's Le Morte d'Arthur* (London, 2010). A somewhat modernised but complete Caxton text, retaining book and chapter divisions, is the Modern Library's *Le Morte D'Arthur*, ed. Elizabeth J. Bryan (New York, 1999).

by its – to most student eyes – off-putting font, offers a fuller text of the Roman
War than does Vinaver because Shepherd makes use of a reconstruction of the
opening of Tale II advanced in the late 1990s by Field in which Field convincingly demonstrates that there are alternating gaps in each witness to Malory's
Tale of "King Arthur and the Emperor Lucius."[85] Readers interested in Malory's
relations to his sources will still need to consult Vinaver's Commentary to his
critical edition, augmented by Field's source-studies, Ralph Norris's account of
the minor sources, and Field's own Commentary where, to take one example,
he finds something new to say about the episode of the Healing of Sir Urry.[86]
Without question Field's text provides the clearest, most readable critical edition
of *Le Morte Darthur*. Further emendation may still be necessary in places,[87] but
Field's *Morte Darthur* should, in our view, now be cited by graduate students
and scholars as the definitive critical edition. It is also to be hoped that, as happened with Vinaver's *Works*, Field's *Morte Darthur* will inspire a further generation of important scholarship, scholarship that continues to take account not only
of Malory's narrative, but of the manuscript and incunable in which that text
survives.

[85] See P. J. C. Field, "Caxton's Roman War," first published in *Arthuriana* 5.2 (1995): 31–73;
revised and reprinted in Field's *Malory: Texts and Sources* (1998), 126–61; and slightly
revised again for inclusion in *The Malory Debate* (2000), 127–67. This last version is thus
the definitive text of Field's important study, but Shepherd (ed.) *Morte Darthur*, in the
opening note of p. 113, is explicit in his adoption of the 1998 version. Obviously Field
himself follows this textual reconstruction in his own edition.
[86] See the Headnote to "Sir Launcelot and Queen Guenivere," at II, 688–9. For sources
in general, including citations of the leading critics, see Norris, "Malory and His
Sources," in this volume.
[87] See, e.g., Ralph Norris, "Once Again King Arthur and the Ambassadors: A Textual
Crux in Malory's *Morte Darthur*," *JIAS* 3 (2015): 102–19; idem, "Errors in the Malory
Archetype: The Case of Vinaver's Wight and Balan's Curious Remark," *Studies in
Bibliography* 60 (forthcoming); and Whetter, *Manuscript and Meaning*, 149–50.

# 4

## Malory in Literary Context

### MEGAN G. LEITCH

When Arthur and Mordred are fighting to the death in the final battle, Malory specifies that Mordred "smote hys fadir, Kynge Arthure."[1] As is well known, this is the only conjoining of "father" and "king" in the *Morte Darthur*;[2] here, Malory foregrounds the catastrophic collocation of personal and political betrayals in the moment that seals the downfall of the Arthurian world. Less well known is the fact that a similar passage occurs in another English romance composed during Malory's lifetime. In the anonymous prose *Siege of Thebes* (c. 1450) – like the *Morte Darthur*, a selective redaction of longer source material into English prose – Oedipus unwittingly but angrily kills his father Layus: "Edippes holding his swerde drawen in his honde, withoute eny more, smote þe king his fader, and þere slowe him."[3] This charged collocation of "king" and "fader" at the point of regicide and patricide does not occur in this prose romance's source, John Lydgate's c. 1422 verse *Siege of Thebes*. Moreover, while Lydgate's version states that Oedipus kills Layus "cruelly,"[4] the (shorter) prose version is more expansive here, indicating that Oedipus acts "in ful grete rage and oute of mesure."[5] Here,

---

[1] Thomas Malory, *Le Morte Darthur*, ed. P. J. C. Field, 2 vols. (Cambridge, 2013), I, 924.1–2; C XXI.4.

[2] Helen Cooper, *The English Romance in Time: Transforming Motifs from Geoffrey of Monmouth to the Death of Shakespeare* (Oxford, 2004), 377.

[3] Friedrich W. D. Brie, ed., "Zwei mittelenglische Prosaromane: *The Sege of Thebes* und *The Sege of Troy*," *Archiv für das Studium der neueren Sprachen und Literaturen* 130 (1913): 40–52 and 269–85, at 48; emphasis mine. The prose *Siege of Thebes* is extant only in one manuscript, Oxford, Bodleian Library, MS Rawlinson D82, along with a prose *Siege of Troy*. These two prose romances appear to be by the same author, and are copied in the same hand (modelled on late fifteenth-century anglicana script with some secretary graphs), occupying the first ten folios and the following fourteen folios of the manuscript respectively. These texts are much shorter re-workings of Lydgate's protracted verse versions of the early 1420s, his *Siege of Thebes* and *Troy Book*, and the prose versions dwell on unresolved or disastrous treason from within kin and community without including much of Lydgate's positive examples of ideal chivalric behaviour or the "consoling" recourse to divine providence that circumscribes treachery and disaster in Lydgate's versions. See Brie, "Zwei mittelenglische Prosaromane," 40–7; David C. Benson, "Chaucer's Influence on the Prose 'Sege of Troy'," *Notes and Queries* 18.4 (1971): 127–30; Helen Cooper, "Counter-Romance: Civil Strife and Father-Killing in the Prose Romances," in *The Long Fifteenth Century*, ed. Helen Cooper and Sally Mapstone (Oxford, 1997), 141–62; and Megan G. Leitch, *Romancing Treason: The Literature of the Wars of the Roses* (Oxford, 2015), 64–84. For full details of the Middle English prose romances, see this last study.

[4] John Lydgate, *The Siege of Thebes*, ed. Robert R. Edwards (Kalamazoo, 2001), 581.

[5] Prose *Siege of Thebes* (in Brie, "Zwei mittelenglische Prosaromane"), 48. It has recently been argued that in parallels such as these the Theban legend influenced the Arthurian

that is, the prose *Siege of Thebes* emphasises problematic intemperance in exactly the same terms as Malory does. "Oute of mesure" is familiar to readers of Malory as an expression for disastrous excess of emotion, or for intemperance that leads to rash or ill-advised action. Pointing out that Arthur has already won the final battle, Malory stresses that the sight of "hys people so slayne frome hym" makes "Kynge Arthure wode wroth oute of mesure" and intent on pursuing the unnecessary confrontation with Mordred (922.33–34 / C XXI.4). Arthur disregards his supporter Sir Lucan's advice to "latte hym [Mordred] be" because Mordred is already defeated (923.15 / C XXI.4); anger "oute of mesure" leads to father and son fighting to the death in the *Morte* as in the prose *Siege of Thebes*.

These resemblances go beyond verbal parallels; they are indicative of the thematic and stylistic affinities that link Malory's *Morte Darthur* with a number of other English prose romances similarly written during the Wars of the Roses and its aftermath.[6] While reading the *Morte* alongside its sources illuminates how Malory reshapes the Arthurian legend (as addressed by Ralph Norris elsewhere in this volume), reading the *Morte* alongside contemporary texts – with which it shares, in part, its genre, themes and/or modes of adaptation – sheds more light on what is particular, and what is conventional, in Malory's literary achievements. This chapter locates Malory in relation to other late fifteenth-century texts: Arthurian cycles in other European languages; romances and chivalric tracts which circulated alongside the *Morte*; and, especially, the other English prose romances produced during the same cultural moment that informed Malory's Arthuriad.

Writing his *Morte Darthur* in the late 1460s while in prison for his involvement in the ongoing Wars of the Roses, Malory re-shaped the Arthurian legend in ways that resonated with contemporary concerns about civil strife, conflicts of loyalties and adverse outcomes. In so doing, he participated in wider literary movements, especially the turn to prose in English romance that generated a number of romances with darker, more admonitory reworkings of the genre's conventional chivalric concerns. Situating the *Morte* in the context of contemporary English and European literary currents, this chapter also returns to the family resemblance theory of the romance genre in order to conceptualise what the *Morte Darthur* has in common with other prose romances, and what sets these texts apart from earlier romance traditions. The second half of this chapter explores such shared interests and shared ways of writing about

---

one: see Paul Battles and Dominique Battles, "From Thebes to Camelot: Incest, Civil War, and Kin-Slaying in the Fall of Arthur's Kingdom," *Arthuriana* 27.2 (2017): 3–28, at 21–2. The possibility that the prose *Thebes* influenced Malory's (slightly later) *Morte* is intriguing, but remains speculative. This chapter is concerned instead with how such shared concerns and ways of writing shaped the literary culture in which Malory participated.

[6] This chapter draws upon material first published in my article "'of his ffader spak he no thing': Family Resemblance and Anxiety of Influence in the Prose Romances," in *Medieval into Renaissance: Essays for Helen Cooper*, ed. Andrew King and Matthew Woodcock (Cambridge, 2016), 55–72, and is used here with permission. See also my *Romancing Treason: The Literature of the Wars of the Roses* (Oxford, 2015), and my entry on "Middle English Prose Romances," in *The Encyclopedia of Medieval Literature in Britain*, ed. Siân Echard and Robert Rouse (Oxford, 2017).

them by addressing fractious families in the *Morte Darthur* and in contemporary English prose romances, such as the *Siege of Thebes*, the *Siege of Troy*, *Melusine* and *Valentine and Orson*. Viewed through these comparative lenses, Malory's Arthuriad appears at once more distinctive, and more distinctively of its time.

## Malory and His Literary Contemporaries

Scholarship has long attended to Malory's literary inheritance and influences, especially in terms of his relationship to earlier verse romances and the English and French Arthurian texts he used as his sources.[7] Criticism has equally focused on situating Malory in relation to the contemporary politics and preoccupations that inform his Arthuriad.[8] More recently, some critics have studied Malory in relation to his literary contemporaries. Of course, that there were other Arthurian cycles and other English prose romances written around the same time as Malory was writing has long been recognised.[9] However, while it was once acceptable to argue that the other fifteenth-century English prose romances "hardly established a tradition of English secular prose on which Malory could draw for his style,"[10] more recent criticism has pursued the insights to be gained from reading the Morte in its closest literary contexts. In the past two decades, Malory's *Morte* has increasingly been treated as a part – though of course a distinctive part – of wider contemporary literary currents. Following a range of recent studies, as discussed below, the *Morte Darthur* can now be read more probingly as one of several late medieval European Arthurian adaptations; alongside other contemporary English reading material such as military treatises and chivalric handbooks; and among the many prose romances and chivalric tracts produced around the same time, a number of which were, like Malory's *Morte*, printed by the first English printer, William Caxton.

One recent contribution has situated Malory among other late medieval Arthurian cycles produced in other vernacular languages. Miriam Edlich-Muth's study of Malory alongside other late Arthurian compilations offers a valuable new perspective on Malory's work.[11] Edlich-Muth brings Malory's Arthuriad

---

[7] See, for instance, P. J. C. Field, *Romance and Chronicle: A Study of Malory's Prose Style* (London, 1971); Larry D. Benson, *Malory's* Morte Darthur (Cambridge, MA, 1976); Felicity Riddy, *Sir Thomas Malory* (Leiden, 1987); Catherine Batt, *Malory's* Morte Darthur: *Remaking Arthurian Tradition* (New York, 2002), esp. 1–35. See also Ralph Norris, "Malory and His Sources" in this volume.

[8] As discussed by Catherine Nall, "Malory in Historical Context," in this volume.

[9] For instance, some of them are mentioned briefly by Elizabeth Archibald and A. S. G. Edwards, "Introduction", in *A Companion to Malory*, ed. Elizabeth Archibald and A. S. G. Edwards (Cambridge, 1996), xiii–xv, at xiv.

[10] Benson, *Malory's* Morte Darthur, 21. The lesser-known fifteenth-century English prose romances are elsewhere referred to less disparagingly, but no less summarily: Derek Pearsall, "The English Romance in the Fifteenth Century," *Essays and Studies* 29 (1976): 58–83, at 73; Douglas Gray, *Later Medieval English Literature* (Oxford, 2008), 180. Mark Lambert mentions a few of them, but only as foils for the *Morte*: see *Malory: Style and Vision in* Le Morte Darthur (New Haven, CT, 1975).

[11] Miriam Edlich-Muth, *Malory and His European Contemporaries: Adapting Late Arthurian Romance Collections* (Cambridge, 2014).

into dialogue with four cycles (in Italian, Dutch, French and German), including two that are closely contemporaneous with the *Morte Darthur*: Ulrich Fuetrer's German *Buch der Abenteuer* and Micheau Gonnot's French compilation extant in Paris, Bibliothèque nationale, MS français 112, both written in the 1470s under the patronage of respective local dukes. Through this comparative study, the combining of common sources such as the thirteenth-century French prose *Lancelot* cycle with local narratives (for instance, in Malory's case, the English Alliterative *Morte Arthure*; in Fuetrer's case, German Parzival stories) to create a distinctive Arthurian cycle emerges as a strategy shared across these late compilations rather than one unique to Malory. Malory's style, narrative voice, chronological and genealogical frameworks, plot and characterisation can be understood as in some ways "fairly typical" of these late Arthuriads.[12] Yet Malory's is one of the more unified Arthurian collections, and one of the most striking divergences noted by Edlich-Muth is that the *Morte* is the only one of these five late cycles to feature Arthur as a protagonist as well as a figurehead. This adds to our understanding of the significance of a source such as the Alliterative *Morte Arthure*, a narrative in which Arthur single-handedly fights a giant and leads his army to victory over the Roman Empire, and which Malory adapts and inserts among the quests of other knightly protagonists such as Gawain, Lancelot and Gareth.

Recent criticism has also analysed the *Morte Darthur* in relation to the concerns of its intended readership, the English gentry, and alongside other texts read by the gentry. For instance, Raluca Radulescu has demonstrated that the *Morte*'s preoccupations with knights' personal "worship" (or publicly recognised worth), friendship, fellowship (in the sense of affiliation and alliance), and good lordship are shared by the fifteenth-century English gentry, whose extant letter-collections give insight into contemporary concerns.[13] Other studies address the *Morte* in relation to fifteenth-century English political discourses or reading material from chronicles and military treatises to pious verse romances, in order to illuminate shared secular or spiritual concerns.[14] For instance, between 1475 and 1491, Caxton printed a variety of chivalric tracts which express concerns about ethics and social cohesion that parallel those in Malory's *Morte*. In *The Game of Chess*, which uses an allegory of chess pieces as representatives of society to explore the integral role that all estates – from peasant or pawn to king – must play to ensure social order, Caxton adds his own comments which sharpen the text's ethical instructions and emphasise its relevance to the contemporary moment. Here, Caxton laments that:

> the verray trewe love of the comyn wele and proffyt nowadayes is selde
> founden. Where shal thou fynde a man in thyse dayes that wyl expose

---

[12] Edlich-Muth, *Malory and His European Contemporaries*, 153.

[13] Raluca L. Radulescu, *The Gentry Context for Malory's* Morte Darthur (Cambridge, 2003); see also Thomas H. Crofts, *Malory's Contemporary Audience: The Social Reading of Romance in Late Medieval England* (Cambridge, 2006).

[14] See, for instance, Sarah L. Peverley, "Political Consciousness and the Literary Mind in Late Medieval England: Men 'Brought up of Nought' in Vale, Hardyng, Mankind, and Malory," *Studies in Philology* 105.1 (2008): 1–29; Catherine Nall, *Reading and War in Fifteenth-Century England: From Lydgate to Malory* (Cambridge, 2012); Raluca L. Radulescu, *Romance and Its Contexts in Fifteenth-Century England: Politics, Piety, and Penitence* (Cambridge, 2013); and Ruth Lexton, *Contested Language in Malory's* Morte Darthur: *The Politics of Romance in Fifteenth-Century England* (New York, 2011).

hymself for the worshyp and honour of his frende or for the comyn wele? Selde or neuer shal he be founden.[15]

The imagined community in which Caxton invites English people to participate by buying his books and following their instruction is a community organised around the secular, inclusive concept of the commonweal, a concept which gained political traction in England during the Wars of the Roses from 1450 onwards and which resonates with the concerns about fellowship and treason in the *Morte*.[16]

Indeed, when printed in 1485, Malory's *Morte* entered wider circulation among a group of other prose romances likewise printed by Caxton and similarly concerned with fellowship, and critics are increasingly reading the *Morte* in this context. Other prose narratives similarly treating distant or legendary history that Caxton's press imprinted in the 1480s alone include *Godeffroy of Boloyne* (1481) on the First Crusade, and *Charles the Grete* (1485) and *The Four Sonnes of Aymon* (1488) on the reign of Charlemagne. Although these and other texts Caxton himself translated follow their French sources more closely than Malory adheres to his, Caxton seems to have selected them in part for their connections to English literature and society. Recent critics have analysed these texts' construction of the reputations of the three Christian "Worthies" – Arthur, Charlemagne and Godfrey[17] – and the texts' treatment of crusading and chivalric conduct.[18] Like the *Morte*, Caxton's prose romances devote a great deal of attention to chivalric bonds and anxieties about trust and fellowships. Malory's Lancelot voices – and seeks to distance himself from – the concerns about betrayed trust and broken fellowships that punctuate the *Morte* when he asserts "I reporte me to all knyghtes that ever have knowyn me, I fared never wyth no treson, nother I loved never the felyshyp of hym that fared with treson" (855.4–6 / C XIX.7). Caxton's own translated prose romances offer similarly anxious statements condemning betrayed loyalties. In *Charles the Grete*, for instance, the noble giant Fierabras declares, "I swere and assure the that neuer while I lyue shal I be traytour to no man lyuyng," and in *The Foure Sonnes of Aymon*, the protagonist Renaud proclaims, "It is the fouleste crafte that a knyght may for to doo treyson."[19] These

---

[15] William Caxton, *The Game and Playe of the Chesse*, ed. Jenny Adams (Kalamazoo, MI, 2009), II. 559–62. Caxton translated *The Game of Chess* from a mid fourteenth-century French version of the Latin *Liber de Ludo Scaccorum*; he first printed it in Bruges in 1475 and dedicated it to Edward IV's brother George of Clarence. After Clarence was executed for treason in 1478, Caxton printed a second edition at Westminster in 1482, marketed more broadly as a book "ful of holsom wysedom and requysyte unto every astate and degree" (Preface, 19–20).

[16] See Leitch, *Romancing Treason*, 160–8.

[17] The Nine Worthies were heroes respected across the Christian West, including three biblical worthies, Joshua, David, and Judas Maccabeus; three classical worthies, Hector of Troy, Alexander the Great, and Julius Caesar; and three Christian worthies, Arthur, Charlemagne, and Godfrey of Bouillon.

[18] William Kuskin, *Symbolic Caxton: Literary Culture and Print Capitalism* (Notre Dame, IN, 2008); J. R. Goodman, "Malory and Caxton's Chivalric Series, 1481–85," in *Studies in Malory*, ed. James W. Spisak (Kalamazoo, 1985), 257–74; Joerg Fichte, "Caxton's Concept of 'Historical Romance' within the Context of the Crusades: Conviction, Rhetoric and Sales Strategy," in *Tradition and Transformation in Medieval Romance*, ed. Rosalind Field (Cambridge, 1999), 101–13.

[19] William Caxton, *The Lyf of the Noble and Crysten Prynce, Charles the Grete*, ed. Sidney J. H. Herrtage (London, 1881), 58.24–26; Caxton, *The Right Plesaunt and Goodly Historie*

statements are paradigmatic of how, in these printed prose romances, exemplary behaviour is defined, interrogated, urged and elegised in part through chivalric paragons' determination "allwayes to fle treson" (97.29 / C III.15) – a stipulation of the Round Table Oath unique to the *Morte*. Here, Malory articulates a standard of conduct that, if less famously codified in Caxton's own prose romances, is equally espoused there, and in an equally admonitory and normative fashion.[20]

Thus, although he drew upon Burgundian literary traditions, Caxton's selection of romances and chivalric treatises was also acutely informed by English literary fashions and concerns.[21] As mentioned previously, Edlich-Muth's work has shown that in relation to continental Arthurian cycles Malory's *Morte* emerges as all the more distinctive for featuring Arthur as both a figurehead for his knights and the subject of his own adventures. By contrast, in the context of other texts printed by Caxton, the *Morte* is one of many prose romances that uses a respected Christian king as both the subject of, and the organising principle for, a series of chivalric adventures.[22] For instance, in *Charles the Grete*, Charlemagne fights wars but also takes a back seat when some of his twelve peers become the protagonists, battling Saracen giants, defeating enemy armies, and marrying ladies they rescue – just as Malory's Arthur, whose biography structures the cycle, takes a back seat when the focus shifts to the adventures of his knights in the middle sections of the *Morte*.

Most of the English romances written in the second half of the fifteenth century were, like Malory's *Morte Darthur*, in prose. While to the modern reader prose may seem an obvious choice for writing narratives, during the late Middle Ages, following the fashion for earlier epics and chansons de geste – and long before the eighteenth-century invention of the novel[23] – verse was still often the standard for literature. Following the twelfth-century genesis of the romance genre at Anglo-Norman and continental French courts, some French romances were written in prose from the thirteenth century onward; however, English romances, first extant from the thirteenth century, remained solely in verse for approximately two hundred years. Moreover, when English romanciers began writing in prose in the middle of the fifteenth century, their shift of form or medium was not merely stylistic. Romances written in English prose offered a significant reworking of the narrative arc of the genre, and were thematically attuned to the climate of social instability in which they were produced and received. These chivalric prose romances flourished in England especially from c. 1450 to c. 1520; that is, during the Wars of the Roses and the first few decades of the Tudor period. They include both adaptations of earlier English verse romances and

---

*of the Foure Sonnes of Aymon*, ed. Olivia Richardson (London, 1885), 234.8–9. See also, similarly, *Foure Sonnes*, 265.19–21, and Caxton, *Godeffroy of Boloyne*, ed. Mary Noyes Colvin (London, 1893), 236.7–8.

[20] Leitch, *Romancing Treason*, 138–74.

[21] Kuskin, *Symbolic Caxton*, 193–235; Leitch, *Romancing Treason*, esp. 140–5.

[22] Goodman, "Malory and Caxton's Chivalric Series," 269–70, and Jennifer R. Goodman, *Chivalry and Exploration 1298–1630* (Woodbridge, 1998), 28–29; Leitch, *Romancing Treason*, 150.

[23] However, for a discussion of the novelistic qualities of Malory's *Morte*, see Cory James Rushton's chapter on "Malory and Form" in this volume.

translations of French prose romances, and were produced in both manuscript form and printed editions.

The Middle English prose romances, then – including, but not limited to, those printed by Caxton – often share their subject matter with romances written in other times and places, but it is their treatment of this narrative material that sets them apart. Helen Cooper's 1997 essay, "Counter-Romance: Civil Strife and Father-Killing in the Prose Romances," adumbrates a way in which Malory's Morte Darthur can be understood as part of a wider sub-genre,[24] and more recent scholarship has further explored the implications of interpreting Malory alongside this most cognate of fifteenth-century reading material.[25] Like Malory's reworking of the Arthurian legend, a number of the other Middle English prose romances rework the familiar legends or histories of figures such as Charlemagne and Melusine, and of the classical sieges of Thebes and Troy, taking a distinctly darker approach to individual success and chivalric cohesion than is found in earlier English romances, which are all in verse. Moreover, the stories re-told in English prose romance were selected and re-shaped from a wider array of possible sources in both earlier English verse romance and French prose romance. Malory's Morte Darthur is distinctive here for the variety of its sources – both English and French, verse and prose – and for the latitude with which it treats them, distilling and recasting into a book that has, if not an entirely consistent narrative, then at least a consistent – and primarily secular – chivalric ethos. Yet other English prose romances do sometimes depart from their sources in ways that demonstrate a significant shift of emphasis and interest, often matching the admonitory chivalric ethos that imbues Malory's text.[26]

## Prose Romance and Family Resemblance

Reading the Morte in its contemporary literary context can give us a better sense of what Malory was doing – or what he might have been perceived as doing – by writing a late medieval (Arthurian) romance in English prose. In order to illuminate further Malory's position as part of a wider literary movement, the rest of this chapter explores how Malory's Morte dwells on the nature and consequences of problematic family relationships and traits such as intemperance in ways that parallel other contemporary English prose romances. The selectivity with which romances produced in other times or places were chosen for translation and/or adaptation into Middle English prose romance from the middle of the fifteenth century onward bears witness to a literary culture particularly interested in narratives of strife and disaster. Whereas the majority of English chivalric verse romances end happily with the success and social (re-)integration of the central characters, these prose romances often have unhappy, disastrous endings, and

---

[24] See note 3 above.
[25] More recently, see also Cooper, The English Romance in Time; Kuskin, Symbolic Caxton, 193–235; Joyce Boro, "All for Love: Lord Berners and the Enduring, Evolving Romance," Oxford Handbook of Tudor Literature, 1485–1603, ed. Mike Pincombe and Cathy Shrank (Oxford, 2009), 87–102; and Leitch, Romancing Treason.
[26] Leitch, Romancing Treason, 64–91.

while they retain the genre's concern with the pursuit of secular, chivalric ideals, they are usually more pessimistic or more admonitory in their didactic treatment of such concerns. For instance, in narratives such as the thirteenth-century *King Horn* or *Havelok the Dane*, the earliest extant Middle English romances, the royal protagonist regains his kingdom and secures a suitably beautiful and high-born bride through his chivalric deeds; and in fourteenth-century romances such as *Guy of Warwick* and *Sir Launfal*, the eponymous knights rise above their station through battlefield prowess and/or marriage. By contrast, the later prose romances often feature protagonists or dynasties undone by betrayal.

Whereas earlier verse romances show unity overcoming divisions within families or fellowships, prose romances such as Malory's *Morte Darthur*, the prose *Siege of Thebes*, and Caxton's *Charles the Grete* showcase what *not* to do by focusing on the disastrous results of divisions within affinity groups.[27] Mapping these parallels in anxieties and ethics across the prose romances foregrounds some of the ways in which the *Morte* fits into its contemporary literary context and participates in wider movements characteristic of the literary culture of the Wars of the Roses. The focus here on anxieties about family bonds, inheritance and influence – on the disjunctions between nature and nurture, and the consequences of intemperate conduct – showcases some of the many concerns that the *Morte* shares with other English prose romances written around the same time. Other case studies of correspondences between Malory and the other prose romanciers – on matters such as distinctive representations of fellowship, treason, chivalry and/or attitudes towards crusading and the wider world following the 1453 fall of Constantinople – can be found elsewhere,[28] though more work remains to be done on this understudied sub-genre.

In the Morte Darthur, family is fragile and flawed. When King Arthur kills and is killed by his son/nephew Mordred (the product of his incestuous relationship with his half-sister Morgause), it is partly because another of his nephews, Gawain, has scuppered any chances of a peaceful reunion between Arthur and Lancelot. Arthur had been prepared to forgive Lancelot for his affair with Guinevere had Gawain not insisted on revenge for Lancelot's accidental killing of two of his brothers. Gawain calls upon Arthur as "my kynge, my lorde, and myne uncle" (888.23 / C XX.9; dialogue not paralleled in Malory's sources),[29] compelling Arthur to make war on Lancelot in France and giving Mordred the opportunity to usurp the throne at home in England. Moreover, it was yet another of these brothers – Aggravain – whose jealousy and ill will led to the publicising of the affair between Lancelot and Guinevere. Aggravain is killed by Lancelot for his pains, but the one brother willing to join him in this endeavour, Mordred,

---

[27] Leitch, *Romancing Treason*. Not quite all of the Middle English prose romances have this emphasis on an unhappy ending: for instance, Caxton's *Paris and Vienne* (1485) and *Blanchardine and Eglantine* (1488) showcase young lovers overcoming parental opposition and/or external enemies to reach a wedding and a happy ending. However, narratives of disastrous divisions do dominate in Middle English prose romance, and resonate with contemporary concerns during the Wars of the Roses.

[28] See studies mentioned in footnotes 3, 6, 18, 22, and 25 above.

[29] *The Works of Sir Thomas Malory*, ed. Eugène Vinaver, 3rd edn, rev. P. J. C. Field, 3 vols (Oxford, 1990), III, 1635.

escapes; the other brothers – Gawain, Gaheris and Gareth – refused to join in this exposure of the adulterous affair. But it is when Lancelot is rescuing Guinevere from being burned at the stake for their adultery that he accidentally kills the two unarmed brothers, Gareth and Gaheris, who are in the crowd surrounding her.

This outline of some of the ways in which family loyalties and traits such as jealousy and the desire for revenge affect the later stages of the Morte can be traced much earlier as well. The characteristic intemperance and recklessness Gawain manifests in insisting on revenge against Lancelot for the accidental killing of Gareth and Gaheris is paralleled earlier when Gaheris rashly slays their mother Morgause for sleeping with Lamorak: Gaheris "cam to there beddis syde all armed, wyth his swerde naked, and suddaynly he gate his modir by the heyre and strake of her hede" (486.19–20 / C X.23). Gawain, Gaheris, Agravain and Mordred all then attack Lamorak (continuing the blood feud that saw Gawain kill Lamorak's father King Pellinor, in revenge for Pellinor's killing of the Orkney brothers' father King Lot). Malory departs from his sources to include Mordred in this murder, and invents the cowardly blow from behind with which Mordred slays Lamorak (554.14–15 / C X.58).[30] There are other reasons for the downfall of Arthur's kingdom, of course, and other ways in which the values and conflicts of loyalties of Malory's Arthurian world are interrogated,[31] but the destructive role of this hot-headed set of brothers looms large in the *Morte Darthur*, and is magnified by Malory's alterations to his sources, such as to blacken Mordred by involving him in underhanded deeds, or to foreground the impact of Gawain's intemperance.

Similarly, in the prose *Siege of Thebes*, intemperance results in Oedipus killing his father, as we have seen; it is also a prominent trait of Oedipus's offspring, Pollymet and Etiocles, who quarrel over their father's throne until their lords convince them to divide the rule of Thebes on an annual basis. Pollymet accordingly leaves Thebes to await his turn elsewhere; when night comes, he shelters from the weather in a porch, and another man, Tydeus, requests to share his shelter. Even though the porch is "large ynogh" for the two of them, and Tydeus speaks to Pollymet "in ful gentil and sobre wise," Pollymet gets so angry that he instigates an unnecessary duel with Tydeus.[32] While this intemperate combat also takes place in Lydgate's version, the prose version gives it more weight, not least by choosing to reproduce it while eliding some episodes and most of the moralising glosses that characteristically augment Lydgate's much longer verse version.[33] Lacking the intervening moral exempla and without the divided parts of Lydgate's version, Pollymet's anger-induced combat reads in much closer juxtaposition to Oedipus's own combat, which the prose version does reconstrue to foreground intemperance.

When King Adrastus interrupts the duel between Pollymet and Tydeus and asks the pair "of wens þei were, and of what lynage twey come of," both answer in a way that reveals anxiety about family relationships:

[30] Vinaver, *Works*, 1513.
[31] For more extended discussion of conflicts of loyalties within the *Morte Darthur*, see the chapters by Lisa Robeson and Dorsey Armstrong in this volume.
[32] Prose *Siege of Thebes*, 49.
[33] "Introduction," in *John Lydgate: The Siege of Thebes*, ed. Edwards, 4; Derek Pearsall, *John Lydgate* (London, 1970), 128–31, 138, 152 and 155.

> Tedeus answhering first and seid, þat he was son vnto king Calydon,
> And shuld be his eyre, And declared unto him þe cause of his exile, and
> of his metyng þere that tyme with Pollymet. Pollymet told þat he was of
> Thebes, son to Jocasta þe quene, but of his ffader spak he no thing.[34]

Tydeus mentions his lineage, and Tydeus speaks "þe cause of his exile," but the text does not voice it: here, the narrator eschews any explicit reminder of the fact that Tydeus has been exiled for (accidental) fratricide, just as the text – and Pollymet – display unease about Pollymet's shameful patricidal and incestuous father: "of his ffader spak he no thing," nor is there any mention of the fact that he is at odds with his own brother. Pollymet, it seems, worries about his reputation and about the influence of his father, from whom he and his brother have inherited their intemperate disposition. The prose *Siege of Thebes*, that is, shows not only betrayal between those who are expected to be loyal to each other, but also betrayal of the expectation – whether genetic or generic, or both – for members of the same aristocratic family to have and/or inherit positive traits. We are told of Pollymet and Tydeus that, after their duel, "thes two knightes by alliaunce, loved so truly togidre alwey during theire lyves, þat þere was never truer love founde bitwixt two breþeren."[35] Here, as often in the *Morte*, friendship or fellowship – which are often forged through combat – offer what family cannot.[36] As a late fifteenth-century reader puts it in an eight-line poem, uniquely appended to Bodleian Rawlinson D 82, the one manuscript in which the prose *Siege of Thebes* is extant: "Unneth a man now may truste his owne broþer."[37] However, in the English prose romances, this lack of trust extends not only to family relationships, but also to family resemblance.

Malory's *Morte*, in its larger arc as opposed to its self-contained Fair Unknown episodes, parallels other English prose romances in their darker attitude towards family bonds and behaviour. In Fair Unknown narratives such as *Libeaus Desconus* and Malory's "Tale of Sir Gareth," we see a conventional attitude towards family inheritance. Regardless of the fact that the Fair Unknown heroes' family origins are, to begin with, unknown or concealed, they convincingly demonstrate their worthy blood through their conduct. Here, noble progenitors produce noble protagonists, and elevated identity is confirmed by good manners and military prowess (as well as good looks). Malory's Sir Tor, for instance, is proven to be the son not of the cowherd Aryes who has raised him, but rather of King Pellinor, because Tor is "passyngly well vysaged and well made"; rejects manual "laboure" in favour of martial endeavour; and wants most of all "to be made knyght" (79.1–9 / C III.3). The Fair Unknown trope demonstrates the successful passing on of positive traits even in extreme circumstances; it shows how the

---

[34] Prose *Siege of Thebes*, 50.

[35] Prose *Siege of Thebes*, 50.

[36] For a discussion of the ways in which belligerence creates bonds in the *Morte*, see Andrew Lynch, *Malory's Book of Arms: The Narrative of Combat in* Le Morte Darthur (Cambridge, 1997), esp. 87–8.

[37] The manuscript is c. 1450 (see note 3 above), and the verse annotation and marginalia are late fifteenth century: Oxford, Bodleian Library, MS Rawlinson D82, fol. 34r; "Deceit, III," *Secular Lyrics of the XIVth and XVth Centuries*, ed. Rossell Hope Robbins (1952; Oxford, 1955), 101.

romance genre often comfortably espouses the *opposite* of anxiety about inherit-ance. Conventionally, that is, romances imply that protagonists' noble traits are due to their nature, rather than to their nurture.

Many of the late prose romances, by contrast, show a concern that positive traits may not be inherited, and/or that negative traits will be inherited. These texts exhibit anxiety about how the previous generation is influencing the new one; their focus on what is – and is not – being inherited therefore betrays a certain anxiety about influence. In this, the prose romances may show an affinity with Chaucerian models of filial inheritance (and of literary inheritance, as dis-cussed later). As A.C. Spearing observes, Chaucer often suggests that good quali-ties are not inheritable, or are not "naturally bequeathed."[38] And as the Loathly Lady in Chaucer's "Wife of Bath's Tale" puts it:

> men may well often finde
> A lordes sone do shame and vileynye.
> [...]
> He nis not gentil, be he duc or erl,
> For vileyns synful dedes make a churl.[39]

Chaucer tends to write of "gentillesse" and "courtoisie" as virtues that are per-formed rather than inherited, that make themselves known in behaviour rather than in bloodlines. Chaucer's courteous Franklin can have a son who does not emulate his virtue, and the clerk in the Franklin's Tale can act with gentility despite not being of gentle birth. For Chaucer (as far as one can ever pin him down to a view), scions of the new generation are shaped at least as much by their nurture (or lack thereof) as by their nature or class.

This "Chaucerian" view of idiosyncratic evolution is sometimes paralleled in the later prose romances, though not always optimistically. For instance, in *Valentine and Orson* (c. 1500), the twin sons of the Emperor of Constantinople are separated from their parents in infancy, and grow into very different adults. Valentine is fostered by King Pepin of France, while Orson is raised by a bear (as his name suggests). King Pepin is Valentine's uncle, but neither of them know it; Valentine seems to prove that he must be of high birth by his combination of battlefield prowess and gentle behaviour. But this romance does not replicate the Fair Unknown meme of inevitable nobility straightforwardly, since Orson shares only his brother's abilities as a warrior, and is otherwise a savage until his brother manages to partially domesticate him.[40] Here, Valentine's twin brother effectively serves as a "control group," demonstrating how little of Valentine's virtue *is* in fact due to inheritance. The example of Orson, who has received the same genetic inputs as Valentine but has missed out on the civilising process,[41] suggests that it is the influence of the French court, rather than Valentine's blood,

---

[38] A. C. Spearing, "Father Chaucer," in *Writing After Chaucer: Essential Readings in Chaucer and the Fifteenth Century*, ed. Daniel J. Pinti (New York, 1998), 145–66.

[39] Geoffrey Chaucer, "The Wife of Bath's Tale," in *The Riverside Chaucer*, ed. Larry D. Benson, 3rd edn (Boston, 1987), 1150–8.

[40] *Valentine and Orson*, ed. Arthur Dickson, trans. Henry Watson (London, 1937), 14.1–2. The late fifteenth-century French source was printed in 1489.

[41] That Middle English literature contributes to what Norbert Elias has termed "the civilising process" has been demonstrated by Ad Putter, in *Sir Gawain and the Green*

that underpins his virtue. Here, character is revealed to be a product of *nurture*; aristocratic *nature*, when left to itself, produces the brutish Orson. Gentility, then, does not necessarily manifest itself where it should. Moreover, like Mordred and Oedipus, Valentine kills his father (the emperor of Constantinople) in battle – though (like Oedipus) without knowing his identity.

While *Valentine and Orson* is unable to eradicate the idea that desirable traits might not be inherited, other late prose romances dwell on the ways in which undesirable traits are inherited. In John Bourchier's *Huon of Burdeux* (c. 1515), treacherousness and cowardice are figured as inherited traits. The foremost traitor of the matter of France, Ganelon – whose betrayal of Charlemagne results in the death of Roland and defeat at the hands of Saracens – is connected with a traitor central to *Huon*'s narrative in a way that suggests that betrayal runs in the blood. When Earl Amaury, an underhanded enemy of Huon's, is described as a "felon traytour" (5.4), the narrator further specifies that he is "son to on of the neuewse of the traytour Ganelon" (5.7–8).[42] This idea of infelicitous familial propensities is given more explicit expression elsewhere in the text. For instance, the traitorous inclinations of the duke of Vienna, who wants to kill Huon and claim his wife Esclaramond for himself, are traced as follows: "this duke Raoull was the untrewest traytoure that ever lyved: the which ylnes procedyd by ye duches his mother/ who was doughter to [...] the moost untrewest and falsest traytour" (315.21–25). Here, treacherous behaviour is explicitly figured as an "ylnes," an inherited condition or ineradicable disease passed on in the genes that influences the conduct of future generations. Contemporary readers might also understand such dispositions as the result of imbalances in the four humours (blood, phlegm, yellow bile and black bile) – the medieval paradigm for understanding links between health and temperament according to which a personal (or familial) tendency towards rash anger, for instance, was attributed to a predominance of yellow bile (or choler).[43] Reprehensible or choleric behaviour, then, demonstrates family resemblance in such cases. In this etiology of inheritance and temperament, even these nobly-born figures cannot escape or rise above the influence of negative traits.

Thus, in these prose romances as in Chaucer's *Canterbury Tales*, negative traits are naturally bequeathed, while positive ones are not necessarily bequeathed. We can see this also in what is perhaps the prose romances' best known example of problematic or perverted inheritance: Malory's Mordred, who is, like Pollymet, the incestuous son of a king. Here, legendary incest again seems to speak to wider anxieties about family inheritance; Mordred, whom Arthur labels "the

---

    *Knight and French Arthurian Romance* (Oxford, 1995), esp. 7; see also Norbert Elias, *The Civilising Process*, trans. Edmund Jephcott, 2 vols. (1939; Oxford, 1978).

[42] John Bourchier, Lord Berners, had a French prose source written in the 1450s and printed by Michel le Noir at Paris in 1513 and 1516. A date of c. 1515 is probable for the first English edition of *Huon*: see N. F. Blake, "Lord Berners: A Survey," *Medievalia et Humanistica* 2 (1971): 119–32; updated by Joyce Boro, "The Textual History of *Huon of Burdeux*: A Reassessment of the Facts," *Notes and Queries* 48.3 (2001): 233–7.

[43] For a discussion of the four humours and their relationship to medieval interpretations of health, temperaments and emotions, see Pedro Gil Sotres, "The Regimens of Health," in *Western Medical Thought from Antiquity to the Middle Ages*, ed. Mirko D. Grmek (Cambridge, MA, 1998), 291–318.

traytoure that all thys woo hath wrought" (923.13–14 / C XXI.4) in a battlefield accusation not found in Malory's sources, does not inherit his father's virtue. While in earlier Arthurian narratives Mordred is characteristically a villain, he becomes especially sinister in Malory's *Morte*. Malory deviates from his sources to create a darker portrayal of Mordred. In addition to inventing the cowardly blow from behind with which Mordred slays Lamorak, Malory also makes Mordred Agravain's accomplice in the exposure of Lancelot and Guinevere at the beginning of Tale VIII, thereby making Mordred partly responsible for widening the fractures in Arthur's community. In both the French *Mort Artu* and the Stanzaic *Morte Arthur* (Malory's two main sources for this part of the narrative), by contrast, this agency is attributed solely to Agravain.[44] Moreover, whereas in the Stanzaic *Morte* Mordred has the admiration and confidence of his peers,[45] and in the *Mort Artu* Arthur "dist que il velt bien que il remaigne et que il la gart" ("said that he wished well that he [Mordred] remain and that he guard the queen"),[46] by contrast, in Malory's description of Arthur making Mordred his deputy, no one expresses trust or respect for Mordred. Arthur's choice of Mordred is instead configured as an obligation induced by blood relationship: "bycause Sir Mordred was Kynge Arthurs son, he gaff hym the rule off hys londe and off hys wyff" (906.9–11 / C XX.19). This motivation is unique to the *Morte*.[47] By stressing that Mordred is Arthur's son, Malory does give Mordred a plausible claim to regency; however, his emphasis is then on how Mordred treacherously exploits this claim, and how family relationships thereby fall apart.[48] And like the prose *Thebes*, the *Morte Darthur* suggests that fellowship between brothers-in-arms, or *chosen* affinity groups such as the Round Table community, offers a potentially more reliable bond than family.[49]

This distinction can be seen especially clearly in the different ways in which Malory's paragon Gareth relates to his family: on the one hand, in his role as a Fair Unknown in The Tale of Sir Gareth, and on the other hand, in his role when divisions instigate the downfall of Arthur and his realm. In his relatively self-contained Tale, even when Gareth avoids publicising his parentage in order to prove his worth as a Fair Unknown, his own merit – his stature, bearing, courtesy and military prowess – demonstrates that he is "com of men of worshyp" (224.19 / C VII.1), en route to this Tale's happy ending with his marriage, the establishment of his chivalric identity, and the revelation of his respectable parentage. However, in his appearances in the *Morte* when the focus is on the overarching Arthurian narrative, Gareth is keen to distinguish himself from his family, who

---

[44] Vinaver, *Works*, 1629.
[45] In the Stanzaic *Morte*, when Arthur is preparing to wage war on Lancelot, he asks his knights who ought to be regent. They reply that "Mordred the sekerest was / [...] To save the reme in trews and pees": "Stanzaic Morte Arthur," in *King Arthur's Death*, ed. Larry D. Benson (Kalamazoo, 1994), 2518–20.
[46] *La Mort le Roi Artu*, ed. Jean Frappier, 2nd edn (1936; Genève, 1954), 166; translation mine.
[47] Vinaver, *Works*, 1643.
[48] For more on Malory's blackening of Mordred, see my *Romancing Treason*, 114–19.
[49] On the importance of non-familial relationships in Malory's *Morte Darthur*, see Elizabeth Archibald, "Malory's Ideal of Fellowship," *Review of English Studies* 43 (1992): 311–28.

are characterised by their collective ill will and intemperance (and their treacherousness, like certain families in *Huon of Burdeux*). This attempt to keep negative
family influence at a distance even inflects the otherwise happy solidarity of the
end of The Tale of Sir Gareth, where Gareth chooses a different affinity:

> there was never no knyght that sir Gareth loved so well as he dud Sir
> Launcelot, and ever for the moste party he wolde be in Sir Launcelottis
> company. For evir aftir Sir Gareth had aspyed Sir Gawaynes conducions,
> he wythdrewe hymself fro his brothir Sir Gawaynes felyshyp, for he was
> evir vengeable, and where he hated he wolde be avenged with murther,
> and that hated sir Gareth. (285.27-32 / C VII.35)

This commentary, as Kate McClune observes, "reveals the dark undercurrents of
an ostensibly optimistic tale";[50] Gareth, then, seeks to distance himself from the
negative traits of his family – like Pollymet in the prose *Siege of Thebes*, though
more successfully. When Agravain's ill will prompts him to plot the betrayal of
Lancelot and Guinevere and he seeks the support of his family, Gareth is one
who responds that he "woll nat be knowyn of your dedis" (870.27–871.1 / C XX.1);
Gareth is anxious not to be influenced or tainted by the familial traits of (choleric)
hot-headedness and ill will that motivate this betrayal.[51]

In the prose *Melusine*, concerns about family inheritance are physical as
well as performative. Whereas Melusine gets her serpent's tail through a curse,
Melusine and Raymond's own sons begin monstrous in shape, and, in some
cases, monstrous in behaviour too. Among others, the sixth son, Geffray, is born
with a singular deformity, as he has:

> in hys mouthe a grete & long toth, [...] and he was moch grete & hye, and
> wel formed & strong, [but also] merueyllously... cruel, In so moche that
> euery man fered & dradde hym when he was in age.[52]

Both Geffray's physical deformity and his cruelty deviate from hereditary expectations. In fact, he gets so angry when he hears that his brother Froymond has
become a monk that he burns down the abbey, killing all the monks, including
his brother. The narrator mentions that before Geffray does this, his ten knights
leave him, "sayeng that they wold not be coulpable of" that deed.[53] Geffray does
repent afterward, but his wicked intemperance in going through with such an
unknightly action despite the censure and counsel of his knights underscores his
moral deformity. He has not inherited his father's nature, but he has inherited a
monstrous disposition and demeanour thanks to the curse laid upon his mother,
and no amount of nurture seems to be able to improve his conduct or temperament. This is also the case for the tenth son, the aptly named Horrible, who:

---

[50] Kate McClune, "'the vengeaunce of my brethirne': Blood Ties in Malory's *Morte
Darthur*," *Arthurian Literature* XXVIII (2011): 89–106; see also Barbara Nolan, "The *Tale
of Sir Gareth* and the *Tale of Sir Lancelot*," in *A Companion to Malory*, 169.

[51] See also Christopher Cannon, "Malory's Crime: Chivalric Identity and the Evil Will,"
in *Medieval Literature and Historical Inquiry: Essays in Honour of Derek Pearsall*, ed. David
Aers (Cambridge, 2000), 159–83.

[52] *Melusine*, ed. A. K. Donald (London, 1895), 104.26–33.

[53] *Melusine*, 309.16–17.

brought at hys birth thre eyen, one of the which was in the mydel of his forhed. he was so euyl & so cruel that at the foureth yere of his age he slew two of hys nourryces.[54]

In fact, family inheritance is so problematised here that the worst offshoot has to be destroyed. Melusine orders Horrible to be killed because "yf he be lefte alyue / neuer man dide, nor neuer shal doo, so grete dommage as he shall."[55] Raymond accordingly has Horrible trapped in a cave and suffocated in smoke. Thus, this family puts two of its own members to death by fire. Geffray killing Froymond and his fellow monks is an example of the deviant nature of Melusine and Raymond's offspring, while the execution of Horrible is a response to their sons' genetic deviance.

In the prose *Siege of Thebes* Pollymet inherits his father's intemperance and engages in destructive behaviour until he and his brother Etiocles kill each other in battle, but family inheritance initially seems more promising in the prose *Siege of Troy*, the other romance which is similarly solely extant in MS Rawlinson D 82. In the prose *Troy*, the first part of the narrative focuses on Jason and Medea, and here Jason's chivalric success in gaining the golden fleece and winning Medea as his bride seems secured by the birth of two strong and attractive sons. However, while Jason's sons inherit their father's physical appearance, this resemblance does not secure their future as it might in a Fair Unknown romance. Here, the sins of the father are visited upon the sons: Jason "left hir in grete myschef, And toke anoþer lady; And he hadde by Medea ij sones, And by cause they were so like Jason, Medea slewe hem bothe."[56] Thus, whereas for many Fair Unknowns, being handsome and well built (like their fathers) earns the characters respect and admiration and lends credence to their elevated origins, here the results of this aristocratic family resemblance are catastrophic rather than constructive. Like Malory's Gareth, these young scions are murdered when trust is betrayed.

In these English prose romances as in others, positive inheritance is insecure, negative inheritance is all too likely, and both of these conditions are cause for concern. The influence that the older generation should or might exert on the younger is often figured as cause for anxiety either way. Both Gareth and Mordred, in different ways, show how anxiety about influence informs the *Morte's* trajectory. In considering the role of this anxiety of influence, my aim has been to draw attention not only to representations of inheritance within the prose romances, but also to the texts' own literary inheritance. The romance genre has been productively understood through the theory of family resemblance, and this old-but-invaluable theory of genre is useful for reflecting on the insights these comparative approaches can offer for our understanding of the ideologies and literary traditions with which the *Morte* engages. This theory recognises that any given characteristic may be absent without obscuring a text's nature as a romance[57] – even the happy ending commonly associated with romance

[54] *Melusine*, 105.9–12.
[55] *Melusine*, 318.17–18.
[56] Prose *Siege of Troy*, 276.
[57] Ad Putter, "A Historical Introduction," in *The Spirit of Medieval English Popular Romance*, ed. Ad Putter and Jane Gilbert (Harlow, 2000), 1–15, at 2; Cooper, *The English*

but absent from texts such as the prose *Thebes, Melusine* and Malory's *Morte*.[58] These are not the only romances that fret about family inheritance; for one thing, the romances I have been discussing were translated from French romances or, in the case of the prose *Thebes* and *Troy*, reworked from earlier English verse romance. However, anxieties about inheritance are characteristic of many of these late English prose romances to an extent that indicates something about them as a sub-generic movement, and Malory's place within them. The fact that the translated prose romances manifest the same attitudes towards or anxieties about family inheritance as the prose romances that are altered from earlier English verse or – like Malory's *Morte Darthur* – partially independent from their French sources suggests the selectivity with which this literary culture sought out, reproduced and/or reworked narratives in order to reflect on these anxieties.

*

For his Arthurian romance, Malory made some of the same choices of form and emphasis as many of his fellow English romanciers – and some of his fellow European Arthurian compilers – during the second half of the fifteenth century.[59] For Malory and his literary contemporaries, writing in prose facilitates expansion as well as elision, creating space for emphasising and recasting. As a medium, prose is flexible; it offers a way of responding to the literary tradition, but at a distance. Prose seems conducive to the registers of these romances through its associations with chronicles and didactic writing;[60] with authenticity, verifiability, realism and perhaps a certain "grittiness." It is partly through the reader's sense of the *norms* of the romance tradition that the deviations here signify, without removing these prose texts from the romance family. The composition and survival of these earliest English prose romances coincides with and was informed by the Wars of the Roses and its aftermath.[61] Over the course of a few decades troubled by multiple viable claimants to the throne in the wars between Lancaster and York (1455–85), and a new dynasty seeking to establish itself in the face of rebellions and fears of returned Yorkist claimants during the reign of the first Tudor king, Henry VII (1485–1509), families and neighbours were often divided against each other and old certainties were unsettled.[62] This

---

    *Romance in Time*, 8–9; Melissa Furrow, *Expectations of Romance: The Reception of a Genre in Medieval England* (Cambridge, 2009), 54. The concept is first articulated by Ludwig Wittgenstein, *Philosophical Investigations*, trans. G. E. M. Anscombe (Oxford, 1953), 31–2, and applied to literary genres more generally in Alastair Fowler, *Kinds of Literature: An Introduction to the Theory of Genres and Modes* (Oxford, 1982), 41.

[58] Cooper, *The English Romance in Time*, 9.

[59] For more on formal aspects of the *Morte*, see Cory Rushton, "Malory and Form," in this volume.

[60] See Cooper, *The English Romance in Time*, 363, and Ian A. Gordon, *The Movement of English Prose* (London, 1966), 53 and 59. A similar argument is made with respect to medieval French literature in H. J. Chaytor, *From Script to Print: An Introduction to Medieval Vernacular Literature* (1945; London, 1966), and French chronicles in particular in Gabrielle M. Spiegel, "History, Historicism, and the Social Logic of the Text in the Middle Ages," *Speculum* 65.1 (1990): 80–2.

[61] Cooper, "Counter-Romance"; Leitch, *Romancing Treason*; Cath Nall, "Malory in Historical Context," in this volume.

[62] Michael Hicks, *The Wars of the Roses* (New Haven, CT, 2010); Charles Ross, *The Wars of the Roses: A Concise History* (London, 1976); Anthony Goodman, *The Wars of the Roses:*

seems relevant to how these romances, in their prose form, their darker take on family, and their narrative arcs, make meaning in part through their tensional relationship to earlier English verse romances.

Like some of the characters these prose romances portray, and a bit like Chaucer when he cites the made-up Lollius rather than Boccaccio as his source for *Troilus and Criseyde*, the writers of these prose romances seek to distance themselves from the influence of their verse-writing forebears in ways that nonetheless reveal the generic expectations they have inherited. In both their prose form and their darker content, Malory and the other English prose romances present themselves as partially independent, in a way that nonetheless emphasises, or makes meaning through, their relationship to the tradition from which they are descended. Since the term "the anxiety of influence" invokes the spectre of Harold Bloom, it might be worth acknowledging his background presence directly, despite the caveats with Bloom's model of literary influence and its anxieties. Bloom's idea of writers responding to other writers through a "clinamen" or swerve is relevant here; this is a model in which influence is shown through difference.[63] Like the tragic killing of Gareth and Gaheris, the disturbing murder of Jason's heirs and the execution of Raymond's son Horrible emblematise the way in which the Middle English prose romances respond to the genre by killing the confidence in proper inheritance that infuses earlier popular romance, lingering instead on delinquents and disconcerting traits. By offering an ethical discourse that perhaps operates more through negative exempla than through the positive examples more customary of verse romance, these prose romances participate in the didacticism of romance, but more forbiddingly.[64] Viewing Malory in this context gives us a better sense of what he was doing – or what he might have been perceived as doing – by bringing an Arthuriad into English prose. In concentrating on literary parallels for the darker aspects of the *Morte Darthur*, this chapter is by no means suggesting that these are the only connections available; after all, the darker turns are inseparably intertwined with the ideals they threaten. This chapter instead seeks to encourage reading Malory alongside other (contemporary) texts more often, in order that we may continue to attune ourselves to the formal, thematic, and ideological insights to be gained by so doing.

---

*Military Activity and English Society, 1452–97* (London, 1981), esp. 8; S. B. Chrimes, *Henry VII* (London, 1977), 68–94.

[63] Harold Bloom, *The Anxiety of Influence: A Theory of Poetry* (Oxford, 1973), 14; I refer to Bloom's model loosely, as I am not primarily concerned here either with poets or with named authors responding to other named authors in ways that are designed to ensure their own immortality; I am concerned, rather, with responses to or within a genre or tradition, in a more flexible, but nonetheless pointed, way.

[64] On romance's didacticism, see Furrow, *Expectations of Romance*, and Phillipa Hardman, "Popular Romances and Young Readers," *A Companion to Medieval Popular Romance*, ed. Raluca L. Radulescu and Cory James Rushton (Cambridge, 2009), 150–64.

# 5

# Malory in Print

SIÂN ECHARD

As the chapter by Thomas H. Crofts and K. S. Whetter in this volume shows, Malory's *Morte Darthur* survives to us in only one medieval manuscript, and because that manuscript – the Winchester manuscript – was not discovered until 1934, its impact on the reading and reception of Malory's text was not fully felt until the middle of the twentieth century. Before that time, the *Morte* was transmitted exclusively in print. This chapter looks at the range of printed versions of Malory's text, from its precarious early print history, represented by only a single surviving perfect copy of the first printing of the text, to the proliferation of editions and adaptations that arose from the medieval revival of the nineteenth century, the fine press movement of the early twentieth century, and the mass production of Arthurian material aimed at children and juvenile readers. Until 1934, every print edition of Malory depended, ultimately, on William Caxton's printing of 1485, and yet the remarkable variety of formats and presentations bears witness to the many audiences to whom Malory's text appealed.

## Early Print

In the preface to his 1485 printing of the *Morte Darthur*, William Caxton writes that he produced the book in response to popular demand, of a very particular type:

> After that I had accomplysshed and fynysshed dyvers hystoryes, as wel of contemplacyon as of other hystoryal and worldly actes of grete conquerours and prynces, and also certeyn bookes of ensaumples and doctryne, many noble and dyvers gentylmen of thys royame of Englond camen and demaunded me many and oftymes wherfore that I have not do made and enprynte the noble hystorye of the Saynt Greal and of the moost renomed Crysten kyng, fyrst and chyef of the thre best Crysten, and worthy, Kyng Arthur, whyche ought moost to be remembred emonge us Englysshe men tofore al other Crysten kynges.[1]

By 1485, Caxton had indeed printed many chronicle histories, many explicitly religious works, and many exemplary and didactic texts. He had also published

---

[1] William Caxton, Preface to *Morte Darthur*, in Sir Thomas Malory, *Le Morte Darthur*, ed. P. J. C. Field, 2 vols. (Cambridge, 2013), II, 854. Further references to this edition will be found in parentheses in the text.

works by Geoffrey Chaucer, John Gower and John Lydgate, the great triumvirate of Middle English poets. As England's first printer, Caxton both created and responded to the market and public taste, and in that light it is significant that Malory's work is presented here as aligning with histories and with exemplary narrative. As the preface continues, Caxton tells us that he protested that Arthur is not historical, and was challenged by his "dyvers gentylmen" until he had to admit that "there was suche a noble kyng named Arthur" (II.855). Furthermore, he assures his readers that in the book he has chosen to print about the king, they will find "noble shyvalrye, curtosye, humanyte, frendlynesse, hardynesse, love, frendshyp, cowardyse, murdre, hate, vertue, and synne. Doo after the good and leve the evyl," he admonishes his readers, "and it shal brynge you to good fame and renommee" (II.856). Part of the packaging of Malory's *Morte*, then, is its presentation as in some sense true, or at least morally useful, as Caxton acknowledges that while some things might not be quite true, nevertheless "al is wryton for our doctryne" (II.856).

Another part of Caxton's packaging has to do with another kind of utility. He tells his readers that "for to understonde bryefly the contente of thys volume" he has "devyded it into twenty-one bookes, and every book chapytred, as hereafter shal by Goddes grace folowe" (II.856). As the chapter in this volume by Crofts and Whetter on the Winchester manuscript and modern editions of Malory shows, Caxton apparently did much more to his source than simply divide it up into books and chapters. What is important here, however, is the emphasis on accessibility. Caxton's pages are clean and clear in appearance, made up of a single column of text, with small decorative letters at chapter divisions, along with chapter headings with some white space, and quite ample margins (Figure 1).

Nevertheless, the overall effect is inevitably of blocks of text, in a very long book. A reader could certainly benefit from some help in locating specific parts of Malory's narrative, and the table of contents, which runs to twenty-nine pages, offers that help. It also offers an epitome of the narrative, one that has the possibility of guiding interpretation. Consider, for example, the first two entries for The Second Book, the tale of Balin and Balan:

> Of a damoysel whyche came gyrde wyth a swerde for to fynde a man of suche vertue to drawe it oute of the scabard
>    How balen arayed lyke a poure knyght pulled out the swerde whyche afterword was cause of his deth.[2]

While the maiden warns Balin of the consequences of his decision to keep the sword, it is not immediately clear to a reader coming to the tale for the first time that he will in fact die. The table of contents is in effect a spoiler. The first two entries also emphasise two things that are central to the beginning of the story,

---

[2] Field's edition of the *Morte*, cited in the previous note, does not include Caxton's table of contents. This text, then, is taken directly from the 1485 printing: Sir Thomas Malory, *[Le morte darthur]*. [Caxton]: Enprynted and fynysshed in thabbey Westmestre, the last day of Juyl the yere of our lord M.CCCC.lxxxv. STC 801. There are two surviving copies of this printing, one of them all but complete (the copy now at the Pierpont Morgan Library in New York), and the other, at the John Rylands Library in Manchester, missing eleven leaves.

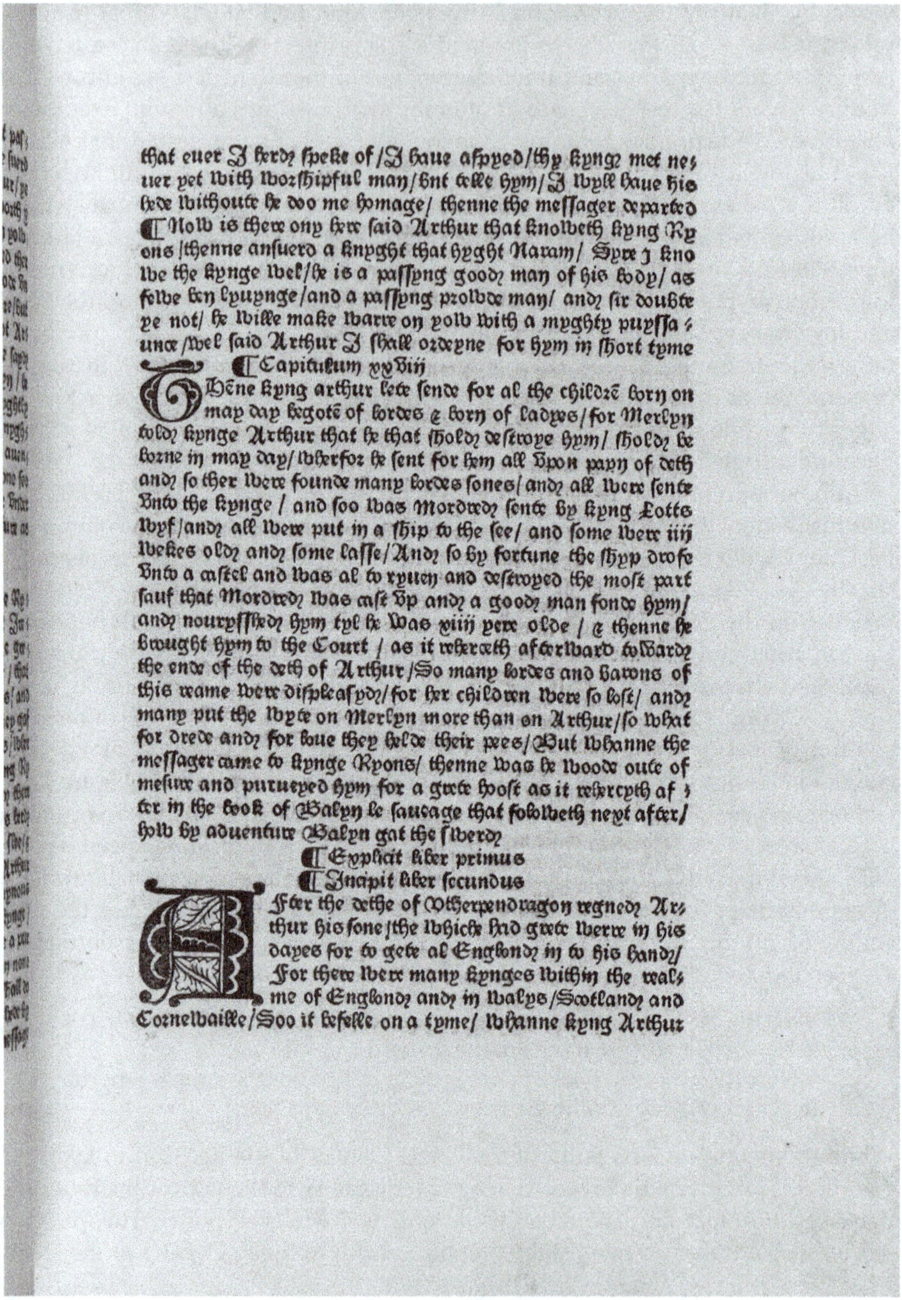

that euer I herde speke of / I haue aspyed / thy kynge met ne∣
uer yet with worshipful man / but calle hym / I wyll haue his
hede withoute he doo me homage / thenne the messager departed
¶ Now is there ony here said Arthur that knoweth kyng Ry∣
ons / thenne answerd a knyght that hyght Naram / Syre I kno∣
we the kynge wel / he is a passyng good man of his body / as
felue ben lyuynge / and a passyng proude man / and sir doubte
ye not / he wille make warre on yow with a myghty puyssa∣
unce / wel said Arthur I shall ordeyne for hym in short tyme
    ¶ Capitulum xxviij

THEnne kyng arthur lete sende for al the children born on
may day begote of lordes & born of ladyes / for Merlyn
tolde kynge Arthur that he that sholde destroye hym / sholde be
borne in may day / wherfor he sent for hem all vpon payn of deth
and so ther were founde many lordes sones / and all were sente
vnto the kynge / and soo was Mordred sente by kyng Lottes
wyf / and all were put in a ship to the see / and some were iiij
wekes old and some lasse / And so by fortune the shyp drofe
vnto a castel and was al to ryuen and destroyed the most part
sauf that Mordred was cast vp and a good man fonde hym / & thenne he
and nouryssed hym tyl he was xiiij yere olde / & thenne he
broughte hym to the Court / as it rehersseth afterward toward
the ende of the deth of Arthur / So many lordes and barons of
this reame were displeasyd / for her children were so loste / and
many put the wyte on Merlyn more than on Arthur / so what
for drede and for loue they helde their pees / But whanne the
messager came to kynge Ryons / thenne was he woode oute of
mesure and purueyed hym for a grete hoost as it rehersyth af∣
ter in the book of Balyn le saueage that foloweth next after /
how by aduenture Balyn gat the swerd

    ¶ Explicit liber primus
    ¶ Incipit liber secundus

AFter the dethe of Vtherpendragon regned Ar∣
thur his sone / the whiche had grete werre in his
dayes for to gete al Englond in to his hand /
For ther were many kynges within the real∣
me of Englond and in Walys / Scotland and
Cornebaille / Soo it befelle on a tyme / whanne kyng Arthur

Figure 1. Opening of Book II, in the John Rylands Library copy of Caxton's printing of the *Morte*, 1485, leaf 81.

but tend to get lost in the mounting fatalism and horror as the tale progresses: that is, Balin's virtue and his poverty. Early in the tale, Balin makes the point that virtue is not necessarily manifested by outward appearance. In a text in which the outward usually *is* presented as a reliable guide – Tor looks nothing like the cowherd who is apparently his father, and Gareth is clearly, to everyone in Arthur's court except Kay, not a peasant despite his request for twelve months' worth of food – Balin's speech is striking, as is the fact that no one else at the court can draw the sword. The brief summary in the table of contents, then, picks out a feature of the story that seems particularly significant, even though it is not truly developed as the tale goes on.

Caxton's text, preface, and table of contents had a persistent influence on subsequent editions, though those editions also made their own innovations. Wynkyn de Worde took over Caxton's business on the latter's death in 1492. He produced his first edition of the *Morte* in 1498.[3] He used Caxton's front matter, including the table of contents. The text is now printed in two columns, and running book titles have been added throughout. Each book begins with a rubric in larger type than the rest of the text. The chapter summaries from the table of contents are now also repeated in the main text, as headings to each chapter. That means, for example, that the Balin entries just discussed are unavoidable, and so we must wonder about their impact on a reader. De Worde's most dramatic innovation, however, is that he incorporated into Caxton's text more than twenty woodcut illustrations – one at the beginning of each of Caxton's book divisions. While early printers often made repeated use of the same, generic woodcuts – standard images of knights on horseback, or of figures of men and women, for example – many of de Worde's woodcuts seem to have been designed as illustrations closely related to the text. These include such scenes as Balin drawing the damsel's sword (Figure 2), Nimue sealing Merlin in the cave, Beaumains arriving at Arthur's court supported by two attendants, Lancelot running naked in his madness, Lancelot riding in the cart, and Mordred attacking the Tower of London with cannons.

There is only a single surviving copy of this printing,[4] and only a single nearly-complete copy as well of de Worde's next printing of the *Morte*, in 1529 (there are also some fragmentary copies).[5] In the previous *Companion to Malory*, A. S. G. Edwards argued

> it is clear that Caxton's edition and its early reprints by de Worde were widely read. Paradoxically, the chief evidence of this is negative: very few copies survive of Caxton's 1485 edition and de Worde's of 1498 and 1529, and those that do are usually imperfect. For such a large work the virtual disappearance of editions is striking. It suggests the degree to which Malory's work, like other early editions of romances, was literally read to destruction.[6]

---

[3] *[Le morte d'Arthur]*, [Westmestre: Wynkyn de Worde, 1498]. STC 802.

[4] There is a fragment in the Bodleian Library; the only mostly complete copy, at the John Rylands Library in Manchester, is missing many leaves, and some of the surviving leaves are damaged.

[5] *[Le Morte Darthur]*, [Imprynted at London: In Fletestrete at [the] sygne of sonne, by Wynkyn de Worde, In the yere of our lord god. M. CCCCC.xxix. the .xviij. daye of Nouember]. STC 803. The copy begins part-way through the table of contents.

[6] A. S. G. Edwards, "The Reception of Malory's *Morte Darthur*," in *A Companion to Malory*, ed. Elizabeth Archibald and A. S. G. Edwards (Cambridge, 1996), 243.

The seconde boke.

Here foloweth the seconde boke of that noble prynce kyng Arthur.

Of a damoysell whiche came gyrde with a swerde for to fynde a man of suche vertue to drawe it out of the scauberde.          Capl'm primu.

After the deth of Uther pendragon regned Arthur his sone/the whiche had grete warre in his dayes for to gete al Englonde in to his honde/ for there were many kynges within the realme of Englonde and in Wales. Scotlonde & Cornewaylle. So it befelle on a tyme / whan kyng Arthur was at London/there came a knyght and tolde the kynge tydynges how that kyng Ryence of Northwales had rered a grete nombre of people/& were entred in to the londe & brente & slewe the kynges true lyege people/yf this be true sayd Arthur/it were grete shame vnto myn astate/but þ he were myghtelywithstande/it is trouth sayd the knyght/for I sawe þ hoost my self Well sayd the kyng/lete make a crye/ þ all the lordes knyghtz & gentylmen of armes sholde drawe vnto a castell called Camelot in tho dayes/& ther þ kyng wolde lete make a coūseyll generall and a grete Iustes. So whan the kyng was come thyder with all his

Figure 2. Balin drawing the sword, from the opening of Book II in the John Rylands Library copy of Wynkyn de Worde's printing of the *Morte*, 1498, leaf 56.

Yet despite the rarity of copies surviving today, both the Caxton and de Worde printings have, as we will see, a very long life, to the extent that they influence many subsequent printings, both in the early modern period and in the nineteenth and twentieth centuries as well. For example, the 1498 de Worde text is the basis for the Shakespeare Head Press edition of 1933, discussed further below.

As noted, de Worde printed the *Morte* again in 1529, and it seems that between 1498 and 1529 some of the original woodcuts had been lost, so some more generic illustrations appear in the later printing.[7] Edward Hodnett writes that the de Worde *Morte* is "the only major work of English literature printed during this early period that contains a substantial number of woodcuts made in England that create for the modern reader a true world of the imagination."[8] He argues that each cut helps to lead the reader into the book to which it is attached, though I would point out that de Worde's design sometimes separates the woodcut from the text to which it refers, with the image appearing in a few occasions on the verso preceding a book change. The visual impact of the illustrations is undeniable, however, as they span the two columns of text and take up almost half of the page (and in one case, two woodcuts are placed on the same page, providing a full page with nothing but illustration).

William Copland printed the *Morte* in 1557,[9] continuing to use ten of de Worde's woodcuts, and adding others, cut to smaller size, that were clearly based on de Worde's programme.[10] Thomas East's edition of 1578 patterned many of its illustrations on Copland's.[11] As Edwards points out, de Worde's woodcuts thus had a lasting effect.[12] Printers often copied programmes of illustration. For example, the many printings of the romance of *Bevis of Hampton* based their illustrations on the very specific cuts first designed for Richard Pynson in 1503, and as was the case with the *Morte* illustrations, when the original blocks wore out, new woodcuts were made based on those old illustrations. If Hodnett is right that de Worde's illustrations create an imaginative response in the reader to Malory's *Morte*, then this visual interpretation of the text had the potential to affect how readers understood the *Morte* for centuries. Indeed, James Spisak's edition of Caxton in 1983 used the Copland illustrations to decorate the text. After 1934 – as the chapter in this volume by Crofts and Whetter on editing Malory makes clear – the contest between the Winchester and Caxton versions of the text could be heated, and the claims of each were vigorously advanced in their various editions. Caxton of course had no illustrations; that the Spisak edition draws on the later print tradition to provide what is missing suggests the degree to which

---

[7] Barry Gaines, *Sir Thomas Malory: An Anecdotal Bibliography of Editions, 1485–1985* (New York, 1990), 9.

[8] Edward Hodnett, *Five Centuries of English Book Illustration* (Aldershot, 1988), 15.

[9] *The story of the moste noble and worthy Kynge Arthur, the whiche was the fyrst of the worthyes chrysten, and also of his noble and valyaunt knyghtes of the rounde table*, [Imprynted at Londo[n]: In Fletestrete at the sygne of the Rose Garlande, by Wyllyam Copland], An. M.D.LXVII]. STC 804.

[10] See Gaines, *Anecdotal Bibliography*, 11.

[11] *The storye of the most noble and worthy kynge Arthur, the which was the fyrst of the worthyes Chrysten, and also of his noble and valyaunt knyghtes of the rounde table*, Imprynted at London: By Thomas East. STC 805. There is some argument over the date of this printing. The *English Short Title Catalogue* gives a tentative date of 1582, and 1585 has also been suggested, but J. A. W. Bennett points to a letter of C. Nathaniel Baxter's (c. 1550–1635) in 1578 referring to a recent printing of the *Morte*; this letter seems to support a date of c. 1578 for East's printing. See J. A. W. Bennett, *The Evolution of The Faerie Queene* (Chicago, 1942), 76 n. 46.

[12] Edwards, "Reception," 241–2.

Figure 3. Title page to William Copland's 1557 printing of the *Morte*, featuring St George. The title-page is a facsimile. This particular copy belonged to William Morris, and also contains his bookplate.

a tradition rooted in early print continued to exercise influence even over the scholarly imagination of the twentieth century.

Another part of Copland's 1557 printing that had considerable longevity was the title page. This page consists of an illustration of St George killing the dragon, in a decorative frame (Figure 3). The St George woodcut was first used in a 1527 edition, by Peter Treveris, of Ranulph Higden's *Polychronicon*,[13] and after Copland deployed it on his *Morte* title page, it was used again in the same way by East. It is not uncommon for some printed books of this period to use generic "knightly" images to illustrate the title pages of romances. Others might use images specific to the text, as for example the versions of an image of a mounted knight with a boar's head on his sword, accompanied by a lion, found in printings of the popular family romance of *Guy of Warwick*. The St George image might fall into either category; that is, it could be a knightly image Copland had to hand, but it also suits a reading of Arthur as an English hero, one who overcomes non-Christian enemies – an association the king had long before Malory, of course. The St George image also came to be one face of Malory's text in the nineteenth century, thanks to its appearance in facsimile on the title page of Robert Southey's edition of 1817, about which I will have more to say below. But first there is one final, black letter (that is, the Gothic-appearing type favoured by early printers) edition of the *Morte* to consider, and that is the text that William Stansby printed for Jacob Bloom in 1634.[14]

Early printers routinely made changes to their texts at the level of word as well as design. While Wynkyn de Worde, for example, used Caxton's edition as his source, he made many small changes to vocabulary, spelling and so on. Oskar Sommer, who edited Malory's *Morte* in 1889–91, estimated that there were "nearly ten thousand variants between Caxton's text and the 1529 text."[15] While Sommer's own accuracy has been challenged, it remains true that a side-by-side comparison of the two editions shows many small changes. Stansby, for his part, based his text on Thomas East's edition, but in addition, it is claimed that the text was deliberately altered to remove material deemed offensive (though in fact changes were minor). The publisher Jacob Bloom provided a preface which explained,

> In many places this Volume is corrected (not in language but in phrase), for here and there, King Arthur or some of his Knights were declared in their communications to sweare prophane, and vse superstitious speeches, all (or the most part) of which is either amended or quite left out, by the paines and industry of the Compositor and Corrector at the Presse; so that as it is now it may passe for a famous piece of Antiquity, reuiued almost from the gulph of obliuion, and renued for the pleasure and profit of present and future times.[16]

This tendency to alter Malory's language crops up again in the nineteenth-century editions to be examined below.

Stansby's text is, like all the editions discussed thus far, printed in a black letter font, but in most other ways, its design clearly signals the tastes of the seventeenth century. Consider, for example, the title. Title pages developed gradually in the history of early print, and because damage to early books often

---

[13] Gaines, *Anecdotal Bibliography*, 10.

[14] *The most ancient and famous history of the renowned prince Arthur King of Britaine...* (London: Printed by William Stansby, for Iacob Bloome, 1634). STC 806.

[15] Cited in Gaines, *Anecdotal Bibliography*, 10. For a discussion of Sommers's edition, see Thomas H. Crofts and K. S. Whetter, "Writing the *Morte Darthur*: Author, Manuscript, and Modern Editions," in this volume.

[16] Stansby, *Famous History*, 4.

involves the loss of outer leaves, we are not always able to know what a title page looked like. The single surviving copy of the 1529 de Worde edition of the *Morte*, for example, has lost leaves from the front, and now opens part-way through the table of contents. But we can compare two sixteenth-century titles with the seventeenth-century one to get a sense of how practices developed. Copland's title page reads, above the woodcut of St George and the dragon, *The story of the moste noble and worthy kynge Arthur, the whiche was one of the worthyes chrysten, and also of his noble and valiaunte knyghtes of the rounde Table. Newly imprynted and corrected.* East's title page and title are the same. But Stansby's printing has no woodcut illustration on the title page. Instead, the whole page is occupied with a much-expanded version of the title: *The Most Ancient and Famous History of the Renowned Prince Arthur King of Britaine, Wherein is declared his Life and Death, with all his glorious Battailes against the Saxons, Saracens, and Pagans, which (for the honour of his Country) he most worthily atchieved. As also, all the Noble Acts, and Heroicke Deeds of his Valiant Knights of the Round Table. Newly refined, and published for the delight, and profit of the Reader.* Like Copland (and East), Stansby declares the fame of his subject, and the quality of the edition. But in addition, Arthur's story has become "ancient," just as the preface designates Malory's work "a famous piece of Antiquity." Medieval texts had begun to seem obscure long before Stansby's edition. Thomas Berthelet presented his 1532 printing of John Gower's *Confessio Amantis* to Henry VIII in a preface that contrasted the "olde vulgars" of writers like Gower with contemporary fashion;[17] while the intent was to praise those old writers, the preface nevertheless opens up a space between the medieval text and the early modern reader. Similarly, the preface to Robert Crowley's 1555 printing of *Piers Plowman* notes that "The Englishe is according to the tyme it was written in, and the sence somewhat darke, but not so harde, but that is maye be vnderstande of such as wyll not sticke to breake the shell of the nutte for the kernelles sake."[18] The popular image of the nut and the kernel suggests Crowley is writing chiefly here about the allegorical and symbolic significances of Langland's language, but the sense that this text is ancient (a word Crowley also uses) does create a distance between the reader and the text. So, for Stansby's title page to declare the antiquity of Malory's text is simultaneously to elevate it, and, potentially, to confine it to the realm of curiosity.

There are other aspects of Stansby's printing that take Malory's text firmly into the seventeenth century. While the text itself is still in black letter – a font which by this time would read as "ancient" (or at least antiquated) to many – the front matter is now set in a mix of italic and Roman type, and the rubrics, running titles and chapter headings are also set in Roman.[19] The text is printed in

---

[17] John Gower, *Jo. Gower de confessione Amantis. Imprinted at London in Fletestrete by Thomas Berthelette Printer to the kingis grace...* (London, 1532), STC 12143, aa.ii.v.

[18] William Langland, *The vision of Pierce Plowman, now fyrste imprynted by Roberte Crowley...* (1550; STC 19906), *.ii v. Metaphors of light and darkness are often found in early modern discussions of medieval texts; see for example Alexandra Gillespie, *Print Culture and the Medieval Author: Chaucer, Lydgate, and Their Books, 1473–1557* (Oxford, 2006), Chapter 3, "Assembling Chaucer's Texts in Print, 1517–1539."

[19] I discuss the associations of various type faces in post-medieval printing of medieval texts in *Printing the Middle Ages* (Philadelphia, 2008). See also Mark Bland, "The Appearance of the Text in Early Modern England," *Text* 11 (1998): 91–154.

King *Arthur* and his valiant Knights of the Rounnd *Table*.
*Sir* Triſtram. *Sir* Launcelot. *Sir* Galahad. *Sir* Perciuall.
*Sir* Gauwin. *Sir* Ector. *Sir* Bors. *Sir* Lionell. *Sir* Griſlet.
*Sir* Gaheris. *Sir* Tor. *Sir* Acolon. *Sir* Ewaine. *Sir* Marhaus.
*Sir* Pelleas *Sir* Sagris. *Sir* Turqnine. *Sir* Kay. *sir* Gareth.

*sir* Beaumans. *Sir* Berſunt. *Sir* Palamide. *sir* Beleobus.
*sir* Ballamore. *Sir* Galohalt. *sir* Lamarecke. *Sir* Floll.
*sir* Superablilis. *Sir* Paginet. *Sir* Belvoure.

Figure 4. Frontispiece to the Stansby/Bloom 1634; copy from the Folger Shakespeare Library (STC 806 copy 1).

three quarto volumes (all the previous printings of Malory's text were the larger, folio size). There are no illustrations beyond the frontispiece – the same in each volume – which features a woodcut of the Round Table, with King Arthur in the centre (Figure 4), and the names of the knights written around the borders, in Roman type. The arms and armour of the knights are resolutely late medieval or early modern, suggesting parade armour of the sixteenth century. As with Copland's St George title page, this frontispiece would go on to have a new life in a later period, as it appeared in one of the two editions of the *Morte* published in 1816, and it is to these editions that we now turn.

## The Medieval Revival, Part I: Editions

Like many medieval authors, Malory fell out of print for a time; in his case, the Stansby/Bloom edition was the last to appear for almost two centuries. The author and his work were not unknown, though it might be fair to say they were not much appreciated. In the entry on Caxton in the *Biographia Britannica* of 1747, for example, a long note on Caxton's printing of the *Morte* dismisses the text quite comprehensively:

> As the author has not made his heroes any great commanders of their passions in their amours, nor rigorously confined them to honour and decorum, in point of fidelity and continence, his book became a great favourite with some persons of the highest distinction for a long time. It had two or three impressions afterwards, and seems to have been kept up in print, for the entertainment of the lighter and more insolid readers, down to the reign of King Charles I.[20]

The note goes on to quote at length from Roger Ascham's condemnation of the *Morte* in *The Schoolmaster* (1570), and certainly Ascham's assessment of the *Morte* as papist and given to violence and bawdiness is reflected in some of the changes and expurgations already mentioned with respect to the Stansby edition. Malory and his work appear in passing in various eighteenth- and early nineteenth-century literary histories. One of the better-known assessments of the author is Walter Scott's, in the introduction to his 1804 edition of *Sir Tristrem*: "... his adventures make a part of the collection, called the *Morte Arthur*, containing great part of the history of the Round Table, extracted at hazard, and without much art or combination, from the various French prose folios on that favourite topic." Scott goes on to note that the *Morte* is to be found "In the hands of most antiquaries and collectors."[21] Indeed the bibliographer and antiquarian Thomas Frognall Dibdin, in his 1810 updating of Joseph Ames's *Typographical Antiquities*, described at length the single perfect copy of Caxton's printing, at that time in

[20] *Biographia Britannica: or, the Lives of the Most eminent Persons Who have flourished in Great Britain and Ireland, From the earliest Ages, down to the present Times: Collected from the best Authorities, both Printed and Manuscript, And digested in the Manner of My Bayle's Historical and Critical Dictionary* (London, 1748), III.1243.

[21] Sir Walter Scott, *Sir Tristrem: A Metrical Romance of the Thirteenth Century* (Edinburgh, 1804), xxxv–xxxvi.

the collection of the earl of Jersey.[22] Still, Dibdin's discussion of the book makes it clear that few antiquaries had seen early printings of Malory's work, and it seems likely, given what we know about the scarcity of the earliest printings discussed above, that Walter Scott has the Stansby printing chiefly in mind when he speaks of "most" antiquaries and collectors owning a copy of the *Morte*. Barry Gaines lists William Hazlitt, Robert Southey, and Walter Scott himself as notable owners of the Stansby printing.[23] And when Malory finally saw print again in the nineteenth century, it was Stansby's version that conveyed the text to its new audience.

In 1816, two different editions appeared in London, one in two volumes and one in three, and both in the very small size known as "duodecimo" (approximately 12.5 x 19 cm). These were newly packaged to appeal to contemporary tastes. The first to appear was a two-volume edition, printed for Walker and Edwards, titled *The History of the Renowned Prince Arthur, and his Knights of the Round Table*.[24] While the front matter is unsigned, it is generally attributed to the literary historian Alexander Chalmers. There were 2,500 sets printed.[25] The illustrations were provided by Thomas Uwins, a watercolourist, and engraved by Charles Warren. There are not many illustrations: each little volume has a frontispiece, and an illustrated title page. These show the Lady of the Lake with Excalibur; Arthur and the questing beast; the vision of Perceval; and Lancelot fighting the dragon from the tomb (Figure 5). The general style suggests contemporary tastes for the picturesque and the exotic; both the Lady of the Lake and the figures seen by Perceval in his vision, for example, suggest Romantic orientalism. The very small size of the books would have made them appealing as gift-tokens.

Despite this wholesale visual and material redesign, the Preliminary Remarks to the Reader assure a purchaser that the text itself is "an exact reprint" of the Stansby printing.[26] It is anything but, of course; the text, too, is modernised, as a comparison of the first few lines will show:

> It befell in the dayes of the noble Vtherpendragon when he was King
> of England and so reigned, there was a mighty and a noble Duke in

---

[22] Thomas Frognall Dibdin, *Typographical Antiquities; or The History of Printing in England Scotland and Ireland: Containing Memoirs of our Ancient Printers, and a Register of the Books Printed by Them* (London, 1810), I.241–54. Ames first published his work in 1749; Dibdin's account of Caxton's Malory expands considerably upon Ames's entry, which seems in fact to have been a description of de Worde's printing, since Ames refers briefly to the "wooden cut" found in each book (Joseph Ames, *Typographical Antiquities* (1749), I.46).

[23] Gaines, *Anecdotal Bibliography*, 13.

[24] This is the form of the title on the engraved title page. That title page is followed by a printed page with a much fuller version: *The History of the Renowned Prince Arthur, King of Britain; with his life and death, and all his glorious battles. Likewise, the noble acts and heroic deeds of his valiant knights of The Round Table.*

[25] Gaines, *Anecdotal Bibliography*, 13. For both of the 1816 editions, see also Barry Gaines, "The Editions of Malory in the Early Nineteenth Century," *Papers of the Bibliographical Society of America* 68.1 (1974): 1–17.

[26] *The History of the Renowned Prince Arthur, and his Knights of the Round Table*, 2 vols. (London, 1816), vi.

Figure 5. Frontispiece and title page to volume 2 of the Walker and Edwards printing of 1816.

> Cornewayle, that held long time warre against him. And the Duke was named the Duke of Tintagil. (Stansby)

> It befel in the days of the noble Utherpendragon, when he was king of England, and so reigned, there was a mighty and a noble duke, in Cornwall, that held long time war against him; and the duke was named the duke of Tintagil. (Walker and Edwards)

The Stansby text was already modernised from Caxton's:

> Hit befel in the dayes of Vther pendragon when he was kynge of all Englond/ and so regned that there was a my3ty duke in Cornewaill that helde warre ageynst hym long tyme/ And the duke was called the duke of Tyntagil. (Caxton)

The Walker and Edwards volumes, in other words, are simply continuing the long process of silent emendation of Caxton's text; still, that practice sits oddly next to assurances about "exact" reprinting.

The second edition to appear in 1816 was printed for R. Wilks, and was the work of the antiquary Joseph Haslewood. Its title page replicates the Stansby title (*The Most Ancient and Famous History of the Renowned Prince Arthur*, etc.) and date, opposite a fold-out facsimile of the Stansby illustration of the Round Table. Despite these initial gestures linking this printing to Stansby, however, for the most part this edition is, visually, very similar to the Walker and Edwards print. The inner frontispiece and title page images, including such subjects as the death of Lancelot and the encounter between Arthur and the Lady of the Lake, are stiff, academic compositions with Italianate features. The artist in this case is William Marshall Craig, described in the *Dictionary of National Biography* as a "mediocre illustrator."[27] It is clear from the Advertisement at the front of the book that this edition appeared after the Walker and Edwards edition, because Haslewood expresses his displeasure at being scooped, characterising the printing of the Walker and Edwards volumes as the "attack" of "some illiberal persons."[28] He goes on to make claims for the superior tastefulness of his text, arguing that the three-volume format preserves "the original division of parts" (while the two-volume format sacrifices this elegance to "pecuniary convenience"), and noting that his text has been pruned to make it "fit for the eye of youth; and that it might be no longer secreted from the fair sex ... But the objectionable and, indeed, obscene passages are certainly preserved in the rival edition of two volumes. In ours, the goatish fancy will seek in vain for the sentence that indelicately describes the feat of the giant."[29] Malory's original line, as represented in Stansby's text, reads "he hath murthered her in forcing her, and hath slit her vnto the nauell."[30] The expurgated version in this edition reads simply, "he hath murdered her."[31] Haslewood also suppresses the use of Christ's name, and condemns the Walker and Edwards edition for including this "breach of moral decorum."[32] Today, despite Haslewood's (justifiable) claims for the superiority of his edition (he also trumpets the inclusion of the facsimile frontispiece), Barry Gaines reports that the Walker and Edwards is the scarcer of the two printings, perhaps, he says, because the latter's popularity "meant that many copies were literally read to pieces."[33] Both editions were central to the revival of interest in Arthurian stories in general, and Malory in particular. Gaines writes that "The importance of these little popular editions with their exciting engravings and low prices should not be underestimated. For the next forty years they remained the most accessible form of Malory's tales of King Arthur and his knights."[34] Alfred, Lord Tennyson (1809–92), whose *Idylls of the* King would become in many ways the face of Malory from the middle of the nineteenth century onwards, as discussed further below, owned copies of both printings.[35]

---

[27] Austin Dobson, 'Craig, William Marshall (d. 1827)', rev. Annette Peach, *Oxford Dictionary of National Biography*, Oxford, 2004: http://www.oxforddnb.com/view/article/6583 (accessed 21 November 2016).

[28] *La Mort D'Arthur. The most ancient and famous History of the Renowned Prince Arthur and the Knights of the Round Table*, 3 vols. (London, 1816), I.iii.

[29] *La Mort D'Arthur*, I.iii–iv.

[30] Stansby, *Famous History*, T i v.

[31] *La Mort D'Arthur*, I.195.

[32] *La Mort D'Arthur*, I.v.

[33] Gaines, *Anecdotal Bibliography*, 14. He also notes, in "Editions of Malory in the Nineteenth Century," that Haslewood's edition does in fact show "obvious editorial pains beyond bowdlerization which are lacking in the two-volume edition," 11.

[34] Gaines, "Editions of Malory in the Nineteenth Century," 12.

[35] Gaines, "Editions of Malory in the Nineteenth Century," 12.

Both of the 1816 printings of Malory were, despite their mutual claims to accuracy, unabashedly popular editions, aimed at a reading public, and not presented as scholarly in our modern sense. But there was work afoot on a scholarly text, and as with the popular editions, the same idea seems to have struck at least two people more or less simultaneously. In this case, at the time that the poet Robert Southey first conceived the idea of working on Malory, Sir Walter Scott, whose novels would have much to do with advancing the medieval revival of the nineteenth century, was already making notes towards his own edition. When Scott learned of Southey's project through an exchange of letters between the two men, he left the field to the latter. It is worth noting that Scott's imagining of the edition included a strong sense of its visual presence; he wrote to Southey that he "'intended to have made it a handsome book, in the shape of a small antique-looking quarto, with wooden vignettes of costume'."[36] The desire to frame a medieval text in design features that heighten the text's antiquity is common in the nineteenth-century medieval revival and indeed beyond, and is not confined to books aimed at bibliophiles. For example, Oskar Sommer's 1889–91 edition, while clearly packaging itself as scholarly, includes woodcut decorative initials throughout.[37]

It was some time after the initial exchange of letters between Scott and Southey before Southey's edition appeared at last, in 1817.[38] As Scott imagined, the Southey edition is indeed a quarto, in two volumes, and while it does not have the suggested vignettes of costume, it does make some visual gestures towards antiquity, through a pastiche of features drawn from earlier printings. As noted above, its title page imitates the Copland St George frontispiece of 1557, here in a redrawn facsimile. The title, *The Byrth, Lyf, and Actes of Kyng Arthur; of his Noble Knyghtes of the Rounde Table, theyr merveyllous enquestes and aduentures, Thachyeuyng of the Sanc Greal; and in the end Le Morte Darthur, with the dolorous deth and departing out of thys worlde of them al*, is taken from the colophon to Caxton's edition. Part of this title is set in black letter type, as are the chapter headings in both the table of contents and in the text proper, and the incipits, explicits and Caxton's colophon. Each book begins with a very large decorated initial, though these engraved initials quote the style commonly found in much later printing, and are quite different visually from any of the initials found in the fifteenth- and sixteenth-century printings of the *Morte*. These are features that suggest the world of the bibliophile, and indeed, the text was advertised in a limited run of 250 regular and 50 large paper copies, but Gaines has established that the records of the publisher, Longman and Co., show that 1,000 copies were printed.[39] Still, the work was clearly cherished by some readers for both its appearance and its

[36] Quoted in Gaines, "Editions of Malory in the Nineteenth Century," 4.

[37] I discuss this ubiquitous habit of signalling "medieval" through visual shorthand in *Printing the Middle Ages*, particularly in the Preface, "The Mark of the Medieval."

[38] *The Byrth, Lyf, and Actes of Kyng Arthur; of his Noble Knyghtes of the Rounde Table, theyr merveyllous enquestes and aduentures, Thachyeuyng of the Sanc Greal; and in the end Le Morte Darthur, with the dolorous deth and departing out of thys worlde of them al*, ed. Robert Southey, 2 vols. (London, 1817). Gaines discusses the various delays in "Editions of Malory in the Nineteenth Century," 3–8 and 12.

[39] Gaines, *Anecdotal Bibliography*, 16.

contents; William Morris, for example, had a copy of Southey's edition, and had it bound in white vellum, sharing a "love and veneration" for the book with his friend and collaborator, the pre-Raphaelite artist Edward Burne-Jones.[40] While Morris's Kelmscott Press never printed Malory's *Morte*, the importance of the work in the projects shared by Morris and Burne-Jones is clear in this anecdote.

The features that align the Southey volumes with the world of the scholarly edition are the introductory essay by Southey, which includes remarks (as was typical at the time for editions of similar medieval texts) about the origins of the romance genre and various remarks about Malory's relationship to his sources, as well as the fairly extensive notes.[41] There is also the expected claim to correctness (and this was an old-spelling edition, unlike the popular editions of 1816) but this is made in a context that also points to the *Morte's* popular future:

> The Morte Arthur was a favourite book among our ancestors. It continued to be printed till the middle of the 17th century, with much alteration of orthography, but very little change of language; and were it again modernized in the same manner, and published as a book for boys, it could hardly fail of regaining its popularity. When I was a schoolboy I possessed a wretchedly imperfect copy, and there was no book, except the Faery Queen, which I perused so often, or with such deep contentment. The present edition is a reprint with scrupulous exactness from the first edition by Caxton, in Earl Spencer's library, that nobleman having, with his wonted liberality, permitted a transcript to be made from this most rare and valuable volume for this purpose.[42]

Southey's suggestion that a version of the *Morte* should be packaged as a "book for boys" looks ahead to the many juvenile adaptations discussed at the end of this essay, and his invocation of ancestral readership becomes an important part of the selling of both the *Morte* and the Middle Ages throughout the nineteenth century.

After the editions of 1816 and 1817, Malory's work regained a significant print presence. Thomas Wright produced a popular edition in 1858 that was much reprinted, through the end of the century.[43] It had two title pages, one declaring Malory a knight and compiler, and listing the many titles of Thomas Wright, and the second, a type facsimile of Stansby's 1634 printing. This edition was part of a series called The Library of Old Authors. From the second half of the nineteenth century, such series proliferated (as did series of simplified and illustrated classics aimed at children, as discussed further below). The prefatory matter included

---

[40] Gaines, "Editions of Malory in the Nineteenth Century," 16; Gaines is quoting from a recollection of Burne-Jones's widow. There is a copy of Southey's edition in the Ashmolean Museum in Oxford, bound in white vellum and with designs painted on its cover by Burne-Jones.

[41] Southey did not actually edit the text itself; that was the work of the antiquarian and collector William Upcott (1779–1845), who transcribed the text and corrected it for the press.

[42] Southey, *Byrth, Lyf, and Actes*, I.xxviii.

[43] *La Mort d'Arthure. The History of King Arthur and of the Knights of the Round Table. Compiled by Sir Thomas Malory, Knt.*, ed. Thomas Wright, 3 vols. (London, 1858). There were versions of this edition in 1866, 1889, 1893 and 1897.

criticism of both 1816 editions and of Southey's edition, about which Wright was particularly scathing:

> The text is a mere reprint of Caxton, without any attempt at editing, and was probably left entirely to the care of the printers. It is, therefore, a book useless to the general reader, and is only useful at all because, for reference, it supplies the place of the original, which is inaccessible. The introduction and notes by Southey display the extensive and indiscriminate reading for which the poet was celebrated, but he has done little towards explaining or illustrating his text.[44]

Wright himself, however, relied on Stansby's text, a choice he defended by saying that

> no particular philological value is attached to the language of Caxton's edition, which would certainly be repulsive to the modern reader, while all its value as a literary monument is retained in the reprint. On the other hand, the orthography and phraseology of the edition of 1634, with the sprinkling of obsolete words, not sufficiently numerous to be embarrassing, preserves a certain clothing of mediæval character which we think is one of the charms of the book.[45]

Again, the emphasis is on appropriate dress for this medieval text, something that will signal its venerability without unduly taxing or challenging a reader. The visual cues include the usual wood initials and separators, wrestling on the page, as is typical in such volumes, with modern type and footnotes.

The year 1868 saw the printing of a single-volume edition of the *Morte*, this one in the Globe Editions,[46] edited by Sir Edward Strachey. Like the Wright edition, the Strachey edition was frequently reprinted throughout the century. The text is plain, printed in two columns, but with large black letter font for book breaks and titles. This edition was the first to notice a passage that Wynkyn de Worde interpolated into his printing,[47] and includes the usual accoutrements of mid-century scholarship, with essays on Malory's sources, the early prints, and on chivalry. At the same time, it is a self-consciously modernising text, presenting itself on its title page as Caxton's edition "revised for modern use." What that means becomes clear in Strachey's discussion of the *Morte's* morality, clearly perplexing to Victorian eyes:

> the perplexed question of the morality of the book demands our notice. If it does not deserve the unqualified denunciation of the learned Ascham, it cannot be denied that the *Morte Arthur* exhibits a picture of a society far lower than our own in morals, and depicts it with far less repugnance to

---

[44] Wright, *La Mort d'Arthure*. I.xiv.

[45] Wright, *La Mort d'Arthure*, I.xiv–xv.

[46] *Morte Darthur: Sir Thomas Malory's Book of King Arthur and of his Noble Knights of the Round Table. The original edition of Caxton revised for modern use*, ed. Sir Edward Strachey (London and Philadelphia, 1868). There were at least a dozen versions of this edition, in several forms, printed between 1869 and 1899.

[47] Strachey, *Morte Darthur*, xiv.

its evil elements, on the part either of the author or his personages, than any good man would now feel.[48]

He goes on to suggest, as others have before him, that the expected readership needs to be protected from some of these elements:

> What is wanted ... is an edition for ordinary readers, and especially for boys, from whom the chief demand for this book will always come, and such an edition the present professes to be. It is a reprint of the original Caxton with the spelling modernised, and those few words which are unintelligibly obsolete replaced by others which, though not necessarily unknown to Caxton, are still in use, yet with all old forms retained which do not interfere with this requirement of being readable ... And for the like reason – of making the book readable – such phrases or passages as are not in accordance with modern manners have been also omitted or replaced by others which either actually occur or might have occurred in Caxton's text elsewhere. I say manners, not morals, because I do not profess to have remedied the moral defects of the book which I have already spoken of. Mr. Tennyson has shown us how we may deal best with this matter for modern uses, in so far as Sir Thomas Malory has himself failed to treat it rightly; and I do not believe that when we have excluded what is offensive to modern manners there will be found anything practically injurious to the morals of English boys.[49]

In referring to Tennyson, Strachey is anticipating what would become common in adaptations aimed at children and youth in the latter part of the century, which often mixed versions of some of Malory's stories with others drawn from Tennyson's *Idylls*. This is also a heavily expurgated version, removing words such as God, Jesus, belly, gut, buttock, and bawdy, along with references to sex.[50]

There were other printings of Malory like those in The Library of Old Authors and Globe Editions; that is, "series" editions aimed at general readership. These include an 1892 edition by Ernest Rhys in the Scott Library (as well as various selected editions by Rhys); a Temple Classics edition of 1897, edited by Israel Gollancz; a 1906 Dent Everyman, and so on. There were abridgements and modernisations, such as Edward Conybeare's 1868 version published by Edward Moxon, and Alfred Pollard's modernised text for the 1900 Macmillan's Library of English Classics.[51] I would like to close this essay by touching briefly on two other contexts for the printing of Malory – the fine press tradition, and adaptations for children. These two strands, set against the visual richness and nostalgia of the Medieval Revival, did much to deliver, not just Malory's text, but an *idea* of Malory, to the twentieth century and beyond.

---

[48] Strachey, *Morte Darthur*, xiii.

[49] Strachey, *Morte Darthur*, xvii–xviii.

[50] Gaines, *Anecdotal Bibliography*, 22. Gaines cites Yuri Fuwa, who calculated that there are almost 400 omitted passages and phrases; see "The Globe Edition of Malory as a Bowdlerized Text in the Victoria Age," *Studies in English Literature* 1 (1984): 3–17.

[51] There is a useful overview of the many nineteenth-century editions in David Staines, *Tennyson's Camelot: The Idylls of the King and its Medieval Sources* (Waterloo, 1982), in the chapter "Alfred Tennyson and Victorian Arthuriana."

## The Medieval Revival, Part II: Fine Press

As noted above, William Morris never did print Malory's *Morte*, though the productions of the Kelmscott Press famously included medieval romances, Morris's own Arthurian poem "The Defence of Guenevere," and the incomparable Kelmscott Chaucer. There were editions of the *Morte* aimed squarely at bibliophiles, however. The Ashendene Press was a personal project of C. H. St. John Hornby, a partner in the large publishing firm of W. H. Smith. It produced small runs of fine books between 1895 and 1935, including a limited edition run of the *Morte*, using Southey's 1817 text, in 1913.[52] The book is a large folio, with wood engravings based on drawings by the brother and sister team of Charles March Gere and Margaret Gere. It was issued in 145 paper copies, eight vellum copies and two Japanese paper copies.[53] The text is printed in a single column in the press's Subiaco type, which was designed for the press by Emery Walker (1851–1933) and Sydney Cockerell (1867–1962) based on a Roman type from fifteenth-century Italy. The use of this clear Roman font distinguishes the book sharply from many medievalising productions of the period; for example, while William Morris designed some lovely Roman-inspired fonts, many of the most famous productions of the Kelmscott press used his black letter types. Chapter headings in the Ashendene *Morte* are printed in red, and the large display capitals are hand-painted in red and blue: calligraphy was one of the medieval arts revived by proponents of the Arts and Crafts movement, and the calligraphers who provided the initials for Ashendene books included Edward Johnston, Graily Hewitt and Eric Gill. The wood engravings occupy about a third of the page on which they appear, and there are also two full-page illustrations, one of the young Galahad's arrival at court, and the other of the dying Arthur with the three queens.

In 1933, twenty years after the Ashendene *Morte* was published, another limited edition printing of the *Morte* appeared, this one under the auspices of the Shakespeare Head Press, which at that time was run by the typographer Bernard Newdigate.[54] There were 370 copies printed of this two-volume edition, and as was the case with the Ashendene *Morte*, a few copies – in this case three – were printed on vellum.[55] The text was edited by Sir Adrian Mott from the 1498 de Worde printing, and a distinctive feature of this edition was that it reproduced the de Worde woodcuts (Figure 6). The designs were based on photographs of the copy of de Worde's printing in the John Rylands Library at Manchester, and the text was printed in double columns, just as in de Worde's own printing. David Riley suggests that the press, which had originally planned a single-column edition, decided, upon seeing the Rylands Library photographs, "to publish something which would reflect as closely as possible the size and design of Wynkyn

---

[52] *The Noble and Joyous Books entitled Le Morte Darthur... Whiche book was reduced in to Englysshe by Syr Thomas Malory, Knyght* (Chelsea, 1913).
[53] Gaines, *Anecdotal Bibliography*, 35.
[54] *The Noble & Joyous Boke Entytled Le Morte Darthur*, 2 vols. (Oxford, 1933).
[55] Gaines, *Anecdotal Bibliography*, 35.

Figure 6. The opening of Book VI in the Shakespeare Head *Morte*, 1933.

de Worde's edition."[56] Still, the influence of current tastes in printing is everywhere in this volume, as de Worde's black letter type is replaced with Caslon, an
eighteenth-century type face that was a particular favourite of Newdigate's, and
had the advantage of suggesting age while also being easier to read than a black

[56] David W. Riley, "'A Definite Claim to Beauty': Some Treasures from the Rylands
Private Press Collection," *Bulletin of the John Rylands University Library of Manchester*
72 (1990): 73–88, at 87.

letter type. De Worde's larger black letter display types are represented instead with red capitals, and the small black letter running titles have been replaced by very large red capitals. So, while the woodcuts themselves are very careful copies (slightly reduced in size) of de Worde's originals, everything else about this book speaks to an aesthetic shared with a work like the Ashendene Malory.

The Ashendene and Shakespeare Head editions of the *Morte* were genuinely limited editions; there were also, however, versions of the *Morte* that aimed to satisfy bibliophilic appetites in a broader public. Take, for example, the Medici Society edition of 1910–11. The first printing of this edition appeared in 500 copies on Riccardi handmade paper; there were also twelve vellum copies.[57] The Medici Society, founded in 1908 and still in operation today, was created to make high-quality colour reproductions available at the lowest possible price. This edition of the *Morte* was illustrated with forty-eight full-page colour plates based on watercolours by William Russell Flint. The text was the modernised text of Alfred Pollard, discussed above (one of the often bewildering features of the proliferation of *Morte* printings in the nineteenth and early twentieth centuries is the way that different texts move around and are repackaged in a variety of formats). While the first printing had deluxe features, and remains both rare and quite expensive today, other formats soon followed, including a two-volume edition in 1920, and a one-volume reprint on thin paper, with twenty-four plates, from 1927, reprinted in 1929 and 1935. Flint's illustrations focus on the women of the *Morte*, and are occasionally mildly titillating, as in the illustration of Percival's sister who, clad in nothing but a diaphanous wrap that has slipped to her waist, cuts off her hair to make the scabbard for Galahad's sword. A review in *The Burlington Magazine*, after praising the typography and design, pronounced Flint's illustrations "grotesquely inconsistent with the style of the book as a whole," and went on to call them "insipid, sentimental, theatrical and entirely lacking in style."[58] Despite this assessment, however, the reprinting and repackaging of the Medici edition to make it ever more affordable, meant that Flint's visualisation of the *Morte* had a lasting influence.

A printing roughly contemporary with the Shakespeare Head edition was the Golden Cockerell Press's three-volume *Morte*, printed for the Limited Editions Club in 1936.[59] The Limited Editions Club, based in New York, began in 1929 to publish illustrated editions of classic works. "Limited" in this sense, however, did not mean quite what it meant to a small hand publisher like the Ashendene Press. At first most Limited Editions Club books were printed in runs of 1,500, and that is the case for the *Morte*. Limited Editions Club books were famous for their illustrations, and the artwork for the *Morte* was provided by Robert Gibbings, a wood engraver and book designer who had bought the Golden

[57] *Le Morte Darthur: The Book of King Arthur and of His Noble Knights of the Round Table*, 4 vols. (London, 1910–11). See Gaines, *Anecdotal Bibliography*, 34.

[58] "Le Morte D'Arthur. By Sir Thomas Malory. In four vols. London: The Medici Society, 1910-11. £10 10s," *The Burlington Magazine* 18.96 (1911): 358.

[59] *Le Morte Darthur: The Story of King Arthur & of his Noble Knights of the Round Table written by Sir Thomas Malory, first printed by William Caxton, now modernized, as to spelling and punctuation, by A.W. Pollard, illustrated with wood engravings by Robert Gibbings* (New York, 1936).

Cockerell Press in 1924. The modernised text – as in the Medici printing, Alfred Pollard's – is illustrated and sometimes framed by Gibbings's engravings. This realisation of the *Morte*, too, became more widely available through reprinting. In this case the book was reprinted in 1955 by the Heritage press, which specialised in large-run reprints of Limited Editions Club books. And the Gibbings *Morte* is not the only "collectible" edition of this type. Like the Limited Editions Club, the Folio Society (founded in 1947 in London) aimed (and aims) to produce beautiful, illustrated books priced within reach of a wide range of readers, and like the Limited Editions Club, it also produced a *Morte*, this one in 1982, with linocut illustrations by Edward Bawden.[60] The design is resolutely modern, and the chunky, black-and-white linocuts are sometimes almost comical.

By far the most famous illustrated Malory in this in-between, limited-yet-accessible category is the Dent-Beardsley *Morte* of 1893–4.[61] This edition was the brainchild of the publisher J. M. Dent, whose particular publishing niche was the production of inexpensive classics, often in series; the eventual culmination of this project was the uniform series known as the Everyman's Library. In addition, Dent wondered if it would be possible to produce books like those being hand-printed by William Morris at the Kelmscott Press, but by mechanical (and therefore much less expensive) means. Brigid Brophy assesses his aims somewhat less kindly, writing that his plan "was to cash in on the medievalizing vogue Morris had created."[62] He settled on the *Morte* for his first experiment, and on the very young Aubrey Beardsley as the artist tasked with producing illustrations, borders, initials and other ornaments for the book. Muriel Whitaker writes that "What Dent had in mind … was the soulful medievalism of Morris and Burne-Jones with a dash of japonesque in the form of bare branches, oriental flowers, and asymmetrical arrangements."[63] What he got was work that has often been characterised as decadent, or even parodic. While Beardsley seems not to have read the *Morte* carefully, and is known to have become bored long before he completed the work, it has been argued that the decadence and ambivalence towards chivalry reflected in many of his drawings sits interestingly next to Malory's own ambivalence, "enacting the text's own criticism of the knights of the Round Table."[64] Dent's desire to make an affordable book (or to cash in) meant that Beardsley was limited to black-and-white line-block illustrations (that could be reproduced mechanically), a limitation that suited his Art Nouveau-inspired style, and was suited to the stretched-out, stylised, often androgynous and ethereal or enervated figures he drew. Dent issued the text in twelve paper

---

[60] *Sir Thomas Malory's Chronicles of King Arthur*, 3 vols. (London, 1982).

[61] *The birth life and acts of King Arthur, of his noble knights of the round table, their marvellous enquests and adventures, the achieving of the San Greal and in the end le morte d'Arthur, with the dolourous death and departing out of this world of them all / the text as written by Sir Thomas Malory … ; with an introduction by Professor Rhys and embellished with many original designs by Aubrey Beardsley* (London, 1893–4).

[62] Brigid Brophy, *Beardsley and His World* (New York, 1976), 60.

[63] Muriel A. I. Whitaker, "Flat Blasphemies – Beardsley's Illustrations for Malory's *Morte Darthur*," *Mosaic* 8.2 (1975): 67–75, at 68. See also her *Legends of King Arthur in Art* (Cambridge, 1990), 265–73.

[64] Lorraine Janzen Kooistra, "Beardsley's Reading of Malory's *Morte Darthur*: Images of a Decadent World," *Mosaic* 23.1 (1990): 55–72, at 56.

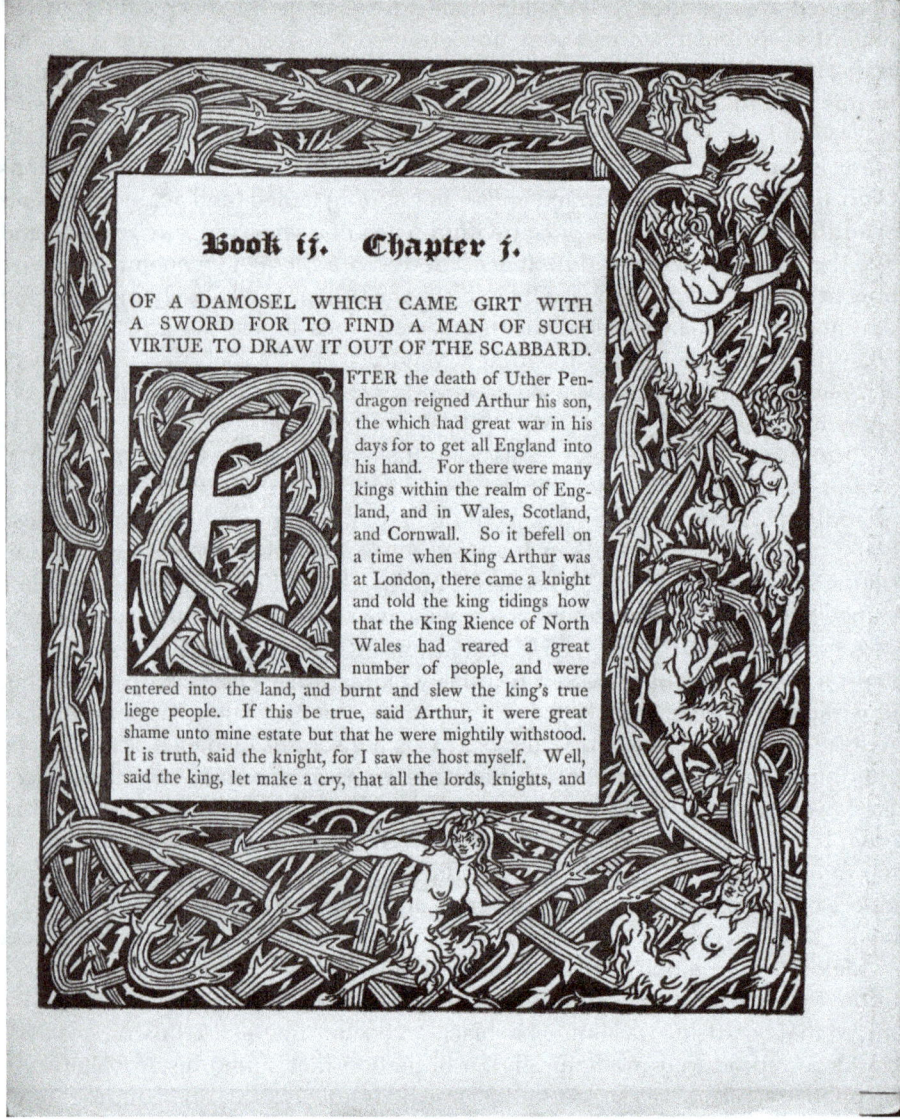

Figure 7. Opening of Book II, from the Dent-Beardsley *Morte*, 1893–1894.

fascicles, in both a "small paper" and a larger, more expensive Dutch paper edition, the latter printed in both red and black. There were 1,500 copies of the small paper edition, and 300 of the Dutch-made paper edition. Buyers could have their collected fascicles bound in two or three volumes, in a binding also designed by Beardsley. While the first edition seems not to have been widely reviewed, it sold well enough for Dent to reissue it in a single volume in 1909, in 1,500 copies, and in 1927, in 1,600 copies.[65] The pictures and designs have since become ubiquitous, often reprinted in other editions of the *Morte*, as well as on their own. Figure 7 shows, again, the opening of the story of Balin, which we have seen several times before in this essay. Here, there is no visual signal about the narrative to follow. Instead, the decorative interlace at the book's opening incorporates satyrs who lounge, play pipes and clamber through thorny vines, in the artist's typically "decadent" style.

## *Malory for Children*

There was one more important channel by which Malory's *Morte* reached many readers in the nineteenth and early twentieth centuries, and that was in versions aimed at children and youth. There is space here to consider only a few of the most notable of these editions. The first is *The Boy's King Arthur*. Produced by the American poet Sidney Lanier, who also published "Boy's" versions of the *Mabinogi*, Froissart's *Chronicles*, and the Percy Folio, it appeared in 1880 in both London and New York.[66] Lanier's Introduction included an account of the development of Arthurian narrative; an extract from Layamon's *Brut*, with interlinear translation; and Caxton's preface to the *Morte*. Lanier presents himself as "a later editor re-arranging the old grown-people's story for many noble and divers boys both of England and America."[67] He writes that "every word in the book, except those which occur in brackets, is Malory's, unchanged except that the spelling is modernized"; the bracketed words are either translations or additions by Lanier to create bridges between parts of his abridged text.[68] The twelve illustrations are black-and-white plates based on paintings by Alfred Kappes, most of them emphasising knightly encounters. They are not remarkable, but Lanier's text was reprinted, in full or in part, many times, and attracted many programmes of illustration.[69] Particularly important among these is the edition illustrated by the American artist N. C. Wyeth, which appeared in 1917. Wyeth studied under Howard Pyle, who had created his own idiosyncratic, illustrated Arthurian adaptations from sources including the *Morte*. Wyeth's colour plates often feature large, muscular knights; his King Arthur, on the book's frontispiece, is heavily bearded and stern in appearance – it would be hard to imagine a starker contrast to Beardsley's figures. Both Pyle and Wyeth drew inspiration from the Brandywine Valley of Pennsylvania, where Pyle had his school, and Muriel Whitaker has suggested that Wyeth's illustrations "[set] romance characters in American landscapes."[70]

---

[65] Gaines, *Anecdotal Bibliography*, 28.

[66] Sidney Lanier, *The Boy's King Arthur, being Sir Thomas Malory's History of King Arthur and his Knights of the Round Table* (New York, 1880).

[67] Lanier, *Boy's King Arthur*, xx.

[68] Lanier, *Boy's King Arthur*, xxii.

[69] A useful resource for tracking the often bewildering reprints of editions like this is Ann F. Howey and Stephen R. Reimer, *Bibliography of Modern Arthuriana 1500–2000* (Cambridge, 2006).

[70] Whitaker, *Legends of King Arthur in Art*, 307. See also Alan Lupack and Barbara Tepa Lupack, *King Arthur in America* (Cambridge, 1999), especially the chapter "Reaction to Tennyson: Visions of Courageous Achievement."

Wyeth was not primarily an illustrator of children's books, but two of the most important children's illustrators of the late nineteenth and early twentieth centuries did take on adaptations of the *Morte*. Walter Crane was one illustrator with an impressive medievalising pedigree; for example, he designed woodcuts for one of the Kelmscott Press productions, and illustrated a lavish, six-volume edition of Spenser's *Faerie Queene*. Crane provided sixteen colour illustrations to Henry Gilbert's *King Arthur's Knights: The Tales Retold for Boys & Girls*, in 1911. This was a collection of thirteen stories, drawn from Malory's *Morte* and from the *Mabinogion*. Gilbert is quite clear about what he thinks his audience wants:

> No doubt many of you, my young readers, have at some time or another taken down the *Morte D'Arthur* from your father's bookshelves and read a few pages of it here and there. But I doubt if any of you have ever gone very far in the volume. You found generally, I think, that it was written in a puzzling, old-fashioned language, that though it spoke of many interesting things, and seemed that it ought to be well worth reading, yet somehow it was tedious and dry. In the tales as I have retold them for you, I hope you will not find any of these faults. Besides writing them in simple language, I have chosen only those episodes which I know would appeal to you.[71]

These episodes include many that concentrate on the youth and education of figures like Arthur, Gareth and Perceval. Many of Crane's illustrations focus on young men, as in his illustration of a very youthful Arthur drawing the sword from the stone. Others emphasise action, as when Beaumains encounters the knight at the ford.

Gilbert's version of the story of Beaumains is drawn from the *Morte*, but other collections for children that featured this story (and it was a popular choice in such contexts) sometimes use Tennyson's version from the *Idylls of the King* instead. An example of this approach is Mary MacGregor's *Stories of King Arthur's Knights* in the Told to the Children series, where, despite the author's assurance that "All the stories in this little book were found in Malory's big book, except 'Geraint and Enid'," the story of Gareth is clearly adapted from Tennyson, even borrowing lines from that poem.[72] Gilbert's retelling of the story of Elaine is, again, based on Malory's, but Crane's illustration of the dying Elaine in her barge lines up visually as well with the many paintings and illustrations from the period drawn from Tennyson's versions of this story, both in "The Lady of Shalott" and in his *Idyll* devoted to Elaine.

Another notable children's book illustrator, Arthur Rackham, took on the *Morte* in 1917 for *The Romance of King Arthur and His Knights of the Round Table*.[73] There was both a trade edition and a limited edition of this printing, the latter

[71] Henry Gilbert, *King Arthur's Knights: The Tales Re-Told for Boys & Girls by Henry Gilbert. With 16 Illustrations in Colour by Walter Crane* (Edinburgh and London, 1911), v.
[72] Mary MacGregor, *Stories of King Arthur's Knights* (Edinburgh, [1905]). The first edition of this book had illustrations by Katharine Cameron, but as often happened with children's retellings, it went through many editions, and in one the illustrations were by Crane.
[73] *The Romance of King Arthur and his Knights of the Round Table, abridged from Malory's Morte d'Arthur by Alfred W. Pollard. Illustrated by Arthur Rackham* (London, 1917).

500 large copies, signed by the artist and bound in vellum.[74] Rackham provided black-and-white drawings and decorations, and full colour plates; in the deluxe copies, the colour plates are separately tipped-in. Rackham had a taste for the fantastic, and admired Beardsley's work in the Dent *Morte*.[75] His colour drawings feature striking, sombre washes over ink outlines, a technique that enhances the moodiness of his illustrations and often sets the central figures against twisting, starkly-realised natural backgrounds or architectural settings. His illustration *How Mordred was slain by Arthur, and how by him Arthur was hurt to the death*, is a nightmarish scene on an apocalyptic battlefield, as the two dark central figures hack at each other against an ominous sky filled with carrion birds. The appearance of the book in 1917 seems particularly apt when one considers illustrations like this one.

All of the editions, modernisations, adaptations and abridgements discussed in this chapter can ultimately be traced back to William Caxton's 1485 printing of the *Morte*. As another chapter in this book shows, the scholarly world of Malory studies experienced an event of seismic proportions with the discovery of the Winchester Malory in 1934, and since that time, there have been scholarly, classroom and facsimile editions of the Winchester text. But Caxton's text continues to have a significant presence in the world of print, thanks to the history I have just traced. The many nineteenth-century popular editions are now in the public domain, so that when a reader sits down to look for an online edition of the *Morte*, one of those printings will invariably be among the first hits. Hard copies of many of these books are still readily available from book-selling sites too, along with dubious print-on-demand "editions" that are often really one of the popular editions of the past, transferred to ebook form with a cover illustration that might be lifted from any of the illustrated editions discussed here. One can also make a digital return to origins, through online facsimiles of both the Winchester manuscript and the Caxton and de Worde printings, all of which are now available in full, for free. There are many Malorys, and new technologies are poised to bring us many more.

---

[74] See Gaines, *Anecdotal Bibliography*, 61.
[75] See the discussion in Barbara Tepa Lupack with Alan Lupack, *Illustrating Camelot* (Cambridge, 2008), 154–5.

# II
## Approaches to Malory

# 6
## Malory and Form
CORY JAMES RUSHTON

Since the discovery of a pre-Caxton *Morte Darthur* at Winchester in 1934 (London, British Library, MS Add 59678), there have been four major theories on the question of what the *Morte* is formally: a series of eight discrete, unconnected (or semi-connected) tales (Vinaver's *Works*, divided into Books I–VIII); Murray Evans's 1979 contention that there are five distinct sections of varying lengths; the Lumiansky School's unified whole, capable of being read as something like a novel across inherently episodic parts; and Stephen Knight's argument that Malory begins with an episodic structure but discovers a means to pursue a more unified conclusion somewhere in the "Tristram," a thesis not widely adopted but which speaks to the widespread critical consensus that Malory gets better as he goes along (which originated with Vinaver himself).[1] The manuscript and its consequences loom so large in this debate that Carol Meale's chapter in the original *Companion to Malory*, the first chapter in the book, does not mention genre or form at all – it is entirely concerned with conflicts over editorial practice from Caxton to Vinaver. This is no criticism of Meale: as she says, "in choosing which version we privilege above the others, we should recognize that we actively participate in the creation of meaning."[2] At a time when Peter Field's new edition has become the standard edition for citing Malory at Boydell and Brewer and Palgrave MacMillan, but while most people who creatively adapt the legend use some variation of Caxton (as everybody did between the fifteenth century and the mid twentieth) or Vinaver's single volume *Works*, Meale's point is something to bear in mind. The problem of form in the *Morte* is inextricably linked to the problem of genre, although it is also connected to a problem of aesthetic or quality. This chapter will interrogate the problem of the *Morte*'s form, and further examine how form impacts interpretation of the work. Can we determine what Malory set out to write? How has Malorian criticism dealt with the existence of two distinct versions of Malory's book? Do Malory's sources dictate what he

---

[1] *The Works of Sir Thomas Malory*, ed. Eugène Vinaver, 3rd edn, rev. P. J. C. Field, 3 vols. (Oxford, 1990), I, lvi; Murray J. Evans, "*Ordinatio* and Narrative Links: The Impact of Malory's Tales as a 'hoole book'," in *Studies in Malory*, ed. James W. Spisak (Kalamazoo, 1985), 29–52; *Malory's Originality: A Critical Study of* Le Morte Darthur, ed. R. M. Lumiansky (Baltimore, 1964); Stephen Knight, *The Structure of Sir Thomas Malory's Arthuriad* (Sydney, 1969). See also the Introduction to this volume on the changing perceptions of Malory's artistry.
[2] Carol M. Meale, "'The Hoole Book': Editing and the Creation of Meaning in Malory's Text," in *A Companion to Malory*, ed. Elizabeth Archibald and A. S. G. Edwards (Cambridge, 1996), 17.

produced, or is he capable of shaping them to his own formal ends? For Malory studies, the question of form has been key.

As Stephen Atkinson has recently remarked, the "Unity Debate" that followed Vinaver's *Works* never ended; it merely "waned," leaving behind an unquestioned and unconscious formalism in which the *Morte* is read as a novel or a proto-novel, the default mode for any discussion of long prose narrative, despite our own overt insistence that it is not one.[3] I want to ask some questions about this, and more, I want to ask whether there is a way to think about what the *Morte* not being a novel says not only about Malory – but about the novel, and perhaps about what the *Morte* looks like not from within Malorian studies but from the vantage point of novel studies. Haunting any discussion of form is the lingering question of whether Malory is, in fact, any good as an artist at all: as Whetter puts it, Malorian studies has long "maligned or been put off by Malory's apparently fragmentary, artless and shoddy form, a form exacerbated by the *Morte Darthur*'s supposed lack of unity."[4] In part, the argument for the unity of the text is also an argument against Malory's perceived artlessness. Wuest argues that Caxton's printed version "reassures readers that this book is a whole, and its interpretive dilemmas – although numerous – ultimately can be resolved coherently, even while withholding solutions to those dilemmas."[5] I make no claim that Malory consciously wrote a novel (for that matter, neither did Caxton), only that what he wrote has been widely taken as a significant part of the history of the novel because it was the best known and most widely read of the long form prose romances which in turn influenced Henry Fielding et al. A further question for this chapter, then, is to what extent it matters if we read the *Morte* as though it were a novel; what are the interpretive stakes?

Form is a notoriously difficult term to define. It morphs into genre very easily, but the distinction is worth making. As Cuddon suggests in the classic *Literary Terms and Literary Theory* dictionary, "When we speak of the form of a literary work we refer to its shape and structure and to the manner in which it is made (thus, its style, q.v.) – as opposed to its substance or what it is about."[6] The form of a sonnet is fourteen lines, in iambic pentameter, regardless of whether it is Shakespeare talking about the Dark Lady or Milton lamenting the massacre at Piedmont (generically, a love sonnet and a political sonnet respectively); the sonnet's formal qualities are how it is built and appears on the page. At root, form can be considered as a term that denotes how a text participates in time and space: how long a text takes to describe things, for example, or how a poem looks on the page. Since story and narrative are separate but connected – story is what happens, narrative how that happening is communicated to the reader

[3]  Stephen Atkinson, "Meaning 'spryngyth, burgenyth, buddyth, and florysshyth': Reading Malory's May Passages," *Arthuriana* 25.3 (2015): 22–32, at 23. See also Thomas H. Crofts and K. S. Whetter, "Writing the *Morte Darthur*: Author, Manuscript and Modern Editions," in this volume.

[4]  K. S. Whetter, *Understanding Genre and Medieval Romance* (Aldershot and Burlington, 2008), 101.

[5]  Charles Wuest, "Closure and Caxton's Malory," *Arthuriana* 27.4 (2017): 60–78, at 63.

[6]  J. A. Cuddon, *Dictionary of Literary Terms and Literary Theory*, 4th edn, rev. C. E. Preston (Harmondsworth, 1998), 327.

– "form" becomes the mechanism by which an author dictates how that story is read. Formal qualities govern the space given to description or dialogue, and the time it takes to read a text by providing more or less detail, and how something like a sonnet's volta – the turn at line 8 – already pre-interprets the text. A further distinction often made is that between organic form and mechanic form, the first being a form that arises from the work itself while the second is a form imposed upon the material prior to the act of composition (a sonnet is the latter). So for this chapter, I am less interested in the generic features of the *Morte* (knights on quests, enigmatic prophecies, etc.) than I am in the structural organization of the text, here primarily the Winchester manuscript (although inflected by Caxton's and subsequent printed editions).

Nevertheless, talking about form does often require talking about content, for they are usually in a tight relationship and can be difficult to disentangle. To take the example of Caxton's edition of Malory's text, his form – atomizing the *Morte* into bite-sized chunks – encourages a certain kind of reading. An historian of the novel, Patrick Parrinder, believes that the *Morte* may be a novel, but not because of Malory: "But Malory's claim owes everything to William Caxton, the Westminster printer and courtier … who divided the romances into twenty-one books and no less than 507 chapters."[7] William Kuskin speaks to Caxton's particular historical moment, a transition – longer than we usually think – between the production of singular manuscripts and the birth of print technology:

> [W]e are met by a paradox: though the printed book appears as an object of unity, it derives from a manuscript tradition premised on knitting together fragmentary parts, and its overall mode of production is a pastiche of techniques. This is the magic of the book: it reduces contradictions in its production process to coherency without resolving them and effectively extends this constellation of ideas to its readers through commercial sale.[8]

While Kuskin is speaking here of Caxton's *Canterbury Tales*, the process likely held for Malory too (and arguably does with Field's new edition); this reminds us that the difference between Malory and Caxton was initially one of medium and not of form. Charles Wuest argues that Caxton's elimination of most of Malory's own explicits "is a form of editing which has become authoring," intended to produce a "book stable and thus appropriate for the Worthies series"; as Wuest notes, Vinaver called the elimination of all but the last explicit a "subterfuge."[9] Further, as Thomas Hanks has argued, Caxton's chapter headings always emphasize Arthur, as he also does in his paratext, leading centuries of readers to see this text as primarily about Arthur, who is therefore the chief protagonist. But the Winchester manuscript has no such emphasis: "Arguably, without Caxton's opening and closing insistence upon the centrality of Arthur, readers might well

---

7   Patrick Parrinder, *Nation and Novel: The English Novel from Its Origins to the Present Day* (Oxford, 2008), 36. See also Crofts and Whetter, "Writing the *Morte Darthur*," in this volume.

8   William Kuskin, *Symbolic Caxton: Literary Culture and Print Capitalism* (Notre Dame, IN, 2008), 127.

9   Wuest, "Closure and Caxton's Malory," 62.

see the ensuing story as focussed chiefly on the rise and fall of the Round Table, with accounts of Arthur, to be sure, but also with accounts" of other knights and adventures (like that of the Grail) in which Arthur hardly features.[10] We call Malory's text the *Morte Darthur* largely because that is what Caxton built it to be. Vinaver's decision to call his edition of Malory *Works*, then, is not just signalling multiple texts, but a significant change in focus. In Foucauldian terms, the "author" of the *Morte Darthur* is in some sense not Malory alone, but Malory/ Caxton – or even Malory/Caxton/Vinaver/Field.[11] The *Morte*'s form seems fluid even before we turn to its relationship with the novel, which has a complicated history of its own.

Michael Schmidt's recent high-profile *The Novel: A Biography* goes back past Malory to Mandeville's *Travels;*[12] Cuddon puts the form's origins in the Egyptian Twelfth Middle Dynasty (c. 1200 BCE).[13] Almost all histories of the novel touch on the Japanese *Tale of Genji,* for its complicated view of human psychology; *Genji* is dated to around 1000 CE. Thomas Hägg's discussion of the late antique Greek novels, while not extensive, is suggestive. Hägg reminds us of several pertinent elements: long form prose literature exists in both Greek and Latin; there is no term for them, possibly because they arise after Aristotle and so remain outside the schemes built on the *Poetics*; they were likely not considered high culture, and thus attracted little discussion despite their clear popularity. Ironically, while scholars have sometimes been reluctant to call these texts novels, they were content to apply a different, equally anachronistic term: romance.[14] This itself has a long history in the seventeenth century, in which prose fiction was increasingly gathered under an umbrella term, the repurposed word romance, first in France and then the rest of western Europe (including England).[15] As Christine S. Lee suggests, "romance" – a word hardly used in the period immediately following Malory, except as a term for an old-fashioned kind of story – was mobilised to fill the very gap that "novel" would one day fill: there was no other "generic term that might invoke the whole list in a single word," a list comprised of a rapidly-expanding interest in fiction as fiction.[16] So there is at least a possibility that we are being precious in our insistence that the *Morte* is not a novel because the novel does not yet exist, when it appears to be a form that can be invented and reinvented over and over in a multitude of cultures. Leaving versification to the side appears to be an almost universal possible narrative strategy across cultures, and that strategy seems to either be prompted by or to allow for the

---

[10] D. Thomas Hanks Jr, "Textual Harassment: Caxton, de Worde, and Malory's *Morte Darthur*," in *Re-Viewing* Le Morte Darthur, ed. K. S. Whetter and Raluca Radulescu (Cambridge, 2005), 27–48, at 30–32.

[11] See "Introduction," in this volume, for more on Foucault's author-function.

[12] Michael Schmidt, *The Novel: A Biography* (Cambridge, MA, 2014).

[13] Cuddon, "novel", in *Dictionary*, 560–600, at 562.

[14] Thomas Hägg, *The Novel in Antiquity* (Berkeley, 1983), 1–4.

[15] Christine S. Lee, "The Meanings of Romance: Rethinking Early Modern Fiction," *Modern Philology* 112.2 (2014): 287–311.

[16] Lee, "Meanings of Romance," 287–98. As Lee rightly suggests, "while the sixteenth century abounded in fiction, its theorists expressed discomfort with the naming of new and mixed literary kinds. If Aristotle didn't mention the genre, it faced a hard fight for legitimacy" (298). From a certain point of view, it was easier to repurpose an old term than to invent a new one.

play of character interiority and psychology. Putter argues that Malory's decision to write in prose would have looked strange to his contemporary readers,[17] but given the number of prose adaptations at the time this seems less stark than we might suppose. Here we might be surprised, because Schmidt, not a medievalist, believes Malory qualifies as a novelist: "The principal characters in *Le Morte d'Arthur* are consistent in speech and plausible in motive. They manifest, as well as character, something like a cast of mind if not a psychology: a sense of motive, in romances of deep love, in tragedies of real perturbation."[18] Something forces Malorians to absolve Malory of even accidental novelness, when students of the novel sometimes count him as at least a progenitor and sometimes more.

If we leave aside the aesthetic and thematic aspects of the novel, and focus on the technology of the novel – and its influence on culture – we do see something which Malory might have bequeathed to that future form. Michael McKeon, in his influential 2002 book *Origins of the English Novel 1600–1740*, addresses the rise of this new technology, printing:

> [M]edieval romance paradoxically is at the height of its dominance and influence in the early modern period; and this is so because it is only then that it can be spoken of "as such" … So print helps transform romance into a self-conscious canon. But it also helps "periodize" romance as a "medieval" production, as that which the present age – the framing counterpart of the classical past – defines itself against. Medieval romance, in which the antecedents of our "history" and "romance" coexist in fluid suspension, becomes "medieval romance," the product of an earlier period and increasingly the locus of strictly "romance" elements that have been separated out from the documentary objectivity of "history" and of print, the technology to which it therefore owes (at least in part) both its birth and its instantaneous obsolescence.[19]

So far, this is not a new strategy, although McKeon shows a healthy awareness that the line between old and new is to some degree artificial. But combined with other factors at work in the fifteenth century, McKeon's perspective looks very similar to the argument that the fifteenth century is "dull," and that it is so in part because printing causes a creative shift to curation rather than creation. This is what Kuskin is talking about in *Symbolic Caxton* when he says that "The English canon is an abstraction that takes place in the concrete," and that "various practices associated with vernacular canon formation – capital, printing, and authority – develop in the premodern past, [and that] modernity does not offer a clean break from this past but is in fact tied to it in material, intellectual, and symbolic ways."[20] The novel, in the English literary tradition, is wrapped up in the modernity of which the printing press is both the prompt and the enabler.

---

[17] Ad Putter, "Late Romance: Malory's Tale of Balin", in *Readings in Medieval Texts: Interpreting Old and Middle English Literature*, ed. David Johnson and Elaine Treharne (Oxford, 2005), 338. See also Megan G. Leitch, "Malory in Literary Context," in this volume.

[18] Schmidt, *Novel*, 26.

[19] Michael McKeon, *Origins of the English Novel, 1600–1740* (Baltimore, 2002), 45.

[20] Kuskin, *Symbolic Caxton*, 117, 13.

The argument that the *Morte* is not a novel relies on at least one deeply problematic assertion: that the generically unstable or hybrid *Morte* is not formally a novel, because we know what a novel is. But from within novel studies, the novel looks every bit as unstable as the romance, and has looked that way for some time:

> Indeed critics seem to take the novel form for granted. At least such are the implications when they assert that a certain book is a novel and that another is not and should be classed in a different category. Such an assessment is only acceptable if it is based on a general principle which takes simultaneously into account the infinite peculiarities of works of this kind, that is to say the freedom they enjoy and the definite requirements dictated by their common form.[21]

In terms of the *Morte*, we Malory scholars declared our unstable object to be unlike another unstable object, and assumed that novel studies did not move or change at all from the publication of Watt's *Rise of the Novel* in 1957. Our definition of "novel" is perversely old. Another problem is that the novel is both genre and form, and when we say Malory's book is not a novel we are talking primarily about genre. With form, the *Morte* is absolutely within the definition of Cuddon's *Dictionary of Literary Terms and Literary Theory*: "As to the quiddity of the novel there has been much debate. However, without performing contortions to be comprehensive we may hazard that it is a form of story or prose narrative containing characters, action and incident, and, perhaps, a plot."[22] Watt had actually been perfectly willing to perform contortions, which is probably obliquely but consciously Cuddon's point; Watt's starting position for the definition of the novel is that it should be "sufficiently narrow to exclude previous types of narrative and yet broad enough to apply to whatever is usually put in the novel category."[23] This will look familiar enough to anyone who has ever engaged in the discussion of what "romance" is.[24] In a way, what we have is a comparison in which the only stable element is that romance is "before" and novel is "after" the originary moment of Defoe, Richardson and Fielding. The *Morte* not being a novel starts to look primarily chronological and not substantive, a trick of literary history.

Malory, then, perhaps requires students of the novel to consider whether their form should be so all-encompassing. Marthe Roberts argues: "For we might ask ... what *The Trial* has in common with *Gone with the Wind*, *Lolita* with *Anna Karenina*, *No Orchids for Miss Blandish* with *Du Côté de chez Swann* or Robbe-Grillet's *La Jalousie*, while stressing the fact that such comparisons, drawn at random from

---

[21] Marthe Robert, *Origins of the Novel*, trans. Sacha Rabinovitch (Bloomington, IN, 1980), 6.

[22] Cuddon, "novel" in *Dictionary*, 561. Cuddon describes the novel as "the hold-all and Gladstone bag of literature."

[23] Ian Watt, *The Rise of the Novel* (Berkeley, 1959), 9–10.

[24] For discussion of this thorny issue, see Helen Cooper, *The English Romance in Time* (Oxford, 2004); Raluca Radulescu and Cory James Rushton, eds., *A Companion to Medieval Popular Romance* (Cambridge, 2009); Ad Putter and Jane Gilbert, eds., *The Spirit of Medieval English Popular Romance* (Harlow, 2000); Melissa Furrow, *Expectations of Romance: The Reception of a Genre in Medieval England* (Cambridge, 2009).

the latest catalogue of our vast universal library, are not by a long stretch among the most ludicrous."[25] Roberts's "ludicrous" would have to contain the distance between *War and Peace* and Bulgakov's *The Master and Margarita*, the first a realistic Russian epic-novel set against Napoleon's invasion, and the latter a Russian novel which includes a magician, witches, the Devil, Pontius Pilate, and a cat named Behemoth who indulges a penchant for firearms. In other words, literary criticism could decide to align the novel as genre (realistic, psychologically correct) with the form, or better still to decide that formally the novel would be better termed "long-form prose" so that a given work's genre – fantasy, magic realism, whatever – would take interpretive precedence. The *Morte*, if Whetter's definition is adopted, is a long-form tragic-romance. In other words, using the case of the *Morte* allows literary historians to provide more secure boundaries at the start of the novel proper's career.[26]

The novel is, at the very least, now seen as ravenously capacious both in content and in its domination of literary criticism. As Robert states, despite the novel's "upstart" nature, "its victories were mainly due to its encroachments on the neighbouring territories it surreptitiously infiltrated, gradually colonizing almost all of literature."[27] For her, the historical power of the novel (for novelists) "resides precisely in its total freedom," a freedom held to be "highly suspect" by critics who desire stronger formal and generic borders.[28] When Bakhtin says all genres are novelised, he partially means this in the sense we all have when we mark undergraduate papers: students call texts as diverse as *Othello* and Maurice Sendak's *Where the Wild Things Are* "novels." They are technically wrong, but at the same time they testify that Bakhtin was prophetic: the novel simply means "text" on some popular and widespread level, and all texts are read as though they are novels unless a conscious effort is made to do otherwise. But Bakhtin primarily means that all literary forms either adopt dialogic principles or accept relegation to an antique canonicity.[29] When Bakhtin talks about the novel's "spirit of process and inconclusiveness," he means that while the novel is a new thing it anticipates literature's turn towards ambiguity and to freedom for existing genres: "novelization implies their liberation from all that serves as a brake on their unique development, from all that would change them along with the novel into some sort of stylization of forms that have outlived themselves."[30] Freed of most explicit formal features by prosification, genre pursues its own internal logic. Whether Malory wrote one book or several, his persistence in both unravelling the formal interlace of the French prose romances and eliminating metre from other sources allows a complexity of narrative rather than form.

Literary criticism still wants to make a distinction between romance, which on one level Malory's work clearly is, and the novel. As Lee says, "Loose and ill-defined as it is, 'romance' still seems the best fit for all those curious older form

---

[25] Roberts, *Origins of the Novel*, 6–7.
[26] Whetter, *Understanding Genre*, 109–10.
[27] Robert, *Origins of the Novel*, 4.
[28] Robert, *Origins of the Novel*, 7.
[29] M. M. Bakhtin, *The Dialogic Imagination*, ed. Michael Holquist, trans. Caryl Emerson and Michael Holquist (Austin, 1981), 7.
[30] Bakhtin, *Dialogic*, 7, 39.

of fictions we cannot quite call 'novels,' distant as they are from the conventions of modern romance."[31] P. J. C. Field, in his chapter on the *Morte* in the seminal *Arthur of the English*, also argues that Malory's work is not a novel (a belief he shares with Vinaver). The reasoning is worth quoting in full:

> Where the novel gives us the world of the probable, the world reported by physical science and individual psychological experience, romance gives us worlds of the possible, sometimes worlds only capable of existing in the imagination. They may be escapist, or nightmarish, or quite different from either of those things. The exact kind of possibility on offer has to be identified from the work in each case.[32]

Field thus agrees with Lee that the novel must contain something like realism, here "the world reported by physical science," but that eliminates many works we comfortably see as novels: *Dracula* is not real, nor are Orcs. Lee's approach is a sophisticated and helpful one, in that she lays out just how the word/generic category "romance" became, and remains, a catch-all for works which experimented with prose form. If Leitch is correct, elsewhere in this volume, that the fifteenth-century prose romances change their "treatment" of earlier romance materials, this has consequences for the history of the novel which have not been explored: "Romances written in English prose offered a significant reworking of the narrative arc of the genre, and were thematically attuned to the climate of social instability in which they were produced and received."[33] Malory writes at a time when romance is fluid and changing, which opens up the possibility that it has already changed into something else.

For David Perkins, the rise of the novel is itself narrative, in that the "possible plots of narrative literary history can be reduced to three: rise, decline, and rise and decline. The reason for this is that the hero of a narrative literary history is a logical subject – a genre, a style, the reputation of an author – and the plots are limited to what actions or transitions can be predicated of such heroes."[34] In order to tell the story of the novel, it must be seen to rise, usually against an immediate literary past which is seen as declining. The hero – in this case, the novel – must have enemies against which its triumph can be measured.[35] For John Richetti, earlier prose texts – going back to the ancient Greek "novel" – were not modern novels because they dealt with "intrinsically significant or heroic events" while the modern novel focuses on the mundane; *Don Quixote*,

---

[31] Lee, "Meanings of Romance," 287. As Karen Sullivan has recently put it in a thorough discussion of the relationship between the novel and its precursors: "Whether romance was considered to be a genre similar to the novel, a genre different from the novel, or a mode within the genre of the novel, it remained a cumulative tradition where new contributions were periodically added to the existing corpus and where the entire category was periodically reconceptualized to encompass its expanded membership." Karen Sullivan, *The Danger of Romance: Truth, Fantasy, and Arthurian Fictions* (Chicago and London, 2018), 33.

[32] P. J. C. Field, "Sir Thomas Malory's *Le Morte Darthur*," in *The Arthur of the English: The Arthurian Legend in Medieval English Life and Literature*, ed. W. R. J. Barron, rev. edn (Cardiff, 2001), 225–46, at 244–45.

[33] See Leitch, "Malory in Literary Context," in this volume.

[34] David Perkins, *Is Literary History Possible?* (Baltimore, 1992), 39.

[35] Perkins, *Literary History*, 32–9.

as a parody of the romance, is one important moment of transition between the two.[36] Parody, at least partially hostile to what it mocks, opens a gap between plot (a knight still rides around the countryside looking for trouble) and tone (he is undermined by the mundanity of his world). There are multiple possible enemies: the romance, of course, but also the sermon and the long-form philosophical or narrative poem. The threat posed to standard literary history by Malory and the other prose romances is safely defused by class, or by their association with an aristocratic genre.

Fielding, as one of the early novel trinity, is himself a complicating factor. Watt stated, in a follow-up article to his classic study, that the book originally had a much more complicated account of Fielding as problematic, which was edited out for length.[37] The long reception of *Rise of the Novel* indeed suggests that *Tom Jones* did not really do what Defoe and Richardson's books did, and Fielding himself (in *Tom Jones*) said that he would have "been well enough contented" to call the book a romance if it were not for the bad name romance had been given by the so-called salon-romances popular in France at the time. These romances were psychologically intense portraits of unattainable women and their hopeless lovers, and Richardson's *Clarissa* is in some sense an attempt to write such a book in English. Fielding thought he was doing something else. Where Richardson turns to the epistolary form to get at a different type of psychological characterization, Fielding consciously borrows the romance structure of texts like *Amadis of Gaul*.[38] The primary difference was not form but subject matter, an emphasis on the low rather than the high (although Jones, it turns out, is very much in the Fair Unknown tradition by the text's end – he is revealed to be of greater social rank than he thought).

One consequence of the perceived "novelness" of the *Morte* is the need to see it as a unified text, with this unity rooted in consistent characterization and a clear order of events. Knight, who calls the *Morte* Malory's "Arthuriad" (perhaps pointing to its epic qualities), operates from the position that "anyone who has insisted that there is a single and uniform structural pattern – whether he sees one or eight units – has been forced into difficulties somewhere or other."[39] The so-called Lumiansky School was dedicated to working through these difficulties, in an ongoing effort to hammer apparent inconsistencies into textual consistency within a unified text. In other words, they focussed on formal negatives that could not be erased, but could even be turned into positives: consistent inconsistency, or the appearance of character interiority rooted in the need to read for a complexity that looked like unpredictability. The areas they chose were largely characterological (especially the apparently inconsistent Gawain inherited from

---

[36] John Richetti, "The Novel before the 'Novel'," in *The Cambridge History of the English Novel*, ed. Robert L. Caserio and Clement Hawes (Cambridge, 2012), 17–21. This idea is what Helen Cooper has in mind when she suggests that *Paris and Vienne* is a step on the way to the novel despite being "still chivalric" (Cooper, "Prose Romances," 226–7).

[37] Ian Watt, "Serious Reflections on *The Rise of the Novel*", NOVEL: A Forum on Fiction 1.3 (1968): 205–18.

[38] Henry Knight Miller, *Henry Fielding's* Tom Jones *and the Romance Tradition* (Victoria, 1976), 11–21.

[39] Knight, *Structure*, 34.

divergent sources) or chronological (Tristram refusing to go on the Roman campaign before his own birth, the death of Bagdemagus, the knighting of Perceval).

Perhaps the most explicit example of this kind of character work is Barbara
Gray Bartholomew's argument concerning Gawain: "In my opinion, Malory creates Gawain as an inconsistent character in order that the knight may (1) serve as
a focal figure, representing a typified image of the Round Table knights and thus
(2) provide basis for Malory's judgment upon the failure of the ideal, specifically
as it is brought to life in the society of the Round Table."[40] Malory is no longer
inconsistent, but deliberately creating textual instability in order to facilitate a
certain vision of the unstable Round Table. Lumiansky's argument concerning
the minor character of Bors, the Grail knight who aids and abets the late stages
of Lancelot's affair with the queen, is both clever and instructive: Bors engages
in virtuous behaviour in pursuit of the Grail, making difficult ethical decisions,
but abandons this behaviour following his return. Lumiansky reads this as Bors
being worse after the Grail Quest, not as an inconsistency but as a consequence
– the return to the world leaves Bors in a state of ethical anti-climax.[41] Lancelot's
total character arc shifts under the influence of Tristram and the increasing prev-
alence of factions in the Round Table, helping to reveal things Malory prefers to
keep oblique – like the beginning of the affair itself.[42] Reading Tristram (and to
a lesser extent Dinadan) as an ongoing commentary on knight-errantry, or even
as creating the conditions for the "tristramization" of Lancelot, requires us to
believe that Malory's *Morte* has an overall architecture of thematic meaning. In
other words, Lancelot getting worse as he interacts with Tristram is part of the
total, planned structure of a single work, in which we as readers are expected to
draw disparate elements together from across the text.

The difficulties of Malory's chronology are numerous. Even Vinaver's argument that the sections of the *Morte* are separate tales does not entirely solve
them. These inconsistencies are many: Bagdemagus dies on the Grail Quest, but
reappears as one of Lancelot's company after the break with Arthur; Perceval
appears as a knight with a well-established reputation in the *Gareth* (Vinaver's
Tale IV), but is only knighted just before Morgause dies (Tale V); Carados is
reported dead in the Book of Lancelot (Tale III), but is killed in *Tristram*. Charles
Moorman produced one of the most extensive revisions to the chronology as
found on the page, arguing that the *Tristram* was co-terminous with Tales II and
III, while arguing both that *Gareth* takes place before both the Roman War and
the book of *Lancelot*.[43] Ellyn Olefsky provides the rejoinder a few years later:
"Moorman's time-scheme is not only an elaborate one, but also one incorporating the bulk of the findings scholars have accumulated on the problem over

---

[40] Barbara Gray Bartholomew, "The Thematic Function of Malory's Gawain," *College English* 24.4 (1963): 262–7, at 262.

[41] R. M. Lumiansky, "Malory's Steadfast Bors," *Tulane Studies in English* 8 (1958): 5–20.

[42] Danielle Morgan MacBain, "The Tristramization of Malory's Lancelot," *English Studies* 1 (1993): 57–65. See also D. Thomas Hanks, Jr., "Foil and Forecast: Dinadan in *The Book of Sir Tristram*," *Arthurian Yearbook* 1 (1991): 149–63.

[43] Charles Moorman, *The Book of Kyng Arthur: The Unity of Malory's* Morte Darthur (Lexington, KY, 1965), 96.

the years. There is only one trouble with it: it will not work."[44] Lancelot cannot have a series of adventures before the Roman War and be considered the best in the world in *Gareth*, whereas he is an untried knight during the Roman War, to take one example.[45] Bagdemagus cannot be solved at all; Percival cannot be "both a new knight at the time of Morgawse's death and a proven one during her lifetime."[46] In some sense, Olefsky's noting that the Tristram's own internal time-scheme may be inconsistent really points to the impossibility of mapping the events of Book V onto the others in any neat and tidy way. Olefsky concludes that "Malory's work is careless and inconsistent" (or that "chronology could not have been one of his major concerns") and that the "cases for and against unity, based on the assumption that inconsistencies must be between books to disunify, or that time schemes must be carried out in minute detail to lend coherence, have been overstated – perhaps grossly so."[47] I would nuance this to suggest that Malory is careless perhaps in that he does not really care: he knows that there is a traditionally accepted chronology of Arthur's reign, and also knows that there is a core group of best-known Arthurian knights (Lancelot, Tristram, Percival, Gawain). Malory seems comfortable with a core group of superlative knights who can be name-checked at any point within that chronology, regardless of when they first appear. He grants himself the absolute freedom Robert says is the core quality of the novel, without knowing it.

The relationship between Malory and his sources also affects what we see as his form. Long seen as uncreative and even slavish when it came to his sources, Malory's departures from them were often taken as signs of ineptitude: as Field argues, Malory "often seems to have trouble" when he moves beyond his sources.[48] In his 1971 study of Malory's prose style, Field warns the reader that he has "been compelled to speak as if the literary characteristics of the *Morte Darthur* were the result of conscious art": "It is no part of my contention that he was a conscious artist: rather the reverse."[49] Vinaver is convinced of Malory's occasional formal and aesthetic failures, except when he is condensing characters and eliminating plots: "Perhaps the fundamental reason why, in spite of all his good intentions, he failed in narrative technique is that his mind was reflective rather than creative."[50] The case against Malory's creativity was easier to make if you do not believe he wrote any of the *Gareth* on his own, but also that having borrowed it, he should have not told it. Citing Edmund Chambers's belief that Malory "would have done better to have left the *Tristan* alone," Vinaver suggests that Malory "would have done better still without the *Gareth*." Indeed, the *Tristram* is precisely where Vinaver says Malory realises he is wasting his time on plots which Vinaver does not consider central to the *Morte*.[51] Atkinson isolates the tension: "… in such cases as Lumiansky's, it is necessary to avoid material

[44] Ellyn Olefsky, "Chronology, Factual Consistency, and the Problem of Unity in Malory," *Journal of English and Germanic Philology* 68 (1969): 57–73, at 60.
[45] Olefsky, "Chronology," 61.
[46] Olefsky, "Chronology," 62.
[47] Olefsky, "Chronology," 67.
[48] P. J. C. Field, *The Life and Times of Sir Thomas Malory* (Cambridge, 1993), 172.
[49] P. J. C. Field, *Romance and Chronicle: A Study of Malory's Prose Style* (London, 1971), 7.
[50] Eugène Vinaver, *Malory* (Oxford, 1970), 42.
[51] Vinaver, *Malory*, 94.

which complicates a simplistic reading; while in Field's, it is easier to blame the author's limitations than the reader's inflexibility."[52] Vinaver's first book on Malory (published in 1929) predates the discovery of the Winchester manuscript, and when it was re-issued in 1970, Vinaver limited himself to a preface, in which he briefly laid out the differences between what he had come to believe and what he wrote in the 1920s. He considered at least some of the artistic problems of the *Morte* to have been solved by abandoning the idea that the text is "one artistic whole, a single unified epic."[53]

For the Lumiansky School, study of the sources was also crucial: *Malory's Originality* is organised around a structure in which each chapter corresponds to one of Vinaver's proposed books, and "includes a statement of the probable source relationship of the 'Tale' under consideration." The changes Malory makes to the sources are now just that: "what Malory borrowed verbatim from the source, what he altered, what he omitted, and what he added." To Lumiansky and his allies, Malory was a conscious (indeed original) artist.[54] Nowhere is this more telling than with the *Gareth*. Faced with a story with no direct known source and which thus challenged the volume's approach, Wilfred L. Guerin broke with what was and to an extent remains the critical consensus that Malory could not have invented the Tale, instead arguing that its central place in the *Morte* (speaking to the happiness of the Round Table at its height) implied that Malory had to have created it after reading several analogues.[55] As seen above, the Lumiansky School's approach left at least a few inconsistencies across the text. Lumiansky argued that all such inconsistencies could be explained by "Malory's probable purposes," and those that could not be reconciled "simply show a need for minor revision, a benefit which was not accorded the book."[56] It is clear that Lumiansky essentially won, in that this close attention to detail across the text, necessary to establish the *Morte* as a unified whole, was closely influenced by the study of the novel and led in turn to novelistic approaches to the text.

Malory has nonetheless long been considered capable of producing effect, usually through dialogue or laconic narratorial comment. Ad Putter argues that "Malory's weaknesses are far from debilitating: indeed, they can paradoxically become sources of strength."[57] Vinaver's theory that the *Morte* gets better as it goes along is quietly central to Knight's view of the *Morte* as evolving from one thing to another: "Much interrupted and unfinished as it is, there is an indication that Malory is here approaching a narrative which is generically different from the episodic style, though the episodic force is so strong in the Tristram that no new structural form can emerge to challenge it."[58] What if we took two moments, not from the best sections but the worst; and not a bad moment and a good moment, but two good moments, to see if there is some change across the

---

[52] Atkinson, "Reading Malory's May Passages," 26.

[53] Vinaver, *Malory*, x.

[54] R. M. Lumiansky, "Introduction", in *Malory's Originality*, 4–6.

[55] Wilfred L. Guerin, "'The Tale of Gareth': The Chivalric Flowering," in Lumiansky, 99–117. For the alternative approach, see Ralph Norris, "Malory and His Sources," in this volume.

[56] Lumiansky, "Introduction," 7.

[57] Putter, "Late Romance," 342.

[58] Knight, *Structure*, 59

book? The moments involve Balin and Palamedes. This in a book traditionally considered clumsy, where Lamorak's all-important death takes place off-stage, and where Malory tells two stories of sons avenging their fathers, one of which we do not see and one of which does not happen. Some of this may be deliberate ambiguity. Some of this may point to the novel.

Bonnie Wheeler argues that "Romance is the genre of parataxis, a form of discourse that subverts the logic of hypotactic, synthetic causality as it amplifies and dilates causalities. The hallmark of romance is its ordering of its basic structural element – the episode – according to paratactic principles."[59] As Wheeler perhaps unwittingly implies, parataxis is a formal quality attached to the genre of romance, parataxis defined as inherently episodic and therefore best interpreted locally, but where a text's overall meaning is produced by contiguity rather than strict continuity. Putter sees Malory's paratactic style as "for the most part well suited to his matter, but his limitations are exposed in passages that demand a more complex calibration of events or propositions," notably around sequence and conjunctions, "his lack of discrimination between analytic connectives (e.g. *for, therefore*) and enumerative ones (e.g. *and*)."[60] Putter's example is the initial description of Balin:

> And the name of thys knyght was called Balyne, and by good meanys of the barownes he was delyverde oute of preson, for he was a good man named of his body, and he was borne in Northehumbirlonde. And so he wente pryvaly into the courte... (48.33–49.1 / C II.2)

Putter points to the ways in which connectives which are meant to suggest causality fail to do so: Balin's release from prison is because some barons support him, but his birth in Northumberland has nothing to do with the reprieve. Malory's style, both concerning events and observations, "gives us one thing after another."[61] In other words, everything in the text piles up, producing effects which can then be interpreted, rather than everything in the text being designed as a whole which is unified from the start. The whole text behaves in the same way the individual sentence does.

Take Balin's pronouncement that the horn he hears blows for him (70.30–1 / C II.16), and then Palamedes' sad, quiet acceptance that his last battle with Tristram is over, as he glances at his dropped sword and chooses not to accept Tristram's offer to let him pick it back up. Both are powerful moments, but one allows the reader to interpret what Palamedes is thinking, and why; as Dorsey Armstrong argues in this volume, "no other knight expresses his grief with such deep interiority and sadness."[62] Recent and sustained work on Balin and Palamedes allows

---

[59] Bonnie Wheeler, "Romance and Parataxis and Malory: The Case of Sir Gawain's Reputation," *Arthurian Literature* XII (1993): 109–32, at 110. The difference between parataxis and hypotaxis is a difference between implicit and explicit: parataxis places the clauses of a sentence into contact with each other, but without explaining the connection (forcing implicit readings), while hypotaxis explicitly joins clauses in a causal way. Field discusses both the context for and Malory's particular use of parataxis in *Romance and Chronicle*, 31–5, 38–46.

[60] Putter, "Late Romance," 340–1.

[61] Putter, "Late Romance," 340.

[62] See Dorsey Armstrong, "Malory and Character," in this volume.

us to perhaps better see Malory's early and later methods, although in a manner that Atkinson warns against. Balin contains a gap within himself that points to but is not interiority, in that he sets out to achieve things but consistently fails; this is less important than that he does those things as, at least temporarily, a central character (he is not Calogrenant to Yvain, in other words). His part in the *Morte* is small, and after his death he is not mentioned again until Lamorak wants someone to blame for Lot's death, and again when his sword finds its way to Galahad. Palamedes, on the other hand, is a crucial character in a very long section, and mentioned frequently after that section; this section, the *Tristram*, is one which Knight identifies as "Malory here approaching a narrative which is generically different from the episodic style, though the episodic force is so strong in the Tristram [sic] that no new structural form can emerge to challenge it."[63] More, Palamedes clearly has one moment – when he laments that he does not know why he acts the way he acts – which is similar to Balin's sense of a personal gap, but which is both vocalised and then picked up without being overtly expressed much later: "A, Palomydes, Palomydes! Why art thou thus defaded, and ever was wonte to be called one of the fayrest knyghtes of the worlde?" He gazes into a well and "sawe his owne vysayge, how he was discolowred and defaded, a-nothynge lyke as he was" (614.19–28 / C X.86). Later, offered the chance by Tristram, who invited him to pick up his sword and resume battle, Palomedes says he has no more desire to fight. He offers reasons, but they are already contained in the melancholy gaze directed towards his lost weapon: "And than Sir Palomydes stood stylle and behylde hys swerde wyth a sorowfull harte" (662.32–663.24 / C XII.14). This is a man who has looked in a mirroring surface and does not recognize himself; but we do, and we do so because the novel has trained us to look for, identify and extrapolate from the gaps in a text. Surely this is one of the passages we might think contain "sympathetic, inward characterization."

This Malorian style can produce good effect, as with the description of the damsel who tests Arthur's court with a sword that can only be drawn by the worthiest knight, in this case Balin again: "Than she lette hir mantell falle that was rychely furred, and than was she gurde with a noble swerde, whereof the kynge had mervayle..." (47.26–7 / C II.1). As Putter says, "Strict logicians would call this careless writing"; the two thans imply temporal sequence, an impossibility because she must already be wearing the sword when she comes into Arthur's presence. "By not resolving the relationship between the two propositions" – lady with fur coat and lady wearing sword – Malory suggests the "marvelousness" felt by Arthur through the syntax itself.[64] The reader is allowed to hold the two parts of the image at once, with a perhaps a tinge of the cinematic as the sword is revealed.

For Brewer, one of the problems was that our familiarity with the novel, its ubiquity as a form, makes it difficult to read texts in any other way: "Many of the differences between critics stem from the fundamental misunderstanding that derives from reading Malory as if he were writing within those criteria

---

[63] Knight, *Structure*, 59.
[64] Putter, "Late Romance," 342.

of literature that have developed since the seventeenth century." Brewer sees
Malory as a "traditional writer" in that he composes in the style "of what has
become common amongst anthropologists to call 'the savage mind' but which I
shall call the 'archaic mind'."[65] Colin Richmond, not a Malory scholar but rather
an expert in the political cultures of the English fifteenth century, might illustrate
the point. Having worked on texts like the *History of the Arrival in England of
Edward IV* (1469–71), a piece of propaganda designed to smooth over Edward's
usurpation of the throne, Richmond turns his attention briefly to the *Morte*, written around the same time and therefore subject to some of the same trends. For
Richmond, the increasingly brutal and chaotic events of the time led to a politics
where "government becomes an end in itself, while the governors are beyond
even their own reproach." The *Arrival* attempts to tell a story of a pragmatic
campaign for the throne, "made presentable by putting [it] into the fancy dress of
the day before yesterday."[66] Richmond connects this to Malory, having – by his
own admission – "read the *Morte Darthur* in something under four weeks."[67] But
this makes Richmond's perception interesting because it is not an expert one, in
that it is not steeped in decades of Malorian scholarship (rather, he sees Malory
as a part of larger intellectual and political world, rooted in his study of histo-
riography). He sees Malory's staying power as the result of his attempts to stay
culturally static or, in Brewer's term, "traditional": Malory is "a writer whose
landmark work set the terms for modern literature in English by holding fast to
those, as he understood them, of the Middle Ages." In doing so, Malory "engendered not a paradox or contradiction, but a tension so creative, a disjunction so
imaginative, that he continues to be read in the twenty-first century as an author
of continuing importance."[68] In other words, Malory transcends not only his era
but his conscious project itself.

Brewer also makes a distinction between "men of action" who have always
read Malory, and "literary critics [who] have despised him," and argues that
this distinction might mean "that nowadays the 'naïve' reader may come closer
to Malory than the sophisticated one."[69] He means in terms of modern literary sophistication, but if the naïve reader sees the *Morte* as a novel and not as a
member of a different category that must be invented, perhaps in this case too
they are "closer to Malory." Vinaver has preempted the discussion of chronology
by suggesting that Malory's allusions and cross-references had to be considered
as they appeared "not to compilers of concordances, not to Ph.D. candidates who
laboriously dig them out and exhibit them," but to casual readers picking up
the *Morte* "for pleasure."[70] Not that non-professional readers could not notice
discrepancies – Roger Ascham realised Lamorak was sleeping with his own aunt

---

[65] Derek Brewer, "Malory: The Traditional Writer and the Archaic Mind," *Arthurian
Literature* I (1981): 94–120, at 94–5.
[66] Colin Richmond, "Malory and Modernity: A Qualm about Paradigm Shifts," *Common
Knowledge* 14.1 (2008): 34–44, at 37. Paul Strohm's is the classic version of this argument
concerning the *Arrival*, in *Politique* (Notre Dame, IN, 2005).
[67] Richmond, "Modernity," 41.
[68] Richmond, "Modernity," 35–6.
[69] Brewer, "Traditional Writer," 95.
[70] Eugène Vinaver, "On Art and Nature," in *Essays on Malory*, ed. J. A. W. Bennett
(Oxford, 1963), 29–40, at 38.

in 1563, which the text itself does not seem to realize – but in most cases, these problems do not loom as large for casual reading. Olefsky agrees there is "a definite sense of the passage of time in Malory that may have a greater effect on the general reader than on the scholar who looks too closely at the work."[71] Malory's enduring popularity is as much the result of readers outside the academic world, who encounter him as a romance in a form that might as well be a novel.

The question of form then seems intractably central to Malory studies because we not only have two distinct witnesses (Winchester and Caxton), we also have an author who tells us nothing about his methods nor makes Chaucerian-style observations about art. Malory's reputation has always included a sense of artlessness, of story over style. Perhaps, then, we could remind ourselves that Malory does tell us something about his motivations for writing, even leaving aside the explicit suggestions of a weary politics in the famous "Englishmen" digression (916.34–917.6 / C XXI.1) or the location of Mordred's support in Kent and other southeastern regions (920.10–12 / C XXI.2). His overt motivation is that he wants his readers to pray and intervene for him. If we take his digressions seriously not as thematic – what business does a thief and a rapist have retelling the story of Lancelot? – but as formal, we might have something new to say about what the *Morte* is.

In Edward Said's classic study of textual beginnings, he argues for a more complicated theory of both beginnings and motivations. A beginning is a thing "designated in order to indicate, clarify, or define a later time, place, or action," containing an author's "intention," meaning "an appetite at the beginning intellectually to do something in a characteristic way – either consciously or unconsciously, but at any rate in a language that … is always engaged purposefully in the production of meaning."[72] This is what Said calls a "transitive" beginning in which "an individual mind wishes to intervene in a field of rational activity."[73] Most contemporary readings of Malory suggest something like this; that the *Morte* is a commentary on his own social and political context. But Said also argues for another kind of beginning, the intransitive: "a *radical* starting point … which has no object but its own constant clarification." The transitive is "projective and descriptive" while the intransitive is "tautological and endlessly self-mimetic."[74] Malory does not start with an invocation of divinity or an address to a listening audience; in his prison cell, he ignores the trope that he is reading to people. His project is always literary and never oral. Malory begins, in Said's terms, not when he calls attention to the time of Uther, but when he embarks on the process of writing through his various anxieties and when he subsequently borrows the books he wants to use as sources.

There is a famous moment in which Thomas Hoccleve writes out a reading list for the Lollard knight Sir John Oldcastle, a list which includes the book of Lancelot and the *Siege of Thebes*, reading that would be safer for a knight in Archbishop Arundel's England. Rather than seeing this as a simple dismissal

---

[71] Olefsky, "Chronology," 63.
[72] Edward Said, *Beginnings: Intention and Method* (New York, 1985), 5–6.
[73] Said, *Beginnings*, 50.
[74] Said, *Beginnings*, 72–3.

of Oldcastle's intellectually spiritual pretensions, a standard critical reading, Melissa Furrow has argued for romance as a thinking exercise, as in Hoccleve's diatribe against Oldcastle or Lydgate's advice to read the Thebes story as a kind of "*contemptus mundi* rather than the celebration of courtly life." Furrow tracks the reception of English romance from the fourteenth century, when serious clerics sought to wean readers away from chivalric stories towards spiritual materials, to the fifteenth, when Archbishop Arundel's *Constitutions* of 1409 essentially outlaws vernacular exploration of theological ideas. In these new conditions, the romance begins to itself be taken seriously as an object of contemplation appropriate to knights especially. Where Chaucer, according to Furrow, really did suffer anxiety about the effects an erotically-charged story like *Troilus and Criseyde* might have on a reader, Hoccleve – only a few years later – suggests a steady regimen of chivalric narrative as a corrective, "vehicles of moral improvement," to Oldcastle's dangerous engagement with spiritual matters which are too much for him. Lydgate's retelling of the Trojan War legend, intended for Henry V, is less a lauding of Trojan or Greek heroism, but rather an insistence that "þer is nouþer prince, lord, nor kyng … Þat in þis lif may have ful surete."[75] In this sense, Vinaver's contention that Malory was "reflective rather than creative" could be seen as a positive: Malory is writing his book in order to reflect on chivalry, English history, himself.

The idea that to keep one's mind from idle thoughts could be a kind of speaking cure for inadequately inhabited chivalry might be applied very well to a knight famously imprisoned. Could Malory have started writing as an exercise in a sort of "mindfulness," and (borrowing Knight's suggestion) did it actually start to work in the "Tristram"? He learned that he liked writing and he learned something about himself, expressed in the famous "all ye Englishmen" passage and, to a less celebrated extent, in the moment where Malory leaves his source to explain why even great knights can fall dangerously sick in captivity:

> So Sir Trystram endured there grete paynem for syknes had undirtake hym, and that ys the grettist payne a prisoner may have. For all the whyle a presonere may have hys helth of body, he may endure undir the mercy of God and in hope of good delyveraunce; but whan syknes towchith a presoners body, than may a presonere say all welth ys hym berauffte, and than hath he cause to wayle and wepe. Ryght so ded Sir Trystram whan syknes had undirtake hym, for than he toke such sorrow that he had allmoste slayne hymselff. (427.10-17 / C IX.37)

Field notes that Malory must have read ahead in his source to include the detail of Tristram's illness, implying that it was something important to him.[76] Malory also absorbed some of the era's pessimism: Lydgate sees Troy primarily as a reminder that nobody can expect perfect security, while Malory's Galahad and Arthur both note the instability of the mortal world as a key condition of

---

[75] Furrow, *Expectations of Romance*, 199. See also Strohm, *England's Empty Throne* (Notre Dame, IN, 2006), 183–85, where Hoccleve's suggested reading list is seen as a means to correct Oldcastle's feminised self.

[76] Sir Thomas Malory, *Le Morte Darthur*, ed. P. J. C. Field, 2 vols. (Cambridge, 2013), Apparatus, 356. Citations in parentheses are from this edition.

human existence (Galahad at 787.34–5 / C XVII.22, Arthur at 927.5 / C XXI.5). It has long been a staple of Malorian criticism that he sees his world reflected in the Arthurian past, and that he considers his own chivalry in light of Arthurian story. But this has rarely been extended beyond a version of authorial interest, whether rooted in enthusiasm or regret.

This would require us to take something we often unconsciously think of as paratext – his requests for prayer and other explicits – and take them seriously as core to the text at the level of form. This is not quite the same things as agreeing with Thomas Hanks that the six explicits which are requests for prayer are a means by which "Malory signals his own presence as an author, and moreover his presence as a Christian author engaging in a Christian act."[77] But elsewhere in the same volume, Fiona Tolhurst argues that these signs of Malory's beliefs may not be deeply felt, but rather can only be taken as evidence to demonstrate his participation and immersion in a culture that understands itself as Christian. Tolhurst notes that Malory asks for "good recover," a word that can mean salvation but can also commonly mean "release from prison and recovery or extrication from a difficult situation": "Such prayers could help the author move toward both political rebirth – through release from prison – and salvation."[78] The *Tristram* illness passage, now seen as perhaps the most personal of Malory's asides rooted in his own experience of imprisonment, can be attached to these requests in that it serves as a kind of evidence for why the prayers are needed: not just to effect his release, but to include the author in a wider community as a way of warding off social isolation. This might dovetail nicely with Catherine Batt's argument that Malory's *Morte* is a site for both the incorporation and interrogation of "English and French constructions of, and literary responses to, the Arthurian world."[79] Malory can be, or become, a conscious stylist while also interrogating himself through the material with which he wrestles; and Batt, too, suggests that Malory's prisoner-author narratorial voice lends itself as a "conflicted element" in the *Morte*'s instability.[80]

The final form of Malory's *Morte Darthur* is therefore an organic one, arising from the process of composing the text itself. To many readers, an argument that Malory begins writing as an exercise in chivalric or spiritual mindfulness will sound like resort to authorial intention. There is, as always, reason for caution there, even with an author who has often been read negatively for his failure to achieve his intentions. I am arguing that Malory intended something close to formless, in that he did begin with few artistic ambitions – what mattered to him was the matter of Britain and how it might be used to interrogate himself (or to take an older version of this argument, to while away those long prison days). The form of the *Morte* emerges as he continues writing, pushing him to

---

[77] D. Thomas Hanks, Jr., "'All maner of good love comyth of God': Malory, God's Grace, and Noble Love," in *Malory and Christianity: Essays on Sir Thomas Malory's* Morte Darthur, ed. D. Thomas Hanks, Jr., and Janet Jesmok (Kalamazoo, 2013), 9–28, at 10–11.

[78] Fiona Tolhurst, "Slouching towards Bethlehem," in *Malory and Christianity*, ed. Hanks and Jesmok, 127–56, at 130–1.

[79] Catherine Batt, *Malory's* Morte Darthur: *Remaking Arthurian Tradition* (New York, 2002), 29.

[80] Batt, *Malory's* Morte Darthur, 34.

consider thematic connections, causes and consequences, and character across the various stories he is folding into his own. The Malorian paradox is this: he did not set out to write a novel, but to all intents and purposes he ended up doing so nonetheless. Or, at least, given the complex terminological history of the terms "romance" and "novel," he wrote something that was both and neither. The novel, eventually, followed him down the path he laid out by chance.

# 7
## Malory and Character
DORSEY ARMSTRONG

The examples of how Malory produces a treatment of his characters unique in the Arthurian tradition are scattered thickly throughout the pages of the *Morte Darthur*. To understand how characterization works in Malory, however, requires that readers engage in retroactive consideration of the total composite accretion of characters' deeds. In order to do this with any degree of thoroughness, one must slowly examine moment after moment in a progression through the narrative, or focus intensely on just one character, and then another, and then another, with the end result that, all too often, the "forest" is obscured by the myriad "trees" that have been identified, classified and categorized; individual taxonomies are easily distinguished, while their inter-relationships are much more difficult to articulate. In this chapter, I take a different approach to Malory's particular style of characterization, beginning with a broad description of his main method(s), and then tracing the deployment of the methodology in terms of five dominant themes in *Le Morte Darthur*: knighthood, gender, kinship, religion and kingship.

With that in mind, I begin this chapter by pointing to two moments in the *Morte Darthur*. The first is one of the most discussed moments in the whole text; it occurs near the end of the narrative, after Arthur has been mortally wounded by Mordred in the battle on Salisbury Plain. Sir Bedevere, following Arthur's instructions, brings him to the water's edge, where waits a barge with many weeping ladies – three of whom are identified as queens – and the loyal knight places the king in the lap of a queen who says: "A, my dere brothir, why have ye taryed so longe frome me? Alas, thys wounde on youre hede hath caught overmuch colde!" (926.31–3 / C XXI.5).[1] Imagine the reader's surprise to discover that the woman who speaks to Arthur with such love and concern is in fact Morgan le Fay, the half-sister who, for most of the narrative, was Arthur's greatest enemy, seeking constantly to destroy him, his knights and his kingdom. When she suddenly re-enters the narrative in a sympathetic and supportive role, all of the past actions of her character are suddenly cast in a new light. We must reconsider, re-evaluate, re-think all of the episodes in which she has played a central role as a villain; with this final appearance, her function – as the figure who supplies

---

[1] All citations are from *Sir Thomas Malory: Le Morte Darthur*, ed. P. J. C. Field, 2 vols. (Cambridge, 2013). All citations to this text will be made parenthetically to volume I.

Arthur's court with necessary challenges against which to fight – suddenly becomes much more potentially complex and nuanced.[2]

We can juxtapose this dramatic and pronounced example of Malory's unique approach to characterization with a more subtle example. On the eve of the Grail Quest, a marvel appears at court: a sword in a stone, floating on the water, with words etched into the rock stating that "Never shall man take me hense but only he by whos syde I ought to honge, and he shall be the best knyght of the world" (668.13–15 / C XIII.2). When Arthur and his knights go out to examine this marvel, the king then asks them each to make an attempt at drawing the sword. Among those is Sir Gawain, to whom Arthur says, "Now, fayre nevew … assay ye for my love" (668.26–7 / C XIII.2). Gawain protests, until Arthur commands that he make an attempt. After Gawain fails – just as he predicted he would – he is chided by Lancelot, who tells him "now wete you well thys swerde shall touche you so sore that ye wolde nat ye had sette youre honde thereto for the castell of thys realme." In response, Gawain points out that: "I might nat withsey myne unclis wyll" (668.35–669.1-3 / C XIII.3).

In the French *Queste del Saint Graal*, Malory's source for his account of the Grail Quest, Gawain says: "je n'en poi mes; se je en deusse orendroit morir, si feisse je por la volenté *mon seignor* accomplir" ["What else could I have done? I would have obeyed *our lord's* command even if it meant dying"] (emphasis mine).[3] At first, this shift from calling Arthur "our lord" (or perhaps "my lord") to describing him as "my uncle" may seem to be a miniscule change on Malory's part, and one hardly worth mentioning. But small as it is, this alteration to Malory's source is critically important and indicative of his larger programme of characterization; the *Morte Darthur*, in Malory's hands, becomes a story that in one respect is dominated by kin loyalty and the vengeance enacted in blood feud. Malory alters this moment as he found it in his source the better to develop a theme that he explores from the opening lines of his text: how kinship can function as a force that has the potential both to support and to destroy a community.

In these two examples – Morgan's care for her dying brother, Gawain's deference to his kinsman rather than his lord – we see the two extremes of approach to characterization that run through the *Morte Darthur*. The one approach is effected dramatically, and is achieved *not* by Malory's alteration to the text, but by his choice to use a *particular* source text and leave it mostly unaltered. The evil Morgan of the early pages of the *Morte Darthur* is drawn from the *Suite du Merlin* and the Prose *Tristan*, while the kind, supportive Morgan of the conclusion is taken from the French *La Mort Le Roi Artu* and the English Stanzaic *Morte*. The fact

---

[2] The simple reason for this contrast has to do with Malory's sources for each section of the text: the Morgan found in the *Suite du Merlin* and the Prose *Tristan* is a malevolent figure, while the nurturing, concerned Morgan at the end of the text is found in French *Mort Artu* and the English Stanzaic *Morte*. Malory seems also to have further enhanced the character of Morgan here by adding the specific detail that "in one of their lapis kyng Arthure layde hys hede"; see *The Works of Sir Thomas Malory*, ed. Eugène Vinaver, 3rd edn, rev. P. J. C. Field, 3 vols. (Oxford, 1990), III, 1652.

[3] The French is from *La Queste del Saint Graal*, ed. Albert Pauphilet (Paris, 1967), 6. The English is Burns's translation: "The Quest for the Holy Grail," in *Lancelot-Grail: The Old French Arthurian Vulgate and Post-Vulgate in Translation*, gen. ed. Norris J. Lacy, 5 vols. (New York, 1993–96), IV, 4.

that when he stitched these texts together Malory opted not to modify Morgan's portrayal in either case is as significant an authorial choice as would be the decision to alter the text so as to make her character more consistent throughout.[4]

The second important way in which Malory creates the unique characterization found in his *Morte Darthur* is by deliberately altering key moments in his source material. Some of these changes may go by as barely-remarked, such as Gawain's explanation for his response to Arthur's demand that he attempt to draw the sword, while others are glaringly obvious – as when Arthur's conquest of Rome ends not in defeat, betrayal and death, but rather, is arguably the apogee of the king's career. In the case of the fight with Rome, the love of Lancelot and Guenevere, and many other key moments, Malory selects moments and episodes from his source texts and rearranges them in a new order within his *Morte Darthur*. For example, Arthur's death at the hands of Mordred is in many ways similar to *how* it occurs in the Alliterative *Morte Arthure*; the critical difference in Malory's text is *when*. So too, although Lancelot and Guenevere's forbidden love is discussed on many occasions, Malory detaches parts of the main source for their relationship as he found it in the Prose *Lancelot* and moves the one instance in which they explicitly consummate their relationship toward the end of the text. He also suppresses all other moments that confirm the adultery as not only existing, but also as continuously ongoing. This strategy affects the tenor of Lancelot and Guenevere's relationship in the early pages of the *Morte*, allowing it to be both devoted *and* chaste; thus, by the end their characters are ennobled and worthy of the readers' sympathy as opposed to deserving scorn or condemnation.

Virginia Woolf famously said of Jane Austen, "that of all great writers she is the most difficult to catch in the act of greatness"; in many ways, the same is true of Malory. His *Morte Darthur* contains episodes long familiar to anyone acquainted with the Arthurian tradition, and the outcome of those episodes remains, in all important aspects, the same. A thousand small changes (a new line of dialogue here, the cutting of an episode there, the moving of the climax of the Roman War to the end of the text as a whole rather than leaving it in its source-text position), and a thousand non-changes (hewing faithfully to the spiritual focus and allegorical tone of the *Queste del Saint Graal*, rather than eschewing it for a more courtly Grail romance as a source), and a thousand decisions that lie somewhere in between: all of these things in combination work to make the *Morte Darthur* an utterly original text that exceeds anything in the Arthurian tradition that has come before it.[5] Taken together, Malory's two primary authorial choices – (1) drawing material from sources with little to no alteration or concern for

---

[4] The best discussion of this remains Terence McCarthy, "Malory and his Sources," in *A Companion to Malory*, ed. Elizabeth Archibald and A. S. G. Edwards (Cambridge, 1996), 75–95.

[5] As McCarthy says of Malory's achievement: "It is his book as a whole that we must assess – the parts he translated (sometimes almost word for word), the parts he borrowed wholesale, the parts he adapted, the parts he rearranged, and the parts which he added himself. Our critical assessment must cover 'the hole book,' as Malory called it, must take into account the overall impact of a literary re-creation for which he is entirely responsible, however little he invented himself"; "Malory and his Sources," 78.

consistency, and (2) changing the source text either by altering a scene or moving it to a location in the narrative far distant from that of his source – has a *cumulative* effect on the narrative, making the whole not only greater than the sum of its parts, but different from any prior Arthurian text.[6]

As I noted above, past attempts to discuss how characterization functions in the *Morte* have generally taken an approach organized in terms of individual characters. There is the classic work of R. H. Wilson, *Characterization in Malory: A Comparison with His Sources*,[7] which is still of vital importance to Malory scholars working on the text today. More recently, Paul R. Rovang has taken up the challenge again in *Malory's Anatomy of Chivalry: Characterization in the Morte Darthur*,[8] a work that explores how certain characters differ in Malory when compared with their characterization in their source texts. Additionally, between the appearance of Wilson's and Rovang's studies, several scholars have addressed the issue of Malory's artistry through a variety of methods.[9]

While the approaches of Wilson, Rovang and others are useful, they do not quite manage to articulate the full range of Malory's achievement. Likewise, other treatments of characterization and originality in Malory tend to focus on key episodes and scenes, making it difficult to attain a *vue d'ensemble* or overall view of the *Morte*. And it is *because* this text is so massive, *because* it uses so many different sources, that the overall depiction of Malory's characters and the episodes in which they appear are both so complex and so difficult to appreciate fully. For example, Malory's decision to use the French Prose *Tristan* as a source for the massive middle third of the *Morte* is a crucial component in the unique development of characterization in the text. In making this choice, Malory had deliberately to set aside the French Vulgate and Post-Vulgate texts that had served him as his primary sources to this point; he opted to turn to a different strand of the French Arthurian tradition, the Tristan material. Although certainly a popular branch of the Arthurian tradition, the tone and the focus of the Prose *Tristan* are dramatically different from the writing found in the Vulgate and Post-Vulgate texts: there is greater emphasis on individual characters, some of whom we meet here and nowhere else; the Prose *Tristan* is also full of moments of lyric poetry, in which characters sometimes literally break out into song; and it wanders further afield from the narrative homeland of the Arthurian court. When this text is inserted into the *Morte,* it provides the text as a whole with a depth that otherwise would be lacking.

---

[6] For a discussion of that tradition, see Richard Moll, *Before Malory: Reading Arthur in Later Medieval England* (Toronto, 2003).

[7] Robert Henry Wilson, *Characterization in Malory: A Comparison with His Sources* (Chicago, 1934).

[8] Paul R. Rovang, *Malory's Anatomy of Chivalry: Characterization in the* Morte Darthur (Madison, NJ, 2014).

[9] See, in particular, *Malory's Originality: A Critical Study of* Le Morte Darthur, ed. Robert M. Lumiansky (New York, 1964), and *Studies in Malory,* ed. James W. Spisak (Kalamazoo, MI, 1985). Other scholars who discuss Malory's unique treatment of his sources include: Catherine Batt, *Malory's* Morte Darthur: *Remaking Arthurian Tradition* (New York, 2002); Kenneth Hodges, *Forging Chivalric Communities in Malory's* Le Morte Darthur (New York, 2005).

In the *Tristram*, the focus has largely moved away from Arthur's court, and we seem in a way to be "starting over": we begin in Cornwall, at the court of a king who is in many ways similar to Arthur (he has a retinue of knights, and his oddly acquired queen is in love with the greatest of these). In the *Tristram* we meet several key characters who will have crucial parts to play as the *Morte* comes to its end. Storylines are fleshed out and in some cases explained or brought to their conclusion – or an origin point is identified. A few examples are: Morgause is murdered by her son Gaheris, a moment that exacerbates the blood feud between the Orkney clan and the family of King Pellinore; Lancelot is deceived into believing he lies by the side of his beloved Guenevere, conceiving the saintly Galahad on Elaine of Corbin in the process; Morgan le Fay increases her attacks on Arthur and his knights, repeatedly seeking to shame and undermine her brother's rule. As Thomas Rumble has pointed out, "to portray the real tragedy of the fall of Arthur's realm, [Malory] had to make clearer than ever before the *causes* of that tragedy. It is just this sense of causality that is missing in the French cyclic *Arthuriad* – no matter in what combination we put together a *Merlin*, a *Quest* and a *Lancelot*. And it is just this sense of causality that is underscored, though implicitly rather than explicitly, by the addition of the 'Tristram' material."[10]

Kenneth Hodges and I have recently argued that an understanding of Malory's text is greatly enhanced when one considers Arthur's realm through the lens of the geographic, as has Meg Roland in the present volume; I contend that this "geographic thinking" is useful, too, if we consider the text of the *Morte Darthur* to be like a map, with borders separating countries that can be at once culturally similar and different, friendly or hostile, toward one another.[11] The various sources of the *Morte Darthur* (some French, some English, some unknown, all drawn from a variety of different literary traditions and often generically jarring when placed side by side) can be symbolically imagined in terms of the Questing Beast, a mysterious, composite creature who roams the landscape of Arthur's Britain and is described thus: "in shap lyke a serpentis hede and a body lyke a lybud, buttokked lyke a lyon and footed lyke an harte. And in hys body there was such a noyse as hit had bene twenty couple of houndys questynge, and such noyse that beste made wheresomerever he wente" (378.28–32 / C IX.11). A Prose *Tristan* butts up against the Post-Vulgate *Quest del Saint Graal*, which sits uncomfortably next to various sections of the *Suite du Merlin*, which is interrupted by the events of the Alliterative *Morte Arthure*, which is itself in turn interrupted by a

---

[10] Thomas Rumble, "'The Tale of Tristram': Development by Analogy," in *Malory's Originality*, 118–83, at 145. D. Thomas Hanks, Jr., echoes and affirms Rumble's statement when he asserts that the "Tristram" is critically important to the narrative movement of the *Morte Darthur* because "[Malory] establishes the context of gentility and valor which shapes the remainder of the *Morte*'s action; develops the theme of the anti-knight; forecasts the fall of Arthur and of his Round Table; prepares the reader for the Grail Quest; paves the way for 'The Knight of the Cart'; and in the love affair of Tristram and Isode, subtly comments upon the affair of Lancelot and Guinevere": "Malory's *Book of Sir Tristram*: Focusing *Le Morte Darthur*," *Quondam et Futurus* 3.1 (1993): 14–31, at 14–15.

[11] See Dorsey Armstrong and Kenneth Hodges, *Mapping Malory: Regional Identities and National Geographies in* Le Morte Darthur (New York, 2014). See also Meg Roland, "Malory and the Wider World," in this volume.

large chunk of the Prose *Lancelot*. The seams between them are visible, but again, they combine to make a unique whole. The same may be said of the territories over which Arthur rules: Wales is not Rome is not Cornwall is not Orkney, yet all of these and more are part of Arthur's domain. Just as the Questing Beast manages to be many animals and one singular Beast, and just as Arthur's realm manages to include many different territories which are all collectively designated as "Arthurian," so too does *Le Morte Darthur* manage to be a single text that is comprised of several texts. And it is these joinings, these unlikely conjunctions, that contribute to the production of unique characters in the *Morte*.[12]

In moving forward with this analysis, I take as an organizing premise something I term "thematic locales," or "nodes of meaning." While one could argue for numerous dominant themes that run through Malory's text, I focus here on what I see as the five most important elements of the *Morte Darthur* listed in descending order of visibility in the text: knighthood, gender/the feminine, kinship, religion and kingship. This thematic approach certainly has its shortcomings – just as a character-oriented analysis does – but I choose it because it allows one to move more freely throughout the text, linking characters to each other, to the source texts from which they come, to other characters and key episodes. What follows is by no means an exhaustive, comprehensive treatment of the subject; rather, it maps the broad contours of how characterization is deployed in Malory's text, and points the way toward further analysis.


## *Knighthood*


I begin with knighthood because it is by far the most important element of the *Morte Darthur* – its *raison d'être*.[13] Without the exploits of the knights roaming the forests and plains of adventure – and the stories they tell upon their return to court – the Arthurian community would have no reason to exist. While one might say this is true of all Arthurian literature, the sheer volume and number of knightly adventures that are contained within Malory's text, plus two key additions made to the narrative – one near the beginning of the text, one near the very end, both of which seem to be Malory's original invention – indicate that defining and testing an "ideal of knighthood" is the primary concern of the *Morte* as a whole.

---

[12] For more on Malory's sources, see, among others: the notes to *Works*, ed. Vinaver and to *Malory: Texts and Sources*, ed. P. J. C. Field, 2 vols. (Cambridge, 1998); *The Malory Debate: Essays on the Texts of* Le Morte Darthur, ed. Bonnie Wheeler, Robert L. Kindrick and Michael Salda (Cambridge, 2000); Carol M. Meale, "'The Hoole Book': Editing and the Creation of Meaning in Malory's Text," in *A Companion to Malory*, 3–17. See also, *The Arthur of the English: The Arthurian Legend in Medieval English Life and Literature*, ed. W. R. J. Barron, rev. edn (Cardiff, 2001).

[13] The books and articles that discuss the function of knighthood in the *Morte Darthur* are almost too numerous to mention. Some of the most important and foundational works of scholarship, however, are: Beverly Kennedy, *Knighthood in the* Morte Darthur, 2nd edn (Cambridge, 1985); Richard Barber, "Chivalry and the *Morte Darthur*," in *A Companion to Malory*, 19–35; Andrew Lynch, *Malory's Book of Arms: The Narrative of Combat in* Le Morte Darthur (Cambridge, 1997); Hyonjin Kim, *The Knight without the Sword: The Social Landscape of Malorian Chivalry* (Cambridge, 2000); and Kenneth Hodges, *Forging Chivalric Communities in Malory's* Le Morte Darthur (New York, 2005).

The simple fact of utilizing so many sources is really what makes knighthood the dominant theme of the *Morte Darthur*. In addition to drawing heavily on the French Vulgate and Post-Vulgate cycle, Malory's use of the Alliterative *Morte Arthure*, his decision to appropriate a large section of the Prose *Tristan* for the middle third of his text, and the choice to include the stories of Gareth and Sir Urry (sources for which have yet to be identified – or which may have never existed)[14] mean that the range of knightly behaviour on display in the *Morte Darthur* is truly comprehensive. Not only that, but certain knights – especially Gawain, Tristram, Palomides and, of course, Lancelot – become more interestingly three-dimensional simply by virtue of there being so many examples of knighthood against which each can be compared.

Additionally, Malory himself makes changes to his knight's characters and stories that "shape" them in particular directions. For example, Sir Gawain in Malory's text is both a good knight and excessively vengeful; early on, he is something of a rogue when it comes to women, but at the end of the text, we learn that his service to ladies throughout his career – none of which we have actually witnessed – is what gives him the special dispensation to appear, after his death, in a dream in which he warns Arthur to wait to march into battle until Lancelot is back at the king's side.[15] As Felicia Nimue Ackerman has succinctly put it: "A foolish consistency is certainly not the hobgoblin of Gawain's mind!"[16] While this complex characterization is primarily a result of Malory's use of sources that differ dramatically from one another in their depiction of this particular nephew of King Arthur, Bonnie Wheeler has argued persuasively that it is Malory's unique paratactic style that contributes significantly to the particular treatment of Gawain in his text.[17] In several places, Malory makes slight changes to lessen the adverse depiction of Gawain and produce a more consistent version of his character. Sometimes Malory cuts actions or dialogue that would leave a negative impression, and in other instances, he offers explanations for Gawain's behaviour – usually related to a fierce loyalty to his kinsmen.[18] And in still others, we are left to surmise or reconstruct events that apparently happen "off stage" and yet still have bearing on the development of the characters within the pages of the text.[19]

Gawain is contrasted repeatedly against his younger brother, Gareth, whose honour, goodness and loyalty to Lancelot above his own brothers are rendered much more emphatic in comparison. Similarly, while Lancelot had always been

---

[14] See especially Field's discussion in his edition of *Le Morte Darthur*, II.185–93.
[15] "'Wellcom, my systers sonne, I wende ye had bene dede. And now I se they on lyve … what bene thes ladyes that hyder be com with you?' 'Sir,' seyde Sir Gawayne, 'all thes be ladyes for whom I have foughten for, whan I was man lyvynge … and God hath gyvyn hem that grace at theire grete prayer, bycause I ded batayle for them for theire right, that they shulde brynge me hydder unto you" (920.32–5 and 921.1–5 / C XXI.3).
[16] Felicia Nimue Ackerman, "'Every Man of Worship': Emotion and Characterization in Malory's *Le Morte Darthur*," *Arthuriana* 11.2 (2001): 33–42, at 36.
[17] See Bonnie Wheeler, "Romance and Parataxis and Malory: The Case of Sir Gawain's Reputation," *Arthurian Literature* XII (1993): 109–32.
[18] On this, see in particular Wilson, *Characterization in Malory*, 69–82; Rovang, *Malory's Anatomy of Chivalry*, 27–38.
[19] One of these would be the account of how Gawain and his brothers ambushed and killed Sir Lamorak, which I discuss below.

the heroic protagonist in Malory's French source texts, in the *Morte Darthur* his prowess and stature are made even more pronounced: Malory enlarges his role in the all-important Roman campaign; he minimizes references to Lancelot's adulterous love for Queen Guenevere, suppressing explicit mention or evidence of it until after the Grail Quest; Malory includes the account of Lancelot's healing of Sir Urry; and the account of Lancelot's death is described in terms most often associated with sainthood.[20] All of these alterations not only contribute to a fuller, more comprehensive picture of what ideal knighthood is and is not, but these changes also work to elevate Lancelot's character once again after it has been badly damaged – both by this greatest knight's failure on the Grail Quest and his accidental slaying of Gareth and Gaheris when he rescues Guenevere from the stake.

Lancelot's decision to rescue the queen is explained and legitimized in much more specific terms than in the source texts, and this is largely due to those two major alterations that Malory made to his text – suppressing most mention of the lovers' adultery until quite late in the narrative and increasing Lancelot's heroic visibility during the war with Rome. Both of these additions are critically important to an understanding of how knighthood functions in the text, but they are also of great importance in terms of the four other dominant themes: gender/ the feminine, kinship, religion and kingship.

The first significant addition Malory makes to his source material is the Pentecostal Oath,[21] which lays out in no uncertain terms what kinds of behaviours are expected of knights, and what kind of actions these agents of the community should avoid. I have argued elsewhere that this addition to the *Morte Darthur*, when compared with other Arthurian literature, means that knighthood in *this* text is arguably considerably more fraught, more structured, more surveilled, than in any of the source texts. After the series of quests that mark his wedding to Guenevere, Arthur:

> stablysshed all the knyghtes and gaff them rychesse and londys, and charged them never to do outerage nothir mourthir, and allwayes to fle treason, and to gyff mercy unto hym that askith mercy, upon payne of forfeiture of their worship and lordship of Kynge Arthure for evir more; and allwayes to do ladyes, damesels, and jantilwomen and wydowes soccour, strengthe hem in hir ryghtes, and never to enforce them upon payne of dethe. Also that no man take no batayles in a wrongefull quarell for no love ne for no worldis goodis.
>
> So unto thys were all the knyghtes sworne of the Table Rounde, both old and yonge, and every yere so were they sworne at the hyghe feste of Pentecoste. (97.27–35; 98.1–3 / C III.15)

This moment comes near the beginning of the *Morte*, when Arthur and his knights arguably stand at the cusp of great things: the lessons learned during the

---

[20] See in particular Karen Cherewatuk, "The Saint's Life of Sir Launcelot: Hagiography and the Conclusion of Malory's *Morte Darthur*," *Arthuriana* 5.1 (1995): 62–78.

[21] As Eugène Vinaver has said of this moment: "This is perhaps the most complete and authentic record of M[alory]'s conception of chivalry. Elsewhere he expresses it incidentally or indirectly, whereas here for the first and perhaps the last time he states it compendiously, in didactic form": *Works*, ed. Vinaver, III, 1330.

quests of Gawain, Torre and Pellinore on the occasion of Arthur's wedding now have become legislated in the Pentecostal Oath; Arthur's conquest of Rome – the moment that will be the apogee of power and status for his community – is just in the offing. The Oath casts an important light – and sometimes, shadow – on all that comes after. Once it has entered the text, the reader is invited to interpret all the actions of Arthur's knights in light of its specific clauses; the Oath is then tested in a variety of contexts to determine if and how successfully it functions as a guide for the Arthurian social project.[22] The answer to this question appears to be: "sometimes." For example, on the Grail Quest, the most courtly of Arthur's knights – with the examples of Lancelot and Gawain being the most memorable – fail in pursuit of this most holy object, while Galahad, Perceval and Bors are the most successful quest participants. The ideals of knighthood expressed in the Oath do not function ideally on the Grail Quest, where they are replaced by more spiritual imperatives.[23] But at the same time, Malory's Lancelot is much more successful in his version of the Grail Quest than he is in the source text. We can make such a determination because we have seen a great deal of Lancelot's character both before and after the Grail Quest and have a plethora of examples from which we can draw a judgement of his character. By contrast, the *Queste del Saint Graal* is (although part of the Vulgate cycle) a stand-alone text, unconcerned with Lancelot's adventures before or after. In the French source, the text ends when the quest ends. In Malory, there is knightly identity *before* and knightly identity *after* the Grail Quest; pursuit of the Grail transforms the knightly agents of the community and in so doing, transforms chivalry as a whole.

The fact that the Oath's clauses embody an ideal of knighthood designed to serve as a foundation and support for the Arthurian community while simultaneously producing the behaviours and episodes that cause that same community to collapse has its clearest expression in the other passage I mentioned at the beginning of this section. This is when, after Lancelot has died in a great aura of sanctity as monk and priest, his cousin Sir Ector offers this threnody for Lancelot. Like the Oath, this passage, too, is sourceless, and most likely Malory's own invention:

> "A, Launcelot! ... thou were hed of al Crysten knyghtes! And now I dare
> say ... thou Sir Launcelot, there thou lyest, that thou were never matched
> of erthely knyghtes hande. And thou were the truest frende to thy lovar
> that ever bestrade hors, and thou were the trewest lover, of a sinful man,
> that ever loved woman, and thou were the kyndest man that ever strake
> wyth swerde. And thou were the godelyest persone that ever cam emonge
> prees of knyghtes, and thou was the meekest man and the jentyllest that
> ever ete in halle emonge ladyes, and thou were the sternest knyght to thy
> mortal foo that ever put spere in the reeste." (939.12–23 / C XXI.12)

---

[22] See Dorsey Armstrong, *Gender and the Chivalric Community in Malory's* Morte Darthur (Gainesville, FL, 2003).

[23] For example, Lancelot famously decides to help the weaker party in a battle he witnesses while in pursuit of the Grail for "incresyng of hys shevalry" (719.35 / C XV.4), only to learn later that what he had witnessed was an allegorical representation of the battle between good and evil, and that his chivalric impulse had caused him to choose the wrong side.

As with the Pentecostal Oath, much of the emphasis here is on martial prowess, courtly manners and service to ladies. Of all the changes Malory made to his source texts, the changes that surround the character of Sir Lancelot are by far the most numerous, and they function to demonstrate that Lancelot's particular knightly identity has been shaped by Malory to place greater emphasis on his reputation for serving ladies. On more than one occasion, Malory has altered his source text to highlight Lancelot's devotion to the feminine; for example, where a castle he rescues from the tyranny of two ogres in the Prose *Lancelot* has a mix of men and women as its inhabitants, in Malory's text he is specifically thanked for rescue by a group of maidens only (206–207 / C VI.10). And when Lancelot fights Sir Brewnys Saunz Pité in the source text, it is because he is "a thorough rotter"[24] who attacks both men and women. In Malory, Sir Brewnys infuriates Lancelot because he focuses his bad behaviour almost exclusively on women: "What … is he a theef and a knyght? And a ravyshher of wymmen? He doth shame unto the Order of Knyghthood, and contrary unto his oth" (205.6–7 / C VI.10), exclaims Lancelot. Thus, good knights are characterized more emphatically by service to the feminine and loyalty to one another in *Le Morte Darthur* than they are in the source texts; how closely a knight hews to the ideal of the Pentecostal Oath is one of the major elements in the expression of his characterization.

It is the sheer number of knights that give the text such depth. Gawain's character seems the more vengeful and irrational when we compare him with Lancelot, with someone like Sir Tristram, and most importantly, with his own brother Gareth. Sir Tristram, the hero of his own text, shifts in stature when his tale is inserted into the middle of the *Morte Darthur*. He is the best knight of Cornwall, yes, but once he enters the orbit of Arthurian knights, his status dims. At the same time, the fact that Tristram is engaged in a love affair with his king's wife – a triangle that parallels the Arthur-Lancelot-Guenevere triangle – and that this relationship is generally viewed in a positive light, means that Lancelot's relationship with the queen is thus ameliorated somewhat by the comparison.

By the same token, the deep grief and mourning of Sir Palomides, the Saracen knight who is "christened in [his] soule," is dramatically arresting in Malory, because no other knight expresses his grief with such deep interiority and sadness. In the Prose *Tristan*, Palomides is unusual in his degree of psychic pain; in Malory's *Morte Darthur*, with a much larger group of knights with whom to be compared, Palomides stands out even more starkly as an unusual specimen of knighthood.[25] And the number of knightly examples to be found in the *Morte* is indeed encyclopaedic; it has long been noted that Malory likes to give his knights identities when the source text supplies none.[26] Thus, in the *Morte Darthur* name-

---

[24] The phrase is borrowed from D. Thomas Hanks, Jr., "Malory's Anti-Knights: Balin and Breunys," in *The Social and Literary Contexts of Malory's* Morte Darthur, ed. D. Thomas Hanks, Jr. and Jessica G. Brogdon (Cambridge and Rochester, NY, 2000), 94–110, at 99. Although he is using it to describe Malory's Sir Brewnys, who focuses his attacks on women, the statement is apt with regard to the source as well.

[25] Bonnie Wheeler, "Grief in Avalon: Sir Palomydes' Psychic Pain," in *Grief and Gender, 700-1700*, ed. Jennifer Vaught and Lynn Dickson Bruckner (New York, 2003), 65–77.

[26] As Wilson notes in *Characterization*: "There exist in the *Morte Darthur* ninety-five characters for whose names … Malory is responsible; six more whose names may come from unknown sources of the episodes in which they figure, but are otherwise of

less knights have identities and sometimes, Malory fuses several different anonymous knights in his sources into a single character, a move that underscores the
importance of the individual knightly career that develops over the course of
the narrative as a whole. Knighthood is the alpha and omega of Malory's text,
and this necessitates a fuller development and characterization of knights – both
individually and collectively – than that which we see in any of his sources.

## Gender/the Feminine

If Malory's addition of the Pentecostal Oath is significant for the way it character-
izes ideal knighthood and thus gives us a template against we can measure such
things, it is even more important for one specific focus that Malory emphasizes in
the clauses of the Oath: service to ladies. As I have argued elsewhere, the specific
instruction "allwayes to do ladyes, damesels, and jantilwomen and wydowes
soccour, strengthe hem in hir ryghtes, and never to enforce them upon payne of
dethe" creates a tension in the narrative that is more pronounced in Malory than
in his source texts.[27] By singling out women for special attention, Malory's text
constructs the feminine as simultaneously essential yet secondary, necessarily
helpless yet contradictorily powerful. The text needs women to be ever in need
of the services of a knight; this gives knights compelling reasons to pursue quests
and to act in certain ways while on those quests. But the *Morte Darthur* unintentionally renders women powerful in that, while they are objects discussed in the
Oath, they themselves are not subject to it. Indeed, women in the *Morte Darthur*
have the power to compel knights to perform favours and put themselves in
harm's way simply by asking, and while the knights have sworn to uphold certain standards of behaviour, ladies need swear no such equivalent oath.[28]

While, generally speaking, the same may be said of Malory's sources, several
changes, large and small, made by Malory in his text demonstrate that he was
interested in the potential power of the feminine; his alterations work variously
to ameliorate, to denigrate and to complicate many of the feminine characters
in the *Morte* – and indeed, in some cases, Malory's changes effectively do all
three at once. As Siobhan Wyatt argues, "Malory embraces every opportunity
to empower his female characters, an unusual attitude in a period that prefers

---

Malory's invention; and sixty-five whose names appear both with source authority
and without it. Thus, out of a total of approximately 425 names of characters to be
found in the work, 166 are affected by Malory's avoidance of anonymity": 38.

[27] See Armstrong, *Gender and The Chivalric Community*, especially Chapter 1.

[28] Siobhan Wyatt, *Women of Words in* Le Morte Darthur: *The Autonomy of Speech in
Malory's Female Characters* (Basingstoke, 2016) offers the most thorough evidence to
date of how significantly Malory altered the depiction of his female characters as
compared with his French sources. Wyatt persuasively supports her "main theory
... that Malory lends credibility to female speech in order to position women as
credible judges of knightly behavior whilst also supplying traits and characteristics
specific to each woman": *Women of Words*, 8. Another excellent overview of the position of women in the *Morte* is Elizabeth Edwards, "The Place of Women in the *Morte
Darthur*," in *A Companion to Malory*, 38–54. Although Edwards specifically avoids an
analysis based on characterization, her arguments about gender and the feminine are
still foundational to Arthurian studies.

to suppress the threat of dangerous women."[29] Thus, his female characters are, generally speaking, better developed and more interesting than their French counterparts, and quite frequently knights are specifically motivated to act due to a desire to serve ladies, rather than to engage in the catchall "pursuit of adventure," an impetus that serves as the prime motivator in most of the source texts.

If we take the example of Guenevere, for instance, we find that the overall impression of the queen in Malory's text is much more positive, and hers is a character that undergoes significant changes over the course of the narrative. When Malory emphasized Lancelot's devotion to the queen, he made Arthur's greatest knight more honourable by ennobling Arthur's wife as well. He does this first of all, as noted above, by suppressing any explicit mention of adultery between Lancelot and Guenevere until quite late in the text; this allows their relationship to be both devoted and chaste for hundreds of pages. We only see the pair commit adultery a single time – during the episode of the "Knight of the Cart" – and after that, Malory tells us specifically on more than one occasion that the queen and knight are together, but the "Freynsshe Booke" does not tell if they were in bed together or simply conversing.[30] In fact, the "Freynshe Booke" is absolutely clear that Lancelot and Guenevere are caught *in flagrante delicto* when a group of knights, led by Aggravain and Mordred, storm the queen's chamber. After the single clear incident of adultery, the behaviour of each (Lancelot sooner than Guenevere) conveys a sense of sorrow and regret for their transgression.

Indeed, when we learn during Guenevere's trial for allegedly poisoning a knight at a dinner party that Arthur needs a champion for his queen – since as king he "cannot have ado in this matter" – it suddenly becomes clear that Guenevere and Lancelot's relationship is not only devoted, but also *necessary*. It would not be fitting for the highest-ranking lady in the land to have no one to defend her; if the king cannot, then by rights it should be the greatest knight.

In the episodes surrounding the explicit instance of adultery, Guenevere comes across as occasionally petulant and demanding. This depiction is more or less true to the source, but her character is improved by two decisions made by Malory: the first is to include an original passage celebrating love "in those days" (i.e., the days of King Arthur) as having been more steady, devoted and chaste, concluding with a comment about how Guenevere, because she was a true lover, had a good end: "And therefore all ye that be lovers, calle unto your remembrance the monethe of May, lyke as did queen Gwenyver, for whom I make here a lytyll mencion, that whylle she llyved she was a trew lover, and therefor, she had a good ende" (842.10–11 / C XIX.1). And that end – which is the second way that Malory ameliorates her character – is significantly and specifically rendered as a narrative of repentance and redemption. After Arthur's death, Malory chooses not to conclude the *Morte* there, but rather, to include some final scenes when Guenevere, sorrowful and penitent, retreats to a nunnery; Lancelot,

---

[29] Wyatt, *Women of Words*, 100.
[30] Prior to the "Knight of the Cart" episode, however, the fact that Lancelot is twice tricked into Elaine of Corbin's bed by a stratagem that persuades him that he is, in fact, being brought to the queen's chamber, suggests that the relationship between Arthur's greatest knight and his wife has been adulterous for some time.

ever the devoted servant, follows her example and joins a religious community. The contrast with her earlier jealousy and possessiveness leaves us with the sense of her character as one that has developed and changed.[31] Indeed, at the end of the text, the only person who argues that the Arthurian project has been a failure is the queen. When, in the aftermath of the death of Arthur and the collapse of Camelot Lancelot seeks to take Guenevere back to his homeland as his wife, it is she who rebukes him, reminding him that their love is in part what has caused Arthur's rule to fail:

> Thorow thys same man and me hath all thys warre be wrought, and the deth of the most nobelest knyghtes of the worlde, for thorow oure love that we have loved togydir ys my ost noble lorde slayne. Therefore, Sir Launcelot, wyte thou well I am sette in suche a plight to gete my soule hele. And yet I truste ... that aftir my deth I may have a sight of the blyssed face of Cryste Jesu ... for as synfull as ever I was, now are seyntes in hevyn. (932.29–35, 933.1–2 / C XXI.9)

The greatest knight of Arthur's realm and its prime exemplar has founded his entire career and identity on service to ladies; at the end of the text, he is unable to abandon the formula that has, for the most part, served him so well. As Guenevere inspired him to perform feats of knightly prowess, so too does she motivate his endeavours in the spiritual realm. This ideal of service to and dependence on the feminine permeates the whole of the *Morte Darthur*, with knight after knight constrained, compelled and motivated to perform great deeds of valour in service to the feminine, in a never-ending performance of heteronormative gender identity.[32]

The intense focus on gender ideals and a construction of the feminine as helpless and needy serves to support Malory's community, but its centrality is such that any manipulation of it can bring that same community crashing down. While several of Malory's female characters are rendered with more complexity in the *Morte Darthur* than they are in the sources (the figures of Guenevere, Nimue, Nyneve, Morgause, La Beal Isode, Perceval's sister, Elaine of Corbin, and the Lady of the Lake comprising just a few such examples) perhaps no single character – male or female – is suggestively depicted with such potentially rich characterization as is Arthur's half-sister, Morgan le Fay.[33]

---

[31] See Edward Donald Kennedy, "Malory's Guenevere: 'A Woman Who Had Grown a Soul'," *Arthuriana* 9.2 (1999): 37–45.

[32] In a moment original to Malory, Lancelot describes how he will always serve Queen Guenevere because of the kindness she showed him on the occasion of his knighting, when she found his lost sword, "lapped" it in her train, and then gave it to him when he needed it (802.13–23 / C XVIII.7). Knighthood here quite literally depends upon the intervention and support of the feminine in a way that it does not quite in Malory's sources; knighthood also is bound in service to the feminine, as we realize when Lancelot promises Guenevere "at that day ever to be her knyght in right othir in wronge" (802.22–3 / C XVIII.7).

[33] The characterization of Morgause, Arthur's other half-sister, is also significant in that, in Malory's text, she behaves more independently, with significant results – Malory describes her as a specifically willing participant in the affair that leads to the birth of Mordred, a slight change from the source text that emphasizes the dangerous power of the feminine in Malory. While neither Arthur nor Morgause are aware that they are

As I discussed in the opening of this chapter, Morgan's appearance at the end of the *Morte* in a nurturing, supportive role comes as something of a shock. No other character more than she has used the power of the feminine to both challenge knights – thereby providing opportunities for the agents of the community to prove their prowess – and also to destroy them. Her power and the malevolence of her attacks on her brother and his kingdom are key elements in the development not only of her character, but also, that of all those who encounter and interact with her. Morgan successfully invokes and manipulates the conventions of femininity as understood by Malory's Arthurian community, but also manages to step outside those conventions when it suits her – demonstrating how central a particular heteronormative construct is to the society, and also, *that it is constructed*. Malory's unique deployment of characterization arises first from his particular conception of knighthood and chivalry; that conception is itself inextricably linked with the feminine. Importantly, the *Morte* does not simply employ women to contribute to the characterization of male characters, but also includes fully characterized women. According to the Oath, the feminine is *explicitly* connected to the foundation and maintenance of the chivalric community; *implicitly*, however, the role of kinship is arguably just as important.

## Kinship

If one could argue that the Pentecostal Oath causes a "ripple effect" in terms of matters of gender and the characterization of the feminine because of what it includes, then one could also argue that what it *omits* functions similarly. In this case, it is the matter of kin loyalty – a force that both supports and contributes to the destruction of the Arthurian community. Although the Oath seems to offer both prescriptive and proscriptive instructions to Arthur's knights, the rules it lays down are both too specific and too vague, and nowhere is the matter of kinship addressed. Again and again, we see knights in Malory's text bend the rules of knighthood – or ignore them altogether – when it is a matter of loyalty to one's cousin or brother. And no one is more centripetally and centrifugally engaged with matters of kinship than is Sir Gawain. Malory stresses this from the very first pages of the text, as when Uwain is banished from court and Gawain declares that "who so banyssheth my cosyn germayn shal bannysshe me"; and of course, at the end of the text, it is kin loyalty that leads Gawain to demand that Arthur take vengeance on Lancelot for the accidental killing of Gareth and Gaheris. Arthur, who becomes increasingly reluctant to exact vengeance, seems helpless in the face of Gawain's wrath to stop him. If, as at the beginning of this chapter, we saw that Gawain is compelled to follow the command of his uncle, even though he wishes to refuse, then at the end of the text, the kin relationship seems to work in the opposite direction – Arthur may not gainsay his nephew, even though he, not Gawain, is the king.

---

committing incest, it is significant that both are willing participants in the adulterous affair. On this see Armstrong, *Gender and the Chivalric Community*, esp. Chapter 1.

Perhaps even more interestingly, on the few occasions when knights do decide to follow the rules of the Pentecostal Oath at the expense of their kin, the results are not good.[34] When, on the Grail Quest, Sir Bors encounters his brother Sir Lionel, naked and a bound prisoner of another knight, his immediate impulse to rescue Lionel is disrupted when he notices a noblewoman who is about to be ravished by a knight: "if I latte my brother be in adventure he muste be slayne, and that wold I nat for all the erthe; and if I helpe nat the mayde she ys shamed, and shall lose hir virginité which she shall never gete agayne" (736.23–6 / C XV.9). Although Lionel survives, his fury at his brother's disloyalty is unrelenting, and he tries on many occasions to kill Ector, on occasion killing others just to get to him.

The contradictory fact that extreme kin loyalty in the *Morte Darthur* can lead to violence against one's own kin is nowhere demonstrated more shockingly than in Gaheris' "honour killing" of his mother, Morgause. The widow of King Lot has taken as a lover Sir Lamorak, son of King Pellinore. When Morgause's son Gaheris finds them in bed together, it is his own mother he kills, rather than the knight, proclaiming, "And now is my modir quytte of the, for she shall never shame her chyldryn" (487.7–8 / C X.24). Gaheris' response reflects the power of the feminine in Malory – both the possibility of it disrupting the order of the Arthurian community, and its position as one of the buttresses of the community's very identity. In turn, this produces a need for the agents of the community to control it emphatically. The fact that the Oath addresses the feminine but does not issue any directives concerning kinship means that one of the central concerns of the Arthurian community – gender – is heavily regulated, while another – kinship – simultaneously exists outside that community's explicit rules. Put another way, matters of kinship so pervade every aspect of the community that they are almost invisible; matters of gender are so visible that they must be explicitly policed. It is the fact that these two elements of characterization are so interconnected – yet treated so differently – that produces much of the tension and narrative movement in the *Morte*.

This concern about kin loyalty as superseding even the clauses of the Oath is most compellingly demonstrated in the interactions of the sons of King Lot and King Pellinore. Although in the killing of Morgause Lamorak is spared, the reprieve is brief. With the exception of Gareth, the Orkney brothers seek constantly to destroy Pellinore's sons, Perceval and Lamorak, as they hold Pellinore responsible for the death of their father, King Lot. The characterization of Gawain, Mordred, Aggravain and Gaheris as exceedingly vengeful is confirmed not just by their actions in the text, but also by a conversation that Malory depicts as taking place between Sir Palomides and Sir Tristram, in which the former reveals to the latter how Lamorak was treasonously slain by the sons of Lot.[35]

---

[34] For more on politics in Malory, see Lisa Robeson, " Secular Malory," in this volume.

[35] "Sir Gawayne and his thre bretherne, Sir Aggravayne, Sir Gaherys and Sir Mordrede sette uppon Sir Lamorak in a privy place and there they slew his horse. And so they faught with hym on foote more than thre owrys bothe byfore hym and behynde hym, and so Sir Mordrede gaff hym his dethis wounde behynde hym at his bakke, and all to-hewe hym..." "Now fye uppon treson!" seyde Sir Trystram, "for hit sleyth myn harte to hyre this tale" (554.10–18).

And indeed, the final conflict between Arthur and Lancelot is precipitated at least in part by kin loyalty – when the Orkney brothers denounce Lancelot and Guenevere, one of the reasons they give is because shame done to their kinsman is also shame done to them; Lancelot, who is held in the highest esteem at court, is not only an outsider – not a relative – but also is engaged in an adulterous affair with the queen: "And we be your syster sunnes: and we may suffir hit no lenger" (872.10–11 / C XX.1). In the end, Arthur himself is helpless against the pull of kin loyalty – it is his inability to say no to the demands of his nephew Gawain that compels him to continue his fight against Lancelot, even when he wishes to be reconciled. Gawain's compulsion to avenge his kin is arguably even stronger than Arthur's; indeed, in his argument persuading Arthur to support his quest for vengeance against Lancelot, Gawain makes a three-fold argument: it was because of the king's direct order that Gareth was present at Guenevere's would-be execution, so Arthur is responsible for the young knight's death; the feudal relationship between Gareth, Gaheris and Gawain means that Arthur must avenge the death of his vassals; and finally – and, I contend, most significantly – the uncle–nephew relationship compels Arthur to seek out vengeance against Sir Lancelot for killing his kin. While the king on several occasions expresses his reluctance to continue the blood feud against Lancelot, Gawain is utterly and unreasonably consumed by this desire, and no amount of pleading, apologizing and atonement on Lancelot's part can dissuade Arthur's nephew from pursuing vengeance. While Arthur's reasons for pursuing Lancelot are a combination of royal responsibility, feudal obligation and kin loyalty, Gawain deliberately invokes these to satisfy his own desire for revenge through blood feud.

## Religion

Like the question of kinship, the question of religion is one that the Pentecostal Oath does not address – except, arguably, in the fact that it is re-sworn every year on the high feast of Pentecost. In fact, not only does the Oath omit any mention of faith or service to God, but several other moments in which Arthur or his knights engage in matters spiritual in the source texts are abbreviated or omitted by Malory altogether. For example, in the Prose *Lancelot*, the young knight receives a sermon from the Lady of the Lake explaining the origins of knighthood: "Above all, knighthood was established to defend the Holy Church, for the Church cannot take up arms to avenge herself or return harm for harm; and this is why knights were created: to protect the one who turns the other cheek when the first has been hit."[36] Likewise, in the *Suite du Merlin*, on which Malory drew for his account of Arthur's pulling the sword from the stone, immediately after Arthur has withdrawn the sword, the archbishop gives him a lecture on

---

[36] "Chevaliers fu establis outreement por Saint Eglize garandir, car ele ne se doit revanchier par armes ne render mal encountre mal; et por che est a che establis li chevaliers qu'il garandisse chelui qui tent la senestre joe, quant ele a esteferue en la destre": *Lancelot: Roman en prose du XIIIe siècle*, ed. A. Micha, 9 vols. (Geneva, 1980), 7:250. The English translation is from *Lancelot-Grail*, trans. Burns, II.59.

proper kingship, to which Arthur replies, "Sir, I entrust myself and everything God gives me to the care and counsel of Holy Church. Please, you be the one to choose and watch over such people as will be best for me in doing God's will for the welfare of Christendom."[37] In Malory, Arthur makes no such declaration of devotion to God and Church but gets straight to the business of waging war against his enemies.

Indeed, in Malory's text religion and spirituality are notable primarily for their absence. The knights do not swear to serve God, and adherence to knightly ideals in Malory means that those earthly knights who participate in the Grail Quest have their experiences cast as partial successes, rather than complete failures.[38] As Eugène Vinaver argues, Malory is not interested primarily in contrasting "earthly" and "divine" chivalry "and condemning the former"; rather, the Grail Quest is seen by Vinaver as an "opportunity offered to the knights of the Round Table to achieve still greater glory in *this* world."[39]

At the very end of the text, Malory tells us that the "Frensshe book maketh mencyon – and is auctorysed – that syr Bors, syr Ector, syr Blamour and syr Bleoberis wente into the Holy Lande ... there these four knyghtes dyd many bataylles upon the myscreantes, or Turkes. And there they dyed upon a Good Fryday for Goddes sake" (940.9-16 / CXXI.13). This turn toward religion at the conclusion of the *Morte* might seem jarring and out of keeping with the characters of these knights up until this moment, but when considered in the light of all the adventures that have gone before, this suggests more a *shift in* these particular characters, rather than a *switch to* a different character with the same name from an alternate text. Malory could easily have ended his *Morte Darthur* on Salisbury Plain – Mordred is dead and Arthur is dying, Excalibur has been returned to the bosom of the water, and Morgan le Fay, done with her performance of maleficence, arrives to help bring down the curtain on the Arthurian drama. But Malory does not end his narrative here – we follow Guenevere into the nunnery and Lancelot to the monastery. We witness the deaths of each which both appear to be "good" ends – both because these characters attempted to adhere to chivalric ideals *and* because, in the end, they have come to recognize that those ideals fall short. It is not that Malory has simply chosen sources at odds with one another in terms of characterization, but rather that in doing so he has created complex – rather than contradictory – characters; they have *evolved*, rather than behaved *inconsistently*. Thus, the turn to religious life by Guenevere, Lancelot and several other knights, and those knights' departure for the Holy Land to serve a religious rather than secular chivalric impulse, is arguably a

---

[37] The translation is from the version of the *Merlin* in the five-volume *Lancelot-Grail*, gen. ed. Lacy; the version of the *Suite* used by Malory most likely included the Merlin proper. Here, I.214.

[38] "Lancelot's apotheosis in 'The Healing of Sir Urry,' where, through his ability to heal the sick knight, he is once again confirmed as 'the best knight in the world,' extends the concept of chivalric prowess as far as Malory dares: secular achievements confer powers usually held to belong to the spiritual world"; Barber, "Chivalry and the *Morte Darthur*," 32.

[39] *Works*, ed. Vinaver, III, 1535.

logical development in the characterization of these figures. At the end of the text they have learned and they have changed.

## Kingship

It might seem odd to rank kingship last of the five key elements that make Malory's characterization unique; for without a doubt, the king is the foundation of the community, the figurehead that helps define that society. But in fact, the characterization of the king and the treatment of kingship in the *Morte Darthur* is seemingly the least significant of the five key themes I have discussed in this chapter. While Arthur is a central figure at the beginning and end of the narrative, to be sure, most of the action in the text takes place away from court. After he has asserted his absolute dominion over almost all of the known world, the court is where Malory's Arthur sits; he is the source from which his knights issue as his agents, and he is the point to which they return to relate their adventures. Arthur is an absent presence in the text; the foundational nature of his kingship so pervasive that it becomes almost invisible.[40] Indeed, what seems like passive "waiting at home" is actually a critical component of Malory's characterization of Arthur, because without an audience to whom they may tell their stories, the activities of the knightly agents would lose all meaning. To signify, adventures must occur twice: once in the having of them, and once in the telling of them.[41]

To be sure, the general arc of Arthur's career – fair unknown to powerful ruler to cuckolded husband to warrior who seeks vengeance on the battlefield – is much the same as it is in the Arthurian tradition before Malory. But once again, Arthur's character is significantly different from that of the source texts due to Malory's "doubled" method of alteration – the linking together of disparate texts plus the alteration of key speeches and episodes in the text. As far as the first sort of change goes, what is key here is both the sheer volume, and the arrangement, of episodes included in Malory's text. Of particular importance is Malory's decision to move the episode of the Roman War to the beginning, rather than

---

[40] Arthur's position here is best understood in terms of Ernst Kantorowicz's seminal argument in *The King's Two Bodies*, in which Kantorowicz argues that the king has a "body politic" and a "body natural": the latter must be safeguarded and protected so that the former may endure. With respect to the body politic, knights and other figures act as the "limbs" of that body, serving as agents and proxies for the king who must remain at home, protected and secure. See *The King's Two Bodies: A Study in Mediaeval Political Theology (with a new Introduction by Conrad Leyser and a Preface by William Chester Jordan)* (Princeton, 2016).

[41] Elizabeth Edwards has called attention to this perpetual movement between these two spaces, noting that "these two locations represent the centripetal force of the attraction of a centralized court (which we might call civilization) and the centrifugal force of adventure (which usually takes place in a wilderness)": "Place of Women," 38. Laurie Finke and Martin B. Shichtman have characterized Arthur's need to stay at home, at court, as necessary to the full functioning of the Arthurian community and its agents: "Arthur himself cannot be involved in the pursuit of value, but must be excluded ... Just as the image of gold, not gold itself, gives value to commodities in the economic sphere, so the image of the king, not necessarily the king himself gives value to his subjects": "No Pain, No Gain: Violence as Symbolic Capital in Malory's *Morte Darthur*," *Arthuriana* 8.2 (1998): 115–33, at 120.

the end of his text.[42] By doing this, and suppressing the account of the betrayal of Mordred while Arthur is on the continent until the end of the *Morte*, Malory gives us a much more glorious, vaunted, impressive Arthur than any to be found in his sources. And because Malory has likewise suppressed any explicit mention of the adultery of Lancelot and Guenevere until near the end of the text, Arthur remains a figure of noble honour and respect – rather than seeming a weak and passive figure – for an extended period of time.

Likewise, Malory's key decision to use the Prose *Tristan* for the middle portion of his narrative has an effect on the reader's interpretation of the character of Arthur. In King Mark, we see Arthur's "dark double": a ruler who has a greatest knight (Tristram) who is in love with the queen (Isolde).[43] As mentioned earlier, the parallels to the Arthur-Lancelot-Guenevere triangle are glaringly obvious. In the Prose *Tristan*, Mark's jealousy, cruelty and treachery serve primarily to create sympathy for the situation of Tristan and Isolde; when those same episodes and behaviours are included in the *Morte Darthur*, it is Arthur's character that is the prime beneficiary. In contrast to Mark, Arthur is restrained, and indeed, seems a much more pragmatic figure; when told by Aggravain and Mordred that Lancelot and Guenevere are engaged in an adulterous affair, Malory tells us that even though the king "had a deemyng" of the truth, he would rather ignore the entire situation, as Lancelot has been such a boon to his rule in almost every way.

In so many important ways, the court of King Mark of Cornwall is different from that of Arthur of Camelot; Mark is jealous, disloyal, conniving and immoral. By placing a version of the Prose *Tristan* in the midst of his text, Malory effectively sharpens and extends the depictions of the characters of King Mark and King Arthur; when compared alongside each other, the character of the former is blackened and that of the latter is improved. As E. D. Kennedy points out, Malory's decision to include the *Tristan* material and its negative depiction of King Mark "contributed markedly to Malory's greater independence in the use of sources by influencing his conception of Arthur in these final tales."[44] But as I discussed above, and as scholars from Wilson to Lumiansky to Rovang and beyond have noted, Arthur's rule is deeply affected by his kin relations and vice versa. The king's "body natural" and his "body politic" have lost the distinction from one another necessary for proper functioning. Arthur seemingly cannot refuse to participate in Gawain's quest for vengeance, nor does he seem to have any power to order his nephew to cease and desist from his unwavering, obsessive quest for retaliation against Lancelot. In Ernst Kantorowicz's theorization of the "king's two bodies," knights such as Gawain should serve as the "limbs" of the body, acting as agents of the body politic and fulfilling its needs. At the end of

---

[42] On this, see in particular Felicity Riddy, "Contextualizing *Le Morte Darthur*: Empire and Civil War," in *A Companion to Malory*, 55–73.

[43] In addition to those scholars already cited, important work on the "Tristram" section includes: Dhira Mahoney, "Malory's 'Tale of Sir Tristram': Source and Setting Reconsidered," in *Tristan and Isolde. A Casebook*, ed. Joan Tasker Grimbert (New York, 1995), 223–54; Larry D. Benson goes so far as to argue that Malory's version of this tale displays "a solidly coherent, even elegant thematic structure" in Larry D. Benson, *Malory's* Morte Darthur (Cambridge, MA, 1976), 109.

[44] E. D. Kennedy, "Malory's King Mark and King Arthur" in *King Arthur: A Casebook*, ed. Edward Donald Kennedy (Abingdon, UK, 1996), 139–172, at 165.

the *Morte*, the limbs are controlling the body of which they should be extensions, rather than the other way around. The ideals of "kingship" and "kinship" have blurred into one another.[45] When the text reaches its crisis point, Arthur's reaction becomes an over-reaction to his prior passivity and acceptance of Gawain's desire for vengeance – he slays and is slain by his nephew and son, and his sister, who so resisted the nurturing bonds of kinship until this point, takes him into her lap and addresses him not as a king, but as her brother. Kingship is an important component of *Le Morte Darthur*, buttressing all other ideals of the text; because it is inextricable from all else (everywhere, so as to be almost invisible) when knighthood, gender relations, kinship and religion become compromised, kingship and how it functions in terms of characterization is similarly affected.

## Conclusion

Characterization in Malory's *Morte Darthur* is effected through changes both large and small, both dramatic and subtle, none of which can be fully appreciated until the conclusion of the work. An analysis of key moments – and characters' actions within and beyond those episodes – demonstrates that in making certain, specific changes (and at times, choosing not to) Malory deploys a vision of the Arthurian community and its main players that is subtle, nuanced, interesting and complex. It is this dual manipulation on the part of Malory – the manipulation of both individual episodes *and* sources – that produces the unique characterization that marks his work as distinct from all that has come before it in the canon of Arthurian literature. In stark contrast to his sources, Malory's characters *evolve*, and as we follow their growth and development, we as readers find ourselves compelled to engage, to ponder, to feel and to care. *Le Morte Darthur* leaves a lasting impact on those who visit its pages, especially those who commit to the long journey from beginning to end; it is a masterpiece.

[45] See note 38, above.

# 8
# Malory and Gender
## AMY S. KAUFMAN

Of all the versions of the Arthurian story available to him in the fifteenth century, Malory seems drawn in particular to those from the pens of Cistercian monks, whose writings betray how much they fear women … In Malory most women are supernaturally malignant or false to their husbands. They bring about the downfall of good knights … A would-be murderer. A thief. A rapist. Would you trust what he tells you about women?[1]

The epigraph above is a fictionalized response from Morgan le Fay to her own portrait in Sir Thomas Malory's *Morte Darthur*. Despite its occurrence in a work of literature, this modern version of Morgan voices a premise not unlike many academic assessments of the *Morte Darthur*, which contend that Malory's own personal misogyny precludes any positive representation of women within his writing.[2] Whereas Chaucer is often touted as having mastered the complexities of the gender debate (for better or for worse), Malory, writing roughly one hundred years later, is often considered the dunce in the medieval schoolroom, blissfully ignorant of – yet simultaneously reveling in – the misogynistic stereotypes he creates and reinforces.

P. J. C. Field's widely accepted theory that the author of the *Morte Darthur* is Thomas Malory of Newbold Revel, a man accused of sexual assault along with a host of other crimes, has provided extensive opportunities for historical and biographical analysis. However, this theory also leaves the Arthurian community with the spectre of a writer whose misogyny casts a long shadow over his text.[3] Malory's biography puts his female characters in an unenviable, somewhat

---

[1] Fay Sampson, *Herself*, Book Five of *Morgan le Fay* (Canton, OH, 2006), 245–7.

[2] Accusations of Malory's sexism range wide. Studies that explicitly voice this accusation include Lisa Robeson, "Pawns, Predators, and Parasites: Teaching the Roles of Women in Arthurian Literature Courses," *Medieval Feminist Newsletter* 25 (1998): 32–6, at 34; along with several contributions to the influential collection *On Arthurian Women: Essays in Memory of Maureen Fries*, ed. Bonnie Wheeler and Fiona Tolhurst (Dallas, 2001), including: James Noble, "Gilding the Lily (Maid): Elaine of Astolat," 45–57, at 45; Elizabeth Sklar, "Malory's Other(ed) Elaine," 59–70, at 62; and Maud Burnett McInerney, "Malory's Lancelot and the Lady Huntress," 245–57, at 250. Cf. Kenneth Hodges, *Forging Chivalric Communities in Malory's Le Morte Darthur* (New York, 2005), at 40–1, who defends *Le Morte Darthur* against these accusations, and Siobhán Wyatt, *Women of Words in Le Morte Darthur* (New York, 2016).

[3] A full description of Field's case for Sir Thomas Malory, as well as a full description of the candidate's criminal record, can be found in P. J. C. Field, *The Life and Times of Sir Thomas Malory* (Cambridge, 1993). For a more concise version, see P. J. C. Field, "The

overdetermined position, their potential agency always already limited by the image of the man who shaped them. Whether Malory's women are deemed "The Good, The Bad, and The Ugly," or "Pawns, Predators, and Parasites," scholars often surrender any hint of a female character's agency to the idea of a woman-hating author and the totalizing weight of historical medieval misogyny.[4] Indeed, most Arthurian scholars are in ready agreement with Maud Burnett McInerney's claim that "Malory's Le Morte Darthur is clearly among the most misogynistic of the major texts of the Arthurian corpus."[5] Those who defend Malory from charges of misogyny do so by arguing that his primary concerns simply lie with the "masculine" and the "martial" rather than with women or their activities, privileging men and their emotions, their internal conflicts, and their social roles.[6]

However, there are good reasons to interrogate our assumptions about the masculinity, and the misogyny, of Malory's text. As readers of this *New Companion to Malory* have likely learned, acceptance of Field's candidate for the *Morte*'s authorship is not entirely universal.[7] Moreover, although Malory may have shaped his brand of Arthurian legend, he was not an omnipotent creator crafting characters from formless clay. Malory worked within a long, complex Arthurian tradition which was centuries old and spanned multiple languages and cultures. And several of the female characters he adapts have amplified roles – and amplified powers – such as the unique passages in which Nynyve protects Arthur and other knights, or defends Guinevere against a false accusation; or Malory's seeming invention of the unusually powerful Lyonet, who creates magical knights (and repairs them when they have been beheaded) in order to safeguard her sister's chastity.[8] Indeed, the *Morte Darthur*'s reputation as a "masculine" text is a surprising predicament for a work teeming with female characters who exhibit a great deal of complexity, along with a vast array of supernatural powers.

The problem with the critical consensus on Malory is not necessarily the assertion that patriarchal structures and modes of thought existed in the Middle

---

Malory Life-Records," in *A Companion to Malory*, ed. Elizabeth Archibald and A. S. G. Edwards (Cambridge, 1996), 115–30.

[4] See, for instance, Mary Etta Scott, "The Good, the Bad, and the Ugly: A Study of Malory's Women," *Mid-Hudson Language Studies* 5 (1982): 21–9; and Robeson, "Pawns," 32–6.

[5] McInerney, "Lady Huntress," 250.

[6] See, for instance, Marion Wynne Davies, *Women and Arthurian Literature: Seizing the Sword* (London, 1996), 61; Andrew Lynch, *Malory's Book of Arms: The Narrative of Combat in* Le Morte Darthur (Cambridge, 1997), 134–57; and Hodges, *Chivalric*, 41. Wyatt argues that Malory's women retain independence even as they largely exist to play positive roles in knightly development: *Women of Words*, 1–2.

[7] See Thomas H. Crofts and K. S. Whetter, "Writing the *Morte Darthur*: Author, Manuscript, and Modern Editions," in this volume.

[8] See Wyatt, *Women of Words*, 3, 15–106. As Hodges notes, "many of the works that begin by assuming Malory's misogyny then proceed to demonstrate that certain female characters are more complex than might be expected from that assumption," *Chivalric*, 31. Elsewhere in this volume, on Malory's adaptation of his sources, see Ralph Norris's chapter; and on Malory's shaping of characters, see Dorsey Armstrong's chapter. On the controversy around the possible creation of *Gareth*, in which Lyonet appears, see both Norris's and Cory James Rushton's chapters.

Ages, which they certainly did, or even the suggestion that misogyny leaks into Malory's text through the author's own biases, a claim about which we can be less certain. The problem is the assumption that such paradigms are totalizing. Taking for granted the effects of Malory's perceived misogyny closes the text in a significant way for women, both as characters and as readers, causing us to analyse his female characters based on the interests of male characters, male readers, and a male writer. Malory's women are rarely evaluated on their own terms: through a definition of agency, and perhaps even activism, that mirrors the means through which they shape the Arthurian world.

### *"Seduced by the Rhetoric of Chivalry"*

Arthurian Studies tends to be conservative in its adoption of theoretical approaches. Feminist theory did not arrive on the Arthurian scene until the 1980s, when scholars began the radical practice of focusing on female activity in medieval romance. At first, critics followed a structuralist approach, dividing women into categories or "types." In 1982, Mary Etta Scott argued that there were exactly three classes of women in Malory: the "good," the "bad," and the "ugly."[9] "Good" characters comment on knights' actions or can be rescued as damsels in distress; "bad" women, such as Guinevere, corrupt men; and the "uglies" are evil sorceresses who lurk in the forest to oppose men and/or to seduce them.[10] Scott's final word on Malory's women is grim: "the women are nearly all pawns in the game the knights are playing, pawns to Malory's great chess game" who "never really take on lives of their own. They are a bloodless lot."[11]

Scott set the standard for feminist analysis until 1992, when Maureen Fries, working from Georges Dumézil's male heroic types, created more nuanced categories for Arthurian female characters. Fries redefines the three types of Arthurian women as heroes, heroines and counter-heroes.[12] Heroines like Guinevere are beautiful and traditionally desirable, whereas Morgan le Fay is the classic "counter-hero" – a magical seductress who works in her own interest "instead of the males'."[13] Perhaps the most interesting of Fries's character types is the female hero: "a woman living with no permanent attachment to a man" who manipulates the world around her through magic and language.[14] However, Fries warns that the female hero "always act(s) only for knightly benefit," and that "her agency ... exists for patriarchal – male rather than female – purposes."[15]

The following decade saw the slow creep of poststructuralist thought into medieval criticism, which enabled feminist scholars to shift their interpretive lenses away from men and chivalry. In a series of essays in the early 1990s,

---

[9] Scott, "Ugly".
[10] Scott, "Ugly," 21.
[11] Scott, "Ugly," 28–9.
[12] Maureen Fries, "Female Heroes, Heroines, and Counter-Heroes: Images of Women in Arthurian Tradition," in *Popular Arthurian Traditions*, ed. Sally K. Slocum (Bowling Green, OH, 1992), 5–17.
[13] Fries, "Heroes," 15.
[14] Fries, "Heroes," 10–12.
[15] Fries, "Heroes," 15.

Geraldine Heng argued that critical readings of Arthurian romance which focus only on knighthood "have been coerced by the rhetoric of chivalry into an incautious complicity, one which identifies particular interests and practices as synonymous with most of the entire text."[16] Rather than prioritize male chivalric narrative, Heng's work identifies "a submerged second narrative" with a "feminine voice" in Malory, one that emerges into the surface text through "disruptive gestures and energies, intrusions and interruptions" – gestures that manifest primarily as magic and enchantment.[17] Arthurian women, Heng argues, have powers that extend far beyond the realm of chivalric interests: they "fix the entire realm of human possibility – good and evil, success and failure, protection or destruction."[18]

In the late 1990s, when feminist theory broadened into gender studies, masculinity reclaimed critical attention. In 1996, Elizabeth Edwards contributed "The Place of Women in the Morte D'Arthur" to the original Companion to Malory. For Edwards, the word "place" in her title serves two purposes: it marks both the role of women and the physical spaces that they occupy. Edwards argues that though landed women like Guinevere "uphold the 'homosocial' bonds between men who uphold the court" and therefore "either disrupt or reinforce masculine identity," unmarried damsels – particularly magical ones – are associated with "the forest or wilderness realm of quest and adventure," which itself has "a symbolically feminine quality" that represents "the mystery that is woman, from the male perspective."[19]

Edwards's reference to "homosocial bonds" between men marks the beginning of a trend in Malory studies that makes widespread use of the Levi-Strauss model of exchange – particularly Gayle Rubin's feminist employment of that model, which argues that the patriarchal "sex/gender system" relies on the exchange of women as gifts – the "traffic in women" – to solidify bonds between men.[20] Such readings, when applied to the Morte Darthur, argue that women serve as both a conduit for the bonds between men and as a gendered Other against which Malory's men fashion their masculine identities.[21] The most prominent and

---

[16] Geraldine Heng, "A Map of Her Desire: Reading the Feminism in Arthurian Romance," in *Perceiving Other Worlds*, ed. Edwin Thumboo and Thiru Kandiah (Singapore, 1991), 250–60, at 251. See also Heng, "Feminine Knots and the Other: Sir Gawain and the Green Knight," *PMLA* 106 (1991): 500–514; and Heng, "Enchanted Ground: The Feminine Subtext in Malory," in *Arthurian Women: A Casebook*, ed. Thelma S. Fenster (New York, 1996), 97–113.

[17] Heng, "Enchanted Ground," 97, 102–3.

[18] Heng, "Enchanted Ground," 98.

[19] Elizabeth Edwards, "The Place of Women in the Morte Darthur," in *Companion*, ed. Archibald and Edwards, 37–54, at 37–45.

[20] Gayle Rubin, "The Traffic in Women: Notes on the 'Political Economy' of Sex," in *Toward an Anthropology of Women*, ed. Rayna R. Reiter (New York, 1975), 157–210. These readings also evoke Eve Kosofsky Sedgwick's *Between Men: English Literature and Male Homosocial Desire* (New York, 1985), whose literary concept of the "homosocial triangle" also shows the ways in which male identity is reliant on the exchange of women.

[21] See, for instance, Davies, *Seizing the Sword*; Laurie Finke and Martin Shichtman, "No Pain, No Gain: Violence as Symbolic Capital in Malory's Morte d'Arthur," *Arthuriana* 8.2 (1998): 115–34; Sheila Fisher, "Women and Men in Late Medieval English Romance," in *The Cambridge Companion to Medieval Romance*, ed. Roberta L. Krueger (Cambridge, 2000), 150–64; Margaret duMais Svogun, *Reading Romance: Literacy, Psychology, and*

influential of these studies – and the first full-length book on gender in Malory – is Dorsey Armstrong's 2003 *Gender and the Chivalric Community in Malory's* Morte d'Arthur. Armstrong highlights the importance of the Pentecostal Oath taken by Arthur's knights at the end of Malory's chapter, "The Wedding of King Arthur," in constructing the masculinity of knighthood. The oath contains a condition known as the "ladies' clause," in which knights promise "allwayes to do ladyes, damesels, and jantilwomen and wydowes socour, strengthe hem in hir ryghtes, and never to enforce them, upon payne of dethe" (97.31–3 / C. III.15).[22] Armstrong demonstrates that a knight's obedience to this oath is a key component of Malory's chivalric vision and the foundation of male identity in the *Morte*, but also reveals that the masculine identity the oath constructs depends upon ladies being "helpless, needy, [and] rape-able."[23] Women in Malory's text thus serve as "the object through and against which a knight affirms his masculine identity."[24] Armstrong makes space for focus on female agency within this system, however, arguing that "feminine figures … are able to use the Pentecostal Oath and its understanding of the feminine as either a defense or a weapon against their socially constructed identities."[25] Later studies that employ the exchange model, such as Molly Martin's *Vision and Gender in Malory's* Morte Darthur, argue for the symbiotic nature of male and female gender performance by demonstrating that masculinity is constructed through public performances that are reliant on the female gaze.[26]

These rich studies of masculinity in *Le Morte Darthur* have been vital for understanding knighthood in Malory: its construction, its fragility and its interdependence, as well as the potential anxieties of the author and his medieval moment. But at the same time, although women play important roles in these analyses, the emphasis on men and their desires can reinforce the image of the *Morte Darthur* as a patriarchal, masculinist narrative. Recent scholarship on women in Malory's text thus tends towards redemptive studies of individual women, arguing for a particular female character's exceptional depth and power as a departure from Malory's patriarchal rules. For instance, Miriam Rheingold Fuller and Kristin Bovaird-Abbo focus on the damsel Lyonet in Malory's "Tale of Sir Gareth" to liberate her from accusations that she is solely constructed as an obstacle to Gareth or as a nagging scold.[27] Jill Hebert's recent book on Morgan le Fay argues that Malory's Morgan is an advisor and a testing figure who points out the flaws in Arthur and his knights.[28] Multiple studies of Malory's Guinevere trace her

---

*Malory's* Le Morte D'Arthur (New York, 2001), and Dorsey Armstrong, *Gender and the Chivalric Community in Malory's* Morte d'Arthur (Gainesville, FL, 2003).

[22] All references to the *Morte Darthur* are from Sir Thomas Malory, *Le Morte Darthur*, ed. P. J. C. Field, 2 vols. (Cambridge, 2013).

[23] Armstrong, *Gender*, 20.

[24] Armstrong, *Gender*, 36.

[25] Armstrong, *Gender*, 44.

[26] Molly Martin, *Vision and Gender in Malory's* Morte Darthur (Cambridge, 2010).

[27] Miriam Rheingold Fuller, "Method in Her Malice: A Reconsideration of Lynet in Malory's *Tale of Sir Gareth*," *Fifteenth Century Studies* 25 (1999): 253–67; Kristin Bovaird-Abbo, "Tough Talk or Tough Love: Lynet and the Construction of Feminine Identity in Thomas Malory's 'Tale of Sir Gareth,'" *Arthuriana* 24.2 (2014): 126–57.

[28] Jill M. Hebert, *Morgan le Fay, Shapeshifter* (New York, 2013).

textual redemption from adulteress to "trew lover."[29] Nynyve has received the most attention for her extraordinarily active role in Malory's text, but scholars have also found models of female empowerment in Elaine of Corbenic, Elaine of Astolat, and even Percival's sister.[30]

Some of the analyses that focus on individual women extend to groups of powerful female "types" or offer paths to expand our view of women in Malory overall: Sue Ellen Holbrook and Jill Hebert connect sorceresses like Nynyve and Morgan le Fay to divine female figures like the Roman goddess Diana, Celtic deities such as the Morrigan, and water and sovereignty goddesses from various traditions, locating a collective unconscious in Malory's text that speaks to female power.[31] Carolyne Larrington's painstakingly-researched and comprehensive study of magical Arthurian women, *King Arthur's Enchantresses: Morgan and Her Sisters in Arthurian Tradition*, broadens our understanding of magical women in Malory by connecting them to their long lineage in earlier romance and medieval history.[32] Other critics demonstrate how women are integrated into chivalry: Kenneth Hodges argues that some women in the *Morte Darthur*, like Guinevere, shape chivalry as judges while others, such as Nynyve and Morgan, act like knights and lords themselves and therefore "must be recognized as participating in knightly culture."[33] Roberta Davidson notes the extraordinary textual influence of certain of Malory's women and sees them as lenses for interpretation, particularly what may have been Malory's own personal interpretation of Arthurian events. My own work has focused on women such as Nynyve, Guinevere, and the anonymous women in Malory's "Alexander the Orphan" to interrogate the primacy of male interests by suggesting that female desire steers Malory's texts – rather than or in addition to male chivalric goals.[34]

---

[29] See, for instance, Fiona Tolhurst, "The Once and Future Queen: The Development of Guinevere from Geoffrey of Monmouth to Malory," *Bibliographical Bulletin of the International Arthurian Society* 50 (1998): 272–308; Beverly Kennedy, "Malory's Guinevere: A 'Trew Lover'," in *On Arthurian Women*, 11–34; Sarah J. Hill, "Recovering Malory's Gueneuere," in *Lancelot and Guinevere: A Casebook*, ed. Lori J. Walters (New York, 2002), 267–89; Sue Ellen Holbrook, "Guenevere: The Abbess of Amesbury and the Mark of Reparation," *Arthuriana* 20.1 (2010): 24–50; and Amy S. Kaufman, "Guenevere Burning," *Arthuriana* 20.1 (2010): 76–94.

[30] Studies on Nynyve include Sue Ellen Holbrook, "Nymue, the Chief Lady of the Lake, in Malory's *Le Morte Darthur*," *Speculum* 53.4 (1978): 761–77; Holbrook, "Elemental Goddesses: Nymue, the Chief Lady of the Lake, and Her Sisters," in *On Arthurian Women*, 71–88; Kenneth Hodges, "Swords and Sorceresses: The Chivalry of Malory's Nyneve," *Arthuriana* 12.2 (2002): 78–96; Hodges, *Chivalric*, 35–62; and Amy S. Kaufman, "The Law of the Lake: Malory's Sovereign Lady," *Arthuriana* 17.3 (2007): 56–73. See also Martin B. Shichtman, "Elaine and Guinevere: Gender and Historical Consciousness in the Middle Ages," in *New Images of Medieval Women: Essays Toward a Cultural Anthropology*, ed. Edelgard E. DuBruck (Lewiston, ME, 1989): 255–72; Sklar, "Malory's Other(ed) Elaine," 59–70; and Kathleen Coyne Kelly, "The Writable Lesbian and Lesbian Desire in Malory's *Morte Darthur*," *Exemplaria* 14.2 (2002): 239–70.

[31] See Holbrook, "Elemental Goddesses," and Hebert, *Morgan*.

[32] Carolyne Larrington, *King Arthur's Enchantresses: Morgan and Her Sisters in Arthurian Tradition* (London, 2006).

[33] Hodges, *Chivalric*, 36–41.

[34] Roberta Davidson, "Reading Like a Woman in Malory's *Morte Darthur*," *Arthuriana* 16.1 (2006): 21–33; Amy S. Kaufman, "Between Women: Desire and Its Object in Malory's 'Alexander the Orphan'," *Parergon* 24.1 (2007): 137–54; "Law of the Lake"; and "Guenevere Burning."

Finally, Siobhán Wyatt's book, *Women of Words in* Le Morte Darthur, emphasizes the importance of female speech in knightly development.[35]

Nevertheless, when today's scholar launches into an examination of women in Malory's *Morte Darthur*, she may find herself at something of an impasse when it comes to defining Malory's portrayal of women qualitatively. Are the *Morte's* women doomed to be limited by authorial misogyny and a narrative that central-izes masculinity and chivalry, or do exceptional women prove the rule, provid-ing models that could disrupt our notions of medieval Arthurian gender and power? Existing scholarship on masculinity, the role of women, and the impact of individual women in Malory creates a strong foundation for reevaluating female agency and activism in Malory's *Morte*, particularly since so much of it suggests that the *Morte Darthur* is a text that searches for meaning through its own composition, and that women help to construct that meaning. Yet female intervention, while widely recognized by critics, is not always construed as female power or agency. Perhaps, then, the definition of agency itself must be interrogated in order to discover new ways of thinking about gender and power in the *Morte Darthur*.

## Towards a New Model of the Subject

Power and agency today are often defined as limitless freedoms belonging to a subject who is unbound by social or historical limitations, capable of expressing her innermost identity to the fullest possible extent. However, recent discourse on the definition of the subject within feminist theory, posthuman thought and new materialism has launched a philosophical shift towards a more complex model of identifying agency. This redefinition, despite its apparent modernity, actually recalls modes of imagining agency in medieval philosophy, and could therefore provide an important framework for examining a text like the *Morte Darthur*.

Elizabeth Grosz argues, in *Time Travels: Feminism, Nature, Power*, that the notion of a sealed, individual, impermeable subject with complete "free" agency is and always has been a flattering illusion. The subject, she argues, is "structured not only by institutions and social networks but also by impersonal or pre-personal, subhuman, or inhuman forces, forces that may be construed as competing micro-agencies rather than as the conflict between singular, unified, self-knowing sub-jects or well-defined social groups."[36] This definition of the subject as permeable and adaptable – as opposed to being a sealed individual with a self-contained mind and soul – emphasizes human connectedness with the environment and with one another. The concept of a "connected" self not only helps us understand ourselves today, but it also gives us access to the self-perception of the medi-eval subject. Though the prevailing myth that "The Individual" was born with the Renaissance is grossly overstated, one might argue that the medieval world nurtured a notion of agency far more pragmatic than our own; so pragmatic,

---

[35] Wyatt, *Women of Words*.
[36] Elizabeth Grosz, *Time Travels: Feminism, Nature, Power* (Durham, NC, 2005), 6.

in fact, that contemporary philosophers find themselves paradoxically advancing backwards toward it. As Jane Bennett points out, medieval philosophers like Augustine did not view human agency as a "clear" or a "self-sufficient" power:

> Augustine, for example, linked moral agency to free will, but the human will is, as Augustine reveals in his *Confessions*, divided against itself after the Fall: the will wills even as another part of the will fights that willing. Moreover, willing agents can act freely only in support of evil: never are they able by themselves to enact the good, for that always requires the intervention of divine grace, a force beyond human control.[37]

What Grosz calls "competing microagencies" might be identified differently in the Middle Ages – medieval philosophy attributes microagency to divine grace, fate, heredity, Nature, astrological influences and the humors; contemporary philosophers prefer to call these forces evolution, positionality, biochemistry or environmental influences. But both medieval and modern materialist philosophers consider the human subject to be composite, made up of invisible and visible forces that flow into and through the self.[38] Human subjects are permeable to the elements of nature, the vicissitudes of social organization, and the indiscernible but reliable influences of metaphysical or scientific forces.

None of this means that agency is an illusion. "On the contrary," Grosz explains, humans "perhaps, have too much agency, too many agents and forces within them, to be construed as self-identical, free, untrammeled, capable of knowing or controlling themselves."[39] Drawing on the work of feminist legal scholar Drucilla Cornell, Grosz identifies agency as "the capacity to make the future diverge from the patterns and causes of the present rather than … an inherent quality of freedom or the availability of unconstrained possibilities."[40]

Using this theoretical redefinition of agency, we might ask ourselves: to what extent are Malory's women free, and realistic, subjects? Do they have the capacity to make the future "diverge from the patterns and causes of the present"? If they make the Arthurian future diverge in a way that is more favourable to women in their world, or that emphasizes the connectedness of human subjects and their environments, and of human subjects to one another, might we even consider their brand of intervention to be feminist activism?

Let us examine, briefly, one of the quests that leads to Arthur's knights swearing the Pentecostal Oath, the textual moment that has been so essential to foundational analyses of gender in the *Morte Darthur*. In "The Wedding of King Arthur," Arthur's celebratory marriage feast is interrupted by "a straunge and a mervailous adventure" that results in three knights embarking upon three different quests (81.16–17 / C III.4). Gawain's particular quest is to retrieve a white hart (which is often, not coincidentally, a symbol of young masculinity).[41] After a series of minor battles that take place during his pursuit of the animal, Gawain

---

[37] Jane Bennett, *Vibrant Matter: A Political Ecology of Things* (Durham, NC, 2010), 28.

[38] See also Bennett, *Vibrant Matter*, 11.

[39] Grosz, *Time Travels*, 6.

[40] Grosz, *Time Travels*, 72.

[41] See Anne Berthelot, "Merlin and the Ladies of the Lake," *Arthuriana* 10.1 (2000): 55–81, at 56 and Kaufman, "Law of the Lake," 58.

locates the hart and sends his greyhounds after it. His dogs chase the beautiful creature into a castle and slaughter it. When Gawain catches up to the carnage, he finds himself facing Sir Blamoure of the Maryse, who cries "A, my whyght herte, me repentis that thou arte dede, for my soveraigne lady gaff the to me, and evyll have I kepte the, and thy dethe shall be evyl bought and I lyve" (84.10–13 / C.III.6). Then Blamoure kills Gawain's hounds. In the combat that inevitably follows, Blamoure begs for mercy but Gawain refuses to provide it, moving instead to strike off his opponent's head. But just as Gawain goes in for the kill, a damsel appears from out of nowhere and throws herself over the knight to protect him, and Gawain "smote of hir hede by myssefortune" (84.32–3 / C.III.6).

Thanks to this misadventure, four knights come after Gawain for his crime. He is gravely wounded during the attack, but four ladies rescue him, proposing an alternative to execution: instead, Gawain must return to court and "bere the dede lady with hym on this maner: the hede of her was hanged aboute hys necke, and the hole body of hir before hym on hys horse mayne" (86.28–31 / C III.8). Gawain obeys and returns to his king and queen burdened by the woman's corpse, so the queen summons a court of ladies to render Gawain's final judgment: that "for ever whyle he lyved to be with all ladyes and to fyght for hir quarels; and ever that he sholde be curteyse, and never to refuse mercy to hym that askith mercy" (87.4–6 / C III.8). Many critics agree that the court of ladies in this episode integrates women into the chivalric code of the Round Table.[42] However, two recent readings of this quest call attention to the woman Gawain murders. Amanda Taylor uses the white hart episode to demonstrate how justice is defined and redefined throughout Malory, arguing that the women involved – both living and dead – "bear witness" to the fact that "women's access to justice is limited in a world where only trial by combat determines justice."[43] Erin Kissick also asserts that the same women "bear witness," this time to "flaws in the chivalric community, especially with regard to the status of women."[44] Both articles suggest, without using these exact words, that women in this tale alter Arthur's kingdom's possible futures: for Taylor, women change the justice system, and for Kissick, they change the definitions of masculinity and knighthood.[45]

Kissick and Taylor both use the term "bear witness" to define the dead woman's agency. Bearing witness is an essential aspect of consciousness-raising, the first step in feminist awareness. But the dead damsel does more than serve as a memorial; she creates a textual transformation – a feminist revision and retelling of Gawain's story. (A female character's struggle within Malory's text is, quite frequently, a struggle of competing narratives, as we can see from Lyonet's constant efforts to reshape Gareth, or Morgan le Fay's defiance of her brother's rule.) Gawain is proud of his actions at first: despite the fact that he has murdered Blamoure's beloved, he sends Blamoure to Arthur's court bearing the

---

[42] See Heng, "Enchanted Ground," 97–8; Armstrong, *Gender*, 39–40; and Hodges, *Chivalric*, 51.

[43] Amanda D. Taylor, "The Body of Law: Embodied Justice in Sir Thomas Malory's *Morte Darthur*," *Arthuriana* 25.3 (2015): 66–97, at 78-79.

[44] Erin Kissick, "Mirroring Masculinities: Transformative Corpses in Malory's *Morte Darthur*," *Arthurian Literature* XXXI (2014): 101–30, at 114.

[45] Taylor, "Body of Law," 84–5; Kissick, "Mirroring Masculinities," 108.

bodies of the dead greyhounds to make the conquered knight, and Gawain's dead dogs, a composite trophy that promotes Gawain's own interpretation of his quest: that Blamoure was "overcom by the knyght that wente in the queste of the whyght harte" (85.11–12 / C III.7). In fact, Gawain's faith in his own success is so impenetrable that he prepares to disarm himself and sleep in the castle where he murdered the damsel. It takes Gaheris, his brother, to remind Gawain that he might now "have many fooes in thys contrey" (85.23 / C III.7). The dead damsel transforms Gawain's narrative of conquest into a grisly murder by forcing his, and the reader's, gaze onto her body and its fate. The knights who attack Gawain at the sight of her body accuse him of both ignoring his responsibility to be merciful and slaying a woman: "Thou new made knyght, thou haste shamed thy knyghthode, for a knyght withoute mercy us dishonoured. Also thou haste slayne a fayre lady to thy grete shame unto the worldys ende, and doute the nat thou shalt have grete nede of mercy or thou departe frome us" (85.26–9 / C III.7). The sentence imposed on him by the four ladies and knights who "read" the message of the dead woman's body – a punishment that requires Gawain to drape her corpse over himself and his horse and wear the woman back to court – clearly both parallels his own "gift" to Arthur and revises Gawain's attempt to turn a barbaric act of violence into a courtly success. Gawain's judges burden him with a very physical signification that fixes their narrative of events and supplants his own. The four ladies also insist that he name and detail his crimes, both to them and to Arthur and Guinevere: he must explain "how he slew the lady, and how he wolde gyff no mercy unto the knyght, wherethorow the lady was slayne," further revising his flawed, short-sighted narrative of events with a version of the story that emphasizes the fundamental responsibility of a knight towards other living beings, especially towards women (86–87.35-1 / C III.8). It is likely no accident that Gawain's judgment is "balanced" – four knights and four ladies confirm his sentence, working together, balancing vengeance and mercy in the same chivalric distribution that the Pentecostal Oath sworn at the end of the episode will codify.

The dead woman's gloss of events continues to circumvent the narrative Gawain wants to impose on his actions, even after he has returned to court. When Gawain faces Arthur and Guinevere, marked by his crime and thus unable to steer the story of his quest in his preferred direction, Guinevere's court of ladies order him to swear upon the four Evangelists "that he sholde never be ayenste lady ne jantillwoman but if he fyght for a lady and hys adversary fyghtith for another" (87.8–9 / C III.8). The dead woman's body, the ultimate "object," shifts from readable object to speaking subject once it can be heard by the "queste of ladyes" set upon Gawain by the queen. The dead damsel "speaks" her interpretation of the event through her corpse, not only redefining Gawain's success as Gawain's failure, but also making a sociopolitical protest; she speaks of the violent disempowerment of women in the most literal sense and comments on an economy in which knights value greyhounds more than women and vengeance more than mercy. Her message unfolds through networks of women as each one "listens" to her corpse: as she speaks, ironically, of objectification – of the process by and through which women, and animals like the white hart and Gawain's dogs, are reduced to quest objects, trophies for knights.

The surviving female readers in this text continue to theorize based on the foundation the self-sacrificing woman has laid. The women who intervene in this episode are readers and interpreters of men, to be sure, but they also create new concepts, not just of chivalry or of masculinity, but of human relations and human identity – a redefinition of the value system that structures the Arthurian world. Their actions have the potential to rewrite preexisting legend, to "gloss" romance tradition in a different way, to create a new narrative of events. The readings performed by women in this Malorian episode thus represent *signifi-cation in process*. Whereas a preexisting ideology would have a predetermined outcome for Gawain's crime, what we see instead is an event and responses to that event that produce a new ideology. Women's readings within the text alter our reading of the text, creating a broader conceptual shift, and inscribing new concepts and new social values in language and law, and in the reader.

Perhaps no character in "The Wedding of King Arthur" enacts this conceptual shift better than Nynyve, the woman who launches the wedding quests – and, by extension, the Pentecostal Oath – in the first place.[46] Though Nynyve eventually earns the title "chyff lady of the laake" in Malory's text, she initially appears as an anonymous damsel during Arthur and Guinevere's wedding feast, chasing a pack of animals: first, a white hart races in chased by thirty black dogs and a white brachet who "boote hym by the buttocke and pulde oute a pece" (81.22–3 / C III.4). The brachet has nearly overcome the stag when her hunt is cut short by a knight who steals her away from court, allowing the stag to escape. Nynyve enters behind the animals and demands that the king send someone to retrieve her brachet.

King Arthur, however, does not exactly cover himself with glory during the events of his wedding feast. He refuses to aid Nynyve. Immediately after he rejects her demand for help, another knight appears from out of nowhere to carry Nynyve herself away. She cries out as she is carried off, and Malory notes that "whan she was gone the kyng was gladde, for she made such a noyse" (81.34–5 / C III.4). Once again, a woman's pleas for her own sovereignty and safety must struggle against a privileged male narrative just to be heard: Arthur dismisses both Nynyve's demands and her cry for help as mere "noyse."

Thanks to Merlin's insistence that ignoring a woman's kidnapping might lead to Arthur's "disworshyp," Nynyve herself becomes the object of a quest. She is to be rescued by Pellinor, a knight with dubious distinction among women; he fathered the knight Torre on a woman "half be force" and stole her greyhound (80.6–7 / C III.3). On Pellinor's path to retrieve Nynyve, he ignores a woman who cradles a dying knight in her arms and cries out to him for help. When he and Nynyve pass the same woman on their return to court, they find that the damsel has taken her own life with her dead lover's sword. Nynyve ensures that Pellinor, like Gawain, will bear the burden of a woman whose life he sacrificed for his own narrow vision of knighthood (96.10–14 / C III.14). When he expresses his regret because she was young and "passing fayre," Nynyve recommends that he bear her head with him back to the king (96.18 / C III.14). But it is Guinevere

---

[46] The following analysis of Nynyve's role in "The Wedding of King Arthur" is adapted from Kaufman, "Law of the Lake." See also Wyatt, *Women of Words*, 77 8.

who judges Pellinor "gretly to blame" for failing to save the dead damsel (97.1–2 / C III.15). As a final critique of Pellinor's treatment of women and his nefarious conduct both as a knight and a father, Merlin reveals that the dead damsel was, in fact, Pellinor's own daughter (97.8 / C III.15).

Like Gawain's victim, Pellinor's victim is also able to speak beyond death thanks to the efforts of women like Guinevere and Nynyve, who use their own agency to disrupt the patriarchal narrative of Arthur's court and insist on the inclusion of female voices. And in fact, Malory made several changes to his sources that conform to a pattern of fashioning roles for women as the judges of their male protectors and the enforcers of other women's autonomy. For instance, Gawain's sole arbitrator in the *Suite du Merlin* was one woman pleading with a group of vengeful knights; in Malory, this becomes a group of women who sit in formal judgment over Gawain with an equal number of men, indicating the importance of a balanced approach to justice. Guinevere has no voice in Pellinor's judgment in the *Suite du Merlin*, but she is the one who accuses him of failure in Malory's *Morte Darthur*. Thus, in Malory's version of events, the adventures Nynyve launches with her interruption of the wedding feast result in the appointment of women as the official adjudicators of knightly conduct. By the end of the tale, she and her quests have been the catalyst for significant changes in Arthur's kingdom.

Nynyve is often read as a passive victim or the object of a quest in "The Wedding of King Arthur," but given the tale's denouement, which remedies the callousness towards women displayed by Arthur and most of his knights, along with this episode's conformity to a pattern of staged abductions in Arthurian romance, it is also possible that she has orchestrated her own kidnapping in order to test the court.[47] Later in the text, Nynyve continues to remedy injustice in *Le Morte Darthur*: she traps Merlin under a rock forever when he sexually harasses her, she rescues King Arthur from Accolon when the king is deceived into fighting with a false version of his sword Excalibur, and she even absolves Guinevere of a false murder accusation. Her appearances in the text shift the narrative in marked ways, and they exemplify both agency and activism as Elizabeth Grosz defines them.

According to Grosz, agency arises in response to an event via the formation of concept: "Concepts are ways of dealing with events ... agency is our capacity to deal with events that we have not dealt with before. Agency is not freely expressing who I am. Agency is the capacity to act."[48] When agency is redefined as the capacity to act in response to an event, and if feminist activism is the use of that agency to create positive social change for women, then every woman in this episode is an activist, including the dead women. Perhaps especially the dead women: their heroic attempts to rescue their lovers will result in dramatic changes to the concepts of chivalry and knighthood in Arthur's court. The oath

---

[47] See Kaufman, "Law of the Lake," 70, n. 9. Hodges, *Forging*, 51, and Holbrook, "Nymue," in *Arthurian Women: A Casebook*, 178, both believe that Nynyve's first appearance is as the passive object of a quest, but that she eventually transcends this status in later episodes.

[48] Elizabeth Grosz, "The Future of Feminist Theory: Dreams for New Knowledges," Duke University Feminist Theory Workshop, 2007.

to protect women that Gawain, Pellinor and all of Arthur's knights must swear, the one that Armstrong's foundational analysis holds as central to chivalric self-definition in Malory, is the dead women's legacy.[49] If we were in a punning mood, we might call the oath the dead women's will.

*

As I hope I have demonstrated, the question feminist theorists might ask in order to advance conversations about women's agency in the *Morte Darthur* is not "What do women signify in Malory's text?" but "What do Malory's women *do*?" Using a definition of agency that involves transformative and interpretive power rather than unlimited freedom of self-definition, Malory's women can be identified as actors, agential forces who create concepts that redefine their world within individual and varied ranges of agency. This approach offers us a chance to negotiate the text openly, to become literary adventurers ourselves, rather than viewing Malory's dark forest through a visor of preconceptions that can obscure the richness of his Arthurian landscape.

Many scholars resist so-called "social" modes of criticism, believing that, with a medieval legend written by a man with a biography like Malory's, one must choose between loving the literature and pitting oneself against the text – that to examine oppression is to condemn the author, to lose the love and passion of the enamoured reader and become the enemy: a *theorist* (shudder) who antagonistically picks literature apart. "Gender" is thus often marginalized as a special interest category, ancillary to criticism in the way that, for so many years, Malory's women have been considered ancillary to his text. Indeed, this companion isolates "Gender" as a single chapter of analysis. And yet, it *must* do so, or it would be accused – and rightly so – of lacking female representation. This double-bind speaks to one of the fundamental challenges facing feminism today: Is it better to have representation, a chapter of one's own, or integration, a full consideration of women that infects all studies of Malory's text? How much, I wonder, will this analysis, or the many gender studies readings that came before it, permeate studies of Malory that are not tagged "gender," "women," or "feminist" in the library's electronic database?

There is plenty of room for scholars to practise generous readings, of Malory and of one another, that will help us transcend our strict critical categories. The *Morte Darthur* itself suggests that the reader who imposes a predetermined narrative rather than seeking a more complex view of events is – like Gawain, Pellinor and even Arthur himself in these early episodes – capable of grievous oversight. Future gender studies theorists might practise our own brand of activism by integrating ourselves into other approaches and changing their concepts of agency and identity, and by allowing new concepts to help us evolve past the limitations of our own work, so that we can move beyond binaries to investigate multiple potential genderings, and infinite models of the subject.

---

[49] Armstrong, *Gender*, 1

# 9
## Malory and Emotion
### ANDREW LYNCH

The *Morte Darthur* is deeply invested in the feelings of individuals – joy, grief, anger, envy, pity, love, shame, hope and fear – and in the shared feelings that negotiate and empower community. In this chapter, I consider the *Morte* in the light of recent critical approaches that treat emotions as simultaneously cognitive and embodied, and as manifested in narrative through interactions of speech, action, event, objects and spatial environment. I also examine the situation of emotions within Malorian structures of power, community and gender, and in relation to ideas of literary genre. I argue that the *Morte*'s emotions, although ideally prescriptive and enlisted for political ends, can also prove to be incompatible and excessive forces, complicating and contesting the behavioural regimes they are meant to uphold, and leading readers into strange and surprising territories of feeling.

The single surviving manuscript of the *Morte Darthur* locates the text's making within an emotionally charged situation. "Syr Thomas Malleorré" describes himself early in the book as "a knyght prisoner" (144.3; W fol. 70v), and in its conclusion he asks readers to pray for his release:

> I praye you all jentylmen and jantylwymmen that redeth this book of Arthur and his knyghts from the begynnyng to the endynge, praye for me whyle I am on lyve that God sende me good delyveraunce, and whan I am deed, I pray you all praye for my soule. (940.21–5 / C XXI.13)

Malory died about a year later. In this famous closing address, characteristically both pragmatic and heartfelt, the reader's forward course through the book from beginning to ending is matched with the course of Arthur's reign and with the inevitable course of the writer's life towards death. The voice is steady; perhaps only the threefold repetition of "pray," with the more intense "I pray you all praye," makes deep feeling overt. There is a confident resemblance drawn between earthly and heavenly communication: it is expected that readers (of the right kind) can address God in the same way that Malory addresses them, and will ask for his salvation just as they will for his freedom. Malory's words first establish, then break, confines of space and time to envisage a community living beyond the walls and after his death, constituted by their close attention to "this book," in his hands now but already imagined in theirs. No particular emotions are named or perhaps even aroused, but the combined effect is surely "moving," at once collective and intimate.

A contrast to Malory's emotional style in this passage can be seen in Caxton's prologue to his print of the *Morte Darthur* in 1485. Caxton presents Malory's book as a narrative catalogue of named specific emotions and emotional situations, and of moral commentary on them: "For herein may be seen noble shyvalre, curtosye, humanyte, frendlynesse, hardynesse, love, frendshyp, cowardyse, murdre, hate, vertue, and synne" (C Prologue).[1] This is not Malory's way of working, yet despite its static and abstract form, Caxton's list generates its own interest through juxtapositions and overlapping of categories – courage precedes love; cowardice is followed by murder and leads to hatred; to put courage in between friendliness and friendship emphasises its practical necessity in turning affective dispositions into the actions that reveal them as true. Despite the difference in discursive treatment, these details show Caxton responding to Malory's own emphases, picking up something of the *Morte Darthur's* basic tendency to treat emotion and action as inseparable, indeed to treat emotions *as* actions, in the manner of modern psychological studies.[2]

Put simply, the "motion" in "emotion" is crucial in Malory. As he represents them, emotions are physiological and psychological movements which are actions in themselves and which cause further actions. As such, they are a mainspring of narrative direction: emotions give the *Morte's* stories and characters their impetus and trajectory, and the stories' most significant outcomes are often the emotional effects that they produce. These can range from simple statements like "Than was the good man and Sir Launcelot more gladder than they were tofore" (715.33–4 / C XV.1), after a fiend relates an edifying story and saves the credit of a dead monk, to a spectacular public demonstration of pain at the last parting of Lancelot and Guinevere:

> And they departed; but there was never so harde an herted man but he wold have wepte to see the dolour that they made, for there was lamentacyon as they had be stungyn [pierced] with sperys, and many times they swouned. And the ladyes bar the quene to hir chambre.
>
> And Syr Launcelot awok, and went and took his hors, and rode al that day and al nyght in a forest, wepyng. (934.5–11 / C XXI.10)

The swooning testifies to the power of the lovers' great hearts to draw the "vital spirits" in the blood to themselves in times of sadness, causing bodily faintness.[3] Embodied and vocal gradations of emotional pain are registered, from the mute weeping of an imagined onlooker to the outcries of the lovers suffering physical agonies. Through these signs, the emotion that tends inwards to their hearts also spreads from the epicentre of heroic grief to embrace witnesses both within and beyond the narrative.

Lancelot and Guinevere's parting is a 'performative' event in various senses. Cognitive and volitional processes are deeply involved, as well as bodily feelings. The queen is formally renouncing her "'mysselyvyng'" – her love with Lancelot

---

[1] *Le Morte Darthur*, ed. P. J. C. Field, 2 vols. (Cambridge, 2013), II, 856.

[2] See W. Gerrod Parrott, "Feeling, Functions, and the Place of Negative Emotions in a Happy Life," in *The Positive Side of Negative Emotions*, ed. W. Gerrod Parrott (New York, 2014), 273–96.

[3] See Simo Knuuttila, *Emotions in Ancient and Medieval Philosophy* (Oxford, 2005), 215.

– before witnesses. Her refusal to give him the kiss he wants seals publicly her separation from him and their former life, in front of the other nuns whom she must rule as abbess. She requires her emotions to serve that political responsibility and her all-embracing aim to achieve salvation (933.9–10 / C XXI.9). In another way, her words and actions can be seen as an "emotional performance," or an "emotive," in the terms of William Reddy. That is, her performance – the term does not imply "insincerity" but an attempt to "do" something with emotions – is "an external means of influencing activated thought material that often enhances the effectiveness of internal strategies of mental control." Guinevere's emotional words and actions are "inputs" to herself as well as outputs. "Emotives can thus be described as tools for arriving at desired states."[4] Guinevere is trying to make herself feel as she knows she should, by acting in a way that empowers the desired feeling. She desires to have the right desire. Her emotional performance rejecting one desire and choosing the other comes "hartely" from her, even though it respects a cognitive preference.

Such a process was familiar to medieval readers, particularly to nuns and lay people, from the self-persuasive vernacular "emotional scripts" available to them in forms like religious lyrics and affective meditations. When Guinevere says that "thorow oure love that we have loved togydir is my moste noble lorde slayne," she is adapting a common self-accusation of guilt for the death of Christ in such scripts, and she continues seamlessly with a reference to her associated hope of salvation "thorow Goddis grace and thorow his Passion of Hys woundis wyde" (932.34–5 / C XXI.9). For all that, the emotional dynamics of this scene are necessarily much more complex in their extended narrative form, with its own long history, than in the self-addressed present tense of a pure "emotion script."[5] Guinevere's desire for Lancelot is equally real; the intense pain she feels at their separation, drawn from their shared past, tells us that. The force of "oure love that we have loved togydir" is inseparable from her need to part from Lancelot; she begs him never to see her face again "for all the love that ever was betwyxt us" (933.2–6 / C XXI.9). As Reddy remarks, the effects of "emotives" are "unpredictable; they represent an attempt at translation that is always inadequate."[6] Another observation is that although Guinevere speaks of "oure love," her feelings differ from Lancelot's. An audience engaging affectively with the scene must also take account of her continuing distrust of his feelings: "I may never beleve thee … but that thou wylt turne to the worlde agayne" (933.21–2 / C XXI.9). An element of critical distance is permitted within the all-embracing effect of sympathy.

In a way that might clash with some modern sensibilities, the public and performative nature of this scene, played out amidst a crowd of the queen's ladies, does nothing to reduce its emotional intimacy – Lancelot and the queen fall into the pattern of several private conversations they have had before – or its

---

[4] William M. Reddy, *The Navigation of Feeling, A Framework for the History of Emotions* (Cambridge, 2001), 322.

[5] See Sarah McNamer, *Affective Meditation and the Invention of Medieval Compassion* (Philadelphia, 2010), 12–13.

[6] Reddy, *The Navigation of Feeling*, 322.

matter-of-factness.[7] For instance, Malory takes full bodily account of the swoons – the queen must be carried away; Lancelot has to wake up, walk to his horse and ride off. The "forest" where he rides weeping for so long externalises his separateness in spatial and temporal terms, but the wider spatial framing of the episode is not purely physical, all the same, but human-centred, based on awareness of physical, personal and cultural surroundings. It starts when Guinevere is "ware of Sir Launcelot as he walked in the cloyster" and ends when he "is ware of an ermytage and a chappel stode betwyxte two clyffes, and then he herde a lyttel belle rynge to mass." In the way of episodic romance, the new location is linked "by adventure" to the previous one and continues an emotional trajectory. Lancelot will become a monk at this place and fulfil the promise he has just made to "take me to penaunce and praye whyle my lyf lasteth" (933.34–5 / C XXI.9). That it should be Sir Bedivere's hermitage where Arthur is buried brings another cycle of feeling closer to its completion.

The parting of Lancelot and Guinevere exemplifies many of the separate elements that give the *Morte Darthur* its emotional profile. It also shows how these elements work together to create emotionally complex narratives which articulate more in effect than the text's relatively limited vocabulary of emotion terms would seem to promise. The text does not describe emotion so much as "make" emotion in the way that Malory's characters "make" sorrow at parting or "make" joy at reunions (e.g. 790.7–8 / C XXI.2): through repertoires of speech, posture and gesture; through continuing narrative impulses of memory and desire; and through entanglements with other people, objects and environments that create an intricate interconnectedness of feeling.

Corinne Saunders has noted how Malory's "emotive terms are frequently accompanied with concisely stated but telling physical effects ... Cognition and affect merge."[8] To use a phrase from Monique Scheer, emotion in Malory can be called the product of "embodied cultural practices," so long as we realise that in the world of the *Morte Darthur* embodiment and cognition are very closely related through action: Guinevere's phrase, "oure love that we have loved togydir," where consciousness of the emotions of love is inseparable from the actions of loving, fits well with Scheer's description: "According to the embodied account of experience, there are no thoughts and feelings that are not manifested in bodily processes, actions, in spoken or written words, or supported by material objects. It is their materiality that makes them available to the senses and to memory."[9]

In Malory's usage, "feeling" is a live metaphor for "understanding" and asserts an embodied form of "knowledge." Gawain writes to Lancelot on his

---

[7] For a comparative study, see Anne Baden-Daintree, "Kingship and the Intimacy of Grief in the Alliterative *Morte Arthure*," in *Emotions in Medieval Arthurian Literature: Mind, Body Voice*, ed. Frank Brandsma, Carolyne Larrington and Corinne Saunders (Cambridge, 2015), 87–104, at 87: "King Arthur exists in a liminal space where the emotions which are normally reserved for private situations can occur in a public setting, while still retaining a high degree of intimacy."

[8] Corinne Saunders, "Mind, Body and Affect in English Arthurian Romance," in *Emotions in Medieval Arthurian Literature*, 31–46, at 43.

[9] Monique Scheer, "Are Emotions a Kind of Practice (and Is that what Makes Them Have a History)? A Bourdieuian Approach to Understanding Emotion," *History and Theory* 51, 2 (2012): 193–230, at 219.

deathbed: "I fele mysself that I muste nedis be dede by the owre of noone" (918.9–10 / C XXI.2). Lancelot's response is "I fele by thys dolefull lettir that my lorde Sir Gawayne sente me, on whose soule Jesu have mercy, that my lorde Arthur ys full harde bestad" (930.13–15 / C XXI.8). The letter itself, "wrytten with myne owne honde and subscrybed with parte of my harte blood" (919.15–17 / C XXI.2), is a striking instance of the mixture of bodily, emotional and cognitive information centred in the cultural practice, and the technology, of writing and reading, as evidenced in the *Morte* itself.

I have been speaking so far about strongly "situated" emotional occurrences in Malory, in which characters and readers "know" what they feel and "feel" it (bodily and cognitively) within contexts of which they are deeply aware, so that emotions generally seem both informative and intelligible, and apparently bear a meaningful relation to the actions in which they arise and which they subsequently cause. For instance, when Lancelot cannot resume his relations with Guinevere, he becomes a monk: "And ever for you I caste me specially to pray" (933.18–19 / C XXI.9). The move makes emotional "sense." Furthermore, these emotions, however extreme, are "performed" (carried out) within familiar institutional settings and sustained by known cultural practices. Barbara Rosenwein's well-known notion of an "emotional community" in its broad version "tied together by fundamental assumptions, values, goals, feeling rules, and accepted modes of expression" fits Malory fairly well, especially as she allows for smaller "subordinate emotional communities partaking in the larger one and revealing its possibilities and its limitations": one thinks of the *Morte*'s kin groups, friendship groups, local affinities, hereditary enemies and people in love.[10] It is also quite easy to think of Malory's Arthurian world as what Reddy calls an "emotional regime," defined as a "set of normative emotions and the official rituals, practices and emotives that express and inculcate them"; in his view these form "a necessary underpinning of any stable political regime."[11] As embodied cultural experiences, emotions can readily be shared – *anyone* would have wept to see the parting of Guinevere and Lancelot. That collectivity of emotion is a vital factor in the establishment of Arthur's reign: "*all* men of worship said it was myrry to be under such a chyfftayne that wolde putte his person in adventure as other poure knyghtis ded" (45.10–12 / C I.25). Malory celebrates this emotional unanimity through the great plenary court scenes that initiate and conclude adventures, and through many public assertions that good people always feel the same way about things: "ever a worshypfull man woll be lothe to se a worshypfull man shamed" (840.5–6 / C 18.24). A main point is that to Malory emotions are spontaneous. So even though they are produced in accord with the feeling rules of his class and period, and allied to literary conventions of speech and gesture, they are presented as like autonomous "affects," which can "range from bodily, cerebral or endocrinal activity (a blush, a glance, a tear,

---

[10] Barbara H. Rosenwein, *Emotional Communities in the Early Middle Ages* (Ithaca, NY, 2006), 24.

[11] Reddy, *The Navigation of Feeling*, 129. For a helpful brief account, see Tanya M. Colwell, "Emotives and Emotional Regimes," in *Early Modern Emotions. An Introduction*, ed. Susan Broomhall (London, 2016), 7–10.

a quickening of mental activity or a heartrate) to broader unconscious desires, or the network of forces that drive, motivate and connect minds and bodies with other minds and bodies in the social world."[12] Malory expects outward markers and utterances of feeling, which he calls "cheer," to tell the truth of inner sensations and desires. Where this does not apply, in cases of "prevy [hidden] hate" (870.13 / C XX.1) or "semble chere" (431.35 / C IX.39) – a false appearance of friendship – we are often dealing with traitors like Mordred and Mark. A dangerous discrepancy between inner feelings and outer appearance also characterises Lancelot's relative failure on the Grail Quest, and his situation on returning to court: "in his prevy thoughtis and in hys myndis so sette inwardly to the quene as he was in semynge outewarde to God" (790.13–14 / C XVIII.1).

All these features show a tendency in the *Morte* to be prescriptive about emotions in political and moral terms, but it is important to remember that Malorian emotions are also distinguished by particular personal histories and attachments, especially in the major characters, those whose feelings matter most in the story. For them, as Robert C. Solomon writes, "emotions are subjective engagements in the world," and essentially relational in nature.[13] So, we can note, the recent conflict between Lancelot and Gawain, in the context of both men's loyalty to Arthur, makes the emotional force of their last exchange different for each of them: Gawain is eager to clear his enmity with Lancelot before he dies, as part of his preparation for judgement, and to reconnect himself with Lancelot in chivalric fellowship. Lancelot, although moved and concerned for Gawain's soul, focusses more on Arthur's immediate predicament because Arthur means more to him than Gawain. Lancelot is always closely attuned to what *he* feels in a way that rules, or even blinds, his responses to the feelings of others. His well-meant offer to the Maid of Ascolat, desperately in love with him, of a dowry to marry someone else is a case in point (826.4–11 / C XVIII.19).

Malorian emotions in these instances can also be considered as what Martha Nussbaum calls "judgments of value," but I wish to emphasise Nussbaum's insistence that these are "judgments in which we acknowledge our neediness and incompleteness before those elements that we do not fully control."[14] While there is a strong sense of emotional evaluation in Malory, and of where emotional loyalties ought to be placed, the capacity to feel deeply always leaves his subjects vulnerable to sudden change. At times, the "adventures" of Malory's desiring romance figures create such an intense volatility in emotional experience that an intelligible connection between emotions and courses of action, and even Nussbaum's core dictum that "emotions are *about* something: they have an object," can become obscured. This is evident, for example, when the intensity of an emotional event causes a departure from reason and projects the subject into an exilic period of madness, beyond the normal emotional collective.

---

[12] Stephanie Trigg, "Affect Theory," in *Early Modern Emotions*, 11.

[13] Robert C. Solomon, "Emotions, Thoughts and Feelings. Emotions as Engagements with the World," in *Thinking about Feeling: Contemporary Philosophers on Emotions*, ed. Robert C. Solomon (Oxford, 2004), 77.

[14] Martha Nussbaum, "Emotions as Judgments of Value and Importance," in *Thinking about Feeling*, 19

The narrative force of such incidents depends directly on Malory's establishment of what can be called the *emotional space* of adventure. For the purpose of analysis, I am adapting Michel de Certeau's simple distinction between "place" and "space" in which place is "the order according to which elements are distributed in relationships of co-existence," but "[a] space exists when one takes into consideration vectors of direction, velocities, and time variables. Thus space is composed of intersections of mobile elements ... Space is a practised place."[15] In de Certeau's view, changes in time, direction and physical mobility are variables that turn "place" into "space." In Malory, I suggest, we find that certain environments not only externalise emotional states, but are transformed into emotional spaces through the emotional labour undertaken within them.[16] Malory's construction of specific emotional spaces – such as the exilic and marginal space of madness – has a potential to disturb normal judgements of value and provide new understandings of the emotional norms depicted in the narrative. Episodes in which an extreme emotional state marginalises the protagonist physically and socially can potentially be read as both supportive and critical of the social and ideological centres from which the hero is temporarily ejected.

We see a main instance of this process in Malory's account of the two-year madness of Sir Lancelot. Typically of Malory, the "wilderness" of chivalric madness is scarcely present as a fixed geographical location or a landscape. Rather, exilic space is realised through emotional experience expressed through a set of embodied actions that run directly counter to knightly norms. These establish an "emotional geography" in which the "first and foremost, most immediate and intimately *felt* geography is the body, the site of emotional experience and expression *par excellence*."[17] The episode's emotional "image-repertoire" of love-exile, to use Roland Barthes's term,[18] includes the following:[19]

  i. social and physical isolation
 ii. a wilderness setting – "forest"
iii. emotional markers: swooning; complaint; fleeing company
 iv. loss of outward signifiers of identity – horse, armour and outer clothing, hence "naked"
  v. lack of direction: no "path"; irregular and frantic movements
 vi. little or poor food, or without cooked food or wine
vii. changed appearance – dirt, scars, leanness
viii. not knowing own name and identity; not known by others
 ix. social degradation: declassed; mocked; physically abused

---

[15] Michel de Certeau, *The Practice of Everyday Life*, trans. Stephen Rendall (Berkeley, CA, 1984), 117.

[16] See Scheer, "Are Emotions a Kind of Practice?", 193.

[17] Joyce Davidson and Christine Milligan, "Embodying Emotion Sensing Space: Introducing Emotional Geographies," *Social and Cultural Geography* 5.4 (2004): 523–32, at 523.

[18] Roland Barthes, *A Lover's Discourse. Fragments*, trans. Richard Howard (New York, 1978).

[19] For a recent study relating Tristan and Lancelot's love madness episodes to the medieval "wild man" tradition and Bakhtinian carnival, see Laura Clark, "There and Back Again: A Malorian Wild Man's Tale," *Arthuriana* 27.2 (2017): 55–71.

When Lancelot is banished from Guinevere's sight "forever," the narrative steadily works through the features I have outlined: Lancelot swoons; he jumps out
the window and runs off "he knew nat whothir" (633.22 / C XI.8); he is "wylde
woode" ("uncontrollably mad") – the phrase aurally connects madness and its
externalisation in the forest environment; he makes "moste pyteuous gronys"
(634.11 / C XI.9); his face and body are torn with thorns so that he is scarcely recognisable and he lives outside his known identity for two years; he "suffird and
endured many sharpe showres" (643.30–1 / C XII.1), "care and woo," "payne,"
"colde hungir and thyrste" (636.25–6 / C XI.10). "Suffer" and "endure" operate
in two senses – Lancelot is caused pain by them, and is able to bear them. The
narrative shows him running aimlessly from place to place, living on fruit and
water, nearly naked, and playing violent pranks on high and low, as if to parody
his former vassalage; in a final traducement of his knightly status, he falls to the
lowest social level – pelted with clods of earth and beaten by mobs, lying on
straw with his food thrown to him (648.9–26 / C XII.3).

Lancelot suffers all this for a love which is causing deep problems to the
Arthurian regime, and will eventually help end it. Nevertheless, all throughout
this period of aberration and anonymity, his centrality to the Arthurian ethos
is preserved through the emotional reactions of others, whether to his known
absence or his anonymous physical presence: at home, his kinship group lament
losing "his noblenes and curtesy, wyth hys beauté and hys jantylnes" (635.18–19
/ C XI.9); in his exile many others, including strangers, deeply pity his sufferings.
He communicates his noble nature even to those he harms: as a "man of grete
worshyp" who has gone mad "for som hartely sorow" – "Jesu defende that ...
[he] sholde be in such a plyght" (645.6–15 / C XII.1); "the goodlyest man that ever
I sawe" (647.32–3 / C XII.3). Even after starvation and violence at the hands of a
city mob, Lancelot's rescuers think "they never sawe so goodly a man" (648.19–20
/ C XII.4). When "arayed lyke a knyghte," even out of his wits he is considered
"the semelyeste man in all the courte, and none so well made" (648.34–5 / C
XII.4). Finally, Elayne finds him in her father's garden as "a goodly man by the
welle slepynge," and falls "on wepynge so hartely that she sanke evyn to the
erthe" (649.5–12 / C XII.4). The Holy Grail itself, employed to bring him back to
knowledge of his identity, witnesses his recovery.

By such emphases, Malory makes Lancelot's time on the margins, physically and socially, a focus for intense emotional support of the central values
he embodies as both a missing premier knight and an unknown "goodly man."
The Arthurian centre is celebrated and its fractures temporarily mended by the
collective sorrow at Lancelot's absence and the collective hope to find him and
help him recover. Elayne and Guinevere, fierce rivals for his love, are joined in
grief: "'Alas!' seyde fayre Elayne, and 'Alas!' seyde the quene, 'for now I wote
well that we have loste hym for ever!'" (634.12–14 / C XI.9). Members of the deadly
feuding families of King Lot and King Pellinore – Gawain along with Perceval
and Agglovale – join with Lancelot's kin in the search.

The episode as a whole occasions and permits a unifying celebration of love,
a oneness of emotional purpose in the Round Table fellowship, and a meld-
ing of the sacred agenda of the Holy Grail with mainstream Arthurian values
that become all but impossible to find again as the *Morte Darthur* continues

– Lancelot's return to the court reconstitutes the same problems that have driven him from it.[20] Arthur does not know but "all Sir Launcelottys kynnesmen knew for whom he wente oute of hys mynde" (657.22–3 / C XII.9). In the long term no one "learns" anything, but Lancelot's adventures on the social and environmental margins of Arthur's world, though a shame to him in ordinary terms, create for a time a distinct emotional space, even a redemptive *political* space, one might say, where his spectacular sufferings and the virtue visible in his "goodly" body provide a unifying focus for onlookers within and outside the story, giving a sense of the holy both to his sorrows and to the pity they arouse.

Another similar episode of love madness in Malory occurs to Sir Tristram: he flees Mark's court after believing Isoud has been unfaithful with his brother-in-law Kehedyns, and fearing that Mark has learned of his presence. Many signs of deep emotional disturbance set up his entry into marginal space: a swoon that lasts three days and nights; being "allmoste oute of hys mynde" – poised on another kind of margin; avoidance of human company – he keeps "escaping" from those who wish to help; sorrowful complaint: "the grettist dole that ever erthely creature made"; refusing to eat and drink (388–9 / C IX.18). All these culminate in an aggressive movement away from knighthood that projects him into new territory without his former social coordinates, and without path or direction: "Than uppon a nyght he put hys horse frome hym and unlaced hys armour, and so he yeode [walked] unto the wyldirnes and braste [broke] downe the treys and bowis" (389.33–5 / C IX.18). Eventually, naked and emaciated, he falls into fellowship with herdsmen and shepherds who feed him but treat him as a fool and beat him when he plays up. He lives six months in this way "and wolde never com in towne" (390.25 / C IX.19).

As with Lancelot's case, Malory does not offer extensive descriptions of the natural environment. The "wilderness" of Tristram's madness is a "wildness" created by a set of bodily and social practices that arise from and articulate intense emotions of anger and sorrow. These emotions put Tristram into a space of aberrance, a world turned upside down, in which everything happens that should not. Within this space, he becomes a clown figure, with his hair docked like a fool's, who souses Arthur's fool, Sir Dagonet, and his squires in a well, while an audience of shepherds laughs (390.14–23 / C IX.19). All this is a degradation of Tristram's knightly identity, but it may also work as a parodic version of the randomly competitive and theatrical life he has been leading as a knight errant and in tournament, a "naked" burlesque performance of chivalric prowess as irregular absurdity. Tristram's time-out in the wilderness can be considered a moratorium on business-as-usual, an uninhibited emotional protest against the impossibly unsettled conditions of his "normal" narrative existence – present/ absent at Mark's court; loyal/not loyal to Mark; married/not married to Isoud Blanches Mayns of Brittany; a vagrant between Cornwall, Brittany and Logres.

As in Lancelot's case, there is also a counter-process of ideological re-centring in the episode of Tristram's madness. It is performed by the emotional labour, again especially the "pity," of those who seek him out. They work as a team to repair the damage to chivalry and love which the narrative of his absence and

---

[20] See Clark, "There and Back Again," 55, 71.

aberrations keeps registering. Tristan's rival for Isoud, Sir Palomides, and Sir Kehedyns, the man he has accused of betraying him with Isoud, join forces to seek him out for the love of her:

> "Alas!," seyde sir Palomydes, "hit ys grete pité that ever so noble a knyght sholde be so myscheved for the love of a lady." (390.29–30 / C IX.19)
>
> ....
>
> and they felyshyppyd togydirs, and aythir complayned to other of there hote love that they lovd La Beall Isode.
>
> "Now lat us ... seke sir Trystramys that lovyth her as well as we, and let us preve whether we may recover hym." (391.34–392.3 / C IX.19)

Tristram can be "recovered," in the sense of being brought back to himself and to elite society. All the same, circumstanced as he is, Tristram's return can do nothing to fix his state, and provides no sense of reunion. Recalled to sanity, his first words to Isoud are "A madame! ... go frome me, for much angur and daunger have I assayed for youre love" (395. 29–30 / C IX.21). Having gone mad on leaving Mark's court, he first re-asserts his name in Mark's presence, and Mark's comment is "A, ... me repentis of youre recoverynge" (396. 5 / C IX.21). ("A" and "Alas" are regular signs of intense emotion in Malory's dialogue). He is immediately exiled from Cornwall, which is itself a margin in this Arthurian world. There is no centre to which Tristram can return from the wilderness, because the wilderness signifies the underlying emotional conditions – anger, sorrow and frustration – of a "normal" life in which nothing is central and steadily directed. His six-months' stay on the margin shows that the emotional centre of his life, his love for Isoud, holds no real place in the world he inhabits as a noble knight; if he were to put Isoud permanently at the centre of his emotional life, his existence as a noble knight would be impossible. Tristram finds his natural environment "in adventure," in chivalric fellowship on the road or on the tournament circuit. His sufferings in the exile of madness embody the intolerable emotional situation of his ordinary life, an unstable compound of desire, anger and sorrow, tending to unceasing activity and change.

Comparing Lancelot's and Tristram's madness stories, one can see multiple and overlapping emotional outcomes resulting from the knight's time on the outside: as parodic displays of aggression against the central norms of knightly life and love; a reaffirmation, through collective pity, of their value; and a celebration of the suffering knightly body as a supreme icon in a medium where collective emotional intensity itself becomes the central value. A structural paradox in the Malorian narrative of emotion becomes apparent here. The deepest emotions of love and grief are only realisable outside normal political life, away from home, yet the narrative still desires the knight's return from exile, to complete the series departure/adventures/return, even when this move will destroy the emotional unity established by his absence. Ideally, the knight's return should close off the sequence of events by bringing him home to the place where he is known, and which the record of his time away then sustains ideologically through its translation into cultural memory and collective identity formation. This "return to identity" is conventionally meant to be "a release from the tyranny of ... [the knight's] collisions with external circumstances,"[21] as we see happen in good "adventures" like Malory's "Noble Tale of Sir Lancelot" and the book of Sir Gareth. Other parts of the *Morte*, especially the very long Tristram section, indulge both tendencies, seeming to want an impossible fusion of extreme emotional adventure and socio-political stability. Within this narrative, intense emotional labour can reverse normal conditions and transform exile into ideological centrality, but the process also involves a tacit admission that deep extremes of emotion, however powerful in the forest, cannot be tolerated for long in the everyday world.

We see also in these two stories, and in many others, the role of gender differ-ence in the emotional structure and expressive resources of the narrative. Men (knights) have more flexible and wide-ranging access to emotional participa-tion in events. Contested love for a woman turns out to be a homosocial bond as much as a source of enmity, as we see with Palomides and Kehydyns, and later with Palomides and Tristram. True, this is not only a masculinist capacity: Guinevere and Elayne of Corbenic can also briefly share their love for Lancelot, and Lavayne, the brother of Elayne of Ascolat, loves Lancelot much in the same way she does: "Sir, what sholde I do ... but folow you, but if ye dryve me frome you?" (826.21–2 / C XVIII.19). Malory has on the whole a very positive view of love as a natural and God-given human faculty, even if it brings trouble. Elayne of Ascolat, speaking as a young maiden in secular life, confidently claims: "I do none offence, though I love an erthely man, unto God, for He fourmed me thereto, and al maner of good love commyth of God" (827.22–4 / C XVIII.19). But gender difference strikes the emotional life most keenly here: Lavayne's desire to be with Lancelot can apparently be fulfilled through close chivalric fellowship; hers, to be either Lancelot's wife or his lover, cannot.

"Fellowship," both in practical and cognitive terms, fulfils very close emo-tional needs for men in Malory, as we see in the "great joy" of their reunions, their deep appreciation of others' prowess, and their laments for deaths and woundings: "hit sleyth myne harte to hyre this tale" says Tristram when he hears of Lamorak's death. (554.17–18 / C X.59). Yet although Malory, possibly citing Chaucer's *Franklin's Tale*, shows Arthur and Lancelot agreeing that "love ys fre in hymselffe, and never woll be bonde" (830.11–16 / C XVIII.20), it seems his great lovers do feel "bound" by their love of women, however willingly, and can regard that as a detraction. Tristram, as noted above, laments the trouble that loving Isoud has caused him. Lancelot tells Guinevere that he would have had as much success on the Grail Quest as Galahad, Bors and Perceval "if that I had nat had my prevy thoughtis to returne to youre love [my love of you] agayne as I do" (791.10–11 / C XVIII.1). The text gives no comparable sense of what she has lost. Even at their parting, he makes much the same claim: "had not youre love [my love for you] bene ... I had passed all the knyghtes that ever were in the Sankgreall except sir Galahad, my sone" (933.24–9 / C XXI.9). He is a true lover, but he never ceases to measure himself as a knight, and in relation to other knights, and his love always has to be seen in that social and gendered context.

---

[21] Northrop Frye, *The Secular Scripture: A Study of the Structure of Romance* (Cambridge, MA, 1976), 54.

As we have seen, there are many emotions named directly in Malory, and, as I have tried to show, many ways of subtly articulating emotions through its complex and extended narrative situations. The *Morte* also has an unusual ability to create emotional effects by leaving out explanations and so provoking further thought. An example is the statement made after Lancelot saves Guinevere from burning and takes her away to Joyous Garde: "Whan they harde that Kynge Arthure and Sir Launcelot were at debate, many knyghtes were glad, and many were sory of theire debate" (885.23–5 / C XX.9). One can understand that knights would have to choose sides, but why are many of them glad about the split? Are they Lancelot's family and friends, or Arthur's, or simply knights of ill will? This uneasy moment moves us beyond the specific "prevy" ("private," "secret") motives of Aggravain and Mordred into the general mood of civil war that characterises the next sections of the book. Malory makes another kind of division there – between those who can subdue their emotional life to the contingencies of the moment and the service of a "party" (a "side") and those like himself, Arthur, Lancelot and Guinevere who give their hearts to an ideal of community and "stabylité" and sustain the long-term memory of "olde jantylnes and olde service" (841.12–19 / C XVIII.25). The *Morte* gives great emotional privilege to the act of remembering: Tristram blames Mark with bitter irony for not calling his service to mind: "well am I rewarded" (397.2 / C IX.22). For Lancelot, perhaps the worst thing about his break with the king is that Arthur seems to be forgetting their past bond: "ye promysed me for ever to be my goode lorde. And now methynkith ye rewarde me full evyll for my good servyse" (891.3–4 / C XX.11). As Raluca Radulescu suggests, these heartfelt feelings are also part of public political addresses designed to stir emotions in the surrounding audience.[22] The characteristic fifteenth-century emphasis on remembering as a point of nobility is an incitement to "gentle" readers themselves to remember the "whole book" as they proceed "from the beginning to the ending," and Malory provides several catalogues to assist the process: the long list of knights and associated stories at the healing of Sir Urré (863–6 / C XIX.11); Lancelot's detailed reminder to Arthur of past service; and his detailed rebuke of Gawain (899–900 / C XX.15).

Another striking emotional effect in Malory, often remarked on, is the recurring difficulty readers can experience in aligning the events of his episodic narrative with an understanding of either causality or thematic coherence, so that we do not know what to "feel," or perhaps, we know experientially what the feeling is but not what to think about it. A classic instance of this is the tale of Balin, where, as Jill Mann says, the assertion of responsibility for a chain of events – Merlin announces that Balin will strike the disastrous "Dolorous Stroke" because of the suicide of a lady he was trying to help – "merely serves to draw attention

---

[22] Raluca M. Radulescu, "Tears and Lies: Malory's Arthurian World," in *Emotions in Medieval Arthurian Literature*, ed. Brandsma, Larrington and Saunders, 105–21, at 106–8. For a further discussion of fifteenth-century literary emotion as political coercion, see Catherine Nall, "Moving to War: Rhetoric and Emotion in William Worcester's *Boke of Noblesse*," in *Emotions and War: Medieval to Romantic Literature*, ed. Stephanie Downes, Andrew Lynch and Katrina O'Loughlin (London, 2015), 117–32.

to the absence of any justification for this event in terms of cause and effect."[23] Ad Putter argues that Malory's "paratactic" style – strings of statements joined to another by "and" or "then" – gives him trouble in distinguishing between a succession of events and a causal chain, citing this speech by Balin:

> "A, fayre damsell," … "worthynes and good tacchis [qualities] and also good dedis is nat only in arayement, but manhode and worshyp ys hyd within a mannes person [body]; and many a worshipfull knyght ys nat known unto all peple. And therefore worship and hardynesse ys nat in araymente." (49.18–22 / C II.2)

Putter points out that an *"entailment"* of the first part of the sequence – a worthy knight may remain largely unrecognised – is suddenly offered as *"proof* of the initial position … Actually the strength of the argument is emotional rather than logical."[24] It could be said that readers' experience of the whole Balin story is clearer in emotional effect than in a grasp of narrative logic. Readers are not in interpretative control of the narrative sequence; we seem to meet events at the same time as the protagonist. Explanations come after the event, too late, and often they are given in terms of what will happen in the future rather than to clarify what has happened. It is not an allegory: ethical motivation, which is paramount in deciding the outcome of "adventures" in Malory's Holy Grail story, for instance, apparently counts for little here; it is not clear that Balin is being punished for anything. Rather, like Tom Stoppard's Rosencrantz and Guildenstern caught in the web of *Hamlet*, he seems to have strayed into a story fraught with other stories unknown to him: intimate enmities and loves; grand histories (the Holy Grail); and future prophecies (of Gawain, Galahad, Tristram and Lancelot); the trajectories of cursed and sacred objects (the sword he draws; the sacred lance); and a host of human habitations: tents, hermitages, houses, castles, gardens, crosses, churches, tombs and bridges. These places turn out not to be neutral for Balin, but already marked with obligations, prohibitions, warnings, conclusions and predictions. Increasingly, as his understanding of narrative signs grows less, the importance of apparently minor details seems to grow more vital, in inverse proportion, so that simply changing his shield becomes a matter of "grete daunger … It is as grete pyté of yow as ever was of knyght" (71.14–21 / C II.17).

In this radical uncertainty, Balin still makes his way as if following a path already laid down for him, and comes increasingly to see that the path leads to death. Importantly, he continually gives assent to continue his journey, but in other ways the feeling of purposive motion is diminished; rather, things seem to come towards him – looming up, then disappearing, as if they were illusory projections:

> Thenne saw he an old hore [white-haired] gentylman comyng toward hym that sayd, "Balyn le Saveage, thow passest thy bandes to come this

[23] Jill Mann, "'Taking the Adventure': Malory and the *Suite du Merlin*," in *Aspects of Malory*, ed. Toshiyuki Takamiya and Derek Brewer (Cambridge, 1981), 71–91, at 82.

[24] Ad Putter, "Late Romance: Malory and the Tale of Balin," in *Readings in Medieval Texts: Interpreting Old and Middle English Literature*, ed. David F. Johnson and Elaine Treharne (Oxford, 2005), 337–53, at 341.

waye, therefor torne ageyne and it will availle the," and he vanysshed
awey anone. (70.26–9 / C II.17)

The emotions that readers feel for, and, to a large extent, *as*, Balin relate to an
apprehension of the forces of "destiny, fate, grace, providence," as Putter says,
and of death: "the reason why he [Malory] takes *aventure* so seriously is that
through it the knight can discover the relationship between these external forces
of causation and the forces that lie under the control of his inner will."[25] The
"knowledge" readers might gain from such a story is not a cognitive mastery,
but an emotional experience, an empathic sharing of wonder, admiration, pity
and grief. This experiential knowledge is neither simply a matter of "empathetic
or sympathetic feelings elicited by figures within the fiction," nor of "feelings of
fascination produced in response to the formal qualities of the text." Rather it
involves "feelings produced by an *interaction* of fictional and aesthetic feelings,
self-modifying feelings 'that restructure the reader's understanding of the textual
narrative and, simultaneously, the reader's sense of self'."[26] The particular form
of Malory's story is crucial to its emotional impact, including its combined evocation and disappointment of the usual generic conventions of chivalric romance.

The *Morte Darthur* is a very big book, built from composite and eclectic
sources, and containing many different kinds of stories. All generalisations about
its emotional character will break down sooner or later. I have not dwelt here
on the emotions of bad characters, on potentially destructive emotions such as
envy,[27] on fear, or on comic elements of the narrative's emotional formation:[28] a
good example is when Lancelot, sleeping by chance in a tent prepared for a love
tryst, suddenly feels "a rough berde kyssyng hym," jumps out of bed to fight the
tent's astonished owner, and wounds him badly: "And than he yelded hym to Sir
Launcelot, and so he graunted hym, so that [on condition that] *he wolde telle hym
why he com into the bed*" (196.19–20 / C VI.5). It is left as an amusement to readers
to judge the proportions of curiosity, alarm and outrage in Lancelot's request.
Malory's skill, and a key to the comedy, is that he lets us intuit what the situation
"feels like" to both men, and literally so to Lancelot, in the surprise touch of the
rough beard. In a different vein, but showing the same skill, he also lets us know
in deep human detail how Arthur, Gawain and Lancelot "feel" about the terrible
and complicated situation that develops after the killing of Gareth.[29] Even today,
Malory does not always receive the credit he deserves as a maker of narrative.
Reading the *Morte* as a book of emotions, in my view, can only increase admiration for his work.

---

[25] Putter, "Late Romance," 344.
[26] Carolyne Larrington, "Mourning Gawein: Cognition and Affect in *Diu Crône* and Some
French Gauvain-Texts," in *Emotions in Medieval Arthurian Literature*, ed. Brandsma,
Larrington and Saunders, 123–42, at 124. Larrington cites D. S. Miall and D. Kuiken,
"A Feeling for Fiction: Becoming What We Behold," *Poetics* 30 (2002): 222–41, at 223.
[27] For envy, see Andrew Lynch, *Malory's Book of Arms: The Narrative of Combat in* Le
Morte Darthur (Cambridge, 1997), 90–133.
[28] See, however, Christopher Cannon, "Malory's Comedy," in *Romance Rewritten: The
Evolution of Middle English Romance* (Cambridge, 2018), 67–82.
[29] For a discussion see Andrew Lynch, "'What Cheer'. Emotion and Action in the
Arthurian World," in *Emotions in Medieval Arthurian Literature*, ed. Brandsma,
Larrington and Saunders, 47–63, at 61 3.

# 10
## Secular Malory
### LISA ROBESON

Caxton's famous guide for readers of the first printed edition of the *Morte Darthur* indicates that he realized the values espoused by Malory's knights and ladies might not be wholly aligned with Christian doctrine. Readers should, he wrote in this preface, "Doo after the good [deeds] and leve the evyl" (C Prologue).[1] Despite the objections of a few Reformation readers such as Roger Ascham, tutor to Elizabeth I, who saw in the romance nothing but "open mans slaughter, and bold bawdrye," audience concerns about Christian values were apparently limited enough to keep Malory's romance steadily in print for the next 170 years (although a version of Caxton's cautionary preface appeared in all black letter editions).[2] After the revival of interest in the *Morte* in the early nineteenth century, editors and adaptors steeped in classical literature began to see the romance through the lenses of Greek epic and tragedy as well as Christian morality. Finally, with the beginning of a professional class of literary scholars and editors in the twentieth century, scholars found the ideologies of Malory's work not in Christianity or classical literature, but in the cultural institutions of Malory's day. Over the last century – from the publication of Vida Scudder's *Le Morte Darthur of Sir Thomas Malory* in 1917 to this writing – critics have returned again and again to an extended conversation about the secular ideals of the *Morte Darthur*. The conversation's threads investigate those communities that shaped the identity of Malory's readers and characters. Malory's noble characters belong to various communities, including those formed by social class, lord's affinity, and regional and national identity. In the past two decades, for example, Andrew Lynch has extended the scholarly discussion of "conflicts in the code of chivalry" that had dominated the first three-quarters of the twentieth century to focus on a more detailed examination of the chivalric values created by the details of combat in Malory's text. Dorsey Armstrong expands the exploration of chivalry by focusing on the role of women in chivalric culture. Hyonjin Kim and Raluca Radulescu examine the influence of the gentry culture of Malory and his readers

---

[1] *Le Morte Darthur*, ed. P. J. C. Field, 2 vols. (Cambridge, 2013), II, 856.

[2] Roger Ascham, "Roger Ascham," in *Malory: The Critical Heritage*, ed. Marylyn Jackson Parins (London, 1988), 56–7. Versions of Caxton's Preface appear in Wynkyn de Worde, *The Noble and Joyous Boke Entytled Le MORTE DARTHUR* (London, 1948; repr. 1934), fol. iiir; Thomas East, *The Storye of the Most Noble and Worthy Kynge Arthur* (London, 1585), fol. iiv; William Stansby, *The Most Ancient and Famous History of the Renowned Prince Arthur King of Britaine*, ed. Thomas Wright, 2 vols. (London, 1634; repr. 1858), 1.26-31.

on the *Morte*'s treatment of chivalry, while Kenneth Hodges and Robert L. Kelly investigate the role of regional identity and communities in chivalry.[3] The ideals of diverse communities, including those of European chivalric culture, a class-oriented English gentry culture, and regional and national cultures, may unify – they may bring the knights and gentlewomen of Arthur's court "holé togydrs" (386.23 / C IX.17) – or they may divide. Central questions of Malory scholarship in the last century concern the tensions within and among the secular ideologies of these communities and whether they are sustainable for a society. In this chapter I outline the process by which it became possible for literary critics and readers to discuss the *Morte Darthur* in terms of secular, rather than Christian, ideologies; explore the critics' analyses of conflicts among values of chivalry, the first cultural institution to be treated as secular in the work; set out ideologies identified by scholars focusing on the social and political communities of Arthur's kingdom; and finally examine the ways in which medieval ideologies of kingship have been applied to the *Morte Darthur*.

## *Vinaver and the Secular Revolution*

While nineteenth-century editors and critics moved away from seeing Malory's work as an effort at Christian didacticism, religious judgement was not abandoned.[4] As Marylyn Parins notes in the introduction to her anthology of Malory criticism, the view that Arthur's incest was a fatal flaw that caused his downfall (because it resulted in the birth of Mordred) was adopted by prominent nineteenth-century editors, literary figures and adapters such as F. J. Furnivall, A. C. Swinburne, William Minto and Ernest Rhys.[5] However, as Malory criticism moved into the twentieth century, scholars acknowledged that religion was a force in the romance, but for the most part treated religion as a cultural phenomenon that, in conjunction with other social forces, contributed to the ethos of chivalry. As with nineteenth-century critics, a major critical question remained the reason for the fall of the Round Table, but rather than focus on the morality of Arthur or other characters, literary critics emphasized the function, or dysfunction, of the "chivalric code." Vida Scudder provided one of the earliest

---

[3] Andrew Lynch, *Malory's Book of Arms: The Narrative of Combat in* Le Morte Darthur (Cambridge, 1997), xiii–xiv; Dorsey Armstrong, *Gender and the Chivalric Community in Malory's* Morte Darthur (Gainesville, FL, 2003), 1–2; Hyonjin Kim, *The Knight without the Sword: A Social Landscape of Arthurian Chivalry* (Cambridge, 2000), 1–18; Raluca L. Radulescu, *The Gentry Context for Malory's* Morte Darthur (Cambridge, 2003), 1–3; Kenneth L. Hodges, *Forging Chivalric Community in Malory's* Le Morte Darthur (New York, 2005), 2–4; Robert L. Kelly, "Malory's 'Tale of King Arthur' and the Political Geography of Fifteenth-Century England," in *Re-Viewing* Le Morte Darthur: *Texts and Contexts, Characters and Themes*, ed. K. S. Whetter and Raluca L. Radulescu (Cambridge, 2005), 79–82.

[4] Andrew Lang, for example, was "impressed" by the "changes that Christianity and the temper of the North have brought into what may be stiled [*sic*] the heroic and aristocratic theory of existence, of duty, of enjoyment," also comparing favourably the "chastity" of Malory's Grail quest to the sexual mores of classical texts (Lang, 2:xvi–xvii).

[5] Marylyn Parins, "Introduction," in *Malory: The Critical Heritage*, 17.

formulations of this approach. She sidestepped the question of didacticism and posited that Malory's purpose was to

> present the controlling interests of the Middle Ages – love, religion, war – in their ideal symmetry and their actual conflict. Malory's way of doing this is to tell the story of the rise and fall of chivalry, with its three loyalties, to the overlord, to the lady, and to God, as symbolized in the fate of that fair fellowship, the Table Round.[6]

Scudder refers to the "interests" of the Middle Ages rather than its "values" or "morals."

Scudder's interpretation did not entirely abandon religious ideology. In her view, Malory's portrait of knights "at once exalt[s] knighthood by their devotion and undermin[es] it by their *sins* and failures" [emphasis mine].[7] However, while her "controlling interests" do not remove analysis based on Christian or moral values – that would be difficult given that one of her identified interests is religion – she helped move analysis of the *Morte Darthur* away from concerns over what moral examples Malory was setting through his characters and focus it more firmly on the tension between the central ideologies of the work, its author and its audience.

It was the influence of the great Malory scholar and first editor of the Winchester manuscript, Eugène Vinaver, that firmly set chivalry at the thematic centre point of the romance and shifted literary criticism further from religious analysis. By 1947, with the publication of his edition of the Winchester manuscript, Vinaver had concluded that Malory's work showed few signs of didactic intention.[8] Rather, Malory's true morality is the "practice and ideals of chivalry." For Vinaver, chivalry is more of a "practice" – a word he repeats several times – than a "doctrine."[9] Moreover, it is a practice that can be examined without reference to religion. The conflicts in the code of chivalry whose tension bring down the Round Table include love and war, but not God. For Vinaver, Malory's *Morte Darthur* tells the story of

> a tragic conflict of two loyalties, both deeply rooted in the medieval conception of knightly service: on the one hand, the heroic loyalty of man to man, ... on the other, the blind devotion of the knight-lover to his lady ... The clash between these conceptions of human love and service is neither an accident nor a caprice of destiny; it is inherent in the very structure of medieval idealism.[10]

To explain Malory's inclusion of the "Tale of the Quest of the Holy Grail," in which the object of the quest is the sight of a holy object and success is achieved through chastity and repentance, Vinaver argued that the story of the quest of the

---

[6] Vida Scudder, Le Morte Darthur *of Sir Thomas Malory* (New York, 1917), 185.

[7] Scudder, Le Morte Darthur *of Sir Thomas Malory*, 186.

[8] Eugène Vinaver, "Introduction," in *The Works of Sir Thomas Malory*, ed. Eugène Vinaver, 3rd edn, rev. P. J. C. Field, 3 vols. (Oxford, 1990), xvii–xviii.

[9] Vinaver, Introduction, xxxii–xxxiii. According to Vinaver, when Malory adapted the *Quest of the Holy Grail* from his French source he detached many of the links between the story of the Quest and the main plots of the romance.

[10] Vinaver, Introduction, xcvi.

Holy Grail had been "tacked on" to Malory's other sources, the French Vulgate and Post-Vulgate cycles, to invite the interpretation that the Round Table collapsed because Arthur's knights had sinned, and so the Quest "provided an additional reason for the fall of the Round Table."[11] For Vinaver, Malory's chivalry is a secular code.

The idea that audiences should read the *Morte* with a sense that certain "sins" were timeless and their representation could be used as moral teaching for contemporary audiences did not die quickly. Several essays in R. M. Lumiansky's *Malory's Originality*, published in 1964, for example, also employ the language of sin and retribution. In this collection a few essays, such as that of Charles Moorman, refer to a "tragic flaw" and "human frailty," but more reflect the language of Thomas C. Rumble, who argues that the Arthurian triangle of Arthur, Guenevere and Lancelot is a "symbol of degeneracy," and the story as a whole shows that "[m]urder ... will out; and so, apparently, will intrigue, adultery, incest, and all the other promiscuities that have come to infect the whole dissolute Arthurian world before its testing in the search for the Holy Grail."[12] Such judgements, however, receded as the century progressed. Larry D. Benson, whose *Malory's* Morte Darthur detailed the fifteenth-century context of the work, argued that chivalry was a "moral code" of the fifteenth century but did not extend the morality of the work to religion or timeless mores; instead, he posited that Malory and his audience would have held the chivalric code to be "a definite set of ideals and practices that defined what they called the High Order of Knighthood."[13] John Leyerle argued in 1980 that chivalric biography and romance functioned as a "*secular* scripture of chivalry" [emphasis mine] for an audience of aristocrats and gentry.[14] Lynch later posited (in 1997) that, while readers cannot ignore such important "ethical and moral statements" as the Pentecostal Oath, "Arthur's celebration of 'fellowship' ... [or] the definition of true love," Malory's "most heartfelt generalisations refer primarily to their local context" and do not provide "unbending rules for interpreting the whole narrative."[15] Only recently has the secular nature of Malory's chivalry been challenged or modified. In their 2013 volume *Malory and Christianity: Essays on Sir Thomas Malory's* Morte Darthur, D. Thomas Hanks, Jr., and Janet Jesmok offer the first argument *for* Christian influence in Malory since the 1960s. Noting the overwhelming effect of Vinaver's commentary and notes on the *Quest of the Holy Grail*, Hanks argues that Vinaver's treatment of the *Quest of the Holy Grail* oversimplified the effects of Malory's changes to his source. He presents good evidence that noble human love and the love of God are intertwined in the *Quest* and elsewhere in the work.

---

[11] Vinaver, Introduction, xciv. Vinaver, of course, believed that Malory had intended to write each tale as a separate story and that the "Tales" were independent of each other.

[12] *Malory's Originality: A Critical Study of "Le Morte Darthur,"* ed. R. M. Lumiansky (Baltimore, 1964): Charles Moorman, "'The Tale of the Sankgreall': Human Frailty," 192; Thomas C. Rumble, "'The Tale of Tristram': Development by Analogy," 145–6.

[13] Larry D. Benson, *Malory's* Morte Darthur (Cambridge, MA, 1976), 146, 148.

[14] John Leyerle, "Conclusion: The Major Themes of *Chivalric Literature*," in *Chivalric Literature: Essays on Relations between Literature and Life in the Later Middle Ages,* ed. Larry D. Benson and John Leyerle (Kalamazoo, 1980), 133.

[15] Lynch, *Book of Arms,* xv–xvi.

Raluca Radulescu takes a different approach to analysing spiritual themes in the *Morte* by placing Malory's work in the literary context of fifteenth-century English penitential romances. These romances combine themes of Christian penance with analysis of the nature of kingship, especially in the motif of the Fisher King.[16] The strength of Hanks's evidence and the literary scholarship of Radulescu's study may not be enough to overcome the influence of Vinaver's secularism on contemporary scholarship, but they do demonstrate that Malory's text resists complete secularization and offers possibilities for future scholars interpreting those sections of the *Morte* that clearly contain Christian reference.[17]

## The Secular Ideologies of Chivalry

### Conflicts in the Chivalric Code

A focus on chivalric culture in its fifteenth-century context moved Malory criticism towards secularism. Its ideologies comprised some combination, depending on the critic, of competing loyalties (to lord, love and/or God). However, as Charles Moorman pointed out, Scudder's and Vinaver's formulation of the major conflicts in the code was simplistic.[18] Vinaver did little to develop the conception of loyalty to king and fellowship of the Round Table other than to define it as "the mutual love of warriors who die together fighting against the odds," a loyalty "more passionate and less ideal than our patriotism." A knight's loyalty to his lady comprised "blind devotion" and "the romantic self-denial imposed by the courtly tradition."[19] However, in Malory's long and complex work, characters play out many versions of conflicts between love and lord. For example, the careers of Sir Tristram and Sir Lancelot both exemplify the conflict between love and loyalty to lord and Malory frequently compares them to each other.[20] Lancelot and Tristram are of royal blood in their own countries, but serve a foreign king: Tristram is from Lyonesse but serves King Mark of Cornwall, while Lancelot is from France but serves King Arthur. Both are in love with their sovereigns' queens, Isode and Guenevere respectively, which certainly causes a conflict between loyalty to their lords and loyalty to their lovers in the narrative. However, the cases play out differently because King Mark is a far different

---

[16] Raluca L. Radulescu, *Romance and Its Contexts in Fifteenth-Century England: Politics, Piety and Penitence* (Cambridge, 2013), 1.

[17] D. Thomas Hanks, Jr., "'All maner of good love comyth of God': Malory, God's Grace, and Noble Love," in *Malory and Christianity: Essays on Sir Thomas Malory's* Morte Darthur, ed. D. Thomas Hanks, Jr., and Janet Jesmok (Kalamazoo, 2013), 9–15.

[18] Charles Moorman, *The Book of Kyng Arthur: The Unity of Malory's* Morte Darthur (Lexington, KY, 1965), 50.

[19] Vinaver, Introduction, xcvi.

[20] Merlin inscribes a rock that refers to Lancelot and Tristram together as the "trewyst lovers" who ever lived (57.2 / C II.8); at the tournament in Ireland, bystanders mistake Sir Tristram for Sir Lancelot (305.22–31 / C VIII.10); King Mark's barons assert that there is no greater knight than Sir Tristram apart from Sir Lancelot (341.8–11 / C VIII.32); at the Tournament of Lonezep Sir Lancelot and Sir Tristram are the knights reported to have won the most worship (604.15–16 / C X.80); Lancelot invites Tristram and Isode to his Castle at Joyous Garde and "charged all his people to honoure them and love them as they wolde do hymselff" (537.33–4 / C X.51).

lord and king than King Arthur. Mark is treacherous, cowardly and so despised that his own knights rebel against him and imprison him because they respect Tristram far more than their king (539.31–540.3 / C X.52). On the other hand, the rumoured affair between Lancelot and Guenevere divides the Round Table in Camelot and engenders a war because many of the Round Table knights demonstrate deep loyalty to King Arthur, but others follow Lancelot because of a closer bond.[21] For Lancelot and Tristram and the knights of their respective courts, the nature of the "loyalty to lord" bond is significantly different. Even in a case where parallels are clear, Vinaver's thesis is too simplistic to explain the conflict.

The work of Moorman and Beverly Kennedy helped to nuance and augment Vinaver's conceptions of the ideals of chivalry. For Moorman, chivalric ideas contained their own internal contradictions that undermined the chivalric court's ability to maintain a stable fellowship. According to Moorman, knighthood in the romance could be divided into two types whose ethics inherently contradicted each other. An older type, illustrated by the feud between King Pellinore's house and that of King Lot of Orkney, is fueled by family tribalism and an ethic of vengeance. As nephews and lords owing allegiance to Arthur, Gawain and his brothers should focus their loyalty on the king's interests. They ignore the royal interest, however, to pursue a family feud. In the wars between the young King Arthur and his brother-in-law King Lot, Pellinore, fighting for Arthur, kills Lot (61.16–23 / C II.10). To revenge Lot's death, Gawain, Gaheris, Aggravayne and Mordred kill King Pellinore, "for we demed that he slew our fadir" (482.32 / C X.21). Because they find their mother with Pellinore's son Sir Lamorak, they also kill her because Lamorak had caused "to much shame for us to suffir" (486.31–3 / C X.23). Eventually Lot's sons also kill Lamorak, causing their other brother Gareth to exclaim "well I undirstonde the vengeaunce of my brethirne … I undirstonde they be murtherars of good knyghtes" (553.28–33 / C X.58). Lot's son Sir Gareth, who alone is primarily loyal to the court, rejects the old chivalry to embrace the new by following Lancelot, a noble knight and the exemplar of the chivalry that the Round Table represents, rather than Gawain. It is the old chivalry, however, embodied by Gawain as he refuses to let King Arthur reconcile with Lancelot at the end of the *Morte*, that contributes to its tragic ending. The older chivalry's commitment to family honour and vengeance ultimately defeats the newer form of chivalry based on loyalty to king and knights, like Lancelot, of noble character.

For Kennedy, "typologies" of knighthood coexisted in the *Morte*. Malory creates three types of knighthood: "True knighthood," exemplified primarily by Lancelot; "Worshipful knighthood," modelled by Tristram; and "Heroic knighthood," embodied by Gawain. As a "True knight," Lancelot excels on the battlefield, in the "forest of adventure," and at court. Tristram, the "Worshipful knight," is primarily concerned with honour. The "Heroic knight," Gawain, is most loyal to family.[22] The varying ethics of the three typologies help build Arthur's kingdom in the early sections, but eventually the different sets of ethics

---

[21] A good exposition of the contrast between King Mark and King Arthur in Malory can be found in Edward Donald Kennedy's "Malory's King Mark and King Arthur," in *King Arthur: A Casebook*, ed. Edward Donald Kennedy (New York, 1996), 139–71.

[22] Beverly Kennedy, *Knighthood in the* Morte Darthur, 2nd edn (Cambridge, 1992), 328–31.

lead each type into collision. A Worshipful knight, Arthur stands on his honour and sense of justice when he condemns Guenevere to the fire for her adultery with Lancelot. Gawain is true to the Heroic typology when he urges Arthur to pursue vengeance on Lancelot after Lancelot has killed Gawain's brother Gareth. Finally, by remaining true to Guenevere, True knight Lancelot wreaks havoc on the stability of Arthur's kingdom.[23]

### Taking the Adventure: Chivalric Ideology as Practice

Critical analyses of the ideology of chivalry in the *Morte* have varied by whether scholars have viewed chivalry more as a "practice" – a set of actions – or as a set of ideals. Vinaver emphasized practice, even though he recognized that there were ethical limits on knightly prowess. In her essay "Taking the Adventure," Jill Mann divorces the practice of chivalry from ideal even more sharply than Vinaver. In comparing Malory's first tale with its source *The Suite du Merlin*, Mann argues that in adapting his source material, Malory eliminated signs indicating motivation and rationale so that readers could not "feel confident in categorising actions or people as right or wrong." Rather, the ideal of knighthood is not a moral principle; it is instead a knight's willingness to put his body in jeopardy in the adventures that come by chance. Balin is a case in point. As far as the reader knows, he is a noble knight, the only one at Arthur's court able to take a sword from a damsel who has declared that the sword is only for one who is a "passynge good man of hys hondys and of hys dedis, and withoute velony other trechory and withoute treson" (48.1–3 / C II.2). He kills the Lady of the Lake in front of Arthur, who seems more offended by the fact that the deed was done while the Lady was under Arthur's safe conduct than by the fact that Balin has killed the Lady of the Lake (51.20–7 / C II.3). For Mann, Balin's subsequent adventures, which culminate in a duel in disguise in which he and his brother inadvertently battle each other to the death, *reveal* his character rather than result from it. If he is a worshipful knight, it is because he has chosen, as he tells the damsel with the sword, to "take the aventure … that God woll ordayne for me" (50.5–6 / C II.3). On the other hand, if Mordred is an example of a destructive knight, it is not because he does not take the adventure, but because he does so to impose his own will on the world.[24] Rather than accept the ordinary rules of medieval succession, for example, which prohibited an illegitimate son from inheriting his father's throne, Mordred "cheats" so that he can become king. He forges letters saying that his father is dead, he summons Parliament and manipulates it into declaring him king, he even tries to marry Guenevere, his father's wife, to strengthen his claim to the crown. Even after his father returns to England and defeats his forces, Mann points out that Mordred does not accept his destiny: Arthur thrusts a lance through him in a last hand-to-hand combat, and Mordred responds by pushing himself up the burr of Arthur's lance in order to give Arthur his death blow in return. Mordred cannot accept even his own inevitable death.

---

[23] Kennedy, *Knighthood*, 331–2.

[24] Jill Mann, "'Taking the Adventure': Malory and the *Suite du Merlin*," in *Aspects of Malory*, ed. Toshiyuki Takamiya and Derek Brewer (Cambridge, 1981), 71–91, at 84, 90.

In *Malory's Book of Arms*, Lynch defines success in combat as the highest ideal of chivalry in the *Morte*. Rather than a "master pattern of divided loyalties and moral conflict," it is the "language of Malory's combat episodes" that "binds 'together' the participants and their actions" to create cohesion.[25] In Malory, success in combat produces "name," or reputation, the most important value of knighthood, and creates a knight's identity.[26] Noble blood is necessary for worship, but blood is also a sign, a "proof of behaviour," that a knight is willing to put his body in jeopardy.[27] Referencing Mark Lambert's explanation of the "shame-honor" culture operating in Malory, Lynch posits that maintaining one's name is the highest good for a knight in the *Morte*.[28] A good example of one's deeds revealing one's name – literally as well as figuratively – would be the case of Sir Gareth. Gareth's tale begins as Sir Gawain sees three mounted men and a dwarf arrive at court just before the feast of Pentecost (often the time to begin an Arthurian adventure) starts. One horseman is remarkably handsome and strong: "the goodlyest yonge man and the fayreste that ever they all sawe ... large and longe and brode in the shuldyrs, well-vysaged, and the largyste and the fayreste handid that ever man sye" (223.24–7 / C VII.1). He informs the court that he has come to Camelot to be given three gifts: first, sustenance for a year, at which time he will ask two more gifts, but he will not tell King Arthur his name (224.3–11 / C VII.1). Although his physical beauty and strength suggests that he is a man of good "blood" and will be a knight of prowess, Gareth is mocked by Sir Kay, Arthur's seneschal, who calls the young man "Beawmaynes" – "Fair Hands" – and, believing the young man is a commoner, puts him to work in the kitchens (224.34-225.20 / C VII.1). When a damsel comes to the king seeking help for her sister, who is besieged by a knight with a name for great prowess, none but Beaumains will agree to undertake the adventure. Knighted by Lancelot, Gareth accompanies the damsel Lynet, who also enjoys mocking him. However, in the course of his adventure Gareth proves his worth by defeating four separate knights and winning the love of Lynet's sister, Lady Lyonesse. Only after his adventure is complete, during a tournament, is Beaumains's real identity revealed to the court: he is Gareth, son of King Lot and Queen Morgause and brother to Sir Gawain (276.1–19 / C VII.30). As he demonstrates his prowess, Gareth demonstrates his worship. His name in the sense of his identity is revealed after his "name" in the sense of his reputation in combat has been established.

Despite the importance of prowess, combat scenes in the *Morte* do show that, as Vinaver pointed out, prowess can be misapplied. While rejecting the idea of a unified code of chivalry in the work, Lynch does identify some repeated themes that indicate "concepts of true justice, or right and wrong quarrels and of proper conduct in fighting."[29] For example, in the Quest section of the *Morte* there is a sense that a knight's spiritual sin is punished by shame. However, the quality most condemned in the work is envy, or "ill will." Since chivalry is a competitive culture – one's name is created by defeating others – envy of

---

[25] Lynch, *Book of Arms*, xiii–xiv.
[26] Lynch, *Book of Arms*, 10.
[27] Lynch, *Book of Arms*, 60–2.
[28] Lynch, *Book of Arms*, 14.
[29] Lynch, *Book of Arms*, 43.

more successful knights is a logical product of that culture. It afflicts most those whose fighting ability does not match their rank (e.g., Gawain and his brothers except for Gareth). When envy is maintained over a long term, the outcome is destructive: "In the honour economy, kinsmen and supporters of the great are like shareholders whose stocks are devalued when another centre of worship – for 'worship' read 'power' – grows stronger."[30] Such is the case for Gawain and his brothers Gaheris, Aggravayne and Mordred. Aggravayne's and Mordred's envy of Lancelot causes them to spread rumours about Lancelot's affair with the Queen. At first Aggravayne says that his anger against Lancelot is caused by the "shame" Lancelot's affair with Guenevere brings to their uncle King Arthur – and of course, to all of Arthur's family members such as Aggravayne and his brothers (870.16–23 / C XX.1). But in Sir Gawain's response to his younger brother there is a hint that he understands that jealousy contributes to Aggravayne's anger. He reminds Aggravayne of the times Sir Lancelot has rescued the king and queen, pointing out that he and his brothers would have been "full colde at the harte-roote had nat Sir Launcelot *bene bettir than we*, and that hathe he preved hymselff full ofte" (871.13–17 / C XX.1; emphasis mine). They would have been even more shamed if their king and uncle had been captured and imprisoned or killed, and Gawain acknowledges that he and his brothers did not have enough prowess to prevent this. As Gawain predicts, Aggravayne's rumours do result in "warre and wrake" among court factions, and thus begins the downward spiral of the Round Table (871.10 / C XX.1).

### The High Order of Knighthood: Chivalry as a Set of Ideals

While in the second half of the twentieth century critical attention shifted from chivalry's role in the fall of the Round Table to a focus on the nature of chivalry and its contributions to motivations and themes in Malory's *Morte*, many scholars still concentrated on chivalry as a set of ideals apparent in Malory's text. Vinaver's discussion was unable to avoid issues of a "great cause" that drove the protagonists' actions. In contrast to the analyses of Mann and Lynch, critics such as Benson and Kennedy developed explorations of chivalry as a set of ideals. These ideals still were considered primarily secular, a product of fifteenth-century European culture. Kennedy argued that each typology of knighthood had its own set of ideals: the Heroic knight (Gawain) valued family loyalty, the True knight (Lancelot) prowess and love, the Worshipful knight (Tristram and Arthur) honour and service. Kennedy's omission of a typology for a "Holy Knight" – exemplified, say, by Galahad – is telling. She considered the religious devotion of the Quest of the Holy Grail an amplification of the portrait of True knighthood; this incorporation of religious knighthood into True knighthood indicates how far critics had come in treating chivalry as a primarily secular cultural phenomenon.

Using fifteenth-century romances and chivalric handbooks to provide context for Malory's work – all of which presupposed an ideological foundation for chivalry – Benson argued that Malory had a moral code, "a definite set of ideals

---

[30] Lynch, *Book of Arms*, 97.

and practices that defined what they called the High Order of Knighthood."[31] In his analysis, loyalty to lord is deemphasized (as it was in fifteenth-century chivalry) in favour of "corporate values": "the sense of honor and integrity, courage and prowess – would remain but would be diverted into socially useful standards." In both historical chivalry of the period and Malory's chivalry, noble blood is necessary and a virtue; manners are important; and an ideal knight had to be a lover. But above all, a knight was a man of worship – of worthiness and prowess.[32] Moreover, as Benson points out, according to Nicholas Upton, the fifteenth-century author of a handbook of chivalry dedicated to Humphrey, duke of Gloucester, jousts "prove [a knight's] strength and manhood; which man-hood and fortitude is a moral virtue; yea, and also one of the cardinal virtues."[33] Upton's conclusion – that physical prowess demonstrates the higher good – is remarkably similar to Lynch's analysis. However, as a fifteenth-century chivalric writer, Upton cannot separate this good from the language of morality: "cardinal virtue." Benson sees the ending of the *Morte* as a "celebration" of the ideals of chivalry, which are listed in Ector's threnody for Lancelot: courtesy, faithfulness to one's lover, godliness, gentleness to ladies, and determined action against one's enemies (939.11–23 / C XXI.12).[34]

### The Pentecostal Oath

The institution of the Pentecostal Oath, sworn by Malory's knights at the found-ing of the Round Table at the feast of Pentecost and renewed each year, seems to attach a set of ideals to the chivalric culture that underlies Arthur's polity. In an original addition to his source material, Malory's Round Table knights swear an oath, renewed every year at Pentecost:

> the kynge stablysshed all the knyghtes and gaff them rychesse and londys, and charged them never to do outerage nothir mourthir, and allwayes to fle treson, and to gyff mercy unto hym that askith mercy, uppon payne of forfiture of theire worship and lordship of Kynge Arthure for evir more; and allwayes to do ladyes, damesels, and jantilwomen and wydowes soccour, strengthe hem in hir ryghtes, and never to enforce them uppon payne of dethe. Also that no man take no batayles in a wrongfull quarrell for no love ne for no worldis goodis. (97.27–35 / C III.15)

For Vinaver, this oath is "perhaps the most complete and authentic record of [Malory's] conception of chivalry." Comparing the first section of Malory's *Morte* with his French source, the Post-Vulgate *Suite du Merlin*, Thomas L. Wright argued that Malory wrenched the French source's Round Table from a fundamentally religious to a secular code.[35] In his essay "Chivalry in the *Morte Darthur*" in the first *Companion to Malory*, Richard Barber sees the Pentecostal Oath as the "purpose" of the Round Table, similar to induction oaths sworn by

---

[31] Benson, *Morte Darthur*, 148.

[32] Benson, *Morte Darthur*, 148–50.

[33] Nicholas Upton, *De Studio Militari*, ed. F. P. Bernard (Oxford, 1931); quoted by Benson, *Morte Darthur*, 168.

[34] Benson, *Morte Darthur*, 246.

[35] Thomas L. Wright, "'The Tale of King Arthur': Beginnings and Foreshadowings," in *Malory's Originality*, 36.

orders of knights, and reflecting kings' awareness of the dangers that knights who need to demonstrate prowess posed to society: "Knights were powerful and potentially anarchic figures ... physically able to dominate their neighbors."[36] Ideologically the Oath confirms a knight's commitment to the larger society: authorized or societally proscribed killing is forbidden, as is betrayal (*treson*) and battle in wrongful cause. It also channels chivalric violence so that it strengthens the vulnerable of society, women and those who are defeated but ask for mercy.[37] The conditions under which the oath is taken even, in theory at any rate, establish economic justice. The tournaments and wars chivalric culture necessitated supported and at times enriched knights, functioning as an economic system, as Barber notes.[38] However, combat for gain is not necessary in Arthur's Round Table community because the king has given his knights riches and lands.

Interestingly, scholars investigating the role of women in the *Morte* were among the first to push back on Lynch's assertion that the Pentecostal Oath was a moral statement that operated in submissive partnership to the themes elicited from analysis of the details of combat. The portion of the Oath pertaining to women, or the "Ladies Clause," is the clearest statement in Malory on the role of women in chivalric culture. Armstrong argues that "knightly combat and its language are, in a sense, produced and giving meaning by Malory's women, or, to put it more precisely, *by the text's understanding and construction of women.*" The Oath does not simply reveal knights' purposes and destiny, but creates it; masculine activity needs the feminine, and so the powerless gender becomes powerful.[39] Felicia Nimue Ackerman points out that in a chivalric world in which truth is demonstrated not through trial by jury but by judicial duel and the success of a knight-defender, the Ladies Clause does not simply raise the status of women (by making them necessary for worshipful combat) but protects those who could have been the victims of misused power.[40] The Ladies Clause provides a role for women in the ideology of chivalry and becomes a driving force for that ideology. Hodges notes that for Gareth to prove himself worshipful, he must prove himself to women. Elsewhere I have argued that women may also earn worship by upholding the High Order of Knighthood and, in the unique case of Perceval's sister, a gentlewoman, like a gentleman, may earn worship by shedding her blood.[41]

---

[36] Eugène Vinaver, "Commentary: The Tale of King Arthur," in *Works*, III, 1335; Richard Barber, "Chivalry and the *Morte Darthur*," in *A Companion to Malory*, ed. Elizabeth Archibald and A. S. G. Edwards (Cambridge, 1996), 22, 32.

[37] I follow the practice of Felicia Nimue Ackerman in calling the aristocratic women to whom the oath refers "women," with the qualifier "noblewomen" or "ladies." As she points out, "nonaristocratic women scarcely even appear in Malory's world," and it is simpler just to use the generic term ("'Always to do ladies, damosels, and gentlewomen succour': Women and the Chivalric Code in Malory's *Morte Darthur*," *Midwest Studies in Philosophy* 26 (2002): 1–12, at 2).

[38] Barber, "Chivalry," 22.

[39] Armstrong, *Gender*, 2 (emphasis original); Dorsey Armstrong, "Gender and the Chivalric Community: The Pentecostal Oath in Malory's 'Tale of King Arthur'," *Bibliographic Bulletin of the International Arthurian Society* 51 (2000): 203.

[40] Ackerman, "Women and the Chivalric Code," 3–5.

[41] Hodges, *Forging Chivalric Communities*, 81; Lisa Robeson, "Women's Worship: Female Versions of Chivalric Honour," in *Re-Viewing* Le Morte Darthur: *Texts and Contexts,*

## Ideologies of Community

### "[H]olé Togydirs": Chivalric Community in the Morte Darthur

In reviewing the history of fifteenth-century chivalry, Benson noted that loyalty to lord had been replaced by "corporate values." Likewise, P. J. C. Field states, "the essence of chivalry, for Malory, was its unity." Critical attention has been paid to the community of knights of the Round Table, with different analyses of how much or how little they resemble a chivalric order, and how the notion of a "fellowship" among knights compares with older critical perceptions of loyalty to lord, love, and God.[42] With some influence from historians following K. B. McFarlane, who analysed fifteenth-century political relationships and developed the theory of "bastard feudalism," the analysis of communities began to extend from simply the fellowship of the Round Table to other communities with which Malory's characters identified: those shaped by social class, geography and nation.[43] Tensions among these groups, just as much as conflict within the code of chivalry, destabilize the Round Table in Malory's *Morte Darthur*.

The Round Table itself is the most prominent community in the *Morte Darthur*. Even though some of Arthur's knights originally fought under his father Uther, the word *chevalry*, which denotes both "cavalry" and "chivalry," is not used in the *Morte* until the young king formulates his court and army (14.33 / C I.10).[44] In the early part of Arthur's reign, the word also is associated with *felyship*, which, like *chevalry*, appears first in the *Morte* as Arthur prepares for the Battle of Bedgrayne (19.18–21 / C I.11).[45] Just after Arthur marries Guenevere, a knight from the North comes to court and asks what tidings come from Camelot. A fellow northerner replies,

> Be my hede … there have I bene and aspied the courte of Kynge Arthure, and there ys such a felyship that they may never be broken, and well-nyghe all the world holdith with Arthure, for there ys the floure of chevalry. And now for thys cause am I rydyng into the northe, to tell oure chyfftaynes of the felyship that ys withholdyn with Kynge Arthur. (95.28–33 / C III.13)

In this passage *chevalry* is clearly linked with *felyship*, which is repeated twice.

---

*Characters and Themes*, 107–18, at 109–12, 115–16.

[42] P. J. C. Field, Introduction to *Le Morte Darthur: The Seventh and Eighth Tales* (London, 1978), 48. For a literature review of scholarly work on the subject of fellowship in the *Morte*, see Elizabeth Archibald, "Malory's Ideal of Fellowship," *Review of English Studies* n.s. 43 (1992): 311–28, at 311.

[43] K. B. McFarlane first formulated his position in "Bastard Feudalism," in *England in the Fifteenth Century: Collected Essays* (London, 1981), 23–43.

[44] Field's Glossary defines "chyvalry" as "horsemen" (14.33 / C I.10) and as "prowess," "knighthood," and "reputation" elsewhere (*Le Morte Darthur*, II, 909). Sir Ulfius and Sir Bracias fight for Uther (6.5 / C I.3–5) and for Arthur at the Battle of Bedgrayne (21.21 / C I.14). *A Concordance to the Works of Sir Thomas Malory*, ed. Tomomi Kato (Tokyo, 1974), 286.

[45] Kato, *Concordance*, 391–2.

For Jill Mann, *felyship* is one of the key terms of the *Morte Darthur*.[46] Elizabeth Archibald points out that referring to the Round Table as a *felyship* is original to Malory. She comments that Malory's French sources generally identify knights "de la maison le roi Artus" and "compaignons/compainz de la Table Reonde." In the *Morte*, knights are not labelled with reference to "Arthur's house" – or to Arthur at all – but rather in relation to the Round Table. Moreover, the word *compaignie* is generally used in the sense of a short-term company of knights and only rarely in a collective meaning, i.e., a term that would be applied to a military order. While *felyship* is often used to refer to the friendship of individual knights, the fact that the Pentecostal Oath is renewed yearly "shows that this is no temporary warband, but a permanent society with formal rituals and rules."[47] The strength of the bond within the fellowship of the Round Table that Arthur has founded is witnessed by Arthur's grief in the last section of the *Morte* when he learns that Lancelot has killed many of his Round Table knights as he rescued the queen from execution:

> Alas, that ever I bare crowne uppon my hede! For now have I loste the fayryst felyshyp of noble knyghtes that ever hylde Crystyn kynge togydirs. Alas, my good knyghtes be slayne and gone away fro me, that now within thys too dayes I have loste nygh fourty knyghtes, and also the noble felyshyp of Sir Launcelot and hys blood, for now I may nevermore holde hem togydirs with my worship ... And much more am I soryar for my good knyghtes loss than for the losse of my fayre quene; for quenys I might have inow, but such a felyship of good knyghtes shall never be togydirs in no company. (886.7–887.1 / C XX.9)

In his speech, it is clear that Arthur believes that the fellowship of knights is the basis of his kingship – "the fayryst felyshyp of noble knyghtes that ever *hylde Crystyn kynge togydirs*." The repetition of collective and plural nouns in the passage, such as "fellowship," "knights," "company" and the adverb "together" emphasize the importance Arthur places on the role the fellowship plays in his kingship.

The clauses of the Pentecostal Oath – as Archibald points out, a statement that is intended to last as long as the Round Table – demonstrate that knights' commitments are to be directed to support the fellowship as well as the vulnerable in their society. For example, the oath enjoins knights to "fle treson." Megan Leitch claims that *treason* in Malory represents "the ever-present opposites to fellowship." The word is used to define the limits of healthy community for Malory's knights and Malory's audience, underlining their responsibility to society.[48] The "outerage" and "mourthir" knights are enjoined to reject may be performed upon other knights as well as upon gentlewomen, and knights who themselves become vulnerable (those who must ask mercy because they have been defeated in battle) must be supported. Those who do not follow these principles, such as

---

[46] Jill Mann, "Malory: Knightly Combat in *Le Morte D'Arthur*," in *The New Pelican Guide to English Literature*, ed. Boris Ford, 9 vols. (Harmondsworth, 1982–8), 1:332.

[47] Archibald, "Malory's Ideal of Fellowship," 311–14, 318.

[48] Megan G. Leitch, *Romancing Treason: The Literature of the Wars of the Roses* (Oxford, 2015), 92, 100–1.

Sir Brewnys Saunze Pité, who lies about his identity, interrupts a combat between Round Table knights, and rides in to try to kill a knight who has been unhorsed, are labelled "false traytoure knyght."[49] Even Sir Brewnys' appellation – "sans pitié," or "without pity" – shows that he has no mercy. His actions place him statutorily outside the community; the fact that he is also a coward only confirms his unworthiness.

### Ideologies of Class and Geography

Certainly individual treason in Malory undermines the Round Table's ideology of fellowship. However, fellowship is also strained by the ties of knights to communities other than the Round Table. In *The Knight Without the Sword: A Social Landscape of Malorian Chivalry*, Kim modifies the assumed definition of chivalry used previously by Malory critics and identifies a somewhat different ideology of loyalty based on historical analysis of the gentry class during Malory's time. Particularly relevant for this review of secular ideologies is Kim's application of fifteenth-century vassalage relationships to the *Morte*. Basing his analysis on the work of McFarlane, Kim summarizes McFarlane's formulation of fifteenth-century "bastard feudalism," a system of vassalage that had replaced formal homage with a more informal set of benefits for retainers and lords:

> [A magnate] had at his disposal "good lordship" or patronage, which entailed not only the recognition and endorsement of the retainers' landed status quo but also the more active roles of protecting their interests in legal disputes and orchestrating their social advancement. The retainers were, in turn, expected to serve in the lord's council, give him political and military support, help him rule his "country," and be an active part of his visual propaganda, riding with him in his livery on various public occasions. They constituted the lord's affinity, together with his family, household staff, tenants, and simple well-wishers.[50]

Tracing the lines of affinities to the major nobles in the work, Kim finds networks of loyalties that eventually conflict. Affinities could comprise direct vassals, blood relations, servants and other knights defeated in combat. As king, Arthur is overlord of all magnates and of client kings like Lancelot. Affinities can be fluid, and knights can be members of several affinities. In this situation, good overlordship matters. Kim points out that knights like Gareth, who is a client of Gawain (by relationship), Lancelot (by choice) and Arthur (as subject) may choose one relationship over the other depending on who is the best lord. Gareth, for example, could choose Gawain as overlord because Gawain is his brother or Lancelot because he is a better lord. He chooses Lancelot.[51]

By examining combat and tournament scenes in Malory closely, Kim is able to demonstrate the destabilization of the Round Table by two different sets of affinities, that of Lancelot (which includes knights associated with Tristram, his own relatives such as Bors and Ector, knights associated with Lamorak who was killed by Gawain's brothers, and those knights such as Gareth and Lavayne

---

[49] Leitch, *Romancing Treason*, 96.
[50] Kim, *Knight without the Sword*, 65–6.
[51] Kim, *Knight without the Sword*, 69–70.

who have chosen Lancelot for his nobility) and that of Gawain (which includes his relatives, except for Gareth, and knights who are jealous of Lancelot). For most of the *Morte*, Gawain's and Lancelot's mutual commitment to King Arthur keeps the tensions of the two affinity networks in check. However, Gawain's sense of injury when Lancelot mistakenly kills his brother Gareth causes Gawain to release the control he had tried to exercise over his family, as, for example, when he abjures Aggravayne and Mordred to stop spreading rumours about the Queen and Lancelot's affair (871.3–12 / C XX.1). In determining to avenge himself on Lancelot for Gareth's death, Gawain allows his commitment to the court to be overwhelmed by grief and anger. Gawain's vengeance leads to a war between affinities. As Kim points out, the affinity led by the best lord, Lancelot, who is noble, generous and persuasive – all the qualities McFarlane sees in the greatest magnates – would have won the conflict if Arthur had not sided with his own blood relative, Gawain.[52] Events lead Arthur to choose between his two principal overlords and the affinities they command – an impossible choice for a king whose greatest love is the "fayryst felyshyp of noble knyghtes that ever hylde Crystyn king togydirs" (886.8–9 / C XX.9). In the end, he is unable to hold the two affinities together with his personal authority, and the realm lapses into civil war. The ideology of unity and fellowship becomes the prey of loyalty to affinity.

Kim grounded his theory of a multivalent chivalry in fifteenth-century gentry concerns for land and for lord. Kenneth Hodges and Kelly note that geography and nationality create intersectional chivalries. According to Hodges, Malory presents chivalry as "dynamic, changing (often rapidly) through time in response to local conditions as knights actively shape chivalry to their own purposes."[53] Hodges notes that most of the hero knights of Malory's story of Tristram are regional: Tristram is Cornish, Gareth from the Orkneys, Lamorak from Wales, Palomides a Saracen (whatever that may have meant to Malory and his audience).[54] According to Hodges, Lancelot is a foreigner from Guienne.[55] Regional knights have goals that overlie those of the national court. For example, combats to counter truage from client kings, such as that between Tristram and Marhalt of Ireland (298.20–300.19 / C VIII.7–8), are regional rather than national (as is Arthur's war with the Roman emperor over truage). Moreover, success by knights of one region may threaten the political influence of knights of other regions: Hodges argues that Lamorak is hated by Gawain's brothers not just because Lamorak's father killed their father but also because Arthur's

---

[52] Kim, *Knight without the Sword*, 88–98.

[53] Hodges, *Forging Chivalric Communities*, 2.

[54] On the difficulty of determining what Malory conceived when he used the term "Saracen" or "pagan," see Peter H. Goodrich, "Saracens and Islamic Alterity in Malory's *Le Morte Darthur*," *Arthuriana* 16.4 (2006): 10–28. On the terms under which Arthur's court could accept Saracens in the *Morte*, see Donald L. Hoffman, "Assimilating Saracens: The Aliens in Malory's *Morte Darthur*," *Arthuriana* 16.4 (2006): 43–64. On the late medieval European perceptions of Saracens that informed Malory's culture, see Jeffrey Jerome Cohen, "On Saracen Enjoyment: Some Fantasies of Race in Late Medieval France and England," *Journal of Medieval and Modern Studies* 31.1 (2001): 113–46 and John V. Tolan, *Saracens: Islam in the Medieval European Imagination* (New York, 2002).

[55] Kenneth Hodges, "Why Malory's Launcelot Is Not French: Region, Nation, and Political Identity," *PMLA* 125.3 (2010): 556.

recognition and reward of Lamorak's prowess as a knight threatens the Orkney affinity's political influence.[56] Likewise, Kelly notes the tension of regional loyalties in the *Morte*, pointing out that Arthur's early wars pit a centralized court sited in the south against border lords of the north and west. In fifteenth-century Britain, only the southeast (the genesis of support for Jack Cade's historical rebellion and Mordred's literary one) had a greater reputation for revolt. Powerful northern lords like the historical Nevilles and Percys could be compared to King Lot, who could keep order in the north but also presented continual challenges to royal authority.[57]

## Malory's Arthur and Ideologies of Kingship

### First among Equals: Ideal Kingship and Chivalric Governance

Chivalry and kingship cannot be separated in Malory. As Arthur says, it is the "felyshyp of noble knyghtes" that has held his Christian kingship together. If Arthur is king, he is also the head of a chivalric order whose prestige depends on the prowess and worship of its knights. At the same time, his success as king depends on the prestige and military power he commands as patron of "the floure of chevalry." As a chivalric king, Arthur must be courageous but does not have to be the most successful of knights – unlike Lancelot, he loses combats to worthy knights such as King Pellinore (42.11–15 / C I.24). Arthur's greater role is to serve as a "heroic knight" in Vinaver's sense rather than Kennedy's, as a nationalistic war leader and conqueror: "Arthur is the 'Conqueror', the English counterpart of Charlemagne," and Vinaver argues for parallels with Henry V.[58]

The emphasis Vinaver puts on Arthur's "heroic knighthood" and his similarities to Henry V suggest that the Winchester editor believed Arthur's most important role was as king, conqueror and general; Kelly is even more explicit in arguing that the chivalric code is not so much a statement of chivalric ideals but a "contract" between king and clients.[59] The fact that the Oath is taken after Arthur has "stablysshed" all his knights with "rychesse and londys" – essential to maintaining prestige, power and affinity for a fifteenth-century knight – shows that the oath cements royal policy. For Kelly, the Round Table is not a fraternal chivalric order but a "royal military order" established primarily to provide for the kingdom's military needs.[60]

In conquest, Arthur earns prestige for himself, his knights and his kingdom, and his knights' satisfaction is palpable. As a chivalric king, he must give his knights opportunities to win worship, and, as Sir Cador of Cornuayle says when he counsels Arthur to reject the Roman emperor's demand for truage, "I am nat hevy of this message, for we have be many dayes rested us and have ben ydle … now we shall have warre and worship" (147.10–14 / C V.1). At the beginning

---

[56] Hodges, *Forging Chivalric Communities*, 87–92.

[57] Kelly, "Political Geography," 79–83.

[58] Vinaver, Introduction, xxx–xxxi.

[59] Robert L. Kelly, "Royal Policy and Malory's Round Table," *Arthuriana* 14:1 (2004): 43–71, at 52.

[60] Kelly, "Royal Policy," 60.

of the story of Tristram, Malory's narrator emphasizes the greatness of Arthur's conquests, delineating all the realms that are under his control, including England, Wales, Scotland, France, Brittany and "all the lordshyppis unto Roome" (289.12–20 / C VIII.1). It is indeed when Arthur is functioning as what Hodges calls a "national knight," a conqueror whose success floats all boats, that political friction in his kingdom is minimal. Hodges notes that Arthur's relationship to his knights is different during the Roman wars, when all who fight for the king against the foreigners are "oure knyghtes," and when the tournament at Lonezep "separates southeast England from the rest of Arthur's lands."[61]

In investigating the question of why Arthur is less effective as a domestic leader than a conqueror, many critics have turned to treatises and handbooks on medieval kingship. Elizabeth Pochoda, for example, highlights medieval theorists' emphasis on the need for the king to protect the kingdom from foreign threats (as Arthur does successfully in the Roman wars) and also maintain law and order at home.[62] Pochoda argues that in both ideology and practice, governance by chivalric order undermines the king's ability to accomplish his goals. Chivalry was a code of "personal perfection" rather than a "social ideal."[63] Essentially competitive, chivalry requires knights to win worship, land and wives at the expense of others.[64] The king's position as leader of a chivalric society Pochoda sees as primarily fraternal does not give him the power or authority to manage conflict and maintain order within his own kingdom.[65] When Arthur's knights engage in fair combat in joust or battle with knights outside the Round Table, such as Sir Tarquin, a killing has no effect on relationships in the court.[66] However, when a Round Table knight kills another Round Table knight or his relative, relationships may become poisonous, as in the feud between the sons of King Lot of Orkney and Lamerok, whose father killed theirs in fair battle.

Subsequent critics applying historical analysis of fifteenth-century politics to Malory's *Morte Darthur* have noticed the same tension between royal authority and aristocratic authority hampering the success of Arthur's government by chivalric order. Focussing on the second part of McFarlane's thesis – that an "undermighty" king could be as dangerous as overmighty nobles – Kelly notes that early in the *Morte* Arthur demonstrates a strong executive will as he subdues regional client kings and conquers southern Europe.[67] By the time of the civil war with Lancelot, however, Arthur's royal will seems diminished. Felicity Riddy notes that after the queen has been returned to Arthur by Lancelot, "Arthur is

---

[61] Hodges, *Forging Chivalric Communities*, 87–8.
[62] Elizabeth T. Pochoda, *Arthurian Propaganda: Le* Morte Darthur *as an Historical Ideal of Life* (Chapel Hill, NC, 1971), 35–52.
[63] Pochoda, *Arthurian Propaganda*, 71.
[64] Pochoda, *Arthurian Propaganda*, 92.
[65] Pochoda, *Arthurian Propaganda*, 108.
[66] A tremendously strong knight, Sir Tarquin has declared vengeance on the Round Table because Sir Lancelot defeated and killed his brother. He encamps by a stream and challenges all who wish to cross to joust. Many Round Table knights, including Sir Gawain's brother Sir Gaherys and Sir Lancelot's kin Sir Lionel, are defeated, humiliated by being stripped naked and tied to a horse, and then thrown into a dungeon. Sir Lancelot eventually finds and defeats Sir Tarquin, to the gratitude of members of Sir Gawain's kin, Sir Lancelot's kin, and all of the court (192–3, 200–5 / C. VI.1, C VI.7–10).
[67] Kelly, "Political Geography," 82–4.

unable to assert his authority over Lancelot."[68] When he loses his will, as I have argued, Arthur allows the rise of what Christine Carpenter has called a "substitute king," a magnate who becomes the *de facto* power of government to fill the vacuum of weak kingship.[69] In the section of the *Morte* between Lancelot's rescue of the queen and Mordred's rebellion, Gawain's mighty will supersedes the king's.

Those applying medieval political theory also note that Arthur does not function ideally by the end of the work. In *The King's Two Bodies*, Ernst Kantorowicz identifies the relationship between the king, the law and the aristocracy as a defining relationship for a polity. The question of when the king could legitimately be above the law and when he should be subject to it was a vexed one.[70] In the last sections of the *Morte*, Arthur often errs in his judgement. Kelly demonstrates that when Arthur condemns Guenevere to the fire without trial he violates law and custom by prosecuting the case himself (since Arthur was the victim, the barons should have decided the case) and by ordering summary judgment.[71] Moreover, as Ruth Lexton points out, in an unkingly way Arthur may have made his judgment in anger, as Lancelot seems to anticipate that the king will act in "hete and malice" in condemning the queen to execution (879.19–28 / C XX.5).[72] For his lapses in sovereignty, Lexton sees Arthur as a king whose weak rule, "unreliable and fluctuating," is compensated for by the Round Table and its members as long as their shared commitment is strong enough to do so.[73] Rather than Kelly's Arthur, who rules a military order as a superior to his fellow knights, Lexton sees Arthur as king who is first below, rather than among, equals.

### Kingship and Counsel

If there is one area in which critics agree that Arthur fails in expectations of kingship, it is in the receiving of counsel. Medieval mirrors of princes, particularly the *Secretum Secretorum*, consider the ability to receive and evaluate counsel as a fundamental process for good kingship.[74] Early in Malory, Arthur seems to receive counsel well and make decisions that are lauded by his barony. In his efforts to subdue the rebellious kings, he takes counsel from Merlin and his barons and ultimately decides to ally with kings Ban and Bors, who help make Arthur's victory over the rebels possible (14.14–15.16 / C I.9–10). Likewise, when

---

[68] Felicity Riddy, "Contextualizing *Le Morte Darthur*: Empire and Civil War," in *A Companion to Malory*, 66.

[69] Lisa Robeson, "Malory and the Death of Kings: The Politics of Regicide at Salisbury Plain," in *The Arthurian Way of Death: The English Tradition*, ed. Karen Cherewatuk and K. S. Whetter (Cambridge, 2009), 136–50, at 142.

[70] Ernst Kantorowicz, *The King's Two Bodies: A Study in Mediaeval Political Theory* (Princeton, NJ, 1957), 143–64.

[71] Robert L. Kelly, "Malory and the Common Law: *Hasty jougement* in the 'Tale of the Death of King Arthur'," *Medievalia et humanistica* 22 (1995): 116–17.

[72] Ruth Lexton, *Contested Language in Malory's* Morte Darthur: *The Politics of Romance in Fifteenth-Century England* (Houndmills, UK, 2014), 165.

[73] Lexton, *Contested Language*, 173–4.

[74] Judith Ferster, *Fictions of Advice: The Literature and Poltiics of Counsel in Medieval England* (Philadelphia, 1996), 39–54. For a summary of discussions of counsel in Malory, see Louis J. Boyle, "Ruled by Merlin: Mirrors for Princes, Counseling Patterns, and Malory's 'Tale of King Arthur'," *Arthuriana* 23 (2013): 52–66, at 57.

Arthur receives a demand for tribute from the Roman emperor, he hears counsel from his barons, who recommend that Arthur go to war, a war which ends successfully (146.20–149.5 / C V.1–2). At the end of the *Morte*, however, he does not show the same ability to evaluate counsel and select the best path. Kelly and Radulescu note that Arthur does not follow Gawain's advice when it is good (when Gawain advises Arthur not to put the queen to summary judgment) but does follow his advice when it is bad (to pursue a vengeful war on Lancelot).[75] Moreover, according to Radulescu, Arthur does not display an ability to evaluate counsel. Arthur fails to recognize, for example, that when Aggravayne and Mordred advise the king to try to surprise the queen and Lancelot together in her chamber, "Aggravain and Mordred are motivated by hatred and envy, and their goal is to destroy Lancelot and Guenevere, at the expense of peace in Arthur's kingdom." When Gawain advises Arthur to go to war with Lancelot, the king likewise does not seem to recognize that Gawain's love of family and desire for vengeance has overruled his desire for stability and peace in the kingdom.[76]

According to Louis J. Boyle, Arthur may fail at evaluating and receiving counsel because he learned from Merlin, who was too ideal a counsellor, and because the traditional teachings of *speculum principis* texts offered conflicting advice. In adapting his French sources for the first part of Arthur's reign, Malory created a Merlin who was all-knowing, a "spokesman for God" rather than the Merlin who warned of impending disaster in the French texts. Because Merlin's advice is always accurate, always good, Arthur never learns to evaluate the motivations of counsellors or anticipate the consequences of recommendations. Finally, Boyle argues that Arthur may have been following the recommendations of the mirrors for princes texts when he takes counsel less and less as the *Morte* develops, since these texts recognize that a king who takes counsel too often may be seen as weak and leave himself vulnerable to aggressive challenges from nobles.[77]

## Ideologies and Communities

Field and Lambert have both commented on the importance of the word "noble" in Malory's *Morte Darthur*. Lambert writes, "In the world of *Le Morte Darthur* virtue consists essentially of living up to a code, behaving in the manner characteristic of (or ... being the best individual according to the defining standard of) one's category."[78] A century of Malory criticism has shown that the ideals that make one noble in the *Morte* vary by community, and that, as members of multivalent communities – the "High Order of Knighthood," the gentry or noble class, region or kingdom – knights and gentlewomen in Malory's work must continually negotiate tensions within and among sets of community ideals. The only institution or person who can reconcile knights' and ladies' competing sets

---

[75] Kelly, "'Hasty jougement," 111; Radulescu, *Gentry Context*, 126.
[76] Radulescu, *Gentry Context*, 134.
[77] Boyle, "Ruled by Merlin," 57–9.
[78] P. J. C. Field, *Romance and Chronicle: A Study of Malory's Prose Style* (Bloomington, IN, 1971), 74–5; Mark Lambert, *Malory: Style and Vision in* Le Morte Darthur (New Haven, CT, 1975), 31.

of identities and ideologies is the king. But the principles of late medieval king-ship may have been too contradictory for one man. If Arthur did not wholly succeed at sustaining a polity in which multiple sets of ideologies compete, he did create a chivalric kingdom in which, at its high points (the Roman wars, the Great Tournament), he brought them temporarily "holè togydirs."

# 11
## Spiritual Malory
RALUCA L. RADULESCU

In Malory's time as in his *Morte Darthur* (and in other romances of the period, Arthurian and non-Arthurian), chivalry encompasses both secular and spiritual ideals.[1] Critical attention to spiritual priorities in the *Morte Darthur* has focused primarily on Malory's adaptation of the "Quest for the Holy Grail," while also including the episode of "The Healing of Sir Urry" – original to him – into the discussion. "The Tale of the Sankgreal" (Malory's title for his Grail Quest; henceforth *Sankgreal*)[2] is his closest translation of any source; it is based on a deeply religious narrative, the Old French Vulgate Cycle *La Queste del saint Graal*,[3] and remains the most religious of Malory's tales. A close comparison with the *Queste* led Eugène Vinaver to consider that Malory's vision of chivalry seemed more secular than that of his primary French source, which was harsher in its judgement of chivalric failure to achieve spiritual perfection.[4] This foundational view has been revisited by numerous critics since then, though the extent to which Malory chose to diminish the importance of religion in the knightly life of the protagonists in his Arthuriad remains open to interpretation. Many devotional and theologically-rich passages from the French *Queste* remain virtually

---

[1] See M. Keen, *Chivalry* (New Haven, CT, 1984); for an application to the romance genre, see the reference at note 34 below.

[2] "The Sankgreal," in Sir Thomas Malory, *Le Morte Darthur*, ed. P. J. C. Field, 2 vols. (Cambridge, 2013), I, henceforth cited parenthetically in the text.

[3] *La Queste del saint Graal*, ed. Albert Pauphilet (Paris, 1967), henceforth cited parenthetically in the text by page number. Malory also knew the Post-Vulgate version of the story; see *La Version Post-Vulgate de la "Queste del Saint Graal" et de la "Mort Artu": Troisième Partie du "Roman du Graal,"* ed. Fanni Bogdanow, 2 vols. (Paris, 1991).

[4] See *The Works of Sir Thomas Malory*, ed. Eugène Vinaver, 3rd rev. edn, ed. P. J. C. Field, 3 vols. (Oxford, 1990), esp. III, 1535: "Malory's attitude may be described without much risk of oversimplification as that of a man to whom the quest of the Grail was primarily an *Arthurian* adventure and who regarded the intrusion of the Grail upon Arthur's kingdom not as a means of contrasting earthly and divine chivalry and condemning the former, but as an opportunity offered to the knights of the Round Table to achieve still greater glory in *this* world" (emphasis original). However, the very phrase that Vinaver focussed on, the Grail knights' assertion that "he shall have much erthly worship that may bring hit to an ende" (731.9–10; my emphasis) is not, in fact, in disagreement with the spirit of the French *Queste*. Field demonstrates that, while Vinaver only compared the *Sankgreal* with Pauphilet's edition, two other extant versions of the *Queste* use "oneur terriens" ("earthly worship"), which makes it likely that Malory took the words from his French source (see *Le Morte Darthur*, ed. Field, II, 549), where the phrase would not have been perceived to be in contradiction to the spiritual worth gained by the knights during the Grail Quest (for more on this, see the discussion in the present chapter).

unchanged – albeit abridged – in Malory's *Sankgreal*; the symbolism of Catholic rituals and of the Grail as the "holy vessel" are similarly untouched.

The cornerstone of Malory's changes to his French sources consists in the joint effect of Lancelot's position in the *Sankgreal* (his repentance leading to his partial vision of the Holy Grail), his surprising success in "The Healing of Sir Urry," and his eventual saintly death. These moments lift Malory's Lancelot from the position of the archetypal sinner he was in the French romances to that of a remorseful, but redeemable, and hence more likeable character in the *Morte*. Alongside Lancelot, other knights and their adventures can also be considered to reinforce a less austere vision of spirituality than that presented in the French *Queste*.

Following studies of Malory's Arthuriad that have highlighted the links between the tales,[5] the *Sankgreal* has been considered an indispensable bridge between the early tales, which establish Arthur's reign and the reputations of his individual knights, and the later ones, when the Round Table fellowship collapses. A significant proportion of recent studies have re-articulated Vinaver's emphasis on "secular chivalry" in the *Morte*.[6] However, the original concerns of the Grail Quest can benefit from a re-examination of Malory's multi-faceted use of "fellowship" in its religious and secular forms.[7] Taking into account classic studies on this topic by Jill Mann and Felicity Riddy,[8] as well as more recent work, this chapter highlights Malory's evident concern for coherence in his adaptation of the original Grail Quest story, its links with the parallel story of the Grail keepers and their bloodlines, and the emotional trajectory of the main Arthurian protagonists, through whom the readers of the *Morte* experience the spiritual import of the adventures, and then the denouement of the Grail Quest.

To start with, Malory's entire *Morte* is marked by religious observance in an unobtrusive way. Arthur and his court regularly hear mass, go to confession and attempt to live by standard Catholic precepts. Unsurprisingly, important courtly events are scheduled to coincide with major feasts in the Christian calendar, as in the original Old French Vulgate romances. Early in "King Uther and King Arthur" we read that Arthur's successful act of pulling the sword out of the stone takes place "upon New Yeres day, whan the servyce was done" (8.1 / C I.3–5). When Arthur's achievement is not accepted by the barons the decision as to

---

[5] Murray J. Evans, "*Ordinatio* and Narrative Links: The Impact of Malory's Tales as a 'hoole book'," in *Studies in Malory*, ed. James W. Spisak (Kalamazoo, MI, 1985), 29–52. For a recent re-evaluation of the linking of the tales and the role played by the *Sankgreal* in this respect, see Raluca L. Radulescu, "The Politics of Salvation in Thomas Malory's *Le Morte Darthur*," in *Romance and Its Contexts in Fifteenth-Century England: Politics, Piety and Penitence* (Cambridge, 2013), chapter 4.

[6] See the essays contained in *Malory and Christianity: Essays on Sir Thomas Malory's Morte Darthur*, ed. D. Thomas Hanks Jr. and Janet Jesmok (Kalamazoo, MI, 2014). Among other studies on the relationship between secular and spiritual chivalry in the *Sankgreal*, see also Raluca L. Radulescu, "'Now I take uppon me the adventures to seke of holy thynges': Lancelot and the Crisis of Arthurian Knighthood," in *Arthurian Studies in Honour of P. J. C. Field*, ed. Bonnie Wheeler (Cambridge, 2004), 285–95.

[7] See also Elizabeth Archibald's classic study of the concept in her "Malory and the Ideal of Fellowship," *The Review of English Studies* 43 (1992): 311–28.

[8] See Jill Mann, "Malory and the Grail Legend," in *A Companion to Malory* (Cambridge, 1996), 203–20, esp. 210–11, for the analysis of the phrase "holé togydirs"; Felicity Riddy consecrated the phrase in her classic study *Sir Thomas Malory* (Leiden, 1987), 116–17.

whether he is worthy of the title or not is put off until Candlemas. Finally, Arthur pulls the sword out of the stone one last time at the feast of Pentecost when all the "lordes and the comyns" (11.7 / C I.7) proclaim him king, irrespective of the will of the barons, who have no choice but to accept him. From here on the reader of Malory's Arthuriad finds that Pentecost becomes the most important date in the calendar of the Arthurian court, along with "Twelfth Day" (that is, Epiphany), Candlemas and Easter; it is not surprising, therefore, to find that Galahad's re-enactment of the feat of pulling a sword out of the stone at the beginning of the *Sankgreal* occurs at Pentecost.[9]

The most important annual reunion of the Round Table fellowship usually also falls on this day, when the Round Table oath is renewed, unifying all under its chivalric precepts. Both in Malory's society and in his sources, Pentecost stood, of course, for the important moment when the Holy Spirit descended on the apostles after Christ's resurrection; symbolically, therefore, the feast stands for the "wholeness" of the fellowship and the first mission traditionally associated with knighthood and chivalry – to defend the Holy Church and the faith, even though Malory chose not to include this specific injunction in his Round Table oath at the beginning of the *Morte*.[10] None of this would surprise Malory's first medieval audiences, for time in medieval narrative – and in Arthurian romance in particular[11] – is often measured following the major divisions in the Christian calendar, pragmatically defined according to periods of fast and times of celebration.

An important premise, therefore, needs to be set from the start of any reconsideration of spirituality in the *Morte*: Malory both reacted to the material he found in his sources and incorporated elements from his personal experience (and that of his contemporaries) that would have sounded and felt true to his first (anticipated or implied) audience. Even from the perspective of a nostalgic recreation of a golden past – since Malory likely combined this approach with the more realistic, politically-inflected narrative that recent studies have uncovered in his Arthuriad – he would have naturally selected the elements that would resonate with his readers' experience, and fulfilled their expectations. In numerous aspects of his narrative style apart from spiritual tenor he always seems to choose to update, rather than archaise, his sources; there is no reason to believe, therefore, that his treatment of religion would be any different. On this basis,

---

[9] For an analysis of the import of this coincidence and the complementarity between the roles played by Arthur and Galahad in Malory's *Morte*, see my "Lancelot and the Key to Salvation," *Arthurian Literature* XXV (2008): 93–118.

[10] In the Old French Vulgate Prose *Lancelot* the Lady of the Lake specifically instructs a young Lancelot that chivalry was established to defend the Church (see *Lancelot: Roman en prose du XIIIe siècle*, ed. A. Micha, 9 vols. (Geneva, 1980), VII, 250; "Above all, knighthood was established to defend the Holy Church" – translation from *Lancelot-Grail: The Old French Vulgate and Post-Vulgate in Translation*, gen. ed. Norris J. Lacy, 5 vols. (New York, 1993–6), II, 59). However, Malory chose not to use these words from the Prose *Lancelot* in his formulation of the Round Table oath (97.28–35). Interestingly, the same injunction is repeated in Ramon Llull's best-selling medieval chivalric treatise; see Ramon Llull, *The Book of the Ordre of Chyvalry, translated and printed by William Caxton*, ed. Alfred T. P. Byles (London, 1926), 24.

[11] See also Miriam Edlich-Muth, *Malory and His European Contemporaries* (Cambridge, 2014).

this chapter starts from the premise that, irrespective of modern critical debate over his treatment of religion in the *Morte*, it remains clear that Malory's own experience of (gentry) religious practice and his creative reflection on the broader intersections between the different emphases on religious devotion in his French and English sources are equally important avenues to explore in relation to spirituality in his Arthuriad. This chapter aims to demonstrate that, far from being Malory's least interesting story, devoid of the excitement and passions of the rest of his Arthuriad, the *Sankgreal* can offer fresh ground for investigations linking this building block in Malory's writing to the rest of his vision, giving it depth and enhancing its appeal. The main parts of this re-examination of spirituality will focus on the links between the tales created through a unified vision of earthly and heavenly chivalry, the importance of swords and lineages, and the indissoluble links between blood, gender and the healing of wounds. These themes will be explored by considering the implications of manuscript study as well as the emergence of a focus on the history of emotions in Arthurian and Malory studies.

*

When the unique Winchester Malory manuscript (London, British Library, Additional MS 59678) was discovered in 1934, the copy of *Le Morte Darthur* it contained clearly displayed a substantially different text than that enjoyed by readers since William Caxton's first edition of 1485.[12] Divided into eight tales that tend to follow the distinct nature of Malory's main sources, rather than the twenty-one books of Caxton's edition, the text could now show the nature and relationships among the constituent parts of the *Morte* as Malory presumably intended them to be read. The *Sankgreal*, which takes up fifty folios in the Winchester manuscript (349r–409r), starts on a fresh page, and the first rubricated word[13] is a Christian feast: "At the vigyl of Pentecoste, whan all the felyship of the Table Rownde were com unto Camelot and there harde hir servyse" (665.3–5 / C XIII.1; fol. 349r).

In a similar fashion to the French *Queste*, therefore, the story starts at the feast that brings the knights together yearly to swear their Round Table oath. The Winchester scribe for this portion of the story chose to present it as a fresh start, leaving space between the end of the Tristram narrative and the Quest.[14] Significantly, the end of this version of the Grail Quest is marked by Malory's precise labelling of the story as "the Tale of the Sankgreal that was breffly drawy*n* oute of Freynshe [into Englysshe] whych ys a tale *cronycled* for *one of trewyst and of þe holyest that ys in thys worlde*. By Sir Thomas Maleorré, knyght" (789.14–17 / C XVII.23; fol. 409r; my emphasis). Malory's precise use of the verb "cronycled," coupled with the qualifying adjectives "trewyst and … holyest" for the whole

---

[12] On the Winchester manuscript, see Thomas H. Crofts and K. S. Whetter, "Writing the *Morte Darthur*: Author, Manuscript and Modern Editions," in this volume.

[13] Rubricated words are written out in red ink, rather than the brown ink used for the main text; this process was expensive, as it required a change of pen. See Crofts and Whetter, "Writing the *Morte Darthur*."

[14] Carol M. Meale, "'The Hoole Book': Editing and the Creation of Meaning in Malory's Text," in *A Companion to Malory*, ed. Elizabeth Archibald and A. S. G. Edwards (Cambridge, 1996), 3–15.

tale, associate the author with both compilers of historical chronicles and authors who penned spiritual instruction during the later Middle Ages. This explicit also draws attention to the presumed veracity of this account of both Arthur's reign and the arrival of Christianity in Britain, heralded long before Malory in the branch of the Vulgate Cycle known as the *Estoire del saint Graal* – a story unavailable in English to most readers apart from the modest poem *Joseph of Arimathea* (in the Vernon manuscript, Oxford, Bodleian Library, English Poet a. 1) and Henry Lovelich's early fifteenth-century translation, neither of which seems to have been known to Malory.[15] Indeed, at several councils of the Church in the early fifteenth century, efforts were made to establish the legend of Joseph of Arimathea as a reliable source for the claim made for the ancestry of the English Church.[16]

John Hardyng, one of Malory's contemporaries, and the author of a Galfridian-inspired chronicle,[17] chose to incorporate the Grail Quest into his *Chronicle*, though his focus was less on the spiritual pursuit of salvation than on the pragmatic appropriation of the legacy of Grail keepers into the establishment of an Order of the Holy Grail by Galahad. Malory used Hardyng's chronicle as one of his minor sources in other parts of the *Morte*, but he did not include Hardyng's innovation, the Order of the Grail, into his *Sankgreal*, although he chose to set the Grail story in Wales, which is where Hardyng says the Grail is found in the second version of his *Chronicle* – a suggestion not made before. Malory used as his primary source the Vulgate *Queste del saint Graal* (henceforth *Queste*), and selected minor elements from the Post-Vulgate *Queste*, the Prose *Tristan* and the *Perlesvaus*.[18] The adventures described in the *Sankgreal* follow the narrative line in the Old French *Queste*, yet the linking of events and objects to earlier episodes in Malory's Arthuriad indicates more careful planning than the comparison with his main source might indicate.[19]

Although Malory's *Sankgreal* remains his closest translation of an existing source, his method of adaptation of the narrative material has led critics to

---

[15] See Radulescu, *Romance and Its Contexts*, chapters 3 and 4. Malory likely knew about this branch of the Vulgate, given his familiarity with and use of the other parts of the Vulgate and Post-Vulgate Cycles.

[16] See Edward Donald Kennedy, "Glastonbury," in *The Arthur of Medieval Latin Literature*, ed. Siân Echard (Cardiff, 2011); *The Chronicle of Glastonbury Abbey: An Edition, Translation and Study of John of Glastonbury's "Cronica, sive, Antiquitates Glastoniensis Ecclesie,"* ed. James P. Carley, trans. David Townsend (Woodbridge, 1985). Some fifteenth-century copies of the Middle English *Brut* chronicles also recorded the importance of the Grail in the context of additions to the main chronicle narrative of the legend of Joseph of Arimathea.

[17] Hardyng's *Chronicle* followed a long-established and widespread tradition of "Galfridian" chronicle writing – that is, chronicles ultimately derived from Geoffrey of Monmouth's twelfth-century *Historia regum Britanniae*.

[18] See P. J. C. Field, "Malory and the Grail: The Importance of Detail," in *The Grail, the Quest, and the World of Arthur*, ed. Norris Lacy (Cambridge, 2008), 141–55, at 147; Ralph Norris, *Malory's Library: The Sources of the* Morte Darthur (Cambridge, 2008), 117. Ralph Norris has demonstrated that Malory drew on John Hardyng's *Chronicle* as a minor source for a number of his alterations to his sources in other sections of the *Morte Darthur*.

[19] For a comparative study of Malory's *Sankgreal* and the Old French Vulgate *Queste* see Sandra Ihle Ness, *Malory's Grail Quest: Invention and Adaptation in Medieval Prose Romance* (Madison, WI, 1983).

significant debate over the nature of his enterprise and the story's place in the architectural structure of his Arthuriad. Without a doubt, the *Sankgreal* poses similar questions to those raised by its predecessor, the Old French *Queste*. Among them are: the problems posed by secular chivalric adventure and prowess in arms as a path to salvation; the relationship between regular attendance and participation in Christian rituals and the degree of success an Arthurian knight can expect in chivalric encounters; the significance of the arrival of the Grail as a disruptive moment in the history of Arthur's court; the role played by men and women in the history of salvation. In this respect the *Sankgreal* can be considered a cornerstone for Malory's Arthuriad. Here Malory shows he understood this to be an opportunity to engage with one of the more difficult aspects of Arthurian romance, the conflict between the pursuit of secular reputation and the humility required in the pursuit of Christian perfection. While the rest of his *Morte* may explore topics as varied as gender, politics and socio-economic pressures on the shaping of personal and collective identity – to mention just a few of the key interests covered in his work – the *Sankgreal* presents a streamlined version of Arthurian "reality," whereby questions of great interest to the reader can be explored almost entirely outside of fifteenth-century constraints. The political feuds of earlier tales are suppressed and "fellowship" – in its multi-faceted aspects – emerges unscathed as a focal point.

The driving force for Arthur's fellowship of knights to undertake the quest is, of course, the Grail itself.[20] As an object of veneration and pursuit, the Grail is a symbol of plenty that accompanies the descent of the Holy Spirit at one yearly celebration of Pentecost at Arthur's court. Indeed, the appearance of the Grail at Arthur's feast signals the traditional association between his chivalric fellowship and the spiritual fellowship of the first apostles that Malory inherited from his French source, but which he chose not to mention until the *Sankgreal*:

> And than the kynge and all the astatis wente home unto Camelot, and so wente unto evynsong to the grete monester. And so aftir uppon that to sowper, and every knyght sette in hys owne place as they were toforehonde. Than anone they harde crakynge and cryynge of thundir, that hem thought the palyse sholde all to-dryve. So in the myddys of the blast entyrde a sonnebeame, more clerer by seven tymys than ever they saw day, and all they were alyghted of the grace of the Holy Goste. Than began every knyght to beholde other, and eyther saw other, by theire semyng, fayrer than ever they were before. Natforthan there was no knyght that might speke one worde a grete whyle, and so they loked every man on other as they had bene doome. Than entird into the halle the Holy Grayle coverde with whyght samyte, but there was none that myght se hit nother whom that bare hit. And there was all the halle fulfylled with good odoures, and every knyght had such metis and drynkes as he beste loved in thys worlde. And whan the Holy Grayle had bene borne thorow the hall, than the holy vessell departed suddeynly, that they wyst nat where hit becam. Than had they all breth to speke, and

---

[20] For a summary of Grail definitions, see Mann, "Malory and the Grail Legend," and Field, "Malory and the Grail."

than the kyng yelded thankynges to God of Hys good grace that He had
sente them. (673.26–674.10 / C XIII.6)

This initial moment of fellowship, understood as the brotherhood among the
Round Table knights now confirmed as elect by the descent of the Holy Spirit,
signals the unity of purpose that has characterised Arthur's vision for his court
in previous tales. The temporary brightness of their faces points not only to a
biblical comparison, but also to the inner composure and stability that each
knight can achieve sitting at Arthur's Round Table and partaking in his ideal
"fellowship." The central focus of the scene is the Grail, mysteriously covered,
but enticing the viewer to speculate on its interpretation in this version of the
story.[21] Temporarily, doubts over the success of Arthurian chivalry in providing
stability in the world are set aside, and the story harks back to the hopeful days
of Arthur's early reign.

Indeed it is at the start of the *Sankgreal* that Malory's changes to earlier por-
tions of his Arthuriad are given full shape, and show his vision. In "King Uther
and King Arthur" he used the Post-Vulgate *Suite de Merlin* to emphasise the role
played by Balin, the "unhappy knight," whose "mis-adventures" Malory chose
to link to developments later in his Arthuriad. It is the sword Balin uses to strike
the dolorous stroke to King Pellam,[22] and which Merlin placed in a stone that
floats down the river that Galahad will pull out; it is the same sword that Merlin
foretold that Lancelot would use to wound Gawain in the final tale:

> "Thys ys the cause," seyde Merlion. "There shall never man handyll thys
> swerde but the beste knyght of the worlde, and that shall be sir Launcelot
> other ellis Galahad hys sonne. And Launcelot with thys swerde shall sle
> the man in the worlde that he lovith beste: that shall be sir Gawayne."
> (74.9–13 / C II.19)

Merlin's prophetic words (not found in Malory's sources) resonate in the rest
of the *Morte*. It is at this point in the Winchester manuscript (in which Balin's
adventures receive by far the largest number of marginalia (side annotations)
and signposting comments by comparison with other tales)[23] that a (final) gloss
reads: "Here ys a pronostication of the Sank Greall" (fol. 31r). While Merlin's
words predict the future of the sword, they signal the passage of the sword
from the hands of an "unhappy knight" (Balin) to the chosen one (Galahad)
and then to the sinful but partially redeemed knight (Lancelot). There is also
a symbolic mission: where Balin gave a stroke that caused a wound, Galahad
heals it, continuing the pragmatic legacy of the Grail keepers; where Lancelot
broke his promise made during the Quest, he is granted a miraculous healing,

---

[21] In Malory's sources the Grail is a dish or a platter and only later does it become a
chalice; see Mann, "Malory and the Grail Legend," for an overview of the significance
of the Grail.

[22] See *Le Morte Darthur*, ed. Field, II, 62, explaining I.68.15–18, where Malory conflates
the characters of (and the wounds inflicted on) King Pellam and King Pelleans; Field
also addresses the streamlining effects of this choice.

[23] See P. J. C. Field, "Malory's Own Marginalia," *Medium Ævum* 70.2 (2001): 226–39
(the article includes an appendix listing all the marginalia and their location in the
Winchester manuscript); for a recent discussion of the marginalia in the Balin story,
see Radulescu, *Romance and Its Contexts*, chapter 4.

and a saintly end, thus fulfilling the symbolic mission of providing a model of behaviour no Galahad ever could.

The opening of the *Sankgreal* in the Winchester manuscript shows the rubrication of "Pentecost" alongside the expected proper names as elsewhere in the manuscript. Winchester's rubrication of proper names and Pentecost on the first page of the tale confirms the importance given to Galahad, the pre-eminent knight, and his father, Lancelot, in the Grail Quest. On the first few folios alone Lancelot is physically present in the rubrication, although his absence is conspicuous from the narrative itself; to this extent it may be argued that the memorialising function of the rubrication acts here to great effect.[24] In Winchester's marginalia, possibly authorial, as P. J. C. Field has argued,[25] the *Sankgreal* draws attention to the meaningful association between Galahad, Lancelot and the spiritual feast of togetherness, Pentecost. Irrespective of the narrative trajectory uncovered in the pages that follow, the reader of Winchester would be encouraged to ponder the links between these two pillars of Malory's version of the story, father and son, who also each prove to be entrusted with a mission. Galahad achieves the Grail vision, and completes the Grail adventures; Lancelot can be said to fulfil the mission of the Grail keepers, in whose line both he and Galahad are placed by tradition (and by Malory), to provide a spiritual path to those of his fellows who might otherwise be too troubled by secular concerns to be able to see any salvation.[26] Indeed, unlike the authors of his French sources, Malory repeatedly reminds his audience that Galahad and Lancelot bear responsibilities that were established long ago. At the beginning of the story an "old man" tells Galahad "ys of kynges lynage and of the kynrede of Joseph of Aramathy" (669.30–1 / C XIII.3; fol. 350r); Guenevere, in a passage original to Malory, confirms that Galahad "ys of the nyneth degré frome Oure Lorde Jesu Cryst" (673.22–3 / C XIII.6; fol. 352r).[27] Galahad's physical resemblance to Lancelot is here noted, and his ability to fulfil the adventures is praised. Malory's readers are repeatedly reminded of the lineage of the Grail keepers and Arthur's greatness in having Lancelot and Galahad as part of his earthly fellowship of knights, even if Galahad's presence among them is brief.

Galahad's arrival at the court may be seen to signal a temporary sense of "wholeness": he takes his place in the "siege Perilous" and thus closes the circle of the Round Table. By contrast, the memorable speech Malory grants Arthur at the start of the quest hints that the "completeness" Galahad has brought to the fellowship is to be contrasted with the fragmentation and divisions it heralds:

> "Now," seyde the kynge, "I am sure at this quest of the Sankegreall shall ye of the Rownde Table departe and nevyr shall I se you agayne holé togyrdis. Therefore ones I woll se you all holé togydir in the medow of

---

[24] For a recent study of Winchester's rubrication, see Kevin S. Whetter, *The Manuscript and Meaning of Malory's* Morte Darthur: *Rubrication, Commemoration, Memorialization* (Cambridge, 2017).

[25] Field, "Malory's Own Marginalia."

[26] See Radulescu, "Malory's Lancelot and the Key to Salvation."

[27] See Field's explanation of this inaccuracy as Galahad cannot be Christ's descendant (*Le Morte Darthur*, II, 557–8). Nonetheless, the importance given by Malory to this connection is evident here.

Camelot, to juste and to turney, that aftir youre dethe men may speke of hit that such good knyghtes were here, such a day, holé togydirs." (672.25–30 / C XIII.6)

Galahad's arrival can only point to the downside of taking pride in earthly chivalry, for reputation does not endure. Galahad never belongs to this world and he does not aim to fulfil Arthur's dream of togetherness for the fellowship. Through Galahad and the other Grail knights (Perceval and Bors), the audience within the *Sankgreal* and outside it learns that completeness can only be achieved on a personal level and through the practice of a different type of worthy service, which aligns the knight with saintly endeavours and is therefore a solitary, rather than a collective, journey.

In the *Sankgreal* Malory pits not only individual knights, but also different types of fellowship, against each other. Apart from the Round Table fellowship and its rules, there are the temporary earthly fellowships (company) the knights enjoy on the quest, and the symbolic fellowship that both Galahad and Lancelot belong to, thanks to their descent from the Grail keepers. These fellowships reflect the nature of chivalry in Malory's sources and in his own Arthuriad (proclaiming unity under fixed ideals, but often failing in medieval practice), and also the disillusioned England of the late fifteenth century. For the latter perhaps only the promise of a spiritual experience of a completely different order could provide any consolation when the country was felt to be falling apart after years of civil war.

For this reason, the fallibility of the ideals upheld by the Round Table knights, and the way in which Lancelot is figured as a redeemable sinner, come together in Malory's story to show that the *Sankgreal* cannot be about either collective success or individual victory for the spiritually fit. Malory's Galahad fulfils all the expectations of an ideal knight. Educated by the nuns, he is uniquely equipped with wisdom and knowledge beyond his years and reassured in his predestined role of Grail knight (670.12–16 / C XIII.4; 671.21–34 / C XIII.4). While modern critics have focused on Malory's evident softening of Lancelot's sinful nature, leading to several opportunities for his favourite knight to fulfil at least some of the requirements of the Quest, less attention has been paid to the character of Galahad, the seemingly perfect knight, whose trajectory may appear less interesting, given its predictable outcome. In fact, Malory's Galahad is much more "perfect" than his French counterpart in the *Queste*. He is more self-assured, more definitive in his decisions, less concerned with the welfare and spiritual fate of those around him. He appears to be more mechanically suited to the role of saintly knight than any other companion on the Grail Quest, but for this very reason he is also the character whose perfection makes him a special case. He inspires admiration among the Round Table knights on the quest within the *Morte* (no doubt among Malory's fifteenth-century readers, too) in the way the protagonists of another popular late-medieval genre, saints' lives, do.

All of Galahad's actions are divinely sanctioned and hence deemed morally right; foreknowledge of the future also elevates him above his Grail Quest companions. Malory and his contemporaries likely admired Galahad's holiness, but his personal model of chivalric perfection could not be emulated by the first audiences of the *Morte*, whereas he could still provide inspiration for others to strive for spiritual perfection.[28] Mann's views on Galahad and the complex religious symbolism Malory preserves from his French sources are relevant here:

> In minimizing the role of ... religious expositions, Malory makes the world of the *Sankgreal* consistent with that of the rest of his work: a world of pervasive enigma, in which explanation or understanding comes, if at all, fitfully and too late to have any bearing on the action – a world in which the knight must engage in adventure without any clear notion of the consequences or character of his involvement. And here as elsewhere, adventure is heuristic: it reveals a knight's pre-existing worth rather than offering an opportunity to acquire it. Galahad's superiority is not a result of his trying harder, ... he is simply not tempted ... His pre-eminence consists in his wholeness, which is his from the beginning, and which the events of the narrative are designed to express.[29]

Mann is right to draw attention to Galahad's pre-existing worth, which cannot therefore be diminished or enhanced through his adventures. However, for other Arthurian knights, acquiring worth requires sustained effort over time, and it is this journey or progress in acquiring worth that Malory's Lancelot so amply demonstrates. Across his development in the *Morte* Lancelot's worth (acquired in the early tales) diminishes as he is shamed for his sins in the Quest. However, the Grail Quest *is* about an opportunity to acquire heavenly worth and the Grail knights are told very clearly how to apply themselves to this task: go to confession and leave sinful behaviour behind. Some, like Gawain, refuse to do any more than go to confession; some, like Lancelot, do both, and are rewarded. Their choices are personal and hence their failures are due to human failure, not predestined fate; on the other hand, Galahad is clearly without sin and his trajectory does not display any effort in acquiring worth.[30]

Malory's Galahad, therefore, does not act as a lynchpin in the story, not in the way he was cast in that leadership role by the authors of the original French *Queste*. He divides and exposes the Round Table fellowship as unworthy of its collective reputation and the knights as impossible to redeem on an individual level unless they give up earthly "fellowship," understood as the overriding clan-based loyalties of the Arthurian world outside the Grail. There are no lessons to learn from Galahad's experiences in the Quest, whereas Perceval's, Bors's and Lancelot's Grail Quests are qualitatively different, edifying in their own right and to different degrees. Emerging from their new fellowship is a sense of spiritual brotherhood similar to that developed by some religious orders such as the Dominicans and the Franciscans in medieval England.

Perceval and Bors defend personal Christian principles, resisting carnal temptation (Perceval) and putting spiritual pursuits and morally upright deeds above loyalty to earthly kin (Bors). The latter might be said to be an illustrative

---

[28] For the opposite view, that Malory altered Galahad's characterisation in the original *Queste* to make him more "earthly," and "lower on the spiritual ladder" in his *Sankgreal*, see Fiona Tolhurst, "Slouching Towards Bethlehem: Secularized Salvation in *Le Morte Darthur*," in *Malory and Christianity*, 126–56.

[29] Mann, "Malory and the Grail Legend," 209–10.

[30] I am grateful for discussions with P. J. C. Field on this topic.

counterpart to Galahad; Bors shows, more than any other knight on the Grail quest, that he has understood the spiritual nature of the adventure and relinquished his attachment to worldly burdens. Bors is reminded by a maiden who is in great danger of being raped that his duty is to defend her, as part of the Round Table oath,[31] and hence chooses to free her and let his brother Lionel, who is simultaneously in need of Bors's help, be taken away, beaten and humiliated, possibly to be put to death. However, later adventures show Bors is not always able to reconcile his feelings with the demands of the Quest. He cannot defend a priest who intervenes on his behalf, and who is decapitated by Lionel (who was threatening to fight Bors to the death), nor can he intervene when Collgrevaunce is similarly defeated and mercilessly slain by an enraged Lionel, although Collgrevance stood in the path of Lionel's anger towards a defenceless Bors. Only divine intervention stops the brothers Bors and Lionel from killing each other in this episode, and the message of the divine voice is clear: "sir Bors, go hens and beare thy brothir no lenger *felyship*, but take thy way anone ryght to the see, for sir Percivale abydith the there" (747.19–21 / C XVI.16; my emphasis). The fellowship Bors is told to forsake is earthly; it pertains to family relationships, and also to the secular chivalry practised in Arthur's court. Bors will not defend himself nor the priest nor Collgrevance because he cannot fight against another knight of the Round Table. In other words, Bors discovers that the spiritual demands of the Grail Quest go against the secular rules of Arthurian fellowship.

Indeed, throughout the testing of Bors the reader of Malory's *Sankgreal* witnesses the genuine suffering of the knight who chooses the morally right path, whose emotional turmoil is for all to see: when he hears the damsel in distress, "he had so much sorow that he wyst nat what to do … Than lyffte he up hys yghen and seyde wepynge" (736.22–3, 27 / C XVI.10); when Lionell his brother runs his horse over him Bors is concerned that he might die without confession (744.19–21 / C XVI.15). Bors shows genuine contradiction in his beliefs and hence is more human in his path to the Grail; he is too injured to defend Collgrevaunce, who in turn is defending him, but that does not stop Bors from the torment of the moral implications of this inaction in this gruesome combat between brothers (in arms, and by blood): "sir Bors sate up all angwyshlye and behylde sir Collegrevaunce, the good knight … Thereof he was full hevy, and thought if sir Collgrevaunce slew hys brothir that he sholde never have joy; also, and if hys brothir slew sir Collgrevaunce, 'the shame sholde ever be myne'" (745.30–5 / C XVI.15).

By contrast, Malory suggests that the best fellowship a knight can enjoy on the path to the Grail is of a spiritual kind – and thus Bors is brought to Perceval and Galahad, in whose company he will experience the mysteries of the holy vessel and will discover individual "wholeness." The experience of fragmentation that

---

[31] The maiden "conjured hym, by the faythe that he ought unto Hym 'in whos servyse thou arte entred, and for kynge Arthures sake, which I suppose made the knyght, that thou helpe me and suffir me nat to be shamed of thys knyght'" (736.18–21 / C XVI.10). In his edition Field removes Caxton's "hyghe ordre of knyghthode" (Caxton's substitution for "by the faythe…"), which is picked up in Vinaver's edition as well, on the grounds, Field believes, of "compositional padding" in Caxton (see *Le Morte Darthur*, ed. Field, II, 620–1).

chivalric duties (fellowship) trigger in the knight is much more complex than that engendered by the journey to salvation, which now seems clear and less complicated, leading to "wholeness." In this episode, perhaps more than anywhere else in the *Sankgreal*, Bors stands as an example of genuine angst in choosing the right path, though he does not hesitate in taking the hardest decisions on each occasion, which lead to violent outcomes (the death of the priest, and Collgrevance's death). His emotional responses form part of a broader movement towards internalising the quest as a spiritual experience, which will be explored in Perceval, and, to an even greater extent, in Lancelot.[32] Bors's adventures during the Grail Quest, like Perceval's, show that the constant moral battle faced by Arthurian knights in their joint pursuit of earthly glory and spiritual salvation continues well after the *Sankgreal* is over.[33] The journey towards spiritual salvation is continued by Gawain and Lancelot, and, to some extent, the Round Table fellowship, even though the latter cannot really achieve wholeness again after the Quest is over, except during "The Healing of Sir Urry" episode.

Gawain and Lancelot are the two pillars of chivalry upon which Arthur's fellowship is built. Gawain jettisons the spiritual opportunity offered by the Grail Quest early on, famously stating, when an old hermit admonishes him to leave his sinful ways, that "hit semyth me by your wordis that for oure [Gawain's and Ector's] synnes hit woll nat avayle us to travayle in thys queste" (730.3–4 / C XVI.4). Gawain, it seems, thinks that there is no point to try. Shortly afterwards, when the hermit reminds him that there is still time to repent, Gawain merely rushes off: "and I had leyser I wolde speke with you, but my fellow sir Ector ys gone and abith me yonder bynethe the hylle" (730.15–17 / C XVI.4). Earlier on Gawain had dismissed the demands of the Quest for penance with the memorable words "I may do no penaunce, for we knyghtes adventures many tymes suffir grete woo and payne" (691.31–2 / C XIII.16), a response that is reminiscent of medieval chivalric manuals in which knights are urged to repent, but only later in life.[34]

---

[32] The rise in studies of the history of emotions in Arthurian romance is a fruitful avenue for further exploration of this issue, both in the *Sankgreal* and elsewhere in the *Morte*. For a ground-breaking collection of essays on the topic, see *Emotions in Medieval Arthurian Literature*, ed. Frank Brandsma, Carolyne Larrington and Corinne Saunders (Cambridge, 2015). See also Andrew Lynch, "Malory and Emotion," in this volume.

[33] It does not seem accidental that Malory's paring down of the *Queste* draws attention to the presence of Bors and Lionel at the beginning of the *Sankgreal*, at the abbey where Galahad is introduced to Lancelot. When Lancelot and Galahad arrive at the court together, Malory does not initially record any reaction to them, but rather, surprisingly, notes "the kynge and the quene were passynge glad of Sir Bors and Sir Lyonel, and so was all the felyship" (667.6–8/ C XIII.2). Field emends the passage, on the logic that Lancelot's arrival must have been intended here; hence he adds "Lancelot" before Bors and Lionel although none of the extant witnesses include him. The French source does not contain an equivalent to this passage (see *Le Morte Darthur*, II, 552). Nonetheless I believe Malory's paring down of the details in this episode leads to added emphasis on the two brothers whose experiences in the quest will test the bonds of both kin and chivalry (two out of several types of fellowship) – which has not been noted before.

[34] For a discussion of Arthurian romance and Christianity in the context of contemporary chivalric manuals, see Raluca Radulescu, "How Christian is Chivalry?" in *Christianity and Romance in Medieval England*, ed. Rosalind Field, Phillipa Hardman and Michelle Sweeney (Cambridge, 2010), 69–83. Malory's hermit admonishes Lancelot to avoid

Gawain's disregard for the demands of the Grail Quest do not disqualify him, however, from gaining God's mercy after his death, as the reader of the *Morte* finds out that service to ladies, as prescribed by the Round Table oath, has earned Gawain a place in heaven. Indeed, Gawain's return to Arthur in a dream, to warn him of the impending disaster of the battle with Mordred (920.30–921.18 / C XXI.3) seems designed to show God's merciful approach to those Arthurian knights who are unable to change their ways, but have still fulfilled some of the requirements of the Church (here defending the weak in their "righteous quarrels") and chivalry. That Gawain does not gain any spiritual understanding during the Grail Quest is due to his stubborn resistance to Christian rules. He is willing to go to confession, but will not make amends or change his life sufficiently to join the ranks of the Grail knights and see the Grail openly.

Lancelot, on the other hand, is the one character Malory clearly favoured, and whose trajectory both before and after the Grail Quest seems to typify the most palatable spiritual journey a fifteenth-century English romance audience would enjoy. Lancelot's pursuit of worldly glory and love of Guenevere are singularly human, and bring him closer to Malory's contemporaries. In Lancelot's conversion from sinner to penitent, fifteenth-century audiences would recognise the rituals and practice of Catholicism to which they were accustomed. As Field, Riddy, Karen Cherewatuk and other critics have shown, the details encountered in Malory's description of Christianity here in the *Sankgreal* and later, during Lancelot's repentance and saintly death, show attention to those elements of his story that would resonate with his readers' late-medieval experience of worship.[35]

Lancelot openly admits his sins, though interestingly he identifies them not only as sins according to Christian rules but also, even more evidently, as transgressions against the Round Table oath which forbids knights to "take no batayles in a wrongefull quarell for no love ne for worldis goodis" (97.34–5 / C III.15). He tells the hermit "how he had loved a quene unmesurabely and oute of mesure longe" and "for her sake wolde I do batayle were hit ryght other wronge. And never dud I batayle all only for Goddis sake, but for to wynne worship and to cause me the bettir to be beloved" (696.19, 21–4 / C XIII.20). While it is not the first nor the last time that the reader sees Lancelot's actions being measured against the chivalric oath sworn every year at Pentecost,[36] the crux of Malory's changes to his source can be summarised in the significantly softer injunction the hermit places on Lancelot, "no more com in that quenys felyship as much as ye may forbere," followed by the reassurance that critics have found most controversial in this section of the *Morte*: "I [the hermit] shall ensure you ye shall have the more

---

the company of the queen as much as possible, and then have more worship in *this* world. This does not obviate either the need for the penance Lancelot will undertake, including the wearing of a hair shirt, nor the punishing regime he subjects himself to after Arthur and Guenevere's death (for a detailed examination of these, see Karen Cherewatuk's "The Saint's Life of Sir Lancelot: Hagiography and the Conclusion of Malory's *Morte Darthur*," *Arthuriana* 5.1 (1995): 62–78).

[35] Cherewatuk, "The Saint's Life"; also, by the same author, "Malory's Lancelot and the Language of Sin and Confession," *Arthuriana* 16.2 (2006): 68–72.

[36] In "The Tale of Sir Launcelot", similar judgements may be explored, as is even more evident in the last two tales, in relation to Lancelot's defence of Guenevere on several occasions.

worship than ever ye had" (696.27–8, 32–3 / C XIII.20). Modern critics, including myself, have often considered this promise to signify more "earthly" worship (as Malory puts it later in the *Sankgreal*), meaning an increase in Lancelot's secular worship or reputation, but not in his spiritual reputation. However, Field's recent discovery that the French equivalent of Malory's phrase "erthly worship" ("oneur terriens") appears in manuscripts of the French *Queste* in a way that does not imply a divergence between secular and spiritual reputation,[37] coupled with the importance of acquiring worship through painful efforts discussed above, suggests this emphasis on worship in the *Sankgreal* still accomodates both spiritual and chivalric merit at this point.

Lancelot admits that the burden of guilt and sin he bears is not just that of an ordinary sinner, but one that is heavier in the light of his responsibilities, such as he has seemingly shirked for some time in relation to his observance of the Round Table oath as well. Such responsibilities are also closely related to the performance of his duty as descendant in the line of Grail keepers, which places upon him a mantle of leadership in spiritual, as well as secular, matters. This is a point rarely tackled by modern critics, but which would matter to Malory's fifteenth-century audiences, given the efforts expended by the English Church in establishing its ancestry by use of the Joseph of Arimathea legend.[38] Malory's insistence on keeping the details of Lancelot's descent narrated in the *Queste* seems to suggest he was keen to remind his readers of the Grail legacy in Britain, and Lancelot's role in bringing greater glory to Arthur's court through the connection to the Grail.

Lancelot had experienced, by this stage, the shame and confusion brought about by missing the experience of the Grail, when at the beginning of the quest he was blinded by his sin at the chapel (at that stage he was told by a divine voice he could not experience the vision of the Grail because of his sins: 694.30–3 / C XIII.19; fol. 362v). There can be no greater contrast between this early episode and Lancelot's final vision of the Grail. For Lancelot the adventures of the *Sankgreal* do lead to spiritual awakening; at the end of his quest he recognises the "holy vessell" without any external help, and correctly interprets it as the chalice of the Eucharist, surrounded as it is by angels, unmistakably proclaiming the mystery of the Holy Trinity in the mystery of transubstantiation that the priest is specifically seen "to show so to the peple":

> And with that he saw the chambir dore opyn, and there cam oute a grete clerenesse, that the house was as bryght as all the tourcheis of the worlde had bene there. So cam he to the chambir doore and wolde have entird. And anone a voice seyde unto hym, "Sir Launcelot, flee and entir nat, for thou ought nat to do hit! For and thou entir thou shalt forthynke hit."
>
> Than he withdrew hym aback ryght hevy.
>
> Than loked he up into the myddis of the chambir and saw a table of sylver, and the holy vessell coverde with rede samyte, and many angels aboute hit, whereof one hylde a candyll of wexe brennynge and the other hylde a crosse and the ornementis of an awter. And before the holy

[37] See above, p. 211, n. 3.
[38] See above, p. 215.

vessell he saw a good man clothed as a pryste, and hit semed that he was at the sakerynge of the masse. And hit semed to Sir Launcelot that above the prystis hondys were thre men, whereof the too put the yongyste by lyknes betwene the prystes hondis; and so he lyffte hym up ryght hyghe, and hit semed to shew so to the peple. (773.27–774.9 / C XVIII.14)

As Field notes, there is no doubt that Malory understood the need to show his contemporaries a version of the Grail that would resonate with their beliefs of the presence of Christ in the Eucharist.[39] In this moment, as in other parts of the *Sankgreal*, an orthodox view of religion and spirituality emerges, one that does not resonate with the more secular concerns of glory and prowess in arms elsewhere in the *Morte*. To be granted a vision of the Holy Grail takes more than abiding by the rules of the Round Table; it implies a deeper, and personal, rather than collective, understanding of faith and a pursuit of holiness and purity. That Lancelot, who only experiences the Grail partially, is granted the privilege of telling the court his Grail adventures, is significant (788.30–5 / C XVII.23).[40] Malory draws attention, once again, to Lancelot's elect status – a status that is reinforced in the later episode of "The Healing of Sir Urry" where he heals the cursed (wounded) knight Urry in an act which mirrors Galahad's "miracles" in the *Sankgreal*. In these later scenes, replete with echoes of the Pentecostal reunions before the Grail Quest, Arthur's fellowship comes together once more, united in humility and obedience to Arthur and God. Is the fellowship once again "holé togydirs" as a healed, religiously-minded company of knights, in the spirit of the Grail Quest, or is the episode to be interpreted as a confirmation that Malory is suggesting a more secular interpretation of God's favour to Lancelot and Arthurian chivalry? Critical opinion is divided on the matter of Lancelot's tears at his successful, though reluctantly undertaken, fulfilment of Arthur's command to "search" Urry's magical wounds (866–8 / C XIX.12). Whether his tears are of relief at saving his reputation, joy at God's presence in the world and at King Arthur's court once again, or simply the typical reaction of one who has "touched" the divine and acted as a channel for God's grace, they signal the importance of exploring and experiencing emotions in Malory's predominantly masculine world, a topic that has only just started to gain more attention from critics.[41]

The emotional impact of service to a spiritual, rather than earthly, cause, is coupled with the link between genealogy, virginity and the healing of wounds elsewhere in the *Sankgreal*. One of the longest passages in the tale is taken up by the encounter between Perceval, Galahad and Perceval's sister on the boat which carries the story and objects that tell of Galahad's descent: the bed made out of spindles from the Tree of Life, the Sword with the Strange Hangings and the story of Solomon and his wife. While modern critics have attended to the adventures of the Grail knights, given their importance in the overall plot of the *Morte*, there is every reason to believe that Malory and his contemporaries, alongside

---

[39] Field, "Malory and the Grail."
[40] He shares this with Bors, who tells of his adventures (and Perceval's and Galahad's), yet Lancelot has been entrusted with telling about those adventures that happened to him directly: "that he had sene." Bors tells of the "hyghe aventures of the Sankgreall such as had befalle hym and his three felowes," including Lancelot.
[41] See Lynch, "Malory and Emotion."

their apparent interest in secular adventures, also found the long *excursus* into the pseudo-history of these objects as fascinating and edifying as the original audiences of the French *Queste* did. Here the ancestry of the Grail story is proven and the virginity of both Galahad and Perceval's unnamed sister is associated with their miraculous healing of wounds. The worship acquired through these characters is of both spiritual and chivalric import; Perceval's sister's sacrifice shows the key role played by female worship in the economy of the Round Table – here, its spiritual economy.[42]

Immediately after the Grail Quest is over, Lancelot "forgate the promyse and the perfeccion that he made in the queste" (790.11–12 / C XVIII.2), primarily the injunction to keep away from the queen as much as he might. For the world of Malory's *Morte*, however, this does not seem to mark the end of religious experiences nor the end of knightly aspiration for a holy end as expected by fifteenth-century readers. That the focus of his Arthuriad shifts to the holy end the crusading knights meet after a life of chivalric worship *and* the period when they follow Lancelot on his path to an ascetic life shows how Malory envisages that more worth can still be acquired on the hard path to spiritual salvation. While the return to spiritual perfection at the end of Lancelot's life may not be Malory's (only) answer to the troubled decades of the Wars of the Roses, his focus on spiritual matters at the end of the *Morte* urges us to consider just how natural religiosity was to his readers, and how deeply connected secular and religious matters were in fifteenth-century England, and in the *Morte Darthur*.

---

[42] For studies of these issues, see Martin Schichtman, "Perceval's Sister: Genealogy, Virginity and Blood," *Arthuriana* 9.2 (*Essays in Memory of Maureen Fries*): 11–20; and Lisa Robeson, "Women's Worship: Female Versions of Chivalric Honour," in *Re-viewing* Le Morte Darthur: *Texts and Contexts, Character and Themes*, ed. K. S. Whetter and Raluca L. Radulescu (Cambridge, 2005), 107–18.

# 12
## Malory and the Wider World
### MEG ROLAND

Malory's great legend of King Arthur and the Round Table appears to be the most English of narratives, with its tragic plot deeply embedded in the English landscape: Tintagel, Camelot, Glastonbury. And yet Malory tells readers that he drew upon many French as well as English sources, occasionally legitimising his account – if not always accurately – with the phrase "as it tellyth in the Frenshe booke" (221.3–4 / C VI.17), immediately identifying a potential gap in the geographic perspective.[1] The work soon reveals a far wider geographical scope than just the action circling around the court at Camelot.[2] The tale with the most explicit foreign references is, of course, The Tale of Arthur and Lucius (also known as the Roman War) in which Arthur leaves England to campaign across Europe, successfully killing the Roman emperor Lucius and, in Malory's version, achieving the crown of emperor at the hands of the pope, in Rome. But references to a wider world – both foreign and otherworldly – are frequent, and journeys to or intrusions from these foreign or otherworldly places underlie the superstructure of the work and the restless quest to define individual and English national identity.

Part of Malory's geographical inclusion of a wider world is attributable to the geography of his sources as well as to the nature of geographical thought during the 1460s when Malory was writing his great synthesis of Arthurian lore. At this juncture between medieval and modern geographical thought, "the world" was undergoing visual and cultural redefinition: from the era of the *mappa mundi*, with its Jerusalem-centred narrative of Christian universal history, to the longitude and latitude coordinates of early modern maps based on the projections of Claudius Ptolemy and Gerardus Mercator. The temporal and spatial developments of the mid fifteenth century are as much a part of Malory's *Morte Darthur* as are Camelot, London and York such that, in addition to English spaces and politics, the work reveals a surprisingly global focus. In *A Companion to Malory*, Felicity Riddy points out that Malory's emphasis on issues of English nationhood give the

---

[1] Sir Thomas Malory, *Le Morte Darthur*, ed. P. J. C. Field, 2 vols. (Cambridge, 2013). All citations are from volume I.
[2] Malory, drawing on his French sources, primarily refers to Camelot as the seat of Arthur's court, whereas other English Arthurian texts favour Caerleon. See Robert Allen Rouse and Cory James Rushton, "Arthurian Geography," in *The Cambridge Companion to the Arthurian Legend*, ed. Elizabeth Archibald and Ad Putter (Cambridge, 2009), 218–34, at 219.

*Morte Darthur* "a specifically English orientation,"[3] but Arthur and his knights not only "take the adventure"[4] in the forests surrounding Camelot but also venture to Rome and Sarras as well as multiple other locations overseas, including France and Ireland. Foreigners also intervene into English territory, including French allies, Saracen invaders[5] and Roman ambassadors, as well as more enigmatic or otherworldly figures such as the Lady of the Lake. Malory had, we might say, a dual focus on England as well as on "the wider world" over which Arthur might plausibly be in command or in contestation. Malory frequently implies that Arthur is destined to be the ruler of "all Crystendom" (100.6 / C IV.1) and, over the course of the work, seeks to articulate the outer boundaries of what that geo-political space might encompass.[6] In addition to its Englishness, then, the *Morte Darthur* sets the concern for English nationhood within a sense of an expanding world and a militant Christendom, over which Arthur is to preside.

## Fluid Geographies

"Malory's geography" is not, strictly speaking, "Malory's." It also belongs to a set of spatial practices during the fifteenth century that looked back to tradi-tions and shaped developing ones. Despite this, Malory's conception of terri-tory and space has tended to be treated as his own individual or idiosyncratic take on the world. For example, in his 1919 edition, Edward Strachey declares that, aside from the Roman War tale, Malory's "geography is fanciful enough."[7] Dorsey Armstrong and Kenneth Hodges describe Malory's geography as "tricky to work with, which is why we say he uses an (il)logic of space."[8] But such read-ings of Malory tend to assess his geographical worldview from the perspective of post-Enlightenment geography. Robert Rouse and Cory Rushton make clear that medieval Arthurian geography is "a complicated mixture of real places and mythic sites" and their careful work with sources and places shows the nuanced methodology needed.[9] In so doing, they note that this mixture is "shaped and reshaped in often idiosyncratic ways for successive authors and competing

---

[3] Felicity Riddy, "Contextualizing *Le Morte Darthur*: Empire and Civil War," in *A Companion to Malory*, ed. Elizabeth Archibald and A. S. G. Edwards (Cambridge, 1996), 55–74, at 64.

[4] On the pattern of fragmentation and integration resulting from the movement of knightly adventure in *Le Morte Darthur*, see Jill Mann, "Taking the Adventure: Malory and the *Suite du Merlin*," in *Aspects of Malory*, ed. T. Takamiya and D. Brewer (Cambridge and Totowa, N.J., 1981), 71–96.

[5] See *Arthuriana* 16.4 (2006), a special issue devoted to the subject of Saracens, ed. Jacquelyn de Weever. While the term "Saracen" could refer specifically to Muslims or Arabs, it could also be used more generally to refer to any group of pagans.

[6] For the seminal works on culture and space, see Henri Lefebvre, *The Production of Space* (New York, 1992) and Gaston Bachelard, *The Poetics of Space* (London, 2014; first published in English 1964).

[7] Sir Thomas Malory, *Morte Darthur*, ed. Edward Stratchey (London, 1919), xv.

[8] Dorsey Armstrong and Kenneth Hodges, *Mapping Malory: Regional Identities and National Geographies in* Le Morte Darthur (New York, 2014), 2.

[9] For the rich symbolism of the landscape of the forest in Malory and in the genre of romance more widely, see also Corinne J. Saunders, *The Forest of Medieval Romance: Avernus, Broceliande, Arden* (Cambridge, 1993), especially 163–85.

narrative traditions."[10] They suggest that the geography of many medieval writers was "idiosyncratic at best"[11] but, in addition to such idiosyncratic geographic experiences and sources, Malory was also writing within the structure of a body of thought regarding geography and space during a dynamic period of change in which Ptolemaic maps developed and our "modern" worldview was set in motion. As an alternative methodology, Malory's geography can be approached as part of a productive process of experimental geography and geocreativity, terms that have arisen over the past decade in reference to transdisciplinary exchanges between geography and the humanities.[12] Aside from a possible campaign to France, what might constitute the geographic imagination of this "knyght-presoner" (144.3 / W fol. 70v) writing in the mid 1400s?[13]

Rouse and Rushton point out Malory's interest in English place names and the way in which he "adds a significant layer of realism to his text when he mentions places he knows."[14] P. J. C. Field identifies Malory's "liking for real places," and his oft-noted penchant for inserting English place names into his text when he can.[15] According to Field, Malory's additional geographical references "tend to be straightforward because the authors of Malory's French sources set their stories for the most part in a vaguely realized Britain that he knew better than they did."[16] The exception to Malory's additive geographical realism is his version of Arthur's Roman War campaign across the Continent, about which Field suggests that "when Malory does not understand [the geography], his story may not fit the landscape it claims to be set in."[17] Certainly, it must be acknowledged that Malory's knowledge of the world during the period of pre-Columbian exploration was fragmentary and incomplete, informed by military experience, word-of-mouth accounts, cultural situatedness and, to a large degree, reading. As scholars grapple with the complexity of "Malory's geography" in a work reliant on centuries of cultural geographies, multiple authors and multinational sources, it is no wonder that "idiosyncratic" seems the only plausible adjective in relation to his world view, geographic imagination and use of place.

In all of these analyses of Malory's geography, his geographic coherence, or lack thereof, is measured against our modern conception of geographical "realism," as we understand it in the twentieth century. However, in the fifteenth

---

[10]  Rouse and Rushton, "Arthurian," 220.

[11]  Rouse and Rushton, "Arthurian," 219.

[12]  *GeoHumanities: Art, History, and Text at the Edge of Place*, ed. M. J. Dear, Jim Ketchum, Sarah Luria and Doug Richardson (London, 2011).

[13]  This self-reference only appears as part of an explicit in the Winchester manuscript; Caxton's text omits the explicit. See the very useful "Index of Proper Names," in *Le Morte Darthur*, ed. Field, vol. II. For a discussion of Malory's incarceration, see Robert Davidson, "Prison and Knightly Identity in Sir Thomas Malory's *Morte Darthur*," *Arthuriana* 14.2 (2004): 54–63.

[14]  Rouse and Rushton, "Arthurian," 219.

[15]  P. J. C. Field, "Apparatus and Commentary," in *Le Morte Darthur*, ed. Field, II, 115. For a further discussion of Malory's geography, see also P. J. C. Field, "Caxton's Roman War," *Arthuriana* 5.2 (1995): 31–73, reprinted in *The Malory Debate: Essays on the Text of* Le Morte Darthur, ed. Bonnie Wheeler, Robert L. Kindrick and Michael N. Salda (Cambridge, 2000), 127–67.

[16]  Field, "Apparatus," II, 115–16.

[17]  Field, "Apparatus," II, 116.

century, geographic thought – when not in service to functional navigation or wayfinding – could be simultaneously operative in literary, spiritual and cultural registers and function as a more fluid, symbolic and creatively-engaged spatial construct, a transitional link between the geographic frameworks of the Middle Ages and the early modern period. The written geographical tradition of the fifteenth century is a textual weaving of "stratification and juxtaposition,"[18] a fusion of literary traditions and personal experiences, visual and mental maps. Reflecting on the geographical accretion evident in the Post-Vulgate Cycle, one of Malory's sources,[19] Field notes that a later adaptor "unfortunately failed to eradicate some of the discrepancies between the new material and the old."[20] From an editor's perspective this may make sense, but from the perspective of cultural geography, such "discrepancies" or ruptures reveal a cultural layering of geographic thought embedded in the movement to and from Arthur's court. After a long disciplinary estrangement that began in the fifteenth century, the intersection of literature and geography is once again being explored as a "zone of creative interaction"[21] such that we can read the geography of the *Morte Darthur* with a fresh perspective. The departures, adventures and returns, crucial to the genre of romance, provide both literary spaces and poetic cartographies at a moment when humanist or "modern" concepts of space and mapping were in formation. The topographical capaciousness of Malory's tales reveals deeply embedded and yet shifting cultural routes, a rumbling of tectonic plates from earlier eras and texts, alongside new spatial practices such as the rise of locational geography and a fascination with place names, both ancient and contemporary. Placing Malory as part of this "in-flux" geographical context rather than merely as a geographically idiosyncratic or illogical or source-driven writer reveals the ways in which his romance anticipated and even shaped geographic thought for his readers. Malory operates within a cluster of aesthetic and geographical conventions which exemplify fifteenth-century geographical thought including the classical geographical writing tradition, medieval *mappae mundi* (see Figure 1), travel narratives,[22] and pilgrimage accounts, as well as eye-witness experience, chronicles, and emerging mathematically-based cartographic practices. Despite this creative amalgam of written and visual culture, visual maps have become the primary signifiers for the purported "break" from medieval to modern geography, overshadowing the gradual intellectual assemblage that led to mathematically-ordered cultural geography and the re-imagination of the relationship between world and geographical self.[23] This process coincided with Malory's great Arthurian project – that is, the linearisation of space and time.

---

[18] A phrase used by Dr Jeffrey Blanchard, Lecturer in Architecture, Cornell University, lecture on Roman architecture, Rome, Italy 2013.

[19] For Malory's use of the Post-Vulgate Cycle, see Ralph Norris, *Malory's Library: The Sources of the* Morte Darthur (Cambridge, 2008).

[20] Field, "Apparatus," II, 2.

[21] Doug Richardson, Sarah Luria, Jim Ketchum and Michael Dear, "Introducing the GeoHumanities," in *GeoHumanities*, 3–4, at 3.

[22] The fourteenth-century *Travels* by John Mandeville, for example, continued to be widely-read throughout the fifteenth century.

[23] For a discussion of the "geographical self," see E. S. Casey, "Between Geography and Philosophy: What Does It Mean To Be in the Place-world?" *Annals of the Association*

## *Ptolemy and New Representations of Space*

The greatest geographical development of fifteenth-century humanist geography was the publication of the *Geography*, comprised of a list of place names, locational coordinates and commentary based on the mathematical projections of the second-century Greek mathematician and cosmographer, Claudius Ptolemy. Ptolemy's calculations formed the basis of late medieval and early modern

Figure 1. Hereford Map, c. 1300.

*of American Geographers* 91.4 (2001): 683–93. See also Steven C. Larsen and Jay T. Johnson, "The Agency of Place: Toward a More-Than-Human Geographical Self," *GeoHumanities: Space, Place, and the Humanities* 2.1 (2016): 149–166.

Figure 2. Ptolemy, *Geographia* [Geography], Florence, c. 1460–70.

editions of *The Geography*, many of which included a folio-size world map and multiple regional maps drawn upon Ptolemy's "projection" or method of converting a spherical world into a two-dimensional representation (see Figure 2).[24] Ptolemy's *Geography*, along with his other works, *Almagest* (a work of astronomy) and *Tetrabiblios* (a work of natural astrology) exerted a powerful influence on European geographical thought in the mid fifteenth and early sixteenth century when Ptolemy's text along with maps based on his projection were first produced as a proto-atlas in manuscript and woodblock print editions.[25] Ptolemy's text was translated from Greek into Latin by Jacobus Angelus in 1406, and produced, first in manuscript editions in Rome and Florence and, subsequently, in print houses in Venice, Bologna, Rome, Florence and Ulm by the late fifteenth century. England has a curious lacuna in its history of map production: while new maps based on Ptolemy's *Geography* were printed on the Continent beginning in the late 1470s, it was not until 1544 that Sebastian Cabot's world map was printed in London, followed by Richard Wright's 1599 *Chart of the World* and John Speed's

---

[24] Translated from the Greek by Jacopo di Angelo da Scarperia, 1406. Donnus Nicolaus Germanus, cartographer. The New York Public Library, Manuscripts and Archives Division.

[25] Patrick Gautier Dalché, "The Reception of Ptolemy's *Geography* (End of the Fourteenth to Beginning of the Sixteenth Century)," in *The History of Cartography*, 6 vols., *Cartography in the European Renaissance, Part 1*, ed. David Woodward (Chicago, 2007), 3:285–364.

1627 *Prospect of the Most Famous Parts of the World*. But copies of Ptolemy's works made their way to England via the book trade.

From the commentary and locational coordinates that form the basis of Ptolemy's "tables," twenty-eight to thirty-two maps were drawn and included as part of the work (no original maps from Ptolemy's text were either made or survive). The maps depicted a spherical Earth displayed in two-dimensional form, typically orientated to the north (as is now our convention). A Ptolemaic map or globe (minus, of course, the American continent) is known to have been part of Columbus' navigational arsenal late in the century. But well prior to that date, the accumulating impact of new geographic thinking as expressed in Ptolemy's *Geography*, in tandem with the long-known discussion of the Earth's sphericity in texts such as Mandeville's *Travels*,[26] in the development of portolan charts and rutters (coastal navigational maps and itineraries), and in first-person pilgrimage and travel accounts, all formed part of the restless geography of the fifteenth century. To understand Malory's geography, then, it is essential to place it within the intellectual and geographical developments at work in the fifteenth century. By the time that William Caxton printed his edition of Malory's *Morte Darthur* in 1485, there can be little doubt that he was well aware of the new geography – by then luxury editions of the *Geography* held "pride of place"[27] in the libraries of northern European nobility, including the Burgundian court with which Caxton had been affiliated.[28] "Malory's geography," we might say, is inflected by the stirrings of Ptolemaic geography even while it is unlikely that Malory ever saw a Ptolemaic-based map.

As a co-agent in the rethinking of space that marks the fifteenth century, Malory assembled an array of sources and episodes regarding Arthur and his knights, then famously unravelled the interlacement of the structure of his source romances, rearranging them in a chronology of the "birth, life, and acts of the said King Arthur."[29] In his final explicit (a brief note to the reader at the conclusion of a tale), Malory asks those who "redeth this book of Arthur and his knyghtes from the begynnyng to the endynge" to pray for him (940.21–2 / C XXI.13).[30] Malory thus creates a new English Arthuriad that progresses "from begynnyng to the endynge," that is, in linear, chronological time.[31] Malory's literary process is a recognisable parallel to the tandem cartographic process of the linearisation of space and time. This potent confluence of spatial practices was accelerated by the introduction of print and the subsequent dissemination of print editions of the *Geography* and *Morte Darthur*.

---

[26] For the impact and dissemination of the fourteenth-century *Travels* by Sir John Mandeville, see Iain Macleod Higgins, *Writing East: The "Travels" of Sir John Mandeville* (Philadelphia, 1997).

[27] Lisa Jardine, *Worldly Goods: A New History of the Renaissance* (New York, 1996).

[28] George Doutrepont, *Inventaire de la "Librairie" de Philippe le Bon 1420* (Geneva, 1977). Note especially Item 199, *Cosmographia Tholomei*.

[29] William Caxton, "Epilogue," in *Le Morte Darthur* by *Thomas Malory*, ed. Stephen H. A. Shepherd (New York, 2004), 819.

[30] The Winchester manuscript is missing its final gathering; thus, this passage is attested only in the Caxton print edition.

[31] For a discussion of literature and time in the context of contemporary geocriticism, see Adam Barrows, *Time, Literature, and Cartography after the Spatial Turn: The Chronometric Imaginary* (New York, 2016).

Malory has long been associated with the taint of medieval geographical naïveté and often portrayed as a nostalgic, backward-looking author. In his essay "Malory and Modernity," for example, Colin Richmond has argued that Malory was "resistant to the vast changes in the politics and culture of his time"[32] and that Malory's text was marked by "paradigm-shift-resistant qualities."[33] However, one of the unrecognised reasons we have continued to find Malory so engaging, I propose, is not only for the way his book looks back to a chivalric code of the past, but for the way it looks forward to an emerging conception of space and time. A methodology by which to approach the geography and spaces of the *Morte Darthur* includes the necessity of considering Malory's geography within the geographic aesthetics and practices of the fifteenth century. With its sweeping geography, Malory's work unravels romance time, provides "double names" for places, and specifies distances in English "myles." Further, Malory's use of polyvalent scale as a tool for analysis is critical to the way in which he evokes a vast sense of space both within and beyond the boundaries of England.

## Unravelling Romance Time

An important way in which Malory's romance participates in the changing cartographic grammar of the fifteenth century is the way his narrative creates what Homi Bhabha discusses as "the structuring process of visualizing time."[34] Malory re-structured his sources to unravel synchronous romance time, an attribute of Malory's work long-remarked upon but never placed in the context of cartographic development. The Vulgate Cycle and Post-Vulgate Cycle, romances upon which Malory drew, operate in a kind of equipollent geometrics of time, similar to the simultaneity of the representation of time on a medieval *mappa mundi*. Malory's Arthurian world, however, partially steps out of this synchronous dream-time and into a narrative where characters also move across space in accordance with chronological time. For example, towards the conclusion of the Fair Maid of Astolat episode Malory writes, "So thys passed on all that wynter" (830.31 / C XVIII.20), followed by a passage that continues this tracking of time: "Thus hit past on tylle Crystemassse"(831.1 / C XVIII.21). The next episode, The Tournament at Winchester, begins with the phrase "So at aftire Crystemas" (832.1 / CXVIII.21) and the following episode, The Knight of the Cart, continues this sequential chronological thread: "And thus hit passed on frome Candylmas [2 February] untyll Ester" (841.1–2 / C XVIII.25). These time-based passages convey a sense of the inexorable, doom-laden movement toward the book's conclusion – a narrative enactment of the astronomical reckoning that forms the basis of cartographic projection – that is, the measuring of time.

Malory further imposes a chronological sequence on his narrative through the use of his famed paratactic style – his continual use of phrases such as "And than,"

---

[32] Colin Richmond, "Malory and Modernity: A Qualm about Paradigm Shifts," *Common Knowledge* 14.1 (2008): 34–44.

[33] Richmond, "Malory," 35.

[34] Homi Bhabha, *The Location of Culture* (New York, 1994), 142.

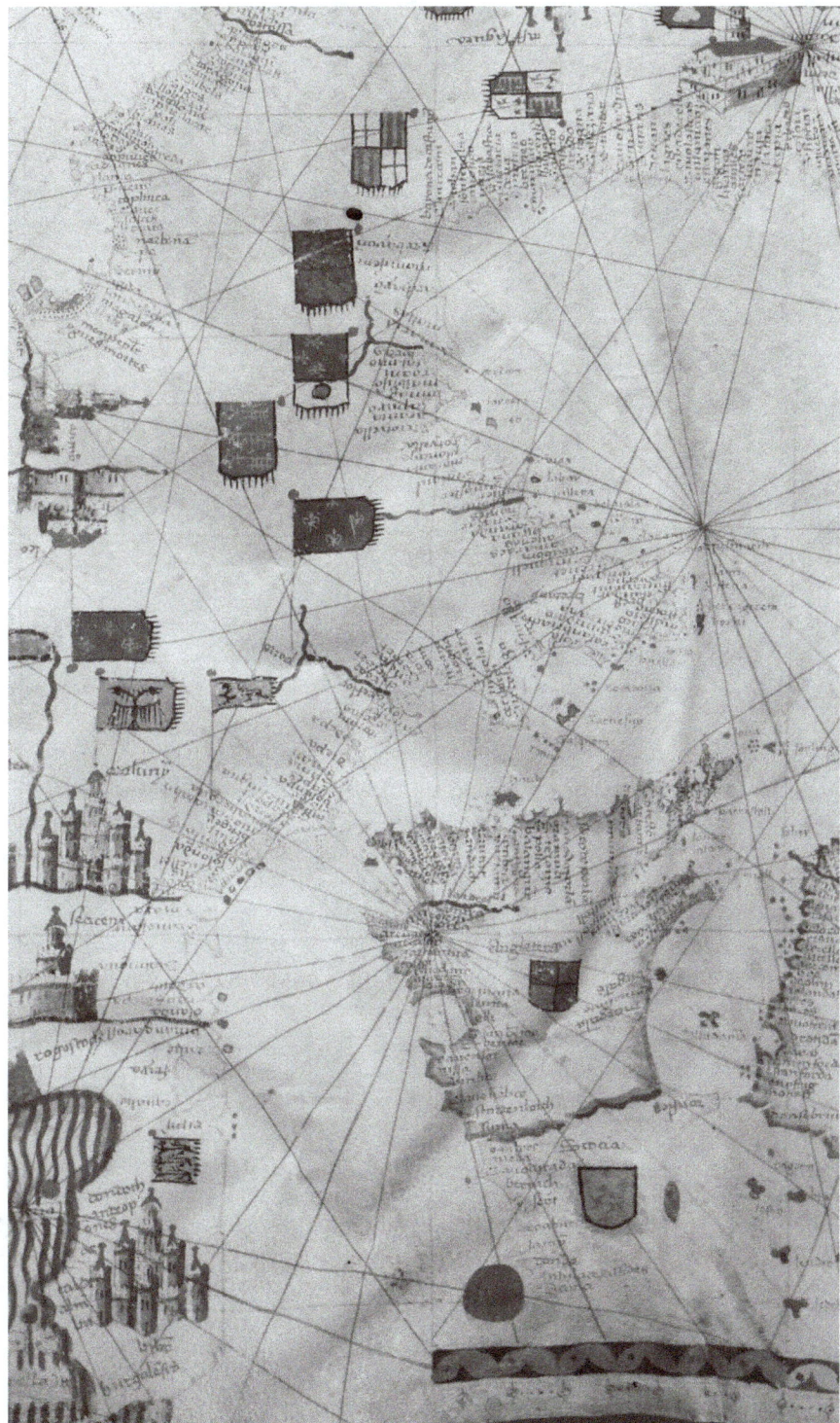

Figure 3. Petrus Roselli, portolan chart, 1466.

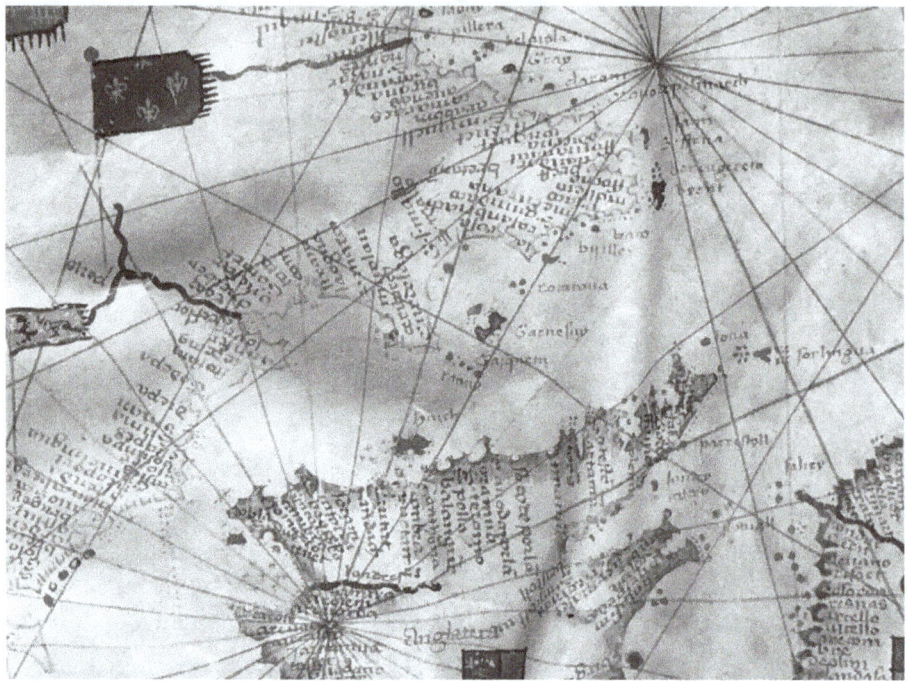

Figure 4. Detail, Roselli portolan chart.

"And so," "So whan this was done" and "Than."[35] Malory's relentless use of these paratactic phrases provides a strong narrative ordering, placing locations and actions in sequential order across the expanse of the page. Malory also frequently notes how long a character journeyed from one place to another, for example, when he observes that Sir Melyas has ridden into an old forest where "therin he rode too dayes and more" (684.20 / C XIII.13). When Gwenyvere realises Launcelot is sleeping with Elayne, for example, "than she … might nat slepe a foure or a fyve owres" (632.31–2 / C XI.8). Subsequently, Launcelot, mad with love grief, abides in Sir Blyaunte's castle "more than a yere and a halff" (645.29 / C XII.2). There are many such examples of the specificity of time passing in the *Morte*. Of course, Malory also uses stock romance "time units" such as "a twelve-moneth" and Christian holy days such as Pentecost or the "utas" (a week, or octave, after a feast day) of Seynte Hyllary (151.34–152.1 / C V.2).[36] The effect of his frequent temporal references is a narrative that unfolds under a persistent attention to the arc of the hours of a day or the turning of a season. As Malory notes in the opening Tale of Uther and King Arthur, "And so the tyme drove on and all thynges redy ipurveyed …" (17.4–5 / C I.10). Malory's romance incorporates equipollent, epi-sodic narratives from earlier romances as well as chronicle-based episodes within a superstructure governed by the passage of linear time. Linearity in the *Morte*,

---

[35] Bonnie Wheeler, "Romance and Parataxis and Malory: The Case of Sir Gawain's Reputation," *Arthurian Literature* XII (1993): 109–32.

[36] See Meg Roland, "The Utas of Seynt Hyllary: Time in the Roman War Campaign," online: www.passionategeography.com [accessed November 2016].

however, was not complete nor homogenous – while the overarching narrative takes place "from beginning to end," there is still ample space for romance time and an amalgamated aesthetic of fluid, passionate geographies.[37]

Keith Lilley has described medieval *mappae mundi* as governed by "center-enhancing space."[38] With the increasing production and use of portolan charts and Ptolemaic-based maps in the fifteenth century, the medieval centre-enhancing space no longer marks the map in quite the same way: portolan charts depict harbours and trade routes with a linearisation of place names (toponyms) fanning out along the coast. Despite this linearisation, portolan charts depict differing scale across sectors of the map[39] in much the way that Malory's text does not maintain "consistent" scale across the narrative. Portolan charts also use red ink to denote toponyms of greater importance to the mapmaker,[40] a rubrication scheme strikingly similar to the scribal practice in the Winchester manuscript of Malory's work in which red ink emphasises names of characters and, occasionally, places.[41] As Armstrong and Hodges point out, many of the knights' names include a reference to their place of origin.[42] Thus, the red rubrication of names in Malory's text *is also a rubrication of place*, a form of gazetteer that invokes the disparate spaces from which the knights hail, including "Alardyne of the Oute Iles" (83.32 / C.III.6), "Peryne de Mounte Belyarde" (64.33 / C II.13) and "Sir Myles of the Laundis" (97.12 / C III.15).

In Malory's sources, Mordred's usurpation during Arthur's Roman War campaign results in the dissolution of Arthur's realm, but Malory's famed deferment of the tragedy so as to stage Arthur's successful return opens up time for Arthur's kingdom to contain the various quests and adventures in a chronologic sequence while simultaneously de-centring the cultural and political power of Rome. David Wallace has argued that Malory's "spaces of play"[43] break into a narrative of imperial conquest, another instance in which combining romance time and chronicle time does not trouble the geographic aesthetics of the work. In Malory's version, Arthur's journey to the center of power does not destroy the periphery, as it does in Malory's ultimate source, Geoffrey of Monmouth's twelfth-century version; instead, an island that had been on the far edge of the *mappa mundi* now holds sway against the centripetal force of Rome.

---

[37] I have adopted the phrase "passionate geography" from the work of Iain Chambers, *Mediterranean Crossings: The Politics of an Interrupted Modernity* (Durham, NC, 2008), 72. See also Meg Roland, "The Rudderless Boat: Fluid Time and Passionate Geography in (Hardyng's) Chronicle and (Malory's) Romance," *Arthuriana* 22.4 (2012), special issue in honor of Edward Donald Kennedy: 77–93.

[38] Keith Lilley, *City and Cosmos: The Medieval World in Urban Form* (London, 2009).

[39] Roelof Nicolai, "The Premedieval Origin of Portolan Charts: New Geodetic Evidence," *Isis* 106.3 (2015): 517–43.

[40] Tony Campbell, "Red Names on the Portolan Charts (1311–1677)," *Map History/History of Cartography*, online: http://www.maphistory.info/RedNamesCommentary.html#conclusions [accessed November 2016].

[41] See Thomas Crofts, *Malory's Contemporary Audience: The Social Reading of Romance in Late Medieval England* (Cambridge, 2006).

[42] Armstrong and Hodges, *Mapping*, 1.

[43] David Wallace, "*Imperium*, Commerce, and National Crusade: The Romance of Malory's *Morte*," in *Medieval Literature: Criticism and Debate*, ed. Holly A. Crocker and D. Vance Smith (London, 2014), 321–32, at 324.

## The Doubleness of Place

Another element that Malory's narrative shares with fifteenth-century geographic practice is the identification of both the ancient, or legendary, name of a city and the modern name. As noted, Malory often adds specific contemporary place names for English locales, as if to ground the vague landscape of Arthurian romance in the soil and cityscape of fifteenth-century England. In the tale of the Fair Maid of Astolat, for example, Malory "geo-rectifies" Camelot as at "that tyme called Wynchester" (807.12 / C XVIII.10; see also 804.5 / C XVIII.9), then tells of King Arthur's stopover at the town of Ascolat "that ys now in Englysh callyd Gylforde" (804.25 / C XVIII.8). Malory infuses the landscape of his romance with a contemporary geographic specificity not found in his French or English sources and, in so doing, disrupts the world of romance with the present, creating a simulacrum of linear history from an ancient past to the political present.

This practice of coordinating local and ancient place names is not idiosyncratic to Malory – it was an integral part of the contemporary humanist fascination with Ptolemy's *Geography*. To be clear, there is no evidence whatsoever that Malory, writing in the 1460s, had access to a manuscript edition of the *Geography*; the first print edition, in 1477, came well after Malory's date of composition. But the zeitgeist of the attention to place names, the Portuguese use of the astrolabe in determining latitude at sea, the development of portolan charts, and the impact of humanist interest in translating and producing maps based on Ptolemy's *Geography* all speak to an ethos of intellectual engagement with the paradigm of latitude and longitude and the inscription and overlay of a grid upon the world. Malory' impulse to layer new geographic knowledge over his source texts results in what we might call a consciousness of the doubleness of place evident in the *Geography*; ancient and local place names provided a parallel reckoning of place as both timeless and bound by the measurements of time.[44]

Cartographic historian Patrick Gautier-Dalché has observed that during the first half of the fifteenth century, Ptolemy's *Geography* "was appreciated by Italian humanists for features other than those we see as constituting the originality of his work," that is, the resulting world and regional maps. "First and foremost," Gautier-Dalché argues, "the *Geography* was seen as a compendium of ancient place-names."[45] In light of humanists' interest in linking ancient and contemporary place names, we can place what has been identified by literary scholars as an individual penchant of Malory's in the context of a developing geographic consciousness attendant to the double-life of place.

### Myles

At times, Malory uses very specific distance to locate his characters. For example, Malory notes that Meleagant's castle was "within seven myle of Westemynster"

---

[44] See Claudius Ptolemy, *Ptolemy's* Geography: *An Annotated Translation of the Theoretical Chapters*, ed. J. Lennart Berggren and Alexander Jones (Princeton, 2000).
[45] Gautier-Dalché, "Reception," 359.

(843.1 / C XIX.1). In Hardyng's *Chronicles*, the *Prose Merlin*, and the *Morte Arthure*, in contrast, distances are typically obliquely articulated, without the specificity we see in Malory. In Hardyng's *Chronicle*, for example, distance is generalised:

> With castels hyegh and toures at every myle
> Endlonge that walle with many other pyle. (Book III, 994–5)[46]

But this is quite different from the specificity with which Malory maps movement across space as he describes Arthur or his knights travelling "ten myle" (17.9 / C I.10 and 106.21 / C IV.6), "within three myle" (103.35 / C IV.4), "half a myle" (134.20 and 26 / C.IV.23), "six or seven myle" (814.33 / C XVIII.13). Malory does not always provide specific distances in miles but when he does so, the effect is to ground the account in contemporary geographical detail as well as symbolic space. In the opening tale, for example, Arthur meets his allies Ban and Bors precisely "ten myle out of London"(17.9 / C I.10), the distance from the city suggesting both the specific distance and the incredible relief and gratitude Arthur feels toward these reinforcements in his bid for sovereignty.

Malory's French sources, if they gave specific distance, would have used the French measurement of leagues[47] and, in this regard, Malory anticipates by decades the 1528 English-language edition of *The Rutter of the Sea*, a navigational log that converted leagues from the earlier French source text (c. 1483) into English miles.[48] Malory's reckoning of miles serves as another layer of his translation of French sources into English vernacular as well as serving as a late medieval GPS (global positioning system), providing detailed directional turns by the "half-myle." Additional studies of the distances articulated in Malory's sources may reveal the extent of his cartographic and symbolic spatial practice as he overlaid his French sources onto English topography.

## Scale

Part of the aesthetic of fifteenth-century geographic practice included variable scale – that is, medieval maps did not necessarily adhere to a consistent spatial register. Typically seen as a form of geographic deficiency from the vantage of post-Enlightenment rationalism, multi-scalar perspective is capacious, open to possibility and simultaneity. Malory's geography includes both "realistic" English landscape and ruptures of consistent scale.

---

[46] John Hardyng, *The Chronicle of John Hardyng*, ed. Henry Ellis (London, 1812).
[47] For example, in the Prose *Lancelot*, a maiden leads Lancelot a generalised distance, "a good league until they came to a shelter." See "Lancelot, Part V," in *Lancelot-Grail: The Old French Arthurian Vulgate and Post-Vulgate in Translation*, ed. William Kibler, gen. ed. Norris Lacy, 5 vols. (New York, 1993–1996), 3:216.
[48] William Copeland published *The Rutter of the Sea* in England in 1528, a translation of an earlier French rutter by Pierre Garcie. In Robert Wyer's editions of *The Compost of Ptolemy* in the 1530s and '40s a rutter was included and the French "leagues" were converted to English "myles."

Theories of non-scalar analysis are a controversial thread in the current "scale debate" within the field of human geography.[49] Such theories of space provide the shock of the familiar to readers of Malory's Arthurian romance where different social processes can be "unevenly and complexly distributed across various scalar levels."[50] Cultural geographers such as Sallie A. Marston contest hierarchical scale in favour of "flat ontologies" as an antidote to the problems of globalism in the twenty-first century. Such non-linear scalar shifts are intimately familiar, however, to readers of Malory's *Morte Darthur* as it moves from "mervylous dreme" to the locational specificity of Launcelot's river crossing "at Westmynster Bridge" in London (846.35 / C XIX.4, not in Malory's source) or Arthur's men "redy on tho bankes" in the bustling port town of Sandwyche (152.30 / C V.2). Indeed, having one's spatial imaginary shaken up is part of the enduring appeal of Malory's work. The text moves across global, local, national, personal and imaginary boundaries in complex yet – if the longevity of the book is any testament – deeply moving ways that stir our emotions and offer multiple if sometimes contradictory perspectives on how to grapple with the complex human problems of government, divided loyalties and familial networks. Malory, arguably, "tackles aggregations of power at multiple scales"[51] and through "micro and macro-processes." In so doing, he defies expectations of consistent scale and uses the "map" of his great narrative as an analytical tool. Cultural geographers such as Marston now provocatively suggest that the rationalist-scientific construct of scale that arose out of late medieval and early modern Ptolemaic and Mercator-based cartography is in serious need of reconsideration. Manuel Castells suggests, instead, the concept of a "space of flows,"[52] which resists categorising spaces as discrete entities but as constituted by the relation of places, selves and objects. Reading Malory's scalar "mash up" invites modern readers to step outside our received paradigms of space and time.

Our own embeddedness in the dominant scalar framework is itself fictive and problematic, and narrows our ability to apprehend the spatial imaginary in which Malory wrote his geography – a world that was expansive and time-space flexible. Armstrong and Hodges argue that "Malory's use of what we like to call an (il)logics of space [is] a fundamental component of his text's structure."[53] Despite the transgressions of what we consider a "realistic" time-space continuum, the fluid geographies and polyvalent scale are uncanny and yet functional in Malory's Arthuriad. After the long dominance of the Mercator projection, contemporary readers can tolerate, perhaps even celebrate, the passionate geographies of Malory's Arthurian landscape, and appreciate the ways in which this landscape is porous rather than fixed. Malory uses scale such that it can function

---

[49] Sallie A. Marston, John Paul Jones III and Keith Woodward, "Human Geography without Scale," *Transactions of the Institute of British Geographers*, n.s. 30.4 (2005): 416–32; John Paul Jones III, Keith Woodward and Sallie A. Marston, "Situating Flatness," *Transactions of the Institute of British Geographers*, n.s., 32.2 (2007), 264–76, and Simon Springer, "Human Geography without Hierarchy," *Progress in Human Geography*, 38.3 (2014): 402–19.

[50] Jones et al., "Situating," 265.

[51] Jones et al., "Situating," 274.

[52] Manuel Castells, *The Rise of the Network Society*, 2nd edn (Oxford, 2000), see 407–59.

[53] Armstrong and Hodges, *Mapping*, 16.

not as a self-evident reality of geographic space but as a methodology for geo-political analysis. As a narrative instantiation of an alternative-scalar analysis, there is so much territory yet to be explored in Malory's *Morte Darthur*.

One of many examples of Malory's use of micro and macro spaces can be seen in the spatial modulations of the opening tale. Arthur must prove himself as legitimate patrilineal heir (in the public space of the Sword and the Stone episode), as a medium between the terrestrial and magical geographies (when Arthur tethers his horse to row across the lake with Merlin to receive the magical sword from the watery Otherworld), as a one-on-one combatant (when Arthur almost slays Pellinore), as a passive dream-state body (when Arthur "slept mae-rveylously sore" (107.24–5 / C IV.6) in the ship of silk), and as global sovereign (when he rebuffs the Roman ambassadors). At either end of the opening epi-sode, Malory toggles between issues of conception (Arthur's and Mordred's) and issues of international standing. It is no surprise that once Mordred survives Arthur's death-by-exposure edict, he is "cast up" upon the seashore (46.17 / C I.27), the embodiment of the internal threat of conception and external threats from across the sea.

Malory's socially-produced political spaces reach from English provincial cen-tres to the power centre of Europe: Rome. He moves the reader from the public space of kingship to the most private spaces – the lover's bedroom, the heal-ing of a wound, the re-counting of a dream. Shifting across macro- and micro-spaces, Malory eschews fixed scale, allowing spaces to border and intrude upon one another as Arthur and those in his network negotiate body, dream, region, nation, Christendom and Otherworld – a pluri-verse of competing spaces. In so doing, Malory proposes a king who can repel threats imposed both by "false treson and by enchauntment" (117.5–6 / C IV.12).

Having contextualised Malory's Arthuriad as an active agent in fifteenth-century geographical aesthetics, let us turn to the opening tale, the Roman War tale, and the concluding tale with an acknowledgement of the necessity of fur-ther inquiries and geo-critical methodologies to deepen our understanding of the multiple geographies and spatial practices at work in the many episodes of the *Morte Darthur*.

## The Tale of Uther and Arthur

The opening tale of the *Morte Darthur* includes the story of Arthur's conception, the Sword and the Stone episode, the travails of Balyn, the wedding of Arthur and Gwenyvere and several additional adventures. The action quickly shifts from the unnamed power centre of Uther Pendragon's court to the western, semi-autonomous region of Cornwall, a site of resistance to the sovereignty of Uther. At the siege of the castle at Tintagel, however, Malory's scale shifts to that of the body, at once the landscape of physical desire and the immateriality of self as Uther shapeshifts to Gorlois, via Merlin's magic. Together, these micro assemblages aggregate and re-negotiate the self, the national, the regional, the international and the Otherworldly.

Once Arthur establishes himself, at least provisionally, as heir and king, Camelot acts as a centripetal locus to which Arthur and his knights continually return for feasts, court life and counsel. Sir Torre, for example, "departed and com to Camelot on the third day by noone" (91.22–3 / C III.11); after wooing Gwenyvere, Arthur "brought her to Camelot" (95.7 / C III.13); and after various adventures Arthur "rode to Camelot – and held there a grete feste with myrth and joy" (100.27 / C IV.2). Widening waves of geographical contestation follow Arthur's coronation – Cornwall, Scotland, and Wales rebel against Arthur's claim to a unified kingdom. Arthur entreats his French allies, Ban and Bors, to assist him, and other references to French locales include Benwick, Nantes and Calais.[54] Amid the focus on the internal ordering of the nation, "mo than fourty thousande" Saracens who made "grete destruccion" invade the north of England; taking over the Castell Wandesborow (33.5 / C I.18) in Scotland.[55] Ban and Bors return to France to fight Claudas; Arthur fortifies the French cities of Surhaute (32.33 / C I.18) and "Nauntres in Bretayne" (33.14 / C I.18) as a bulwark against future invasions by Saracens; and the advance party of the Roman ambassadors that will subsequently set Arthur's Roman War campaign in motion "com into the courte twelve knyghtes that were aged men, which com frome the Emperoure of Rome"(39.34–5 / C I.23). It is a kingdom in continual motion.

Within this flux, five kings harry the northern boundary, entering "into the londis of Kyng Arthure" (100.33 / C IV.2), causing Arthur to exclaim in sheer frustration, "Alas! … yet had I never reste one monethe syne I was kyng crowned of this londe. Now shall I never reste tylle I mete with tho kyngis in a fayre felde" (101.1-3 / C IV.2). With his defeat of the five kings, Arthur presumably also expels the Saracen invasion just as he had repudiated the claim made by the Roman ambassadors (40.5–6 / C I.23), foreshadowing his "extended extra-territorial" Continental campaign.[56] The terrain of these early episodes stages an intense geographical restlessness and gauges Arthur's capacity to respond. Despite this bone-wearying unrest, the promise is held out that Arthur "hath the floure of chevalry of the wordle with hym" (101.26–7 / C IV.2); and that it will be his destiny to quell the pagan forces of the East as well as supplant the imperial authority of Rome. The scale of the geographical framework is vast – nothing less than all of Christendom and exending into the Mediterranean and Middle East. Even Arthur's cruelty in condemning all male babies under four weeks old to exposure "in a shyppe to the se" (46.14 / C I.27) contributes to the "transoceanic"[57] nature of Arthur's ascendancy to power. Within this global framework, there is the local scale of forest and hermitage as well as micro-spaces where individual knights hack and hew their unknown assailant at the level of the body. The

[54] Peter Field identifies the author Thomas Malory as a knight from Newbold Revel, born in 1415: see P. J. C. Field, *The Life and Times of Thomas Malory* (Cambridge, 1993). If so, Malory was likely part of an English campaign in Bayonne, in the Gascony region of southwest France, which accounts for his familiarity with French geography.

[55] See Barry Gaines, "Malory's Castles in Text and Illustration," in *The Medieval Castle: Romance and Reality*, ed. Kathryn Reyerson and Faye Powe (Dubuque, IA, 1984), 215–18.

[56] Wallace, "*Imperium*," 325.

[57] Armstrong and Hodges, *Mapping*, 9.

struggle between Arthur and Morgan le Fay, Camelot and Avalon provides symbolic alternative spaces of territory and flow. The "samyte"-covered arm offers Arthur a potent sword from the watery Otherworld below, an object crossing from one spatial register to another. Thus, Arthur's drive to dominion is local, global and Otherworldly.

For Malory, the geography of the Otherworld, including Avalon, Christian mysticism and the terrain of dreams, creates alternate geographical spaces from that of English political space. Arthur's negotiation of such multiple scalar frameworks is essential to the establishment of his fitness to rule, as well as to the fragility of that rule. Malory offers a nuanced and affective response to what is perhaps more incredible than any questing beast, white hart or water-born sword – that an individual who stands, at one moment, precisely ten miles outside of London also possesses the capacity to cross the scalar delimitations of spatial hierarchies. Thus, the king who "loked aboute the worlde" (106.34; C IV.5) in Malory's opening tale is multi-faceted, both powerful over and vulnerable to intersecting spatial imaginaries.

Part of the work of the first tale is to establish Arthur, not only as the ruler of all of England, but as one whose success against masculine military incursions and feminine magic ensures that "all Crystendom shall speke of hit," a phrase reiterated in the first tale (100.6 / C IV.1; 115.21-22 / C IV.1; 121.29 / C IV.15). Arthur's renown, in the future tense, will reach the edges of the known world. As the "whole book" unfolds, Arthur's conquests and that of his knights include Rome, Sarras and, at least aspirationally, Jerusalem. While Rome functions symbolically as the seat of power for Christendom and imperial power, Sarras, which Malory locates as "in the partis of Babilonye" (788.21–2 / C XVII.23), is the site where the Grail will be achieved in the tale of "The Sankgreal," a place both of Eastern mysticism and Christian spirituality. The international and otherworldly allusions magnify the scale of Arthur's realm to that of world-atlas proportions and inoculate the drive for national sovereignty with imperial and spiritual aspirations.

At the end of the Tale of Uther and Arthur, Malory's explicit declares his identity as a knight but also his location in prison: "Who that woll make ony more lette hym seke other bookis of Kynge Arthure or of Sir Launcelot or Sir Trystrams; for this was drawyn by a knyght presoner, Sir Thomas Malleorré, that God sende hym good recover" (144.1–4 / W fol. 70v).[58] Confined to a room or set of rooms in Newgate prison,[59] Malory effects a dramatic telescoping of the scale of the preceding tale: the confinement of a prison cell in contrast with multiple global incursions and forays magnifies the epic scale at which Arthur has operated. Intriguingly, Malory suggests that all of the action he has just relayed might not be all that transpired or all that is known: "lette hym seke other bookis," he suggests, at once declaring his limited textual resources but also that Arthur's geographical space might encompass even more territory than has just been related. The confined space of the author, speaking across unknown time and space, provides a momentary counterpoint to the restless geography, a narrative

---

[58] The explicit is omitted in Caxton's edition.
[59] Anne F. Sutton, "Malory in Newgate Prison: A New Document," *The Library*, 7th ser., 1.3 (2000): 243–62.

pause, replete with the implicit hope that Arthur has, at least temporarily, stabilised the kingdom before taking up the campaign against Rome.

## The Geographies of the Roman War

Arthur's campaign to Rome, "The Noble Tale of Arthur and Lucius" (Caxton's Book V), largely coincides with the well-travelled pilgrim route of the Via Francigena, linking Canterbury and Rome. Over the centuries, as England Christianised and Rome solidified as the central power of Christendom, pilgrims and papal legates traversed the arduous route between London and Rome, including a sea crossing, a lengthy journey across France, and a strenuous ascent of the Alps, before entering Italy and undertaking the south-easterly journey to Rome. Pilgrims sought out Rome in the thousands, especially in jubilee years: it is estimated that over 200,000 pilgrims gathered in Rome in the jubilee of 1300,[60] a spatialised enactment of the centrality and authority of Rome in relation to Christian Europe. In Malory's and Caxton's lifetimes, the Great Pentecostal Jubilee of 1450 was also attended by thousands of European pilgrims.[61] Just as pleasure and penitence intermingled in pilgrimage journeys, a "seson" in Italy offered Arthur and his men its own recompense: revelling in his victory over Lucius, Arthur rests in the "Vale of Vysecounte"[62] with "vynys full plenteuouse" (187.18–19 / C V.12) and, after his acclamation as emperor, "suggeourned that seson tyll aftir that tyme" (188.5–6 / C V.12). A season in the wineries of southern Italy certainly offered Arthur and his men a welcome respite from military campaigning.

That pilgrimage or cultural routes formed part of the underlying geography of the Roman War route is attested early in the tale by the Lord of West Wales when he affirms his willingness to support and join Arthur on the campaign against the Emperor Lucius: "For onys as I paste on pylgrymage all by the Poynte Tremble, than the vyscounte was in Tuskayne, and toke up my knyghtys and raunsomed them unreasonablé" (148.12–14 / C V.2). Malory's route for Arthur through France and Luxemburg (Barfflete, Parys, Sessoyne, Lushburne, Flaundris, Lorayne, through Almayne (154.6–7 / C V.4; 164.18 / C V.7; 175.23–4 / C V.9) and south through Italy (Lumbardy, Myllayne, Porte Tremble, Tuskanye, Vyterbe) (187.10–18 / C V.12) generally follows that of the Via Francigena, substituting the mountain pass at "Godarte" (186.16 / C V.12, the Saint Gotthard pass) for the Grand Saint Bernard Pass, and reflective of route changes by Malory's lifetime. Thus, Arthur is not merely travelling *to* Rome; he is traversing a deep cultural route across the Continent that reveals long-recounted textual and physical itineraries, spatial relations, cultural memory and symbolic geographies.

Malory's account of the Roman War is derived primarily from the English Alliterative *Morte Arthure* and supplemented by Hardyng's *Chronicles*[63] along

---

[60] Robert Hughes, *Rome: A Cultural, Visual, and Personal History* (New York, 2011), 58.

[61] Hughes, *Rome*, 58.

[62] Field suggests this may be "an error for Vale of Viterbo." See "Apparatus," II, 892.

[63] For Malory's use of Hardyng as a source, see Edward Donald Kennedy, "Malory's Use of Hardyng's Chronicle: A Reconsideration," *West Virginia Philological Papers* 54 (2011): 8–15.

with other minor sources.[64] In the Alliterative *Morte Arthure*, Arthur traverses the Continent from Normandy to Burgundy, where Arthur kills the Emperor Lucius. After the decisive victory, the Arthurian army moves north to Luxemburg, then begins its southward trajectory to Metz, Lucerne, the Gotthard pass, Lake Como, and Milan. The route in Italy then passes through Spoleto, and on to Viterbo, never quite reaching Rome. In Malory's version, the site of the mortal battle between Arthur and Lucius is set in the "Vale of Sessoyne" (169.27 / C V.8), long thought by scholars to suggest a northern France location. This incongruous location, far north of the rest of the route, contributed to Malory's reputation as hazy on European geography. William Matthews' linguistic and geographical identification of Siesia,[65] near Dijon, as Malory's intended battle site untangled this geographic crux. Such an example points out the importance of careful attention to place names, source texts and cultural routes along with a tempering of judgement regarding Malory's multi-faceted cultural geography.

In addition to the overland Continental geography provided in the Roman War tale, the catalogue of allies of the emperor reveals a multi-layered and inherited geography.[66] In the Alliterative *Morte Arthure* and in Malory's re-working of the tale, the ethnographic enumeration of Eastern kings begins to change in ways that can best be described as *cartographic*.[67] While *mappae mundi*, such as the Hereford Map, were rich in ethnographic detail and populated with exotic animals, races and monsters,[68] manuscript and print versions of Ptolemaic maps and portolan charts of the mid to late fifteenth century not only radically re-shape the representations of landmass and coastlines, they also sweep clear the ethnographic quality of the *mappa mundi*. There are no people on the map. The focus, instead, is on topographical features such as mountains and rivers, and on city locations. It is not necessary that Malory actually saw a copy of Ptolemy's edition; instead, it is clear that the conceptual linearisation and cultural processes that underlay the development of Ptolemaic maps were similarly at work in literary culture.

The catalogue of Eastern adversaries in the Roman War tale reveals a century-long shift away from an ethnographic *mappa mundi* version of the tale and towards a version more akin to a geodetic, topographical world map. For example, "Irtac,

---

[64] Ralph Norris, *Malory's Library: The Sources of the* Morte Darthur (Cambridge, 2008).

[65] William Matthews, "Where was Siesia-Sessoyne?" *Speculum* 49.4 (1974): 680–6, at 685. For a further discussion of Malory's geography, see also *The Works of Thomas Malory*, ed. Eugène Vinaver, 3 vols. (Oxford, 1967), 3rd edn, rev. P. J. C. Field (Oxford, 1990), 1396.

[66] Rouse and Rushton, "Arthurian," 219. Regarding Caxton's editing of Malory's geography, see Meg Roland, "From 'Saracens' to 'Infydeles': The Recontextualization of the East in Caxton's Edition of *Le Morte Darthur*," in *Re-viewing* Le Morte Darthur: *Text and Contexts: Characters and Themes*, ed. K. S. Whetter and Raluca Radulescu (Cambridge, 2005), 65–77.

[67] For a discussion of the "convergence of the three conceptual frameworks" of *mappaemundi*, portolan charts, and Ptolemaic maps, see David Woodward's extensive essay, "Medieval *Mappaemundi*," in *The History of Cartography*, 6 vols., *Cartography in Prehistoric, Ancient, and Medieval Europe and the Mediterranean*, ed. David Woodward (Chicago, 2007), 1:286–320; see especially 314.

[68] See Asa Mittman, *Maps and Monsters in Medieval England* (New York, 2006), and Naomi Reed Kline, *Maps of Medieval Thought: The Hereford Paradigm* (Woodbridge, 2001).

King of Turckie"[69] in Layamon's eleventh-century *Brut* becomes a strictly geographical reference, "To Tartary and Turkeu", in the Alliterative *Morte Arthure*.[70] Resisting his usual penchant for adding character names to unnamed figures in his source text,[71] Malory is similarly geographic, referencing an anonymous "Kyng of Tars, and of Turkye" (151.5 / C V.2). Just as maps in the fifteenth century begin to transition from cultural ethnography to spatial projection, so too does the catalogue of Eastern rulers.

In the Allliterative *Morte Arthure*, the allied forces of Lucius are described as "a full gret nombyre," "legyons ynewe" and as "summes full huge,"[72] but in Malory, Lucius' allies become partly monstrous: "fyffty gauntys that were engendirde with fendis" (151.19 / C V.2). Malory's version morphs into a loathsome, miscegenated horde, both a racial and territorial threat. The harrowing of the boundaries of Latin Christendom by Lucius' "horryble peple" (151.24 / C V.2) highlights concerns that a Muslim invasion of Europe was imminent. The Turks sacked Constantinople in 1453 and Mehmet II advanced into Turkey, just shortly before Malory wrote his romance. Malory's account of Lucius' defeat, therefore, provides a potent revenge narrative and a cathartic, if fictive, release from fears of Turkish incursion into Europe. Arthur's ultimate coronation in Rome in Malory's version, another departure from his source text (in which Arthur never actually reaches Rome), affirms an aspirational unity for Christian Europe as well as Arthur's territorial and spiritual supremacy.

## The Morte Arthur

In the concluding tale, "The Morte Arthur," Arthur's global significance is again affirmed as the "floure of chyvalry of alle the worlde" (870.9 / C XX.1), but this global claim will shortly be undone by the adder that emerges from under "a lytyll hethe-buysshe" (922.13 / C XXI.4), a micro-scale disruption of the hoped-for world order. The ensuing battle results in Arthur's (presumed) death and sets the final dissolution of the kingdom into motion. The military, secular and spiritual geographies contained within the king's body – Cornwall, London, York, Ireland, Wales, France, the Alps, Rome, Sarras and all the Eastern principalities that succumbed to Arthur or his knights – are now fragmented. Malory suggests three alternative geographies in the wake of unrealised English imperialism: territorial England, Avalon and Jerusalem. With the passing of the realm to Arthur's cousin Constantine, the geographical referent for Constantine's power is no longer the world, nor all of Christendom but only "Kyng of Englond" (939.30 / C XXI.13). By the time Malory was writing the *Morte Darthur*, English territorial losses in France were such that only Calais remained as an English toehold on the Continent; the bitter reality of English territorial contraction following the Hundred Years War

---

[69] *Laȝamon's Arthur: The Arthurian Section of Laȝamon's Brut (Lines 9229 – 14297)*, ed. W. R. J. Barron and S. C. Weinburg (Austin, TX, 1989), line 12659.

[70] *The Alliterative Morte Arthure: A Critical Edition*, ed. Valerie Krishna (New York, 1976), line 582.

[71] "Index of Proper Names," in *Le Morte Darthur*, ed. Field, II, 862–92, at 861.

[72] Alliterative *Morte*, lines 602, 605, 606.

was clear.[73] Along with Constantine's rule comes the reestablishment of English Roman-Catholic order – the bishop of Canterbury, previously in hiding in a hermitage under threat from Mordred, is "restored unto his bysshopryche" (939.33 / C XXI.13). With this narrower focus on the core geography of England and its spiritual centre of Canterbury, the implied obedience and loyalty of the bishop to his spiritual and temporal leader – the pope in Rome – is made clear. Thus universal Christian order, at least until the reign of Henry VIII, is restored in a humbled, diminished England.

Malory offers two additional geographies, however, as antidotes for the territorial diminishment of the island nation. At Arthur's mortal wounding, an alternative to the global space Arthur occupied in the first two tales now moves to the fore: the fluid, watery terrain of the feminine "vale of Avylyon" (927.6 / C XXI.5). This Otherworld, with its "residual mysteriousness,"[74] is obliquely located by the arm that rises from the lake to reclaim Arthur's sword. The agent of the unknown irruption "vanysshed awaye the honde with the swerde into the watir" (926.16–17 / C XXI.5) and, in so doing, intimates an alternate realm beyond the bounds of ordinary space and time. Arthur's passage in the "lytll barge wyth many fayre ladyes" (926.24 / C XXI.5) will bring him to Avalon, a world parallel to England, but veiled. If Arthur was initially posited as the hope for all of Christendom, the transport of his body from the terrestrial to the alluvial realm of Avalon suggests that the geography symbolically contained within the body of the king has been transubstantiated. In this key existential moment, Sir Bedivere laments, "A, my lorde Arthur, what shall becom of me, now ye go frome me and leve me here alone amonge myne enemyes?" (927.1–3 / C XXI.5). Arthur offers only an enigmatic aphorism, "for in me ys no truste for to truste in. For I wyll into the vale of Avylyon" (927.5–6 / C XXI.5), a topographical referent that merges the register of landscape and water and that cedes the territorial boundaries of England he had laboured to establish.

In the last lines of the book, a third alternative geography is offered. Although the final pages of the Winchester manuscript do not survive, in Caxton's print version the rumour that Launcelot's remaining four knights lived out their days as hermits is refuted and the claim put forward that they went to the Holy Land where they "dyd many bataylles upon the myscreantes or Turkes" (940.14–15 / C XXI.13). The intention Arthur mused upon earlier in the Roman War tale – that of going over the "salte see" to revenge "His deth that for us all on the Roode dyed" (187.33–5 / C V.12) is now partially fulfilled. Malory (or Caxton)[75] goes on to say that the knights "dyed upon a Good Fryday for Goddes sake" (940.16 / C XXI.13). Cartographically, the culminating space of Jerusalem suggests a return to the centre-enhancing space of the medieval *mappa mundi* but it is only a fragile

---

[73] Wallace argues that the Roman War campaign's "fantastical projection" includes English re-territorialisation of France, *"Imperium,"* 326.

[74] A term used by Catherine Batt in "Malory and the Questing Beast and the Implications of Author as Translator," in *The Medieval Translator: The Theory and Practice of Translation in the Middle Ages,* ed. Roger Ellis (Cambridge, 1989), 142–66, at 152.

[75] The final gathering of the Winchester manuscript has not survived; for a discussion of the reference to "Turkes" as a possible Caxton addition, see Meg Roland, "Arthur and the Turks," *Arthuriana* 16.4 (2006): 29–42.

and temporary hold for, as Malory's and Caxton's reader well knew, Jerusalem was slipping from realisable Crusade aspirations.[76] The era of the *mappa mundi* was passing.

## Caxton as Cartographic Reader

A testament to the cartographic potency in Malory's narrative is evident in the response by the book's printer William Caxton when he published the *Morte Darthur* in 1485. Caxton's most vigorous editorial intervention occurs in the Roman War account with interventions in routes and city names. By the time Caxton printed the *Morte Darthur*, he had already published the geographic encyclopedia *Mirror of the World* (1481, with a subsequent edition in 1490) with both medieval T-O maps and illustrations of globes, as well as the geographic *Description of Britain* (1480) and the larger work from which it was excerpted, the *Polychronicon* (1482). Although Caxton's much shorter version of the Roman War account has been largely viewed as a drive for concision and modernisation, part of the rationale behind Caxton's editorial work in this tale can be attributed to his reading of the work within a geo-political context, including national identity and an attentiveness to the geographies of place names and routes.

Malory's text, as I hope I have made evident, was reflective of the co-constitutive nature of the emerging constructs of space and time and the way in which medieval and early modern geographic frameworks operated in an aesthetic and scientific synthesis. Late medieval Arthurian romance, along with other narrative and visual cultural productions, was part of the diffuse cultural development of early modern geographic thought, a role obscured retrospectively because of the cultural ascendancy of the visual map. The amalgamated geo-aesthetic of tradition and innovation, of simultaneity and chronology, of romance time and poetic geography are manifest in the equal regard for "Poetes and Astronomyers"[77] just prior to the ascendancy of the visual map, mathematically-based cartography, and the discipline of geography. In the context of the cross-disciplinary fields of GeoHumanities and historical cartography, we can now bracket the term "idiosyncratic" in reference to Malory's geography. Western geographical culture has "loked aboute the worlde" (106.34 / C IV.6) from various perspectives and, in this moment of "post-humanism" geography, Malory's work can provide a lively, alternative model to our dominant geographic worldview.

---

[76] Near the conclusion of the Roman War tale, Malory refers once to Rome as "the cité of Syon that is Rome callyd" (187.27), a poetic but perhaps also spiritual-cartographic de-centring of Jerusalem.

[77] A phrase from an edition of the popular fifteenth- and sixteenth-century almanacs initially known as *The Kalendar of Shepherds*, here as *The Compost of Ptholomeus*, Robert Wyer, printer, 1530?, STC 20480, sig..O(2)r.

*Explicit: Wormhole of Time-space*

Field notes that the eighth and final tale of Malory's *Morte Darthur* in the Winchester manuscript "suffers from the wormhole that began in the final pages of the sixth tale."[78] This physical attribute of the manuscript brings to mind an element of contemporary theoretical physics which posits dark-matter-like connections, or wormholes, between disparate space-times. While Malory's text suffers from the effect of a determined book worm or two, gnawing, letter by letter, through the *Morte Darthur*, Malory's Arthurian world moves easily between the intimate space of a half-mile or prison cell, to the far reaches of Rome, Sarras and Avalon, and to inexplicable other spaces of natural and supernatural registers, the terrain of "depe foreste" (136.28–9 / C IV.25) and dreams. Field has remarked that Malory's frequent references to other texts create a sense that "the *Morte Darthur*, substantial as it is, gives a mere epitome of an Arthurian world too big for any one author to grasp."[79] With its time-space "wormholes," Malory's geography creates an experience of an expanding universe, a topography large enough and mysterious enough within which the full range of human experiences can unfold, a narrative of expansive geographic space.

[78] Field, "Apparatus," II, 768. For a detailed description of the manuscript wormholes, see ibid., II, 689.
[79] Field, "Apparatus," II, 689.

# III
## Malory's Afterlives

# 13
## Malory in Wartime Britain
### ROB GOSSEDGE

Medievalism in general, and Arthurian romance in particular, exercised a powerful influence on many writers and artists at work during the World Wars of the last century. Some of the uses were simply propagandist – as in the utilisation of Sir Galahad, St George and anonymous crusader knights in numerous recruitment posters.[1] Sometimes medievalism provided myths of consolation, as in the deliberate archaisms and chivalric cadences of eulogies and, later, memorials to the fallen.[2] They could also offer hope, as in such popular myths as the Angel of Mons, wherein a regiment of spectral archers from the Battle of Agincourt was supposed to have protected British soldiers under German fire (a legend that began life as a short story by Arthur Machen, but quickly became a widely held belief).[3] Occasionally, medieval studies just went on happening out of a sense of duty: hence J. R. R. Tolkien, who had fought in the First World War, supplemented his Oxford tutorials by teaching *Sir Orfeo* to naval cadets in 1943–44;[4] and, in France, Emile Pons spent the years of the Occupation (1940–44) preparing his translation of *Sir Gawain and the Green Knight*, known as *Sire Gauvain et le chevalier vert* (1946), dedicated to his brother, who had been killed at the Great War battle of Verdun.[5] Often, some sense of the medieval past was invoked in order to attempt some sort of – personal or historical – understanding of the horrors of conflict, as is powerfully evident in David Jones's writing (discussed below), but which is also apparent in so many accounts of soldiers who saw themselves, or were seen by others, as latter-day knights. Though an anachronism in an age of mechanised warfare, as Paul Fussell wrote in his classic study *The Great War and Modern Memory* (1975), "the experience of a man going up the line to his destiny cannot help seeming to him like those heroes of medieval romance if his imagination has been steeped in actual literary romances or their equivalent."[6]

Of those romances, it was Malory's *Morte Darthur* that proved to be the most profoundly influential. In some ways, this was to be expected: the *Morte Darthur* had secured a prominent position in the English literary canon in the course of

---

[1] Mark Girouard, *The Return to Camelot: Chivalry and the English Gentleman* (New Haven, CT, 1985), 275–93.

[2] Jay Winter, *Sites of Memory, Sites of Mourning: The Great War in European Cultural History*, 2nd edn (London, 2014), 85.

[3] David Clarke, *The Angel of Mons: Phantom Soldiers and Ghostly Guardians* (Oxford, 2005).

[4] Humphrey Carpenter, *J. R. R. Tolkien: A Biography*, 2nd edn (London, 1987), 146.

[5] *Sire Gauvain et le chevalier vert*, trans. Emile Pons (Paris, 1946).

[6] Paul Fussell, *The Great War and Modern Memory*, 2nd edn (Oxford, 2000), 135.

the nineteenth century, due to the endeavours of multiple editors of both popular and scholarly editions.[7] Yet as a book about war and other forms of violent
conflict, the *Morte Darthur* had often prompted ambivalent, if not outright hostile, responses. One of Malory's earliest critics, the sixteenth-century humanist
and educationalist Roger Ascham, condemned it for (amongst other things) its
depiction of "open man slaughter," wherein the "noblest knyghtes … do kill
most men without quarrel."[8] Later scholars had similarly tended to read the text
as the expression of a "barbarous" age.[9] By the mid nineteenth century, however,
there was a tendency to gloss over the *Morte*'s militarist values, or else to treat
the near-continuous violence of the text as quite distinct from what the critics
often saw as the "deeper interests and structures" of the text – a critical practice
that continued until quite late into the twentieth century.[10] A renewed interest
in the language, narrative and social meanings of violence has redressed this
critical imbalance in the past twenty or so years (as discussed in Catherine Nall's
chapter in this volume). And the violence of the text has again become central to
readings of the *Morte*, whether as a series of discursive relations to other writings
on war in the fifteenth century,[11] or as an expression of a contemporary "nihilistic
energy" that culminates in the fulfilment of a "death-wish of a[n aristocratic]
class" at the final battle of Camlan.[12]

Yet, while Andrew Lynch is surely right in claiming that "Malory's readers
are obliged to find terms in which his bloodshed is meaningful," for many *Morte*-
carrying soldiers of the First and Second World Wars, the ambiguities and logic
of the *Morte Darthur*'s depiction of war needed little critical negotiation.[13] In spite
of the elision of violence from critical readings of the *Morte* from the mid nineteenth century until the last quarter of the twentieth, wartime readers of Malory
were powerfully influenced by its articulation of warfare and soldiery. As this
chapter explores, Malory's retelling of the rise and fall of Arthurian civilisation
could shape a soldier's immediate sensory perception, as it did for David Jones;
inspire a notion of chivalry, as it did in Rupert Brooke's wartime sonnets; inform
a later memoir, as it did T. E. Lawrence's; or even supply an antidote to war, as
T. H. White understood it.

[7] See Siân Echard, "Malory in Print," in this volume, for discussion of such editions.
[8] Roger Ascham, *The Scholemaster*, in *The English Works of Roger Ascham*, ed. W. A.
Wright (Cambridge, 1904), 231.
[9] Samuel Johnson, "Preface," *The Plays and Poems of William Shakespeare*, ed. Samuel
Johnson, 7 vols. (Chiswick, 1814), II: liii–iv; anon., Review of *Le Morte Darthur* ed.
Thomas Wright, *Dublin University Magazine* 55 (April 1860): 497–512, at 497, 511.
[10] Andrew Lynch, *Malory's Book of Arms: The Narrative of Combat in* Le Morte Darthur
(Cambridge, 1997), xiii. For a survey of nineteenth-century views of *Le Morte Darthur*
see Marylyn Parins, *Sir Thomas Malory: The Critical Heritage* (London, 1987).
[11] Lynch, *Malory's Book of Arms*; Catherine Nall, *Reading and War in Fifteenth–Century
England: From Lydgate to Malory* (Cambridge, 2012).
[12] Felicity Riddy, "Contextualizing *Le Morte Darthur*: Empire and Civil War," in *A
Companion to Malory*, ed. Elizabeth Archibald and A. S. G. Edwards (Cambridge,
1996), 55–74, at 71.
[13] Andrew Lynch, "'Thou Will Never Have Done': Ideology, Context and Excess in
Malory's War," in *The Social and Literary Contexts of Malory's* Morte Darthur, ed. D.
Thomas Hanks, Jr, and Jessica Gentry Brogdan (Cambridge, 2000), 24–41, at 24.

While previous studies of wartime Arthuriana have commented on the paucity of texts produced during the World Wars of the last century,[14] this chapter argues that combatant and non-combatant writers affected a profound and lasting reshaping of the modern Arthurian myth. In particular, it concentrates on how they came to understand their own wartime experiences in terms of the breadth of the *Morte Darthur*'s narrative cycle – a sequence of tales that contained, in Caxton's words, "chyvalrye, curtosye, humanyté, frendlynesse, hardynesse, love, frendshyp, cowardyse, murdre, hate, vertue, and synne" (as well as the all-important sense of tragedy).[15] But the *Morte* had a further sense of cyclicity that appealed to wartime writers, as it was itself but one manifestation of a series of retellings of the Arthurian tragedy, itself produced by a soldier in the midst of civil war. For many combatant writers, the *Morte Darthur* contained an uncannily familiar history of war and soldiery – and they used its literary materials to tell their own similar stories.

### *"A most chuckle-headed trade": Malory and Nineteenth-Century Conflict*

Although the legend of Arthur remained largely dormant in the seventeenth and eighteenth centuries, the story was still of use to poets and dramatists commemorating contemporary British military victories. The Nine Years' War with France was given epic treatment in Richard Blackmore's much-ridiculed *King Arthur* of 1697, which in twelve would-be Virgilian books recounted how, "with wondrous Toyl, and mighty Fortitude, / the valiant King the haughty Frank subdued."[16] In the next century, both William Hilton's verse-drama *Arthur, Monarch of the Britons* (1759) and Joseph Warton's poem "To His Royal Highness the Duke of York" (1760) linked Arthur's story to British victories during the Seven Years' War with France. And the onset of the Revolutionary and Napoleonic Wars produced a flurry of – albeit minor – patriotic Arthurian verse, as Stephanie Barczewski has discussed.[17] Arthurian narrative was also invoked more generally to frame British imperial ambitions, as in Richard Hole's *Arthur; Or the Northern Enchantments* (1789), wherein Merlin outlines Arthur's military-historical mission, validated by protective liberalism, in the poem's final lines:

> Crush stern oppression, and the wrong'd redress;
> Fight to protect, and conquer but to bless.[18]

---

[14] Norris J. Lacy, "King Arthur Goes to War," in *King Arthur's Modern Return*, ed. Debra N. Mancoff (New York, 1998), 159–69; and Donald L. Hoffman, "Arthur, Popular Culture and World War II," in *King Arthur and Popular Culture*, ed. Elizabeth S. Sklar and Donald L. Hoffman (Jefferson, NC, 2002), 45–58.

[15] William Caxton, Preface to *Morte Darthur*, in Thomas Malory, *Le Morte Darthur*, ed. P. J. C. Field, 2 vols. (Cambridge, 2013), II, 854. Further references to this edition will be found in parentheses in the text.

[16] Richard Blackmore, *King Arthur: in Twelve Books* (London, 1697), 12:343.

[17] Stephanie L. Barczewski, *Myth and National Identity in Nineteenth-Century Britain: The Legends of King Arthur and Robin Hood* (Oxford, 2000), 32–39.

[18] Richard Hole, *Arthur; Or the Northern Enchantment: A Poetical Romance in Seven Books* (London, 1789), 7:252.

The source for each of these militarist Arthurs lay in the figure of history and ultimately in Geoffrey of Monmouth's *Historia regum Britanniae* (c. 1138), rather than
Malory's fifteenth-century romance. Nonetheless it was during the Napoleonic
Wars (1803–15) that the *Morte Darthur* began its gradual re-emergence, with three
editions appearing at the war's close.

Even before these publications, Malory remained well-known to some readers, chiefly through extant copies of the 1634 Stansby text still in circulation in
antiquarian circles. One notable use of the *Morte Darthur* in a wartime context
was John Hookham Frere's incomplete satire *The Monks and the Giants* (published
in 1816, but written several years earlier), which connected Malorian romance
with the recent Peninsular Wars. With its author already possessing a reputation as a sharp parodist, this Arthurian satire features a few passing references
to Wellington (Frere, who had enjoyed a promising political career, had been
replaced by Wellington's brother as ambassador to Spain, amid much criticism).[19]
But the chief focus is on the early years of the Napoleonic Wars, during which
ill-discipline and questionable leadership (including Frere's own) culminated in
the disastrous retreat from Corunna. Gawaine and Tristram, lifted from Malory,
receive especially rough, possibly allegorical, treatment. The former's "success
in war was strangely various":

> In executing schemes that others plann'd,
>     He seem'd a very Caesar or a Marius;
> Take his own plans, and place him in command,
>     Your prospect of success became precarious.[20]

Gawaine's and Tristram's various battlefield mishaps culminate in a poorly
executed attempt to relieve a castle of Spanish maidens, besieged by a group of
giants. By "good luck" they finally succeed: "When those vile cannibals were
overpower'd / Only two fat Duennas were devour'd."[21] Fearing his veiled satire
had been perceived too directly, Frere did not complete his retelling.

In 1830 another poem that juxtaposed Malorian romance with the Peninsular
conflict appeared anonymously in *Blackwood's Edinburgh Magazine*. Titled "Lines
Written after Reading the Romance of Arthur's Round Table," the poem begins
by praising Arthur and his knights. But it is praise qualified by the limited range
of their knightly activity – these were men who gave "England's service [to]
English hearts," and who "Ne'er left their countrymen in want and pain / To
soothe the woes of Portugal or Spain."[22] In contrast, those who sit at "Arthur's
table now" only bring shame upon themselves in "meekly follow[ing] each
supreme behest." The context was the deep unpopularity of Wellington's pre-
miership; he would be forced to resign in the autumn of the year in the face of
widespread social and political unrest.[23]

---

[19] Rory Muir, *Britain and the Defeat of Napoleon, 1807–1815* (New Haven, CT, 1996), 64.
[20] John Hookham Frere, *The Monks and the Giants*, ed. R. D. Waller (Manchester, 1926),
     canto 2; verse 28.
[21] Frere, *The Monks and the Giants*, canto 2, verse 53.
[22] "An Oxonian," "Lines Written after Reading the Romance of Arthur's Round Table,"
     *Blackwood's Edinburgh Magazine* 27 (May 1830): 705, lines 6, 9–10.
[23] "An Oxonian," "Lines Written after Reading," lines 12, 37.

When the Arthurian revival came to fruition thirty years later, the reception of Malory's *Morte Darthur* was conditioned by the enormous influence of the poetically and ideologically rich *Idylls of the King* by Alfred Tennyson.[24] Violence is central to Tennyson's Arthuriad in a way quite distinct from Malory's. The opening idyll depicts Arthur fighting only in noble, metaphorical terms, striving against the abstracted "heathen" and "beast" amidst the "great tracts of wilderness" in order to establish his new civilisational "order."[25] Yet by the *Idylls'* conclusion, when all "reels back into the beast," the order has collapsed into the "last, dim, weird battle of the west," in which "friend and foe were shadows in the mist / And friend slew friend not knowing whom he slew."[26] Whereas Malory's narrative, as Lynch has shown, frequently elides its heroes' potential culpability for military violence – nearly every major character in the *Idylls*, save the King alone, is in some ways responsible for that final calumny, as "a moral decline in individuals is translated back into their common military and political disaster."[27]

Tennyson's "world-war of dying flesh"[28] would furnish several poets with suitably apocalyptic images in the war years of the twentieth century; in particular, many of Wilfred Owen's most famous verses find their origins in Tennyson's *Idylls*.[29] But it was another nineteenth-century writer – from the other side of the Atlantic – who would pave the way for modern readings and retellings of Malory in wartime. As with Frere's *The Monks and the Giants*, the mode of connecting an Arthurian past with contemporary notions of war in Mark Twain's *A Connecticut Yankee in King Arthur's Court* (1889) is satire – but the focus here is sharply focused on social structures, rather than personal vendettas. The chief conceit of the novel is a time-travel narrative: Hank Morgan, a munitions engineer and the Yankee of the title, receives a blow to the head and is mysteriously relocated to a sixth-century Britain that is almost wholly rendered from Malory's *Morte Darthur*.[30]

The *Morte* is the major intertext of the novel – *A Connecticut Yankee* frequently repeats and paraphrases its adventures wholesale, and even has the Yankee's lady and later wife, Demoiselle Alisande a la Carteloise (nicknamed "Sandy" by Hank), quote entire episodes directly from the early books of the *Morte*. And though Hank sardonically criticises Sandy's (and therefore Malory's) style as

---

[24] For a survey of Tennyson *Idylls* and their relation to Malory's *Morte Darthur*, see Rob Gossedge and Stephen Knight, "The Arthur of the Sixteenth to Nineteenth Centuries," in *The Cambridge Companion to the Arthurian Legend*, ed. Elizabeth Archibald and Ad Putter (Cambridge, 2009), 103–19.

[25] Alfred Tennyson, "The Coming of Arthur," *The Idylls of the King*, ed. J. M. Gray (Harmondsworth, 1983), lines 11, 518, 10, 508.

[26] Tennyson, "The Passing of Arthur," *The Idylls*, lines 26, 95, 100–1.

[27] Lynch, "Ideology, Context and Excess in Malory's War," 26.

[28] Tennyson, "Merlin and Vivien," *The Idylls*, line 191.

[29] Compare, for instance, Wilfred Owen, "Hospital Barge at Cérisy," in *The Poems*, ed. Jon Stallworthy, 2nd edn (London, 1990), lines 9–14, with Tennyson, "The Passing of Arthur," lines 361–71.

[30] Time-travel narratives were popular in the years immediately preceding *A Connecticut Yankee*'s publication. Prominent examples include the Arthurian-inflected *The Fortunate Island* (Boston, 1882) by Max Adeler (pseudonym of Charles Heber Clark), "The Chronic Argonauts" (1888) by H. G. Wells (reworked as *The Time Machine* seven years later), and *Looking Backward 2000–1887* (New York, 1888).

"archaic," "monotonous" and "limited," he reads the romance's honour system well, saying of Sir Marhaus's overcoming of a duke's six sons, who later swear fealty to Arthur: "it was a good haul ... and will breed a handsome crop of reputation in Arthur's court."[31] Nonetheless, for the nineteenth-century Hank, "knight-errantry is a most chuckle-headed trade" (98); and with his mixture of "knowledge, brains, pluck and enterprise" (40), he sets about transforming the Arthurian past. He swiftly deflates Merlin's wizardry, confronts the Catholic Church and reorganises the whole kingdom through a mixture of technical skill, practical knowledge and a good dose of showmanship. He counters superstition with science, usurps feudalism through capitalist business models and bypasses the influence of church and state through aggressive print-media manipulation.

Yet the novel soon departs from being a straightforward celebration of American, industrial contemporaneity over a comically barbarous Arthurian age. If the Yankee abolishes slavery, it is replaced only with a particularly aggressive form of exploitative capitalism; and if the feudal monarchy is brought to an end, it is only exchanged for a technocratic dictatorship, as industrial modernity becomes as brutal as the "medieval" world with which it contends. This brutality is nowhere more apparent than in the novel's closing battle, waged by Hank, his sidekick Clarence and fifty-two "fresh, bright, well-schooled, clean-minded young British boys" against the whole nobility of Britain, to whose side the populace – "sheep" to Hank's mind (247) – have flocked. With several miles of electrified fencing, a few pistols and thirteen Gatling guns "vomit[ing] death" (255), the Yankee's victory is assured, and twenty-five thousand lie dead by the novel's apocalyptic conclusion. Yet there is a coda: Merlin – "that cheap old humbug, that maundering old ass" (28), whom Hank had humiliated and replaced at the novel's opening – returns and, with the sorcery that had been dismissively derided, condemns the Yankee to a centuries-long sleep, from which he will awakes only to madness and death.

Views on the novel have traditionally been divided between "hard" critics, who see in the novel a satire on the sentimentality towards the past, and those "soft" critics who perceive it as an attack on the belief in American political and material progress.[32] Though many nineteenth-century readers in both America and Britain believed that *A Connecticut Yankee* was purely a satire on the "Old World," Twain had been careful to map many of the "sixth century's" failings onto contemporary America – the most powerful of which intersections is the equivalence of the "historical" slave-owners with the "slave-lords" of the pre-Civil War southern states, who are opposed, of course, by the abolitionist Yankee (172). The time-travel conceit is key to understanding the text's political and historiographical ambivalence, as it profoundly challenges the prevailing philosophical notion that western history was essentially progressivist – that history was little more than a chronicle of moral, political and intellectual improvement. Indeed, the opening of the novel, as the Yankee seeks to transform "this

---

[31] Mark Twain, *A Connecticut Yankee at King Arthur's Court*, ed. Allison R. Ensor (New York, 1982), 74–5, 99. Further references are to this edition.

[32] Both views are summarised in Everett Carter, "The Meaning of *A Connecticut Yankee*," *American Literature* 50 (1978): 418–40, at 418–19.

dark land" of Arthurian England (51) into a "strangely altered" but "happy and prosperous country" (228), repeatedly demonstrates that idea of historical perfectibility. Yet as the novel progresses, distinctions between "civilisation" and "barbarism" become fuzzy, increasingly challenged by the problematic contiguity of past and present, as feudalism and capitalism, superstition and science, Old and New Worlds collide and reveal themselves to be increasingly indistinct. At the novel's close, historical difference – and with it, causality – appears to dissolve; as Clarence says, even if Guinevere's adultery had not been discovered, Hank's reinvented Camelot would have collapsed "by-and-by" (237); just as, a few pages later, "by-and-by an adder bit a knight's heel" (240). And a sense of historical cyclicity is complete by the time Merlin taunts the unconscious Yankee: "Ye were conquerors, ye are conquered" (256).

In the mass slaughter that closes the novel, as thousands of cavalry and infantry storm Hank's near-impregnable position, defended by electrified wire and machine guns, the novel offers one last complex historical vision: to a past, nightmarish evocation of an American Civil War battle that, unintentionally, looks towards the mechanised, yet still strangely chivalric, future conflicts of the Great War.[33]

## *The* Morte Darthur *and the Great War*

For Rupert Brooke, the idealistic soldier-poet who had once written a dramatic treatment of the Arthurian story based on Malory, the Great War would restore a chivalric ethos to England's aristocracy, as he wrote a year before his death in 1915:

> Blow, bugles, blow! They brought us, for our death,
> Holiness, lacked so long, and Love, and Pain.
> Honour has come back as a king, to earth,
> And paid his subjects with a royal wage;
> And Nobleness walks in our way again;
> And we have come into our heritage.[34]

But the heritage ended, as David Wallace has written, "with the Somme and associated slaughters of the First World War: that massive loss of a chivalrically minded youth that, had they not stumbled into the age of barbed wire and

---

[33] Twain was not the only American author to associate the *Morte Darthur* with the antebellum South, and the violence of the Civil War. In 1872 an anonymous author published a short pamphlet, *The Morte d'Arthur: its Influence on the Sprit and the Manners of the Nineteenth Century* (Baltimore, MD), dedicated to demonstrating how the Southern commanders shared "the spirit of ancient Chivalry" that warranted them a place "at Arthur's Round Table" (40). See also Daniel Helbert, "Malory in America," in this volume.

[34] Rupert Brooke, "The Dead," in *Collected Poems* (Cambridge, 2010), lines 9–14. The fragment of Rupert Brooke's "King Arthur: a tragedy" is contained in a notebook among Brooke's papers, at King's College, Cambridge (MS King's/PP/RCB/2/D; fols. 1–2, 4, 10–13, 34, 47–8).

machine gun, might have sustained English global *imperium* for a little while longer."[35]

As Mark Girouard first discussed at length, during the Great War medieval and neo-medieval chivalric tropes and figures were heavily drawn upon by numerous poets, artists and propagandists.[36] Images of the crusades and St George were especially prominent. Malory's heroes, initially, were seldom called upon; their histories were too complex for easy iconographic representation in recruitment posters, and their stories were too bound up in the *Morte Darthur*'s tragic arc to be of much ideological utility. One Arthurian exception was Sir Galahad, who appeared across a wide variety of wartime writings. Malory's depiction of the maiden knight may have been an influence, but Tennyson's pre-*Idylls* poem, "Sir Galahad" (1842), was the more likely inspiration. Tennyson's depiction of a pure youth, whose physical and martial strength flowed causally from his moral and sexual health – "My strength is as the strength of ten / Because my heart is pure" – became emblematic of questing youth.[37] Newspaper reports often seized upon the figure, as did Christian propagandists.[38] Galahad also featured – with and without the Grail – in several memorials to the fallen, especially at public schools.[39] The letters of one dead soldier to home were collected by his mother under the title *My Galahad of the Trenches* (1918).[40]

These uses of Galahad – alongside other manifestations of patriotic chivalry – engendered a hostile reaction from soldier-poets in the later years of the war. In his 1917 poem "Babylon," Robert Graves dismissed Galahad as a figure of childhood imagination – one of several "ghosts of a timorous heart ... Weeping for a lost Babylon."[41] His close friend, Siegfried Sassoon, echoed similar sentiments in "The Poet as Hero" (1917), in which he admits to having once dreamed of finding "the Grail, / Riding in armour bright, serene and strong" – but now he has "said goodbye to Galahad."[42] The contemporary poem "They" poured further scorn on such notions and, with not untypical misogyny, heaped contempt on those mothers who "believe / That chivalry redeems the war's disgrace."[43]

This turning away from a Victorian Camelot was simultaneous with a new trend for looking again at Malory's *Morte Darthur*; the tragic narrative arc that

[35] David Wallace, "Sir Thomas Malory," in *The Cambridge Companion to Medieval English Literature 1100–1500*, ed. Larry Scanlon (Cambridge, 2009), 229–41, at 229.

[36] Girouard, *The Return to Camelot*, 275–93; see also Paul Fussell, "The Fate of Chivalry and the Assault upon Mother," in *Killing in Verse and Prose and Other Essays* (London, 1990), 217–44.

[37] Tennyson, "Sir Galahad," lines 3–4.

[38] Anon., "A Fisher Galahad," *The Times*, 27 May 1916: 3; Anon., "Quiet Friends. In an Old Picture Gallery," *The Times*, 14 June 1918: 9; C. Brown, "The Modern Call to Knighthood," *Quiver* 51 (May 1916): 653–4; J. D. Jones, "Sir Galahad," *Quiver* 51 (May 1916): 661–3.

[39] Christine Poulson, *The Quest for the Grail: Arthurian Legend and British Art 1840–1920* (Manchester, 1999), 112–3.

[40] Mary Dearing, *My Galahad of the Trenches: Being a Collection of Intimate Letters of Lieut. Vinton A. Dearing* (New York, 1918).

[41] Robert Graves, "Babylon," in *Complete Poems*, ed. Beryl Graves and Dunstan Ward, 3 vols. (Manchester, 1995), lines 17–18.

[42] Siegfried Sassoon, "The Poet as Hero," *The War Poems*, ed. Rupert Hart-Davis (London, 1999), lines 5–6, 9.

[43] Sassoon, "They", *The War Poems*, lines 3–4.

had kept Arthur away from the propagandists began to resound with newly war-weary readers. For instance, although Arthur W. Pollard's 1917 retelling of Malory for children is replete with nineteenth-century ideas of muscular chivalry – Arthur is described as "a typical sportsman," Lancelot, "the most splendid study of a great gentleman in all our literature" – Arthur Rackham's accompanying illustrations convey a series of hauntingly brutal wartime images.[44] As Barbara Tepa Lupack and Alan Lupack have written, this "wartime book commissioned to reflect the nation's mood of patriotism, [ultimately] provided a portrait of failed idealism that revealed Rackham's enormous sadness over the tragedy of war."[45] Frequently, Rackham's images marry Arthurian warfare to the dark tones of the contemporary Somme. In one plate, illustrating Mordred's siege of the Tower of London (wherein Guinevere has sought sanctuary, following Mordred's usurping of the crown), artillery men, some clad in armour, some not, scramble about the scene, preparing to fire two cannon at the walls. For Malory, the inclusion of the "grete gunnes" (*Morte*, 915.24 / C XXXI.1) – up-to-date equipment in fifteenth-century England – presented a temporal rupture in his otherwise "historical" text (and would have recalled to contemporary readers the Yorkists' use of cannon when besieging the Lancastrian forces garrisoned in the Tower). For contemporary readers of Pollard and Rackham's text, the image of "grete gunnes" might have inspired a similar transhistorical breach. In another, full-colour, plate, a wearied, horseless Arthur drives his lance through his traitorous son, Mordred, in the final act of Camlan's bloody field. Above them is a leaden, crow-filled sky; beneath them, inked in sepia and black, are the countless corpses of the fallen. Pollard's description of Arthur as "a typical sportsman" is nowhere to be seen in this evocatively contemporary scene.

Soldiers too began to read the *Morte* in light of their wartime experiences. Robert Graves, at Oxford after the war, later commented on how only the medieval texts he studied there seemed relevant to his generation:

> I thought of Beowulf lying wrapped in a blanket among his platoon of drunken Thanes in the Gothland billet, Judith going for a promenade to Holofernes' staff-tent; and the Brunanburgh with its bayonet-and cosh fighting – all this came far closer to most of us than the drawing-room and deer-park atmosphere of the eighteenth century.[46]

When he came to compose an introduction to Keith Baines's abridgement of Malory in 1960, Graves was still reading such texts in terms of soldiery, battle tactics and strategy.[47] Like Graves, many former combatants found a curious affinity between their own wartime experiences and various forms of medieval literature – prose and verse romance, elegies, *chansons de geste*. As the Great War began to be recorded in personal memoirs, and memorialised in fiction and verse, the recollection of modern warfare became increasingly infused with medievalist

---

[44] A. W. Pollard, *The Romance of King Arthur and his Knights of the Round Table*, illus. Arthur Rackham (London, 1917), vi, ix.

[45] Barbara Tepa Lupack with Alan Lupack, *Illustrating Camelot* (Cambridge, 2008), 155.

[46] Robert Graves, *Goodbye to All That*, 2nd edn (London, 1958), 239.

[47] Robert Graves, "Introduction," to *Malory's Le Morte D'Arthur*, abridged by Keith Baines [1962] (London, 2001), xi–xx, at xiv.

strains. John Masefield – a non-combatant who worked briefly as a hospital orderly in 1915 – produced an account of the disastrous Gallipoli campaign from the point of view of the private solider, and prefaced each of his chapters with moving quotations from the *Chanson de Roland*.[48] His later cycle of Arthurian poems, *Midsummer Night* (1927), drawn from both Malory and earlier Welsh versions of the myth, offered a series of haunting depictions of the effects of war on soldiers and non-combatants alike.[49] J. R. R. Tolkien's *Fall of Arthur* (abandoned sometime in the 1930s), imitated the form of the fourteenth-century Alliterative *Morte Arthure*, but eschewed the war with France and Rome, in favour of an ever-eastward war against Saxon lords and the king of Gothland.[50] And though he had "said goodbye to Galahad" in his war poetry, there are several noticeable Malorian passages in Sassoon's fictionalised memoir, known collectively as the George Sherston Trilogy (1937).[51]

Another soldier-medievalist was T. E. Lawrence. In his youth an aficionado of William Morris's neo-medievalism, he had also written his undergraduate thesis on the crusader castles of France.[52] He famously carried a copy of the *Morte Darthur* (as well as a collected Aristophanes and the *Oxford Book of English Verse*) in his saddlebags throughout his campaigns in Arabia.[53] Dressed in resplendent samite Arab dress (a personal gift from Prince Feisal), fighting on camelback, and with cavalry charges still a decisive tactic in his battle plans, Lawrence's war could seem very far from the mechanised soldiery of the Flanders trenches – and seemed to draw ineluctable comparisons with Malory. Indeed, he alluded to the *Morte* several times in his memoir, *The Seven Pillars of Wisdom* (1922), and understood the nomadic Bedouin among whom he fought as latter-day Arthurian knights, with a familiar code of chivalry.[54] Indeed, Lawrence's biographer, Lawrence James, has argued that the *Morte Darthur* was the very model on which the *Seven Pillars* was based.[55]

Lawrence also had a part to play in what was perhaps the most important discovery relating to the *Morte Darthur* of the last century. When in 1934 Walter Oakeshott discovered what turned out to be the sole surviving manuscript copy of the *Morte Darthur* at the Fellows' Library at Winchester College, it was Lawrence who motorcycled from Oxford to verify it. He also hoped to edit it, but that endeavour fell to Eugène Vinaver, who would eventually publish the work in a three-volume edition that took thirteen years to prepare. He famously chose the deliberately provocative title *The Works of Thomas Malory* to reflect his belief that Malory had not produced a single, unified text, but a series of eight related but ultimately separate tales. It was a thesis that preoccupied Malory studies for

---

[48] John Masefield, *Gallipoli* (London, 1916).
[49] John Masefield, *Midsummer Night and Other Tales in Verse* (London, 1927).
[50] J. R. R. Tolkien, *The Fall of Arthur*, ed. Christopher Tolkien (London, 2013).
[51] Siegfried Sassoon, *The Complete Memoirs of George Sherston* (London, 1937).
[52] Later published as *Crusader Castles* (London, 1936).
[53] T. E. Lawrence, letter to Robert Graves, 28 June 1927, *T.E. Lawrence to his Biographers*, ed. Robert Graves and Liddell Hart (London, 1938), 55.
[54] T. E. Lawrence, *The Seven Pillars of Wisdom*, ed. Angus Calder (London, 1997), 96, 476.
[55] Lawrence James, *The Golden Warrior: The Life and Legend of Lawrence of Arabia* (New York, 1990), 344.

several decades.[56] While many readers, critics and authors remained committed to their single-volume, "hoole" copies of the *Morte Darthur*, Vinaver's expensive scholarly edition was hugely popular; and a second impression, with corrections, was made available the following year.[57] Whereas the taste for Victorian neo-medievalism did not survive the 1914–18 conflict, that same conflict had transformed the *Morte Darthur* into a book about war, a literary testament to the past that had become strangely and powerfully reanimated in the present.

### *"The landscape spoke with a 'grimly voice'"*: David Jones's In Parenthesis

Of the post-war memorialists, it was David Jones who most profoundly "read" his experiences of the war in terms of Malory's romance. In his own words "a Londoner, of Welsh and English parentage, of Protestant upbringing, of Catholic subscription," Jones enlisted in the Royal Welch Fusiliers at the outset of the war, and served throughout its duration.[58] He made his artistic reputation in the 1920s, primarily as an engraver and painter, and published *In Parenthesis*, which concerned the things he "saw, felt, & was part of" as a soldier on the Western Front, in 1937.[59] Divided into seven parts, *In Parenthesis* chronicles seven months of the war between December 1915 and July 1916, beginning with his Anglo-Welsh battalion's embarkation to France, and ending with its attack on Mametz Wood, as part of the Somme offensive (an attack that also involved Graves and Sassoon, who served, as officers, in the same regiment as Jones).

A multi-layered, densely allusive and sometimes "difficult" literary work, which is neither quite poem nor prose, *In Parenthesis* symbolically links its narrative of the experiences of the non-commissioned soldiers of "B" Company with representations of war and soldiery drawn from a vast and diverse range of sources, ranging from Welsh elegies and English prose romances to *Henry V* and *La chanson de Roland* – often evoked via an allusion to Lewis Carroll's Cheshire cat or Coleridge's *Rime of the Ancient Mariner*. Two of the most important of these intertexts are the early Welsh heroic lament, *Y Gododdin*, a sixth-century series of elegies commemorating the disastrous raid by three hundred northern Celts on the Angles of Deira, and the story of Arthur, which is drawn from a number of accounts, French, English and Welsh, though the *Morte Darthur* has an especial significance to the work, as Jones made clear in his preface:

> I think that the day by day in the Waste Land, the sudden violences and long stillnesses, the sharp contours and unformed voids of that mysterious existence, profoundly affected the imaginations of those who

[56] For a discussion of Vinaver as editor of Malory, see Thomas H. Crofts and K. S. Whetter, "Writing the *Morte Darthur*: Author, Manuscript and Modern Editions," in this volume. For a comprehensive overview of the issues involved in the "hoole book" debate, see *The Malory Debate: Essays on the Text of* Le Morte Darthur, ed. Bonnie Wheeler, Robert L. Kendrick and Michael N. Salda (Cambridge, 2000).

[57] Barry Gaines, *Sir Thomas Malory: An Anecdotal Bibliography of Editions 1485–1985* (New York, 1990), 40–1.

[58] David Jones, *The Anathemata* (London, 1952), 11.

[59] David Jones, *In Parenthesis* (London, 1937), ix.

suffered it. It was a place of enchantment. It is perhaps best described in
Malory, book iv, chapter 15 – that landscape spoke "with a grimly voice."
(ix)

Jones felt a strong affinity with Malory – he understood both himself and the
author of the *Morte Darthur* to be writing in "the late autumn" of their respective
epochs (whereas Malory's sources were "of the springtime").[60]

As a result, *In Parenthesis* is steeped in Malorian allusions. Some are seemingly incidental, even humorous: one Welsh soldier is known to his comrades as
"Dai de la Cote male taile" due to his oversized greatcoat (70), and the attack on
Mametz wood is described both as another Camlan, and "a first clarst bollocks"
(138). Other references are ennobling, most notably in the climactic seventh part
when numerous soldiers in "B" Company are killed in the assault, the troops falling to the earth like others who have "fructif[ied] the land": Tristram, Lamorack,
Alisand le Orphelin [sic], Beaumains, Balin and Balan and Peredur (160–2). They
die on a second "wycked day of desteny" (*Morte*, 923.22–3 / C XXI.4), one in
which "[p]roperly organized chemists can let make more riving power than ever
Twrch Trwyth" (155), the raving giant boar that nearly destroys the Island of
Britain in the earliest piece of vernacular Arthurian prose, the Welsh *Culhwch
ac Olwen*. This admixture of Welsh and English traditions is typical in the work.
For Jones, the Arthurian legend was a unifying myth; as he wrote in *Epoch and
Artist*, "there is no other tradition at all equally the common property of all the
inhabitants of Britain."[61]

One of the most notable features of Jones's use of the Arthurian myth is that
– unlike the work of Graves, Sassoon and Lawrence – it is exclusively concerned
with the comradeship of ordinary soldiers, rather than commissioned officers.
This extension of chivalry to the working-class soldiers is apparent in one of the
most celebrated sections of *In Parenthesis*: Dai Greatcoat's speech in the fourth
part of the poem, wherein he mythologises the Welsh's martial past – whether
fighting for his own people's freedom in glorious defeats, or embattled in other
nations' wars. It begins:

> This Dai adjusts his slipping straps, wraps close his misfit outsize
>     greatcoat – he articulates his English with an alien care.
> My fathers were with the Black Prinse of Wales […]
> I was with Abel when his brother found him,
> under the green tree.
> I built a shit-house for Artaxerxes.
> I was the spear in Balin's hand
>     That made waste King Pellam's land. (79)

He was present at Badon Hill; witnessed Arthur, "The Bear of the Island," break
the land "in his huge pride, and / over-reach of his imperium"; saw the "repul-
sive lips" of "Lord Agravaine" urge Arthur's court to doom; fought at Camlan
and was "the adder in the little bush / whose hibernation-end / undid, / unmade
victorious toil" (80–2). This eternal Welshman also marched with Roland in

---

[60] David Jones, *Epoch and Artist: Selected Writings* (London, 1959), 245.
[61] Jones, *Epoch and Artist*, 216.

Charlemagne's wars, was present at the defeat of the Gododdin and was even "in Michael's trench when bright Lucifer bulged his / primal salient out" (84). The theme of this section, Jones's note informs the reader, is "the repeated spoliation of the Island by means of foreign entanglement and expeditionary forces across the channel" (209, n. 37). Both Welsh tradition and Arthurian myth have plenty of instances. In this historical pattern, the Great War was yet another equally destructive expeditionary war, which would spoil the land once more.

But the use of Malory extends beyond allusions and quotations; the *Morte Darthur* forms the very language of Jones's depiction of the war, as in the description of "B" Company's night-time advance, observed by Jenkins:

> Past the little gate
> Into the field of upturned defences
> Into the burial yard –
> The grinning and the gnashing and the sore dreading –
>   nor saw he any light in this place. (31)

The "grymly voyce" of Malory is powerfully present here. The relevant passage is Launcelot's approach to the Chapel Perilous (*Morte*, 215.5–28 / C VI.15), with its "lytyll gate" and "chapell-yerde." The "upturned defences" find their root in the "ryche shyldis turned up-so-downe" of (dishonoured) knights who had been to that place before Launcelot – and had been defeated by the "thirty grete knyghtes" who "grenned and gnasted" Launcelot's approach. As John Ball and his platoon repeat Launcelot's uncanny journey one further time, the scene acquires an additional sense of *das unheimliche*. As language of the Front and the *Morte Darthur* blend – beyond the paraphrases and quotations of Twain; and beyond the allusions of Lawrence and Sassoon – time itself seems to become "malleable, heterogeneous and indefinite," which Favret describes as that all-too-familiar sense of writing about modern war in relation to past conflicts.[62]

W. H. Auden claimed that David Jones's *In Parenthesis* was "the greatest book about the First World War" he had read – a view repeated by many other poets and critics, though the book has also had some sharp detractors.[63] The chief charges against Jones are that, in contrast to the intimate immediacy of so many of the affective lyrics that emerged from poets writing at the Front, *In Parenthesis* is unnecessarily difficult and learned – Paul Fussell calls him a "turgid allusionist," and describes the thirty-four pages of notes that accompany the work as a manifestation of "the literary insecurity of the autodidact."[64] The second charge, also made by Fussell, is that the poem seeks to place the Great War in a great tradition of warfare, when the exceptionalism of that conflict means that it cannot be understood in traditional terms:

> *In Parenthesis* poses for itself the problem of re-attaching traditional meanings to the unprecedented actualities of the war. ... The poem is a deeply conservative work which uses the past not, as it often pretends to do, to shame the present, but really to ennoble it. The effect of the

---

[62] Mary A. Favret, *War at a Distance: Romanticism and the Making of Modern Wartime* (Princeton, NJ, 2010), 41.

[63] Keith Alldritt, *David Jones: Writer and Artist* (London, 2003), 108.

[64] Fussell, *The Great War and Modern Memory*, 144, 155.

poem, for all its horrors, is to rationalise and even to validate the war by implying that it somehow recovers many of the motifs and values of medieval chivalric romance.[65]

The difficulty of writing about war – what Margot Norris describes as "art's incommensurability to war: its inability to respond with adequate and appropriate gravity, scale, and meaningfulness" – is evidently true.[66] And yet it seems difficult to read Jones's use of Malory – or other medieval materials – as attempting to validate the conflict in the way Fussell has here claimed. As Mary Jones noted, the heroic battles Jones calls upon are not the imperial campaigns of Waterloo, Trafalgar or the Boer War, but tragic battles, historical and mythic – Catraeth, Roland's death at Roncesvalles, Llewelyn's fall, Camlan.[67] The "motifs and values of medieval chivalric romance" are not so much recovered by the war, as made explicable by the experience of it. The sheer temporal stretch between Jones's medieval sources and his contemporary subject matter itself registers the extreme difficulty in attempting to understand an experience that lies almost beyond the scope of human comprehension. Yet, in this world of modern and medieval waste lands, sometimes the experience of war is too much even for Jones's mythic, Malorian system. After all, when "skin [has] gone astrictive … who gives a bugger for / the Dolorous Stroke" (162)?

## "An antidote to war": T. H. White, Arthurian Myth and the Second World War

As with previous major conflicts, the Second World War brought about another cycle of Arthurian texts. Dramatic retellings were prominent. Charles Rann Kennedy's Christian-apocalyptic play *The Seventh Trumpet* debuted in New York in 1941. Its plot centring on the aerial bombardment of a British monastery, the play focuses on the need for faith as Armageddon approaches, with the recovery of the Grail offering some spiritual comfort.[68] Less religious in tone, and more direct in its nationalist use of the trope of the Arthurian return, was *The Saviours* by Clemence Dane (the pen-name of Winifred Ashton). A series of radio plays produced over twelve months from November 1940, it begins in Arthurian mode with Merlin recounting his role in the war against the Saxons, before he narrates the dramatic biographies of six further "saviours": Arthur, Alfred, Robin Hood, Elizabeth I, Nelson and finally the "Unknown Soldier." Each figure is a manifestation of a single hero "who helps his [and her] people to become strong and civilised, and then disappears," itself a variation on Arthur's role as the king who would return in the time of his people's greatest need.[69] Another variation on the theme of Arthur's return is Marcel Varnel's little-remembered 1942 film, *King Arthur Was a Gentleman*, a patriotic vehicle for the popular comedian

---

[65] Fussell, *The Great War and Modern Memory*, 145, 147.
[66] Margot Norris, *Writing War in the Twentieth Century* (London, 2000).
[67] Mary E. Jones, "Heroism in Unheroic Warfare," *Poetry Wales* 8.3 (1972): 14–21.
[68] Charles Rann Kennedy, *The Seventh Trumpet* (New York, 1942).
[69] Clemence Dane, *The Saviours* (London, 1942), v.

Arthur Askey – though here, as Kevin Harty has discussed, the mode is slapstick comedy and some mediocre musical numbers.[70]

More recent fiction focused on the Second World War has also treated the trope. Arthur returns again in Dennis Lee Anderson's *Arthur, King* (1995), this time as a RAF pilot who confronts Mordred (now flying for the Luftwaffe) during the Battle of Britain.[71] More sophisticated is Donald Barthelme's *The King*, published posthumously in 1990, which blends knowledgeable details from Malory with a reimagined Second World War, as Launcelot, Gawain and an ill-equipped Arthur become enmeshed in the world of Lord Haw-Haw, Ezra Pound and Winston Churchill. Both sides undertake the quest for the Grail, here potently imagined as a metonym for the atom bomb. Eschewing time-travel, fantasy and comedy, *The King* avoids any narrative explanation for the historical collapse of time frames. Beginning with an extended parody of Malory's prose style, it ends as Launcelot's *aventures* in the *Morte Darthur* began, with the greatest knight in the world sleeping under an apple tree, dreaming perhaps of "no war, no Table Round, no Arthur, no Launcelot," or perhaps of "the softness of Guinevere ... the sexuality of Guinevere."[72]

The dominance of the novel form in Arthurian literary production in the second half of the twentieth century rested, generally, on the success – popular and critical – of the series of novels by T. H. White that came to be known as *The Once and Future King*. Born in India to a family of colonial administrators, White knew the *Morte Darthur* intimately, and understood it idiosyncratically. He went up to Cambridge in 1926 (unlike contemporary Oxford, not then a centre of medieval studies), and wrote his undergraduate thesis on Malory – though it has not survived. White then worked as a schoolmaster at the progressive public school of Stowe, where he wrote short novels and other popular works in his spare time. He published his first Arthurian novel, *The Sword in the Stone*, in 1938.

Like so many of the most influential Arthurian writers, White took the *Morte* as his frame narrative, but composed his narrative in the lacunae of Malory's romance. Troubled as a child, and often frustrated as an adult (Sylvia Townsend Warner's magnificent memoir deals with the causes), White provided Arthur – known here as Wart – with an *enfance* unknown in the medieval tradition.[73] And in Merlyn he created an ideal educator with a broad curriculum that prepared the young Arthur for kingship through lessons taken from the natural world. Initially intended as a standalone novel, it was soon followed by *The Witch in the Wood* (1939), which provided further *enfances* for Gawain and his brothers, though these are darker, even sadomasochistic (and often misogynistic), in tone. *The Ill-Made Knight* followed the year after. This followed Malory more closely, but with twists that revealed the novelist's psychological interest in character. Here, Lancelot, the ill-made knight of the title, is gay: his illicit love for Guinevere

---

[70] Kevin J. Harty, "King Arthur Goes to War (Singing, Dancing and Cracking Jokes): Marcel Varney's 1942 Film *King Arthur Was a Gentleman*," *Arthuriana* 14.4 (2004): 17–25.

[71] Dennis Lee Anderson, *Arthur, King* (New York, 1995).

[72] Donald Barthelme, *The King* (New York, 1990), 158. Both Barthelme's and Anderson's novels are discussed in Lacy, "King Arthur Goes to War," and Hoffman, "Arthur, Popular Culture and World War II."

[73] Sylvia Townsend Warner, *T. H. White: A Biography* (Oxford, 1967).

(usually known as Gwen) little more than a heteronormative transference of his desire for Arthur. In the following novel, unpublished during the war, but later known as the *Candle in the Wind*, an ageing Arthur and Lancelot devise the Grail quest as a spirited – if not spiritual – means of inspiring a younger generation of knights to uphold the law of chivalry and to support Arthur's pursuit of right over might. But the novel ends, as the Arthurian tragedy always must, with devastation, and with Arthur, now weary, on the eve of the battle of Camlan.

When White began his Arthurian sequence in 1938 it was, in his own words, "rather warm-hearted – mainly about birds and beasts. It seems impossible to determine whether it is for grown-ups or children."[74] Yet, this was a book that was forced to grow up, as White's rewriting of Malory could not escape the context of the ensuing years. As Stephen Knight has written: "White was writing as fascism, Stalinism, and war gathered force, and he is the first Arthurian writer to turn his mind firmly onto the politics of international violence, making explicit what is implied in Twain."[75] Violence and aggression soon became the core issues of the sequence. Early in the second volume, Merlyn, not unlike Twain's Hank, interrogates the very meaning and value of chivalry:

> What is all this chivalry, anyway? It simply means being rich enough to have a castle and a suit of armour ... Look at all the barns burned, and dead men's legs sticking out of ponds, and horses with swelled bellies by the roadside, and mills falling down, and money buried, and nobody daring to walk abroad with gold or ornaments on their clothes. That is chivalry nowadays. (237–8)

Much of Arthur's education and early rule focus on the need to control such violence and redirect might to the service of right. He does this by force ("a good reason for starting a war"), and undertakes the conquest of the Gaels. Merlyn, troubled, says that he knew such a man when he was young, "an Austrian" who "tried to impose his reformation by the sword and plunged the civilized world into misery and chaos" (284).

Merlyn's anachronism is explained by the fact that he is living backwards in time. But the novel plays with history in an almost postmodern style throughout the narrative. For instance, while the events of the Arthuriad take place according to Malory's chronological order, they are superimposed across the whole later English Middle Ages: the coming of Uther takes place in 1066; Arthur succeeds to the throne in 1216 (as did the nine-year-old Henry III); his early battles coincide with the reigns of Edwards I and III; and Camlan takes the place of Bosworth in 1485. Similarly, the novel utilises White's varied and detailed knowledge of medieval life with a whimsical penchant for anachronism that is quite different from Twain's. Here "manchets" (small loaves of bread) and "pennoncels" (triangular flags, usually attached to a lance's tip) sit alongside references to the *Morning Post* and *Humberland Newsman* (281, 343, 5, 23). The historical collapse becomes even more apparent in the final novel, as Mordred leads a party of black-shirted Thrashers, a fascist group, whose symbol is a "scarlet fist clenching a whip," and

---

[74] White, Letter to L. J. Potts, 14 January 1938, *Letters to a Friend*, ed. Françoise Gallix (Gloucester, 1984), 86.

[75] Stephen Knight, *Merlin: Knowledge and Power Through the Ages* (Ithaca, NY, 2009), 196.

who are dedicated to "some kind of nationalism, with Gaelic autonomy, and a massacre of the Jews" (646). In a manner that recalls both Twain's *Connecticut Yankee* and, more directly, Jones's *In Parenthesis*, war in White's Arthurian cycle appears as temporally wayward. It simultaneously represents one specific war (the Second World War), an echo of a past war (here, Malory's insular campaign and, later, Camlan) and an idea of war understood in a transhistorical way: a war as all wars, each a platonic shadow of an ideal, devastating war.[76]

White, however, resisted Twain's borderline-nihilism and was not, unlike Jones, an actual combatant who sought to understand his own experiences in light of Malory's model. He read – or at least tried to read – in the *Morte Darthur* something of a treatise on war, as he wrote to his old Cambridge tutor, L. J. Potts, after he had nearly completed what he had thought was the final volume of his Arthurian quartet. In his letter written from Ireland in December 1940, when Britain was suffering the worst of the Blitz, White claimed that he had discovered that the "central theme of the *Morte d'Arthur* is to find an antidote to war."[77] It was a typically idiosyncratic reading. While the *Morte*'s heroes may lament the death of great knights, and while there are several, isolated expressions of guilt for Gawain's, Lancelot's and Guinevere's respective roles in the final tragedy, the text expresses no such desire for such an antidote to the martial values that so dynamise and dominate the *Morte Darthur*'s narrative arc. The closest moment to an anti-war sentiment in Malory is articulated by the "comyn" people after they tire of Arthur's long, unsuccessful war against Lancelot:

> than was the comyn voice among them that with kynge Arthur was never othir lyff but warre and stryff, and with sir Mordrede was grete joy and blysse. (*Morte* 916.28–31 / C XXI.1)

The text is clear, however: Arthur is here "depraved" (meaning "defamed") by the "comyn" people, whose inconstancy is a perpetual "defaughte" (failing) of "us Englyshemen" (*Morte* 917.5 / C XXI.1). White, however, was convinced, and so he ploughed on with a fifth book that whisked the old and disillusioned Arthur away from the battlefield, and back to Merlyn and the animal teachers of his youth. What ensues is an extended Socratic dialogue on the causes of war, as well as two more lessons of the sort he experienced in his youth: a visit to a fascist colony of ants (whose anthem, "Antland, Antland Over All," is not hard to decode as a reference to the "Deutschlandlied"); and an extended flight with a flock of peaceable geese. His experience with the totalitarian ants yields a lesson on the dangers of communal property; from the geese he learns the value of globalism – a world without "tariff barriers, passports and immigration laws" (781). But the book is messier than this implies, and there are tensions and contradictions throughout the novel-cum-political treatise: Merlyn announces himself to be both a "staunch capitalist" and "an anarchist" (722, 801); and though a spirit of anti-nationalism pervades much of *The Book of Merlyn*, Arthur's seminar on

---

[76] Cf. Favret, *War at a Distance*, 42; and David A. Bell, *The First Total War: Napoleon's Europe and the Birth of Warfare as We Know It* (Boston, 2007), 3.
[77] White, Letter to L. J. Potts, 5 December 1940, *Letters to a Friend*, 115–16.

war and peace ends with a flea-ridden hedgehog singing Blake's "Jerusalem" in a thin Cockney accent (790–1).

*The Book of Merlyn* ended with a call to pray for both "Thomas Malory, Knight, and his humble disciple, who now voluntarily lays aside his books to fight for his kind" (812). But White never managed to enlist, and his *Merlyn* would be another casualty of the war: his publisher, Collins, declined to print his sincere but inexpert political treatise. Nonetheless, when White came to revise the whole work for publication in 1958, he took the episodes with the pacific geese and the fascist ants and imported them into what had originally been *The Sword in the Stone* (several episodes from that earlier work were excised to make Wart's education more emphatically political). The *enfances* of Gawain and his brethren were much reduced in what was now called *The Queen of Air and Darkness*; the queer material in the *Ill-Made Knight* was made more opaque (though it is still legible in the final version); and the anti-war material, no longer constrained to an Oxbridge seminar in a badger's den, was worked through the entire four-book sequence, now given the title of *The Once and Future King*. The novel now ended with Arthur, in his tent before Camlan, "looking back at his life and despairing" (685).

But the text has one last bold textual flourish – one that echoes the textual process of cyclicity that this chapter has argued was the marker of the Malorian readings and rewritings of the war years. For a page enters – a young Tom Malory of Newbold Revel. The king commands him to flee the battlefield, in order to record the greatness of the Round Table, and its mission to transform Might into the vessel of Right. Having so instructed the young Malory – and, in the process, commissioned the *Morte Darthur*, complete with new pacific significance – Arthur is prepared for the destruction of the next day, and draws himself up, "to meet the future with a peaceful heart" (697).

# 14
## Malory in Japan*
### MASAKO TAKAGI

The topic of King Arthur and the Round Table was not regarded as suitable for serious research in Japan until some decades ago, but today the situation looks rather different. Why are so many Japanese interested in Malory, and what kind of cultural background lies behind that interest? Malory is an intriguing topic for many outside European culture in regard to its literary, linguistic and cultural context, and for many Japanese, questions about Malory have often been questions of language, from its interpretation in the broadest sense to a mere stroke on a letter, like a difference between the letter "t" and "c." Toshiyuki Takamiya proved, based on palaeographical evidence, that the long-inherited mistake of "Astolat" in place of "Ascolat" was due to the habit of scribe A of the Winchester manuscript, as this scribe recurrently wrote *sc* in a ligature that looked like *st*.[1] This type of focus on the language may be related to the peculiar situation of Japan where, since the dawn of its era of modernization, Japanese people have had to struggle continuously to acquire the English language and Western culture. This chapter surveys the history of Malory's reception in modern Japan, including the development of Malory's *Morte Darthur* as an academic subject.

After the Edo period came to an end in 1868, the Meiji restoration began, bringing many rapid and fundamental changes to Japan. In the field of literature, the movement to introduce and translate Western works began on account of the urgent need to catch up with Western civilization and establish it in Japan. Japan had almost no exposure to the West until then because of *sakoku*, the isolationist policy which banned most Westerners from entering Japan except for the Dutch. During the Edo period, translation in Japan had primarily meant the art of translation between Chinese and Japanese, which made use of the Chinese characters shared by both languages. While Chinese-Japanese translation had

*My special thanks go to Takako Kato for giving me the opportunity to tackle this interesting topic, and Osamu Yamada, who wrote a dissertation on the reception of Malory in Japan in 2008. I am grateful to P. J. C. Field, whose opinion on Malory scholarship in Japan has been insightful. My gratitude also goes to Yoshio Konuma for giving me the suggestion of looking into the reception of Wagner. I also thank Kiyokazu Mizobata for answering my questions on concordances. Finally, I am grateful to Toshiyuki Takamiya, Yuri Fuwa and two anonymous readers for going through the early drafts of this chapter and giving me useful suggestions.
[1] Toshiyuki Takamiya, "'Ascolat' in the Winchester Malory," in *Aspects of Malory*, ed. Toshiyuki Takamiya and Derek Brewer (Cambridge, 1981), 125–6, 211–12.

become a finely-tuned art,[2] Dutch was also learned because that language was considered necessary for trading purposes. When the Black Ships from North America[3] arrived and the Japanese government was left with no other option but to open its ports to the United States, vigorous new attempts to improve the art of translation from European languages, particularly English into Japanese, began to be made: many schools which had taught Dutch changed their language to English. It also meant the Japanese language was obliged to change; it is symbolic that many new words which express modern, Western concepts were coined after the influx of Anglophone Westernization. With this urge to acquire Western civilization, the curious Japanese audience reached out for, embraced and enjoyed extraordinary stories from the West. In this atmosphere, Malory's *Morte Darthur* was introduced by foreign instructors, hired by the Japanese government to teach Western culture, into literature and language classes at a very early stage. Its popularity then grew on its own with various translation attempts. In 1905, Sōseki Natsume even created a Japanese version of the Arthurian legend. He took several motifs of Arthurian literature from Western writers and used them as storylines in his fiction. At about the same time, many stories from Malory began to be introduced into Japanese children's literature in various forms, though most of them remained fragmentary adaptations. Among the critical approaches to Malory, studies focused on Malory's language and the textual development of his work caught the attention of Japanese scholars, particularly after the Second World War.

## Lafcadio Hearn (1850–1904)

Many foreigners were engaged in the Meiji restoration movement, including an Irish newspaper journalist born in Greece, Lafcadio Hearn (1850–1904). Later known as Yakumo Koizumi, Hearn is representative of an early generation of such teachers from the Western world. While he famously collected interesting, eerie Japanese ghost stories in his spare time, he taught Japanese students English and Western literature and thought, including the *Morte Darthur*.

On one occasion, Hearn chose Malory as a good source for teaching about Western morality. In his essay, "With Kyūshū Students," Hearn reminisced on his days in Kumamoto with the pupils of the Fifth Higher Middle School, where he taught and discussed various Western stories from Orpheus to Edgar Allan Poe's short fiction. He found to his dismay that Mary Shelley's *Frankenstein* held no appeal for them and wondered whether the story's fundamental "peculiar horror" was not shared by the Oriental mind, which felt "no distance between

---

[2] The art is known as *kakikudashi-bun*: translation of Chinese classics by applying Japanese phonetics and grammar while retaining the original Chinese characters and meaning.

[3] The Black Ship was a common term applied to Western vessels arriving in Japan during the Edo period, but between 1852 and 1854 it referred to the different types of warships commanded by Commodore Matthew Perry when he forced the opening of Japanese ports to American trade.

God and men."[4] After this experience, he decided to throw in Malory, in order to suggest a "strong Western moral." He introduced a section from the Holy Grail adventure, where Sir Bors abandons his brother Sir Lionel, who is being badly beaten with thorns, to rescue an unknown maid who is about to be taken away. After the rescue, Bors is told that Sir Lionel had since died (736–7 / C XVI.9).[5] Because Hearn began without any basic explanation of the idealism of Western chivalry (due to his curiosity about how the pupils would initially react), they freely expressed their feelings of disagreement and resentment after he introduced the narrative. It was striking that all but one of the students disagreed with the conduct of Sir Bors for helping the maid who was a stranger to him, and condemned the knight for leaving his suffering family member. They simply could not understand that a mightier cause than family love could even exist. Since the students had more problems in understanding Christianity and religious morals, their discussion deviated from the heroism that Hearn originally intended to teach. In the end, Hearn had to sum up, "[Y]ou should also know that the sentiment obeyed by Sir Bors is one which still influences the conduct of brave and noble men in the societies of the West, – even of men who cannot be called religious in the common sense of the word."[6]

It is questionable whether a thorough explanation of Western chivalric heroism in advance would have helped these students react any differently. Evidently for them the episode appeared contrary to the basic teaching of Confucius, that one must put the family in order before putting the nation in order if one wishes to put the world in order. This value still pertains in Japan today, so it is no surprise that the attempt more than a century ago to teach Japanese students the concept of Western chivalry provoked such counter-reaction.[7] As Hearn was a careful observer of the Japanese, he probably partially foresaw what might be a crucial dividing point between Western and Eastern morals before drawing upon the Sir Bors example.

Hearn taught at Tokyo Imperial University from 1896 to 1903.[8] The first generation of famous future leaders in English literature and language all studied under him: Wasaburō Asano, a spiritualist and translator; Moto Kurihara, a teacher at Hiroshima Higher Normal School (later integrated into Hiroshima University); Sadajirō Kobinata, the author of *English Literary History* (1923) and later a professor at Hiroshima Bunri University; Bin Ueda, a literary torchbearer, translator and eventual successor of Hearn; Bansui Doi, a poet and a translator of Homer; Rinshirō Ishikawa, a linguist and a compiler of English-Japanese

---

[4] Lafcadio Hearn, "With Kyûshû Students," *Out of the East: Reveries and Studies in New Japan* (Cambridge, MA, 1895), 51–2.

[5] Sir Thomas Malory, *Le Morte Darthur*, ed. P. J. C. Field, 2 vols. (Cambridge, 2013).

[6] Hearn, "With Kyûshû Students," 55.

[7] It has to be noted, however, in the light of Japanese *Samurai* ideals, that there are many occasions when *Chū*, or loyalty, and *Gi*, or righteousness, are put before family love. Sacrificing family for righteousness, and the agony suffered for this sacrifice, is a common theme in Japanese popular epics such as the famous Kabuki play, *Chūshingura*, or *the Story of 47 Lordless Samurai*. Although the story is not a parallel for the world of Malory's *Morte*, there is certainly common ground between the Japanese *Samurai* ideals and Malory's chivalric ideals in terms of loyalty and righteousness.

[8] He then taught briefly at Waseda University, but died in 1904 from angina pectoris.

dictionaries; Hakuson Kuriyagawa, a professor at Kyoto Imperial University, to name but a few. Kuriyagawa's son, Fumio, later became a professor of Old and Middle English literature at Keio University, which had been founded by Yukichi Fukuzawa, one of the most prominent liberal ideologists of early modern Japan.

Hearn's lectures were later compiled and published as *A History of English Literature* in 1927, revised in 1932 and 1934 and then reissued in 1938.[9] In this *History*, he bestowed the highest possible praise on Malory.[10] Malory was essential reading in his bibliography, and he recommended as the best cheap edition Sir Edward Strachey's *Le Morte D'Arthur* in the Macmillan Globe Library, although it was a bowdlerized text. Hearn commented, "It is one of the books that ought to be in a part of everybody's library."[11] So the students in his class at Tokyo Imperial University were well acquainted with the *Morte Darthur* thanks to Hearn. He simply loved it so much that he could not help emphasizing its greatness:

> There is no book in English prose more delightful to read than this 15th century text; and we do not need any glossary or dictionary of Middle English to help us in reading. Even such unfamiliar words as "truller" are easily understood from the context. Nor is the charm of the book merely a charm of fine-sounding and beautiful English. The immense charm of the book is in the idea which it expresses—the idea of perfect knighthood, in the conduct of the warrior, the conduct of the retainer, the conduct of the leader, the conduct of the friend. There is not very much about the conduct of lover and husband; but it is sufficiently implied.[12]

Hearn also constantly lectured on common aspects between the Japanese *bushi-do* (*Samurai* spirit) and Malory's idea of chivalry. One may be induced to speculate that the first reaction Hearn had received from the pupils in Kumamoto remained in his mind, as in the example below he points out the difference between Malory's ideas and those in Old Japan. He certainly, from time to time, compared and contrasted the Japanese *bushi-do* and European knighthood:

> And all those ideas of the West and the East – of Mediæval [sic] Europe and Old Japan – are in some respects very different indeed; nevertheless I cannot imagine that any Japanese student could read this book without pleasure. All that the old *Samurai* idea implied in this country, was expressed in England by the idea figured in this wonderful book. The

---

[9] The original edition in 1927 was in two volumes, containing lectures given by Hearn between 1896 and 1903, taken down by his students, then compiled and edited by R. Tanabe and T. Ochiai. It was revised under the title of *Complete Lectures on Art, Literature and Philosophy, by Lafcadio Hearn*, in 1932, edited by Ryuji Tanabe, Teizaburo Ochiai and Ichirō Nishizaki. The subsequent revised edition appeared in 1934, however, under the original title of 1927, *A History of English Literature*, and then the popular edition based on the third edition was published in 1938, all by Hokuseido Press, Tokyo. Citations are from the 1938 edition.

[10] When discussing romance, Hearn described Malory as the "last great production in the mediaeval spirit (I am speaking of only mediaeval romance) [which] has been justly termed the greatest of all romances, of any age or country." See Hearn, *A History of English Literature*, 113–14.

[11] Hearn, *A History of English Literature*, 114–15.

[12] Hearn, *A History of English Literature*, 114.

English knight and the Japanese knight had not the same idea of duty as to detail; but the fundamental idea was certainly the same; – and if you read the volume, you will feel that the two were, after a fashion, ghostly brothers.[13]

Hearn, who married a Japanese woman and led his later life as a Japanese national,[14] may have found his own ideals overlapped with Japanese ones when he wrote about the merging of Western and Eastern chivalric ideals. It was fortunate for future Malory scholars that Hearn was such an enthusiastic reader of Malory. In a sense, he was more advanced than typical literary historians of the West at the time because he paid attention to Malory before many Western literary historians did. His influence on the literary sphere in Meiji Japan was enormous and easily surpassed the bounds of the field of English literature. Therefore, it is no surprise that his inclination fortunately helped nurture the next generation of Malory scholarship, and this influence is still visible today.[15]

As Japan opened various channels to connect to the West, information on early Arthurian texts was brought by those who studied in Germany. In 1888, a philosopher and literary critic, Sadahiro Hisamatsu (1857–1913), introduced the medieval story of *Tristan und Isolde* as popular literature in verse which had developed in the Middle Ages.[16] Another famous author connected to Germany was Ōgai Mori (1862–1922), who was also an army surgeon: he had been dispatched to Germany to study hygiene from 1884 to 1888. He referred to the Arthurian legend as one branch of medieval romance in 1889, while discussing the difference between the romance and the novel.[17] Mori supervised the publication of the Arthurian

---

[13] Hearn, *A History of English Literature*, 114.

[14] It has been pointed out by Shūko Takeshita that Hearn may have lived with dual nationality because the British government did not allow him to discard his British nationality. Shūko Takeshita, "Meiji Zenki no Gaikokujin Nyūfu Kon-in ni Kansuru Ichikousatsu: Koizumi Yakumo no Jiken kara [Intermarriage in the Meiji Era: A Case Study of Lafcadio Hearn]," *Aichi-Gakuin University Review, Ningen-Bunka* 31 (2016): 274–265.

[15] Some argue that an English scholar, John Lawrence, who taught at Tokyo Imperial University from 1906 to 1916, had a bigger influence on later Japanese medievalists. See, for example, Toshiki Hashikawa, "Ogawa Sanshirō ga <Eibun Gakusha> to Naru Mirai—Jon Rorensu no Gakutou to "Jokyōju B" Chiba Tsutomu no Kouseki ni Terashite [Sanshiro Ogawa's Future as an *Anglicist*: In the Light of the Academic Heritage of John Laurence [sic] and the Trail of 'Assistant Professor B,' Tsutomu Chiba]," *The Kyoritsu Journal of International Studies* 30 (2013): 125–44. It is probable that John Lawrence influenced those who pursued academic paths, while Hearn became more famous among the general public as a lover of Japan.

[16] Osamu Yamada, *Meiji / Taisho Āsā Oh Rouman—Entaku Kishi Monogatari no Nihon ni okeru Juyō to Tenkai* [Meiji and Taisho Period Arthurian Romances: The Reception and Development of the Stories of the Knights of the Round Table in Japan], unpublished BA thesis, Keio University, 2008, at 15. Sadahiro Hisamatsu published the article as "Doitsu Shousetsu no Enkaku [Development of German Novels]," in a journal, *Jogaku Zasshi*, issue 104, 7 April 1888.

[17] Rintarō Mori, "Ima no shoka no Shousetsu ron wo yomite [Upon Reading the Current Literary Criticism on Novels]," *Ōgai Zenshū* [Complete Works of Ōgai], 38 vols. (Tokyo, 1937), 12: 85. The article was originally published in a literary journal, *Shigaramisoushi* 2 (November 1889). Rintarō was Ōgai Mori's real name, while Ōgai was his nom de plume. Ōgai was the editor-in-chief of this journal, which advocated Romanticism and lasted for five years, from 1889 to 1894. For a reconsideration of the *Morte*'s relationship to romance and the novel, see Cory James Rushton, "Malory and Form," in this volume.

legend for children compiled by Shun Uchiyama in 1914, but this edition included many bowdlerizing changes, such as banishing adulterous love and women's jealousy from the story. The element of Christianity was also stripped away, so Galahad did not achieve the quest of the Holy Grail. Under the new regime, it was safer to depict women as stereotyped, ideal housewives, and Christianity as an ephemeral dream. Even though there was no written consensus, emphasizing what the society was presumed to want was a common practice of its people. The Restoration government was united under the state religion of Shintoism, and the strictness of the Edo government which had controlled Christianity for over 300 years was not yet forgotten. The fifteen years of the Taisho era is generally regarded as a short happy period of freedom, but people barely liberated themselves; instead, they followed the new rules of Westernization shaping the government's intent. Consequently, what remained as a popularized Arthurian legend was just the frame of the knights and their strange adventures.[18] It was published as one of a series of collected world masterpieces for children, which came into fashion during the Taisho era.[19]

## Bin Ueda and the Wagnerian Boom

Bin Ueda (1874–1916) is considered to have been one of the best students of Lafcadio Hearn. He acquainted himself with various European languages, and covered a vast field of European literature, but he himself tended towards modernism. He is best known today for having introduced the French symbolist poets, such as Mallarmé and Verlaine, in *Kaichō-on*, the collection of poems he translated and edited.[20]

In his youth, he wrote on various literary topics mainly by summarizing the newly published literary reviews in the West. In 1896, he reviewed Algernon Charles Swinburne's newly published Arthurian poem, *The Tale of Balen*, in the literary journal *Teikoku Bungaku*.[21] There he listed Chrétien de Troyes from French

---

[18] Yamada discusses the peculiarity of Uchiyama's edition in detail. For example, Igrene is a young princess of Cornwall before she meets Uther, and she gradually opens up her heart to him. Merlin's magic seems to play no part in their union. The Lancelot and Elaine episode takes no account of Guinevere's jealousy, so there is no triangular love. In the quest of the Holy Grail, Galahad "awakes" after a long prayer, so there is no achievement of the quest. Yamada, [Meiji and Taisho Period Arthurian Romances], 15 and 52–9.

[19] *Sekai Meicho Monogatari 4 Āsā Oh Monogatari* [World Masterpieces: Four Stories of Arthur], supervised by Ōgai Mori and Hōgetsu Shimamura, translated and compiled by Shun Uchiyama (Tokyo, 1914). The Taisho era saw at least four major translations of Arthurian legends. Uchiyama's edition was published in 1914, Kiyoshi Fukunaga's edition in 1917, Naomi Baba's translation of "Gareth and Lynette" from Tennyson in 1924, and the edition by a team of editors called Kagai Yomimono Kankō-kai also in 1924. Both 1917 and 1924 editions rely on Waldo Cutler's *Stories of King Arthur and his Knights* (1904) with Tennyson occasionally interspersed. See Yūzō Tamaki, "<Nōto> Meiji Kouki to Āsā Oh Monogatari—Hān, Rōrensu to Marorī [<Note> The Arthurian Stories at the End of the Meiji Era: Malory in Hearn's and Lawrence's Lectures]," *Sakai Women's Junior College Review* 32 (1997): 61–74, at 62.

[20] *Kaichō-On*, trans. and compiled by Bin Ueda (Tokyo, 1905).

[21] "Suinbān no Shincho [New Publication of Swinburne]," in *Teihon Ueda Bin Zenshû* [Authentic Text: Complete Works of Bin Ueda], ed. Ueda Bin Zenshû Kankōkai (Ilōjin

literature, and Wolfram von Eschenbach's *Parzival* and Gottfried von Strassburg's *Tristan* from German literature,[22] and preached that even a student of English literature should be familiar with these names because the "Celtic thoughts" that underlie the base of European cultural heritage are expressed in them.[23] It is doubtful to what extent he was acquainted with these works, but it was certainly one of the earliest discussions of this kind by a Japanese academic. In July 1897 he introduced some recent publications in England, and listed the new Temple Classics version of *Le Morte Darthur*.[24]

Although Ueda's knowledge of the Arthurian legend was rather shallow, some related themes began to spread through the aid of his followers, sometimes in an astonishing way. One scandalous event occurred in a manner which captivated the Japanese public, and it was related to Wagner's *Tristan und Isolde* as depicted by an Italian novelist, Gabriele D'Annunzio (1863–1938). The decadent author and poet was obviously one of Bin Ueda's favourite writers, as the fact that the first poem in *Kaichō-on* was D'Annunzio's "Tsubame no Uta [The Swallow's Song]" shows.[25] On 23 March 1908, an author and a follower of Bin Ueda, Sōhei Morita, attempted murder-suicide with a woman called Haruko Hiratsuka, later the prominent feminist Raichō. When they were saved by the hotel owner in a snowy spa resort in the north of the Kantō region, Nasu-Shiobara, they explained that they had imitated the couple's footsteps as depicted in D'Annunzio's *Il trionfo della morte* [The Triumph of Death] (1894).[26] This incident was reported widely in the newspapers, and caught the curiosity of people who were eager to reach out for any Western literary concept, so publication of its translation was planned immediately. *Il trionfo della morte* is a gloomy story in which the protagonist Giorgio becomes obsessed with Wagner's opera *Tristan und Isolde*, and longs for the love and death experienced by Tristan with his lover. Instead of frowning at the decadence, the Japanese public happily wallowed in its ambience. The

---

Yano et al.), 10 vols. (Tokyo, 1978), 3: 230–5.

[22] Ibid., 231. The article was first published anonymously in a section entitled "Kaigai-soudan," in a literary journal *Teikoku Bungaku*, September issue, 2.9 (1896). *Teihon Ueda Bin Zenshû*, 3: 618.

[23] Ueda, [New Publication of Swinburne], 232. It must be admitted that what Ueda expresses as "Celtic thoughts" (Keruto Sou) is unclear.

[24] "Kinkansho sen [Selected New Publications]," *Teihon Ueda Bin Zenshû*, 3: 437–40, at 438. This article was first published anonymously, entitled "Dokushokai no Kinkansho [Recent Publications in the Literature World]," in the "Kaigai Soudan" section of *Teikoku Bungaku*, July issue, 3.7 (1897). *Teihon Ueda Bin Zenshû*, 3: 645.

[25] Bin Ueda was not versed in the Italian or Provençal languages, so "The Swallow's Song" is likely to have been translated from the English version of *Francesca Da Rimini* by Arthur Symons. Jirō Ozawa reveals that Ueda translated most of the poems not from the collections he mentioned, but from widely-circulated verse collections and review journals. See Ozawa Jirō, "*Kaichō-On* no Seiritsu Haikei [Background of the Development of *Kaichō-On*]," *Geibun Kenkyu: Journal of Arts and Letters* 52 (1988): 1–27, at 18–19.

[26] This story appears in a collection of essays *Shinchô-sha Yonjû-nen* [Forty Years of Shinchō-sha Publishing] (Tokyo, 1936), by Giryō Satō (1878–1951). Satō was the founder of Shinchō-sha publishing company, and wrote up the memoir of his firm in 1936, to commemorate the company's fortieth anniversary. The text is available at the website of Japan P.E.N. Club Digital Library under the title of *Recollecting Stories of Publishing* [Shuppan Omoide Banashi] in <http://bungeikan.jp/domestic/detail/355/>, created 16 February 2008.

novel first appeared in Japanese in the literary journal *Subaru* in 1909, translated not from the original Italian but from French and English by Gian Ishikawa.[27] It was published in 1913 by Dai Nihon Tosho in book form. The young Chōkō Ikuta, another of Bin Ueda's followers, also translated it from French and English, and when his version was published by Shinchō-sha in 1913, it was so successful that it achieved record sales for the publisher.[28] However, the story did not connect the Japanese reader in any way to the original Tristan legend or to Wagner's original music.

In 1896, a novelist and translator (notably of Shakespeare), Shōyō Tsubouchi (1859–1935), translated Alfred Tennyson's "The Lady of Shalott" into Japanese with ample commentary.[29] It circulated widely as a supplementary textbook for students of English literature because Tsubouchi taught English at what would later be known as Waseda University. The poem's popularity is clear from the fact that by 1926, it had been translated by three other people, all of whom based their work on Tsubouchi's translation, each attempting to emphasize different aspects of the poem.[30] It is questionable, however, whether Tennyson's source, Malory, was paid as much attention as he deserved, although his importance was accurately mentioned by those who introduced it. For the majority who learned the poem, it was no more than a gateway to contemporary Victorian and English literature, and Tennyson's deep interest in his own cultural heritage was not recognized until Sōseki Natsume appeared.

By the early stages of the Meiji restoration, therefore, elements of the Arthurian legend had found their way into Japan, but they were intertwined with other phenomena and aspects, and rarely came to the surface. For instance, during the same period, the Art Nouveau movement was zealously appreciated by the Japanese public, and many book designers actively copied the state-of-the-art style.[31] Ironically enough, their products were simply regarded as fashionable; people generally failed to appreciate the concept of the arts-and-crafts movement as a revival of the spirit of Western medieval craftsmanship. The Wagnerian boom can be cited as another example. The German composer Richard Wagner acquired many enthusiastic fans in the Meiji and Taisho periods, although his

---

[27] An English translation by Arthur Hornblow had been available since 1896, but the text Ishikawa used remains unidentified. See Ikuho Amano, *Decadent Literature in Twentieth-Century Japan: Spectacles of Idle Labor* (New York, 2013), 71. See also the Japanese translation of Gabriele D'Annunzio, *Shi no Shōri* [Il trionfo della morte], trans. Isao Waki (Kyoto, 2010).

[28] Giryô Satô, "Hon'yaku Shuppan – *Chichi to Ko, Shi no Shôri* [Publishing Translation Works: *The Father and the Son*, and *The Triumph of Death*]," in [Forty Years of Shinchō-sha Publishing], 88–90.

[29] Shōyō Tsubouchi published his translation as "Eibun Arufureddo Tenison no saku, Sharotto no Youki [English Alfred Tennyson Makes The Lady of Shalott]," in three issues of *Kokugakuin Zasshi*, 2.3–5 (January–March 1896). This was the first complete translation, although the first introduction of the poem preceded it by four years, by Masahisa Uemura, in *Nihon Hyōron* 46, 15 October 1892. See Yamada, [Meiji and Taisho Period Arthurian Romances], 18.

[30] Tengen Kataoka in 1905, Riu Takada in 1904, and Seimyou Iguchi in 1926, respectively. See Yamada, [Meiji and Taisho Period Arthurian Romances], 32.

[31] Goyô Hashiguchi's design of Sōseki Natsume's novel, *Wagahai wa Neko de aru* [I Am A Cat] (1905–07), and Takeji Fujishima's design of a verse collection, *Midaregami* [Tangled Hair] (1901) by a female poet, Akiko Yosano, are well-known examples.

operatic works were seldom available on records, let alone performed live by orchestras. Wagner's social philosophy was appealing to Japanese society, as it was in Europe, and it was believed that his ideals could have the power of making a breakthrough in the stagnant situation in Japan.[32] Most people learned about him as an ideologist rather than a composer through literary reviews in journals. Therefore, although Wagner's name reverberated so much, his plots (based on Germanic and Arthurian legends) were simply too distant for the Japanese audience to connect to, just like his music, which was hardly played.

Thus, people were enthralled by various kinds of Western art forms, but mostly they received them shallowly, as something exotic and new, or at times tried to apply them as immediate solutions to their current problems. Seeing through to the Western medieval period behind these works was certainly not the primary concern of the Japanese in the Meiji and Taisho periods.

## Sōseki Natsume (1867–1916)

In Great Britain, Alfred, Lord Tennyson died on 6 October 1892. Without delay many literary critics in Japan commemorated, introduced and translated works of his in Japanese literary journals. It is notable that Sōseki Natsume, who later wrote such masterpieces as *Wagahai wa Neko dearu* [I Am a Cat] and *Kokoro*, while still a student at Tokyo Imperial University, translated a long obituary on Tennyson written by an American lecturer, Augustus Wood (1855–1912).[33] Wood seems not to have been a respectable teacher in the long run due to his heavy drinking habit, but he had a fabulous early career: a BA at Brown University, he studied at Johns Hopkins University, and received a PhD from the University of Heidelberg in August 1892 in German philology. The record at Johns Hopkins shows that, while enrolled in its doctoral programme, Wood had signed up for courses such as Middle German and Old Norse in the Teutonic seminary, and also for *Beowulf*, Anglo-Saxon Poetry, Anglo-Saxon Prose, Historical English Grammar, Elements of Phonetics, *Piers the Plowman* and Early Scottish Poets in the English seminary.[34] After obtaining his PhD, he took up a position at Tokyo Imperial University in September 1892. It was only one month after his arrival in Japan that he learned of the passing of the renowned poet laureate. In writing his obituary, Wood's profound knowledge of old languages led him to position Tennyson's *Idylls of the King* and "The Lady of Shalott" properly in relation to Malory's *Morte Darthur*. For Natsume, the experience of translating the obituary must have been a cornerstone for his two pieces of chivalric fiction based on Malory thirteen years later.

[32] Tōru Takenaka, "Meiji no Wāgunā Būmu [Wagner Boom in Meiji Japan]," *Memoirs of the Graduate School of Letters, Osaka University* 48 (2008): 33–65, esp. 46–55.

[33] Jun Etō, *Sōseki to Āsā Oh Densetsu* [Sōseki and the Arthurian Legend] (Tokyo, 1991; originally published in 1975), 108–10. The person who translated Wood's English into Japanese is not mentioned in the original article, but scholars have assumed it to be Sōseki's work, and now the hypothesis is generally accepted. See ibid., note 1 at 125–6.

[34] Yoshikazu Nakagawa, "Ōgasutasu Uddo Kou [Dr Augustus Wood: A Man and his Work]," *Historical English Studies in Japan* 21 (1989): 129–41, at 130.

Sōseki Natsume was born in 1867, read English literature at Tokyo Imperial University, and graduated in 1893. He was seventeen years younger than Lafcadio Hearn, but was not taught by him, as Hearn started teaching at the university three years after Natsume's graduation. Natsume first worked as an English instructor in Shikoku and then in Kyūshū. In June 1900, by the appointment of the Meiji government, he was sent to London and became an overseas student at the age of thirty-three. Acquisition of Western languages was still considered an urgent issue, and Natsume was expected to deepen his knowledge of English language and literature. It is well known, however, that during the two years of his student life in London Natsume was not so keen on learning the English language teaching methods for which he had been dispatched, but indulged himself in reading English literature instead.[35]

Among other literary subjects, Natsume pursued his interest in Arthurian romances and medieval English studies. His diary testifies that he attended W. P. Ker's course on medieval literature in the autumn of 1900 for two months at University College, London, and he purchased the second edition of the Macmillan *Morte Darthur*.[36] His two pieces of fiction related to Malory's chivalric theme were written in 1905, a couple of years after his return to Japan: one about a knight with a phantom shield and his lover, broadly reminiscent of other stories of the Round Table, the other based on Elaine's tragic unrequited love for Sir Lancelot. "Maboroshi no Tate [The Phantom Shield]" was published in the literary journal *Hototogisu* (April issue) and "Kairo-kō" (the Lancelot/Elaine story) in *Chūō-Kōron* (November issue) of the same year; both were gathered together in a collection of short stories, *Yōkyo Shū* [Fugitive Pieces], published in 1906.[37]

These Arthurian fictions make a stark contrast with Natsume's later works. The first point is that Natsume ungrudgingly reveals his education in English literature, perhaps because they were written while he was still occupying his brief teaching position as lecturer of English literature. The reputations of "Kairo-kō" and "Maboroshi no Tate" remain controversial, however. They are much less read than other works of Natsume, which are written in an easy, modern, colloquial and occasionally comic style. The serious, medieval setting of Malory's world also seems unapproachable compared with the familiar Japanese everyday setting at which Natsume later excelled. Due to this unique position, paradoxically, more academic attention has been paid to these pieces of Arthurian fiction than the other short stories in *Yōkyo Shū*.

Jun Etō said that Natsume "breathed the air of London where people such as William Morris and Burne-Jones had revived the Arthurian legend" before he concluded that it was appropriate to classify "Kairo-kō" in the category of

---

[35] See also the introduction which precedes the translation of "Kairo-kō: A Dirge," trans. Toshiyuki Takamiya and Andrew Armour, *Arthurian Literature* II (1982): 92–126, at 92–8. The introduction also explains that the meaning of the word *Kairo* in fact literally means "dew drops on a shallot leaf" (95), a shallot being a kind of green onion. This works as a hidden pun on "The Lady of Shalott," whose storyline Natsume partly traces.

[36] Etō, [Sōseki and the Arthurian Legend], 130–2.

[37] A collection of seven short stories written and published in various literary journals from January 1905 to January 1906.

Victorian revival literature of the Arthurian legend.[38] For Etō, regardless of the archaism Natsume pursued, "Kairo-kō" remained a modern fiction which mirrored Natsume's life. In order to prove that, Etō allocated one chapter of his thesis to the question of how Natsume had read Malory. This focus was possible only because his supervisor was Fumio Kuriyagawa,[39] for Etō could not have read the text of Malory without his guidance. Etō traced all the writings that Natsume had scribbled in the Macmillan edition he had possessed,[40] and found that the notes and underlinings were mostly concentrated on Sir Lancelot's failure to achieve the Holy Grail. It seems obvious that Natsume was particularly interested in the adulterous love between Guinevere and Lancelot, which served as the backdrop of "Kairo-kō" as well as Tennyson's *Idylls* and "The Lady of Shallot."[41]

Another unique aspect of both "Kairo-kō" and "Maboroshi no Tate" is the author's own remarks about experimenting with the themes borrowed from Tennyson and Malory. In the short introduction which precedes "Kairo-kō," Natsume hinted at the influence of Tennyson's *Idylls*. He begins by deploring Malory's characterization of Lancelot and Guinevere because "the Lancelot depicted by Malory resembled a rickshaw man, Guinevere being his light-o'love,"[42] and in contrast praises the vivid characterization in Tennyson's *Idylls* because "the character portrayal succeeds in making nineteenth-century men and women act out their parts on the medieval stage."[43] This may be due to the fact that Natsume had been well versed in Tennyson before he read Malory.[44] Most significantly, Natsume underlines that although he does not remember the story clearly, he decided *not* to reread *Idylls of the King* upon writing "Kairo-kō" because he wanted to be free from the temptation of borrowing from the great poet. The insinuating preface seems like more than an innocent feeling of an author and it reveals, either beyond the writer's recognition or on purpose, that his conscious motivation to write the piece *was* at least partly to trace the path Tennyson had laid out. "Maboroshi no Tate" also has a short introduction in a similar manner, and there Natsume explains that although he could have, he did *not* attempt to rewrite the original story of Malory

---

[38] In his doctoral thesis, submitted in 1975, Etō concluded that "Kairo-kō" in fact depicted Natsume's secret love for his sister-in-law. According to Etō, the works of Art Nouveau artists such as Pre-Raphaelites, who had been influenced by Japanese art such as *Ukiyoe*, enabled Natsume to perceive both Japan and the Western Middle Ages through their work. Etō speculates Natsume's artistic impulse was cultivated in London while he acquainted himself with the illustrations by Aubrey Beardsley in the Dent edition: Etō, [Sōseki and the Arthurian Legend], 211–15.

[39] As discussed further below, Kuriyagawa was a prominent scholar of Old and Middle English at Keio University, and he translated part of Oskar Sommer's edition into Japanese.

[40] Etō, [Sōseki and the Arthurian Legend], chapter 5, 128–66.

[41] Etō in his dissertation interprets this as Natsume's "personal" experience, implying the love between Natsume and his sister-in-law. These scribbles by Natsume are undated, so it is not known whether they were written prior to the creation of "Kairo-kō."

[42] "Kairo-kō: A Dirge," 103.

[43] Ibid.

[44] From presumptive evidence, Etō considered that Natsume had read Tennyson's Arthurian poems in Japan by 1897, while his acquisition of Malory was after 1900 in England. Etō, [Sōseki and the Arthurian Legend], 111. Natsume also accuses Malory of some incoherence and discursiveness in the preface, which may be due to his penchant for Tennyson. See "Kairo-kō: A Dirge," 103.

in a Japanese medieval setting because he was afraid the effect would be "unhar-
monious." However, the fact remains that Natsume *was* tempted to replace the
Knights of the Round Table with Japanese *Samurai* lords before he began to work
on this piece. Therefore, these short explanations that precede both works testify
that Natsume thought carefully before he consciously experimented with writing
the Western medieval short stories in Japanese, in his own style.

The second unique factor which should be mentioned about "Kairo-kō" and
"Maboroshi no Tate" is their language. In both works, Natsume intentionally
adopted the lavish, archaic writing style which was quickly becoming obsolete
during the Meiji era. Toshiyuki Takamiya, as well as Etō, argues this *gabun-tai*
– pseudo-medieval style – was Natsume's choice as a Victorian pseudo-medievalist; Natsume should have chosen a simpler and sturdier style of classical
Japanese if he had truly sought to revive the archaic world of Malory.[45] But this
certainly was not the case with Natsume. Rather than just being a hastily prepared pseudo-medievalist, Natsume seems to have had a more profound authorial intention for choosing this style of writing.

Natsume's choice of *gabun-tai* seems to show not simply his penchant for the
stylishness of Japanese archaic writing; it also reveals how difficult the era was
for Japanese language and society, which was going through intense fluctuation.
Arinori Mori, a radical Meiji intellectual, had asserted in 1872 that the English
language should be adopted as Japan's first language instead of Japanese.[46]
Regarded as anti-patriotic for many reasons, he was assassinated in 1889. Within
just a few years, two separate styles of writing developed in the Japanese literary sphere. One was the beautified pseudo-classical style – *bibun-tai* – which
became very popular among the younger generation in the Meiji era.[47] Many
young writers zealously wrote something between prose and verse, particularly
on nature, in a style adapted from the classical Japanese writing. Three poets,
Keigetsu Ōmachi, Hagoromo Takeshima, and Ukō Shioi published a literary
journal emphasizing *bibun-tai*, called *Hana Momiji* [Flowers and Foliage] in 1896
and it became one of the best-sellers of the time. Numerous publications, and
almost every literary journal, came to have a column of *bibun-tai* and encouraged
the contributions of young writers.[48] On the other hand, some writers started a

---

[45] He argues that, for Natsume, Malory remained an interest as a philological, linguistic,
as well as stylistic object. Toshiyuki Takamiya, "Chūsei Bungaku to Sōseki [English
Medieval Literature and Sōseki]," in *Asā Oh Monogatari no Miryoku: Keruto kara Sōseki
e* [The Attraction of the Arthurian Legend: From the Celtic Studies to Sōseki] (Tokyo,
1999), 212–21, at 218.

[46] According to I Yeonsuk, it is wrong to take this remark of Mori as anti-nationalistic
sentiment because Mori had more practical reasons to advocate English. I Yeonsuk
asserts that Mori rather wanted to criticize current educational practice, which placed
great emphasis on Chinese reading (*Kanbun*) rather than on the Japanese language. I
Yeonsuk, "Kodoku na Gengo Shisouka Mori Arinori [A Lonely Language Philosopher
Arinori Mori]," an essay contributed to the homepage of the Mori Arinori Center
for Higher Education and Global Mobility, June 2016. <http://arinori.hit-u.ac.jp/wp-
content/uploads/2016/02/97b0994cce4ad2c1278104a32e936073.pdf> [accessed 10 March
2017].

[47] *Bibun-tai* (beautiful letters style) and *gabun-tai* (elegant letters style) are the same style
of writing which flourished in Japan at the turn of the century. They are also called
*gikobun* – pseudo-classical letters.

[48] Satô, "Bibunhayari [Bibun Trend]," in [Forty Years of Shinchō sha Publishing].

movement towards unification of the written and spoken language.[49] The latter finally became the major trend among modern writers, particularly with the surge of Naturalist writers. In response to this movement, the *bibun-tai* trend waned quickly and eventually was pushed aside as empty and purposeless.

It is notable that both "Kairo-kō" and "Maboroshi no Tate" were written at the moment when *bibun-tai* was decaying. Natsume's choice of the pseudo-classical style pointed at what was on the verge of extinction there and then – not in the Middle Ages but in his own era. He seems to have been aware that he was the very witness of the rise and fall of *bibun-tai*. This fading style also suited stories focused on romantic love in the faded, forgotten past.[50] The primary theme of both stories was tragic love: in "Maboroshi no Tate" William loses his lover Clare in a battle and in "Kairo-kō" Elaine reaches Camelot in a boat as a corpse. Tragic love has deep roots in Japanese literature, and the romantic touch of *gabun-tai* was ideal when Natsume wrote within this universal and nostalgic theme of love and loss. The Japanese lost much of Edo culture after the influx of Western civilization, while Japan fought the Japan-Qing War (First Sino-Japanese War) in 1894–5, the first Anglo-Japanese alliance was formed in 1902, and the Russo-Japanese War broke out in 1904–5. The Japanese people may have become wealthier, but at the cost of change in every corner of society, and some among the Japanese literary sphere realized they were about to lose even that particular archaic writing style of the Edo period as they passed through the turbulent era towards modernity. The *bibun-tai* movement of which Natsume was conscious in the literary sphere resembled the last cry of those who loathed parting with the good old days in the face of – often brutal – Meiji restoration, which changed most of the former Japanese lifestyle, including the language.[51]

Natsume remarked on the Japanese language in his speech on English language education in 1911. When discussing the decline of English ability among young Japanese students, Natsume commented that it was a matter of course as more textbooks for learning various subjects were now available in Japanese. He said he was even "happy" to see Japanese remain as Japan's first language because its usage testified to Japan's status as a proud independent nation.[52] Although one cannot see the strife between *bibun-tai* and the Naturalist style

---

[49] Traditionally, since the medieval period, Japanese differed greatly between the spoken and the written languages. Shōyō Tsubouchi, who translated "The Lady of Shallot," and Teishimei Futaba, the author of a Japanese novel *Ukigumo*, were the first of such writers to pursue this movement of unification of spoken and written Japanese.

[50] In this context, the Japanese *bibun-tai* movement itself can be contrasted with the Victorian revival movement in the West, rather than solely focusing on Natsume.

[51] One example is the contrast between chivalry and *bushi-do*. The archaic writing style inevitably resurrects *bushi-do* when it comes to the description of knights and knightly deeds.

[52] Natsume Sōseki, "Gogakuryoku Yousei hou [How to Cultivate the Language Ability]," in *Shiryou Nihon Eigakushi* [Documents of Japan's English Language History], ed. Tetsuo Kawasumi, supervised by Takao Suzuki (Tokyo, 1978), 94–106. Therein, Natsume made a few practical suggestions to improve the English education environment. The point of his suggestion was to learn every subject in English, and respond to every question in English. See also Yūichirō Yamada, "Sōseki 'Gogakuryoku Yōsei' Saikou [Reconsidering Sōseki's 'How to Cultivate Language Ability']," *Hiroshima Shūdai Ronshū (Jinbun)* 43.2 (2002): 1–49.

from this remark, Natsume seems to have been aware of the cost and pain for the Japanese language to survive and be reborn as a modern one. He could certainly write and think in English, but instead he chose to write in Japanese, borrowing materials from Western settings and adapting them for the Japanese. His experiment with *gabun-tai* in the two pieces of Malorian fiction thus seems to witness the writer's lament for the traditional, formalistic beauty which would be doomed to extinction in the Japanese language.

## *Yaeko Nogami (1885–1985)*

A variety of Arthurian legends adapted for children were published from the Meiji to the Showa periods, but many of them tended to be light adventure stories and often from heavily adapted versions by writers such as Waldo Cutler and Andrew Lang. Apart from such works, Yaeko Nogami's 1942 translation of Thomas Bulfinch's *The Age of Chivalry, or Legends of King Arthur* (1858) should be mentioned in relation to Natsume.[53] In 1906 Yaeko married Toyoichirō Nogami, later a scholar of Japanese *noh* plays, who studied English literature under Sōseki Natsume at Tokyo Imperial University. Toyoichirō had recently graduated when they married and the marriage was kept secret at the beginning. Through this union, Yaeko had the chance to learn from Natsume directly with other members of his loose literary circle, called the Thursday Club. After the passing of Natsume, she commented that she was lucky to have been close to the literary giant.[54]

Yaeko Nogami's first published translation was part of a book of Greek myths, Thomas Bulfinch, *The Age of Fable, or Stories of Gods and Heroes* (1855), which appeared in 1913 with a complimentary letter from Natsume as a preface. Nogami reminisced in an interview that she had been encouraged to acquire the knowledge of "Greek and Roman myths, stories of the Middle Ages such as the Arthurian legend, and the Bible," if she wished to know Western values to their roots.[55] Although she did not name the person who taught her these things, it makes sense to speculate that this suggestion came from either Natsume or her husband, Toyoichirō.[56]

---

[53] Yaeko Nogami was born into a wealthy family in Ōita, Kyūshū. She translated several other children's stories including Charles and Mary Lamb's *Tales from Shakespeare*, and Eleanor Porter's *Pollyanna*. Her best known literary work is *Hideyoshi to Rikyū* [Hideyosi and Rikyū] (1964) which she started writing at the age of seventy-four: the story about the development of the Japanese tea ceremony during the medieval period. She was awarded many literary prizes, including the Order of Culture in 1971.

[54] Akiko Sasaki, "Nogami Yaeko no 'Sensei': Sōseki to iu Taiken [Nogami Yaeko's "Teacher": Sōseki as an Experience]," *Kyōyō to Kyōiku, Aichi Kyōiku University* 5 (2005): 19–28.

[55] Yoshiko Enomoto, "Nogami Yaeko to Seiō [Yaeko Nogami and the West]," *Ferris Studies* 27 (1992): 25–41, at 33.

[56] The fact that Yaeko Nogami graduated from Meiji Jogakkō [Meiji Girls' School] should also be taken into account in determining who had the most imperative voice. See, for example, Naoko Nakamura, "Nogami Yaeko to Meiji Jogakkō [Yaeko Nogami and Meiji Girls' School]," *Annals of the Institute for Comparative Studies of Culture, Tokyo Woman's Christian University* 69 (2008): 1 18.

Almost thirty years after her translation of *The Age of Fable*, Yaeko Nogami's translation of *The Age of Chivalry* was published by Shōbundō.[57] This work has long remained popular, and helps spread an overview of the Arthurian legend to this day. It cannot be denied that it is a little outdated as many other translations are also available, but it is still widely read as an orthodox edition today, and is a convenient gateway to the Arthurian legend for general readers. It describes the famous heroes and heroines of legends and operas as paragons of chivalry, from King Arthur to Tristan and Iseult to Perceval, and it also refers to Geoffrey of Monmouth, Malory and the *Mabinogion* for those who wish to know the legend further.

## Hakuson Kuriyagawa[58] and Fumio Kuriyagawa

Bin Ueda's emphasis on Celtic studies was taken up and expanded amply by Hakuson Kuriyagawa (1880–1923). He graduated from Tokyo Imperial University in the presence of the Emperor Meiji with the honour of receiving a silver watch as the best student.[59] Hakuson began research at graduate school under Sōseki Natsume on "the expressions of love in Western poetry," but his family situation worsened dramatically so he had to abandon his studies and he began working as an English instructor in Kumamoto, as Hearn and Natsume had done. While there, he wrote and published *Kindai Bungaku Jukkou* [Ten Lectures on Modern Literature] (1912), a collection of lectures dealing with the preceding fifty years (1860–1910) in the field of European literature. Chapter 4 was centred on the English literary sphere. He drew on Matthew Arnold's *On the Study of Celtic Literature* (1867) to graphically illustrate the Northern, Teutonic pathos and the Southern, or Mediterranean, gay lyricism in modern English literature.[60] Arnold sought Celtic "delicacy and spirituality" in the English people, and although it was impossible to specify where Celtic people originated, he could refer much to Roman and French influences, so Hakuson used this contrast for the sake of convenience. He remarked, "we do not need to go back to the pre-Chaucer English" in order to understand such fusion between the South and North,[61] but this sounds a little ironic today because going "back to the pre-Chaucer English" was exactly what his son Fumio would do. The book was an instant success in the publishing world, running into eighty-eight printings in twelve years. Many later writers copied Hakuson's style.[62] Thus becoming a popular author and

---

[57] Thomas Bulfinch, *Densetsu no Jidai: Kamigami to Eiyū no Monogatari* [The Age of Fable, or Stories of Gods and Heroes], trans. Yaeko Nogami (Tokyo, 1913).

[58] Hakuson was his nom de plume; his autonym was Tatsuo.

[59] Zhaohui Chen, "Zouge no Tou wo Deru Kumon [The Agony of Leaving the Ivory Tower]," *Tokyo Daigaku Chūgokugo Chūgokubungaku Kenkyūshitsu Kiyō* 10 (2007): 49–76, at 51.

[60] Tatsuo Kuriyagawa, "Chapter 4: Bungei-jō no Nan-oh, Hoku-oh, oyobi Eikoku [Literary Characteristics of Southern Europe and Northern Europe, and Britain]," in *Kindai Bungaku Jukkou* [Ten Lectures on Modern Literature] (Tokyo, 1912), 206–38.

[61] Kuriyagawa, [Literary Characteristics of Southern Europe and Northern Europe, and Britain], 220.

[62] Zhaohui Chen, [The Agony of Leaving the Ivory Tower], (2007): 51–2.

scholar of Western literature, he was appointed as the successor to Bin Ueda at Kyoto Imperial University upon Ueda's sudden death in 1916.

Naturally, many of Hakuson's ideas were influenced by Lafcadio Hearn, whose lectures he had attended in his student days. He later recollected with much affection his days in Hearn's classroom, describing him as "a person of feelings."[63] Hakuson later discussed the Celtic revival movement even more extensively, and this time introduced W. B. Yeats and the Irish literary revival movement in particular.[64] Drawing again upon Matthew Arnold, he approximated the Celtic melancholy to the Japanese feeling of "Mono no Aware," "which Lafcadio Hearn had translated as 'Ahness of things.'"[65]

Hakuson not only served as an intermediary between the West and Japan: as a writer in the Taisho Democracy period, he also wrote on many social matters to criticize the old Japanese style and tried to instigate a new lifestyle among the Japanese people. His *Kindai no Ren-Ai Kan* [Modern Views of Love] (1922) is just one example, written while arranged marriage was still prevalent in Japan. It too became a best-seller, and romantic love became a social phenomenon. The book praised the bond between man and woman based on mutual love, which is the acme of human spirituality. It also stressed that love is strengthened by marriage with chastity.[66] Despite the successful career, his life him brought much hardship, and when he died at the age of 43, his son Fumio was only sixteen years old.[67]

The brilliant career of Hakuson's son, Fumio Kuriyagawa (1907–1978), started when he translated *Beowulf* from Old English into Japanese as an undergraduate at Keio University. He had read *Heike Monogatari* many times, working to invent a classical translation style befitting the poem.[68] While his father occasionally wrote on themes related to Japanese culture and society and was at times a vehement critic, Fumio stayed out of any cultural politics, and calmly stuck to literary

[63] Hakuson Kuriyagawa, *Koizumi Sensei Sonohoka* [Professor Koizumi and Other Essays] (Osaka, 1919), 35.
[64] Hakuson Kuriyagawa, "Keruto Bungaku Fukkou Gaikan [Introduction to the Celtic Revival Movement]": this essay was first published in the journal *Bunshō Sekai* in January 1915, and reprinted in [Professor Koizumi and Other Essays], 332–58.
[65] Ibid., 339.
[66] Hakuson Kuriyagawa, *Kindai no Ren-Ai Kan* [Modern Views of Love] (Tokyo, 1922), 133–4.
[67] Hakuson Kuriyagawa suffered misfortune in his personal life: he had to have one leg amputated due to infection in 1919. He died the day after the Great Kanto Earthquake struck on 1 September 1923, because he was late in escaping from the tsunami that hit his villa on the shore of Sagami Bay. Hakuson's achievement was forgotten in Japan after his death, but his reputation grew posthumously in China through Lu Xun's translation. Kuriyagawa's works first acquainted Chinese people with basic Western literary concepts such as "symbolism" or "decadence" in Chinese. Leo Ou-fan Lee, *Shanghai Modern: The Flowering of a New Urban Culture in China, 1930–1945* (Cambridge, MA, 1999), 315-16. See also, Takamasa Kudō, *Chūgokugoken ni okeru Kuriyagawa Hakuson Genshō—Ryūsei, Suitai, Kaiki to Keizoku* [The "Kuriyagawa Hakuson Phenomenon" in the Chinese-Speaking Region: The Rise, Decline and Regeneration of His Reception in Mainland China, and the Continuation of His Popularity in Taiwan] (Kyoto, 2010).
[68] *Heike Monogatari* is an epic war chronicle dating from around 1220. Kinjirō Oshitari, "Kuriyagawa Fumio Sensei to Beowurufu Yaku [Professor Fumio Kuriyagawa and the *Beowulf* Translation]," in *Kaisō no Kuriyagawa Fumio* [Recollections of Fumio Kuriyagawa], ed. Yasaburō Ikeda et al. (Tokyo, 1979), 67–9, at 68.

texts. Much of Fumio's career can be contrasted with that of his father. He consciously chose Old English and Middle English literature, while his father's field had broadly covered the whole of modern European literature.[69] Fumio refrained from speaking about social phenomena and seemed to confine himself to the ivory tower.[70] While his father was often regarded as an object of envy among his literary associates, Fumio was liked by everyone for his gentle manners and was regarded as having no enemies.[71]

Fumio's supervisor at Keio University was the internationally renowned poet Junzaburō Nishiwaki (1894–1982), who was short-listed for the Nobel Prize in Literature several times.[72] He became the leader of the Modernism, Dadaism and Surrealism movements in pre- and post-war Japan. Since his youth he had been well versed in the Western classics, and his versatility in ancient languages was unquestionable, not least as he submitted his graduation thesis on economics in Latin.[73] He stayed in Oxford and in London between 1922 and 1926, during which time T. S. Eliot's "The Waste Land" was published. He himself published his first collection of poems, *Spectrum*, in 1925 in London.[74] Nishiwaki's initial experience in Britain was full of disappointment, however, because he found that the poetic style in England had changed so dramatically from the Edwardian style he had studied and made his own. He is said to have thrown all of his previous poems in the River Thames when they were swept aside as old-fashioned.[75] After his return to Japan in 1926, Nishiwaki started teaching Old and Middle English at Keio University, where Fumio was "the only" student who enthusiastically followed him, according to Nishiwaki.[76] Fumio was interested in the

[69] Hakuson ruthlessly described the study of *Beowulf* and Cædmon as "artistically with no value," in his obituary essay, "Koizumi Sensei," in [Professor Koizumi and Other Essays], 20.

[70] Hakuson confessed he was ashamed of his own timidity in his collection of essays on Japanese society. People like John Ruskin and William Morris who chose to leave their ivory tower to fight against society's contradictions were apparently his heroes: see Hakuson Kuriyagawa, *Zouge no Tou wo Idete* [Out of the Ivory Tower] (Tokyo, 1920), 1–2, 66, 68, 241, 252. On Fumio's career, Junzaburō Nishiwaki reminisces that Fumio himself may have consciously chosen a path different from his father. While Nishiwaki was interested in the spiritual phase, Fumio was interested in the practical phase. Junzaburō Nishiwaki, "Kuriyagawa-kun no Omoide [Memory of Mr. Kuriyagawa]," in [Recollections of Fumio Kuriyagawa], 22–3.

[71] Many testify Fumio's placid gentleness and calm stoicism in [Recollections of Fumio Kuriyagawa]. Yoshio Nakano confesses he once joked to Fumio's face that he seemed to be a reincarnation of his father with all his bad elements filtered out. Yoshio Nakano, "Touseki [Mourning]," in [Recollections of Fumio Kuriyagawa], 20–2, at 20.

[72] Nishiwaki was nominated eight times: six times by Naoshirō Tsuji (in 1958, 1960, 1962, 1964, 1965 and 1966), once by the Japanese Authors' Union in 1961, and once by the Japanese Academy in 1963. In the nomination database, the 1958 nominee is wrongly spelled as Janzaburo Nihiwaki: <http://www.nobelprize.org> [accessed 13 April 2017].

[73] Nishiwaki's first major was economics, and his supervisor was Shinzō Koizumi, who is known to have taught the 125th Emperor, Akihito, who reigned from 1989 to 2019.

[74] It was published at his own expense by Cayme Press.

[75] Yukinobu Kagiya, "Shō-den [A Biographical Sketch]," in *Kaisō no Nishiwaki Junzaburo* [Recollections of Junzabuō Nishiwaki] in *Webu de shika Yomenai Nishiwaki Junzaburo*, archive of Keio University Press, <http://www.keio-up.co.jp/kup/webonly/art/kaisou/vol1.html> [accessed 23 March 2017].

[76] Nishiwaki recollects the memory of Kuriyagawa as "the only person who followed [his lecture on OE and ME] with interest": Nishiwaki, [Memory of Mr. Kuriyagawa], in [Recollections of Fumio Kuriyagawa], 22.

study of sources and manuscripts, and what Nishiwaki had learned in England aroused much of his academic interest.[77] In 1931, upon graduation, Fumio was appointed to a post at Keio University and became Nishiwaki's junior colleague, while Nishiwaki continued filling the roles of both a professor and a poet. In 1933, Nishiwaki published *Ambarvalia*, a revolutionary collection of poems which changed "the concept as well as the language of modern Japanese poetry by boldly incorporating a language of translation."[78]

Nishiwaki's poetic output ceased during the Second World War, however. His concentration on classical studies during the war partly reflects the severity of political control during this period, when many Surrealist poets were interrogated and imprisoned.[79] One of his fellow poets and students, Shūzō Takiguchi, who took Nishiwaki's classes with Fumio, was also interrogated.[80] It was after those days that Nishiwaki zealously started working on his doctoral dissertation, later published as *Kodai Bungaku Josetsu* [An Introduction to Ancient Literature]. Undoubtedly Fumio and Nishiwaki supported each other as colleagues and research associates during the darkest period of war, and it seems Fumio encouraged his former teacher to concentrate on purely academic work. When American air raids swept across Tokyo towards the end of the Second World War, all of Fumio's collection of books in Meguro was burned, and he saved only the manuscript of Nishiwaki's dissertation, which he had borrowed from its owner and returned afterwards.[81] That he saved only Nishiwaki's manuscript shows Fumio's deep attachment to Nishiwaki's work: he genuinely wished Nishiwaki to complete his doctorate even in the context of a devastating war. They would not extinguish the beacon of the pursuit of learning; both received their PhDs after the war: Nishiwaki in 1949, and Fumio in 1950 on *Beowulf*.

Nishiwaki published his translation of *The Waste Land* in 1952, and it won high acclaim. He was also active as a critic, and published a biography of T. S. Eliot and analysis of his poems in 1956.[82] Fumio never seems to have changed his scholastic style, which may be called "*mutekatsuryū* [winning without fighting]" in his own words.[83] He did not have ample resources for his research when he decided to take up *Beowulf*, so the only and the best guide was his curiosity and what

---

[77] Ibid.

[78] "Nishiwaki Junzaburo," *Poetry Kanto* 25 (2009) <http://poetrykanto.com/issues/2009-2/nishiwaki-junzaburo> trans. Hosea Hirata [accessed 17 March 2017].

[79] Hosea Hirata, *The Poetry and Poetics of Nishiwaki Junzaburo: Modernism in Translation* (Princeton, NJ, 1993), 198.

[80] Nishiwaki later testified that thanks to Takiguchi's verbal evidence, he narrowly escaped being imprisoned. See Kenkichi Yamamoto, "Nishiwaki Kyōshitsu no Omoide [Recollections from Nishiwaki's Classroom]," in [Recollections of Fumio Kuriyagawa], 31–4, at 33.

[81] Nishiwaki, [Memory of Mr. Kuriyagawa], 23.

[82] Nishiwaki's *Arechi* [The Waste Land] (Tokyo, 1952) was the second Japanese translation of the work, the first one being Tamotsu Ueda's translation in 1938 of "The Burial of the Dead," which inspired many poets. Although the poem was translated by other people, Nishiwaki's was the most read in post-war Japan. The Japanese title was the same as several precedent poetic journals, *Arechi*, one of whose editors was Nobuo Ayukawa, another famous Modernist poet influenced by T. S. Eliot.

[83] *Mutekatsuryū*. It was one of the key words in his retirement speech in March, 1973, at the annual meeting of Keio Institute of Cultural and Linguistic Studies. Kuriyagawa Fumio, "Omou Koto to Omoidasu Koto [What I Think and What I Remember]," in

was available to him then.[84] When the war took everything away from him, he learned anew that purely following his own instinctive curiosity was not a bad research method at all.[85]

After obtaining his PhD, Fumio chose to let his curiosity take him further instead of dwelling on *Beowulf*. Caxton's edition of Malory in Japanese was published in 1966 by Fumio and his wife Keiko Kuriyagawa, in an abridged form.[86] They translated Caxton's Books I, V, XII, XVIII, XIX, XX and XXI (based on H. Oskar Sommer's edition), omitting most of the Tale of Tristram and the Quest of the Holy Grail. Fumio explained that he omitted the Tale of Tristram because it was "the most verbose section of Malory."[87] His commentary reveals they also consulted the first edition of Eugène Vinaver's *The Works of Sir Thomas Malory* (1947) and highlights the essential points of Vinaver's discussion: his controversial argument of eight separate romances, the major sources for each tale, and the identity of Sir Thomas Malory.[88] The linguistic aspect of Malory, which would be taken up many times by later Japanese scholars, was also of interest to him. Shun'ichi Noguchi recalled that Fumio Kuriyagawa had discussed as early as 1958 the problem of Book V, where Malory's northern dialect (derived from his source, the Alliterative *Morte Arthure*) was changed into the Midland dialect in Caxton's edition, and made some speculation based on the aspect of language.[89]

It was only in 1995 that the Winchester manuscript was published in a full Japanese translation by Kunio Nakashima and others.[90] It was even later, in 2004–7, that a complete translation of Caxton's edition in Japanese became accessible.[91] Thus, even to this day, Kuriyagawa's translation remains one of the most trustworthy academic versions of the *Morte Darthur* available in Japanese. It may be partly due to Fumio's commentary that the Japanese market wished to have a complete translation of the Winchester manuscript before Caxton's

---

[Recollections of Fumio Kuriyagawa], 291–311, at 302–9. It seems that he thought of this style as "winning with no style," or "winning without any specific method."

[84] Kuriyagawa, [What I Think and What I Remember], 302.

[85] Ibid., 309.

[86] It was first published by Chikuma Shobō in 1966 entitled *Āsā Oh no Shi* [The Death of King Arthur] as no. 66 in *Sekai Bungaku Taikei* [World Literature Series]. Chikuma Shobō published a new series by the same name in 1971, this time *Āsā Oh no Shi* was no. 10 in the series.

[87] Sir Thomas Malory, *Āsā Oh no Shi* [The Death of King Arthur], ed. and trans. Fumio Kuriyagawa and Keiko Kuriyagawa (Tokyo, 1986; first published in 1971). See ibid., Fumio Kuriyagawa, "Kaisetsu—Marorī to Āsā Oh Monogatari [Commentary: Malory and the Stories of King Arthur]," 461.

[88] Kuriyagawa explained that he made the decision because he wanted to express the grand design Malory had drawn in this concise edition. He emphasized that, until the discovery of the Winchester manuscript, only Caxton's edition or editions which derived from it circulated and all of them, including Caxton, regarded it as a single work. See [Commentary], 466.

[89] Shun'ichi Noguchi, "Kuriyagawa Sensei no Omoi-de [Memories of Professor Kuriyagawa]," in [Recollections of Fumio Kuriyagawa], 106–9, at 108.

[90] Sir Thomas Malory, *Kan'yaku Āsā Oh Monogatari* [Complete Translation of the Stories of King Arthur], trans. Kunio Nakashima, Mutsuko Ogawa, and Sachiko Endō, 2 vols. (Sagamihara, 1995).

[91] Sir Thomas Malory, *Āsā Oh Monogatari* [Stories of King Arthur], trans. Kimie Imura, 5 vols. (Tokyo, 2004–7). Vol. 1 was published in 2004, vols. 2 and 3 in 2005, vol. 4 in 2006, and vol. 5 in 2007, by Chikuma Shobō. It contains numerous illustrations by Aubrey Beardsley, originally from the Dent edition.

edition because Fumio emphasized the importance of the discovery in 1934 of the Winchester manuscript and Vinaver's assertion that the Winchester manuscript preserved better what Malory had originally written, although the author's revision was not always enough.[92]

## Towards the New Age

Jun Etō was already a well-known writer and critic when he submitted his doctoral thesis, later published as *Sōseki to Āsā Oh Densetsu* [Sōseki and the Arthurian Legend], under the direction of Fumio Kuriyagawa; he received his PhD from Keio University in 1975. In his thesis, Etō referred to the possibility of Sōseki Natsume's secret love for his sister-in-law, one possible interpretation of "Kairo-kō," and another literary critic, Shōhei Ōoka, vehemently refuted this. The resulting literary controversy is the famous Etō-Ōoka Debate.[93] Etō virtually lost the debate (although he never admitted it), but the general public learned from Etō's theory that Sir Thomas Malory's *Morte Darthur* cast an enormous influence through Tennyson on Sōseki Natsume.[94]

Popularized children's versions of the Arthurian legend also became more and more abundant after the Japanese started recovering from the wounds of the Second World War. In addition to Yaeko Nogami's translation of *The Age of Chivalry*, Fumio and Keiko Kuriyagawa's translation of R. L. Green's *King Arthur and the Knights of the Round Table* was published in 1957. Two films adapted from T. H. White's *The Once and Future King* were released: *The Sword in the Stone*, an animation by Disney, in 1964, and *Camelot*, based on the Broadway hit musical by Alan Jay Lerner and Frederick Loewe, in 1967.[95] The two-volume translation of T. H. White appeared later, in 1991 and 1992.[96]

---

[92] In his commentary, Kuriyagawa discusses Vinaver's theory that Malory had written eight separate romances rather than one book: [Commentary], 461–5. Kuriyagawa gives an example of how, in the Winchester manuscript, a knight who dies in the previous chapter is alive in the subsequent chapters, and explains such defects as the change of Malory's authorial intent while writing, when separate romances were put together as a coherent whole (465–6).

[93] The Etō-Ōoka debate officially started when Ōoka criticized Etō's hypothesis published in a literary journal at a lecture held at the Institute of Christian Culture, Miyagi Gakuin Women's University, in July 1974. Ōoka published an article in the *Asahi* newspaper on 21 November 1975 and the publication of Etō's doctoral dissertation followed. Etō published his refutation in December, but he remained silent on the topic for the next fifteen years. Makoto Sekizuka, "Natsume Sōseki 'Kairo-kō' Ronsō-Ōoka Shōhei to Etō Jun no Kenkai [Sōseki Natsume's 'Kairo-kō' Debate: The Opinions of Shōhei Ōoka and Jun Etō]," *Gumma Kenritsu Joshi Daigaku Kokubungaku Kenkyū* 20 (2000): 50–62, esp. 54–5.

[94] Makoto Sekizuka summarizes the point of the debate as a discussion of the morality of research when one tries to interpret a text. Sekizuka, [Sōseki Natsume's 'Kairo-kō' Debate], 59.

[95] The release date of *The Sword in the Stone* in Japan is recorded as 18 July 1964 and that of *Camelot* as 2 December 1967, according to the Internet Movie Database, < http:// www.imdb.com/ > [accessed 12 April 2017].

[96] T. H. White, *Eien no Oh – Āsā no Sho* [The Once and Future King (The King Forever: Book of Arthur)], trans. Yumiko Morishita, 2 vols. (Tokyo, 1991–2).

In 1979, a Japanese-made animation TV series titled *Entaku no Kishi Monogatari, Moero Āsā* [King Arthur and the Knights of the Round Table: Hold on Arthur!] was broadcast, originally scheduled to run for a year. The project was initially launched to fulfil overseas demand for supernatural anime, but the story, whose basic plot is about how Arthur rebuilds his country of Camelot and brings peace to the surrounding seven kingdoms of Logres, had little to do with Malory's, although it is mentioned as the source. It was not popular among Japanese children, so Fuji Television had to finish the series earlier, after seven months (thirty weeks). The sequel was further removed from the original story, and was even less popular, so it lasted only for five months (twenty-two weeks). The Japanese television company was willing to choose the Arthurian legend as entertainment for children, but the makers themselves may not have been familiar enough with the legend of King Arthur in order to adapt it to the degree required. It was a mixture of elements of battles, quests and magic, but the scenes were rather subdued compared with other modern fictional anime, and the audience had difficulty in deciding whether to view it as realistic battles or as a fantasy series. Because its plot was a product of weak compromise, the Japanese audience was not attracted to it.

Perhaps it was a good lesson that the Japanese public needed a more serious introduction to the world of King Arthur before they were given a complete commercial entertainment. Kimie Imura and Shiro Yamamoto are among the researchers who have been active in publishing basic and easy introductions for the Japanese reader.[97] Such publications are on the rise, and the *Mabinogion*, a collection of medieval Welsh narratives (some of which are Arthurian), has been added to the list thanks to the translation from the original Welsh language by Setsuko Nakano.[98]

On the other hand, scholarship on the language of Malory alone has developed steadily, particularly as Fumio Kuriyagawa had laid out the field. Shun'ichi Noguchi is a model example: educated at Hiroshima University, he studied Chaucer under Michio Masui, but Noguchi changed his research field to Malory because he wanted to try to go beyond his teacher.[99] It was pure luck that Kuriyagawa was one of the examiners of Noguchi, who had applied for a study-abroad programme offered by the British Council.[100] After Noguchi went to the

---

[97] Some of Tolkien's works, such as *The Hobbit* and *Sir Gawain and the Green Knight*, and Rosemary Sutcliffe's King Arthur series have been translated by Shirō Yamamoto. Kimie Imura was known for many publications on Arthurian romances, Celtic mythology, and fairies even before the complete translation of Caxton's edition in 2004–2007.

[98] *Mabinogion: Chūsei Wēruzu Gensō Monogatari shū* [Mabinogion: A Collection of Medieval Welsh Fantasy Stories], trans. Setsuko Nakano (Tokyo, 2000). This is a complete translation of the Welsh reprinted edition. Akemi Itsuji translated the edition by Lady Charlotte Guest in 2003. *Mabinogion – Keruto Shinwa Monogatari – Shārotto Gesuto ban* [Mabinogion: The Celtic Mythology Based on the Edition of Charlotte Guest] (Tokyo, 2003).

[99] Toshiyuki Takamiya, "Ganko-Ittetsu no Samurai: Noguchi Shun'ichi Sensei wo Shinonde [The Headstrong Samurai Lord: Obituary to Professor Shun'ichi Noguchi]," in *Hon no Sekai wa Hen-na Sekai* [The Absurd World of Books] (Tokyo, 2012), 96–8, at 96.

[100] Takamiya, "[The Headstrong Samurai Lord]," 96.

University of Birmingham, where he studied under Derek Brewer, Kuriyagawa kept sending letters encouraging his research.[101] Noguchi prepared useful *corrigenda* from the Winchester manuscript which contributed to Eugène Vinaver's second edition of *The Works of Sir Thomas Malory* in 1967. Through Noguchi's sedate but steady contribution, the presence of Japanese academics began to be recognized in international Arthurian studies.

Tomomi Kato was the centre of attention at the International Arthurian Congress in Exeter in August 1975, because he had published *A Concordance to the Works of Sir Thomas Malory* (a full 1659 pages) based on Vinaver's second edition of the *Works*. An attempt to utilize computer technology with the "Key Word in Context" (KWIC) format in the field of English literature of the late medieval period was successful, and another attempt in the same field of studies was made by Kiyokazu Mizobata, who published *A Concordance to Caxton's Own Prose* in 1990.[102]

In response to William Matthews's "Question of Texts," posthumously read at the Exeter Congress of the International Arthurian Society in 1975, Noguchi published "Winchester Malory" to refute the theory of Matthews based on his own research into "Caxtonian" vocabulary and diction.[103] This was the beginning of the long journey of Japanese Malory scholars for the next few decades to prove "scientifically" who revised Book V in Caxton's edition.

Toshiyuki Takamiya, a lifelong research associate of Noguchi and a gifted student of Kuriyagawa, studied in Cambridge with Derek Brewer between 1975 and 1978. His first foray into Malory studies was to edit *Aspects of Malory* (1981), intended to examine all questions of sources, order of composition, palaeography and bibliography, and authorship surrounding Malory's text.[104] In the bibliography, he mentioned that articles on Malory written in Japanese had to be omitted.[105] This implied the existence of Japanese-language academic articles written on Malory, but it was also a vexation to Japanese scholars who only published in Japanese and who were therefore unable to share their views with international academia. Indeed, Takamiya strongly encouraged the next generation to publish in English.

After returning to Japan, Takamiya published his translation of Richard Barber's *King Arthur in Legend and History* in 1983, and of Mark Girouard's *Return to Camelot: Chivalry and the English Gentleman* in 1986 (with Yuri Fuwa). Takamiya inherited the rigid collation style from Kuriyagawa; to it, however, he added state-of-the-art bibliographical methods of his own account. In particular, he emphasized the distinctly different production processes between manuscript and print when he discussed Malory and Caxton. He translated Lotte Hellinga's

---

[101] One piece of Kuriyagawa's advice was that, when consulting a manuscript, one should read the same one beforehand on the microfilm and take note of the colour, or blurred characters. Noguchi, [Memories of Professor Kuriyagawa], in [Recollections of Fumio Kuriyagawa], 106.

[102] *A Concordance to Caxton's Own Prose*, ed. Kiyokazu Mizobata (Tokyo, 1990).

[103] Shun'ichi Noguchi, "Caxton's Malory," *Poetica* 8 (1977): 72–84.

[104] Toshiyuki Takamiya and Derek Brewer, "Preface," in *Aspects of Malory*, ix–x.

[105] Takamiya wrote, "It should be noted that as far as Japanese contributions are concerned works written in English alone are listed." See Toshiyuki Takamiya, "A Bibliography," in *Aspects of Malory*, 179.

*Caxton in Focus* in 1991, which was a textbook at Keio Graduate School when Takako Kato, the author of *Caxton's* Morte Darthur: *The Printing Process and the Authenticity of the Text*,[106] and Satoko Tokunaga, a medievalist and translator of Hellinga's *William Caxton and Early Printing in England*, studied there.[107] Attention to minute differences between editions, order of texts, additions and omissions, words, and letters with and without flourishes using digital technology seems to have become a Japanese specialty through Takamiya's graduate classes.

From the 1980s, internationally prominent Arthurian scholars such as P. J. C. Field and N. F. Blake were invited one after another by the English Literary Society of Japan, and by the Japan Society of Medieval English Studies and their affiliations, and the linguistic discussions held therein led to many fine articles in English.[108] The Japanese researchers who read papers with those scholars received warm and generous encouragement to continue their research. In 1993 Takamiya published a groundbreaking article, "Editor/Compositor at Work: The Case of Caxton's Malory."[109] This article developed Lotte Hellinga's hypothesis on compositors' copy-fitting techniques and proved that recovering the supposed text of a lost exemplar used at the printer's was to some extent possible.[110]

Yuji Nakao from Nagoya University was a philologist who focused on grammar in Middle English, and like Noguchi was interested in the authorship question of Malory. He noticed that the frequency of the disjunctive connective "ne" in Caxton's Roman War episode was similar to that in Caxton's own preface,

---

[106] Takako Kato, *Caxton's* Morte Darthur: *The Printing Process and the Authenticity of the Text* (Oxford, 2002).

[107] Lotte Hellinga, *William Caxton and Early Printing in England* (London, 2010). *Shoki Ingurando Insatsushi – Kyakusuton to Koukeisha tachi* [Early English Printing History: Caxton and his Successors], trans. Satoko Tokunaga, supervised by Toshiyuki Takamiya (Tokyo, 2013).

[108] At the 57th annual meeting of the English Literary Society of Japan in Komazawa University on 18 May 1985, a symposium entitled "Malory and Caxton" was held, chaired by Toshiyuki Takamiya. It comprised four papers, by Shun'ichi Noguchi, Yuji Nakao, Tsuyoshi Mukai and Toshiyuki Takamiya, and P. J. C. Field was the commentator. The papers by Noguchi and Nakao concentrated on the refutation of the late William Matthews's paper read posthumously in 1975 at the International Arthurian Congress in Exeter. They argued in favour of Vinaver's hypothesis that Caxton revised Malory's original writing, reflected in the Winchester manuscript, for his edition of 1485. Noguchi's discussion was published as "Caxton's Malory Again," *Poetica* 20 (1984): 33–8, and Nakao's as "Does Malory Really Revise His Vocabulary? Some Negative Evidence," *Poetica* 25–26 (1987): 99–109. P. J. C. Field accepted Nakao's view, in his third edition of Vinaver's *Works* in 1990. On 24 May 1999 Toshiyuki Takamiya organised and chaired another symposium, "New Perspectives in Malory Studies," with William Snell, Valerie Wilkinson, Takako Kato and Norman Blake as speakers at the 71st Annual Meeting of the English Literary Society of Japan at Matsuyama University. Kato's paper focused on the textual differences between Malory and Caxton, and was received favourably by Blake.

[109] Toshiyuki Takamiya, "Editor/Compositor at Work: The Case of Caxton's Malory," in *Arthurian and Other Studies: Presented to Shunichi Noguchi*, ed. Takashi Suzuki and Tsuyoshi Mukai (Cambridge, 1993), 143–51.

[110] With the identification of San Marino, Huntington Library, MS HM 136, as Caxton's exemplar of the *Chronicles of England*, I have collated three lines from every page of Caxton's edition against HM 136, and proved that Hellinga and Takamiya's theory is generally applicable in extracting and differentiating compositor's copy-fitting techniques. "Research Note-3/4 : Study on the Prose *Brut* MSS in relation to William Caxton's *Chronicles of England* (1480)," *Kyorin University Review* 24 (2012): 111–211.

and cast doubt on the hypothesis that the episode's vocabulary was revised by Malory. He was also the first to suggest Caxton's *Chronicles of England* as a handy source Caxton could refer to. His continual research on negative particles between the Winchester manuscript and Caxton's edition accumulated enough data to show that Caxton was a likely reviser of Book V, and marked a crucial dividing point of the discussion started by Matthews.[111] It was the moment when the research style that Japanese philologists had long developed was rewarded internationally.

It may not be a coincidence that in Japan, publishing history has recently become a popular field of study. Not only is it interesting, but it also reveals the practical aspect of publishing as a business, and that quite often an author or a piece of work would not be received favourably by the general public without the support of a successful publishing company. Yuri Fuwa, the first student and research associate of Takamiya, has recently published reprints of the three editions of the *Morte Darthur* from 1816 and 1817, and revealed the fierce battle between their editors: Walker, Wilks and Southey.[112] For those who are interested in the differences between the texts of Malory and Caxton, many useful hints for further study can be found in Fuwa's article, where she discusses the editor's decision-making concerning the book's size and page layout, the order and speed of printing, and publishing as a shrewd business.[113]

Organized by Takamiya, the HUMI (Humanities Media Interface) project was launched in 1996 for the purpose of creating a digitized archive of rare books and manuscripts when Keio University acquired the 42-line Gutenberg Bible. Among other examples of digitizing rare books and manuscripts in libraries around the world, digitization of the Winchester manuscript (British Library, Additional MS 59678) took place in November 2003 for two weeks at the British Library in London.[114] The manuscript is now available to Malory scholars online, in 16-mega-pixel images, on the British Library website.

---

[111] Nakao's article, originally published in *Poetica* 25-26 (1987), was revised as "Musings on the Reviser of Book V in Caxton's Malory," in *The Malory Debate: Essays on the Texts of* Le Morte Darthur, ed. Bonnie Wheeler, Robert L. Kindrick and Michael N. Salda (Cambridge, 2000), 191–216.

[112] *The Morte Darthur: A Collection of Early-Nineteenth-Century Editions*, ed. Yuri Fuwa (Tokyo, 2017). Walker's edition is in vols. 1 and 2, as *The History of the Renowned Prince Arthur, King of Britain; With his Life and Death, and All his Glorious Battles. Likewise, the Noble Acts and Heroic Deeds of his Valiant Knights of the Round Table. In Two Volumes*, by John Walker/Longman in 1816. Wilks's edition is in vols. 3–5 as *La Mort D'Arthur. The Most Ancient and Famous History of the Renowned Prince Arthur and the Knights of the Round Table. By Sir Tho$^s$ Malory, Knt.*, by R. Wilks, Simpkin & Marshall in 1816. Southey's edition is vols. 6 and 7, as *The Byrth, Lyf, and Actes of Kyng Arthur; Of his Noble Knyghtes of the Round Table, Theyr Merveyllous Enquestes and Aduentures, Thachyeuyng of the Sanc Greal; And in the End Le Morte Darthur, with the Dolourous Deth and Departyng out of Thys Worlde of Them Al.*, with an Introduction and Notes by Robert Southey, Esq., by Longman et al. in 1817.

[113] Yuri Fuwa, "Reprinting Malory: Walker, Wilks, and Southey," introduction to *The Morte Darthur: A Collection of Early-Nineteenth-Century Editions* (Tokyo, 2017).

[114] Masaaki Kashimura and Toshiyuki Takamiya, "Kichōsho no Dejitaru Ākaibu no Genjō to Mirai eno Tembō [Digital Archiving of Rare Books: Present and Prospect]," *The Japanese Society of Printing Science and Technology* 41.3 (2004): 149–58.

With technological developments, efforts to produce concordances continue. Kiyokazu Mizobata, who had made his first concordance out of *Caxton's Own Prose*, published his second, *A Concordance to the Alliterative* Morte Arthure in 2001 and his third, *A Concordance to Caxton's* Morte Darthur *(1485)* in 2009.[115] With Tomomi Kato's concordance to Vinaver's *Works*, a thorough comparison of the Winchester manuscript and Caxton's edition using these concordances and the British Library's digital archive is now possible. In particular, the addition of the Alliterative *Morte Arthure* to the concordance collection aims at the comparison of Malory's supposedly closest source for the Tale of Arthur and Lucius (the Roman War episode). Although the debate on the reviser of Book V of Caxton's edition has been settled in favour of Caxton, many questions remain regarding Malory's own text and now lost sources, so the cross-referencing which these concordances make possible will be a useful guide for further scientific research on textual traits and derivations.

While academics are working hard, attempts to reach the general audience go on. One such example is shown by a fantasy writer, Reiko Hikawa, who has written a trilogy about Arthur's kingdom through the eyes of a maid who has the magical power to turn into a jenny wren.[116] The first volume describes the evil attempts of Morgan le Fay to disrupt Arthur's kingdom, the second the Quest for the Holy Grail, and the third the death of King Arthur and the destruction of the kingdom. It follows the basic outline of Malory faithfully, and can be regarded as an orthodox Arthurian fantasy. Thus, Japanese Arthuriana is expanding in various directions, questioning aspects of languages, imagining new fantasies, merging East and West and connecting past and future with state-of-the-art technologies.

---

[115] *A Concordance to the Alliterative* Morte Arthure, ed. Kiyokazu Mizobata (Tokyo, 2001); *A Concordance to Caxton's* Morte Darthur (1485), ed. Kiyokazu Mizobata (Osaka, 2009).

[116] Reiko Hikawa, *Āsā Oh Kyūtei Monogatari 1. Kyamerotto no Tak*a [Stories of King Arthur's Court 1. The Hawk of Camelot]; 2. *Seihai no Ōh* [2. The King of the Holy Grail]; 3. *Saigo no Tatakai* [3. The Last Battle] (Tokyo, 2006).

# 15
## Malory in America
### DANIEL HELBERT

> "Sir Thomas Malory's History of King Arthur and the Round Table ...
> must some day come to be known more widely than now as one of the
> sweetest and strongest books in our language."
>
> Sidney Lanier, *The Boy's Froissart* (1879)

Although Thomas Malory was widely respected by Victorians, their praise of
Malory's writing is generally more subdued than comparable statements by
contemporary American writers like Sidney Lanier. The eminent British scholar
F. J. Furnivall, for instance, memorably characterized the *Morte Darthur* as a
"most pleasant jumble and summary of the Arthurian Legends."[1] Furnivall's
assessment is not derogatory, but it stops well short of Lanier's superlatives.
This difference in Malorian ardour is noteworthy, especially given that Lanier's
America – with its historical emphasis on social democracy and revolutionary
republicanism – was considerably more incompatible with Malory's stratified,
aristocratic dreamscape than was the Victorian Empire in which Furnivall and
his contemporaries lived. And, yet, Lanier's ardent endorsement of Malory's
writing and influence on the world is largely in harmony with the assessments
of most other American literati in the nineteenth and twentieth centuries. We
are, thus, left with what Barbara and Alan Lupack have called the "paradox" of
American Arthurian literature: "the tremendous appeal of the Arthurian legends
in America ... [is] seemingly at odds with American ideals and values."[2]

To understand *why* Malory in particular was so venerated among American
authors, we must first understand *how* these authors shaped the legend for
their own contemporary uses. Malory's translation into American society did
not come without some considerable adaptation and justification. The following
chapter examines some representative examples of American authors from about
1800 through the High Modernism of the early twentieth century. For the sake
of brevity, but also for the sake of consistency with this volume's subject matter,
I direct my primary attention to those authors who can reasonably be shown to
have directly consulted and considered Malory's *Morte Darthur*. However, since
uses of Malory in American literature are obviously part of a much wider context
of American interpretations of the Middle Ages in the nineteenth and twentieth

---

[1] F. J. Furnivall, *Sir Thomas Malory: The Critical Heritage*, ed. Marylyn Parins (London,
1987), 165.
[2] Alan Lupack and Barbara Tepa Lupack, *King Arthur in America* (Cambridge, 1999), xi.

centuries, I will first trace some of the more dominant trends of medievalism in America before examining how American Malorians fit into these contexts.

## A Brief History of American Medievalism

The history of "American" medievalism begins, indeed, with the first British endeavours upon the shores of the continent which would eventually become the United States. After his return from the first English colony in America, Roanoke Colony, Thomas Harriot's meticulous natural and anthropological notes were combined with woodcuts made from fellow colonist John White's illustrations of the Algonquin Indians to be published as *A Briefe and True Report of the New Found Land of Virginia*.[3] Harriot's notes and White's illustrations constituted the most in-depth description of Eastern Woodland Indian culture, religion, society and environment to date, and the work would be consulted by colonists for decades well into the height of the colonization era.

Interestingly, at the end of this work – after Harriot and White's primitive ethnography – the publishers included another series of woodcuts that purported to depict early medieval people (specifically the Picts) in strikingly similar appearance and dress to the Algonquin Indians. The stated reason for this impromptu lesson on medieval history? "For to show how the Inhabitants of the great Bretannie haue bin in times past as sauuage as those of Virginia."[4] Thus, from the outset, the descriptions and visual representations of Native Americans were contextualized by explicit comparisons to the British Middle Ages. While modern historians may have very good reasons to characterize this era of New World colonization as a cultural watershed of transition and change for Western culture, the first colonists saw in the New World only their troubling medieval past.

There are some interesting moments in the study of medievalism in the Colonies. After the British Colonies became the United States of America, however, there is a notable increase in artistic and political interest in the Middle Ages. The reasons for this intensified emphasis have much to do with finding legal precedents for a constitutional government and for justifying the radically different style of legislative bureaucracy being practised by the United States. But perhaps the most pressing reason for this burgeoning interest in the medieval past had to do with a collective anxiety in the newly "American" people. As an active territorial extension of the British nation, the British colonists had few reasons to be perturbed about the stature of their heritage. For a new nation that had recently thrown off both ties to Britain and the enduring institution of monarchy, however, links with an authorizing past had to be constructed.

Some of the more remarkable of these constructions were made by Thomas Jefferson, the author of the Declaration of Independence, third American president, and founder of the University of Virginia. Jefferson, unlike many of his day,

---

[3] Thomas Hariot, John White, and Richard Hakluyt, *A Briefe and True Report of the New Found Land of* Virginia (1588) (New York, 1871).
[4] *A Briefe and True Report*, 67.

did not perceive the American experiment to be a clean break with British history as a whole but rather he saw it as a revival of some very important and recently neglected medieval British principles: the (supposed) proto-parliament of Anglo-Saxon England (the witenagemot) and the distribution of monarchial authority to the gentility and people by the Magna Carta (1215). Famously, in recognition of these revivified Anglo-Saxon principles, Jefferson suggested that the verso of the Great Seal of the United States depict Hengist and Horsa, the mythical patriarchs of the Anglo-Saxon people. Because of Jefferson's prominence, and also because of the success of the University of Virginia, we must credit him with nothing less than the foundations of Anglo-Saxon studies in the United States and the prestige of medieval studies within the early American academy at large.[5] Though Jefferson and revolutionary America are often enshrined as examples par excellence of nouveau-Enlightenment thought, Jefferson perceived much of early American culture and politics as more of a return to conservative, medieval principles than an experiment in novel extremism.

Jefferson, as with most things, was a bit before his time in his medievalism. The century following Jefferson's death saw a veritable frenzy for all things medieval both in America and England; and the medieval zeitgeist is discernible in the period's architecture, visual art, opera and literature on both sides of the Atlantic. The causes of this widely recognized trend are far too nuanced for a full explanation here; but it is worth pointing out that the combination of changes to social and political structures instigated by the French Revolution and the Industrial Revolution played a major role. Suspicions about the nature of this "Progress," or perhaps just an understandable nostalgia for a perceived stability of the pre-modern period, appealed to a wide range of people in this period who found their surroundings much less stable than in previous generations.

One of the most important direct inspirations for medievalism of the literary variety was Sir Walter Scott's immensely popular novel, *Ivanhoe: A Romance* (1820). Scott's popularity crossed the Atlantic quickly and American medievalism shifted from Jeffersonian elitism to bourgeois avidity. Much like in England, there were jousting and ring tournaments held throughout the States in imitation of Scott's version of the Middle Ages. However, unlike in England, this newfound "popular" medievalism also found its way into the most contentious political debate of the era: slavery and race relations in the United States.

There are some important exceptions to this perceptible connection between race relations and American medievalism: Henry Longfellow, for instance, published an exemplary essay on Anglo-Saxon literature in 1838 without a hint of contemporary politics; and much of the early Arthurian literature (such as Wilmer, Emerson and Lowell, discussed below) seems, ostensibly at least, to be largely removed from questions of slavery.[6] In other areas, however, artistic debates about medievalism became a proxy war for race debates in the United

---

[5] John Niles discusses all of the above elements of Jefferson's medievalism and many more. See John D. Niles, *The Idea of Anglo-Saxon England, 1066–1901: Remembering, Forgetting, Deciphering, and Renewing the Past* (Chichester, 2015), esp. 265–301.

[6] Henry Wadsworth Longfellow, "Anglo-Saxon Literature," in *Prose Works of Henry Wadsworth Longfellow* (Boston, 1873), 384–111.

States. Walt Whitman, a prominent opponent of slavery who famously penned very eloquent verses about African Americans in his *Leaves of Grass*, barely disguised his opposition to medievalism in the preface to that same work: "Let the age and wars of other nations be chanted and their eras and characters be illustrated and that finish the verse. Not so the great psalm of the republic."[7] On the other extreme, the extraordinarily inflammatory (if rhetorically skilful) social theorist George Fitzhugh advocated for slavery (of both poor whites and blacks) as a humanistic endeavour; and he promoted the Middle Ages as a shining example of what America could potentially become: "In the balmy days of royalty, of feudal nobility, and of Catholic rule, there were no poor in Europe."[8] Though Fitzhugh's assessment hardly stands up to the historical record, it is at least consistent within his uniquely anti-capitalist, anti-communist theory of an ideal society – a society which was largely but quietly modelled on a romanticized view of the Middle Ages.

Though the Civil War may have resolved some of the legal issues of slavery, the larger questions about race in American society that were present before the war only loomed larger following Lee's surrender at Appomattox Courthouse. And the idea of the Middle Ages would continue to be a forum for these questions for decades to come. On one side of the debate were critics like Mark Twain (discussed below), who diagnosed the South as a whole as having contracted "the Sir Walter [Scott] disease"; Twain felt that were it not for the "modern and mediaeval mixed" character of Southerners, then the nation as a whole would be much more progressive.[9]

On the other end of the ideological spectrum, however, some authors promoted nostalgia for the Middle Ages as a means of enforcing a retrogressive patriarchal society which intimidated non-white populations and women into political subservience. Thomas Dixon's popular novel, *The Clansman: An Historical Romance of the Ku Klux Klan* (1905), and the even more popular movie-version of his book, *Birth of a Nation* (1915), are perhaps the most prominent representations of this inflammatory medievalism. Both versions of the story revolve around the rape of a white woman by a freed black man and the rise of "white crusader knights" on horseback (i.e. the KKK) to avenge injustice. They used, to great effect, the imagery and language of popular medievalism to both sympathize with the supposed plight of the chivalric white male and authorize racial violence in order to "protect" and infantilize white women.

Twain and Dixon are polar examples of the uses of and reactions to medievalism in the post-Civil War era; most others, including the vast majority of authors who were inspired by Malory in this period, fell somewhere in between. Most American adaptors of Malory comment on social issues and race in only the most oblique or inferential manner – or, by explicitly choosing to ignore those issues, invite another range of commentary on the matter. Regardless, their use of the Malorian medieval will ultimately need to be considered within this larger social context. To represent the Middle Ages at all during this period carries some

---

[7] Walt Whitman, *Leaves of Grass* (Brooklyn, 1855), iv.
[8] George Fitzhugh, "Southern Thought," *De Bow's Review* 24 (1858): 27–32.
[9] Mark Twain, *Life on the Mississippi* (New York, 1883/1901), 328.

ideological baggage; whether American representations of the *Morte Darthur* engage in these debates or succeed in avoiding them is a question that must be asked of each individual work and author.

After the First World War, the social dynamics surrounding race and medievalism took a back seat to questions about the viability of society as a whole. Of course, questions of race and social structure do not disappear with modernist receptions of medieval culture, but the damage inflicted by the war created some broader, existential questions. Medieval literature, again, proved to be an appropriate venue for exploring such questions; authors consistently adapted themes, characters and language from Malory and other medieval authors (especially Dante, Boccaccio and the Anglo-Saxon poets) in order to frame the cacophony of abstract, cerebral literatures that high modernism is known for. Despite Ezra Pound's modernist mantra, "make it new," it was the very, very "old" which would define his (and many others') writings. As Patricia Ingham has recently said, "the era of high modernism was also an era of high medievalism."[10]

### Pre-Tennyson Malorian Authors: Romantic Arthur and Civic Arthur

Authors who were inspired by Malory played a great variety of roles in the broader historical contexts traced above, as anyone familiar with the diversity of earlier American literature would surely expect. In accordance with other genres of American literature, the works which depict Arthurian characters follow the trajectories of Western Romanticism until the later nineteenth century, transition to realism through the early twentieth century, and to modernism after that – all of which is as we should expect. However, if we ask a more specific question about what roles these works play within the more narrow study of medievalism, we can begin to classify Malorian American works into two broad camps: those which cast Malorian elements in a Romantic sense of nostalgia, and those which revive themes from the *Morte* for civic reformation.[11]

Of the former camp, the medieval Arthurian legend was a source of nostalgia for, especially, the supernatural. Although supernatural events occur throughout other genres of classical and medieval literature, those genres generally offer a much more laboured and less ambiguous connection to either classical mythology or Christianity. Certain elements of the Arthurian legend, on the other hand, are notoriously obscure about the relationship between supernatural power and traditional Christianity. That obscurity, especially as it is manifested in the figure of Merlin, was attractive to certain early American authors whose literary endeavours were more secular in orientation.

The first, though by no means the foremost, American author to revive Malorian characters in American literature was Lambert Wilmer, whose three-act play

---

[10] Patricia Clare Ingham, *The Medieval New: Ambivalence in an Age of Innovation* (Philadelphia, 2015), 54.

[11] I owe the terms "Romantic" and "Civic" medievalism most directly to David Matthews's similar division of British medievalism in his *Medievalism: A Critical History* (Cambridge, 2015), 26–30.

*Merlin* (1827) plays fast and hard with Arthurian traditions.[12] Evidently, Wilmer wrote the play with the noble intention of cheering up his lovelorn friend, Edgar Allen Poe. Poe had recently (and involuntarily) ended his engagement with Sara Elmira Royster and many of Poe's friends, including Wilmer, considered Poe to be despondent and possibly suicidal.[13] Accordingly, *Merlin* centres around a problematic relationship between a beautiful young woman named Elmira and a lusty young explorer from whom she has been separated because of the workings of the Greek Fates. At one point, this shipwrecked lover, named Alphonso, is pulled from the brink of a cliff and lectured on the immorality of suicide. Merlin, a god-like prophet in a revolving battle with the Fates, intercedes on behalf of the couple to reunite them.

Despite the title and the above summary, *Merlin* is not set in the pre-modern period but instead jumps around from the banks of the Hudson River in New York to an unnamed shipwreck site and then to an unspecified location that houses "Merlin's Cave." The New York setting (if nothing else) suggests a setting in Wilmer's era or the recent past. Merlin is the only recognizable allusion to the Arthurian legend in the play, and even then the character seems only a distant memory of the Malorian antecedent. There are only a few fleeting references to the medieval version of the legend, most of which are thrown into Merlin's final speech:

> With charms of force, a brazen wall I'll rear
> Around Cairmardin, -that in the future there
> Unharm'd by foes, I may pursue that lore
> Which erst hath been the source of all my power.
> Those dark, mysterious volumes that contain
> The scrolls of fate, I will peruse again;-
> And still to human kind a friend I'll prove,
> Man the chief object of my care and love![14]

Wilmer alludes, here, to the long association of Merlin (or, in Welsh, Myrddin) with Carmarthen/Cairmardin, probably invented by Geoffrey of Monmouth as a creative etymology for the town's name: Caer [fort]- Myrddin.[15] Additionally, Wilmer here nods to Merlin's ability to implement large-scale constructions through supernatural powers and he alludes to the character's thematic connections with bookish hermits and clerics in the Middle Ages. Even so, this Merlin – with his humanistic love for humble people and his willingness to use his non-Christian, supernatural powers to intercede charitably on their behalf – represents a wholly different style of character than Wilmer's medieval inspiration. This Merlin is the *Odyssey*'s Athena for all of humanity, willing to intervene against the antagonistic pantheons of secular fate and Christian morality. Wilmer's sole

---

[12] Lambert A. Wilmer, *Merlin: Baltimore, 1827; Together with Recollections of Edgar A. Poe*, ed. Thomas Olive Mabbott (New York, 1941).

[13] Lupack and Lupack, *King Arthur in America*, 4.

[14] Wilmer, *Merlin*, 3.4.

[15] In reality, the second part of the town name is likely an Early Welsh corruption of "Moridunum," which was the Roman name for the town.

interest in Malory's Merlin is his supernatural traits that are largely free from classical mythological or Christian history.

Ralph Waldo Emerson also perceived Merlin as representing a "third way," or at least an alternative, under-explored tradition of wisdom and transcendence within Western culture. Emerson was an enthusiastic reader of Malory and his journals occasionally spell out his reactions to certain sections of the *Morte Darthur* (the Merlin-Vivien subplot is clearly his favourite).[16] However, in his three Merlin poems, Emerson depicts the character outside of the narrative arc in the *Morte*. In "Merlin II" (1846) for instance, Emerson begins with "[t]he rhyme of the poet / Modulates the King's affairs" and goes on to describe Merlin's advice to King Arthur in terms of the grand, natural order of universal ideals.[17] This sage, cerebral, and yet tragic figure is clearly an embellishment of Malory's Merlin, who is venerated in the *Morte Darthur* for his political advice. In this poem, however, Merlin moves beyond the political into the transcendental and philosophical, telling Arthur that thoughts of great inspiration "come also hand in hand; / In equal couples mated ... Perfect-paired as eagle's wings, / Justice is the rhyme of things."[18] Emerson shapes Malory's Merlin into a composite character who shares Emerson's opinions on poetic inspiration and the necessity of balance in Nature and spirit.

In his other two Merlin poems, Emerson blends Malory's Merlin with his widely-recognized antecedent in the Welsh tradition, Myrddin. Myrddin, along with other traditional, semi-historical bards in Celtic language traditions, was undergoing something of a revival in the early nineteenth century as a result of James Macpherson's extraordinarily popular *Ossian Cycle*. Even more so than Malory's Merlin, Myrddin the prophet and singing bard appealed to Emerson's construction of a nature-based, poetic transcendentalism.

These assumed connections between the Arthurian legend and the natural world are also important to James Russell Lowell's adaptation of Malory, *The Vision of Sir Launfal* (1848).[19] In the poem's preface, Lowell explicitly frames the work as an addition to the Grail Quest found in "the seventeenth book of the Romance of King Arthur" by Malory. It should be noted, however, that Sir Launfal – best known from Marie de France's Anglo-Norman lay, *Lanval* (c. 1190), and Thomas Chestre's adaptation thereof, *Sir Launfal* (c. 1480) – does not make an appearance in Malory's *Morte Darthur*.[20] Lowell warns his readers, however, not to expect a close rendition of Malory, as this story apparently takes place in "a period of time subsequent to the date of King Arthur's reign."[21]

---

[16] Lupack and Lupack, *King Arthur in America*, 7–8.
[17] Emerson, "Merlin II," *Poems by Ralph Waldo Emerson* (Boston, 1846/1904), 123.
[18] Emerson, "Merlin II," 124.
[19] James Russell Lowell, *The Vision of Sir Launfal and Other Poems* (Boston 1868/1910).
[20] It should be noted that Field has located a possible reference to Launfal in the *Morte*, in a brief mention of the Arthur's knights: "Sir Lamyell of Cardiff that was a grete lovear." Indeed, Field has emended this reference to "Sir Lanvall" in his edition, p. 865, line 33. See his argument for this identification in P. J. C. Field, "Malory and Cardiff," *Arthuriana* 16.2 (2006): 45–8. Lowell, of course, would not have been aware of this argument or emendation.
[21] Lowell, *The Vision of Sir Launfal*, 11.

Lowell does not elaborate further, but more than one reader has detected an eerie similarity between Sir Launfal's "North Countree" setting and the vivid New England countryside made famous in other works by Lowell and his contemporaries.[22] The poem begins, for instance, with a description of the day Launfal remembers his vow to find the Holy Grail, on an exultant "day in June" when "maize has sprouted," "the robin is plastering his house," and "the soul partakes the season's youth."[23] It is not only the presence of New World flora and fauna in Lowell's description of the spring day that "Americanize" this Arthurian setting, but here and throughout the poem we are given to understand that the natural environment is playing an active role in the development of Launfal's character. Much more so than in Malory, American literature often depicts the wilderness as a guiding force for characters, as a crucible, instructing characters and shaping their moral evolution; Lowell's "Vision of Sir Launfal" conspicuously takes part in this tradition.

In a serious departure from medieval literature (and from Malory in particular), the actual physical adventures Launfal encounters on his quest are not described at all. After the description of the June day, Launfal gallops out of the castle gate while being lectured, unsuccessfully, by a leper on the importance of charity. The narrative then jumps forward to a description of a winter day outside the same castle many years later. Launfal, now a bedraggled, grey-haired knight, is refused entrance to the castle and goes to sit beside a frozen brook (meticulously described by Lowell) to eat his meal of bread crust and water. The same leper approaches and Launfal offers to share this meal with him. The leper reveals himself to have been a divine test for Launfal, which he has passed, and the leper gives the knight the coveted Holy Grail. Lest we miss the moral of this story, the leper then explains to Launfal that the Grail represents heartfelt Christian charity and (like the serene frozen brook or the enjoyable June day) it is accessible to any who seek it. Launfal suddenly wakes up from a dream (apparently before all of this had ever happened), and decides not to go on a Grail Quest after all, but to do God's work at home instead.

It is in this last, overt appeal to homely Christian morality that Lowell begets a new era of American adaptations of Malory. Like Emerson and Wilmer (and many other American authors who do not consult Malory), Lowell sees the Arthurian Middle Ages as a precedent for American natural and supernatural motifs. But, unlike these more romanticized, secular works of medievalism, Lowell employs Malory as a means of explicit civic reform, as a venue for the progressive, Christian rehabilitation of a flawed society.

The notion that the Arthurian world offered examples which might inform the changing society of nineteenth-century America appealed to many other American Arthurian writers. The choice of Malory in this regard is hardly surprising, given the wide range of stories Malory provides and his vague presentation of theology. American readers were at liberty to adapt from Malory's array of Arthurian stories and choose their perception of his ambiguous moral

---

[22] Howard Maynadier, *The Arthur of the English Poets* (New York, 1966), 381. See also Lupack and Lupack, *King Arthur in America*, 10.

[23] Lowell, *The Vision of Sir Launfal*, lines 33, 71, 73 and 90.

code. Two readers of Malory in particular, Frank O. Ticknor and Moncure Daniel
Conway, found that Malory's text had implications for the American Civil War –
implications which differed drastically between the two authors.

Moncure Daniel Conway was both a wealthy ante-bellum Virginian and a
prominent abolitionist – an unusual combination which ultimately forced him
northward as tensions around slavery mounted in Virginia. He was very out-
spoken about the ills of slavery before and during the Civil War and was one
of many prominent abolitionists who ultimately convinced Abraham Lincoln
to issue the Emancipation Proclamation in 1863. Before that, however, Conway
published a strange but intriguing piece of Arthuriana following the death of
famed abolitionist and insurgent John Brown, who was executed in December
1859. The story, which came out in the journal Conway edited, *The Dial*, is titled
"Excalibur: A Story for Anglo-American Boys" (1860).[24]

Set at the Christmas of 1859, the story features a jovial and loving uncle by
the name of Paul recounting stories to his niece and nephews – one of whom is
named Arthur. Prompted by the boy's name, Paul tells the story of King Arthur's
sword, beginning conventionally with the sword's withdrawal from the stone
by a young Arthur and quickly moving to Bedivere's casting of the sword into
the water. It is at this point that Conway goes "off-script," and narrates how
Excalibur was eventually brought to Frederick the Great for his Austrian campaigns "against tyranny" by a peasant fisherman who found the sword in
the ocean. Excalibur serves Frederick well and, on his deathbed, the emperor
bequeathed this sword to the recently retired General George Washington with
the inscription, "from the oldest general in the world to the greatest."[25] Finally,
Excalibur is taken up by John Brown in the cause of freeing the American slaves;
Uncle Paul says, "in [Brown's] hand it conquered a whole nation ... as he died
he was more victorious than he had ever dreamed of being; he melted a million
hearts and poured them into the moulds of Freedom." Uncle Paul notes that
though Brown had not yet killed the "Dragon" of Slavery, "[Excalibur] has made
its wound, piercing beneath the scales of the Dragon; and that wound can never
be healed."[26]

Conway's portrayal of Excalibur's use by America's first president and a leading abolitionist is, as far as I can tell, unique within Arthuriana; and it is easy
to dismiss as a bizarre (if noble) attempt to politicize the legend. However, we
should note that this pastor, historian and would-be diplomat was not otherwise
prone to fantasy writing, and his strange children's story did not fall out of thin
air. It is a historical fact that when John Brown raided on Harper's Ferry in 1859,
the abolitionist kidnapped Lewis Washington (the great grand-nephew of the
first president) and stole one of George Washington's swords from Lewis's estate;

---

[24] "Excalibur: A Story for Anglo-American Boys," *The Dial: A Monthly Magazine for
Literature, Philosophy and Religion* 1.1 (1860): 384–9. The magazine, which only ran for
the 1860 year, was edited by Conway, but the publication of this piece was originally
anonymous. Conway claims authorship and describes his research and writing process in his autobiography: *Autobiography: Memories and Experiences of Moncure Daniel
Conway in Two Volumes*, vol. 1 (Boston, 1904), 310–11.
[25] Conway, "Excalibur," 45–6.
[26] Conway, "Excalibur," 49.

Brown wore this sword until he was captured a few days later. And, indeed, it was widely reported in the press at the time that this very same sword had been bequeathed to Washington by Emperor Frederick II.[27] If there were also a rumour circulating that the sword had been King Arthur's Excalibur, it would not be surprising given the amount of Arthurian propaganda that surrounded Frederick's court.[28] The sword (which is very much not medieval, in origin or even style) is currently on display at the State Library of New York.[29] Conway, for his part, seems to have thought he was merely serializing and embellishing an otherwise largely true story, though he later realized that he had been inaccurate.[30]

On the other side of the Mason-Dixon Line was Frank O. Ticknor, a Georgian physician and sporadic poet. Ticknor is probably most famous for his poem "Little Giffen," in which he recounts nursing a sixteen-year-old Confederate soldier back to health, only to watch the boy run back headlong into battle and – we are given to understand – to his death. Ticknor valorizes this Southern patriotism with hyperbolic medievalism: "I sometimes fancy that were I King / Of the courtly Knights of Arthur's ring ... I'd give the best on his bended knee – the whitest soul of my chivalry – For Little Giffen of Tennessee."[31]

Such idealization of "Southern chivalry" as being "medieval" is hardly unique to Ticknor, but few poets I am aware of employ that rhetoric with such consistency and avidity as he did. For the most part, Ticknor's use of the theme is, as in "Little Giffen," furthering what W. J. Cash has called the "Cavalier myth of the Old South" – the idea that noble Virginian families were the direct descendants and heirs of medieval chivalry.[32] This mythology is perhaps best represented in Ticknor's early poem "The Virginians of the Valley," where he praises Virginia's defenders as "the knightliest of the knightly race" and implies a more or less direct descent from the Grail knight of yore to the Virginia cavalryman of his own day.[33]

The medievalism of Ticknor's poetry takes on a darker air after the war, however, and it also betrays some thematic influences from Malory. This is especially evident in Ticknor's poem dedicated to Jefferson Davis (the president of the Confederacy), titled "Arthur, the Great King." The poem, as one might expect, invites a metaphoric comparison between the two leaders, but Ticknor goes beyond obsequious flattery. Set as the "sun of battle smolders low" (i.e., after the war is over), King Arthur is depicted as "gaunt" and "grizzled," covered

---

[27] "The Negro Insurrection. Origin and Objects of the Plot. Capt. Brown, Of Kansas, Originator of the Disturbance," *The New York Times Book of the Civil War: 1861–1865*, ed. Harold Holzer and Craig L. Symonds (New York, 2010), 19 October 1859.

[28] See Donald L. Hoffman, "Was Merlin a Ghibelline? Arthurian Propaganda at the Court of Frederick II," in *The Social Implications of the Arthurian Legend*, ed. Martin B. Shichtman and James P. Carley (Albany, NY, 1994), 113–38.

[29] "The Steel Hilted Smallsword," *George Washington's Mount Vernon*. Accessed 9 May 2017. http://www.mountvernon.org/preservation/collections-holdings/washingtons-swords/the-steel-hilted-smallsword.

[30] Conway, *Autobiography*, 311.

[31] Francis Orray Ticknor, "Little Giffen," in *Southern Poems, Selected, Arranged and Edited with Biographical Notes*, ed. Charles William Kent (Boston, 1913), 32–3, lines 31–7.

[32] W. J. Cash, *The Mind of the South* (New York, 1941), 3–6.

[33] "The Virginians of the Valley," in *The Poems of Frank O. Ticknor, M.D.*, ed. K. M. R. (Philadelphia, 1879), 12–13, line 1.

in battle dust, and yet all the more noble. Excalibur gleams in anticipation of another battle, and Ticknor notes that there is more than a shared sense of "nobility" to this comparison between Arthur and Davis: "And were his smile King Arthur's own, / Of all that met his kindling eyes / Not one should marvel did he *rise!*"[34] In a notably complex construction, Ticknor offers the defeated Arthur at the end of Malory's *Morte Darthur* as a metaphor for the beaten, war-ravaged South embodied by Jeff Davis. They are both, implies Ticknor, representations of an unfairly lost golden age, both are considerably more dignified than their victorious opponents, and (most importantly) both are fated to "rise" again.

The last Arthurian poet of the Civil War era covered here is Sarah Bridges Stebbins (nom de plume, Sallie Bridges).[35] She is of particular importance to Malory's American heritage for a couple of reasons: first, Bridges is a talented and underappreciated poet who takes up the Arthurian theme with critical insight and a nuanced understanding of the legend's implications. Second, and perhaps more to the point, she is the first American author of either sex to truly *adapt* and *interpret* Malory's text as a comprehensive literary enterprise. While other authors (such as those above) use Malorian characters, settings, or themes as a springboard for poetic enterprises largely unrelated to Malory, Bridges consistently demonstrates a solid comprehension of the *Morte Darthur* and she responds to that work's implications in her own unique, vivid style.

The majority of Bridges's Arthurian poems in *The Marble Isle* (1864) recount a scene from Malory and then elaborate on the characteristic emotions conveyed by the scene. This "reader response" style of approach to Malory somewhat modernizes the medieval text while it also personalizes and reinterprets the work – all without overtly changing the story. For instance, in her poem "Sir Lancelot's Slumber," Bridges reworks the scene from Malory's Book VI when Morgan le Fay and three other queens kidnap Lancelot. In the *Morte*, the scene is one of many that Malory includes to emphasize Lancelot's infinite desirability as a male knight and his unwavering allegiance to Guinevere. In Bridges's adaptation, however, the story is told, rather, from the perspective of the four queens. At one point Bridges emphasizes the emotional turmoil that Lancelot's refusal causes: "There is no cause like this on earth / to rouse a woman's slumbering ire, / To turn her fondest love to hate, / And kindle pride's enduring fire."[36] Characteristically, Bridges humanizes some of Malory's stock "evil female" characters while simultaneously building on Malory's theme of Lancelot's desirability and tenacity.

Her final poem of the collection, "Avilion," is worth special mention both because of its novelty and because of its implied commentary on contemporary

---

[34] "Arthur, The Great King: To Jefferson Davis," in *The Poems of Frank O. Ticknor*, 53–55, at 54 (emphasis in original).

[35] Sallie Bridges, *Marble Isle: Legends of the Round Table and Other Poems* (Philadelphia, 1864). Various sources indicate that Sallie Bridges is the pseudonym of Sarah Bridges Stebbins of Philadelphia, who is also the author of *Galgano's Wooing and Other Poems* (New York, 1890), among other books. See William Cushing, *Initials and Pseudonyms: A Dictionary of Literary Disguises*, vol. 1 (New York, 1885), s.v. Stebbins, Mrs. Sarah (Bridges).

[36] Bridges, "Sir Lancelot's Slumber," in *Marble Isle*, 171–4, at 174.

events. The poem narrates an imagined journey by the poet herself to Avalon to meet King Arthur and, as it happens, many other members of Malory's text who have been summoned to Avalon by Arthur himself after the ending of the *Morte Darthur*. After Arthur finds out from when and where the poet is coming, the king inquires into the state of worldly affairs. Bridges explains to him "how the nations groan'd," and Arthur decides to return from Avalon "To lead the way to truth through seas of blood!"[37] The poem closes with Bridges waking up from the dream and looking forward to Arthur's return.

It is clear enough in this final poem that, like Ticknor and Conway, Bridges sought to connect the events of the Civil War to Malory's Arthurian landscape. Bridges's parallelism here, however, strikes me as being of a different sort altogether from the more openly factional uses of the legend by the two former poets. To Ticknor and Conway, the Arthurian realm represented the heritage of a golden age and virtuous idealism that they were keen to align with their political goals. Bridges's relationship with Malory was more comprehensive and nuanced: she recognized Malory's *Morte Darthur* as a literary elegy for the death of a chivalric age and she may very well have recognized the *Morte* as an elegy for all the chivalric individuals who had died in Malory's own civil war. Such a connection of Malory's watershed historical moment to the one she was actively witnessing in America is an observation which is both astute and poignant.

## Post-Tennyson, Post War

It is typical to utilize the American Civil War as a dividing line in studies of United States history and literature, given the war's violent redirection of the shape and structure of American society. My own brief exploration of American literature, here, divides American Malorian literature at around the same time (mid 1860s), but for a much different reason. As I note above, many of the central questions explored through medievalism in America before the Civil War continued to be explored afterwards. The emphasis on Malory and the Arthurian legend as having an emphatic role in those discussions increases considerably, however, after Alfred, Lord Tennyson's intermittent publication of the *Idylls of the King* between 1859 and 1885. Because of the immense popularity of the *Idylls*, Tennyson drew his fair share of imitators and satirists in the United States. Many, perhaps even *most*, of the authors who wrote reactions to Tennyson were content to accept the Arthurian narrative of the *Idylls* at face value. Others, however, such as the ones I discuss below, were inspired by Tennyson to study Malory before penning their own versions.

Sidney Lanier was one such American reader of Malory, and he is important not only for his own unique artistic representations of Malory but also for his role in ensuring that future generations had easy access to the *Morte Darthur* itself. Lanier is best known to scholars of American literature for his poetry and literary criticism; his poem "The Marshes of Glynn," in particular, has solidified

[37] Bridges, "Avilion," in *Marble Isle*, 223–38, at 231.

his reputation in American letters. However, in the final months of his long battle with tuberculosis (contracted in a Union prison during the war), Lanier was most predominantly concerned with a task that would make a less obvious statement for his legacy – editing medieval literature for children. *The Boy's Library* editions (which were intended to be followed with an equivalent for young women) were promoted as young adult versions of medieval canonical works; but unlike how that task might be approached today, Lanier's adaptations of the texts kept much of the original spelling and only removed sections of the text for abbreviation and modest censorship. Though he finished a total of four editions (Froissart, the *Mabinogion*, the Percy Folio, and Malory) before he died, Lanier clearly promoted his version of *Le Morte Darthur* (1880) as being the most important for young boys to read, based on his assessment of its literary merit and its potential to instill positive values for the American youth.

The reason for this emphasis on Malory's importance is derivative of Lanier's unique interpretations of Malory, which were notably advanced for his day. Lanier, for instance, is particularly aware of (and fond of) Malory's anachronistic construction of chivalry: "Froissart's Chronicle [ca. 1400] is, in a grave and important sense, a sort of continuation of Malory's novel."[38] Though this statement may seem to be chronologically impossible, Lanier goes on to explain that though Malory is writing in the late fifteenth century, his portrayals of knighthood derive mostly from Malory's idealization of chivalry in the twelfth and thirteenth centuries. Froissart is, of course, writing a somewhat less romanticized portrayal of chivalry in the fourteenth century. Most adaptors of Malory in Lanier's day were content to accept the *Morte Darthur* at face value – that Malory was relating a history which, even if embellished, is nonetheless accurate in its portrayal of chivalry. Lanier, on the other hand, recognized Malory's anachronistic manufacture of knightly ideals. This was not a fault, however, in Lanier's assessment, because Lanier saw himself as being engaged in a very similar project.

Another writer who approached Malory from an anachronistic perspective was Mark Twain, though in this case Twain himself supplied the anachronism. *A Connecticut Yankee in King Arthur's Court* (1889) is arguably the most important work of American Arthuriana, and it certainly ranks as one of the most striking adaptations of Malory in the modern era. The plot, as implied by the title, revolves around a nineteenth-century Connecticut man named Hank Morgan who is transported back to the sixth-century world of Camelot after being knocked out by a man with a crowbar. Within hours of arriving at King Arthur's court, Hank vows to become the "boss of the whole country inside of three months" – his rationale being that he, an American industrialist caught in the Middle Ages, is de facto the most intelligent person in the kingdom.[39] Twain consistently confirms his protagonist's assessment and Hank quickly becomes a special minister to the king and is dubbed "The Boss." The remainder of the plot, then, derives from the inherent tension between Hank's attempts to "invent" modernity and the conservative, superstitious elements of medieval society resisting these changes.

---

[38] *The Boy's Froissart*, ed. Sidney Lanier (New York, 1879), x.
[39] Mark Twain, *A Connecticut Yankee in King Arthur's Court* (New York, 1889), 15.

Though Merlin is Hank's most frequent opponent, Hank regularly outwits him with nineteenth-century technology. Among other instances, Hank destroys Merlin's tower with gunpowder and a lightning rod and wins tournament mêlées with a lasso and a set of revolvers. At the height of Hank's power, he installs railway lines, telegraphs, modern factories and public schools while simultaneously eliminating slavery, curtailing the power of the Catholic Church in Britain, and turning the Round Table into a venue for stock-broker meetings between former knights turned investors. Twain's skills as a humourist glisten in this novel, and the modern, Protestant, republican-capitalist Yankee repeatedly humiliates his ignorant, superstitious and culturally retrograde medieval hosts.

Such is the central theme of the novel – and one that Twain had been stewing over for some time before writing the book. Twain was adamantly opposed to the flurry of American medievalism brought about by Scott and Tennyson; in his previous writings Twain derides neo-Gothic architecture and Southern pretensions to "chivalry," and makes a not-so-subtle case that Southern medievalism significantly contributed to the outbreak of the American Civil War.[40] *A Connecticut Yankee* is, thus, the culmination of Twain's anti-medieval diatribes, in which his protagonist lives out a fantasy to "exterminate the whole chivalry of England" in order to install American, quasi-egalitarian republicanism in its place.[41] Twain never directly addresses the irony of adapting a canonical medieval text to demonstrate America's supposedly irreconcilable differences between the British Middle Ages and American modernity.

And yet Twain's relationship with the Middle Ages in this novel is more complex and nuanced than he is generally given credit for. His treatment of the *Morte Darthur*, for instance, indicates he had no small amount of respect for Malory's abilities as an author. Twain includes a long passage from "Sir Lancelot du Lak" in its original language at the beginning of the novel and he writes dialogues in Malorian English with some skill throughout the book. Whatever Twain might have felt about the naive and potentially dangerous attempts to revive Malory's world in nineteenth-century America, Twain treats Malory himself as an authoritative and accomplished storyteller, and he enshrines Malory's language in a way that only a gifted observer of dialects like Twain could do.

Furthermore, the ending of *A Connecticut Yankee* also throws some cold water on the assumed premise, implied throughout the novel, that American modernity is infinitely better than the medieval past. Hank fails to prevent King Arthur's death, despite his futuristic knowledge and technology, and the Catholic Church and the knights of England eventually rise up against Hank. Hank gleefully sets up a state-of-the-art defence system and tricks the enemy army of eleven thousand knights into attacking him. With powerful electric fencing, controlled dams, landmines and Gatling guns, Hank and his small force mow down an entire generation of young men in the space of a few hours. Then, as victims of their own success, Hank's crew is trapped by a wall of rotting corpses for fear of leaving their technologies in order to venture outside the perimeter. While we are given to understand that the rest of Hank's party dies from disease spread

---

[40] Twain, *Life on the Mississippi*, 328–29.
[41] Twain, *Connecticut Yankee*, 432.

by the corpses, Merlin puts a spell over Hank that causes him sleep – and dream – for 1,300 years. By the time Hank wakes up, back in the nineteenth century, he has been tortured by nightmares of his actions for over a millennium. Merlin gets his revenge by, ironically, sending Hank to the future he had tried to create at Camelot. Malory's portrayal of the chivalric Middle Ages may have fuelled Twain's skills as a satirist, but Malory's world seems, in many ways, still preferable to modern barbarity posing as honourable Progress.

Twain's younger contemporary Madison Cawein shared all of Twain's respect for Malory and few of his qualms about glorifying the Middle Ages. The Louisville native and prolific poet (with over thirty book-length collections) was well regarded as a writer while he was alive, but his legacy has lapsed into obscurity in the century after his death. Cawein would never be described as being as avant-garde or innovative as the following generation of poets; he was much more interested, instead, in reviving traditional poetic forms and antique literary subject matter. In these particular goals he demonstrates exceptional competence; I can only imagine that the unenthusiastic reception of Cawein's poetry is more a reflection on the rapidly changing tastes of his day than on any lack of substance or talent in Cawein as a writer.

Though Cawein's poetry is filled with allusions to many eras and traditions, his emphasis on the Arthurian legend stands out, and Thomas Malory is by far Cawein's most important source for that legend. Cawein claimed that he had read Malory and had considered the *Morte* as a subject for his own work before discovering Tennyson, but that the *Idylls* were the catalyst for his renewed interest in Malory.[42] His adaptations of and allusions to Malory are spread widely throughout his extensive corpus, but they form an especially core component in his *Accolon of Gaul with Other Poems* (1889) and *Lyrics and Old World Idylls* (1907).

Cawein has far too many Arthurian poems to discuss comprehensively here, and his approach to Malory does not conform to any singular model. Many of his Arthurian poems are similar to Sallie Bridge's approach, in which Cawein summarizes a section of Malory and then reacts to that story – a sort of reader response in verse. In other poems, such as "A Guinevere" and "Morgan le Fay," Cawein writes Malorian fan fiction, expanding the *Morte Darthur* with scenes that fit the characters as he conceived of them.[43] Other poems by Cawein are closer in style to the British Romantics – whom he emulated often enough to earn the title "The Keats of Kentucky." That comparison is especially appropriate for Cawein's poem, "To One Reading the Morte D'Arthure" (*sic*). Rather like Keats' "On first looking into Chapman's Homer," Cawein gives the impression of becoming physically immersed within this life-altering work of literature. And, as in the Keats sonnet, bookish adulation evolves into artistic emulation: "Dost walk with stately, armored men / In marble-fountained closes? / So speak the dreams within thy gaze, / The dreams thy spirit cages."[44] Malory's *Morte*

[42] See Lupack and Lupack, *King Arthur in America*, 110–11.
[43] Madison Cawein, "A Guinevere," in *Blooms of the Berry* (Louisville, 1887), 95–7; "Morgan le Fay," in *Myth and Romance: Being a Book of Verses by Madison Cawein* (New York, 1899), 33–5.
[44] "To One Reading the Morte D'Arthure," in *The Poems of Madison Cawein Volume V: Poems of Meditation and of Forest and Field* (Boston 1907), 213–14.

*Darthur* is, thus, not merely a box of stories and characters for Cawein to draw from, but a canonical work of art to be modelled by contemporary artists. Given the frequency with which the *Morte* shows up in Cawein's poetry, it would seem that Cawein followed his own advice in that matter.

One other Arthurian poem by Cawein deserves mention because of the influence it had on the following generation of poets. Cawein's "Waste Land" is a vivid emotional and visual description of the Wasteland motif that is common to many Arthurian tales. Malory puts less emphasis on this motif than other Arthurian authors, but given its importance to Cawein and later writers, I will quote the section in full:

> And hit was in the realme of Logrys, and soo befelle grete pestylence, and grete harme to both realmes. For sythen encrecyd neyther corne ne grasse nor wel nyghe no fruyte ne in the watir was no fysshe, wherefor men callen hit, the landes of the two marchys, the Waste Land, for that dolorous stroke.[45]

As with so many other allusions in the *Morte*, Malory's brevity leaves something to be desired; Cawein thus saw fit to expand upon Malory's terse description.

> And then—I saw the trees.
> Skeletons gaunt that gnarled the place,
> Twisted and torn they rose—
> The tortured bones of a perished race
> Of monsters no mortal knows,
> They startled the mind's repose.[46]

Cawein is known for his poetic descriptions of the natural world, but his description of this mythical plane of desolation and despair strikes a much more disturbing tone than in his other works. The poem is, at its core, a textual and emotional expansion of the medieval original which lingers on the impacts the scene might have had on Malorian characters.

Cawein published this poem in *Poetry* magazine in 1913, in a publication that included an essay by Ezra Pound – who also happened to be on the editorial board for the magazine. It is widely believed that T. S. Eliot encountered Cawein's poem in this publication because he would have been interested in Pound's essay. Given that T. S. Eliot's "The Waste Land" (1921) shares a title, an inspiration, and (broadly) some of the same themes as Cawein's poem, Cawein warrants mention as a possible direct influence on Eliot.

However, even if Eliot had been consciously or unconsciously influenced by Cawein's poem, it is important to note that the Eliot poem is of a decidedly different ilk than Cawein's more traditional piece. Whereas Cawein's poem is a direct

---

[45] *Caxton's Malory: A New Edition of Sir Thomas Malory's* Le Morte Darthur *based on the Pierpont Morgan Copy of William Caxton's Edition of 1485*, ed. James W. Spisak (Berkeley, CA, 1983), XVII.iii. I have cited Caxton's edition of Malory since the Winchester manuscript had not, as yet, been discovered and American authors were working from editions based solely on Caxton.

[46] Madison Cawein, "Waste Land," *Poetry: A Magazine of Verse*, ed. Harriet Monroe, 1.4 (1913): 104–5.

engagement with Malory's passage, Eliot is much more interested in the wider construct of the Waste Land as a folkloric motif and in transferring that motif to Eliot's own contemporary society. Much like the "grete pestilence" which creates infertility in Malory's distant realms of King Pelles, Eliot sees the First World War as having supremely wounded Western society, to the point that it is unable to regenerate itself from that damage. Like his medieval Arthurian precedents, Eliot links the viability of the land to the viability of the persons inhabiting that land. Thus, the languid and hopeless characters who speak in "The Waste Land" are as barren and atrophied as the repugnant "dull canal" on which the Fisher King of Eliot's poem sits:

> A rat crept softly through the vegetation
> Dragging its slimy belly on the bank
> While I was fishing in the dull canal
> On a winter evening round behind the gashouse
> Musing upon the king my brother's wreck.[47]

As Eliot himself notes, his interest in this myth is derivative of Jessie Weston's *From Ritual to Romance* (a very early anthropological reading of the medieval folk-lore surrounding the Grail Quest) and James Frazer's *The Golden Bough*. Malory's *Morte* and other medieval works are, thus, once removed from Eliot's poem.

Nonetheless, Eliot's application of the Fisher King mythos to modernity is compelling and has resonated with generations of readers. The central, driving difference in the motif in "The Waste Land" and medieval literature, however, is the ending of the story: in Eliot's Waste Land there is no magic lance to revive the emotionally famished land, no redemptive ideology to stir meaningful life within the desolate masses. In medieval Grail literature this story is a comedy, a story of how a small unit of medieval Christian knights triumphed over wide scale adversity; Eliot, instead, presents the myth as comprehensive cultural trag-edy with no perceptible resolution.

Eliot's "The Waste Land" is often cited as the work which instigated the Anglophone literary transition into high modernism, owing especially to his experimentation with form, his intentionally chaotic use of diverse speakers, and his self-conscious pessimism about post-war society. Another core element that "The Waste Land" bequeaths to literary modernism is its dependence upon a medieval, Arthurian motif to conceptualize these ideals. As other scholars have noted, the most well-known practitioners of high modernism in American lit-erature, like Eliot, drew connections between early twentieth-century society and broad themes in medieval folklore. Ernest Hemingway personalized the myth of the Fisher King in *The Sun Also Rises* (1926), which follows a castrated American soldier living among a meandering, desolate, and often-intoxicated group of expats in post-war Paris. F. Scott Fitzgerald created a modern American version of Arthurian aristocracy in *The Great Gatsby* (1922), with Jay Gatsby as the idealistic courtly lover, Nick Carraway as the chivalric moral compass, and Tom Buchanan as the problematic king-husband. Taking his cue from Eliot, Fitzgerald

---

[47] T. S. Eliot, "The Waste Land," in *The Waste Land*, ed. Michael North (New York, 2000), lines 187–91.

even creates a hyper-modern Waste Land in the Valley of Ashes between the privileged Camelot of the Long Island Egg communities and the degenerate setting of New York City. William Faulkner experimented with Arthurian themes more overtly (and less successfully) in his early novella *Mayday* (1926), in which a knight named Sir Galwyn of Arthgyll pursues a quest in search of his true love. Later in his career, Faulkner employed these themes of chivalry and nobility more subtly in his creation of the romantic, "half-baked Galahad" figure of Quentin Compson in *The Sound and the Fury* (1929).[48]

As the above brief description illustrates, however, the direct connections between Malory and these most celebrated of modernist authors are allusive at best and tangential at worst. Malory supplies little more than the title to Eliot's poem; in his excessively copious notes to "The Waste Land" Eliot references a range of major and minor authors from antiquity to the poem's present, but Malory is never mentioned. Similarly, while it is readily apparent that Faulkner, Hemingway and Fitzgerald had read Malory, they were largely content to draw, instead, on broad structural themes and archetypal characters that Victorian authors like Tennyson had already stereotyped. The Malorian heritage of these authors is undeniable, but their direct use of the *Morte Darthur* in their own writing is so homogenized with more contemporary versions of the legend that Malory himself is rarely distinguishable.

John Steinbeck is the notable exception to that rule, however. The California-born Nobel Prize winning author was positively obsessed with Malory for most of his life. Steinbeck even developed a friendship with Eugène Vinaver and visited the professor and his wife in Manchester on some occasions. The instigation for Steinbeck's cultivation of this friendship was his research for one of his final projects in life, a modernization of Malory for contemporary audiences: *The Acts of King Arthur and his Noble Knights* (published posthumously in 1976).[49]

The book in its unfinished state reads something like an update and modernization of Malory which corresponds, structurally, to the Winchester manuscript. The language is modernized (though Steinbeck does include some older words here and there for aura) and there is more depth to the characterization than in Malory. Judging from his letters to his editors and to Vinaver, however, Steinbeck seems to have had two much more grandiose goals in mind. The first is much in accord with the other adaptors of Malory that the current chapter examines: Steinbeck wanted to make Malory relevant for his own time; he wanted to revise the legend for a modern setting and a modern audience. As he wrote to Vinaver in 1955: "Malory writes and thinks of a 15th century Arthur – Chrétien speaks of his time and I, heaven help me, can only think of the Round Table as having existed in Salinas, California around the turn of the 20th century."[50]

This move to Americanize Malory's characters can be seen throughout his adaptation, where he interpolates characters within an implicitly modern,

---

[48] See Lupack and Lupack, "Beyond *The Waste Land*," in *King Arthur in America*, 134–82. The Lupacks discuss Arthurian allusions in various works by Hemingway, Fitzgerald and Faulkner in much greater detail.

[49] John Steinbeck, *The Acts of King Arthur and His Noble Knights*, ed. Chase Horton (Oxford, 2007).

[50] Letter dated 6 July 1955, quoted in Lupack and Lupack, *King Arthur in America*, 203.

American context – even when the textual setting never changes. Consider, for instance, Steinbeck's treatment of Sir Kay who, in Malory, is consistently portrayed as boorish, rude and petty; he serves largely as a foil for the paragons of knighthood in whom Malory is more interested. Steinbeck, however, has Kay explain to Lancelot *how* and *why* his attitude changed when Arthur gave him a largely bureaucratic role in the court: "To you war is fighting. To me it is so many ashen poles for spears, so many strips of steel – counting of tents, of knives, of leather straps – counting – counting ... Look, sir, did you ever know a man of numbers who did not become small and mean and frightened – all greatness eaten away by little numbers as marching ants nibble a dragon and leave picked bones?"[51] It is not only that Steinbeck gives Kay a depth of character he lacks in the *Morte Darthur*, but Kay's depth of character here stems from an American working man's contempt for bureaucratic bean counting – a sentiment prominent among many other Steinbeck characters.

Steinbeck also had another goal in his adaptation of Malory: he wanted to expand on Malory's own fifteenth-century conception of the *Morte Darthur's* characters; to explicate, as it were, Malory's deeper understanding of Malorian motifs and characters as only a fellow "novelist" could.[52] In order to accomplish this, Steinbeck read extensively into the Arthurian scholarship of the 1950s, consuming both prominent and obscure theories of Arthuriana and ultimately getting lost in the competing theories of medieval history and Arthurian literature. Referring to the scholarly debate on the etymology of Arthur's name, Steinbeck writes: "I can see how a man, if he wanted to, could get bogged down here and spend many happy years fighting with other specialists about the word bear and its Celtic Arthur."[53]

Steinbeck's object in this lengthy study, however, was not to contribute to academic scholarship but to write Malory's characters and themes appropriate to a medieval person's conception of them: "I think it is possible through knowledge and discipline for a modern man to understand, and, to a certain extent, live into a fifteenth century mind."[54] Obviously, the goals of presenting Malory's *Morte Darthur* simultaneously in the context of its original fifteenth-century conception *and* in the cultural milieu of twentieth-century hometown America are largely antithetical to one another and Steinbeck's adaptation suffered from this admirable but schizophrenic approach. I suspect that it was as a result of his inability to reconcile these two goals that Steinbeck abandoned *The Acts of Arthur and His Noble Knights* in 1959 and did not return to it.

Though Steinbeck's intense study and attempted adaptation of Malory late in life is his most explicit engagement with the *Morte Darthur*, it is neither his first nor his most important engagement. From the outset of his literary career, Steinbeck modelled his work on Malorian themes and translated the Arthurian world into American fiction. Indeed, Steinbeck's very first novel, *Cup of Gold*,

---

[51] Steinbeck, *The Acts of King Arthur*, 321–2.
[52] Steinbeck, "Letter: March 14, 1957," in "Appendix" to *The Acts of Arthur*, 326. For a discussion of the perception of Malory's *Morte* as a "novel," see Cory James Rushton, "Malory and Form," in this volume.
[53] Steinbeck, "Letter: January 3, 1957," in "Appendix" to *The Acts of Arthur*, 321.
[54] Steinbeck, "Letter: March 14, 1958," in "Appendix" to *The Acts of Arthur*, 341.

overlays the adventures of the historical Welsh pirate Henry Morgan with themes and symbolism from the Grail Quest in some novel and creative ways.[55] However, it would be Steinbeck's later and more familiar subject matter which would solidify both his legacy as a canonical American author and his important role in Americanizing Malory's magnum opus.

Steinbeck found his first critical and financial success in the 1935 novel *Tortilla Flat*, which centres around a group of "paisanos" (Mexican-Indian-American rustics) living in Monterey, California. The war veteran Danny inherits two houses in town from his grandfather and invites a rag-tag group of small-time criminals and partiers to live with him. This lively group of endearing ruffians drink and philosophize their way through a series of humorous adventures, including an elaborate heist of picnic food, a quest to pillage a wrecked Coast Guard ship, and befriending a reclusive, dog-loving homeless man named "The Pirate." The novel culminates in an epic house party at Danny's house in which the inebriated host challenges the whole town to a good-natured brawl and ends up plummeting to his death in a nearby ravine. Though there are few references to Malory or even broadly Arthurian characters and events in the novel, the structure and theme of the work was explicitly intended by Steinbeck to mirror Malory's *Morte Darthur*: "The form is that of the Malory version, the coming of Arthur and the mystic quality of owning a house, the forming of the round table, the adventure of the knights and finally, the mystic translation of Danny."[56]

In his following works, as in *Tortilla Flat*, Steinbeck maps the nobility of Malory's Arthurian aristocracy onto America's forgotten masses: the paisanos, the dust-bowl migrants, and the exploited ranch-hands of the mid-twentieth-century American West. These events and characters, in a less competent author's hand, might seem mundane and unimportant, but Steinbeck infuses these with subconscious Malorian precedents to turn their everyday struggle in rural and suburban America into epics and legends of canonical proportions. Critics of Steinbeck's fiction (especially *The Grapes of Wrath*, *The Winter of our Discontent* and *Of Mice and Men*) have variously demonstrated Steinbeck's dependence on key Malorian themes – such as knightly camaraderie, mystical translation and spiritual quests for adventure – to elevate some of America's most unfortunate and disabused people into a state of reverence within the American conscious.[57] Although Steinbeck's abandoned *Acts of King Arthur* did not achieve the literary success of his earlier work, it serves as a useful reminder of the importance of the *Morte Darthur* to the remainder of his literary corpus.

---

[55] Lupack and Lupack, *King Arthur in America*, 186–90.

[56] John Steinbeck, "Letter: 1934," in *Steinbeck: A Life in Letters*, ed. Elaine Steinbeck and Robert Wallsten (New York, 1975), 96–7.

[57] The essays collected in *Steinbeck and the Arthurian Theme*, ed. Tetsumaro Hayashi (Muncie, IN, 1975) are a good starting point for this scholarship, as is Andrew Welsh's "Lancelot at the Crossroads in Malory and Steinbeck," *Philological Quarterly* 70.4 (1991): 485–502. More recently: Lupack and Lupack, *King Arthur in America*, 183–209 and Barbara A. Heavilin, "'Parallels with Our Own Times': Ethan Allen Hawley as Lancelot Grotesque," *Steinbeck Review* 5.1 (2008): 49–61.

## Conclusion

Steinbeck serves as an appropriate conclusion to this (admittedly incomplete) compendium of American adaptations of Malory for a few reasons. The first reason is that Steinbeck, unlike most of the authors covered in this chapter, is hardly at risk of critical neglect. If Malory's direct influence on American literature were limited to the many minor authors discussed above (such as Sallie Bridges and Madison Cawein), and similar authors who were not discussed for reasons of space and theme (such as John Erskine and Edwin Arlington Robinson), it might be argued that Malory's impact on American fiction was only tangential, and that Twain and Emerson's references are the exceptions rather than the rule. However, when these authors are taken into context with Steinbeck's consistent emphasis on Malory throughout his career, such a suggestion is far less viable. Instead, Steinbeck's emphasis highlights Malory's *Morte Darthur* as a central text in the American literary heritage; and this is despite the seeming incongruity between the stratified society that Malory glorifies and the American libertarian-republicanism that rebelled against that same society. American authors, thus, paradoxically, seek to distance themselves from medieval culture while simultaneously drawing on and adapting some of the most important texts created by medieval culture.

Furthermore, the way in which Steinbeck adapts Malory into American literature speaks to one of the answers to that seeming incongruity between the Malorian Middle Ages and American Modernity: much like Malory himself, American authors are almost always willing to "translate" the Arthurian legend for contemporary audiences; with no small amount of adaptation, Malory's *Morte* becomes surprisingly relevant to the populist, democratic values with which American readers have been concerned. From James Russell Lowell's Grail knight of Protestant Christian charity to T. S. Eliot's democratized Fisher King, Americans were even more creative than British authors at adapting and reinterpreting the legend. In terms of direct influence on American literature, the Holy Bible is one of the very few texts which exceeds Thomas Malory's *Morte Darthur* – but the *Morte* is far less sacred to Americans, which is perhaps why it has been so enduring and adaptive to American culture.

# Select Bibliography

This bibliography is not comprehensive, but rather reflective of key topics and debates in Malory studies. It offers a representative overview of both seminal works and recent trends in the field, and for ease of browsing, it is organised according to type of resource (monographs, edited collections, articles, and works of reference). For additional references, see the chapters in this volume and the essays in the Collections of Essays cited below (which have not been separately listed).

## Monographs

Armstrong, Dorsey, *Gender and the Chivalric Community in Malory's* Morte d'Arthur (Gainsville, FL, 2003)

Armstrong, Dorsey, and Kenneth Hodges, *Mapping Malory: Regional Identities and National Geographies in* Le Morte Darthur (New York, 2014)

Batt, Catherine, *Malory's* Morte Darthur: *Remaking Arthurian Tradition* (New York, 2002)

Benson, Larry D., *Malory's* Morte Darthur (Cambridge, MA., 1976)

Cherewatuk, Karen, *Marriage, Adultery and Inheritance in Malory's* Morte Darthur (Cambridge, UK, 2006)

Crofts, Thomas H., *Malory's Contemporary Audience: The Social Reading of Romance in Late Medieval England* (Cambridge, UK, 2006)

Edlich-Muth, Miriam, *Malory and His European Contemporaries: Adapting Late Arthurian Romance Collections* (Cambridge, UK, 2014)

Edwards, Elizabeth, *The Genesis of Narrative in Malory's* Morte Darthur (Cambridge, UK, 2001)

Field, P. J. C., *The Life and Times of Sir Thomas Malory* (Cambridge, UK, 1993)

Field, P. J. C., *Romance and Chronicle: A Study of Malory's Prose Style* (London, 1971)

Gaines, Barry, *Sir Thomas Malory: An Anecdotal Bibliography of Editions, 1485–1985* (New York, 1990)

Hodges, Kenneth, *Forging Chivalric Communities in Malory's* Le Morte Darthur (New York, 2005)

Ihle, Sandra Ness, *Malory's Grail Quest: Invention and Adaptation in Medieval Prose Romance* (Madison, WI, 1983)

Kato, Takako, *Caxton's* Morte Darthur: *The Printing Process and the Authenticity of the Text* (Oxford, 2002)

Kennedy, Beverly, *Knighthood in the* Morte Darthur (Cambridge, UK, 1992)

Kim, Hyonjin, *The Knight Without the Sword: A Social Landscape of Malorian Chivalry* (Cambridge, UK, 2000)

Kuskin, William, *Symbolic Caxton: Literary Culture and Print Capitalism* (Notre Dame, 2008)

Lambert, Mark, *Malory: Style and Vision in* Le Morte Darthur (New Haven, CT, 1975)

Larrington, Carolyne, *King Arthur's Enchantresses: Morgan and Her Sisters in Arthurian Tradition* (London, 2006)

Leitch, Megan G., *Romancing Treason: The Literature of the Wars of the Roses* (Oxford, 2015)

Lexton, Ruth, *Contested Language in Malory's* Morte Darthur: *The Politics of Romance in Fifteenth-Century England* (New York, 2014)

Lynch, Andrew, *Malory's Book of Arms: The Narrative of Combat in* Le Morte Darthur (Cambridge, UK, 1997)

McCarthy, Terence, *An Introduction to Malory* (Cambridge, UK, 1991)

Martin, Molly, *Vision and Gender in Malory's* Morte Darthur (Cambridge, UK, 2010)

Nall, Catherine, *Reading and War in Fifteenth-Century England: From Lydgate to Malory* (Cambridge, UK, 2012)

Norris, Ralph, *Malory's Library: The Sources of the* Morte Darthur (Cambridge, UK, 2008)

Pochoda, Elizabeth T., *Arthurian Propaganda:* Le Morte Darthur *as an Historical Ideal of Life* (Chapel Hill, NC, 1971)

Radulescu, Raluca L., *The Gentry Context for Malory's* Morte Darthur (Cambridge, UK, 2003)

Radulescu, Raluca L., *Romance and its Contexts in Fifteenth-Century England: Politics, Piety, and Penitence* (Cambridge, UK, 2013)

Riddy, Felicity, *Sir Thomas Malory* (Leiden, 1987)

Rovang, Paul R., *Malory's Anatomy of Chivalry: Characterization in the* Morte Darthur (Madison, NJ, 2014)

Whetter, K. S., *The Manuscript and Meaning of Malory's* Morte Darthur: *Rubrication, Commemoration, Memorialization* (Cambridge, UK, 2017)

Whetter, K. S., *Understanding Genre and Medieval Romance* (Aldershot, 2008)

Wyatt, Siobhan, *Women of Words in* Le Morte Darthur: *The Autonomy of Speech in Malory's Female Characters* (New York, 2016)

## Collections of Essays

Archibald, Elizabeth, and A. S. G. Edwards, eds., *A Companion to Malory* (Cambridge, UK, 1996)

Brandsma, Frank, Carolyne Larrington, and Corinne Saunders, eds, *Emotions in Medieval Arthurian Literature* (Cambridge, UK, 2015)

Cherewatuk, Karen, and K. S. Whetter, eds, *The Arthurian Way of Death: The English Tradition* (Cambridge, UK, 2009)

Field, P. J. C., *Malory: Texts and Sources* (Cambridge, UK, 1998)

Hanks, D. Thomas Jr., and Jessica G. Brogdon, eds, *The Social and Literary Contexts of Malory's* Morte Darthur (Cambridge, UK, 2000)

Hanks, D. Thomas Jr., and Janet Jesmok, eds, *Malory and Christianity: Essays on Sir Thomas Malory's* Morte Darthur (Kalamazoo, MI, 2014)

Lumiansky, Robert M., ed., *Malory's Originality: A Critical Study of* Le Morte Darthur (New York, 1964)

Spisak, James W., ed., *Studies in Malory* (Kalamazoo, MI, 1985)

Takamiya, Toshiyuki, and Derek Brewer, eds, *Aspects of Malory* (Cambridge, UK, 1981)

Wheeler, Bonnie, and Fiona Tolhurst, eds, *On Arthurian Women: Essays in Memory of Maureen Fries* [*Arthuriana*, 9.2] (Dallas, 2001)

Wheeler, Bonnie, and Robert L. Kindrick and Michael N. Salda, eds, *The Malory Debate: Essays on the Texts of* Le Morte Darthur (Cambridge, 2000)

Whetter, K. S., and Raluca L. Radulescu, eds, *Re-Viewing* Le Morte Darthur: *Texts and Contexts, Characters and Themes* (Cambridge, UK, 2005)

## Articles

Archibald, Elizabeth, "Malory's Ideal of Fellowship," *The Review of English Studies*, NS 43 (1992): 311–28

Armstrong, Dorsey, "Postcolonial Palomides: Malory's Saracen Knight and The Unmaking of Arthurian Community," *Exemplaria* 18.1 (2006): 175–203

Cannon, Christopher, "Malory's Crime: Chivalric Identity and the Evil Will," in *Medieval Literature and Historical Inquiry: Essays in Honour of Derek Pearsall*, ed. David Aers (Cambridge, UK, 2000), 159–83

Cecire, Maria, "Barriers Unbroken: Sir Palomydes the Saracen in 'The Book of Sir Tristram," *Arthurian Literature* XXVIII (2011): 137–54

Cherewatuk, Karen, "'Gentyl Audiences' and 'Grete Bokes': Chivalric Manuals and the *Morte Darthur*," *Arthurian Literature* XV (1997): 205–16

Coleman, Joyce, "Reading Malory in the Fifteenth Century: Aural Reception and Performance Dynamics," *Arthuriana* 13.4 (2003): 48–70

Cooper, Helen, "Counter-Romance: Civil Strife and Father-Killing in the Prose Romances", in *The Long Fifteenth Century*, ed. Helen Cooper and Sally Mapstone (Oxford, 1997), 141–62

Field, P. J. C., "Sir Thomas Malory's *Le Morte Darthur*," in *Arthur of the English*, ed. W. R. J. Barron (Cardiff, 2001), 225–46

Francis, Christina, "Reading Malory's Bloody Bedrooms," *Arthurian Literature* XXVIII (2011): 1–20

Gaines, Barry, "The Editions of Malory in the Early Nineteenth Century," *The Papers of the Bibliographical Society of America* 68.1 (1974): 1–17

Harris, E. Kay, "Evidence against Lancelot and Guinevere in Malory's *Morte Darthur*: Treason by Imagination," *Exemplaria* 7.1 (1995): 179–208

Heng, Geraldine, "Enchanted Ground: The Feminine Subtext in Malory," in *Arthurian Women: A Casebook*, ed. Thelma S. Fenster (New York, 1996), 97–113

Hodges, Kenneth, "Wounded Masculinity: Injury and Gender in Sir Thomas Malory's *Le Morte Darthur*," *Studies in Philology* 106.1 (2009): 14–31

Hoffman, Donald L., "Assimilating Saracens: The Aliens in Malory's *Morte Darthur*," *Arthuriana* 16.4 (2006): 43–64

Huber, Emily Rebekah, "Delyver Me My Dwarff!' Gareth's Dwarf and Chivalric Identity," *Arthuriana* 16.2 (2006): 49–53

LaFarge, Catherine, "Conversation in Malory's *Morte Darthur*," *Medium Ævum* 56 (1987): 225–38

Kaufman, Amy S., "Between Women: Desire and its Object in Malory's 'Alexander the Orphan'," *Parergon* 24.1 (2007): 137–54

Kaufman, Amy S., "The Law of the Lake: Malory's Sovereign Lady," *Arthuriana* 17.3 (2007): 56–73

Kaufman, Amy S., "Guenevere Burning," *Arthuriana* 20.1 (2010): 76–94

Kelly, Kathleen Coyne, "The Writable Lesbian and Lesbian Desire in Malory's *Morte Darthur*," *Exemplaria: A Journal of Theory in Medieval and Renaissance Studies* 14.2 (2002): 239–70

Kelly, Robert L., "Wounds, Healing, and Knighthood in Malory's Tale of Launcelot and Guenevere," in *Studies in Malory*, ed. James W. Spisak (Kalamazoo, MI, 1985), 173–97

Kennedy, Edward Donald, "Malory's *Morte Darthur*: A Politically Neutral English Adaptation of the Arthurian Story," *Arthurian Literature* XX (2003): 145–69

Kissick, Erin, "Mirroring Masculinities: Transformative Corpses in Malory's *Morte Darthur*," *Arthurian Literature* XXXI (2014): 101–30

Leitch, Megan G., "'of his ffader spak he no thing': Family Resemblance and Anxiety of Influence in the Prose Romances," in *Medieval Into Renaissance*, ed. by Andrew King and Matthew Woodcock (Cambridge, UK, 2016), 55–72

Mann, Jill, "Malory: Knightly Combat in *Le Morte Darthur*," in *The New Pelican Guide to English Literature*, ed. Boris Ford, 9 vols (Harmondsworth, 1982–88), I, Part I, 331–39

McClune, Kate, "'The Vengeaunce of My Brethirne': Blood Ties in Malory's *Morte Darthur*," *Arthurian Literature* XXVIII (2011): 89–106

Meale, Carol, "Manuscripts, Readers and Patrons in Fifteenth-Century England: Sir Thomas Malory and Arthurian Romance," *Arthurian Literature* IV (1985): 93–126

Nall, Catherine, "Malory's *Morte Darthur* and the Rhetoric of War," *Medium Ævum* 79.2 (2010): 207–24

Peverley, Sarah L., "Political Consciousness and the Literary Mind in Late Medieval England: Men 'Brought up of Nought' in Vale, Hardyng, *Mankind*, and Malory," *Studies in Philology* 105.1 (2008): 1–29

Phillips, Helen, "Bewmaynes: The Threat from the Kitchen," *Arthurian Literature* XXVIII (2011): 39–56

Putter, Ad, "Late Romance: Malory's Tale of Balin," in *Readings in Medieval Texts: Interpreting Old and Middle English Literature*, ed. David Johnson and Elaine Treharne (Oxford, 2005), 337–53

Rushton, Cory, "Absent Fathers, Unexpected Sons: Paternity in Malory's *Morte Darthur*," *Studies in Philology* 101.2 (2004): 136–52

---. "'Of an uncouthe stede': The Scottish Knight in Middle English Arthurian Romances," in *The Scots and Medieval Arthurian Legend*, ed. Rhiannon Purdie and Nicola Royan (Cambridge: Brewer, 2005), 109–19

Simpson, James, "Violence, Narrative and Proper Name: *Sir Degaré*, 'The Tale of Sir Gareth of Orkney,' and the *Folie Tristan d'Oxford*," in *The Spirit of Medieval English Popular Romance*, ed. Jane Gilbert and Ad Putter (Harlow, 2000), 122–41

Sutton, Anne F., "Malory in Newgate Prison: A New Document," *The Library*, 7th series, 1.3 (2000): 243–62

Taylor, Amanda D., "The Body of Law: Embodied Justice in Sir Thomas Malory's *Morte Darthur*," *Arthuriana* 25.3 (2015): 66–97

## Works of Reference

Kato, Tomomi, ed., *A Concordance to the Works of Sir Thomas Malory* (Tokyo, 1974)

Mizobata, Kiyokazu, ed., *A Concordance to Caxton's* Morte Darthur *(1485)* (Osaka, 2009)

# Index

In those cases where individual chapters disagree in spelling or there is no standard spelling in the criticism, this index privileges the spelling found in the most extensive discussion.

# ARTHURIAN STUDIES

www.ingramcontent.com/pod-product-compliance
Lightning Source LLC
Chambersburg PA
CBHW060621100726
47907CB00006B/1715

* 9 7 8 1 8 4 3 8 4 6 7 5 8 *